This novel is entirely a work of fiction

The names, characters and incidents portrayed in it are the work of the author's imagination. Historical names have been used as 'coat-hangers' for the fictitious characters and any resemblance to actual persons, living or dead, events or localities is entirely coincidental.

Written by: Christopher Savage

Edition 1.9 - 20/07/2017

Front cover designed by: Nick Savage - Xi Design

Cover model: Anna Subbotina

Dedication

This book is dedicated to my wife Jackie and close family. If you look, you will find yourselves in here. If ever you need me and I am not there, you will find me also in these pages.

Books in the Angels & Shadows series:

Book 1: Angels & Shadows

Book 2: Forsaken

Book 3: Scorned

Book 4: The Assassin

Angels & Shadows

Prelude

England. September 2013.

Elizabeth left her aunt's house a in a blind rage. She was absolutely livid. It was supposed to have been her first *official* date with Mike and a monumental moment in her 18 year life. She had planned a romantic evening with her first true love and he had ruined it. Elizabeth had spent the whole of the day in anticipation of it and most of the afternoon making herself look irresistible for him.

As she boarded the bus for town she tossed her mane of golden locks away from her face defiantly.

"I will enjoy tonight despite him," Elizabeth thought and almost said the words out loud as she paid the conductor.

Her large emerald eyes, set in a broad brow and high cheekbones, shone with the rage within her. An old lady, who was sat in one of the aisle seats, placed her hand over her mouth and whispered conspiratorially to her friend.

"I wouldn't want to cross that one tonight."

Despite the old lady's attempt to muffle her whisper, Elizabeth's special inborn skills picked up every word as if she had shouted them out loud. The withering look that she gave in return silenced the pensioner, who averted her eyes and didn't look up again.

Elizabeth took her seat at the back of the bus and sat there with a face like thunder. Her full red lips were set in a massive petulant pout and she bristled with attitude. The tickets to the cinema were pre-booked. Elizabeth had decided that she would watch the movie anyway; at least it might distract her from her venomous thoughts, she had decided.

Elizabeth knew that she was dealing with the situation badly and hadn't even given Mike the chance to explain himself. There had to be a good reason, he simply wasn't like that. It was so out of character. Weeks of sleep deprivation had taken its toll on Elizabeth and she was being irrational, she knew it. But she just couldn't sleep. The menacing stalker in her repeating nightmares was real to her now, even more so since actually seeing him *live* in the video clip that Mike had taken. He was the same despicable man as in her dreams; even down to how he dressed and the cane that he carried. It was the cane that concealed the blade that would inevitably take her life. She even had a name for him now; it was 'Sir William Withey Gull', more popularly known as 'Jack the Ripper'.

Inexplicably, Elizabeth was being stalked by a monster from the past. She knew that he would eventually get her, just as he always did in her dreams. It was simply her destiny. She daren't sleep; for fear that he could harm her even there.

Elizabeth stepped off the bus. The night had a chill to it and the moist summer air was condensing into a light mist that swirled mystically around her legs as she walked. She was deep in thought and it came as a surprise when she arrived at the cinema. There were only two movies to choose from. One was the latest in the series of *A Nightmare on Elm Street* and the other a Disney adventure. Elizabeth chose the Disney option for obvious reasons.

"I already have one freak in my dreams," she thought, "the last thing I need right now is another!"

The film was about to start. Elizabeth hurriedly collected her ticket along with some comfort food and took her seat just as the film began. Binging on chocolate and Coca-Cola would cheer her up, or so she thought. An hour later, she had neither gained comfort nor diversion from it. Instead it had fuelled the guilt that she was already feeling about her disproportionate reaction to being side-lined by Mike.

It was warm and snug in the gloomy cinema and the music of the soundtrack, soothing. The many sleepless nights had left Elizabeth tired to the point of desperation. She was caught up in a circle of thoughts that she could neither break free of, nor solve. Despite her effort to resist, Elizabeth was slowly succumbing to her tiredness until finally she drifted into a confused, almost feverish sleep.

Her feeling of guilt fuelled her dreams. One after another the faces of her friends and family were appearing in her head, each scalding her about her attitude.

"You've really done it now Elizabeth," one said, looking hatefully at her.

"He won't be coming back!" said another.

It was all becoming frenzied. She was apologising to them and begging for another chance, but nobody would listen. Suddenly, her brother's face was in hers and he was shouting at her.

"You spoil everything for me Lizzie, you always have. He would've been a good friend but you've ruined it!"

Elizabeth was still apologising and pleading with him when his face began to transform. Now he was leering at her through cold eyes with lips pursed like a woman's. Ben spoke but it wasn't his voice; it was squeaky, almost feminine.

"It's alright my little precious, I will free you soon," it was the same face, the same voice and the same words that her stalker had used in her nightmares. It was Withey!

Elizabeth cried out in pure terror of it. She stood up in the middle of the cinema and screamed hysterically until the lights came on and ushers came running down the aisles to assist her. When they reached out to calm her, she couldn't separate their actions from her dream. Elizabeth cowered away from them, whimpering like a whipped puppy.

"Please no, don't hurt me please, I'll do anything… "

As the dream receded, Elizabeth realised her predicament and began to feel foolish.

"I'm so sorry, really I am… I don't know what… I mean, please excuse me."

Elizabeth turned away with her head bowed low in shame. She clutched the collar around her throat as if she was cold, but the chill was only a physical manifestation of her fear and vulnerability. She ran out passed the ticket office into the now fogbound street, unable to breathe. Eventually, Elizabeth stopped and leant against a wall for support. She was gasping for air, trying unsuccessfully to regain her composure. Elizabeth's nerves and emotions were completely in tatters, and her terror coiled and writhed like a snake within her.

She looked around her to find that the mist had now turned into a thick fog. Even though Elizabeth knew the area quite well, she had difficulty in orientating herself. Lack of sleep and anxiety had dulled her wits. The direction of the traffic in the one-way street confirmed which way she had to go. She headed against it, towards where she knew that the pedestrian area would be. Distance is a hard thing to reconcile in fog, Elizabeth knew that it was a left turn ahead somewhere, but she couldn't tell which one. To make matters worse, the street names were set at the first floor level of the buildings, too high for Elizabeth to read in the ever thickening fog.

"I must have already gone too far," Elizabeth concluded.

She took a left anyway, thinking that at least she would be heading in the right direction. She could soon tell that she was, because the roads had become narrow and traffic free, just as she had expected. Elizabeth came unexpectedly to a dead end. She hadn't seen the the cul-de-sac sign that was obscured by the fog and the darkness. Cursing her luck, she doubled back on herself taking the first right to work her way around the block. She was desperately hoping to meet someone who actually knew where they were in the almost total black out.

The sound of Elizabeth's stiletto shoes on the pavement was the only sound that she could hear. They seemed to ring out disproportionally in the still night air, as if calling attention to her; calling Withey. Calling the Ripper!

"I'm here, come and get me," they were saying and the thought of it sent a frisson down her spine.

It felt chilly to Elizabeth now; really chilly. A choking feeling of dread began to consume her. It was just as it was in her nightmare. Now she was listening out for those other footsteps, the Ripper's. The feeling of *déjà vu* in her deepened, taking over her mind, driving her inexorably towards insanity.

If it was possible, the fog became even denser and the night darker. Elizabeth nearly missed the right-hand turn. She took it at the last second and quickened her pace as she did so. She was becoming increasingly disorientated in the fog, bumping against the wall constantly and grazing herself as she tried to steer herself along the narrow pavement. Her panic was rising to breaking point. Irrationally, Elizabeth imagined that someone might jump out on her from one of the doorways and stepped out into the middle of the road. She immediately regretted it. Her high heel shoes now made even more noise on the polished cobblestones, shattering the silence of the night, pinpointing her position to any predator. Instinctively she reached down, unhooked the backs of them and kicked them off. She ran on bare footed terrified, driven to the very edge of despair.

Elizabeth's bare feet padded softly against the cobblestones now. She ran on blindly in the night, with no idea of where she was or running to; not even what she was running from. Then she heard it. Rubber soles were slapping the cobbles at the same tempo as hers. Behind her, all around her, she wasn't sure, but ever closer by the second. Elizabeth forced herself to stop and listen to place them. She knew that her life would depend on the decision that she was about to make. She was all alone at a crossroads in the blackness, turning in circles, just as she was in her dreams. Trying to work out which way to run for safety; for her life!

Sir William Withey Gull was already sat in the cinema when Elizabeth entered and took her seat, four rows in front of him. It was obvious to him which film she would choose. He smiled with self-satisfaction at his own perception. He had even guessed where she might choose to sit. The rows between them were empty and Withey could clearly smell Elizabeth's fragrance. He tasted the air and it excited him, enhancing the anticipation of the perverse things that he was going to do to her. He was a nondescript sort of man, fairly short and a little rotund. Dapper would adequately describe his dress style. His grey jacket sported generous lapels over a neat waistcoat with gold watch chain draped in catenary. He wore a bow tie, brimmed hat and carried a short, broad cane which completed his Poirot-esque style.

When Elizabeth left her seat screaming, Withey was in rapture over the powerful physical manifestation of terror that he had instilled in her. Years of careful grooming and planning had led up to this point and he knew that it would all be perfect, just as it had been so many times before. Withey's womanly mouth was salivating as he fondled the handle of the knife concealed in his ornate cane. It was as if it was a living thing, calling him to expose it and bathe it in young virgin blood to quench its thirst. But the knife was insatiable, as it had been over the centuries, and would be for centuries to come.

Withey followed Elizabeth out of the cinema, just outside of her vision. He maintained that close proximity as she stumbled her way towards the bus station. When Elizabeth came to the cul-de-sac and doubled back, she almost walked straight into him. Withey had to side-step to avoid her but, in her fear, Elizabeth remained totally unaware of his presence.

"Not yet my little precious, you are not nearly ready for me. I will only release you when you have lost all control; when you are paralysed by the fear that I have created within you."

Withey was in delicious anticipation of the final act.

"No, not until you are begging me for your worthless life. Only then will I free you Elizabeth Robinson, only then...."

Withey was just yards behind Elizabeth when she kicked off her shoes and began to run up the middle of the road. He was panting with the exertion of trying to keep up with her, and worried that he was about to lose her. His little mouth was working like a baby's sucking at a bottle. Beads of acrid sweat formed like raindrops on his pudgy face. It came as quite some relief when she suddenly stopped at the crossroads.

Elizabeth had started to circle in confused terror, ever conscious of what might be behind her. She moved jerkily, looking over her shoulder just as much as in front. Withey knew that she was listening for him and it fuelled his excitement. He knew too what she was going through, what they had all been through; countless women over countless years.

"Elizabeth would be special though," Withey thought.

He slipped silently by her to take up his position at the place where he knew that she would finally be; the place where he would take her life.

"Soon now Elizabeth," Withey whispered, caressing the handle of his cane, "very soon my little precious," his anticipation was a tangible thing, almost painful and he needed to exorcise it.

As Elizabeth circled at the fogbound crossroads, she thought she heard footsteps. Her head jerked from side to side as she tried to place her stalker, but he had stopped. The silence was deafening. She set off again running blindly, with no idea of whether she was running towards him or away. Elizabeth's fear had risen past terror, shocking her body into paralysis until her legs no longer responded to her commands. It was like she was wading through treacle, just as it was in her dreams. Elizabeth knew that she would meet him very soon now. It would all end for her here, alone in this cold and nameless street. Despair filled her heart. She knew it was hopeless to try and run from him; he would catch her, he always did. This was her destiny and she was resigned to the inevitability of it now, already wishing it over and done with. Elizabeth stopped and capitulated, totally broken. Her head was bowed and she sobbed uncontrollably. It was as she had always known it would be.

Elizabeth looked up and he was there, her master. The man was immaculately dressed with his little waxed moustache, carrying his cane, leering at her through the coldest eyes that she had ever seen. It was Elizabeth's last chance. Even in her numbness she knew that. She began to strike out at him desperately, but just as in her dreams, her fists landed like caresses on him. Withey just smiled cruelly at her and offered his womanly mouth as if to kiss her. Elizabeth could smell the acrid stench of him now and pulled her head back, heaving the contents of her stomach out onto the pavement. Withey showed Elizabeth the ornate cane and slowly withdrew the knife, deliciously watching her as the horror of it twisted her delicate features into a grotesque mask.

Withey's voice sounded shrill in the still night air.

"You have waited patiently for this moment Elizabeth, but it's alright my little precious, I will free you now. You are ready at last".

As he pressed the knife into Elizabeth's throat, her perfect white skin opened, letting the first blood run down her neck. There was only one more thing that he wanted of her that would make it all perfect; it was for her to beg him for mercy.

He knew that he wouldn't be disappointed and it began as Elizabeth stammered her words.

"No, please no. Don't take my future I beg you, I will do anything, anything! Please, just don't hurt me please… "

Withey was fully aroused now. He paused in the cutting stroke to savour the moment. Elizabeth could see by his cruel smile that her plea was futile.

In those last moments that she had left, her short life flashed before her. There were images of her parents smiling down at her when she was small. She knew now that she would never use her special talents to bring them back from their premature and violent deaths. She had failed them and the pain of it hurt more than the knife that was cutting into her throat. Then there was Ben looking so proud after winning the cup for his team, knowing too that he would never survive against the Shadows without her. She saw Mike with his special smile and deeply regretted that they could never be together as one.

All the people she loved flashed through her mind in milliseconds. She felt crushed by their love for her and desolated at how she was letting them all down. Not even fighting for her life; just capitulating to be yet another victim of this despicable man. Elizabeth sought solace from her final thoughts, the ones that would take her into oblivion. In her mind she was riding Beauty, galloping bareback through fields of corn with the wind in her hair. Her final memory was the image of Edith and Brady, her unborn children that she had been given the gift to 'glimpse' in the future. How could she just accept death and not let them be born to her? How could she be so weak as to fail to unleash those awesome powers that lie within her and save them? How could so much hope, so much possibility end in this ultimate submission to this despoiler of women?

Chapter 1

Foothills of Mount Olympus, Greece. Summer 2007 (6 years earlier).

Although it was past mid-summer in the foothills looking out towards Mount Olympus, the fabled Seat of Zeus king of gods, the temperature had not dipped below 30 degrees.

The two maidens bathing naked in the fresh mountain pool were in many ways closer in kind to the Nymphs and Deities of the myths, which formed the history of this very Greece, than their flesh and blood suggested. In fact they were in part responsible for them. But that comes later.

Mortal lifetime typically spans three score and ten, seventy years. These beauties however, were not mortal and had been on our Earth for more than 5,000 of our years yet they were still in the very prime of their lives. They were among the last of their kind and carried with them the burden of having witnessed man's atrocities to man over the millennia. They were the regulators but were gradually becoming disillusioned and powerless to prevent man's eventual decline into the abyss.

They were not entirely free of guilt themselves. It was their people who had brought the *Shadows* with them to live amongst long ago, and they who had lost control of them. The responsibility to restore the balance was now almost entirely in the hands of these two nubile girls as they were the last remaining full-blooded Matriarchs of their race.

It was easy to walk amongst us then, in the primitive times of the early colonial days, when they had control of the Shadows. All that man needed were gods to fear, and worship and rules to obey in order to create a conscience within us. They had provided that. These were simple tools to guide us to the good side of our being and there was no need to constrain our lives further. It was the creation of our humanity, a beautiful gift that they had given us. It brought with it peace, love and compassion.

But that was before they lost control...

The maidens bathing in the cool waters were sisters. Only five of their years separated them but Maelströminha was the eldest and with that came the responsibility of her birth-right. She was Principal Matriarch and responsible for the future of her race, although incongruously, she appeared to be only in her early to mid-twenties of our years. Her sleek black hair was plaited in a rope and swept over her shoulder falling down her naked breast to her slim waist. She was petite and athletic in build, but not at the cost of her feminine curves. Her face was finely sculpted with high cheekbones and large startling blue eyes, that reflected the sun as it danced on the chop of the clear mountain waters. Her full mouth and perfect white teeth gave her the most captivating smile and her laughter was lyrical and kind to the ear.

She was chatting animatedly to her sister, although there was an underlying tension about it all. Maelströminha was evidently teasing her about something, judging by the way that Crystalita suddenly stood up with her hands on her boyish hips in mock disdain. The innocent act displayed her nude svelte body that glowed with the health of youth in the bright Grecian sunshine. Her long platinum blonde hair tumbled down her back and caught the light and shone like a halo around her head. She was bronzed and beautiful and shared the same startling blue eyes as her sister, but unfortunately not her temperament.

Something was said and Crystalita stormed out of the pool stamping her feet in temper. She turned her back to her sister and sat on a rock with her arms folded and chin jutted out as she seethed in a black rage.

Maelströminha let her be for a while, knowing how head strong she was and the pointlessness of trying to talk to her too soon. After a few minutes, she stood up and walked over to her. As she left the pool, water ran in rivulets down her naked body following her feminine contours, encouraged by the natural and unaffected sway of her hips. It was a scene that would have become iconic had it ever graced the silver-screen.

She stood behind Crystalita and began to brush her shining blonde hair. As she did so, she began to sing to her but the song was more than words and a tune, it was on another level of communication that man has yet to evolve to. It was a song of emotions and deeply spiritual. It was a song of love and hope and trust and forgiveness. After some minutes, Crystalita gave that forgiveness unconditionally and turned to her sister for the consistent comfort that she had given her selflessly over the millennia. Maelströminha had not only been her sister but her mother and father too, since both had died when they were little more than children.

Crystalita sobbed like a child in her sister's arms and words were not necessary for Maelströminha to understand her. She knew that her sister was dying by degree, fading like an orchid untended in the desert. They had been living an exile of their own making for centuries, preserving their genes for the rejuvenation of their kind. It had become too much for Crystalita to bear. They were waiting for the pivotal moment when compatible siblings were born of their race, a happening that last occurred over 2,000 years ago but had at last happened again. Those rare and precious siblings, Elizabeth and Ben Robinson, were unaware of their birth-right and of the mortal danger that they were in.

Seeing these maidens alone in the wilderness locked in an urgent and tearful embrace, you would be forgiven for assuming that they were exposed and vulnerable. But these highly evolved women held an awesome power over Nature within them that could match that of even Zeus himself, king of gods, god of the sky and thunder and ruler of Olympus!

Crystalita found her voice and begged her sister's consent.

"You have to let me be the one to go to them, you have to. I can't stay here any longer May. I can't."

She often spoke to her sister in the diminutive form *May*, particularly when she wanted something.

"Please, the loneliness is killing me, can't you see that?"

"Of course I can see it, just as you can see that it's killing me too. But you don't have the skills to survive in their world Crystalita. The

Shadows will seek you out and kill you. The children that we need to protect will be used as bait to draw us to them. We are their greater goal and the only thing that now stands in their path to total domination."

"But we have agreed that they need protection May," Crystalita protested, "Our civilisation depends on them reaching maturity. Another birthing of more than one child to the Patriarch bloodline may never happen in our lifetime and then it will be too late."

Maelströminha remained defiant.

"There are others of us from Angelos who are better placed to do this; Angels who have integrated and become more adapted than us. It is they must watch over the children until the time is right for them to come to us."

Crystalita was beside herself with anger over the injustice of it.

"But integration has diluted their bloodline and cost them most of their powers, how can that be the right way when I have far superior ability?"

"They are streetwise Crystalita and you are naïve. Besides the mirrors tell me that you have little or no chance of surviving the mission and I have looked in them for most all possible outcomes..."

Crystalita turned petulant and vented off at her over-protective sister.

"You and your damned mirrors May. Take them to the Greek markets and join the other soothsayers. I can choose my own destiny."

It was just venom as Crystalita knew that the mirrors never lied. They had predicted the atom bomb attacks by the Americans against the cities of Hiroshima and Nagasaki during the Second World War. This atrocity and countless others were orchestrated by the Shadow organisation. They had become the war-mongers comprising of a coalition of oligarchs, corrupt politicians, zealots and megalomaniacs.

"Don't let me die without even feeling the touch of a man's hand on me or what is life? Must I remain here until I'm a childless old maid with a bitter heart?"

Crystalita's plea struck a chord in May; it was just as she felt herself. She yearned for love too. It was a cruel denial and her long life had been more of a curse than a blessing. May knew that it would be futile and unfair to try and stop her sister. She capitulated.

"I will have Emanuel place you close to them immediately."

Crystalita screamed out in unrestrained delight. She danced around which stimulated the natural bioluminescence within her and she literally shone like a beacon. May's skin however just greyed by comparison. There was no joy in her heart to stimulate her receptor gene, for she knew that she had probably sentenced her sister to death.

It was the last desperate throw of the dice.

Chapter 2

Pakistan. Saturday, February 14th 2009 (2 years later).

The dun coloured twin engine Boeing CH-47 Chinook flew out of Karachi, heading north over Godap Town and out towards Pakistan's Khirthar National Park. The Dureji Road was below them. They followed it until it up to the Hub Dam reservoir and then headed northwest along the Hub Tributary to where it met the main road five miles southeast of their final destination; Goth Allah Bakhsh.

Sean O'Malley dropped the Chinook down low over the Pakistan desert whipping up a sandstorm as the powerful rotors thumped the still night air. Ralph Robinson checked his watch; it was 2030 hours Zulu time, 0130 hours local time. They were on schedule. It left them one and a half hours to make the five mile overland trek to Goth Allah Bakhsh.

Ralph was the most senior of the squad, both in rank and years, even though he was still in his late thirties. The very nature of his business dictated that few commanders made it much into their forties. Ralph had been increasingly riding his luck and could easily be destined to be one of them. He was a little less than six feet tall, strongly built and ruggedly handsome with a broad smile and vivid blue eyes. The strain of the last five years in command was beginning to tell on him though. His fair hair had started to grey at the temples and his dimpled smile had deepened into creases in his bronzed face. But he wore it well. Ralph was leading a group of ex-SAS soldiers and Mossad agents, formerly of Israel's National Intelligence Agency. Together they made up an elite squad of twelve highly trained counterterrorist experts. This unit, and others like it, worked covertly outside of any government authority although, off the record, they were internationally endorsed by them. It allowed *certain things* to be done without fear of recrimination.

Ralph's mission was another 'search and destroy' assignment. The target was an Al-Qaeda terrorist training camp. Ten Taliban insurgents, commanded by the Mullah Ismael Alansari, were conditioning a group of some 30 young students taken from the madrasahs of Pakistan. They were being radicalised for another suicide bomb campaign in Tel Aviv. The scope of Ralph's mission was to assassinate the Mullah and neutralise the camp, whilst limiting student casualties to an acceptable level. When Ralph was given the task he had wondered at the ease at which politicians could use expressions such as acceptable level when referring to the death of vulnerable, innocent people. It just showed how disassociated from reality they had now become.

The Chinook touched down for less than 30 seconds, in which time Ralph and nine of his squad had disembarked with their weapons and supplies. The tail gunner and medic, Craig Jamieson, stayed on the Chinook preparing the on-board trauma unit for the pickup scheduled at 0400 hours local time; one hour after the planned raid. They had chosen the time of their attack to coincide with both the darkest phase of the desert night and the hour when man is at his lowest ebb. At this ungodly hour, men are easily confused and vulnerable. Craig was a personal friend of Ralph and had accompanied him on several missions. Unfortunately it had become almost an expectation to suffer casualties. Craig was wondering how many of the brave ten had got return tickets this time.

For safety reasons, Ralph had chosen the drop site to be five miles from the target. The characteristic thumping beat of the Chinook's twin rotors could be heard for several miles in the still desert air and surprise was essential to the outcome of their mission. He had allowed 90 minutes for the ensuing five mile run across rough desert terrain, with backpacks, weapons and webbing totalling 60 pounds in weight. They would then have another 60 minutes to fulfil their mission and get themselves, including the wounded, to the pickup point half a mile due west of the terrorist camp.

Ralph took out his handheld DAGR GPS to orientate himself, then struck out at a fast jog with his men falling in behind. He would increase the pace once they had accustomed themselves to the task. Only one hydration break had been planned at the three mile point, giving his men the psychological boost that they would have at least broken the back of the run at that stage. The break would be their final opportunity to go through their plan. It had been meticulously put together using satellite technology, Nimrod and Unmanned Aerial Vehicle reconnaissance data. They were as ready as they could be but lacked first-hand, up to date intelligence. There was a real risk that conditions could have changed in the last 24 hours and that they could be walking into a trap.

The going was heavy. They were running over sand and scree that gave under foot and it was telling on two of the heavier men. Ralph had to re-think his strategy. A unit attacks as one so Ralph had to reduce the pace rather than increase it. There was no point arriving for combat with part of his team already blown. When they reached the rest point, they were all thankful for their isotonic drinks and to stretch out and relieve the build-up of lactic acid in their muscles.

Ralph looked at his squad critically. They were all highly trained and experienced men but only three were from his original command; the others had fallen in duty over the last eighteen months. He knew it was unlikely that they would all be going home and the duty of telling the next of kin was his as Officer in Command. Ralph wondered how much longer he could carry that burden. He was battle fatigued himself and had ceased to care whether he made it back or not. It was only the thought of the impact on his young family that kept him going.

There were two new faces in the squad, replacing those fallen in the last mission, both in their early twenties. Although young, they were exemplary soldiers. Only the best of the best were considered for the elite task force. On top of that, there were certain other credentials that were necessary to satisfy the Top Secret status of the mission, including all those associated with it from government officials to ground crew and pilot.

One of the new faces was Corporal Michael Goldberg-Jackson. He was the son of one of Ralph's closest friends, Emanuel Goldberg. The responsibility of his safety weighed heavily on Ralph and increased his foreboding towards the task ahead. Ralph had been over every aspect of the intelligence gathered for this mission and it didn't quite stack up in his mind. A big fish like the Mullah Ismael Alansari protected by only ten Taliban insurgents? It was unlikely at best, despite the photographic evidence appearing to support it. He decided on attacking in two waves, the second only going in if they had walked into a trap. This served another purpose for Ralph. He would put Corporal Jackson in command of the second squad. In that way, if he was wrong and there was no trap, then the Corporal's unit would be safely out of the fray.

"OK men stand down and listen to," Ralph checked his wristwatch. "We rest here for ten minutes."

That was five minutes more than his men had expected and they looked grateful for the extra respite. Ralph continued,.

"Change of plan, same tactics but we go in two squads. 'A' squad, that's Mossad with me. You SAS boys, 'B' squad, go on standby with Corporal Jackson. 'B' squad, you only go in if we are walking into an ambush. Understood Corporal?"

"Roger," confirmed Corporal Jackson.

He didn't show it but the young Corporal knew that Ralph was strategically excluding him from the game. That had to be because of his friendship with his father; he assumed and was seething about it. What Mike didn't know, was the depth of Ralph's real concerns over an Al Qaeda ambush. Ralph laid the A1 size plan out on the sand and they huddled attentively around it. Ralph orientated them.

"As you know we're coming in from the south and we meet the chain link fence here and we synchronise watches then."

He took them around the already familiar map pointing out the landmarks to refresh their memories.

"There are two guard towers with machine guns, here and here. 'A' squad, with me, circle to the west. I take out the lookout in the tower here using sound suppressed sniper rifle, then we cut the chain link fence."

Ralph had their absolute attention. They all knew that even the smallest mistake would cost lives.

"Corporal, you go east with 'B' squad and take out the lookout in this tower here in the same way. If possible we are looking at simultaneous hits at exactly plus three minutes after we go. If we're lucky, the kills will go unnoticed for longer than our mission."

Ralph paused to let them assimilate what he had said.

"At this stage we're fully committed. If anything goes wrong our first duty is to neutralise the towers. We will have lost the element of surprise, so it's all guns blazing boys. We can't go in with their guns overhead on us, or we'll be mown down. In this scenario you follow your instincts a little and pray a lot."

Although Ralph was making light of the situation in typical military manner, they all knew they would be dead in the water if even one of the machine guns was to open up on them.

"OK. 'B' squad then move to the western fence and cut an escape hole there. A bloody big one too, as we could be running through carrying casualties," that was a sobering thought for them. "And then you wait there. Got it?"

Ralph fixed Corporal Jackson with his stare. He didn't want any half-baked heroics. He got the submissive nod that he was hoping for. Ralph could instinctively sense his reluctance though, and hoped that the young corporal wouldn't become hot-headed when the time came.

"If the intel we have is right, and there's only the Mullah plus ten Taliban, then two will already be dead in the towers. That leaves us just eight to deal with. We go in with flash-bangs to disorient them and then kill them in their beds. That leaves the Mullah but don't underestimate him; he is of another breed and infinitely more deadly than his ten men put together. We kill him as a unit; every gun, understood?"

Most of Ralph's men had been involved with others of the Mullah's *breed* before and had lost lives heavily to them. They knew exactly what he meant and were nodding in full understanding of it.

"Corporal, if this goes to plan we'll be out in less than three minutes. You and your squad will be the fresh legs to get us to the rendezvous if we are carrying casualties. Pickup is half a mile due west at 0400 local time. Nobody gets left behind, not even the dead. Are we all clear on that?"

Ralph looked around him and there was a consensus among them. Every soldier wants to make it home, even after death.

"Chief," began Corporal Jackson, "and if it doesn't go to plan?" he cocked that quizzical sideways glance that always struck a humorous chord with his mates, and not least the girls in his life.

"From the first shot give us four minutes. If you're still hearing return fire in five, then get ready. If it's still going on in six, come and get us, 'cos it's gone tits up."

18

Corporal Mike Jackson nodded his understanding.

"So 'A' squad," Ralph continued, "our job is to get it right and make sure that 'B' squad don't have to carry us for half a mile, they're not your mothers and quite frankly, they don't look up to it either."

Ralph had an easy way of command and enjoyed his men's deep respect. There wasn't a man among them who wouldn't have laid down his life for him and they were smiling at his jibe. He drew their attention back to the job in hand.

"We go through the fence here. The students are billeted here; Taliban here and we think the Mullah, here. Don't take that as gospel though, it's only based on the relatively high standard of the building compared to the others. He could be anywhere."

Ralph pointed out his men, "Agent Ben-David, you take these two. Flash-bangs go in to disorientate the Taliban here, then go in and kill everything that moves. They will be concussed, disorientated and vomiting everywhere so take advantage in those early seconds."

He turned to his remaining man, Corporal Sam Jakobson, a young but able agent.

"OK Sam, we deliver flash-bangs at exactly the same time to the Mullah here and here, and then go in. We lay down blanket fire room by room until the rest of our team come in here."

Ralph pointed at the back entrance.

"We flush the Mullah out through the back door here. His only escape is through you three. OK?"

Ralph could see that they were all on board and added some cautionary advice.

"Don't miss. This man has escaped dozens of attempts on his life before and he will not be afraid, disorientated nor consider himself beaten. He'll be like a cornered lion and just as resourceful. If you give him even the smallest opportunity then he will kill you, be sure of that. He has already killed scores like you. There's no room for any compassion and he will afford you none either."

The warning was acknowledged but their morale was already high. They had absolute commitment and positive expectations. Each man knew his task and trusted his life implicitly to his mates. It was with total belief and commitment, that Ralph and his men ran forwards to execute their duty at the Al Qaeda terrorist camp located at Goth Allah Bakhsh.

Adrenaline is an amazing stimulant. They ran at almost an attack pace for the next two miles, without pain or fatigue. Nothing concentrates your mind more than the fear of death. Ralph stopped them 200 yards short of the fence so that they could control their breathing and begin to focus their minds.

"Alright lads, activate your comms equipment now. We only break radio silence if it's all gone FUBAR though, not just because you're feeling insecure, got it?" Ralph raised his hand and waved his men forwards. "May the Angels be with us!"

He led them on over the floodlit killing field towards the fence. The terrain was flat and without cover and so they spread out, keeping low and slow to dilute their visual presence. The squad made it undetected to the fence, despite one guard having seemingly looked right at them. Ralph's decision to attack at this ungodly hour, when a man's wits are at their dullest, had already paid off. Ralph was unaware of having held his breath over the last 50 yards to the fence and exhaled audibly such that he had to stifle the sound with his sleeve. Adrenaline was coursing through his veins such that his hands were shaking as he synchronised watches with his men. A silent nod of his head was all that was necessary for his men to split east and west to execute their tasks.

Both squads arrived at their respective towers within two minutes, giving them another to assess the situation. It was as they expected; both guards were there under duress rather than professionally fulfilling their duties. Neither guard had his weapon at arms and one was drawing heavily on his cigarette, not even looking out across the fence-line.

Ralph and Corporal Jackson loaded bullets into the breaches of their sniper rifles and took aim while their separate supports counted down to the plus three minute mark.

"...3,2,1 fire!"

Both soldiers were recognised marksmen in their own right and both trained in this type of kill. There was only tenths of a second between the enemy lookouts being dispatched with head shots, both falling unnoticed onto the decking of their towers.

Instantly, the other three soldiers of 'A' squad began cropping the fence. It took only one minute and they were in. As they went through, Corporal Jackson and 'B' squad ran silently by to take up their position on the western fence to prepare for the exodus.

Ralph had familiarised himself with the photographs from the gathered intel to such a degree that it was like walking in his own neighborhood. The task ahead was crystal clear in his mind. When they arrived at the Taliban quarters, he split off the three men to deal with that and then pressed on to the Mullah's billet with Sam. They were in sight of each other when they threw the flash-bangs in unison through the unglazed windows of the buildings.

The explosions split the night with a thunderous bang and a blinding flash. They kicked the doors in immediately afterwards and stormed in with their 9mm Heckler & Koch submachine guns blazing, delivering lead at a rate of 800 rounds per minute, decimating everything in sight.

The Mullah Ismael Alansari was in the student's quarters with 38 heavily armed Taliban insurgents patiently waiting for the attack. He was watching the guard on one of the lookout towers, through an open window, when his neck suddenly snapped backwards and his corpse dropped to the floor. The Mullah smiled cruelly through his dense grey beard and gappy teeth. The loss of a man's life meant nothing to him and he was implacable as he addressed the waiting militia.

"The infidels have arrived."

The insurgents lined up in two rows with their weapons at the ready, waiting for the Mullah's command.

The sound of five flash-bangs detonating simultaneously was deafening even in the students' quarters 100 yards away. The insurgents reeled at the force of the shockwave. Moments later, machinegun fire opened up and Mullah screamed out his order.

"Kill the infidels!"

The insurgents burst out through the doorway and charged towards the two stricken buildings. The Mullah followed at a safe distance with his shalwar kameez billowing around his rangy frame in the stiff desert breeze.

As the smoke from the submachine guns cleared in the two targeted billets, the enormity of their situation also became clear. Both buildings were deserted; they had walked right into a terrorist trap.

"FUBAR!" Ralph cursed.

Ralph's comms activated as if agent Ben-David had heard him.

"Chief do you copy? Nobody home, repeat nobody home," Ben-David's voice was urgent.

"Roger that; same here. It's a trap! Go to the middle of the block and get down. Taliban will be ripping it to bits with their AK-47s imminently."

Ralph's worst fear had impacted. He needed to call in 'B' squad but was still reluctant to deploy until he knew more. He pre-empted his Corporal's call.

"Wait on Corporal, until you hear heavy incoming fire that will give us an idea of their number, their position and what we are up against."

"Roger that Chief."

Corporal Jackson's response was clinical. It didn't even begin to convey his frustration of not being called straight into action and for that, he was furious beyond measure.

As Ralph and Sam dived to the floor they dragged mattresses from the beds just as the rifle fire tore into both of the buildings.

Corporal Mike Jackson had heard the message exchange and turned to his men. A contingency plan was already forming in his head as the rifle fire began.

"OK, listen on men. If those two billets were empty, then we can assume that they were all in the student quarter waiting for us. That means that we can assume that the 30 students are Taliban insurgents and armed to the teeth."

It wasn't contested. Mike Jackson continued.

"Their strength is therefore 38 now, plus the Mullah. They will already be circling the huts to trap them there. Take your positions 20 yards outside of their circle as I tell you."

Corporal Jackson pointed at each man in turn giving them their compass position.

"North, East, South and West as you stand. I'll fill in according to what we see or take over from a fallen man. Open fire as soon as you see one of us to your left and right, not before. OK? Now go!"

There was no cover nor time to take it even if there was. 'B' squad had no choice but to run totally exposed to their stations. Fortunately the insurgents were in frenzy, focussed on their own kill. They were too busy strafing the buildings with their AK-47s. As the fabric of the buildings began to give way to the relentless fire, the insurgent's bullets entered deeper and deeper into it getting ever closer to their defenceless prey.

It took a valuable 50 seconds before they were all in place at their given compass points. Their enemy had their backs to them and were completely unaware of their predicament. Corporal Jackson's squad opened fire with their machine guns reaping the enemy like a scythe through corn, sending them into a state of mindless panic. Those still standing turned to flee but were met by the Mullah screaming fanatically at them.

"Turn and fight you worthless Drones!"

The Mullah grabbed the AK-47 from one of his dead men and shot three others in the back that dared to disobey him. He spun around to face the SAS soldier directly behind him and yelled vitriolically as he emptied the magazine into him. The Mullah knew there and then that it was over. All that he could do now was survive to fight another day. With strength that defied the Mullah's wiry frame, he hefted up the corpse of one of his men and ran backwards into the darkness using it as a shield. 'B' squad's bullets simply thumped harmlessly into it as the Mullah Ismael Alansari disappeared into the night.

Ralph was pinned down. At first it was only the occasional bullet that made its way through to their inner sanctum, but as the walls failed and gave way under the relentless fire, the air around him began fizzing with them. It would only be a matter of seconds now, before the bullet-ripped walls would offer no protection at all. Ralph was about to stand and make a futile effort to escape, when he heard the familiar sound of the Heckler & Koch machine guns. As they opened up, the assault on their building immediately ceased as the enemy turned their attention to the new threat.

"Well done son!" Ralph yelled aloud with immense relief.

"Come on Sam, let's give them a hand!" Ralph shouted to the Mossad agent lying next to him.

Ralph retched as he saw his comrade's sightless stare and the blood flowing out of his open mouth.

"God no, not another," he lamented as he knelt by him, gently closing his eyes for the last time. "Go in peace Sam."

The rage mounted inside him. Ralph burst out of the billet through the shredded door with murderous intent but it was already over. Taliban bodies were strewn around like macabre puppets in hopeless positions of death. Ben-David appeared at the doorway of the other building clutching his stomach, then fell face down into the sand. One of the SAS soldiers was at his side in seconds ripping his blood soaked shirt from him while another searched his backpack for a field dressing and morphine.

Ralph and Corporal Jackson ran inside the building to look for the other two Mossad agents. After a couple of minutes they returned with their two lifeless bodies slung over their shoulders. Ralph turned to Corporal Jackson with tears of rage forming in the corner of his eyes.

"What a shambles Corporal, what a bloody shambles," he was shaking his head in despair. "We've been set up again! Someone's giving us false information. There's a traitor amongst us, it's the only explanation."

There were no words that the Corporal could have possible said to relieve any of the pain and responsibility that Ralph was feeling and so he didn't try.

"There's still the Mullah, what do we do Chief?"

"He'll have already gone to ground, forget him. The dead and wounded are our priority now Corporal."

Ralph looked at his wristwatch. It was 0310 local time. He could hardly believe that all this loss of life had taken place in less than ten minutes. He focused back on their task, thankful for the diversion.

"Attention men! We've got less than 50 minutes to rendezvous and six men to carry four bodies, come on let's get to it; on the double!"

The half mile over rough terrain to their rendezvous was gruelling. Two were carrying the unconscious Ben-David leaving four of them to shuttle the three dead. It was gut busting. They heard the Chinook several minutes before it appeared in the night sky. Thankfully Sean O'Malley's keen eyes caught sight of them saving them the torture of the last few hundred yards.

O'Malley swung the Chinook around so that the tail gunner was facing the direction of Goth Allah Bakhsh in case the enemy were in pursuit. He dropped the Chinook to the ground, whipping up a dust cloud that stung the eyes of the broken and weary soldiers. It only took them a minute to load their sorry cargo before the big copter lumbered back into the air. Craig, the medic, had carefully prepared the operating theatre and was put immediately into action. The fight for Ben-David's life had begun, even before the last of the squad had found his seat.

The Mullah Ismael Alansari was only 100 yards behind the remains of Ralph's elite task force. He was hidden in the dust cloud as the last of the bodies was loaded into the cargo area of the Chinook. He ran on another 20 paces before dropping to the desert floor levelling his rifle at the open tailgate of the Chinook, waiting for sight of his quarry. The whole training camp scenario had been staged just to kill one man, Ralph Robinson, a high ranking Angel. He thought that his chance had passed but as the Chinook began to swing around to head back to Karachi, he had him unmistakably in his sights.

"Praise Allah!" he yelled and squeezed off a full magazine of 30 rounds into the open cargo area.

The Chinook tail gunner had the Mullah sighted as soon as the flame plume from the rifle gave his position away. Bullets were ricocheting around the cargo hold and one took the gunner in his left foot. He screamed out in agony, missing his chance to return fire and cursed as he fought to regain his self-control.

The Chinook gained altitude, then circled and came back over the area where the Mullah had been. The injured gunner laid down his vengeful fire from the M60D machine gun at a rate of 550 rounds per minute, ploughing the ground with lead. The Chinook turned and repeated this several times until an area the size of a football pitch had been strafed and the ammunition spent. Satisfied that nobody could have lived through that Hell-fire, O'Malley headed the Chinook out southwards back towards Karachi.

Corporal Jackson was still looking out into the gloom of the desert when he called to Ralph over his shoulder, "Do you think we got him Chief?"

When there was no reply, the Corporal turned to shout his question out above the din of the powerful rotors. He was only just in time to break Ralph's fall as he collapsed bleeding profusely from his neck.

"Medic! Man down!"

Ralph was clutching his neck, blood spurting out between his fingers. His shirt was already soaked in his own blood.

"Quickly he's going into shock!" Corporal Jackson already had his fingers jammed into the hole in Ralph's neck, hopelessly trying to stem the flow of blood.

Craig worked quickly and professionally. After a couple of minutes he looked up in despair, "I can't stop the bleeding Corporal; we're losing him."

Corporal Jackson had the deepest respect for the man dying on the floor beside him. He took his hand, so that he wouldn't pass alone.

"Wait!" Craig was shaking his head in disbelief. "It's not possible, I don't know how or why but the bleeding is stopping. Get me some plasma, he needs a transfusion quickly! The Angels must truly be with him today Corporal."

As the Chinook slipped into the southern sky, the Mullah Ismael Alansari stood up from the desert floor, caked in debris from the heavy machinegun fire. He was known as the un-killable man. The Mullah raised his gun over his head and shook it in defiance at the receding helicopter. He knew that his bullet had found its mark and roared in triumph before turning east back towards Goth Allah Bakhsh.

Chapter 3

Ralph Robinson arrived at the family home at a little after four o'clock on Sunday afternoon. The house was empty as he had expected it to be. Jodie, his wife, would be picking up the kids from their activities. He had travelled a third of the way around the world for Ben's twelfth birthday the next day. Ralph was under pain of death to be there before the kids came home and he had only just come in under the bar. His trips away were becoming more and more frequent and were impacting heavily on his family but the situation was way out of Ralph's direct control.

He eased the kitbag from his shoulder and winced as the stabbing pain in his neck that took his breath away. He heard a car outside and looked out of the window, fully expecting to see his family arriving. It was just a green sports car passing by slowly as if looking for some elusive house number. Ralph walked to the drinks cabinet and poured himself a large Jack Daniels and downed it in one.

"Purely medicinal," he assured himself, poured another then slumped into his La-Z-Boy recliner. He was asleep in moments.

When Jodie pulled up on the drive, Elizabeth and Ben saw Ralph's Porsche.

"Daddy's back!" they shouted in unison.

They piled out of the car, both desperate to get to him first and burst through the front door, calling him as they ran into the lounge. Ralph was already dead to the world and oblivious to the commotion going on around him. Even the children kissing him and pulling at his arms made no difference. Jodie came into the room and called them away.

"Leave Daddy. You know what he's like when he's been away. Let him sleep a while."

Jodie was both cross and disappointed. It was such a let-down to them all when Ralph did this. She noticed, as if for the first time, that his hair was greying at the temples. Even in relaxed sleep, his dimples were becoming deep creases in his face. The last few years had taken their toll on him and he was burnt out. No matter what Jodie said, she couldn't make him listen or convince him to slow down.

She decided finally, that despite this recent attrition, he was still handsome and in some ways perhaps even more so than ever. She felt momentarily cross at the unfairness of how men seem to somehow improve with age, and that time seemed to be on their side.

"Look Mum, Daddy's hurt again."

Elizabeth rolled down the neck of her father's shirt revealing a rudely tied and blood-stained bandage. Jodie put her fingers inside the bandage revealing a deep hole at the base of Ralph's neck, near his collar bone. She did the same at the back of his neck exposing the exit wound. It was still fresh and hot to touch.

"Is it bad Mummy?"

Ben's hands were over his mouth and he looked frightened.

"No Ben, a lot of blood but it's just a scratch, she lied. We'd better leave him to sleep. He'll be fine in the morning for your birthday, you'll see."

Jodie drew the curtains and they left the room. He had been shot again. Jodie wondered just how long it would be before he didn't return to them at all. A frisson ran up her spine as she felt the dread of how empty their lives would be without him. That dreadful thought consumed her and she had to dig deep to shake it off. Jodie knew only too well that it would be eighteen to twenty hours before Ralph would wake. It was the same every time he was injured, some kind of shock reaction. She also knew that when he did he would be on top of the world and up for anything. It was inexplicable. Even the children had grown used to this pattern and had resigned themselves to wait until he had recovered before making their demands of him.

Jodie had known for some time that Ralph was caught up in something dangerous that he wouldn't share with her. She had let him get away with it so far, because of her own fear of facing the truth, whatever that might be. The last bullet wound had been down-played as an accident on the ranges during a Territorial Army training exercise. She had given him the benefit of the doubt on that occasion but he invariably came home with some injury or other. The fear of losing him was suffocating her. Jodie decided there and then to have it out with him, once and for all, as soon as they were alone.

It was late morning when Ralph awoke. He looked around the darkened room wondering where he was and smiled with relief when he realised that it was home. Jodie had taken his shoes off and covered him with a blanket. He felt guilty for collapsing on them again and pulled the blanket off getting up stiffly. There was the sound of a car outside. Ralph assumed that it was the family giving up on him and going out for the day. He hurried to the window and looked out, but it was just the same green sports car passing by slowly again.

"Jodie must have taken the kids off school for the day," he thought.

Even half-awake, he knew that it wasn't the weekend. He became aware of the sound of happy voices coming from the kitchen and the evocative smell of bacon cooking. It was a scenario that he had missed dearly over the last six weeks. When Ralph let himself into the kitchen he was instantly mobbed by his excited children. Jodie could only smile at him and wait patiently in the background for her turn.

Ralph looked appreciatively at Jodie as the children fussed over him. Jodie was in her early thirties, boyishly slim and elegant with long blonde hair in a high ponytail. She was bare-footed wearing loose-fitting faded blue dungarees and a pink and white chequered shirt with the sleeves rolled up above her elbows. Her only make-up was eye-liner and red lipstick. That was all she ever needed to look stunning. Ralph was desperate to hold her but that wouldn't be until the night. For now it was all about the children.

Elizabeth and Ben managed to ask dozens of questions and start several stories without Ralph actually saying anything. He was just happy to have them in his arms and was savouring the moment. When the sweet assault started to fade he took the opportunity.

"Can I give Mummy a cuddle now?"

The children reluctantly let him go. Ralph knew that he wouldn't have long; two minutes at best. He wrapped his arms around Jodie and swung her around in circles as if she weighed nothing and kissed her.

"Girl have I missed you," he whispered and was lost in her.

When he leaned back to look at her face he could see that she was crying. Silent tears of happiness and relief were streaming from the palest of blue eyes.

"Don't ever leave me for that long again," she scalded, "or it won't just be a bullet that you get in the neck."

Jodie tried to force a smile but it was unconvincing. Ralph knew that it was a rebuke and knew just how much she had suffered. He kissed her again tenderly.

"I will try," he promised just as unconvincingly.

"Right," Jodie was business-like now. "Sit down and let me look at that neck of yours."

The children gathered around in the ghoulish way that kids do. Jodie untied the blood-caked bandage and eased it free.

"God!" she exclaimed. "I married a freak."

His neck was still strangely hot but there was only light scaring to both sides of it. Elizabeth and Ben looked visibly disappointed over the anti-climax.

"Good genes perhaps?" Ralph countered with a lopsided grin.

"But not from this planet that's for sure," Jodie was dismissive and turned her back on him.

"What happened to you Dad, where did all the blood come from?"

Ben asked, in expectation of another one of Dad's wild stories.

"From fighting the tigers and giants again Ben; it gets harder as you get older and slower you know?"

Ralph's voice was conspiratorial and full of intrigue. He looked around him as if he might be overheard.

"Their numbers are on the rise again and I have to cull them."

"No Dad I'm too old for that now, I'm twelve!" Ben protested. "What really happened?"

He was wide-eyed in delicious anticipation. Ralph continued with his version of the story despite Ben's protestation of being *too old now*. Ben and Elizabeth wouldn't have had it any other way though. For the next half hour, they were enthralled and hanging on his every word. It was all a load of rubbish and they knew it. But, when it came to rubbish, nobody could tell it better than Dad.

"...and that is why I was nearly late for your birthday Ben," the shaggy dog story ended.

"Well that has to be the most elaborate excuse of all time!" Jodie laughed clapping her hands enthusiastically. She had enjoyed the story too.

"Fetch my kitbag please Ben, I've got something for you."

Ben was gone before the sentence ended. Moments later he handed the bag to his father, waiting in eager anticipation.

"Strange, I could have sworn that I put it in here."

Ralph looked puzzled faking a thorough bag search until he had achieved just the right amount of disappointment.

"Ah here it is. I wrapped it myself."

"Happy birthday Ben!"

Ralph proudly produced something taped up in a Dixons' duty-free airport shopping bag. Ben's face lit up. It was patently obvious what it was by the shape of it and by the shop name.

"Can you guess what it is?" Ralph asked.

Ben shook it, "A football?" he smiled and gave his father a big hug before ripping the bag off. "Wow a laptop, you did remember! Thanks Dad it's exactly the one that I wanted."

"How could I forget number one son, particularly as you haven't stopped talking about it since Christmas?"

Ralph acknowledged Jodie's approving look knowing that she was expecting him to forget too.

"Thank God for last minute shopping at the airport," thought Ralph and he could tell that Jodie thought so too.

Jodie had already planned the day. After breakfast they went to the stables, saddled up and took the bridle path to the Ridge; their favourite family ride. From the Ridge back to the stables was a two mile downhill gallop through country and woodland demanding a high level of rider skill. The Robinson family were all competent equestrians and the race was on. None of them had any intention of losing.

Elizabeth and Ben's horses were colt and filly from a union between their parents' horses and were now near full grown. The weight advantage they had over their parents, compensated for the stamina advantage of the older horses. The race was therefore evenly matched and they were all competitive spirits. The gallop was breath-taking, if not a little dangerous, but that only added to the thrill of it.

First over the fence into the paddock was Elizabeth on Beauty, with Ralph right on her shoulder. Jodie and Ben jumped the fence in unison only a matter of feet behind. They dismounted breathless and elated; particularly Elizabeth who went into the little victory dance she had done ever since she was a toddler. It was a dance that particularly annoyed Ben.

They tended the horses, showered and headed for Frankie and Benny's restaurant to eat before watching a movie. It was after nine o'clock when they finally got back to the house. They were all shattered but Elizabeth and Ben wouldn't give in. The day had been far too much fun to end.

Ben took the opportunity to load the software into his new laptop, while Elizabeth played the piano. It was her latest conquest; *Bridge over Troubled Water* by Simon and Garfunkel. Her music teacher, Miss Crystal, had worked tirelessly with Elizabeth to perfect it and she had chosen it because it was one of her Dad's favourite songs. Ralph listened intently, bursting with pride. Elizabeth was a natural and hearing her play was one of his greatest pleasures. At the end she spun around on the piano stool to face her mother. Elizabeth's face flushed with excitement.

"Mum, will you play while I dance with Daddy?"

It wasn't so much a question as a demand but one that Jodie was happy to oblige. She and Ralph were talented dancers and Elizabeth had watched on over the years and taken to it with a passion.

"Wait Mum, I need to do something," Elizabeth ran upstairs excitedly.

The minutes passed.

"What is she doing up there? She's been gone ages?"

Jodie knew, as mothers do, and smiled back at him.

"Be patient Ralph, you will see."

When Elizabeth swept into the room she was wearing a full length white dress and gold high-heeled shoes. She had made her face up and piled her thick golden curls high on her head. When she walked towards him, the walk was well-practiced and confident.

Ralph had never seen her like this before and *shocked* didn't quite describe it. She was only in her fourteenth year but she looked like a young woman to him now. It had all happened so quickly. Ralph was suddenly saddened about just how much of her growing up he had missed.

"My God," he uttered in a whisper.

Ralph's chin had dropped and Jodie kindly lifted it for him. Just for a moment, Elizabeth looked crest-fallen. She didn't understand her father's reaction. Seeing her plight, Ralph quickly recovered his composure.

"You look beautiful Lizzie, truly beautiful. It's just, well, where did my little girl go?"

She smiled at him innocently, "I'm still here."

Ralph took her in the classic closed hold as Jodie struck the opening chords to Johann Strauss' *Vienna Waltz*. He led her through the turns, step changes and fleckerls that are the Viennese Waltz. Elizabeth was light on her feet and responded to her father's subtle guidance as she changed smoothly from natural to reverse turns while travelling counter-clockwise around the floor. Her fleckerls were well spotted and Jodie had to concede that she couldn't have bettered them herself. It was a feast to watch. The Viennese Waltz is one of the most elegant and challenging of dances. Elizabeth acted it well and confidently, with elegant poise. Even Ben found it more consuming than setting up his laptop and abandoned it. There was no question of sibling jealousy, Ben simply watched on in admiration.

Ralph was the perfect partner and led her through each mood and change of rotation expertly. It was a pivotal moment in Ralph's life. Although he had danced with his daughter on countless occasions, this was the first time that he had danced with her as a woman. It was one of those happy-sad moments where his pride was battling with his guilt. He realised right then, that he needed to enjoy her for those few years left, before she would be completely her own person.

When it was over Elizabeth, still flushed with the exertion of the dance, threw her arms around her father's neck.

"I love dancing with you so much Daddy!" she was holding him desperately. "It's not the same when you leave us. You are staying a while aren't you?"

The desperation in her voice touched Ralph deep within his soul. It confirmed that he had to change things and be there for them while they still needed him. He needed an exit plan now, before it was too late. He needed to be around.

"Yes I will be staying Lizzie, long enough for you to get fed up of me."

Ralph kissed the top of her head. It was a pivotal moment and Jodie could sense it too.

"That just couldn't happen Daddy."

Elizabeth was acutely conscious of the fact that she had never been happier in her life than she was at that moment. From now on life would be just perfect, she just knew it.

Ralph looked at Jodie and nodded at her. She knew by the look on his face that at last he meant it, or at least he would try. She left the piano with tears of relief filling her eyes as she joined the huddle and whispered softly in his ear.

"Thank you Ralph. I love you."

Ben couldn't believe what he had heard his father say; it was everything that he had ever wanted. He left his seat with child-like enthusiasm and threw himself into the group. It was a monumental family moment, life-changing for all of them; the tears and laughter was testament to it.

Somehow Ralph had managed to encompass all of them in his embrace and he pulled them all into him, crushing them with love. A wry smile crossed his face as he considered how the hell he could ever keep that promise.

When the children were finally persuaded that it really was bed time, they retired reluctantly. Jodie was bursting to say all the things that she simply couldn't while they were around. She poured two large Jack Daniels and nestled beside Ralph on the sofa. His arm fell naturally around her shoulders and she felt truly safe for the first time in weeks. They looked into the open fire enjoying the peace and calm, words weren't necessary right then. It was several minutes before Jodie broke the silence.

"That was a bullet hole in your neck wasn't it?" the question didn't need an answer. "I can't take it anymore Ralph. I don't know what you do, where you go or who's trying to kill you. I don't know how you heal so quickly and that just *can't* be right."

Jodie turned her head and looked at him searchingly, testament to the fact that she didn't really know him.

"I don't even know if you're going to bring danger back home to me and the children."

Jodie paused for the response that never came and then continued.

"Every time you leave, I prepare myself for you not coming back. I've even practiced what I would tell the children if that were to happen."

Jodie had to stop talking. She couldn't trust herself not to cry and desperately didn't want to do that and lose her objectivity and credibility. Ralph turned her face to his and held her gaze. He was taken aback by her beauty and vulnerability which made his guilt even more intense.

"You're right. It's time that you knew at least some of it."

Ralph was struggling to know where to start. It would all sound preposterous to anyone on the outside.

"To begin with our property development business just gives me the legitimacy to conduct other activities without attracting, should I say, *unwanted attention*."

Even that came as a bombshell and Jodie was knocked sideways by it.

"You mean that we don't actually have our own business. It's a fraud?"

Jodie had worked part-time in it for years. The very thought that it wasn't real was beyond her imagination.

"No Jodie, we have a thriving business, mostly thanks to you. But for me it's just a convenience. I only need the credibility of it. We have more money than we need."

Ralph was matter of fact and Jodie stunned. His mind was in turmoil. He owed it to Jodie to come clean but there was a limit to *how* clean he could be. The whole truth would be way beyond Jodie's comprehension and would give her more fears than she already had. He decided on an abridged version.

"The world isn't quite as you may think Jodie. There are two secret global organisations, or *societies* would better describe them; and they have been at war culturally, economically and philosophically for thousands of years."

Jodie could feel her fear begin to squirm like a snake in her belly and had to consciously try to suppress it.

"I belong to one of those societies and the other is our enemy. They are an enormously corrupt and ruthless creed that have infiltrated and have ruling power over many international organisations. They reach into the very heart of governments and religions all over the world. Their objective is total economic and governmental control whatever the human cost. That *cost* has often involved escalation to war and genocide."

Ralph held Jodie's hands and never took his eyes off hers so that she would see the truth in what he was about to say.

"Since the early days our enemy has recognised that man can be controlled in many cruel ways. They have used corrupt governments, war, religion, superstition, genocide, poverty, fear and greed. The list goes on; even using our own capacity for love against ourselves.

This evil society has managed to use its own vast resources or infiltrated other organisations to manipulate outcomes to their own purpose. History is full of examples but they are often down-played, because that control is still on-going. The corruption runs deep, even into what are perceived to be respectable governments and businesses."

Ralph could sense that Jodie was already dreading what she was about to hear. She encouraged him on despite herself.

"Don't stop Ralph. I need to hear this; all of it."

Ralph squeezed her hand to give them both the strength that they needed.

"To give you an example; one of the most despicable things that mankind has ever suffered was the Catholic Inquisitions. The Roman Catholic ecclesiastical court, infiltrated and dominated by our enemy, literally forced their will throughout Europe for six centuries. All those people who spoke out, or even thought differently to the Catholic Church, were relentlessly persecuted and branded as heretics. They were then tortured and killed in the foulest and most inhumane of ways.

The execution of this crusade was the perfect cover for our enemy to carry out their own agenda, the genocide of our kind and the legitimate removal of any opposition. Nobody truly knows how many were killed. The records are held in the Vatican archives and privy only to a select few, but it was probably in the millions."

Jodie interrupted.

"Are you saying that your enemy, this *creed*, is responsible for the coordination of all of the major atrocities across the world and history? Surely that would demand a highly sophisticated central organisation, global communications and advanced travel ability? You are talking about events long ago when there was little or none of this."

Jodie's logic was undisputable and Ralph felt guilty that he hadn't shared the truth with her before. She was clearly analytical enough.

"Not all events Jodie, but certainly most all of the major ones. That includes the two World Wars and the on-going problems in Africa and the Middle East. You will just have to trust me that organisation, communications and travel have never been a problem for them, not even thousands of years ago.

In the modern world they have infiltrated most major organisations. Globalisation has played in their hands and their kind can be found ruling in the governments and conglomerates. They are the oligarchs;

they can be Senators, religious leaders or media moguls. Between them, they sell war for personal gain and death is their currency.

Terrorism and destabilisation is their current favoured tool. They use it relentlessly and without compassion through fundamentalists and zealots. Al-Qaeda is almost completely under their control. Iran is provoking Israel to the point of military retaliation and both has been infiltrated by our enemy. They are orchestrating this political impasse, taking us ever closer to global nuclear war, Armageddon."

Ralph saw Jodie's pupils dilate with the shock of the threat of nuclear war. She was shaking her head as if denial would make it all go away. She gathered her composure.

"So if they are the bad guys then who are the good guys, the other secret society that you referred to?"

Jodie's voice had the slightest of tremors which gave away her anxiety. She had already guessed the answer.

"Well, we are the *Regulators* if you like."

Ralph smiled in an attempt to under-play the statement but Jodie was quick to make him expand on it.

"What do the Regulators do?"

This was Ralph's last chance to lie and he considered doing just that. It would have been the easy way out for him. He was in a dilemma but he owed it to his family to share at least some of it. Jodie's fear of him bringing the danger home was well founded. The enemy were getting closer to him and to the other Patriarchs. It was only a matter of time now before his cover would be breached and his family at risk.

Ralph took a deep breath and committed himself.

"Many centuries ago the Regulators were still in control and were able to moderate the expansionism of those who were later to become our enemy by using our political and economic influences. Unfortunately over time the balance of power shifted away from us and now we have to employ more hostile methods to control them. It has never been our way but it was borne out of necessity and justified by the net saving of lives."

"The net saving of lives?" questioned Jodie. "You mean you kill them?"

She was profoundly shocked at the statement and even more so in the matter of fact way that Ralph had delivered it.

"And what is your part in all this Ralph? What exactly do you do?"

Her tone was curt. It was an accusation rather than a question and Jodie was clearly getting annoyed about the lifetime of deceit.

"Well," Ralph was struggling with the wording. "I'm an equaliser, I give the oppressed a better chance."

"Oh my God you are an assassin!"

Jodie's eyes opened wide with shock. She covered her mouth with the palms of her hands. Her head was spinning and then she tore into him.

"I've lived with you for fifteen years and I don't even know you! You go away; kill people then come home as if nothing has happened, make love to me and play with the kids. What kind of monster are you?"

She began to sob uncontrollably, pummelling Ralph's chest with her fists in futile anger and disappointment. Ralph encircled her in his powerful arms to suppress her struggles. Eventually Jodie became submissive but she continued crying for a long time afterwards. She felt bereft, something inside her had died. It was trust and that simple inner peace and contentment. She feared that she would never know it again.

They talked long into the evening about the detail of the double life that he had led; how his targets were selected, how he got in to make the assassinations and out again safely. She learnt about the sophisticated back-up team that worked with him. This at least gave her some reassurance about his personal safety. He told her how his society had strong but unofficial support from high-ranking officials in all the international intelligence organisations and the military, not to mention industry, commerce and the government.

Ralph told of his last mission, a joint venture with the Israeli Mossad and the SAS, to take out an enemy cell of terrorists that were schooling young vulnerable Muslims for another suicide bombing campaign in Tel Aviv. Ralph didn't tell her though, that this had gone badly and that they had lost one third of their contingent to enemy fire. Over recent years the mortality rate for people like him had risen to one in four.

He told her in graphic detail of the many atrocities that their enemy had inflicted on mankind over the centuries and how his kind had fought for the oppressed. As the last of the embers died in the fireplace, so did Jodie's faith in good prevailing over evil. She was tired and dispirited but she now fully understood why Ralph couldn't give up the fight even if he wanted to. It wasn't a matter of choice, it was his obligation by birth and it prompted her next question.

"And what of Elizabeth and Ben when they grow up, will this be their curse too?"

The fact that it took several seconds for Ralph to reply answered her question unequivocally.

"In time they will become as me, as will their children; should we be so lucky."

That was as much as Jodie could take in one night. She forced a brave smile and cupped Ralph's face in the palms of her hands. She looked up into his deep blue eyes and her voice was husky as she kissed him, "Carry me upstairs and make me forget all of this."

Ralph swept her up into his arms as easily as if she were a child and carried her upstairs. She looked scared and vulnerable. The enormity of his responsibility towards his family was captured in that moment and he whispered to her softly.

"I will try and change things, even if that's only until the kids are grown up, I promise."

There were two people that he needed to contact to help make this happen; Maelströminha and Emanuel Goldberg and that would be first thing in the morning.

When Jodie awoke, she reached across for Ralph but he was already up. She checked the time. It was only just turned six o'clock. The sleep was the best that she'd had in weeks and she felt on top of the world. Even the dark news that she had heard from Ralph the night before hadn't dampened her spirits, for now all she was focussed on were the positives.

Jodie took her robe and went downstairs to find Ralph. When she entered the lounge he was stood in front of their old ornate mirror, deep in thought and unaware of her presence. She had seen him do this on many occasions. It was almost like he was in a trance. It really was quite bizarre. He had said that it helped him organise his thoughts, so she decided to leave him. There was certainly enough on his mind to need organising. She slipped out and made some coffee.

It was another fifteen minutes before Ralph left the mirror. When he walked into the kitchen he was somewhat startled to see that Jodie was already there.

"I didn't hear you get up, honey," Ralph's expression was that of genuine surprise.

"When you are doing your *pretty poly* impersonation in front of that old mirror, you don't hear or see anything. You never have," she teased. "Coffee?"

"I'd love one."

Ralph walked over and put his hands on her hips as she poured.

"That's as far south as you go Romeo," Jodie said chastisingly as she cupped her free hand against his cheek. "The kids will be up in a minute."

"You do me an injustice," he grinned at her impishly, "anyway I've decided to join you on your run to the shopping centre this morning. I can drop you in town after taking the kids to school for some retail therapy, while I see someone about those changes that we talked about."

Jodie swivelled around to face him almost upsetting the coffee.

"You really mean it Ralph. You will stop it for us?"

The joy on her face was a picture and it squeezed Ralph's guilty heart so that he had to force himself to add the caveat.

"As much as I can, but only until the kids have finished their schooling. I've already had high level clearance this morning so now I just need to sort out the detail with Emanuel."

"With Emanuel Goldberg? But he's just a financier...," Jodie suddenly became painfully aware of her own naivety. Her shoulders slumped in resignation. "He isn't just a financier, is he?"

"No Jodie he's not, he's the Senior Patriarch in our society. I will need his help to reallocate my field work and see if he's got a desk that I can drive for a few years."

"A few years! Oh Ralph."

It was actually going to happen. Jodie threw her arms around his neck. She was blown away and every kiss that she planted on his face was testament to that.

The family breakfast was relaxed and the conversation flowed freely. Ralph needed bringing up to speed on the six weeks of family life that he had missed which included a number of significant sporting successes for Elizabeth and Ben. Elizabeth had competed with Beauty at three equestrian events and had nailed two firsts and a second. She animatedly took Ralph through all three and her retention for detail was quite remarkable. Ralph was sad that he had not shared these special moments with her and it reinforced the correctness of his decision to take time out for the family.

Ben was waiting impatiently for Elizabeth to finish so that he could expound his achievements too. Ralph had encouraged him in archery and fencing, two sports that he had learnt to a high standard himself. They were essential skills that he had used in anger in his more covert capacity. Ben had been selected to represent his county in both and had boldly challenged his father to a duel, such was his confidence. Ralph would look forward to that and wasn't about to detune his own efforts to appease Ben.

"You can literally live and die by your own sword," he justified.

It would be a lesson that he might need to draw on one day.

Elizabeth and Ben left to get themselves ready for school which gave Jodie a chance to run through some of the more mundane things like correspondence, planned social events, medical appointments and the like.

"I've booked another appointment for Lizzie with Doctor James. I'm really worried about her nightmares. They're increasing in regularity and she's not coping well Ralph, not well at all," Jodie looked despairingly of it, "When she gets them she wakes up screaming, it's totally real to her Ralph and she never sleeps afterwards. She's become afraid to sleep at all in fact and I often find her still reading in the early hours of the morning. Now she thinks that she has premonitions. It's too much for her Ralph, she will have a breakdown I just know it."

"When is the appointment? I want to go too but I think that we need to get a route through to a specialist. There must be an underlying problem, something that we need to deal with."

Ralph was really concerned. He had suffered these as a child too and could still vividly remember how terrifying it was. It ran in the family and Ben would be likely to suffer the same at some stage.

"Not until a week Friday," Jodie replied.

"Too long Jodie. I have some contacts that we can use."

Jodie could not have imagined how far reaching his society was.

"We will have her at a specialist's within a couple of days, not just the local GP."

Ralph would make it happen and Jodie was pleased that he was back in the driving seat.

Elizabeth and Ben elected to go to school in Ralph's classic Porsche 968. It was a bit of a squeeze in the back but they loved the old sports car and it was worth the struggle. Jodie slipped into the passenger seat while Ralph locked the house. As Ralph got in, Ben asked:

"Can we take the bendy road down to the canal, Dad?"

He loved the way that his father would gun the powerful Porsche engine and take the racing line through the tortuous bends right from the Ridge down to the sweeping right-hander by the canal. He got the affirmative sign and sat back nodding conspiratorially to Elizabeth; job done.

Ralph put the key in the ignition and adjusted the rear view mirror. He was about to start the engine, when his eye caught sight of the green sports car that had been around lately. It slowed to an almost stop as it passed their drive. Ralph released the ignition key suddenly, as if it was scalding hot. Something was wrong he could sense it. Years of covert experience had sharpened his awareness and there was something definitely wrong. It was that same green sports car driving by too slowly and too often!

He swung himself out of the low coupé and sprinted up the drive towards the gate. The car accelerated immediately and was gone by the time he reached the road.

"Damn!" Ralph cursed himself for his own stupidity. "Shoddy, very bloody shoddy."

He was better than that and knew it. He was off-guard and lucky this time. It could have cost the lives of his family. They were looking at him puzzled and slightly alarmed.

"It's just somebody that I've seen paying too much attention to our house. Don't worry they won't be back."

Much to Ralph's relief it appeared to be accepted, well at least by the kids. There was a certain amount of *standard procedure* that went with this type of scenario. He needed to check the car thoroughly. Ralph disappeared from their view. It was a low car and Ralph had trouble squeezing his muscular chest under the door sill but it was there, exactly where he would have put it himself. Eight pounds of C4 explosive with a detonator set to pick up the electrical activity of the starter motor. He disarmed it as if it was just a part of his day job, which ironically it was.

When the enormity of the situation hit him he began to shake. It was a totally new experience for him, but then he had never faced losing his family before. Ralph fought to regain his composure, breathed out then eased himself out from under the car. As he slipped into the driver's seat, he dropped the device discretely by his feet and started the engine. It roared like a caged lion, much to Elizabeth and Ben's pleasure. When he glanced in his mirror the contrast between Elizabeth's and Jodie's expressions couldn't have been greater. Elizabeth was smiling in anticipation of an exciting ride and Jodie had a face like thunder. It was never going to be that easy.

"What the bloody hell is that!" demanded Jodie.

She was pointing accusingly at the device.

"Oh just something left on the drive," Ralph said lamely.

Jodie knew exactly what it was. The naïve housewife had left town last night.

Because of the event earlier, Ralph wanted the family to stay together. He dropped them all at the shopping centre and parked outside Emanuel Goldberg's town house. He rang the bell and looked up into the security camera. Facial recognition software granted him access and the door released. Emanuel's office was on the ground floor at the back, the rest of the building was his very grand family home.

The door into Emanuel's office was open. Drinks had already been prepared in readiness on the old oak table. It was like walking back in time. The room was dowdy, with rows of bookcases along three of the walls and an enormous antique mirror facing Emanuel's desk. Displays of antique guns, axes, swords and cutlasses filled all other available gaps. Old weapons were one of Emanuel's passions.

"Good to see you Ralph, now tell me that it's all nonsense about you quitting on us."

It was only half-jokingly. Emanuel valued Ralph's contribution over and above all others. He wasn't going to find such an able replacement easily.

"Emanuel my good friend, I'm doing you a favour! There are none as good as you were in the field. I'm just giving you a chance to come out of retirement and get away from the wife for a while."

Ralph gave that easy dimpled smile of his.

"As good as I was, she would kill me and you know that."

They fell into a welcoming embrace as best friends do. It was Ralph who got down to business first.

"We're losing the battle Emanuel. On my last mission they were ready for us. It was only good soldiering, particularly by your son, which got us out of it. Either we're being given false information, or there's a traitor amongst us," Ralph shook his head despairingly.

"The latter, I'm afraid Ralph, but we are on it."

Emanuel was the most senior of the Patriarchs and as such enjoyed the confidence of Maelströminha herself. He consulted with her almost daily. It was through close contact with her that he administered her vision. With respect to Ralph's request there was no ambiguity. He was to give Ralph and his family all the support and protection they needed. They were pivotal to her long term plan.

"Things have escalated since I spoke to Maelströminha this morning Emanuel," Ralph placed the explosive device on the oak desk. "This was under my car."

Emanuel exhaled with a whistle.

"That's the sort of early morning call that you can do without," he ran his fingers through his mane of curly white hair as he thought about it. "So they have found you at last. We always knew that they would, just not this soon. You have to leave the house tonight, there's no question of it," Emanuel was thinking on his feet. "I have a safe house that you can go to. It's not so big but it's heavily guarded around the clock. Of course your children will need special schooling arrangements and you will need a reason for leaving your house so quickly."

Emanuel paused as he considered his options then raised his hand.

"I have it! Your development plans with me have fallen through and you are on hard times, bailiffs and all that. I will see to the schooling and your possessions. Oh, and you will need to change your cars. That should do for a start," almost as if in hind-sight Emanuel added. "Of course you must immediately get the old ornate mirror transported to your brother's house for safety. Its value to us is beyond measure."

"Yes, of course right away and thanks Emanuel, but that's the easy bit," Ralph had his head in his hands. "How do I break this to Jodie and the kids? How do I tell them that their world's been turned upside-down and that they have to leave everything they know and all of the people that they love?"

Ralph's mobile phone gave the message alert. He looked at the display, it was from Jodie and it simply said, "Love you x"

Chapter 4

Present day. Saturday, February 2013. Four years later.

Elizabeth Robinson stood in her Uncle's hallway in front of the magnificent full-length mirror. She examined herself closely as she had done so many times over the last four years. She had an athletic build, perhaps a bit lacking in curves but at last Elizabeth decided and with some pride, that she was growing up well. She was nearly eighteen now and the girl in her was all but gone.

Elizabeth had missed out on the last four years of her childhood; circumstances had dictated that. But who could have foreseen such a tragic accident? In just one moment all that joy and happiness was taken away from her. A cold chill went down her spine at the thought of just how devastating a single telephone call can be and had dreaded the phone ringing ever since. Of course she had to grow up immediately there was her younger brother Ben to consider.

"It's time for you to be a big girl now."

They had told her and she had never questioned it. Elizabeth recalled with regret that she hadn't properly grieved her parents' death, nor in truth, accepted it. Everything was all bottled up inside her and it was growing like a cancer.

Elizabeth tousled her shock of curly blonde hair and pulled it back harshly so that she could examine her face in the old ornate mirror more closely. Large green eyes shone like cut emeralds from her tanned face and her features were full and prominent. At last she concluded that she had something of her mother's beauty.

The truth was that she had inherited that and more. Elizabeth was charismatic and coupled with her father's focus and determination, was a force to contend with. But of course the accident had changed everything and she needed to be all those things, if not for her then for Ben. Benjamin was her younger brother by two years. Although nearly sixteen now, he was still very young for his age and Elizabeth had done her best to keep him so. The accident had affected him so badly that she protected him like a lioness does her cub. He hadn't yet come to terms with his loss and Elizabeth was determined to fill the gap left behind. After all she was now the only one he could really turn to.

"And I will be there," she vowed out loud to her reflection.

Elizabeth remembered the first weeks after the accident, how Ben wouldn't leave her side for fear of losing her too. Night after night she soothed and reassured him that everything would be alright. She never allowed herself to cry, so as not to show Ben how hopeless it really was.

Elizabeth remembered how her Aunt and Uncle and their friends used to praise her courage.

"Isn't Lizzie coping well? She's such a strong little thing and so good with Ben, you must be really proud of her."

None of them could see the emptiness in her soul, the desperate loneliness and despair that she was suffering in silence. Even before her parents had died, Elizabeth had the reoccurring nightmares but these had increased in regularity and severity since then. Now she couldn't even find solace in her sleep.

Then there was school. Nobody seemed to know what to say or do but then how could they? At first everybody tried but it soon became too much trouble and they got bored of it, all except Laura that is, lovely Laura, her only true friend.

She could feel that everybody was just waiting for her to get on with it, so she did.

"But that wasn't possible for Ben," Elizabeth reflected.

The two years difference in their ages was monumental. Ben just went into himself and took refuge in his own thoughts and memories, safe from any more pain and suffering; or so he thought.

Elizabeth's jaw hardened and a scowl took the beauty from her face. She recalled how the other children had seen his weakness and cruelly exploited it, making his already wretched life even more unbearable. She had even resorted to fighting the bullies in the playground, but then they just did it when her back was turned. Ben regressed still further into the emptiness of his own world. The pain of it all was just too much for her to bear. Sleep deprivation from the constant nightmares had weakened Elizabeth and her strength suddenly dissolved into fits of sobbing. She questioned her image in the mirror.

"But who's there to help me, I was a child too? I didn't deserve this and I just can't do it anymore. I can't be strong, not for me not even for Ben."

Desperation was mounting within her like the pressure in a volcano. Finally, Elizabeth broke down and the emptiness in her soul consumed her. She had never felt so alone, so desperate for someone to turn to.

After some time, Elizabeth's shoulders stopped shaking and she choked back her sobs. When she looked into the mirror once again, she was aghast at the transformation that had come over her. The womanly strength that she had seen only minutes before was all gone. Her green eyes had lost their shine and were limpid in red swollen sockets. A lost girl was looking back at her vulnerable and afraid. The room started to spin and Elizabeth began to lose consciousness. She reached forwards to support herself against the old mirror but felt no resistance there; her hands just seemed to pass through the glass.

Caring hands inexplicably grasped hers on the other side and Elizabeth thought she heard a familiar voice.

"You will be alright Lizzie and you will know what to do."

In her last moments of consciousness she looked up at the reflection in the mirror, but it wasn't hers.

"Mum!" she called out and then the darkness came.

It was late evening when Elizabeth awoke on the floor in front of the old mirror scrolled in gold, with carvings of cherubs clutching their bows and harps beaming down at her. A feeling of calmness and serenity came over her. She felt strong again, ready to go on but something had changed, changed forever and Elizabeth wasn't sure what that was.

"Lizzie, Ben, come down. Breakfast is ready and I am not calling you again!"

Aunt Jillie was not to be disobeyed. She was caring but rules were rules. There was no latitude to bargain and certainly none to be late. Elizabeth pulled back Ben's bedclothes and scalded him.

"Why do you do this to me every morning Ben? You know how much it upsets Aunt Jillie to be late."

Elizabeth was furious. It was always the same, just like being stuck in *Groundhog Day*.

Jillie and George were the closest family that Elizabeth and Ben had. Since the accident, George had adopted his brother's children out of duty but that had disrupted their own plans. Loving as they were, life was hard and Jillie was always conscious of how much she wanted her own children. Caring for someone else's just wasn't in her plan. George was constantly reminded of that.

"At last! Sit down the pair of you and eat your cereal. Eggs will be ready in a couple of minutes and George needs to leave in fifteen. That is with or without you."

George was the peacekeeper and responded as was expected of him.

"Come along you two and make haste, do as you are told," but he caught Elizabeth's eye and winked conspiratorially.

Elizabeth smiled back and remembered that it was just what her father used to do to keep the peace. The similarity was poignant and the emptiness and loss consumed her so that she had to turn away to hide her tears.

When they had finished breakfast, George was already in the car with the engine running. They were late as usual. Elizabeth was unusually quiet on the journey to school and George gauged how long to leave her before he spoke.

"I couldn't help but see your tears at breakfast this morning Lizzie, what's the matter?"

"It's nothing really Uncle just that sometimes, well sometimes I miss Mum and Dad so much that I just don't know what to do. It's simply horrid and I feel so guilty."

"Why should you feel guilty Lizzie, nothing's your fault."

"It is. I knew that they shouldn't have gone to see that house. We were happy where we were. I knew it and I didn't stop them so it's my fault."

Elizabeth burst into tears of remorse and George waited until she brought herself under control. He knew her well enough not to try reasoning with her until she was ready to listen again.

"Lizzie we've been over this time and time again, it's not your fault. Your father needed to find a smaller house, his business was struggling in these hard times and he was forced to look at down-sizing. It was unfortunate that's all."

George could see that his words were close to useless. Elizabeth was in a place of her own but he continued none the less.

"The big contract that he was depending on for the new town development would have made him a millionaire. It was such bad fortune that the man behind it, Emanuel Goldberg, died so unexpectedly. That money would've changed everything and they wouldn't have been driving to search for a new home. It's this dreadful economic downturn to blame Lizzie not you, definitely not you."

"Yes, of course Uncle, I know you're right."

Elizabeth capitulated to end the conversation but she didn't believe it; not at all. It would be four years ago tomorrow that her parents had taken them to be looked after at Uncle George's so that they could view their new house. She remembered her father enthusing about it to make them feel better, but she knew too that it was only window dressing.

"It's not as big as the house we have now but you will love it Lizzie. You will still have your own room and the garden is beautiful. Ben will sleep on a sofa-bed in the lounge until we can afford to extend the house and that won't be long. Things will get better soon I promise."

But it was an empty promise. Elizabeth could still clearly recall the dreadful feeling of foreboding that came over her, a premonition of disaster. It had filled her with dread and she had blurted out her fears to them.

"Don't go to see this house, don't go please! There's something terribly wrong about it all, I can't explain but you mustn't go, trust me please!"

Her father had tried to placate her.

"Lizzie it's understandable that you don't want to leave the house you've grown up in with all of the memories, but it's just a house. Nothing terrible is going to happen I promise. We'll make new memories in the new house, you'll see. Uncle George will look after the stables, nothing will really change."

She remembered her mother's embrace and what she had said.

"Don't fret darling its seven o'clock now and we'll be back in an hour or so. We'll talk all about it then so let's have no more nonsense."

With that her mother had kissed them goodbye, turned and walked with her father down the grand hallway to the open door. Elizabeth remembered that she was still mumbling the same words helplessly over and over again.

"Please don't go, please..."

Elizabeth had then turned her back to them to face the old ornate mirror that her father had hung there for safe keeping. The last time that she ever saw her parents alive, was their reflection in the mirror as they smiled back and walked towards the car and their deaths.

When Ralph and Jodie Robinson left their brother's house, Elizabeth was in tears and young Ben, completely bewildered by it all. Jodie was trying to stay upbeat for the children's sake, but when she had looked back at Elizabeth sobbing her heart out, it was more than she could bear.

"Oh Ralph, we can't leave her like this, I've never seen her so upset."

Ralph had to be firm. He had their security to consider now. He could no longer assume that they would be safe in their family home.

"Jodie, we have to. It breaks my heart too, but if we don't get the safe house set up quickly, then the consequence is unthinkable."

Ralph was insistent. Reluctantly Jodie turned away and they walked on to the car waving back at their children. They were silent for several miles. Ralph was deep in thought about how he was going to transition their lives to the new secure regime and Jodie, the eternal mother, how she could keep the family positive and happy.

She looked up at Ralph and saw his pained expression. He was exhausted by the guilt of what he had brought on the family but she knew that it was not of his making. He was only a chess piece on the board of a much greater game. They were just collateral damage in the grand scheme of things.

"Ralph, I do have faith."

Jodie had always supported Ralph's decisions and they always turned out to be good ones, in part because of her unerring support.

"I know that you will turn all this around and times will be good for us again. Stay strong for us Ralph. We need you to be that and more."

Jodie leaned across to kiss his cheek. Ralph turned his head to face her. She looked up into his deep blue eyes for the last time. Ralph was distracted and never saw the green sports car coming up behind them at breakneck speed. Just as they were taking the tight right-hand bend, along the canal bank, the green car veered in front of them clipping their front wing. It sent the Porsche spinning into the trees. The broken car somersaulted roof first into the canal, the glass burst and the car sank to the bottom of the canal instantly.

Chapter 5

Ben was at his desk. It was his third year at the Northlands Secondary School and he still hadn't fitted in. Academically he was top of his class, top of his year in fact. Ben excelled in sports too, well individual sports to be more precise. Here he was without challenge and had won numerous awards for field events, swimming, tennis, fencing, archery and the like. In fact, Ben's swordsmanship and archery skills had earned him a place in the county teams, where he would be competing against the under-sixteen's.

Team sports however were altogether a different thing. The problem was integration. Since the accident, Ben had become withdrawn and unable to relate to his classmates. They in turn had sensed a new weakness in him and in and exploited it. At first it was just unkind remarks but soon this turned into goading and pushing.

One day Luke Hemphry, Captain of the school under-sixteen's football team, took it a stage further. He forced Ben into a fight, expecting an easy win. He lost miserably and wore a pair of black eyes for two weeks afterwards. They kept their distance after that but then came the current phase, exclusion. Ben would have preferred that they continued to want to fight him, at least he could respond or deal with the pain afterwards, but this was the cruellest tactic of all and it deepened Ben's feelings of isolation. There was no possibility of joining in team games with these boys, so Ben put all his effort into what he could do and lost himself in his science, maths and individual sports, blotting out all else.

Ben's thoughts turned to Elizabeth. She had been so strong right from when they first received the terrible news of their parent's deaths.

Although Aunt Jillie had tried her hardest to fill the void, Ben had naturally turned to Elizabeth for comfort which had been a monumental burden on her.

There are moments that only happen occasionally in life where you suddenly see things clearly and in perspective. This was one of them for Ben. It was an epiphany. He was already two years older than Elizabeth was when the accident happened, but he was still depending on her for support. He conceded that it was time he stood up for himself and took on some of the responsibility. The decision lifted a great weight from his shoulders and Ben felt energised and positive by it. As he walked past the noticeboard on his way out of school, he put his name down on the football team list for the next day's Cup Final against Kingston.

"Fat chance of being chosen though," he thought, "but that'll shock the bastards!" Ben's sardonic smile said it all.

"Are you sure about this Ben?" Elizabeth questioned as she packed his football kit, "you hate all team sports, and anyway you can't play football. You'll make a fool of yourself in front of everybody including Auntie and Uncle."

Elizabeth knew that this was going to end badly and was cross with Ben for putting his head in the lion's mouth.

"Lizzie, I can play football, I just don't. It's never been about the football; it's been about the boys. They hate me, you know that."

Ben was completely matter of fact about it, not emotional as he always had been in the past.

"I don't want you to worry about me anymore Lizzie I can deal with this now."

Elizabeth fixed him with her big green eyes and challenged him.

"So what's changed Ben?"

"I have Lizzie; I've grown up at last. Believe it or not I just don't care, they can all go to Hell," Ben was resolute and clear minded. "If I don't play then they win anyway, like they always have."

Elizabeth studied him a little more closely than usual. Ben was strikingly handsome with blonde hair and the deepest blue eyes framed in a strong brow and high cheekbones. He was already showing muscle shape from his commitment to his individual sports. Yes, there was no doubt about it she concluded.

"Her girlfriends were going to just love him in a year or so."

She quickly decided that a certain amount of *management* would be necessary when that time came.

There was a difference in him though. His jaw was set purposefully and the boy in him seemed to have gone. Somehow Ben had suddenly matured. Elizabeth liked this newfound confidence in him and said no more. She just prayed that Saturday wouldn't be quite the disaster that it would likely turn out to be.

When they arrived at the Kingston football ground it was immediately apparent that this was regarded as an important event for the school. Kingston had won six out of the last eight Cup Finals, which was reflected in the amount of preparation that had gone into the day. Local businesses had contributed for a share of the prestige and a site for their advertising banners. This in turn, helped to fund their coach, who was a semi-professional footballer. All this put together, ensured that the Kingston supporters had turned out in strength, dwarfing the 30 or so from Northlands. It gave the home side a strong psychological advantage.

Elizabeth took her place on the Northlands' stand, along with her aunt and uncle while Ben went to join the other boys in the plush Kingston changing rooms. Mr Murphy, the senior sports master had succumbed reluctantly to the flu, so all responsibilities had fallen on David Williams, his junior. This had pleased the boys enormously. It was not that they disliked Mr Murphy, but everything about getting to the final was because of Mr Williams' hard work and devotion to the boys throughout the season.

The team congregated in the changing room, twelve of them. They were fielding a strong eleven so there was no chance that Ben would play. He got changed anyway and tried to ignore the whispering and sniggering.

"Stevie what a relief, I wasn't sure you were going to make it mate. How's your ankle?"

Luke wasn't expecting to see him and was more than just a little relieved. Stevie Moore was their midfielder and star player; to field a team without him would be unthinkable.

"More or less Luke, but I couldn't miss today's match could I? Otherwise you would've had to play *no-hoper* Ben."

A raucous laugh went around the changing room. Ben just busied himself tying his boots so that they couldn't see his pained expression. When Mr Williams entered he sensed the boy's anxiety. Pre-match nerves were setting in and there were no visible signs of confidence and self-belief.

"Well boys, the last time I saw you play you were a team with your eyes firmly set on winning the cup. Looking around now I just don't see that, perhaps you can tell me what's changed Luke?"

"Well sir Kingston look so professional, everything about them I mean, the ground, their supporters, even these changing rooms and they mostly win don't they sir?"

"Well they certainly will if you believe half of what you're saying Luke," Mr Williams needed to re-chip them. "Things aren't always as they seem boys. At the end of the day, it's how you stand up to them man for man and as a team. Don't let a fancy display of pomp and circumstance with money fool you into believing that they are your betters, they're not. I want you to think about how it felt to win the semi-final, about how well prepared you are; how hard you have trained and how much you want this."

Mr William's face changed and the boys were expecting him to say something profound.

"And after all that and you still feel that they are your superiors, just imagine them all sat on the toilet. That usually works for me!"

The boys fell about in laughter and the tension was immediately relieved. Luke took the moment and shouted his team on but somehow managed to exclude Ben in the doing of it. As Ben left the changing room, he had an inexplicable feeling that something had entered his spirit, buoying him up. He instinctively looked back at the smiling Mr Williams who seemed to say, without the need for words:

"You'll do just fine Ben."

A supernatural shiver went up Ben's back as he ran to take up his position on the substitute bench. He felt energised and positive, but he hadn't a clue why.

David Williams was acting as a Linesman for the day. He was immaculately turned out in his black kit and looked every inch an athlete. His muscular legs drove him effortlessly up the touchline, ready to take his position for the kick off. He was a tall, strongly built man with broad shoulders and a trim waist. Without any exaggeration, he was strikingly handsome. He sported a strong chin, black hair, engaging smile and the most amazing blue eyes. All the young mothers in the Northlands' stand were watching him and turned to each other conspiratorially, giggling like they were schoolgirls themselves. Aunt Jillie turned to Elizabeth discretely.

"Your Mr Williams is a bit of a hunk isn't he?"

"Auntie!" exclaimed Elizabeth, "what a thing to say!"

Then she paused, smiled guiltily and whispered over the back of her hand.

"Yes, he is rather," and blushed in her shame which made Jillie laugh openly.

Kingston came on at the outset with unstoppable force and scored in the first minute. It was only good goal keeping and dependable Stevie, dropping back from midfield to lend support that kept the opposition at bay. The inevitable happened. Kingston broke through yet again to get their second goal in the 20th minute. It all seemed pretty hopeless by then.

Northlands had no answer to the unrelenting force of Kingston, particularly for their centre forward. He was a brute of a boy that cut through the Northlands' players like a charging bull. He was breaking through again, when Stevie went in bravely for the tackle. It was like

David meeting Goliath. Stevie's already weakened ankle gave way and he cartwheeled over and over screaming as he went. The spectators could see instantly that it was a serious injury and a hush came over them.

"Dammit!" Luke Hemphry was stamping around and cursing. "That's the cup gone for sure. There's no coming back from 2-0 down in the first half and certainly not without a midfielder like Stevie."

"Is your substitute ready Northlands?" the referee shouted across to the bench.

At the wave of David Williams' hand, Ben got up and jogged over to his team.

"Christ, don't pass the ball to him," was all that Luke could offer by way of comment to his crest-fallen mates.

Ben had been watching from the bench as the minutes of his opportunity ticked by. His decision to play had been huge for him and it had to be now or never. He had seen the big centre forward breaking free again, and the slim, agile frame of Stevie running gallantly in to stop him. Ben immediately saw Stevie's predicament.

"Don't meet him head on Stevie he's huge, take his flank!"

It was too late. Stevie had already committed himself to the tackle and the noise of the collision was heard at all four corners of the field. The difference in their sizes was too great. Stevie looked like he'd been hit by a truck andhe crowd went silent.

As Stevie's broken body was carried off, David Williams waved Ben on to take up the midfield position. Kingston immediately came on with new vigour, knowing that they had taken out a key player. They were breaking through yet again. Their winger's pass into the Northlands' penalty area was precision, finding their centre forward in mid-stride.

Ben saw the move as it started and raced in for the tackle. His turn of speed, honed from the track events that he excelled in, was incredible to watch. He went in full slide, taking the ball cleanly from the burly centre forward's boot and safely out of play, saving an inevitable goal.

Ben was covering two thirds of the pitch, running into free spaces in the Kingston's side to attack, then back to reinforce the struggling defence when needed. It was futile though, as they had united in excluding him from the game.

Two minutes before half time, Kingston pushed all their players forward to go for a killer goal, knowing that Northlands would never come back from three down in the first half. It was then that Ben intercepted the ball and saw his chance. In their will to inflict the final blow, Kingston had left themselves exposed. Ben had only two players between him and the goal. His turn of speed was too much for the Kingston backs as he raced through them. When Ben struck the ball, it was with all the pent up anger and frustration of four years of bullying. The shot was unstoppable and the goalkeeper's arms never even left his sides.

Ben was immediately mobbed by his team. They were ruffling his hair, slapping his back and shouting praise.

Luke pushed through and took Ben in a bear hug.

"That was awesome Ben, we can still win this!"

Ben looked Luke in the eye as his equal.

"That depends if you want to carry on playing ten men against eleven, doesn't it?"

When Elizabeth saw Ben take to the field, she clasped her hands so tightly that her nails drew blood. She saw how eagerly he took up the call to play, but wondered how she would pick up the pieces afterwards.

To her amazement Ben's authority was immediate. His sliding tackle against the Kingston centre forward was breath taking and a pivotal moment in the game. It was inspirational and it rallied the other players.

"Where did all this suddenly come from?" she puzzled.

Elizabeth was even more dismayed when Ben broke through the Kingston defence to score a spectacular goal. Then it simply beggared belief when he was subsequently mobbed by his ecstatic team. She furrowed her brow and turned to her Aunt Jillie.

"I just don't understand the male of the species, Auntie. Four years of persecution all ends in a game of football?"

Jillie put her arm around Elizabeth shaking her head.

"Lizzie, you never will. If you ever do, then please tell me!"

They looked at each other and burst out laughing, just as the half-time whistle blew.

Mr Williams huddled his team in a circle. They had their arms around each other's shoulders.

"Right boys," he began. "That was a fantastic finish to a miserable first

half. You let Kingston dictate the game and it cost you two goals and

quite possibly the match."

Mr Williams had their full attention, every boy was eager to go back out there and turn the game around.

"Go back out and take control. Their strength is all in their forward play. If you take the game into their half then you neutralise that big centre forward of theirs. Come at them hard straight from the whistle and get the ball up to Luke and Ben."

The team talk proved inspirational and Northlands did just that and Kingston had no answer for it. Ben's cross from the right wing was perfect and it found Luke head who headed it in effortlessly. The scores were even. Apart from a few worrying moments, and a near miss when the Kingston centre forward hit the Northlands' crossbar, the game stayed with Luke's side. In the final moments Ben broke free in much the same way as before and thundered the ball into the back of the Kingston net. The goalkeeper kicked the ground petulantly and the final whistle blew.

What ensued took Elizabeth's completely by surprise. The Northlands' boys ran to Ben and hoisted him in the air carrying him off the field chanting their victory song. Mr Williams let the boys have their moment and went around selflessly congratulating the proud parents. When he got to the Robinsons he had nothing but praise for Ben.

"Man of the Match, you must be delighted," Mr Williams offered. "If ever we needed a boy to find form it was today and Ben timed that pretty well."

George answered for them all.

"Yes we're very proud, and quite honestly, staggered. Ben's shown no interest in any of the team sports before, so quite how this has come about is quite a shock really."

Mr Williams flashed his brilliant smile.

"I think his interest in team sports is about to change and I can't wait to see what he does on the cricket pitch this summer."

Mr Williams left them with that perfect smile. Like all those that had enjoyed his special way of engaging with them, they felt just slightly bereft. There was something inexplicably different about this un-extraordinary, gentle man.

The Robinsons pulled out through the grand wrought iron gates onto the main road heading home. Traffic conditions were light for the time of day and George was able to relax and enjoy the drive. The post-match atmosphere in the car was distracting. George inadvertently chose the route home that took them by the site of the fatal accident, down by the canal. Normally he would have avoided this road because of the sad memories and heartache. George was listening intently to Ben's story as they approached the tight right-hand bend down by the canal bank. He never saw the green sports car coming up rapidly behind them.

David Williams opened the door of his white hot-hatch, threw his kit bag onto the passenger seat and slid in behind the steering wheel. The Robinsons had just turned out of the car park and he was about to follow. A green sports pulled out suddenly from one of the parking bays and sped off after the Robinsons. He'd only seen the drivers face for a split second but it was a face that he knew only too well. Mrs Hyde. It meant that the Robinsons were in mortal danger.

The powerful turbo-charged engine caught at the turn of the key and revved eagerly. He shifted into first gear and left the car park with light wheel spin in pursuit of the other cars. The traffic lights turned red. Mr

Williams cursed his luck, losing considerable ground to the green sports car. It wasn't until he cleared the town that he could use the brute power of the rally tuned engine to close the gap between them. The Subaru responded eagerly to the throttle and the sure-footed sports suspension made light work of the torturous bends as Mr Williams took the racing line through each. As he mounted the brow of the hill that lead down to the canal, he could see the green sports car ahead tailgating the Robinson's car. He dropped down the gearbox and redlined the engine closing the gap rapidly.

The green sports car pulled out to overtake the Robinsons and execute the same killer move that it had done to perfection four years earlier. At that moment, Mr Williams rammed into its rear kerb-side quarter at over 100 mph. The green car spun round several times with tyres smoking until it came to rest in the middle of the road facing the other direction, Then, with wheels burning rubber, it sped off back towards the town.

The impact put the Subaru into an uncontrollable skid that Mr Williams fought hopelessly to control. His car left the highway at over 80 mph, ramming into the canal bridge abutment. Seconds later it burst into flames. Mr Williams was killed outright.

The Robinsons arrived at the family home totally unaware of the fatal accident and the danger that they had been in. Ben ran on ahead to take a shower, dropped his kit-bag in the entrance hall and walked up to the old mirror. When he looked at his reflection, he hardly recognised himself. The boy looking back at him was happy and confident.

Ben's thoughts turned to his parents. He smiled and spoke out loud as if they were there.

"You would've both been proud of me today."

He turned and walked away but could've sworn that he heard his father's voice.

"We are Ben, we are."

He spun around startled and looked back at the old mirror. Instead of seeing his own reflection he saw his parents. They were walking out through the front door towards their car, smiling back at him, just as they had done the last time that he had seen them four years ago.

The remembrance service was held on the following Sunday. The Robinsons attended, along with most of the families from the school. Such was the popularity of this gentle man, that many from the village had turned out to pay their respects too. Most everybody had been touched by the grace of David Williams in one way or another. The only noticeable absentee was Mrs Hyde, Elizabeth's much hated music teacher.

Chapter 6

It was Sunday morning four years to the day after the accident. They had breakfasted early and driven to the cemetery to place flowers at Elizabeth and Ben's parents' well-tended graves.

Elizabeth was arranging the flowers in the silver vases whilst the rest of the family knelt by her side. Each was deeply involved with their personal thoughts and memories. There was a feeling of deep calm and finality about the place and, although their hearts were grieving, soft caring smiles were on their faces. When she had the flowers to her liking, Elizabeth looked up at Uncle George. Her voice was soft and soulful.

"Where did the old mirror in the hallway come from Uncle? I mean I know that it was in our house until the day of the accident but where before then?"

"What a strange question to ask Lizzie, especially at a time like this."

Uncle George's response was slightly guarded, as if he knew something, but was reluctant to say.

"Well, as you know it was your father's. It's been in the Robinson family for generations and dates back to the late 17th century, apparently."

Elizabeth was already intrigued, absorbing every word.

"It's believed to have been crafted by Grinling Gibbons, a famous sculptor of his time."

George was beginning to enjoy the telling of the story. There is something deeply satisfying about being authoritative.

"Gibbons was a master carver to King George the first. He worked for Sir Christopher Wren on St Paul's Cathedral and for many other famous people of that time. It's worth a small fortune actually."

Uncle George was clearly proud of its heritage, not to mention his knowledge of it.

"Traditionally it's been passed on to the first born in the family. That makes it yours now Lizzie. I was only keeping it until such time that you have your own house. I just hope you get one with a room big enough to take it!"

It was almost as big as a doorway and few places other than a grand hallway could ever support it.

"Your father hung it in our hallway for safe-keeping the morning before the accident. One day it will belong to you and your children Lizzie."

Elizabeth was struggling with the logic of her father having to down-scale their family home when he was sitting on such a valuable antique.

"If it's worth so much, then why didn't Dad sell it to have money to keep our home?"

"Well I 'm not sure that it is worth quite that much Lizzie. Besides, your father would never have parted with it. The old mirror was very special to him. I can remember as a boy, after our father died, that he would sit for hours in front of it, almost in a trance. He seemed to be lost somewhere deep in thought and you couldn't talk to him at all, it was very strange."

Elizabeth was putting the first pieces of the puzzle together. There was something very special about the mirror she knew that for sure now. Her father was the mirror's Guardian as were his forefathers for many hundreds of years. She deduced that this responsibility, whatever it was, had now passed to her.

"It will be my responsibility but why and what must I do?" Elizabeth wondered. Her eyes widened in astonishment as the enormity of it hit her. "So I did see something!"

Elizabeth had a feeling of great foreboding. It was a strange mixture of excitement and deep dread. She needed to know more but she kept her tone nonchalant.

"Have you ever found anything strange about the old mirror Uncle?"

"No Lizzie it's just a very old and very beautiful mirror. Come on we must be going now it's getting late."

Elizabeth could tell that Uncle George was holding back but she decided not to push it and followed him obediently to the car. Nobody had seen the look on Ben's face when Elizabeth had asked Uncle George about the mirror. The colour had drained out of him at the very shock of it.

"What have you seen Lizzie! Why are you asking these questions?" Ben wondered.

If Lizzie had seen something too, then there was more to his experience with the old mirror than just his imagination playing tricks on him. The exchange between Elizabeth and George had caused all but Jillie to reflect on the possibilities. The journey home afterwards was in virtual silence.

When they arrived at the Robinson's house Jillie gave them their orders.

"Get changed and straight down for dinner please. It's already prepared. We can eat and then relax over some rubbish TV and maybe watch a film together?"

Ben was desperate to talk to Lizzie alone but what he had to say was private and couldn't be rushed. The long leisurely family evening was almost more than he could bear. It was nearly ten o'clock before they all retired and went to their separate rooms. Ben waited until his Uncle and Aunt were asleep before creeping along the corridor to Elizabeth's room. He pushed the door open and whispered cautiously.

"Lizzie, are you awake?"

"Yes Ben, I can't sleep either it's been an emotional day hasn't it? You can lie down and fall asleep here if you're upset."

"I'm not upset Lizzie. Today was sad but it's not that, it's not that at all."

Ben didn't know how to even begin to explain. It was all so preposterous. Elizabeth was going to think that he had gone stark raving mad.

"What is it Ben?" Elizabeth was becoming concerned and panic was starting to stir in her stomach. "What have you done? Come on Ben tell me!"

"I haven't done anything Lizzie. It's about you and the old mirror. What did you see?"

The shock of Ben's question hit Elizabeth like a physical blow that rocked her sensibility, reducing her to a mumbling fool. She hadn't expected her private thoughts to go public.

"Well nothing really; I mean something but I'm not sure Ben. I was dizzy and it was probably nothing at all. Just nonsense I suppose."

"What did you see Lizzie? Focus please, I need to know."

Ben was forcing her to come clean about it. She began to cry as she tried to come to terms with it.

"Well I was standing in front of the old mirror looking at how much I had changed since the accident," the tears were streaming down her face, "I started to think about how much I missed Mum and Dad and how I couldn't cope any longer..."

The tears turned to sobs and it was a while before she could speak again.

"Yes, and?" Ben prompted.

"And the room started to spin. I felt feint and reached out to steady myself against the mirror. Then, the strangest thing happened. My hands just went through it somehow, like it was water, not glass."

Ben took Elizabeth gently by the shoulders. He could see that she was in distress. The colour had gone from her face. She looked tragic, totally lost, but he needed answers.

"Come on finish it Lizzie; you'll feel better afterwards I promise."

Ben felt guilty for pressing her but he had to make her go through with it. He had to know.

Elizabeth took a deep breath.

"Just before I passed out I felt Mum take my hands and saw her face in the mirror, not mine. She said that I would be all right and that I would know what to do."

Ben held her for some time while she fought to recover her calm. Eventually the shadows in her mind receded and she was lucid again.

"Thanks for listening Ben and I do feel much better for telling you. Now it's your turn, tell me why you asked the question in the first place."

Ben collected his thoughts. His emotions were running high too and it wasn't going to be easy for him either, particularly after experiencing Elizabeth's emotional outburst.

"Well like you Lizzie, I'm not sure what I saw. When we got home from the football match I was still really excited about the game and how everything seemed to have changed for me. As I walked up to the old mirror I felt a compelling urge to stop and look into it. I remember saying out loud that Mum and Dad would've been proud of me and then I turned away."

Ben welled up at the memory of it. Elizabeth stroked his hair and waited patiently for him to recover enough to continue. She appeared calm but her head was also in turmoil. The big sister inside her instinctively came out to soothe her brother.

"As I walked away I thought I heard Dad's voice. I turned around but the reflection in the old mirror wasn't me, it was Mum and Dad that I saw. They were smiling at me from the doorway just like they did when they left the house for the very last time, four years ago."

They lay in silence for some time. Each wanted to talk more about their experience but the telling of it had drained them. They eventually slipped into a deep dreamless sleep.

Chapter 7

Elizabeth was sat at her desk in the music room. She hated Monday mornings as they started with a double lesson of music. Three hours of pure misery. It wasn't that Elizabeth hated music, far from it. Four years ago, music was her passion. Her music teacher, Miss Crystal, was an inspiration to her and she lived for music then. Elizabeth had thrived off the positive energy and nurture that Miss Crystal brought in abundance.

Elizabeth could still clearly picture her. She was petite, blonde and extremely pretty with the amazing blue eyes that shone with joy and energy. Miss Crystal had recognised the musical potential in her. She had dedicated a lot of her personal time in and out of school to tutor her. It wasn't for money, just for the pleasure that it gave her to teach. Miss Crystal had managed to breach that divide between tutor and pupil to become one of Elizabeth's most favourite and valued friends.

Miss Crystal had left the school suddenly and with no explanation. Her house had been rudely emptied, rent left unpaid and nobody had heard from her again. Her replacement turned up the very next day, Mrs Hyde. An obnoxious, women direct from the jaws of Hell. The very moment that she entered the classroom, her eyes had sought out Elizabeth fixing her with an almost satanic glare. That was about as good as it got. This was the bitch that couldn't even be bothered to go to Mr Williams' funeral.

"Elizabeth!" Mrs Hyde had sought her out again, "I don't know why you bother turning up; I really don't. You have the musical talent of a deaf oaf and this homework could've come from a child with severe learning difficulties. I shall recommend yet another spell of detentions and have your parents made aware of the futility of your education."

Her cold dark eyes were like those of a killer shark and were fixed on Elizabeth. Even the class could feel the hatred that she had for her.

"Whatever you say Mrs Hyde."

Elizabeth returned her glare with equal hatred. She had to concede though, that Mrs Hyde was a strikingly beautiful and elegant woman. This undeniable fact only served to make her hatred even more intense.

She had come to terms with the fact that she could never change things but vowed that Mrs Hyde would pay for it one day. Elizabeth relaxed her face and just smiled back. The rage in Mrs Hyde mounted to demonic at Elizabeth's unashamed insolence which made Elizabeth's smile just that little bit wider.

As Mrs Hyde turned and stomped back to her desk Elizabeth felt a prod in her back. She turned to see Laura, her best friend. She was pulling a face with her fingers up by her ears portraying an ugly devil. They got the giggles and had to press their mouths into their sleeves and didn't dare look at each other again. Laura had befriended Elizabeth after the accident and helped her through the initial hard times. Elizabeth simply didn't know what she would have done without her. They were totally different but complimented each other well. Laura was a free spirit, spontaneous and never considered the consequence of things.

"She was surely going to be a nightmare for her parents and soon," Elizabeth had to admit.

In contrast Elizabeth was more mature and responsible but this was as she had to be. She needed Laura's carefree and unconditional love to give her the strength to go forward; just as Laura needed Elizabeth's stability and loyalty to keep her on the rails.

It was in the early hours of the morning that Elizabeth woke to the same reoccurring nightmare. She grabbed the bed-side table lamp and fumbled for the switch. Elizabeth breathed a sigh of relief when the harsh light flooded the room. It was always the same dream. She was being stalked through dark foggy streets by some sinister man. Each dream that she had took her closer and closer to being caught by him.

Elizabeth was dreading the night that would surely come, when he would get her in her sleep, the only place that she couldn't protect herself. The dreams were so real. Elizabeth even knew what he what he would look like, how he would smell and how he would speak. She even believed that she would die when that happened, if not from the event, then the fear of it.

The house was silent, but the silence was deafening. Elizabeth's head was in turmoil but not just from the dream; she had to talk more about the old mirror with Ben. Neither she nor Ben had mentioned it again during the past week. Both were trying to come to terms with the phenomenon. Elizabeth slipped out of bed, took her dressing gown and left her room. As she turned around in the corridor she came face to face with Ben.

"Jesus Ben! You frightened the life out of me."

It was more than a normal fright, as the memory of the stalker in her dreams was still vividly on her mind.

"Sorry Lizzie but we have to talk. Are you ready to do that yet?"

"Yes Ben, more than ready. I was on my way to see you in fact. Let's go downstairs so we don't wake up Auntie and Uncle."

Elizabeth and Ben stood in front of the old mirror not knowing what to expect. They were strangely relaxed though but held hands to give them a bit more courage. Elizabeth broke the silence.

"It's really beautiful isn't it Ben? Just look at the cherubs with their harps and bows and the ornate scrolling. It looks too perfect to be cut and shaped by man. How much love and care must have gone into carving it?"

"Yes it is perfect Lizzie, but maybe too perfect," something about its perfection was worrying Ben. "I know it's hundreds of years old, because Uncle George said so and the style of it. But there's not a mark or blemish on it Lizzie. Not a chip or a crack to the guilt frame and the glass is so clear that it could be new, or not even there at all." Ben's hand tightened on Elizabeth's in awe, "That can't be possible Lizzie, can it?"

"Do you feel safe Ben?"

Elizabeth was unable to take her eyes off their reflection in the old mirror.

"I think so, but only because I have you with me, I'm not sure I'd want to be here alone though."

Elizabeth was serenely calm.

"Good because I think we're about to go on a journey Ben. I don't know how, where or why but we are going; you can be sure of that," Elizabeth paused for a moment while she thought on it. "And I think it's going to be a roller-coaster ride!"

Chapter 8

Elizabeth never went back to bed that night for fear of the menace that stalked her in her dreams. Instead she went down to the stables to tend the horses, just as she had done most every morning since she was eight years old. The Robinson brothers had been keen equestrians even as children and had inherited the stables upon their father's death, before Elizabeth was even born.

Jodie, Elizabeth's mother, had devoted much of her spare time into developing her children's horsemanship. It wasn't without some success. They had earned numerous awards, rosettes and trophies.

Elizabeth had instantly shown natural aptitude and soon became a known rider in the local community. It had become an expectation that she would be in the top three at almost any event.

Ben had his successes too but he was more drawn to his sword fencing and archery. More recently kart racing and motorcycles had become his passion, and any aspirations of horsemanship had gone by the wayside.

Tending the horses was no task for Elizabeth though. To her, it was an act of pure love that gave her peace and satisfaction. George and Jillie had decided to keep the horses after the accident as a distraction for the children. To Elizabeth she still had a complete family in them and she looked fondly at her charges. There was her father's magnificent black stallion. Like him, *Knight* was a risk taker; focussed and independent.

"You are he," she whispered in his ear.

Knight nuzzled her, seeming to sense her thoughts. Then there was *Ellie* a gentle, dependable and loving Bay.

"Just like Mother."

Elizabeth concluded and hugged her neck, causing Ellie to whinny and shake her elegant head.

Then there were the young mare and stallion born of them. They were almost cloned to look at and in their nature. Elizabeth remembered how she and Ben had been given the enormous honour of naming them.

"A very important responsibility," she had told young Ben. "They will be blessed or cursed with the names we give them for all of their lives, we must choose well."

Elizabeth had named the mare *Beauty* after much thought and had to discourage Ben from choosing names such as *Megatron* and *Terminator*. Eventually he settled on *Laser*, which was about as much as she could have hoped for really.

Elizabeth took some apple slices and tempted them over.

"And you are us and all that could have been my darlings."

A tear ran down Elizabeth's cheek at the family comparison and she wiped it away with the back of her hand.

Elizabeth led Beauty to the stables and tacked her up, paying great attention to every detail. All the kit had been meticulously prepared as if ready to show, such was Elizabeth's total devotion to Beauty. She mounted in one fluid move and trotted her out of the yard towards the bridle path that led down to the canal. Elizabeth was wearing her well pressed jodhpurs and riding jacket, looking every inch the consummate equestrienne.

It was almost a twenty minute canter down to the canal. Elizabeth did this route when she was feeling sad. It took her past the bend in the road where the fatal accident had taken place. The ride helped her to come to terms with the finality of it all. Elizabeth stopped by the water's edge, as she had done many times before and dismounted. She set Beauty free to graze while she collected her thoughts. It was normal at this point that her emotions would well up inside her and she would find release in the tears that followed. To Elizabeth's surprise the tears never came. Instead, she had that same feeling of total calm and serenity she had felt when she had woken on the floor in front of the old ornate mirror, and again when she had stood in front of it with Ben.

It was three o'clock Saturday afternoon, the week following David Williams' remembrance service. Elizabeth had done her duties at the stables. Today though, she had treated herself to an exhilarating hours gallop with Beauty along the Ridge, a scenic bridle path overlooking the Robinson's stables.

The thrill had gone some way to relieving the sadness that was in her soul, since the death of Mr Williams. Elizabeth's face was still flushed with the exertion and exhilaration of it, as she and Ben stood in front of the old ornate mirror. Uncle George and Aunt Jillie had gone out for the afternoon, so they had the house to themselves.

They were both charged with a heady cocktail of fear and excitement. It was Ben who took the lead this time.

"Mum said that you would know what to do Lizzie."

"But I don't Ben, I've no idea."

Elizabeth touched the mirror gently and traced her reflection with her finger. She pressed harder and harder until she feared that the glass might break.

"It's solid Ben and all I see in it is us."

Ben started to feel around the frame. His hands were exploring the scrolls and features but there was nothing strange about it except its cleanliness.

"Nothing could possibly be this clean Lizzie and your fingers haven't even left even the faintest fingerprint on the glass."

Elizabeth leaned forwards and breathed out heavily on the mirror.

"It doesn't mist either Ben."

Ben was trying desperately to summon the logic that he'd gained through numerous scientific experiments that he had excelled in at school.

"So we need to know what the difference was when we had our experiences compared to now, then we will have the key."

"What we both had in common Ben!" Elizabeth exclaimed it was all coming together in her head. "That's it. We were both highly emotional at the time. Our emotions are the key Ben, you were really happy and I was really sad. It has to be that."

Ben nodded in agreement and Elizabeth continued.

"OK let's try happy Ben. I'm going to try to fill my head with the joy that I felt this morning galloping Beauty along the Ridge, you try reliving the Cup Final and how it felt to win."

They closed their eyes and let the memories and feelings come rushing back to them. Their relaxed happy faces looked just like the cherubs looking down on them from the mirror's frame. Elizabeth placed her hand on the mirror and it responded to her touch. It started as a light vibration increasing in intensity until the surface of the mirror felt fluid but it still resisted her.

"It's not enough Ben we need to do this together take my hand," it was intuitive; two minds being stronger than one.

Ben took Elizabeth's hand with complete faith. The mirror simply melted away and they walked through it."

Chapter 9

They found themselves in a brightly lit corridor with a highly polished metal floor, walls and ceiling. There were mirrors on both sides identical in size but differing in styles, many dozens of them. They turned to face their mirror and looked back into the empty hallway of the Robinson's house. They had no reflections themselves, it was just like looking through a window. Elizabeth touched the glass and was reassured when she felt the vibration increasing the longer that she did so.

"I think we can get back Ben," Elizabeth said more confidently than she actually felt, "but we're here for a reason and we have to find out what that reason is."

They explored the corridor. It was open at both ends and they could see the sky at each. There were exactly 100 mirrors but 60 of them were broken; no glass just gaping black holes. They could feel the air rushing into them and sensed that they shouldn't get too close. Elizabeth took Ben's arm protectively.

"Stay away from the broken ones Ben, I have a bad feeling about them."

The others were like windows into rooms of contrasting types, some looking like a bygone era and others futuristic in style. In some they could see people going about their daily lives. Ben waved at two children dressed in cotton smocks. They were playing on a scrubbed stone floor in front of an open fire, but there was no response.

"They can't see us Lizzie."

Ben touched the mirror and felt the glass start to vibrate. He took his hand away quickly and felt the hair on the back of his neck stand up with the fear of it.

"Don't touch anything Ben, not until we understand more."

Elizabeth could see that the experience had scared him and he nodded back at her in silent agreement.

It was fascinating. They soon concluded that each mirror was looking into a different time and place. There were oriental rooms with magnificent drapes and carvings, a stone hallway with suits of armour and weaponry of the time of the Crusades. Another looked into an Egyptian temple in the time of the Pharaohs, where a Priestess was anointing a bearded man dressed in a gold embroidered loin cloth. There were many more besides, each with its own story to tell.

It was like living history with a glimpse of the future. One of the mirrors looked into a room that could have been set in a science fiction movie. It was geometric in style, with the simple use of black, white and grey decoration. Strong primary colours had been strategically used to create warmth and depth to the room and the furniture was contoured to fit the shape of the human body. The family were dressed in one-piece loose garments in pastel colours and seemed to be talking to each other with expressions rather than words. Ben was particularly impressed as it appealed to his love of science. He was trying to work out what the electronic game was that the children were playing as they seemed to be *in* the game themselves and not just watching it. He looked on in awe.

"I wonder where and when they are Lizzie."

Elizabeth simply shrugged and shook her head in astonishment. She couldn't even begin to guess. They continued their circuit of the mirrors, standing well back from the broken ones, until they came back to the old ornate mirror. Elizabeth looked in and gasped with shock at what she saw and the colour drained instantly from her face.

"It's me Ben, it's me!"

They could see Elizabeth looking back at them in the mirror with her hair scraped back deep in thought. She looked sad and lost, and then began to cry. She was shaking her head and muttering something. Elizabeth already knew what she was going to say. They were the same words that she had used being repeated back to her.

"But who's there to help me, I was a child too?" the girl in the reflection said. "I didn't deserve this and I just can't do it anymore; I can't be strong, not for me not even for Ben..."

"Oh my God Lizzie it is you! Look you're heartbroken."

The image of Elizabeth started to sway. Her head began to roll around as she began to pass out, falling towards the mirror. To their disbelief, the image's hands passed through into the corridor. Elizabeth calmly took them and said soothingly and without thought, the same words that she had heard herself that day.

"You will be alright Lizzie and you will know what to do."

Elizabeth's image looked Elizabeth directly in the face and shouted back at her.

"Mum!"

Then she passed out and slid to the floor in the Robinson's hallway.

Elizabeth's jaw dropped in astonishment.

"Ben that was exactly what happened to me a few weeks ago. Maybe it was my face that I saw in the mirror and my voice not Mum's. Oh God Ben, what's happening to us?"

They looked back into the old mirror and saw only the empty hallway of the Robinson's house.

"I don't know Lizzie, I really don't know."

They held hands for strength and walked down the corridor towards the fading light outside. They were both charged with dreadful anticipation.

When they stepped out into the balmy night air it was filled with the most beautiful music and singing that they had ever heard. The night sky was lit by a storm of colours rolling in waves from the ridge in front of them where the music coming from. They were no longer afraid. The spectacle was somehow comforting and they were drawn to it. When they looked over the ridge they were met with the most wondrous vision imaginable.

A young woman was sat on the rock in front of them. The skin on her naked and lithe body was encrusted with jewels that emitted light in every colour of the rainbow. The light pulsed with the beat of the music, increasing and decreasing in intensity according to the mood. Her black hair was like a thick rope swept over her shoulder, falling to her slim waist. Her face was finely sculpted with high cheekbones and her eyes changed to every possible hue of blue with the music. From her full mouth, came a song so lyrical that it was enchantment itself. Her long fingers were playing an instrument that was not unlike a lute, but had strings of light.

The maiden slid from the rock like a serpent and began to dance. Her sinuous movements blended with the music, song and lights to become the greatest show on Earth, if indeed that was where they were.

Elizabeth and Ben were totally absorbed in the woman's performance and watched in awe. When the girl finally stopped, they felt bereft; both wanted it to go on. She came towards them without a hint of shyness, despite her nakedness. She was smiling openly at them and her walk had a natural sway about it, like that of a sensuous supermodel.

"Hello Lizzie, Ben. I've waited a long time to meet you," her voice was sweet and she purred like a cat. You can call me May; my given name would be too hard on your tongue at this stage."

"You have waited," questioned Elizabeth, "for how long?"

The girl answered with a dismissive wave of her bejewelled hand as if time had no consequence.

"In your years, more than 300; ever since one of your ancestors first became Guardian of the old mirror."

"Why would you have waited for us and for so long?"

Elizabeth could sense that they were in no danger from this creature and felt both in awe and at ease to talk with her.

"Because you are our hope for the future; a phenomenon such as you is a rare occurrence among us."

The intense light from her skin of jewels had calmed to an aurora that cycled through the spectrum of colours. Elizabeth pondered the implications of May's use of the word *us* but that was for later.

"And who are you May and why are we your hope for the future?"

"I am just one of the many visitors that have been coming to your planet for more than 100 million years; since times before man, when the dinosaurs walked your Earth. Our civilisation now faces destruction unless we have renewal. Your part in that renewal will become clear in time."

Ben was already mesmerised by this woman and it was his love of science that prompted his question.

"A visitor from where and why were you interested in our planet?"

"We are from the planet Angelos in the Galaxy of Andromeda, 2.6 million light-years from your Earth."

May's voice was musical even in speech.

"At first it was only curiosity, but your planet had such possibilities for us. It was like ours, only in its infancy. Our planet was in an asteroid belt and so we were constantly scanning the universe for planet killers; asteroids that could take out our world. In our search we found one that was on a path to destroy yours."

Elizabeth suddenly realised that May had stopped talking but the words were arriving in her head without the movement of her lips. For some reason that didn't seem strange at all. May continued with her lyrical story.

"An asteroid called Baptistina, measuring 100 of your miles across, was on collision course with Earth. It would have taken your planet out of orbit and into deep space, killing all life. We couldn't let that happen, so we used nuclear warheads to destroy Baptistina. Only fragments of her impacted your Earth, but with catastrophic effect; the dust cloud chocked the atmosphere blocking out your sun's rays, cooling the Earth and ending the reign of the dinosaurs. That was 60 million years ago."

"And you have been here since then?" Ben asked incredulously.

May looked sad and she immediately stopped emitting light.

"No Ben, we came and went over the millennia. Ironically, some 5,000 years ago our planet Angelos was in the path of an unstoppable asteroid called Obsidian. It was another planet killer the size of your moon. Before Obsidian hit, 300 of us were sent to your Earth where we have lived amongst you ever since. Orphans, all of us."

Elizabeth could feel the sadness that had come over May in the telling of her story. The fact that her skin had stopped transmitting light was clearly linked to her mood. Elizabeth instinctively took her in an embrace. Somehow that act of intimacy seemed quite natural.

"Can you tell us about the old mirror May?"

May considered her response carefully before she spoke.

"Before you can understand the present and the future, you must first understand the past and where you came from."

The light was returning to her skin and the smile to her face.

"I have much to tell you but humans receive information too slowly. You use only a narrow band of communication through your voice and ears. We must do it as Angels from the lost planet of Angelos have done for millennia. At first you will not follow the data flow but I will show you how."

May began to dance and sing to the music of her lute. Her body began to glow and it lit the night sky like the aurora borealis. Elizabeth and Ben began to feel the information entering their minds as May performed 5,000 years of history in just five hours.

She told of happy times on her planet where all things were in balance. There were two species of man on Angelos; the Angels of whom she was one, a light hearted and compassionate people, and the Shadow, or Shadows as they became to be known. They were refugees selected from the doomed planet Shado in their solar system. They were much fewer in number and had a dark-side to their personality that the Angels had kept in check through millions of years of correction.

The power in their sun was burning low and so expeditions into deep space were necessary to find a suitable planet and secure life for the future. Earth was only one of the possibilities but her sun would suffer the same fate too soon and so they were still searching for a long term solution.

The mood of May's performance changed and she told of the desperate years after the destruction of Angelos, the loss of their families and how integration with Earth people had begun. The Angels and humans were genetically compatible and shared the same power of love and freedom of spirit although intellectually Angels were far superior.

The integration was at a price though. To be compatible, the visitors had to adjust their physiology and make the gene that rejuvenated their DNA dormant. This physical change reduced their life expectancy from thousands of years to little more than mortal expectations. 5,000 years of cross-breeding through happy unions and some *technical assistance,* had accelerated the human's development to become suitable and indeed loving partners. However, extremely rarely, would more than one child be conceived in the union which was a threat to their continued existence.

She told of how the Angels genes were dominant but this mixing of bloods over time had diluted their special abilities and weakened their race. In another thousand years, integration would be complete and those special abilities would be lost completely. May explained that she was the only pure blooded Angel left from the lost expedition. Her role was to be the mother of the new race when the time was right. She told of how she had lived with only her sister and without love for over 5,000 years; two thirds of her life expectancy.

The sadness returned to May and she broke the information transfer briefly to regain strength. The sky darkened once more into night. Elizabeth took May's hands and waited for her to compose herself. At last she began again and the sky lit up once more as the colours coursed through her body. The music and dance began to flow again and her story filled their minds once more.

Along with the 300 visitors, came another 50 of the Shado race. This was regarded by the Angels as being a safe number to control in the environment of their regimented mission to Earth. The Shado race was subdivided into two distinct bloodlines, the Senate that were the dominant and significantly more intelligent beings and the Drones, more dull-witted but malleable and hard-working. The Drones were under the direct control of the Senate and performed the day to day manual tasks essential to the survival of the colony. The destruction of Angelos and their forced exile and integration had changed that and control was lost. The Shadows reverted to their true elemental beings. Their dark-side naturally took over and the Drones became the Soldiers of the Senate.

The Shadows did not embrace the integration policy. They kept their bloodline pure, maintaining the gene that rejuvenated their DNA, enabling them to outlive the Angel race. Whist the Angels' special abilities were diminishing through thousands of years of couplings, the Shadows maintained theirs and the balance of power had tipped their way. Taking the opportunity, the Shadows had begun their policy of ethnic cleansing targeting and eliminating the Angels.

When May's performance came to an end, she was completely drained and her skin had stopped transmitting light. She slumped down against a tree and whispered softly to them.

"You must go now because you are not safe, not until you have learned your skills."

Ben couldn't help showing his alarm.

"Not safe, why and what skills are you talking about May?"

"Not safe, because you have Angel blood in your veins. You are one of us and your skills are those that I have told you of in my dance. The Shadows will have been watching you, waiting for you to lead them to me. You will not remember for some days as your minds will be processing and organising this information but this will pass and you will recall. Now go!"

With that the slim being curled up on the grass beneath the tree and drifted into a deep sleep. Her colours began to change like a chameleon and she blended into her background so that you would never have known that she was there.

Elizabeth and Ben ran back to the old mirror, held hands and stepped back into the Robinson's hallway.

"What time is it Ben we've been gone for hours?" Elizabeth was panicking. "Auntie and Uncle will be furious with us!"

Ben looked at his watch and what he saw was incredulous.

"Well it's still three o'clock, the same time that we walked through the mirror."

"It can't possibly be Ben. Don't be silly, your watch must've stopped."

They were shocked when they saw that the hall clock showed exactly the same time and wondered how that could be? It was too much for them to try and fathom. Their heads were fatigued and confused from the sheer mental effort of receiving all the information that May had given them. They needed to sleep now, desperately. When they got to their rooms, both fell asleep the very second that their heads touched their pillows.

George and Jillie returned to the house at seven o'clock that evening. They were amazed to find Elizabeth and Ben in their rooms asleep and dead to the world. It was nearly lunchtime the next gay when Jillie finally decided that they had spent long enough in bed.

Elizabeth and Ben were sat at the table having a very late breakfast indeed but neither was hungry and both had the mother of all headaches. They were trying to be interested in what Aunt Jillie was saying, but they simply couldn't keep up with it. Jillie finally gave up and conceded that they were both unwell and should go back to bed whilst she and George went and did something useful with the day.

Ben woke several hours later refreshed and went to Elizabeth's room to see her. His headache was gone and he felt on top of the world. Somehow, he felt completely different but for no reason that he could put his finger on. He could tell that Elizabeth was already awake because of the music blaring out from her radio. It was a really upbeat piano piece and Elizabeth was laughing gaily as she listened to it. In fact the music was so loud that he had to knock harder to be heard. Finally Elizabeth called out above the music.

"Come in Ben, come in and listen!"

When Ben entered the room, his jaw dropped at what he saw. It wasn't the radio playing at all. Elizabeth was sat at the piano vamping out the most amazing piece of music.

"It's *The Circus Gallop* by William Groscurth Ben! Nobody plays it, it's just too hard," Elizabeth was laughing as she played the piece with ease. "And I don't even have the music Ben. I just heard it on the radio and somehow I know how to play it."

"Wow Lizzie that's really cool but how can that be?"

Ben was stunned by the speed that Elizabeth's hands were going up and down the keyboard, and she wasn't even looking at them!

"It must be to do with the skills that May said that she'd given us, but isn't this just the best fun ever?"

"Angel's blood," Ben thought to himself, "we really do have Angels blood!"

Elizabeth stopped playing instantly and looked at Ben wide eyed with shock, "Yes it must be that."

A frisson ran through Ben's body. It ran up his back to his neck and scalp.

"Lizzie, I didn't say anything", he said, nonplussed.

"Yes you did Ben, you said *Angel's blood* I heard you."

"No Lizzie, I only *thought* it!"

The enormity of what was happening to them began to sink in and Elizabeth covered her mouth with her hands.

"OMG Ben; wait until Mrs Hyde gets a load of this, that'll really piss her off!"

"No Lizzie, nobody can know anything about this, not even Aunt and Uncle. Remember what May said, we're not safe and if there are Angels, then there must be Shadows too."

"Point taken Ben, get dressed I expect May is waiting to see us."

Chapter 10

They were stood in front of the old mirror. Elizabeth noticed that Ben was looking unusually smart, his hair was brushed and gelled and he was even wearing his best Nike trainers. "Smitten," she thought and saw Ben flush with embarrassment. She smiled realising that he had clearly read her thoughts and she knew that from now on there could be no secrets between them. They held hands instinctively and walked confidently into the mirror.

They found May asleep by the tree just as they had left her, perfectly concealed in her camouflage. Her bejewelled skin had mutated into blades of grass and only the gentle rise and fall of her chest gave her away. They watched for some minutes both in awe and in fear of waking her, knowing that yesterday's performance had exhausted her so.

As they watched a transformation came over her, the lush skin of grass turned to thousands of green emeralds that shone brilliantly in the sunlight. At last, she opened those intense blue smiling eyes.

"Hello my friends," she cooed, "have you rested well?" May stretched out her long limbs like a cat awaking from a deep sleep.

"Yes thanks," Elizabeth returned her welcoming smile. "Whatever you did to us put us to sleep for 24 hours and I had the most amazing dreams."

"Me too," reinforced Ben, "they were literally out of this world!"

May was clearly pleased about what they had said and her smile broadened, dimpling her emerald crusted cheeks.

"Those were not dreams, it was your brains trying to make sense of all the information that I have given you and then filing it in logical order. The dreams will go on for many weeks, months even, and you will discover things about yourselves that will truly amaze you."

"We already have," enthused Elizabeth. "This morning I could play the piano like a maestro with no music it was awesome."

"Yes and we can read each other's minds too!" Ben blurted.

Elizabeth could see from his awkward body language that he was besotted with this exotic young lady and noted too, as women seem to be able to, that May was finding that quite flattering.

"Ah so it has started. That's good, you will need to discover all the skills that I have taught you if you are to have a chance against the Shadows. They have been waiting patiently for you and now they will come. You can be sure of that, they will come."

"So we are in real danger then May, will we know who from?"

Ben was trying to be matter of fact but the wobble in his voice gave away his fear and May picked it up.

"It's entirely natural to be afraid of the unknown Ben and I would be deeply worried if you were not. Without fear there is complacency and complacency can be fatal."

May's words were well chosen and Ben no longer felt foolish or inadequate but emboldened and positive. It was only for a split second but he sensed that this creature could affect his feelings in whatever way she chose. May averted her gaze from him suddenly, as if in guilt. Ben now knew for sure that she could. She quickly created the diversion that she needed to distract from the fact that she was listening in to Ben's private thoughts.

"Come with me to the corridor of mirrors and I will explain all that you need to know for now, but by voice this time. It may take some time yet before your brains have organised themselves enough for you to access the information that I've given you. There are some things though, that you must know immediately to protect yourselves from the Shadows. They will already know that you are maturing."

"Protect themselves from the Shadows?" It was a daunting and surreal thought. Elizabeth and Ben exchanged nervous glances.

May took their hands and walked between them towards the corridor of mirrors. She was a vision, petite with an appealing mixture of woman and child. Ben couldn't take his eyes off her. He could feel his heart beating in his chest and felt clumsy and confused. Elizabeth could sense it all and it confirmed her earlier suspicions.

"Standard symptoms of a huge crush," she smiled knowingly at him.

Ben averted his eyes and flushed red, much to Elizabeth's delight.

The corridor entrance was like the mouth of a cave set in the side of the hill. It passed through to an identical opening on the other side. As they entered the corridor, May began to explain.

"The mother ship that brought us here over 5,000 years ago is below and above us. It's hidden by its cloaking device so that all you see is a grassy hill. The corridor is a module within the ship and the mirrors are portals into other times in space. Keep away from the broken mirrors as they will consume you."

May's expression reinforced the message, in fact May's expressions were a complete language in themselves and words were an unnecessary accessory.

Ben's curiosity was getting the better of him. It was a distraction that helped him to manage his clumsiness.

"How did they become broken?"

May began to explain what the mirrors really were and what had happened to some of them.

"The portals enable movement within the space-time continuum, which allows us access throughout the four dimensions of the universe. The forces involved in creating these openings are immense. If broken, the portal implodes and consumes all matter within it, gathering in density and mass until its gravity is so massive that not even light can escape and a black hole is born somewhere in the universe."

"An attractive girl talking physics, it just doesn't get better!" Ben thought.

May shot him a glance that left him in no uncertainty that she had read his thought; what he didn't see was her inner amusement. May continued as if nothing had happened and Ben simply cringed inwardly.

"The broken mirror becomes a conduit to that black hole and they are the absolute limit of safety. If you were to put even your hand through the portal you would be consumed by the black hole that lies beyond."

May paused to allow the malevolence of the broken mirrors to sink in, so that they would respect their power.

"Each of these mirrors has a sister mirror somewhere else in space and time and they work as a pair. They even look the same. The Shadows have been trying to take control of the sister mirrors that are distributed around your planet, in order to take control of the future. Where they fail to take possession of the sister mirror, they destroy them along with their Guardians so that they can no longer be used by the Angels.

The broken mirrors that you see, represent the evil work of the Shadows and each has involved the death of its Guardian and often their family. There are now only 40 portals open of the original 100 and the Shadows already control ten of those. Their strength is increasing compared to ours. Unless we can find a way to reinforce our abilities, it's only a matter of time before they dominate and take control of your world and complete the genocide of the Angel race."

It was heady stuff. Elizabeth and Ben subconsciously took a step further away from the broken mirror next to them. Ben could feel Elizabeth's unease.

"I know what you're thinking Lizzie and I'm thinking it too," he said sadly.

Ben then asked May the most difficult question that he had ever had to ask in his life.

"Were our parents murdered by Shadows?"

May didn't really have to answer, the look of desolation on her face said it all and her brilliant emerald skin turned to slate grey. She put her arms around Elizabeth and Ben and started to sing soothingly. Her skin began to encrust with rubies and the irises of her eyes turned into rings of the purest sapphires. They could feel energy flow from her touch into their bodies bringing comfort strength and hope. May was literally re-charging them.

Elizabeth spoke for both of them both.

"We're ready May you can tell us everything now."

May smiled reassuringly and led them further down the corridor.

"Come to the sister mirror of the late Emanuel Goldberg. Did you know him?"

"Yes he was our father's friend and was to be his business partner on a new development. He committed suicide though, for no apparent reason."

Elizabeth still had fond memories of him. May sensed it and squeezed her hand supportively as she pointed to the mirror in front of them.

"Look into the mirror for they can give you access to all the images that they have reflected. Soon you will be able to navigate freely in time and space but for now you must just picture Emanuel and your father in the room at the same time close to the date of his death. Can you do that?"

"I'll try," Elizabeth said with uncertainty.

She put her hand on the black glass that had no reflection, unlike all the others, and searched for the images in her head. The minutes passed but she couldn't quite create a strong enough likeness of them. At last she turned to her brother.

"Ben I need your help, hold my hand and join my thoughts please."

The power of their two minds together had immediate success. The mirror misted and then cleared showing the reflection of two men. They were sat at opposite sides of a big oak table. The room was dowdy, with rows of bookcases along the walls and displays of antique guns, axes, swords and cutlasses. Elizabeth immediately recognised the room; she had been there once with her father. The man facing the mirror was Mr Goldberg, exactly as she remembered him. The other man had his back to them and was holding his head in his hands. He took something out of his pocket, it was a mobile phone. Whatever the message was, it had clearly upset him further.

Mr Goldberg was a big affable man with smiling blue eyes and a full head of curly white hair. He stood up and embraced his friend in a supportive, fatherly way. They shook hands and the visitor turned to leave the room, momentarily facing the mirror as he did so.

"Dad!" Elizabeth and Ben shouted together.

Both instinctively touched his reflection lovingly as he left the room. Emanuel Goldberg remained, looking at some device on the table.

"Keep watching but be strong," May urged them, "it is not over."

Her vibrant ruby jewels were dimming and her eyes had lost their rings of sapphires. Elizabeth and Ben had already learnt that this was the harbinger of bad news and braced themselves for what was about to come.

Emanuel Goldberg's broad back was turned so that he didn't see the hooded figure that entered his office through the open window. The intruder quietly took down one of the swords and crossed the room towards him. With a powerful thrust the man drove the sword through the back of Mr Goldberg's neck and out through his mouth.

Elizabeth and Ben flinched at the violent act and Elizabeth had to hold back the bile that had risen to her throat. The killer withdrew the sword, caught the falling corpse and dragged it to the corner of the room. He man-handled Emanuel's slack corpse into a kneeling position facing the walls, reversed the sword and drove it back through his open mouth. Finally he lodged the handle where the two walls met the floor to give the illusion of suicide.

The hooded man took one of the heavy antique axes from the wall, walked across to the mirror and hefted it overhead. For some seconds he was looking directly into the mirror and they could see his face plainly. Emanuel's hooded killer had brown hair swept across his pale forehead and a close-cropped jowl beard. He was wearing mirrored aviator sunglasses that hid his eyes so that he looked sinister and implacable. He was just about to strike the mirror, when something distracted him stopping the act of destruction.

Hastily, the man relocated the axe on the wall, took the device from the oak table and slipped out through the open window. Moments later their father entered the room as if looking for something that he had forgotten, it was his mobile phone there on the table. He saw the slumped body of Mr Goldberg and ran across to him. After checking for life, he picked up his phone and made a call. There was a look of devastation on his face and their hearts went out to him.

Elizabeth lost her concentration with the shock of what she had seen. The image of her father receded and the mirror turned black again, hiding its secrets from them. Somehow May's energy was still keeping them objective. Even so, Elizabeth had paled and was shaking like a leaf.

Ben stepped in to let Elizabeth regain her composure. When he turned to face May, he was suddenly acutely aware of the fact that she had been watching him. It made him feel self-conscious such that he fumbled his words.

"W-was Emanuel the Guardian of this mirror and well, where is it? Now I mean."

Ben hated himself for his clumsiness and even more so when he felt the hotness flushing up his neck to his cheeks.

May smiled back at him but it wasn't a mocking smile, it was something else but whatever it was it immediately took away his self-consciousness. He felt confident and articulate again.

"Had she done something?" he wondered but his thoughts were cut off by her response.

"Yes he was the Guardian Ben and one of the Patriarchs. His knowledge and guidance will be missed by us all. Your father returned shortly afterwards and took the mirror to a place of safety. It's now in the roof space of your Aunt and Uncle's house."

"That explains why this mirror is black and has no image, there's no light in the loft," Ben deduced. "So who was the man that killed Mr Goldberg?"

Ben was enjoying the exchange now with his newly found confidence.

"His name is Adolphius, the leader of a cell of Shadows and one of the most violent and evil beings that your Earth has ever known. He has manifested himself throughout your history and some of these manifestations you will already know. He was known as Vlad the Impaler, a cruel Hungarian man, who brutally murdered tens of thousands of people in the 15th century. Then as Ivan the Terrible, a Russian Czar in the 16th century; among other atrocities he ordered his bodyguards to kill thousands of his own countrymen. More recently, he appeared as Adolph Hitler, history's most chilling tyrant. He was responsible for the genocide of six million Jews and others that he described as *undesirables* which included our kind."

Elizabeth was now fully recovered from the mirror ordeal. She had studied the Second World War at school in some detail and contested what May had said.

"That can't be so May. History tells us that Hitler committed suicide in his bunker with his wife, Eva. He shot himself and she took cyanide. Their remains were subsequently burnt in the garden outside."

Elizabeth felt pleased with herself over her authoritative contribution, but May rebuffed it.

"Ah, how convenient that their remains were burnt don't you think Elizabeth?"

It wasn't meant in a mocking way, but May could see Elizabeth's annoyance and continued more tactfully.

"But you are right Lizzie. That is how it would seem; how it was meant to seem. Years later in 2009, DNA tests on the skull that the Russians had believed to be Hitler's, turned out to be from a 40 year old woman. Hitler had faked their deaths and left the bunker through his portal."

The time was right and May had to tell them what they wanted to know.

"I think you are at last ready for the full story. What I have to say will be very sad for you, but in your hearts you already know it to be true."

May held their hands to ease their pain in the mystical way that she could.

"Your parents' car crash was orchestrated by one of Adolphius' Senators who drove them off the road killing them. We don't know for sure who, but this person will be someone close to you, or close to someone that you know. That is simply how they work. That person, or persons, will be watching you on a daily basis hoping that you lead them to me. Adolphius has centuries of experience of genocide and continues his campaign against us. Now that you have found me it will include you and your family."

Strangely, being told that their parents had been murdered didn't come as a shock to them. They became aware of the warmness of May's hands and a sensation that something within them was leaving their bodies into hers. She was somehow soothing them and taking away their pain.

May could sense that Elizabeth and Ben needed time to come to terms with it all so she diverted their attention to another of the mirrors.

"Have you met my family yet? See here they are."

Ben was really impressed it was the same futuristic room that he had been looking into.

"This is your family and your home? Wow, yes I've been watching the children play, who are they?"

May's face was a picture of love.

"Yes my home. The bigger of the two girls is me and the little one is my sister Crystalita. Isn't she beautiful?"

"Oh she is so beautiful May," Elizabeth interjected. "Just look at her mass of curly blonde hair. Wow! Somehow she looks strangely familiar to me. It's peculiar, like I already know her."

Elizabeth turned to May but she didn't pick up the sombre change that had come over her that was prompted by what she had just said.

"You are beautiful too May. How old were you then?"

"I was in my ninth year and Crystalita in her fourth, life was so happy then. I look into this mirror often, it comforts me to remember them and from where I came."

Although she was sad the love kept May's skin of rubies sparkling even more brilliantly than before and her sapphire eyes shone with the fond memories that she was feeling. At last May's colours subdued and she continued her story.

"Some years after these images that you have been watching, we learned that Angelos was to be destroyed by the asteroid, Obsidian. Crystalita and me were chosen for the expedition to Earth. I think our father had friends in high places and was able to save us. We took the sister mirror from our home with us so that it wouldn't be destroyed and we could then re-visit our memories of our family."

Two people entered the room and May suddenly recovered her brilliance.

"Look, there's my Mother and Father!"

They watched as May and her little sister ran to meet them the very moment that they entered the room. They cuddled them and smothered them with kisses. The act was so emotional and poignant that Elizabeth and Ben's hearts went out to her at the sadness of it.

"These are happy memories, please don't cry."

May put her hands on them and again their sadness seemed to be drawn out until they could only feel the heat of her touch. She had a distant look in her eye and a proudness that was palpable.

"My Father was one of the most famous surgeons on Angelos. He was consulted on all areas of medicine and cryogenics; there were none to compare to him."

May tore herself away from her fond memories.

"Enough of my world, we still have much to talk about yours. Shortly before your parents were killed, we could see from the mirrors that you needed protection until you were old enough to learn your Angel skills and become Guardians of the mirror. That's why we sent your music teacher, Miss Crystal to look out for you. She would have been your mentor."

May looked upset again, her eyes began to stream with tears of liquid gold and again the lustre began to fade from her skin. May chocked over her next words.

"Miss Crystal was my little sister Crystalita, I sent her to protect you. That's why she looked familiar to you Lizzie, but the Shadows took her sweet life."

Elizabeth and Ben took May's hands. It was their turn to comfort her and Elizabeth felt humbled by the sacrifice that she had made for them.

"You risked your little sister to keep us safe, why would you do that?"

"I couldn't stop her. You will understand in time and then you may judge me."

"Perhaps but we do understand your grief May. We know how crushing it is to lose someone that you love," Elizabeth said reflecting on her fond memories of Miss Crystal. "I remember your sister clearly May. She was kind and gentle with the most astonishing blue eyes that I have ever seen."

May made her best attempt at a smile.

"You will always know who the Angels are as they will always have vivid blue or green eyes, as that is genetic. You will also feel their grace and goodness just as you did Crystalita's."

May's face suddenly hardened and she looked dangerous. The transformation was a shock to them. There was a side to her that they had never seen until then and it was scary. May continued.

"And you will sense the presence of Shadows; they transmit evil from their very being and absorb power from darkness and negative thought. If you are ever uncertain, then look to see if they cast a shadow in sunlight. If they do, then they are not Shadows. You must remember this as it might save your lives one day."

Ben had been considering the bigger picture and was putting the pieces of the puzzle together, which prompted his next question.

"Mr Williams didn't have an accident either did he?"

May knew how fond Ben was of Mr Williams and replied as gently as she could taking his hands as she did so to give his pain a conduit to her.

"No you're quite right Ben, he didn't. David Williams sacrificed his life saving yours. We think it was the same Shadow that drove your parents' car off the road and was about to do the same to you at the same place by the canal. David gladly gave his life for yours as the future of all the Angels and all our hopes depend on you now."

Ben still hadn't got over his death and couldn't find his words. Elizabeth had read his mind and knew what he wanted to say.

"Why are two young people like us so important to the future of the Angels?"

May could see that they were at last ready to know their destiny.

"You and Ben, as siblings, are a rare occurrence in the earthly family tree of the Angels. Although Angels and humans are genetically compatible, as I have told you, there is a fertility problem. Often unions are childless and multiple children by the same parents are truly exceptional. Multiple children born to the Patriarch bloodline, the elite of the Angels, has not happened in the last two millennia; well not until you were born that is."

"Father was a Patriarch?"

The pride of it was clearly evident in Ben's voice.

"Yes Ben, there's much about your father that you would be proud of. These things I have already told you but you have not yet found them amongst the plethora of information that you have received. Not even your mother knew the half of it. Ralph was pivotal in our survival plans and those plans were founded on the uniqueness of you and Lizzie."

"Uniqueness?" Elizabeth challenged assertively.

Ben noticed for the first time, that Elizabeth had gone through a physical change in these last days since meeting May. The turn of her head, the cast of her eyes, everything was entirely adult about her. She was confident and there was an indescribable energy about her, such that she exuded strength from her very being. Ben looked even more closely and realised that she had become a woman, a powerful woman no longer in adolescence. But more than this she was beautiful beyond his recollection of her, absolutely stunning.

"Was that Angel, or was that just where she was going anyway?" Ben wondered.

May answered Elizabeth's challenge.

"Yes uniqueness. Without questioning you naturally joined your mind with Ben's to enter the old mirror for the first time. Then you invited Ben to join your thoughts to access the reflections of your father and Emanuel when you couldn't do so yourself. Don't you see Lizzie?"

Elizabeth was nodding her head at the realisation of it.

"Yes May, I think I do see now. As siblings we are stronger together; what I can't do alone, then Ben and I can if we unite."

"Yes, and it is only yet an embryo Lizzie! You have no idea of what you can achieve together. For generations we have been weakening as a race, our abilities fading over the centuries with our multiple blood dilutions. Now we have the rare situation of siblings of a strong blood group, the Patriarch blood group, able to unite their powerful minds multiplying their abilities to that of our forefathers. Once again we will be able to threaten the rise of the Shadows. That is why you and everyone that you love are in such mortal danger. The Shadows need you dead to gain total control."

It was a mind-blowing scenario for them to take in but it didn't quite equate to Ben's logical way of thinking.

"Why has this responsibility fallen on us and not our father before he was killed? He could have worked together with Uncle George."

"It would have if they were full blood brothers Ben, but they were only half-brothers. Your Grandmother was married to a soldier before she met the Grandfather that you know. He was killed in active service, leaving her with an unborn child. That child was later named George and your father Ralph was born two years later. Your Mother and Father chose not to tell you and Lizzie this."

It now all made sense to Elizabeth.

"That explains why Uncle George knew of nothing strange about the mirror when I asked him at the cemetery, and why it was only our father who spent hours looking into it. Uncle George could see nothing, he doesn't have Angel blood."

The responsibility of their birth-right hit Elizabeth and Ben like a physical blow and they reeled at the shock of it. May realised that she had already gone too far for their young minds and beckoned them to follow her.

"That's enough for now and I've been a really bad host. Let's leave this place and all our troubles. You must be starving! I'll make you a meal the like of which you just cannot imagine and then, when you're sated, I will sing and dance for you but this time just for your pleasure."

May's smile was positive again and energising.

"You will be refreshed and content afterwards and able to begin to understand who and what you are and you will gain strength from it. Then you will be able to go forwards and realise your destiny, our destiny, as we are of the same family."

When they left the corridor of mirrors and walked out into the Grecian sunshine, they noticed that May had changed again. If it was possible, she was even more vibrant than they had seen her before. May had exchanged her ruby skin for brilliant diamonds and sapphires and her hair was of finely spun-gold filigree that reflected the sunshine. Her face, a mixture of innocence and temptress and her laugh was simply a stairway to heaven.

She had prepared a meal that was literally out of this world in colour, smell and taste. It was like it could be whatever you wished it to be. May sang and danced for them and played her lute and the sound that came from it, was more complete than any orchestra could ever be. The colours that she was emitting seemed to caress them and Elizabeth and Ben were lost in her. They felt safe and content and without realising it, informed. May had not missed her opportunity to continue their education and felt a little guilty for having taken advantage of them so.

It was almost dark when she finished and put down the lute. Both Elizabeth and Ben felt completely relaxed and at ease with all things. They felt somehow organised and ready to take on their quest, whatever that might be. May had prepared them well and it was time to return home.

There was a question however, that Ben had been waiting to ask since they had first met May. He was looking at her beauty. Admiring her skin of diamonds and sapphires, her finely spun golden hair, full red lips and lively eyes that shone like the stars. He suddenly realised that she had noticed him watching her and shyly asked his question.

"You said that we are genetically compatible with you, but how can that be? You're made of metals and minerals, gem stones of all kinds that you change as you please and we are just flesh and blood."

May had that mischievous look in her eyes again.

"Ah Ben, you see me as I want you to and I do so love dressing up as any girl does. Wouldn't you agree Lizzie?"

May's question just received a conspiratorial smile from Elizabeth in return as Ben waited patiently for his answer.

"So what do you really look like May?"

Ben was afraid that he would be disappointed and his face was an open book to her.

"Why just like you and Lizzie." she smiled. "Shall I show you?"

Her jewels melted away revealing smooth, suntanned skin that shone with perspiration from the exertion of her dance. Her hair was long black and lustrous, falling over her shoulder to her narrow waist. Her face was fresh with flawless skin, full lips and brilliant blue eyes set above high cheekbones. May's naked body was athletic, with good muscle definition but not at the expense of her womanly curves. She stood in front of them smiling unashamedly with a mischievous look in her eyes.

"I think you can stop staring now Ben," Elizabeth said with a knowing smile.

The guilt on Ben's face sent her and May into rapturous laughter. Ben was feeling awkward but the laughter was so infectious that he quickly forgot his embarrassment and joined them.

"I think this is a bit too much for you just now Ben."

"This is the body that will mother the new generation one day Ben, with the right man and at the right time. When the Shadows are once again under our control it will happen then Ben."

May fixed him teasingly with her big blue eyes.

"If it's in your lifetime would you do that for me Ben? Would you be my lover?"

May let the jewels flow back over her skin, until she had recovered her modesty.

Ben didn't know if May was asking a serious question, or just playing with him. Either way, both girls were clearly finding it most amusing, as tears of laughter were rolling down their faces.

Chapter 11

There were four of them sat in the ill-lit room. They were more comfortable in the dark as it complimented their nature and they drew power from it. The atmosphere was menacing. Three of them sat together were men and the other, sat apart from them, was a hard faced woman who appeared to be in her early to mid-twenties. The men's demeanour showed respect for the woman, or if not respect, then it was fear. Her fair hair was piled above a high forehead, she was reasonably pretty but her scowl and ice cold eyes took away any illusion to that.

Adolphius looked back at the others through his mirrored, aviator sunglasses. His soft brown hair was swept sideways across his forehead and the stereotypical toothbrush moustache was now exchanged for a full jowl beard that framed his thin lips. He addressed the woman coldly.

"So Fraulein Grese you have failed me again. You failed me in the concentration camps in the Second World War, where you allowed yourself to be caught by the Allied Forces, and you have now failed twice to kill the Robinson brats. Explain yourself."

Irma Grese was one of the cruellest women in history, known in those days as the *Bitch of Belsen*. Grese was the second highest ranking female in the concentration camps of Auschwitz and Belsen. It was there that she administered torture and death to tens of thousands of people, as part of Adolph Hitler's campaign of ethnic cleansing. Grese's love for her work included sexual assault, torture and murder. She administered death by the pistol that she carried with her and used with sadistic enthusiasm. Her particular joy, was selecting those for the gas chamber. In that duty she was merciless, separating wives from their husbands and children from their mothers.

Grese was captured, tried and convicted for her crimes against humanity and sentenced to death. She was transferred to Hameln prison where she was hanged in December 1945, or at least a carefully selected and prepared lookalike was. Adolphius had made the substitution and Grese now owed her life to him.

"Adolphius."

Grese began, her voice was without emotion. She was unscathed by Adolphius' verbal assault and could see him falter at her total lack of fear of him. Fear was the ruling hand over the Shadows and Adolphius was playing a losing one with Grese.

"You so easily discount the dozens of Angels that I have culled where you and your men have failed. It seems you need a woman to do a man's job these days."

Her look was cruel and disdainful. Grese thought that she saw Adolphius flinch involuntarily under her attack and the apparent chink in his armour spurred her on.

"I think that you're losing your stomach for the job Adolphius. As for the Robinson siblings, it was unusual and just unfortunate that they were not in the car with their parents when I cleansed them. On my second attempt it cost Williams his life to save them. One less Angel as far as I see it."

Adolphius was fuming. He was losing face in front of the other two Senators who were quietly enjoying the exchange. Infinitely worse, the Supreme Senator herself had read him the Riot Act. He had been left in no doubt that to fail to neutralise the Robinson siblings, would ultimately result in his retirement, a euphemism commonly used by the Shadows for death. Their Supreme Senator or *the Hydra* as she was known, received funding in the order of £100 billion annually through her global network of cells. This money was essential for funding instability programmes and the power struggle against the Angels. This was under extreme threat if the Robinsons were allowed to develop into their natural beings.

"Your failings have allowed them to meet with the Matriarch Maelströminha. Already she will have shown them how to access their abilities and their strength will be growing by the day. When the brats have learned to work together and combine their forces fully, the balance of power will once more tip the Angels' way. If that happens, then our time left on this earth will be measured in centuries. If the boy is allowed to spawn with the Matriarch, then a new generation of Angels with renewed abilities will be born, and our expectancy will then be decades at best."

The older by far of the other two men, Alexis, was nodding in agreement. He was hunched with thin, wispy white hair and face like the map of the moon. Alexis was approaching his 8,000[th] year and so was reaching the end of his life expectancy. But with great age comes great experience and knowledge. Alexis was always consulted in matters of State and strategy.

Alexis had the accolade of killing Crystalita, the Matriarch's sister. To kill an Angel with true blood and full abilities needed skill and immense cunning, as full blooded Angels had the ability to sense and foresee events even before they happened. Over his 8,000 years, he had learnt to cloak his dark thoughts and emit an illusion of deep religion, peace and compassion. So perfect and well-practiced were his skills, that he could even cast a shadow without absorbing the darkness of it.

He had waited outside the school where Crystalita was working late in her guise of Miss Crystal, the music teacher. As she approached him, he had controlled his emotions so that Crystalita could not sense him.

Alexis had clutched his heart, letting out an agonised scream as he collapsed theatrically against his van. Crystalita, seeing his plight, ran towards the ancient man to help him. As she reached out for him, Alexis pulled a stiletto knife from under his jacket. It was one of his favourite killing tools; he had driven it up from below her ribs, deep into her heart, killing her instantly.

Crystalita had slumped into his arms and Alexis dumped her corpse into his van as if it was garbage. He had not been certain of such an easy kill, so he had secreted six armed Drones in the back of the van as insurance. These sadistic men immediately began to strip abuse and mutilate her body, inflicting Crystalita's final indignity. After the kill Alexis and the Drones had cleared her home of all possessions and faked her sudden and unexplained disappearance. Alexis had exploited Crystalita's only weakness, her humanity.

Alexis now looked at his fellow Shadows through dull, rheumy eyes and addressed them.

"What you say is right Adolphius. The boy is in his seventeenth year now. The knowledge he has received from Maelströminha, will stimulate his evolution both mentally and physically. So we can assume that a union is already possible, however I would judge that to be unlikely, given the youth's moral upbringing. Realistically we have one year maximum before a union between them might happen and that defines our window of opportunity."

Alexis fixed his audience with his cold eyes.

"We have two possibilities as I see it. The first is to cull the siblings within the year and the second is to eliminate the Matriarch. The latter has proven impossible for us over millennia because of her immense power and cunning. An assault on her would cost us dearly and we would have no certainty of success. She will be doubly on her guard now, since I killed her sister. We have little choice other than to stay with our long-term strategy and wait out her lifespan."

They all nodded in agreement and recalled only the last fiasco only too well. They had sent a squadron of 100 highly trained and armed Drone assassins through the portal to eliminate Maelströminha. She had anticipated their every move, using her ability to glimpse the future through the mirrors with crushing effect. As the Drones had filed into the corridor of mirrors, Maelströminha had taken over their minds and set them one upon the other, ripping themselves to bits with their bare hands and teeth. When only one remained standing she had ordered him to tie the 99 dead and dying together and commanded him to throw the end of the rope through one of the broken mirrors into the black hole beyond it. All 99 were then sucked into oblivion like spaghetti into a child's mouth.

Maelströminha had then sent the last man back through the portal to report back to the Senate. Alexis had peeled the skin off him like a plum with his stiletto and then staked him out to dry in the hot sun. It was as a lesson to others about what failure looked like.

"This leaves the termination of the siblings as our only option. You already have a plan I presume?" Alexis directed his question at Grese.

"It is in hand Alexis. My daughter, Katya, has been enrolled at the school and I have already milked the poison from my Black Mambas. Their venom is a highly potent and fast acting neurotoxin. Once introduced into the bloodstream, it causes certain and excruciating death within hours or even minutes."

Grese allowed herself a cruel smile before continuing.

"I have checked at the local hospital for the availability of antivenom. As the snakes are not indigenous, there is none in stock. Katya will have the venom applied under her fingernails and wait her opportunity to strike."

Grese was subconsciously running her tongue along her upper lip with the exquisite ecstasy of her anticipation. She was oblivious to the effect that it was having on her audience.

The fourth member of the cell was Dada, an immense black man with a cannonball head and eyes as black as the night. He rose from his seat and glared at her menacingly.

"Don't fail us again Grese. If you do then I will deal with the brats personally and return for you. You've already cheated the hangman's noose once but your frail neck will not escape my hands."

Grese met his stare with equal malevolence. The Shadows were a selfish, greed driven people whose rule was by fear and control. Any weakness was preyed on. Loyalty and support were not characteristics shared or even understood by the Shadows, only opportunity and self-preservation. Duelling between them in the pursuit of power was commonplace.

In recent history, this notorious Shadow was known as Idi Amin Dada, or *the Butcher of Uganda*. Half a million people suffered under his brutal and despotic rule as president after he seized power in 1971. He had finally fled for his life in 1979 when he joined Adolphius' cell of ruling Shadows. Dada had already made his own plans as to how he would seize power from Adolphius. Grese would simply become a casualty of that coup and he would only then be answerable to the Hydra herself, as all Shadows were. Dada's lips twisted into a sadistic smile as he considered how he would then deal with the Hydra and usurp the role of Supreme Senator.

Chapter 12

It was Monday morning in the music room. Elizabeth and Laura were talking animatedly and the subject was Laura's first truly meaningful kiss. It had happened at the weekend and was clearly a monumental moment in her life. Their heads were close together in conspiratorial manner.

"Lizzie he's just adorable," Laura's green eyes sparkled mischievously and her skin was flushed with the excitement of it. "Mother of course does not approve. He's from the wrong side of town *apparently*."

Elizabeth could see how much it had meant to Laura and was truly happy for her.

"Are you going to see him again?" she asked.

"Am I? You bet I am. He's picking me up tonight in his car. And he's twenty don't you know, with a job and everything. His name's Matt. Isn't that just the best name Lizzie, so manly don't you think?"

Laura was going at 100 miles per hour.

"Woo slow down girl, and you are not twenty. No wonder your Mum's worried about you."

"Oh Lizzie don't be so old fashioned. I'll be eighteen soon and anyway I can look after myself, besides you'll be on the date with me. He's bringing a friend."

Laura's smile was as innocence itself.

"Oh no Laura, don't bring me into this. I've got enough trouble already thank you very much."

"That settles it then, we'll pick you up at six thirty. Don't be late!"

Before Elizabeth could argue further, Mrs Hyde entered the room. She was leading a rather plain, slightly plump girl with short cropped mousy hair.

"Take your seats. Come on quickly now, we haven't got all day!" Mrs Hyde was looking particularly pleased with herself and it had danger written all over it. "We have a new girl joining us and her name is Katya. She will be sitting at the desk next to you Elizabeth but do try not to infect her with your stupidity, there's a good girl."

"Patronising bitch," Elizabeth thought and glared back at Mrs Hyde in contempt.

Katya weaved her way through the desks towards Elizabeth without taking her eyes of her. There was a mocking look on her face and Elizabeth felt ill at ease and somehow vulnerable. Something was wrong. Elizabeth could sense it, but she couldn't think what it could possibly be.

Katya extended her arm towards Elizabeth as if to shake her hand. Elizabeth stood up politely to reciprocate but at the last second Katya withdrew it and quickly sat down leaving Elizabeth stood with her arm out looking stupid in front of the whole class.

"You're dead you bitch!" Laura hissed.

She was immediately protective of Elizabeth but the new girl simply ignored her.

After what seemed an eternity to Elizabeth, the bell finally rang ending the painful and humiliating lesson. They all poured out into the crowded corridor, making their way towards the exit. Elizabeth didn't see Katya coming swiftly towards her with her arms raised high and hands clawed. Katya slashed her venom infected fingernails at Elizabeth's face but Laura had seen it coming. She threw herself between them to protect her friend.

Katya's fingernails sunk deep into Laura's neck, rupturing the flesh and finding the vein. Deep red venous blood pumped from the open wound and ran down her neck, drenching her white blouse. The venom from Katya's fingernails entered Laura's bloodstream and spread its death quickly through her body. Laura fell heavily to the ground in trauma shaking uncontrollably.

Maddened by what she had done, Elizabeth lashed out at Katya in pure rage, catching her hard in the chest. Somehow Elizabeth had summoned up a force from deep within her that she had never experienced before. Katya's breast bone broke under the impact with a loud crack and the air rushed out of her body like the sound of a snorting bull. The force of the blow sent Katya flying across the corridor into the wall where she slumped to the floor, gasping for breath. With monumental effort the terrified Katya picked herself up clasping her broken chest and flew out of the open door into the sunlit yard.

Elizabeth's mouth dropped from the shock of what she saw, or rather from what she didn't see. The fleeing Katya didn't cast a shadow in the bright morning sun, which could only mean one thing. She was a Shadow herself!

The ambulance arrived in only minutes, but by then Laura had lost consciousness and was convulsing on the floor. Her veins had become swollen purple snakes as the poison spread through her body. The paramedics were clearly unsure about what they were dealing with. One of them was tending to Laura's breathing difficulties while the other was radioing ahead to prepare the Intensive Care Unit at the hospital.

The school secretary had successfully contacted Laura's parents, but they had gone to London for the day and it was going to take them at least two hours to return. The Head Mistress and Elizabeth accompanied Laura to the hospital to give whatever support they could until they arrived. They wheeled Laura into the Intensive Care Unit exactly thirty minutes after the assault but she had already slipped into a coma and was no longer breathing of her own accord. The medics had her on life-support and were waiting for the blood test report to give them some idea of what they were dealing with.

There was the sudden sounding of an alarm as Laura went into cardiac arrest and the medics fought frantically to re-establish her heartbeat. At the third attempt with the defibrillator and injections of adrenaline,

Laura's heart began to beat again but weakly and erratically. Elizabeth could see four doctors in the room with her through the window. They were all shaking their heads. One of them turned away from the bed and walked out of the room to where Elizabeth was sitting. His expression was grave.

"Have the parents arrived yet?" the question was unnecessary as he knew that they were already in transit, "only I'm afraid that Laura will only last a few more minutes at best. I'm so sorry but there's nothing more we can do for her. The symptoms are like those associated with a snake bite but that can't be. It really is most strange and very, very sad."

Elizabeth forced herself to be calm for Laura's sake. She would need her now in these last moments.

"Can I go to her so that she doesn't die alone, please?"

Tears of grief and guilt were running down her face and her heart was bursting.

"That would be entirely appropriate, her parents are not here and they would want that too. Come with me but prepare yourself, this will be very difficult for you."

When they entered the room, only one of the doctors was still with Laura. Elizabeth took Laura's hand and knelt beside her.

"I'll leave you together for these last moments. You have my deepest sympathy," the doctor said solemnly.

Laura was unrecognisable. Her face was twisted with pain and her skin was transparent through loss of blood. The dark swollen veins over her body showed through and had spread over her like the roots of a tree. Elizabeth began talking softly to Laura. She told her how proud she was of being her friend and that she could never have got through losing her parents without her. She talked of the happy times that they had shared together and that would live in her heart forever. Elizabeth told her how much her parents adored her and how they would all meet on the other side and be happy again one day.

Elizabeth could feel her slipping away. She looked at the dials and gauges on her life-support machine and watched as they wound their way backwards towards zero. The cardiograph flat-lined and the shock of it stirred a memory deep within her, something that May had put there. Then those familiar words came into her head, the same words that she had heard when it all began.

"You will know what to do."

Elizabeth worked quickly, stripping the bandages from Laura's neck and re-opening the wound. She took a scalpel from the tray of instruments, closed her eyes and slashed the palm of her own hand then cupped it over the angry gouge in Laura's neck. Elizabeth emptied her mind of the pain and all other things. The only thing left in Elizabeth's consciousness, was the heat and wetness of Laura's wound. She imagined that her body was one with Laura's and a receptacle for the poison within her.

"It's me that should be lying there Laura not you. The poison was meant for me. I'll take it from you so that you can go on and enjoy your sweet life. I only ask that you remember me as your best friend."

Elizabeth kissed Laura on her forehead and as she did so, felt the first stab of pain as the venom began to enter her body through the cut in her hand. The minutes passed and Elizabeth watched in awe as Laura's heart began to beat again and the travel of the gauges on the life-support machine reversed until all were in their green zones. The colour slowly returned to Laura's face and the thick purple snakes of death receded until her skin was once more unblemished. Laura's eyes flickered then opened wide in shock.

"Lizzie!"

The doctors outside the room were alerted by the most dreadful scream. They ran to assist, but were stopped in their tracks at what they saw. Laura was sat up in bed with her hands over her face sobbing inconsolably. They turned to Elizabeth who was at the point of collapse. Thick purple snakes had covered her body and her eyes were sunken in her head. As they reached her she uttered something with her last conscious breath.

"Ben come to me quickly I need you!"

Elizabeth was suddenly gripped by the first of the many violent convulsions that would follow along the path to her death.

That afternoon marked the beginning of the cricket season for Northlands. Ben and the other boys had changed into their whites and were waiting for Mr Murphy, the senior sports master. He was about to introduce them to his new assistant, Corporal Michael Jackson. Ben had heard that Elizabeth had gone to the hospital with Laura. He hadn't been told the gravity of Laura's condition and so was reasonably unconcerned about it all. The boys were feeling quite negative towards meeting and being coached by the new man. The relationship that they had built with Mr Williams was still very special to them and his replacement had some big shoes to fill.

Mike Jackson looked relaxed and confident as he approached. He had the build of a typical runner with all excess flesh burned off him. Mike had joined the Army on his 17th birthday. Although now, still only 22, he had recently returned from his second tour of active service in Afghanistan.

Mike had served covertly in 28 Engineers, living native with the Afghans on covert operations. His squadron had suffered heavily under Afghan fire and Improvised Explosive Devices, or IEDs as they were popularly known. 28 Engineers' missions were a notable success and had significantly weakened the Taliban's hold on the Province. Mike was a Physical Training Instructor in his day job for the Army and had been seconded to the school to help out with their sports until David Williams' replacement was procured.

"Boys, I would like you to meet Corporal Michael Jackson, he's our temporary replacement for the late Mr Williams."

Mr Murphy had his hand on Mike's shoulder in supportive manner, as he made the presentation. There was a general mumbling along the lines of, "Pleased to meet you sir," and Mike Jackson sensed their awkwardness.

"Well, I'll leave you to it then Mike. Papers to sort and all that you know?"

Mr Murphy walked back to the main building. He was always glad to leave the *doing* bit to others.

Corporal Jackson began his own introduction to the boys raising an eyebrow and cocking a sideways, quizzical look at them. It was a characteristic that the boys would come to love.

"Firstly I have no intention of being David Williams' replacement. He has earned a special place in your hearts and deserves to stay there. What I want is to build on his and your success, to help you realise your full potential and honour David's memory. Are we going to do that?"

The reply was a resounding, "Yes sir!"

"And the second thing; unless we are in the presence of masters or parents, I am just plain Mike. Is that also understood?

"Yes sir, Mike sir!"

The boys were immediately put at ease and began laughing and chattering. That was going to be his nickname now, *Mike sir* the boys decided. Corporal Mike Jackson had won them over, body and soul.

"Right then let's get on with it. Split into two squads, this side puts up the practice net and the rest of you get the bowling machine and kit from the store room. Then we'll see if you footballers are any good at cricket!"

Corporal Jackson was clearly a leader in true military style and the boys ran off obediently to execute their tasks.

When the nets were set and the boys padded up ready to bat Mike called them to attention to brief them on their mission.

"You will be facing the enemy, they will throw all they've got at you but you will prevail," Mike took a bat from one of the boys. "You will take your stance so. Sideways on but with your head facing them, knees slightly bent and eyes level, always level. Like a Lion waiting for his prey. You don't move until you know where the ball is going and you do not take your eyes off it."

The boys were firmly engaged and had never pictured the game as a *battle* before. Mike took them through the basics of cricket and within two hours he had the bones of a team showing good promise. Ben had produced a particularly impressive batting performance in the nets and had won the admiration and respect of his friends. When it was over Corporal Jackson called them to attention.

"OK boys debrief time," he used the typical military approach. "We have learned a lot today, me and you. We have a squad, a good one, a winning one. If you work at it, the Cup could be yours but I want commitment; that means every Monday and Saturday you will practice and dedicate yourselves to each other as a squad. The strong ones will support the weaker ones and we cross the line together as a unit. Understood?"

"Yes Mike sir!"

"And we need to elect a Captain, nominees please?"

Luke put his hand up immediately.

"Ben sir."

Corporal Jackson looked around but there were no other offers.

"No takers then? OK Captain Ben organise your men, nets down and kit away."

Ben put his team to work but was suddenly stopped in his tracks. Corporal Jackson was the first to see his stricken face and jogged over to him.

"What is it son you look like you've seen a ghost?"

"I can't really explain but I know for sure that something terrible has happened to my sister and she needs me now," Ben was clearly desperate. "Can you take me to the hospital sir? She went there with her friend. Something must have gone seriously wrong I can sense it."

Ben was shaking like a leaf. The colour had drained out of his face, such that the other boys could see his distress.

"What is it Ben, what's the matter?" Luke asked, clearly genuinely concerned.

"I don't know really Luke, something's happened to Lizzie and I have to get to her."

Corporal Jackson took control again in military fashion.

"Luke, I'm putting you in charge. See that the tasks are done then go to the office and tell them I'm taking Ben to the hospital on compassionate grounds. Tell them not to worry but to contact Mr and Mrs Robinson immediately and ask them to go straight to the hospital. Got that?"

"Roger that Mike sir," Luke replied as if he was his military subordinate.

"Ben, I'm parked in the main car park, let's go."

Corporal Jackson broke into a run that Ben easily matched. They ran shoulder to shoulder to Mike's black Jaguar parked in the school yard.

The Jag left thick black snakes of rubber on the asphalt as Mike accelerated onto the main road. Something caught Ben's eye as they left the car park, it was a green sports car pulling out onto the road at speed. The hospital was seven miles away, out on the canal road. Ben knew at once that they were in danger and that it could be the same Shadow that killed his parents and Mr Williams. Ben had to warn Corporal Jackson of their situation, but it was going to sound preposterous.

"Mike. I don't even know how to explain this and you won't believe me anyway but...."

Mike completed the sentence for him with a wry smile on his face.

"But there's a Shadow on our tail, yes? Well we'd better see what they've got under the bonnet of that little green car."

Mike shifted down two gears and red-lined the powerful engine. The road blurred in front of them and they gained a few car lengths on their pursuer.

"Not bad on the straight," conceded Mike, "but let's see how they do on the bends down by the canal!"

His jaw was set firmly in concentration.

"The canal again," Ben thought.

A feeling of dreadful foreboding came over him.

"How do you know about the Shadows?"

"David Williams was my brother. He only adopted that name to make himself less visible to them."

Mike stopped talking as he fought the Jaguar around the tight bends using every inch of the road.

"I've come here to help you survive this cell of Shadows. Your job is to avenge those Angels that have been murdered by them and you can't do that without Lizzie."

Ben was both surprised and shocked at what he heard.

"I'm sorry about your brother Mike. He changed and saved my life, I'll always remember him for that."

"He changed and saved many lives Ben. Now will you just shut up and let me drive?"

Mike raised his eyebrow and shot Ben that sideways, quizzical look of his.

After they left the outskirts of town, the road began to snake its way down towards the canal. Mike's natural touch on accelerator and brake would have matched any Formula One racing driver as he drifted the eager Jaguar through the bends and chicanes. They were steadily gaining distance on the other car and Ben began to feel a little more at ease. As they took the deadly canal bend that had already cost the lives of their loved ones, Ben glanced at the speedometer; it read 100 mph and the tyres were screaming impossibly. Mike gunned the motor on up the hill and Ben looked backwards to assess the situation.

"They're pulling up Mike! They've given up the chase!"

Ben was shaking with the thrill and fear of the race. He looked back at Mike and all he got was that characteristic cheeky grin.

They ran down the hospital corridors without asking which ward Elizabeth was in. Somehow Ben already knew exactly where he was going. When they burst into the ward, Elizabeth was already on life-support. They could see her being tended to by a nurse through the window of a private room. Four doctors were outside in deep consultation. Laura and the Head Mistress had been moved out of intensive care to an isolation ward. Ben went straight to the doctors, interrupting them in mid conversation.

"I'm Ben Robinson, Elizabeth's brother. I need to go in and see her now," Ben said urgently.

As Ben hurried past, he felt a hand on his shoulder stopping him. It was the senior doctor.

"I'm sorry son, but that won't be possible. Elizabeth is seriously ill and in quarantine. She's some highly infectious and virulent disease that she contracted after only minutes of exposure to her friend. I'm afraid nobody can enter until we know what we're dealing with."

Mike called Ben over and whispered to him.

"I'll create a diversion. When I have their full attention you can slip in and lock the door. Do whatever you have to, but be quick. I can only stall them for a few minutes."

Mike walked over to the opposite end of the room, nodded to Ben then threw himself unceremoniously to the floor taking a table and chairs with him. He began to fake a convulsion, thrashing around and banging his head against the tiled floor. The doctors ran over to restrain him and prevent him from injuring himself. Mike was secretly thankful for their assistance but continued his defiant struggle nonetheless.

Ben took the opportunity and let himself into the room where Elizabeth was wired and plumbed into the life-support system. He locked the door and turned to go to Elizabeth. He was met by the nurse who frantically tried to usher him back out. Ben instinctively put his hand in front of her face.

"Stop, you will do nothing!"

The nurse immediately responded to Ben's command. She dropped her arms to her sides and stood there motionless, oblivious to all around her. Ben crossed to Elizabeth's side and stepped backwards at the shock of what he saw. Elizabeth was grotesque beyond imagination. Her skin was like clear plastic, with purple snakes that seemed to writhe beneath it. A tube was rudely taped to Elizabeth's mouth and her spittle was frothing and running from the corners. Her sightless green eyes were fixed, staring up at the ceiling. Ben took her bandaged hand and forced his mind to empty and reach out to hers.

"Come on Lizzie focus, clear your mind. Tell me what I have to do!"

Ben put all his mental effort into reaching out to her, to break the chains of her coma.

"Lizzie come back to me you can't die not now, we've got too much to do. The Angels are counting on us."

Silent tears rolled down Ben's face. It seemed futile but somehow, after several seconds, Elizabeth's irises responded momentarily. Her dilated pupils contracted then relaxed back to their comatose state but Ben had seen it and was encouraged.

"Lizzie you can do it for me, come on Lizzie!"

Somehow, Ben felt energy flow from his hand into hers. Elizabeth blinked myopically, she was physically too weak to talk but he could hear her loud and clear in his mind.

"You've come to me Ben, thank God you're here," Elizabeth was pitifully weak but alert. "I only have the strength to say this once Ben and you must do it without question. Do you understand?"

Elizabeth felt Ben squeeze her hand urging her on.

"Unwrap the bandage from my hand and force it to bleed, then take the scalpel and slash your own and cup your wound over mine. Use your mind to draw the poison out of me into your body, but don't take more than you must. With less poison in our bodies maybe we have a chance to beat the venom. We're stronger now with our Angel genes but you must be quick. Do it now Ben, do it!"

Ben worked efficiently and exposed the congealed gash in Elizabeth's hand that had been neatly stitched together. He braced himself and then ripped open her flesh until the blood ran freely. Ben took the scalpel, averted his eyes and slashed his palm down to the bone. He felt no pain, only the wetness of the gushing blood. Ben clasped his hand over Elizabeth's and bound them together using Elizabeth's blooded bandage. He felt the first sting of the poison as he drew it out from her and watched in awe as she regained her life force by the minute. Ben was so focussed on his sister, that he hadn't noticed the sickness that was coming upon him. It was Elizabeth's terrified scream that brought him to his senses.

"Stop it Ben, you're killing yourself!"

Ben was close to collapse as the sickness consumed him. In those last lucid moments Elizabeth had to summon all her strength to catch him and pull him across the bed to her. Then the blackness came over her. Even in her unconsciousness, Elizabeth had Ben in a vice-like grip. It was as if to let him go would be to lose him for eternity. In their fevered minds, they found themselves walking towards a light so bright that they had to avert their eyes. They stopped to bathe in the warmth of it, as if it were sunshine.

"Are we dying Lizzie?"

Elizabeth's reply was even and fatalistic.

"I think so Ben but we will face it together."

She squeezed Ben's hand to give him strength as they walked ever closer to the light. In the middle of the glare was a golden star that seemed to change shape as they approached it. When they got close, they could see that it wasn't a star at all, it was a golden woman with outstretched arms beckoning to them. Elizabeth recognised her at once.

"May! How can it be you? I know we're dying, have you come to take us?"

Elizabeth was weak and near death. She couldn't take her eyes off the vision of beauty before her. May was like a shimmering gold statue with eyes of the clearest blue exuding calmness and strength but it was Ben that she addressed assertively.

"Ben you are the stronger right now as the poison has not yet ravaged your body so. All that you need to create antivenom is within you, within the chemicals and molecules of your body. All you have to do is open your mind to it. The universe is infinite with infinite possibilities. I have shown you how to use those possibilities, go back into your mind and find the way. You have but minutes Ben, don't fail your sister, yourself or your destiny."

May's golden image receded slowly into the brightness behind her.

Ben wasn't sure whether the vision was just something conjured up by the ramblings of a sick mind. He was still pondering that thought in his delirium when he sensed that Elizabeth had slipped back into the darkness that was consuming her for the final time. She was no longer able to resist the destructive venom that was decimating her body and Ben could no longer feel her pulse. Only the last flickers of her humanity remained, like the dying embers of a fire. The shock of it sparked the final release of adrenaline in his own body and Ben forced his mind to recall the 5,000 years or learning that he had been blessed with. His mind became a computer searching the data by category until his mind went into free-flow. The programme was running without his effort, all he had to do was refine the search criteria as the programme ran to find the solution. Only seconds later Ben's body had identified the nature of the poison within him. Antivenom was being created from the basic building blocks within him, much like how antibodies are generated on demand to consume harmful bacteria.

Ben's wounded hand was still bound with Elizabeth's. As the antivenom grew in concentration in his body, he forced it into Elizabeth. At last he felt her pulse in his hand as her heart re-started, followed by the shock when her mind once again joined his.

"Ben, I knew you'd be there for me when I needed you. I just knew it. May will be so proud of you."

"I draw from your strength Lizzie. We are a team. I can't tell you how much I need you to be there for me, I can't do this alone."

Ben was completely used up. He drifted into a dreamless sleep as his mind searched for solace. When the doctors finally gained entry to the room, they found two young people in perfect physical health but driven to the very edge of exhaustion. Neither woke until the following day. The doctors were dumbfounded and unable to make any sense of what had happened. Even the nurse, who was with them throughout, was unable to contribute anything. When George and Jillie Robinson finally arrived at intensive care, they thought that they were being talked to by a load of bumbling fools.

Irma Grese spun the wheels of her green sports car as she followed the black Jaguar out of the car park. Grese had only one thing on her mind, the elimination of the two Angels in the car in front. Her hatred had been exacerbated by the recent mutilation of her daughter Katya at the hand of Elizabeth. The crushing blow to her chest would cripple her for life, leaving her with permanent breathing difficulties and a hunched body. Ironically, Katya was in another ward at the same hospital undergoing surgery. She would require follow up treatment and convalescence for some time ahead and Grese knew that she would never truly recover.

A grim, cruel smile flickered on Grese's lips as she thought about Elizabeth lying in intensive care without hope of survival. She had been in the waiting room when Laura had arrived close to death and had cursed Katya's misfortune that this worthless being had taken the poison to protect Elizabeth. She had been waiting her chance to administer the venom from her own fingernails when Elizabeth had taken the poison from Laura's ravaged body of her own free will, sentencing herself to death. Grese couldn't believe her luck.

"It's this irrational compassion for others that the Angels suffer from that will finally destroy them," Grese concluded.

It had prompted her to return to the school in anticipation of Ben's response and the opportunity to take him while he was still disorientated.

Grese had not anticipated that Williams' brother would be allocated the task of babysitter so soon. Nor that he would have the driving skills of Ayrton Senna! She cursed her car as it failed to keep pace with the Jaguar and had to concede defeat. Grese turned and drove back to town.

"There will be more favourable occasions," Grese conceded.

She comforted herself with the thought that at least she will have secured the death of Elizabeth today.

Chapter 13

Elizabeth and Ben were kept together in quarantine until the Friday. They underwent numerous tests and scans until the doctors finally admitted that they hadn't got a clue what they were looking for, or indeed what had happened. Laura had also been confined but in a separate room and Corporal Jackson had been dismissed as a red herring in the whole affair. The time that Elizabeth and Ben spent together allowed them some thinking space to try and make sense of it all.

Firstly, they considered the attack on Laura. They quickly concluded the obvious, that Elizabeth was the target and Laura was just unfortunate to have taken the venomous strike. Elizabeth shed a few tears over how it had nearly cost her best friend's life and the vision of Laura's life ebbing away in front of her was horrific and something that she would never forget. It opened their eyes as to just how easily they could lose their own lives and those of their loved ones, in this dangerous game between Angels and Shadows that was unfolding before them. This led their thinking on to, "Who was Katya and who had placed her in the school?"

Elizabeth would have liked to have believed that it was Mrs Hyde, but there was no evidence to support this. It just remained a possibility that needed to be explored later. When Elizabeth told Ben about how, in Laura's defence, she had thrust out at Katya unleashing an incredible force from within her propelling Katya across the hallway, he was stunned.

"Awesome!"

He had exclaimed, then jumped out of bed and proceeded to make Kung Fu moves with the associated sound effects, imagining that he was a Japanese Ninja.

"Ben this is serious! Stop behaving like a child, you're not one anymore."

The poignancy of this casual remark hit them profoundly and saddened them. It was the truth; they would never be free again. Nor could they ever afford to be in this dangerous new world that they now lived in.

Elizabeth told of how Katya had not thrown a shadow when she ran out into the sunlight, so she had to be a Shadow herself. It was further evidence of the truth of all that May had told them. They decided that they needed to trap Mrs Hyde in the sunlight to establish if she was a threat or not but they would plan that later. In any event, they needed to know where Katya had come from and how she was placed at the school.

Ben countered this incredible story by the telling of his adventure with Corporal Jackson. He described the race to the hospital with Mike and how they had outrun the Shadow, or Shadows that were chasing them. When Ben told Elizabeth that Mike was also an Angel, sent by May to help protect them, she was elated. She had been struggling with the burden of the responsibility that they had been given. This news was a breath of fresh air, they were no longer alone. But then negative thoughts and doubt consumed her.

"So Mike is an Angel." Elizabeth's tone was down-beat. "That means he will be targeted by the Shadows too and we will lose him. Just like Mum, Dad, Crystalita and David Williams…"

"Not this one, he's a soldier back from the war in Afghanistan. He's used to killing people and stuff. Wait till you meet him Lizzie, he's really cool!"

Elizabeth smiled at Ben's simple boyish faith in Mike.

"Go on Ben, tell me more about Mike and what happened at the hospital."

"He wasn't evenly slightly scared of the Shadows following us and wow can he drive a car, just like Dad could! When we got to the hospital Mike created a diversion by faking a fit so I could get into your room."

Ben's enthusiasm was infectious and Elizabeth was intrigued.

"When I turned from locking the door a nurse tried to stop me and I just held out my hand and said, "Stop, you will do nothing." She just stood there in a trance, motionless doing exactly as she was told."

Another power logged that they had to explore. Then they considered how Elizabeth had taken the poison from Laura's body.

"How did you even know that you could do that?"

Ben couldn't begin to understand where that had come from.

"I didn't but when I was desperate, those words, "You will know what to do," came to my mind again and I reached back into May's teachings, and I just knew. Anyway May had said that we would discover these abilities within ourselves."

Next they considered their communication skills. Elizabeth had reached out to Ben when she needed him across many miles and May had reached out to them from the Mirror World, wherever that was, when they needed her. They spent some time investigating this new found skill until they could even search each other's memories or hide their thoughts. They practiced on the cleaner from Mozambique when she came in and discovered that her thoughts were in Portuguese. Inexplicably, they understood them and were able to chat to her comfortably in her language. The same was true when their doctor, Hans Schmidt. When he visited, they were able to talk to him in German. They discovered from his mind that he was discharging them from the hospital before he even told them.

The thing that amazed them the most was how their bodies had the ability to create the antivenom. They realised that fully understanding how they could self-heal could prove to be the difference between them surviving against the Shadows or not. This was possibly the key and something that they needed to discuss further with May.

Elizabeth and Ben went over and over every detail of what had happened to them since their first meeting with May on the other side of the mirror. They agreed that they needed to see May as soon as they returned home. They wanted to tell her what had happened to them and learn more about their abilities and how to control them. Most importantly, they wanted to plan how they could take the initiative and become the hunters and not the hunted. They knew that if they didn't, it would only be a matter of time before they were eliminated.

At last they were too tired to think clearly. Ben was pulling at his chin as you do when you are exhausted and trying to concentrate at the same time. Elizabeth noticed it for the first time.

"Ben you need to shave, badly!"

Ben rubbed his chin and the astonishment and pleasure was plain on his face.

"My God Lizzie I do!"

He crossed the room to the mirror and admired his stubble. When he turned to face Elizabeth his proud smile went almost from ear to ear. The acceleration in their development, both physically and mentally, was so evident that Elizabeth feared what Aunt and Uncle would say, or indeed their teachers and friends.

Ben read her expression and thoughts and his answer was quite simple.

"We will control their thoughts Lizzie, just like I did with the nurse."

"Yes of course," Elizabeth's reply was equally as matter of fact.

When they arrived home on Friday morning, Aunt Jillie had taken the day off to look after them. She had clearly suffered from the episode and the thought of having nearly lost them was a shock to her and a realisation of just how much she had grown to love them. She was faffing over them like a mother hen.

"Auntie we're just fine, really we are. Don't worry about us. The hospital got it all confused, it was nothing really. Honestly!"

Elizabeth was firm and Aunt Jillie had to concede.

119

"Well OK but I want you to take it easy and call me for anything that you want. The doctor said that you must rest and rest you will. I'll be back shortly with lunch."

Aunt Jillie was just about to walk away when she stopped and looked at them more closely. A look of consternation came over her face.

"You seem to have changed so much so quickly. Lizzie you've got busty and where did *those* hips come from?"

She turned her attention to Ben.

"And you Ben, you're broader at the shoulder and you need a shave too. Come to think of it, your voice has changed. Deeper isn't it?"

It wasn't natural and Ben could see that Aunt Jillie was questioning her sanity. He put his hand on her shoulder and spoke to her softly but firmly.

"And this is normal and as it should be, isn't that so Auntie?"

Jillie answered as she was told.

"Yes it's how things should be," she hesitated for a moment and looked confused. "Where was I? Oh yes, I'll bring lunch shortly."

She left the room smiling happily, unaware that she had been conditioned. *Easement* or *smoothing* was going to be a fundamental skill from this day onwards and they both felt slightly sickened at the thought of it. Later, when Uncle George joined them for dinner, he required the same smoothing and afterwards he thought nothing of their changing appearance. The conversation was vibrant and after steering it away from the hospital episode, good family catch-up time.

Ben and Uncle George were enthusing about the start of the karting season and were planning the complete overhaul of Ben's kart. It soon became apparent that Ben had outgrown it.

"I can't believe you fitted in this just a year ago Ben. Looks like we will have to swop it in for something significantly bigger," George looked quite puzzled.

Aunt Jillie was planning the next day to be a girl's day. It would start with a canter across the Ridge on the horses and then lunch in town followed by a shopping spree.

"I don't know how you're getting into any of your clothes Lizzie? Jillie said thoughtfully. "You'll have to borrow some of mine for now, until we get you sorted."

Aunt Jillie left the room and returned with some of her most feminine clothes for Elizabeth to try on.

"First we'll have to get you into a bigger bra. You can try this one that George bought me. I haven't used it; it's just a bit too young for me."

Jillie shot George a sideways look and a knowing smile. George grinned back awkwardly and was glad to turn his back as Elizabeth tried it on.

Elizabeth turned to face her audience proudly and Jillie looked genuinely shocked.

"Oh my God Lizzie, you've certainly filled that up!" Aunt Jillie was slightly miffed. "You're bigger than me already. You have your mother to thank for that."

Elizabeth just beamed back innocently.

"Come on Ben, let's go online and have a look for your kart. This could get slightly embarrassing."

The girls took no notice of the comment and gaily carried on with their clothes party. As they left the room, Elizabeth looked up and caught Ben's eye, she had read his thoughts and transferred hers.

"Yes Ben it is good to feel normal again, even if only be for a while."

Chapter 14

Saturday had turned out to be an exceptional day for the girl's. Their canter across the Ridge was invigorating and Aunt Jillie had been far too generous with the lunch and shopping. They had agreed not to be too honest with Uncle George about the bill, justified by not wanting to spoil his day. They bundled through the front door dripping with shopping bags and went straight upstairs to hide the evidence.

Ben had spent the morning at cricket practice with his mates under Mike's instruction. Although he was enjoying it, Ben was dying to tell Mike about their adventure. It seemed forever, but last Ben managed to get some one on one time with Mike. He explained all that had happened to them so far and was surprised when Mike already appeared to know most of it. Ben wondered if May had already given Mike a full brief. If so, then she must have accessed both his and Elizabeth's minds to do so. That was something that they needed to consider further.

"So what do you plan to do next then Ben?" Mike cocked his eyebrow in the inquisitive.

"We'll go and see May again today, if Aunt and Uncle leave the house that is. Either that or we will have to *suggest* that they go out."

Ben accidentally cocked a sideways glance at Mike, mimicking his mannerism. It was infectious and hard not to do so. Ben hoped that Mike hadn't noticed. He moved on quickly.

"We have a lot to tell her and we need advice and training on how to get the most out of our new skills. But more than this we need a plan Mike. Lizzie and I agree that if we don't take the fight to the Shadows, they will just pick us off when the time is right for them."

Corporal Jackson was impressed with the maturity of what he was hearing.

"There's a soldier in you Ben and Lizzie too I wouldn't wonder. The best form of defence is often attack and you're right to take the initiative. It will unbalance them for sure and force them to use their lines of command, something that's very weak with the Shadows. By nature they are lone hunters and there's too much rivalry between them to unite effectively."

Mike could see the difference that had come over Ben in only a few days. May had told him that it would happen and he was ready to consult and trust the young man in front of him.

"Is there anything I can do to help?" Mike asked.

Ben's answer was authoritative, as if he had always been used to giving out instructions.

"I want you to find out where Katya came from and where she is now. When you know that I want you to follow Mrs Hyde and see if she casts a shadow. Elizabeth suspects that she is our enemy."

"OK Ben, consider it done."

They were already friends and shook hands before going their separate ways.

Chapter 15

George and Jillie left the house around mid-afternoon on the Saturday and Elizabeth and Ben wasted no time getting ready to see May. Ben had once again taken more care than usual in his appearance. Elizabeth couldn't help smiling at him, secretly enjoying his awkwardness over it. They stood in front of the old mirror holding hands, took a deep breath and then stepped in.

"I wonder where we are," Ben pondered as they walked down the corridor of mirrors, "or even when?"

"That's another question to ask May," Elizabeth replied.

She shuddered as they walked past one of the broken mirrors, subconsciously steering Ben into the middle of the corridor. Her protective instinct for him was ever present.

They could see May further down the corridor. She was looking into one of the mirrors. It was her mirror. May smiled back at them and then turned her gaze back to the mirror. She was dressed in a crisp white cotton shirt and black pencil skirt with black elegant high-heeled shoes. Her hair was tied up slightly wildly completing the secretarial look. Elizabeth could plainly see that she was looking for Ben's approval when she turned back to them.

"I've been expecting you."

She smiled her angelic smile and kissed them both on the cheek which brought an immediate flush to Ben's.

"I have been spending a little family time while I've been waiting for you. Crystalita is celebrating her fifth birthday here today. I remember that dress she's wearing so clearly that it could have been only yesterday, but that was over 5,000 years ago."

Ben looked at May's face in wonderment. She looked serene, gorgeous and human!

"You will help bring her back to me Ben. One day you will do that for me, I know it."

She smiled up at him in a way that only a woman can. When he looked into her eyes, they seemed to have a depth to them that went on beyond eternity. Ben struggled to find his words.

"But..."

May put her finger on his lips to silence him and spoke to him softly.

"Not now Ben, that is for another day. You are here to tell me about your adventure and for me to help you. Some of it I already know. I have prepared some refreshments, won't you join me?"

May linked arms with them and walked them out into the warm summer sun. She kicked off her heels to walk on the soft, cool mountain grass. A table had been prepared and laid out with a typical English tea. Cucumber sandwiches, Danish pastries, scones with strawberries and cream and the Earl Grey tea was served piping hot. While they ate, Elizabeth recounted the story about her new wardrobe to fit her newly found curves. May was enthralled by it and enjoyed all the detail.

"You must have looked stunning and you must wear that little black dress for me next time you come, I just can't wait to see you in it!"

May's face became conspiratorial and she winked at Elizabeth.

"You're going to get a lot of male attention from now on Lizzie and I can't even imagine what Emanuel Goldberg's son, Michael, will make of you when he sees you!"

The name meant nothing to Elizabeth but they were giggling like schoolgirls nonetheless.

"It's my eighteenth birthday party next Saturday, I bought it for that. It's going to be very posh with a marquee in the garden, evening dress and a butler! He has been hired in especially to present the guests as they arrive, isn't that posh?"

Elizabeth was positively beaming at the thought.

"Auntie and Uncle want it to be a very special occasion, but it will get more relaxed later with live music, dancing and karaoke," Elizabeth paused and then asked seductively. "Could you come May?"

124

"You know that I cannot Lizzie. I would love to, but it would be so unwise. Too big a risk. It would be like a calling card to the Shadows."

May looked deeply saddened and Elizabeth crest-fallen. It would have made her night, the icing on the cake.

"I'm so sorry Lizzie, I truly am. Perhaps you could stand in front of the old mirror for a while so that I could admire you and send you my thoughts?"

Elizabeth immediately responded with her best smile but it was hollow. They moved on to address the tea that had been so carefully prepared. Elizabeth and Ben ate ravenously, they hadn't eaten well during their confinement in hospital and their bodies seemed to demand more food lately. Ben asked why.

"It's because of your physiological changes Ben, like a Ferrari needs more fuel than a Skoda."

May had explained which led naturally on to discussing their newly found powers.

Ben took the lead and described his own experiences in detail and Elizabeth joined in where they had experienced the same phenomenon and finally she added her own individual ones. Ben voiced their joint concern.

"Our worry is May, that we have these talents but we don't know how to control them to their fullest or what other possibilities we may have that we've yet to discover. Our lives may depend on us getting things right first time, so we need your guidance."

May paused to collect her thoughts and was assessing their development so far. There were dangers associated with accelerating their learning and development too quickly that could have permanent physical and mental consequences. May had to balance these possibilities with the clear and present risk that the Shadows would now be attacking them relentlessly and that they were not yet ready.

"Indeed you do. In time your abilities will show themselves naturally, as will your power to control them. But I concede that we don't have the time for this consolidation of your new being to take place. For that is what you are now, new beings.

Angels have experienced a hundred million years more evolution than humans. The knowledge that I've given you has allowed your bodies to slowly rebuild your DNA to replicate as closely as possible that of the Angels. The most significant physiological change will be to your brains. Modern man only uses one sixth of the brain whereas yours will soon be working at close to full capacity.

What appear to be powers to you are just manifestations of where humans would be a hundred million years from now. For example telepathy, mind control and hypnosis. Your kind already has some elementary experience of this, but you will be able to call on these abilities to their fullest. Increased senses like hearing, sight, smell, touch are all things that increase with evolution. Your strength will become five times that of normal beings as your bone density increases by almost double. Your ligaments and tendons will thicken and become more load spreading and your muscle fibre will change to a denser, super-fast twitch type that uses anaerobic metabolism to create fuel. This will greatly increase your power, particularly your short burst power."

May turned to Elizabeth.

"This is what you subconsciously called on when you struck out at Katya Lizzie. We call these *basic skills*."

May stopped to allow them time to consider all that she had said while she poured more tea and replenished their plates.

"Then we come on to *complex skills*. You have already begun to experience some of these. You will discover that you have psychokinetic skills; this is using your mind to directly influence a physical system. This could manifest itself in the movement of objects, self-levitation, shape-shifting, teleportation, creating force-fields and biological healing."

May had the absolute attention and wonder of her young audience.

"Take healing for example. Our bodies have all that we need within ourselves to cure most diseases, poisons and afflictions. We only need to search for the right template. You can create the necessary antibodies, stimulate regeneration through stem cells, or re-route your synapses where brain or nerve damage has occurred."

This time May turned to Ben.

126

"This is how you saved Lizzie. Another facet of healing is using your mind to control things such as blood flow in yourself and in others by controlling their minds. It's a lot to take in isn't it?"

Elizabeth nodded in agreement.

"Absolutely; and the Angels gave all this up and thousands of years of life expectancy to live with mortals. Why?"

May's reply was empirical.

"For love; only for love. Don't measure life in time Lizzie, measure it in how much you have loved and have been loved. That is the only reason for us to be. When the end of your life finally comes, you will think only of your loved ones, not of your wealth and certainly not of your age."

"Can we expect more special abilities? Flying would be a good one."

Ben's question was only half in jest.

"Yes more indeed, but Superman you will not be!"

May's smile was a wondrous thing but it was more than a visual experience. They realised for the first time that with it came a feeling of happiness and joy that she somehow stimulated within them through her thoughts as part of her evolutionary skills. They were in completely uncharted territory.

"The next group we call *perceived skills*. As the name suggests, these are only perceived abilities, not real ones and they are only limited by your imagination. For example you can appear to be invisible by controlling other people's perception of you through mind control using auto-suggestion and hypnosis. You could appear to change form into a lion, again by controlling people's perception of you."

Elizabeth and Ben left their seats in shock as May roared at them. She shook her shaggy mane and bared her long yellow teeth, then quickly dropped her deception and reassured them.

"It's OK relax it is just an illusion. I hope I didn't scare you too much?"

"No, no not at all it just made me jump," Ben lied.

He was trying to compose himself and look cool about it. Elizabeth was smiling to herself. "Holy Crap!" was the thought that she had read loud and clear. May must have done too, as the girls exchanged glances and smiled knowingly at each other. Next, May picked up a rock and threw it into the air with unbelievable force. It began to form a trail of fire behind it until it finally burnt itself out.

"What did you just see?" May asked.

"I saw you create a meteor from a small rock May. It was amazing!"

Ben was now fully recovered from the lion affair.

"I threw a rock Ben that's all. Nothing more than that. You saw what I wanted you to see. My mind is much stronger than yours you see and your thoughts were under my control. I'll do it again but this time unite your mind with Lizzie's and resist me, then tell me what you see."

May picked up another rock and threw it in the air. Elizabeth and Ben linked their minds and concentrated on the missile.

"What did you see this time Ben?"

May was teasing him and had an impish grin on her face.

"Just a rock May, nothing more."

Ben was truly astounded, not to mention a little disappointed.

May continued with her enlightenment.

"Don't you now see how powerful that you are together?" May was clearly pleased with the result of the demonstration. "Your combined force is enough even now to counter mine!"

The message was clear and profound. They now knew without any doubt. If they were going to survive against the Shadows, it could only be by working together and multiplying their ability.

"What can we expect of the mirrors and how do they work?" asked Ben.

"They exploit the theory of relativity and quantum mechanics," May began and Ben's attention re-doubled at her reference to science, his favourite subject. "If you accept that a particle can exist in multiple places at the same time, without actually being anywhere at all. And if you accept that it's only the observer that defines the boundaries in the first place, then suppose that there are no boundaries at all. In that scenario you have infinite possibilities. Yes?"

Ben was keeping up and May continued.

"There are infinite realities and we are all living and looking at things in our own individual reality tunnels. We believe what we see then we believe our own interpretation of it. This is known as naïve realism."

Elizabeth had never studied quantum physics but somehow it was making sense to her too. This could only have been through May's knowledge transfer and she could see where it was all leading to.

"So what is real?" May posed the question. "Scientists have mathematical models that demonstrate that light travels as particles called photons and they have instruments that prove and measure that. They also have mathematical models that support that light travels in waves, not photons and instruments and experiments that prove that too. So which reality is true?"

Ben was still contemplating the question when May answered for him.

"The answer is both or even neither. Something is only true relative to the instruments that you are using and where those instruments are in space-time. In a way, you only find what you're looking for in the first place.

The model of the universe is dictated by the instruments that we choose to define it with and our capability to understand it at that time. The mirrors, or portals, exploit those infinite possibilities as do some of your psychokinetic Angel abilities. If you skilfully use these portals you can navigate backwards and forwards in time and space to change the order of things. I have already told you that the universe is infinite with infinite possibilities, you simply create another possibility."

May's tone became very serious as she continued, evident that what was coming would be profound and essential knowledge for them. Elizabeth and Ben sensed it.

"There are some constraints about these mirrors that you must be aware of. You can only return to your own time by returning through the sister mirror to yours. If either the mirror that you enter or its sister mirror are broken while you are in transit, then you will be consumed by the black hole that is created.

An easy way for a Shadow to kill you is when you are in transit by destroying your mirror, so always be aware of this. Finally you cannot co-exist in the same space and time. The molecules of your body and those of your counterpart would become unstable and try to merge, which would destroy both life forms."

"How close is too close?" asked Ben.

"If you can see your counterparts then you are already too close. It's tens of metres only."

"So how accurately can we arrive at a time that we want to?"

"Good question Lizzie. Initially, you will need to go back to a specific memory or event, the chapter of a book if you like. When you become more practiced, you will be able to move freely between days or even discrete times in that day. The pages or sentences of a book would be an analogy. With experience you will also be able to arrive at a specific place, not just at the location of the sister mirror.

At first, until you have developed your skills, you will always return to the exact moment that you left so that anything that has happened to others while you are away will never have happened, erased if you like and a new possibility created. Our portals are set so that when you come to me you will be in my time or we will never create memories and you will take your experiences back to your time when you leave me."

"Can we stop time?" asked Ben.

"Another good question Ben and the answer is yes, although nobody has ever managed to do that yet. Some of those long since dead were able to slow time down but the *how* was lost with the destruction of my planet Angelos."

"How might they have done that May?"

Ben's enquiring mind was stimulated.

"Scientists have always debated whether time was continuous or built up of discrete moments, the latter proved to be true despite the greater lobby to the contrary."

May looked convincing as a lecturer in her white shirt and black skirt. She noticed that Ben was looking at her and pulled her hair grip out shaking her long black hair loose until it fell around her slender neck and shoulders. Ben was distracted and needed to get back on track which was helped considerably by the sharp stab in the ribs that he got from Elizabeth.

"I can't answer that question as I'm not sufficiently practiced in time travel. But I imagine that it would be by manipulation of those discrete moments.

You must understand that it has always been too high a risk for me and Crystalita to leave this place. We were the only true blooded Angels left from the original 300, chosen to secure the bloodline as I have told you. It was only in desperation that I let Crystalita travel to watch over you and it cost her precious life. If I was to do the same and was also killed by the Shadows, then there would be no future for the Angel race and your world would fall under their rule. That is why I cannot go to your party Lizzie. You must believe me when I tell you that in these last centuries, nothing could have pleased me more."

May brought them back on track.

"Travelling backwards in time is the easiest direction, as there is much more stability in the portal. That is because there is only one possibility, which is what has actually happened in your reality. Travelling forwards in time is infinitely more complex, as the future is not dictated by fate. Your destiny is not pre-ordained. Freedom of choice means that there are multiple possibilities so which path would you take?"

May's question was only rhetorical.

"My only advice to you is to look at multiple paths. If the happening is consistently in each of the paths that you explore then it is likely to happen that way."

May looked sad again and continued.

"During the final stages of the Second World War, in 1945, we foresaw the atom bomb attacks by the Americans against the cities of Hiroshima and Nagasaki in Japan. No matter which path we investigated through time, we couldn't find a way to avoid this happening. Consequently, we failed to save some 200,000 men, women and children."

They could plainly see that May's failure still hurt her deeply.

"Sometimes we must accept that we can only do our best," Elizabeth said.

She put her arm around May and placed a gentle kiss on her cheek, in an effort to distract her.

"Where and when are we now?" Ben asked.

He wanted to move the conversation onwards and desperately wished that he had thought of the comforting arm and the kiss first.

"We are where we landed 5,000 years ago. The time is almost as yours but for the addition of our meetings to allow us to create those memories, and the place is Greece near Mount Olympus. The Angels chose it for its isolation and rich flora that we wanted to study. It has since become a National Park and one of the World's Biosphere Reserves. It's remote here and I'm as safe as I can be. Sometimes I take a risk and go to some of the beautiful places but until the Shadows are once more under control, my life is here."

May became reflective again and her grief was immense. It was Ben's chance to be positive now.

"Then what must we do to help you? We already know that we can't hide from the Shadows, which would only delay the inevitable. We need a plan of attack, we need to strike at the very heart of them but we don't know who they are, where they are, or how to do it. We need you to tell us that May."

"Brave words Ben and I know that you have already followed them up with actions. Your friend Mike has told me of his orders and he's executing them right now."

May's reply was spoken with respect for his proactive intent and Ben felt a rush of pride and a flush of blood to his cheeks again.

"You both need me less than you think you do. You are maturing and working it out for yourselves now by accessing the knowledge that I have given you. All I can say is get to know your enemy and get to know them well. Mike will help you and show you where they are. Remember that with the mirrorsm you can change the order of things and your special abilities together are far more advanced than those of the Shadows."

"And what are the strengths and special abilities of the Shadows then, what can we expect?" Elizabeth asked.

She wasn't sure that she really wanted to know what they were up against quite yet.

"Firstly Lizzie, you can expect no compassion or mercy. They are ruthless killers."

May's answer was deliberately firm. She wanted there to be absolutely no doubt in their minds as to what they were up against.

"If you have the chance to kill a Shadow and you hesitate even for one moment, then it will probably cost you your life and risk those close to you. In the worst case, it could cost the lives of all Angels, including me."

May let them consider the magnitude of their situation further. Her eyes were particularly focussed on Ben and she was trying to reinforce the message in his mind. Over the centuries she had seen many brave men lose their lives to the Shadows through compassion or just plain male ego. She could sense that he had that flaw in his nature too.

Elizabeth and Ben silently communicated their understanding of the importance of this with a brief mental exchange and mutual promises to each other. May continued.

"As for the Drones, their strength is only in their numbers and their inventiveness in killing techniques. Their physical ability is only that of an all-round human athlete, no more. They are only well coordinated as a unit when commanded by one of the Senators, so if you can cut the head off the beast by destroying the Senator, then the Drones are impotent. Fortunately Drones only number thousands over the whole planet because the Senate restrict their population through birth control and by culling them."

Ben was both shocked and puzzled at what possible benefit that could be to the Shadows.

"Why would they do that May, why would they cull their own?"

"Fear of mutiny and losing a power struggle to them. The Senate themselves only number a few hundred globally and so they need a regime of strict control.

Their plan to not integrate with the human population was flawed. Inbreeding slowly reduced their fertility and their numbers have ceased to increase effectively for several hundred years. This has been exacerbated by their mortality rate. There are regular killings associated with feuds both between cells and within cells. The Shadows are in decline but they still hold sway over the Angels."

Elizabeth was stunned.

"My God, so they hate each other almost as much as they hate us?"

"Yes Lizzie. I have told you that they are devoid of any compassion. It will be difficult for you to understand just how empty their souls are and the terrible things that they are capable of doing to achieve power. Many of the wars in history have been as a result of Shadow in-fighting.

The Senate have divided your world into States, each with its own Senators working independently within cells across the State. The cell that has been chosen by the Supreme Senator to destroy you and your family is led by Adolphius. His other senior Senators are Alexis, Dada and Grese whose daughter Katya you have already met.

You will already know the history of these other Shadows from my knowledge transfer to you. Would you rather that I go over it again with you?"

"No," Elizabeth replied for the both of them, "we already understand who they are."

"It is sufficient to say that you couldn't be up against a more dangerous cell of cutthroats. These are some of the most despicable people across all of time."

Even May shuddered at the thought of what was waiting out there for Elizabeth and Ben to face.

"So what powers can we expect from the Senate, the elite?" asked Ben hesitantly.

"None superior to yours on a one to one basis and certainly not if you and Lizzie develop your skills and work together; however they have several thousands of years of experience and cunning to call upon. They will have similar physical strength to you, so don't try and confront them in this way, particularly at night when they are at their most dangerous. They have well developed brains analytically, but lack the ability to form an integrated approach as I have said. They are masters of all weaponry as they have practiced and used them in anger for thousands of years. As old as he is, there is no man yet born that can match Alexis' swordsmanship nor his cunning."

Again May directed that comment directly at Ben.

"So don't let your bravado play you into their hands."

Ben acknowledged her warning with an almost dismissive nod that sent a frisson of dread down May's back and scalp. Ben was indeed likely to be hot-headed and risk all, she surmised. May continued her brief.

"But these are only the basic skills that I talked about earlier. Their complex skills are night based and they mostly come at night, when they want to do their killing that is. At night they can draw power from the darkness to enhance their basic skill set. They can see perfectly in total darkness and become physically much stronger and can better cloak their thoughts so that you cannot sense them. In effect they become almost invisible to you so that you cannot defend yourselves so easily. This is why we have sent guardians such as Crystalita, David and now Mike to watch over you so that they think twice about coming for you at night when you sleep."

"Great," thought Elizabeth, "not only have I got a stalker in my dreams to keep me awake and terrified at night, now I've got Shadows..."

It was Ben however that voiced his concerns, clearly alarmed at their vulnerability.

"I don't think that I'll ever sleep again. Is there anything that we can do to protect ourselves?"

"Remain vigilant and don't sleep in your usual beds until this is over, and always sleep in defence mode. When you found me sleeping beside the tree, I was camouflaged by changing your perception of me. You must do this too. It's a skill that comes with practice and that is what you must do tonight and every night until you have it to perfection."

This was simply not enough to allay Ben's fears.

"That's just passive defence May, isn't there something that we can actively do?"

"Your greatest defences and your ability to attack are through your acute senses, particularly your hearing and sense of smell. Shadows have a double heart beat and a slightly acrid smell about them."

May began tapping the table to mimic the Shadow heart rhythm so that they would recognise it when the time came.

"With practice you will be able to place them accurately in a room even with your eyes shut. Trust your senses, you will even feel their acrid breath against your skin."

Elizabeth winced at the thought of Shadow breath upon her and nodded in agreement to the thoughts that Ben was transmitting to her. They would no longer sleep in their own rooms. In future, they would room together on the floor in the spare room. From now on, they would practice their new skills every night until they could tell where each other was blindfolded. That had an added advantage for Elizabeth, in that she wouldn't have to be alone to face the dreadful nightmares that were increasing in severity by the night.

"Do you have a dog?"

May's question seemed off-track and took them both by surprise. Elizabeth responded.

"No, Aunt Jillie's more of a cat person and won't hear of it. Why do you ask?"

"Dogs will sense them first and give you an early warning. Mike was also a dog-handler in the Army and has two trained Huskies. I will tell him to have Santini stationed in your garden at nights from now on. He will make sure that Tini's gone by the morning, so that your aunt doesn't fret. But you must listen out for him as your lives may depend on it. Is that clear?"

"Crystal," Ben confirmed.

His reply had an air of relief about it. The thought of a guard dog was a comfort to them and their faces showed it.

"You must go now and spend time with each other, practicing your skills. As these grow, so will your confidence and self-belief. If you are ever in doubt just trust your instincts, they will never be wrong."

May smiled at them lovingly and touched Ben's shoulder absentmindedly. "Have a lovely party Lizzie and look after Ben for me."

The touch on Ben's shoulder filled all of his senses and completely removed his power of speech. He fumbled for some words that never came. Elizabeth rescued him.

"I will and thanks for our teas and your help today May. We'll pose for you in front of the old mirror on Saturday, just as you've asked, so that you can see my dress and how dashing a man Ben looks in his tuxedo!"

Elizabeth gave May a knowing smile and it was now May's turn to look just a little embarrassed.

Chapter 16

That night, they arranged their beds to look slept in with cushions under the bed sheets and open books on their pillows. When they were perfectly happy with the deception, they moved into the spare bedroom. They chose to sleep in separate corners of the room directly on the carpet, with Ben behind the door and Elizabeth by the window furthest from it.

Ben had taken the two 19th century French naval cutlasses from Uncle George's study wall and conditioned him not to miss them. He had hidden them under the two corners of the double bed closest to where they would sleep, so that they would be directly at hand if needed. The logic of their chosen sleeping positions was that if an attack came from the door, then Ben would have the advantage of surprise from his position emerging from the back of it. On the other hand, an attack from the window would suit Elizabeth's position.

Their biggest fear was an attack from the other wing of the house where their aunt and uncle slept, placing them in danger first. They agreed that this was unlikely, as there were no stairs at that end and the windows faced the road. They were as sure as they could be that an attack would come from downstairs, through the hallway, then taking the staircase passing Ben's room. Elizabeth's room was the next then the intruders would have to pass the guest room, where they were now before going on to where their aunt and uncle slept. They hoped to God that this would be true, the consequences of it not being so, was unthinkable.

They took turns in controlling the other's perception and finally, when they lay on the bedroom carpet, they appeared to be part of it. After only a few hours all that the other could perceive was a slight irregularity in the shade of the carpet, almost like a stain. This turned into a game. They played hide and seek around the house blending with the curtains, sofas and even the challenge of the black and white chequered tiles of the kitchen floor. This eventually became too easy for them so they tried to find each other blindfolded. Each put the smallest spot of vinegar on their foreheads to simulate the faint acrid smell of the Shadows and then they hid in turn.

Ben was first to be the seeker. He moved silently around the house blindfolded. He was surprised that his memory of the layout of each room was so accurate, that he rarely even touched the furniture. It was as he passed the open doorway of the dining room that he first tasted the sour odour of the vinegar. It was at a concentration of only a few parts in a million but he tasted it nevertheless. Ben allowed the air to pass through his open mouth to savour it and he sniffed the aroma. He immediately had the direction and oriented himself to it. Then there was the heartbeat. Elizabeth had controlled it down to less than ten beats a minute but each was a thunderclap to his sensitive ear and her shallow breathing, like the rush of wind filling a sail. In moments he had her face in his hands. Ben tore off his blindfold and began to brag.

"Yes Lizzie! Three minutes, I got you in just three minutes. You'll never beat that!"

Ben was prancing and whooping around the room jeering at her.

"My turn," Elizabeth said, taking the blindfold.

Much to Ben's chagrin, she did; and comfortably.

"Don't mess with your big sister sucker," Elizabeth taunted.

She did that little childhood victory dance that never failed to annoy Ben, and it didn't on this occasion either. He faked a yawn. The game was no longer amusing.

"Boring, let's play something else."

Elizabeth and Ben went back to the guest room and practiced all the possible scenarios of how a Shadow might enter the room. They considered which way he would turn and how they would administer death in each case. Both were concerned that in the darkness and confusion, they could injure or kill each other. Their plans, therefore, had to be well thought out, robust and well-practiced.

They agreed that they would not communicate mentally with each other prior to the assault for fear of the Shadow tuning in on their thoughts and revealing their plans and positions. This would make it even more essential that the killing was so well rehearsed, as to be done automatically at the time and with no emotion.

Finally they considered that, when the time came, could they actually thrust their swords into the Shadow's living flesh and take his life? Practice and reality being so far apart, it would be massively outside of any of their life-experience and nature. At last they agreed that they could. Any doubts were cast aside when they thought of the Shadows killing their parents, Crystalita, Emanuel Goldberg, David Williams and countless nameless millions over the last 5,000 years. They were ready; well as long as it was only a single Shadow entering the house, coming up the stairs that is...

That night, Corporal Jackson concealed a triple strand of piano wire along the edge of the lawn. It ran the full length of the Robinson's garden and was securely anchored at both ends. Finally he attached a nine foot braided wire runner, that he would clip to Tini's collar. Huskies are notorious escape artists and Tini was no exception. Mike was taking no chances. Satisfied with his work, Mike returned to his car to fetch the dog. Tini was a magnificent specimen of his type, powerfully built with an intelligent expression. As was common in the breed, he had one blue and one yellow eye, which gave him a quizzical expression not too dissimilar to Mike's.

Mike clipped Tini to the runner and fussed him for a while.

"Do your duty soldier, we're all counting on you."

Tini's response was as if he had completely understood the command. With no more fuss he moved into the shrubs and laid down in waiting. He was willing and alert with ears pricked up and eyes searching in eager anticipation. Tini began sniffing and tasting the air for that familiar acrid smell that would always bring out the madness in him.

Mike returned to his car and set off for his second task of the evening, he needed to find out where Katya lived. He arrived at the Northlands school at around nine o'clock in the evening and it was deserted as he expected, well apart from the caretaker doing his evening rounds that is.

"Good evening Corporal Jackson, can I help in any way?"

"Hello Jim. Yes I was hoping to find you. Can you let me in, I have some papers to prepare for tomorrow?"

Mike's reply was cheery and secured the response that he wanted. Jim opened the side entrance for him.

"Do you want me to lock up when I leave Jim?"

"No just pull the door to and I'll pop back later, but thanks anyway."

Jim turned away and left Mike unsupervised, just as he had anticipated.

The Secretary's office was unlocked as Mike had expected but the filing cabinet was not.

"The keys will be in the top right-hand drawer of the desk if I am not mistaken," Mike assumed and they were. He wondered at the pointlessness of locking it and his face fell naturally into that quizzical look of his. "Why do they always do that?"

Mike shuffled through the folders until he came to the personal files of the students. They were filed alphabetically by surname, by year. He came to Grese, Katya and let out an unintentional whistle.

"A big fish indeed," he mused, "and the daughter of Irma Grese, one of the Senate."

He memorised the address, closed the file and put everything back as was. When he walked out into the corridor he already had his next move planned.

Adolphius had called an extraordinary meeting of the cell. The usual Senators were there but with the addition of Katya, who was now being groomed for the future. The Hydra had heard of the numerous failed attempts at disposing of the Robinsons and had given him the roasting of his life. That included very real death threats unless it was sorted. Adolphius was anxious to pass this on to his subordinates. You could have cut the atmosphere with a knife. Grese and Katya were purposefully separated from the other members, so as to be facing them. Any similarity to a trial was absolutely intentional.

"So Grese," began Adolphius removing his aviator sunglasses and forcing Grese to look into the blackness of his eyes, "you have some explaining to do. The fiasco of your failed endeavours to kill mere children has escalated to the attention of the Hydra. She wants results or blood, but it will not be mine Grese, you can be sure of that!"

"And who has delivered this information to the Hydra?"

Grese shot an accusing look at Dada that would have withered even the hardiest flower.

Adolphius avoided the question and defended both himself and the rest of the Senate.

"The Hydra has her sources and her expectations. You have failed her and worse than that, you have failed me!"

Adolphius' fist smashed on the table at the word *me* and his tyrannical eyes spelt death. Grese was unbalanced. Before she could articulate a response Dada was on his feet, his arm was extended pointing accusingly at her.

"The woman is a habitual failure. You entrust her with simple but vital tasks and she consistently fails to deliver, you might as well send in the Drones. She is not worthy of the Senate and you risk our reputation with the Hydra every time you use her. It must stop Adolphius!"

He was a massive man towering above Grese. Beads of sweat were forming on Dada's bald pate making his black skin shine like ebony and his white teeth cut a fierce gash in the blackness of his face.

"If the Senate agrees, I will go to the Robinson's house tomorrow night myself and kill them in their beds."

Dada kissed his fist and pointed at Grese. It was the Shadow's symbol of death. Everyone in the room, including Grese, knew that her days were now numbered. Adolphius looked at Alexis for his ratification and he simply closed and opened his rheumy eyes. It was done, Grese's future as a Senator was now as precarious as was her life expectancy.

The atmosphere in the room was passed hostile. Adolphius chose to relieve it by pointing out the obvious.

"Of course they will have a dog stationed at the house."

Dada nodded in silent agreement but his eyes never left Grese's.

Mike parked his car a couple of streets from the Grese household and approached it from the back garden. The house was in darkness and a brief search proved that nobody was home. Mike wanted to be sure that they still lived there so he climbed up the side of the flat-roofed garage, laid down, and prepared himself for a long wait.

It was after midnight when a car turned into the drive and pulled up in front of the garage. Mike dared not raise his head as Shadow's night vision was impeccable and he would've been seen for sure. Grese would have scaled the wall to his position on the roof in seconds. Even with his Angel strength, Mike knew that he would be no match against her hand to hand, particularly at night. He was forced to glean what he could from his acute sense of hearing and he cursed himself for not being armed. It was a rare occurrence to find members of the Senate out in the open and unguarded. The conversation between Grese and Katya was explosive.

"Damn that Dada to Hell, how dare he?" Grese was spitting fire, "Shaming me in front of Adolphius and Alexis, like I was an incompetent child. When did that black oaf do anything useful, tell me? I've killed ten times as many Angels as he has!"

"Then kill him Mama. If you don't then he will kill you. It's only a matter of time."

Katya was struggling to get her broken body out of the car. She winced as the painful spasms racked her body.

"He said that you failed the Senate and that he will kill the Angel siblings himself. You know where he will do it and when he will do it. Make him fail Mama. You can kill the siblings another day and take the glory."

Katya was every inch as vicious and sadistic as her mother.

"Besides, I want the revenge to be ours. I want to kill Elizabeth for giving me this mutilated body which must I must bear for millennia. But I will only kill her after she has watched me mutilate and kill her brother."

142

Katya's face was a mask of pure evil.

"And when Dada's gone, I will have a full seat on the Senate!"

Katya was silently wondering how she would then displace her mother; such is the way of the Shadows.

"Katya you remind me of me, only you are much sweeter and more sensitive."

Grese laughed at the blatant falseness of the statement but it was not a laugh of joy, it was empty and chilling.

"It will be done as you say Katya and we will make those plans tonight."

Mike heard the car doors close but waited until Grese and Katya were in the house before raising his head. He looked down at the car and gasped, it was a green Lotus. He realised right then that it must have been Grese who had killed his brother and the Robinsons. He was now even more furious with himself for missing his chance of revenge.

"I hope you die screaming you evil bitch. And your crippled sprog, sired by the Devil himself!"

Mike jumped from the roof, landed lightly and was gone in the darkness.

Mike arrived at the Robinson's house just after six o'clock the next morning. The excited welcome that he got from Tini, almost took him off his feet. An onlooker could not have doubted the love that one had for the other. Mike unhooked the runner and hid it in the shrubs ready for his return that evening. He left without disturbing the household.

After school that day, Mike joined Elizabeth and Ben at the school gate. It was the first time that Elizabeth had met Mike. After the initial introduction Mike began to recount his story of the previous night. Neither Ben nor Mike noticed that Elizabeth was a bit withdrawn and hardly contributed to the conversation. It wasn't that Elizabeth lacked interest, far from it, it was just that she felt somehow awkward and didn't know why or what to say.

"The conversation was running between the two boys anyway," Elizabeth thought.

She was looking for something in the way of self-justification. Mike continued.

"OK to sum up then. The Shadows have already planned their attack on you, including who is going to do it, how, where and more or less when. We also know that Grese wants this Shadow, Dada, to fail for reasons of her own personal power struggle. She was driving a green sports car, so we now know that Grese was the killer of our loved ones. Not bad for a nights work is it?"

Mike ended the summary with his lop-sided grin. The question didn't require an answer. Both he and Ben knew though, that it was a missed opportunity to kill Grese and Katya. But then hind-sight is a wonderful thing. Ben chose to respond positively.

"It's a fantastic start Mike. May said to get to know your enemy, and you've done just that and taken us a big step forward. We can follow Grese now, and that will lead us to the others. Then we can kill them all!"

Ben was caught up in the excitement of the moment and made it all sound so simple. Mike on the other hand, was still feeling that he'd failed to complete his own personal mission. Ben's enthusiasm didn't fill that emptiness.

Their exchange gave Elizabeth the chance to find her tongue.

"I'm glad that you didn't kill them Mike. It would have been an unnecessary risk and it wouldn't have made any difference to us if you had."

Ben was flabbergasted. What she had said made no sense to him at all.

"What the hell are you talking about Lizzie, have you gone out of your mind?"

"Mum said that I would know what to do and I do now Ben. At last I clearly and most definitely do," Elizabeth had regained her composure and was serenely confident. "They must all die Ben, horribly if necessary, but they must all die at the right time and that is not now."

"The right time, what do you mean the right time?"

Ben was now even more puzzled. Elizabeth enlightened him.

"What purpose would Grese's death yesterday have achieved for us?"

"Revenge!"

Ben and Mike's answers were simultaneous.

"And what would it achieve if we did it a little more than four years ago?" Elizabeth prompted with a smile.

"Using the mirrors?" Ben was catching up. "We could stop the murders from happening in the first place!"

"Yes Ben, using the mirrors and it's not just Mum, Dad and David. It could be Crystalita and many others that we don't even know of, that she has killed over the last four years."

It was Mike's turn to lose his tongue. He was absorbed in all that Elizabeth was saying but more than that, he was totally absorbed in her. He couldn't take his eyes off her. He felt clumsy and inarticulate and found himself nodding like a toy dog on the back shelf of a car on a bumpy road. Elizabeth rescued him gently.

"Of course Mike, we will need you to help us do what we have to do."

Mike just nodded a little bit more.

It was dinner time at the Robinson's. They were all animatedly discussing the final arrangements for Elizabeth's birthday party, or Ball, as it was swiftly becoming. George and Jillie wanted it to be a day to remember for Elizabeth, but they would of course have some business colleagues and clients attend. Money was no object and they were working on the final guest list.

"Can I invite Corporal Mike Jackson, our new sports master please? Only he's turned out to be such a friend," Ben asked hesitantly.

"Oh yes Auntie, you will love him. He's Mr Williams' brother and just as dashing."

Elizabeth added the *dashing* bit, certain that Aunt Jillie would experience the same love at first sight as she did when she met him.

"Ah well that sounds promising, even if he only turns out to be half as dashing. I'll need his full title though so that we don't announce him incorrectly when he arrives. I will call the school today for it and get his place name printed too."

Jillie was already curious about Corporal Jackson.

"Where would you like him to sit Ben?"

"Next to Lizzie would be good."

Ben looked for Elizabeth's response and he wasn't disappointed in the slightest, she went as red as a beetroot and looked furious.

"Gotcha!" he thought to himself, looking quite smug.

"You bastard!"

Was the transmitted reply.

Chapter 17

It was eight o'clock in the evening when Mike clipped Tini to his runner in the Robinson's garden. He went through his usual settling routine with the dog and then made a wide search of the area, including checking all the parked cars. One of them was a black Range Rover with tinted windows.

Mike looked into the car and sensed that something wasn't right but he couldn't quite work out what. He was confused and the more he looked, the less concerned he became. He felt the engine hood and it seemed cold to him although he could hear the exhaust manifold crackling, but never questioned the contradiction of it. Finally, satisfied that there was no threat, he moved on to the next car. Mike had no idea that he had been staring Dada directly in the face and that his mind was being controlled to see only what Dada wanted him to see. All seemed as it should be. Mike returned to his car and left for an early night to catch up on some lost sleep.

Dada was pleased with his deception. It saved him having to take the risk of killing the young man in the street. He reclined his seat and settled himself for the long wait until the early hours of the morning, when he would have some killing to do.

Later that evening Elizabeth and Ben set up their bedrooms to look occupied as was now their routine. They drew the curtains, switched off the lights, and retired to the guest room. They checked that the cutlasses were still under the bed where they had left them, and took their sleeping positions on the floor. The curtains were left open to let some light in, but the moon was new and it only made the faintest difference. They would have to rely almost totally on their other senses if an attack came. Elizabeth and Ben ran through their plans and *what if* scenarios until they were as happy with them as they could be then drifted off to sleep.

It was three o'clock in the morning when the door of the Range Rover opened. Dada stepped out into the cold, unlit street and shook the stiffness out of his powerful limbs. Dada had chosen this hour as it is the time when humans are at their lowest ebb, and least able to respond to a situation. He noted that even the moon was in his favour, and was invigorated by the near total darkness that it afforded him. Dada's good fortune was short lived though. A police squad car entered the road and the two officers spotted his enormous frame at the side of the Range Rover and pulled over behind it. They exited the squad car donning their hats and approached Dada from opposite sides of his car.

"Your vehicle is it sir?"

Offered the senior of the two officers. He was a tall, thick-set man with broad shoulders, the sort that looked like he worked out a lot. His tone was derisive.

"Is that yours?"

Dada replied through his teeth slanting his head towards the squad car. His eyes never left the officer's.

"We've got us a wise guy Joe, thinks he's somebody."

The officer withdrew his police issue X26 Taser from his belt.

"Not really your kind of neighbourhood is it sir?"

The officer was goading Dada to make him retaliate.

"It was until you just downgraded it."

147

Dada countered, as he decided how he was going to kill him.

"Easy Dave, back off mate," Joe, the junior officer, was trying to defuse the situation. He turned to Dada, "Can I see your driving licence please sir?"

Dada decided that this polite one would die a little less painfully than the other. He opened the Range Rover door and reached in taking the Zulu broad-bladed stabbing spear in his right-hand and his silenced pistol in his left. As Dada turned to face the officers he squeezed the trigger. A bullet hole appeared in the front of Joe's head, just a split second before his brains left the back of it.

It was already too late to save his colleague but not himself. The other officer shot the Taser into Dada's chest delivering 50,000 volts right across his heart, enough to stun a large horse. The big officer's face paled then twisted with horror as Dada casually pulled the electrodes out like it was just the sting of a bee. The police officer realised at that moment that he was a dead man.

Dada rotated the spear into the classic Zulu upward stabbing grip. He thrust it up through his victim's abdomen, into his lungs, ripping through his aorta on its way. The force of the upward stabbing movement, brought the officer's face within inches of Dada's. The final memory that he took with him to eternity was that of Dada's cruel and sadistic grin.

Dada opened the tailgate of the police car and discharged the officer from his spear into the back of it and then returned with the other. He covered the bodies with a survival blanket, locked the car and tossed the keys into the nearby bushes. It was the perfect appetiser and Dada now felt ready for the main course. He had already seen where the dog was tethered. He circled the Robinson's home from a safe distance until he arrived at the other side of the house. The night breeze was blowing from the direction of the dog towards him and he could taste the rank odour of it, an odour hated by all Shadows. It would be impossible for the dog to sense or smell him with the wind in that direction. Everything was falling nicely in his favour.

Dada was dressed in a black overall and black boots making him almost invisible in the gloom. He had the pistol tucked in his belt on the left side and the Zulu broad-bladed stabbing spear was in his right hand. It was the same iron spear that he had used in the Anglo-Zulu war at the Battle of Isandlwana in 1879. Dada along with 20,000 Zulu warriors had attacked and killed 1,300 of the 1,800 British and colonial troops that were camped there. This was despite them being heavily armed with Martini-Henry breech-loading rifles and seven pounder canons. It was the same stabbing spear that he had used at the battle at Rorke's Drift that followed. A mere 150 troops, led by Lieutenant John Chard, had impossibly defended the tiny garrison against 4,000 of Dada's Zulus in an intensive assault. On this occasion, Dada had killed more retreating Zulu than were killed by any single man of the British and colonial troop. Lieutenant John Chard and ten others were awarded Victoria Crosses for their bravery; the most ever received in a single action by one regiment. Chard was an Angel as were three others that were commended. Dada cursed this wretched part of the memory. He kissed the steel blade that he had meticulously sharpened to a razor edge and muttered under his breath.

"You will drink blood once again tonight," he murmured.

Dada began his approach. He had already surveyed the area and had observed that the electricity to the house was fed by an overhead cable. Dada shinned up the post effortlessly and slashed at the cable with his stabbing spear, plunging the house into darkness. Although he was some twenty feet in the air, he jumped to the ground and landed almost silently, which was an incredible feat for such a massive man. Dada had carefully planned his entry route through the glazed panel of the window by the front door. This opened into the grand hallway that would give him access to the main staircase leading up to the bedrooms. He had studied the layout of the house from Council building records and was reasonably sure that Elizabeth and Ben's rooms would be near the top of the staircase. Logically this would have given the adults the more private back wing of the house where he would find and kill them afterwards.

Dada produced a diamond cutting tool and a suction cup from his small backpack. He wetted it with his own spittle then pressed it to the glass. Dada scribed a generous circle with the glass-cutter and waited patiently for a passing vehicle. It was almost fifteen minutes before a milk wagon turned into the street and the jangling bottles gave him just the cover that he needed. As the wagon passed Dada tapped the glass with the butt of his pistol and simultaneously pulled at the suction cup. The glass snapped with a loud crack and the opening was made. Not even the dog had detected the noise. Dada was in making his way silently to the main staircase.

It was a little after midnight when Grese parked the hired BMW at the top end of the street that led to the Robinson's house. She had chosen the position well. It gave her a clear line of sight to Dada's Range Rover, but was far enough away that neither Dada nor the dog would sense her presence. It also gave her a view of the front entrance and the power cable feeding the house. Shadows like to hunt in darkness, so this was an obvious target for Dada. Grese waited in the gloom licking her upper lip, as was her habit when deliciously anticipating death.

At three o'clock, her waiting was over. Dada opened the door of the Range Rover and stepped out. Grese cursed as the police car turned into the street and stopped behind Dada's Rover. If Dada was to abort his mission then she may never get her chance again. She held her breath and looked on in trepidation. When she saw him dispatch the officers effortlessly, she had to admire his professionalism despite her own personal hatred of him. Grese watched as he made his way towards the power supply to the house. Moments later she saw the cable drop and Dada re-appear at the front of the house, where he busied himself at one of the windows.

"Predictable," Grese thought with contempt.

Grese waited until he had entered the house before leaving the cover of the BMW. She ran lightly down the road to the Robinson's house, comfortably vaulted the neighbour's six foot fence, then ran along the boundary to where the dog was likely to be tied. Grese wasn't disappointed. Tini got scent of her immediately and was maddened by it. He began howling, barking and straining to get off his lead. His killer instinct was excited and his fangs, bared. The acrid smell of Shadow was driving him mad.

"Good luck with the Angels Dada!" Grese muttered through clenched teeth, "and may you rot in Hell!"

Dada was half way up the staircase when he heard the dog. He knew instantly that it must have been Grese that had set him up.

"Damn you bitch! I'll deal with you too before this night is out, I swear it."

He continued up the stairs, pistol and spear at the ready. Ben's bedroom was the first room that he came to. Dada had to act quickly now, as the dog was raising such bedlam that the whole house would be awake soon. He thrust the door open, aimed his pistol at the sleeping body under the blankets and the silenced gun spat three bullets into it. Dada dragged the blankets back to confirm his kill. He cursed under his breath as he saw the cushions arranged to dupe him. He stepped back into the corridor and crashed into Elizabeth's room emptying his gun into the shape under the covers. Dada ejected the spent magazine from the pistol and reloaded in an instant. He pulled the covers back and his rage boiled over as he exposed the same carefully arranged cushions.

"I will find you and you will feel the cold steel of this spear tonight," Dada vowed.

He approached the guest room and sensed them inside. It was only a brief exchange but one had linked with the other, giving their position away.

"Now I have you!"

A cruel smile flickered on his broad lips as he prepared himself to burst into the room.

Ben heard Tini first. He was in a deep sleep and it took valuable seconds for him to come to his senses. The floorboards in the corridor were creaking like never before, under some unusually heavy weight. He heard three thuds then the creaking again but this time much closer. Ben was desperate, Elizabeth wasn't waking up. He knew that to break silence, would be suicide. Three more thuds came from Elizabeth's room next door and something clattered to the floor.

The intruder was in the corridor again and Ben couldn't wait any longer. Despite the dangers, he linked with her mind.

"Wake up Lizzie, wake up! There's a Shadow outside in the corridor!"

Elizabeth woke and focussed immediately. She could hear Tini barking frantically now and that could only mean one thing. She grabbed her cutlass from under the bed, taking up the crouching position as she did so. She was ready to spring, just as they had practiced so many times. The intruder had unaccountably stopped outside their door and long seconds passed. Even though their fear was so great as to be almost palpable, they controlled their breathing and heart rates down to almost zero, minimising their visibility to their attacker. They waited in terror of what was sure to come. They hoped to God that they could do what they had planned and practiced, or they would die here this very night.

Dada moved back as far as he could from the door and bent double, then charged head first like a marauding black bull. The solid oak bedroom door shattered like matchwood under the force delivered by Dada's thick scull. He was in and his gun was spitting bullets randomly around the room, hoping for a lucky kill. The crouched positions that Elizabeth and Ben had adopted, saved their lives and the bullets fizzed harmlessly above their heads.

Dada's perfect night vision detected nothing in the room and his acute hearing was giving him no clues either. He spun around scanning the room as he skilfully ejected and replaced the spent magazine. Then it happened. The carpet around him erupted and they were on him. The cutlasses were driven in unison, up through his abdomen and out through his back. Elizabeth and Ben recoiled from the strike withdrawing their swords for the next assault. They were navigating by their senses. The Shadow's heart was beating like a drum and he was breathing heavily under the trauma of his wounds, making their visualisation easy.

Dada was far from disabled though. He recovered his senses quickly and aimed his pistol directly at Elizabeth's face. Ben picked up the smell of cordite in the barrel of the gun and was able to place it accurately. He immediately realised that Elizabeth was in the direct line of fire and he had no time to warn her. Ben brought his cutlass down from above his head with all the Angel power within him, severing Dada's gun hand. The trigger finger of the severed hand went into convulsive spasms and bullets were flying randomly around the room. What would have sent any other being into a rigid state of shock, only served to enrage the bull. Dada was fighting for his life now and it concentrated his mind ten-fold. Elizabeth was trapped between him and the bed with no place to go. He brought his stabbing spear up, in that typical Zulu fashion, from low right upwards, aiming to pierce Elizabeth below her ribs and up into her heart. The faintest glimmer of moonlight reflected from the blade of Dada's spear, betraying his intention. Ben saw it.

"Lizzie!" he screamed out in vain.

It was too late. Ben threw his body into the arc of the spear to protect her. Dada's stabbing spear took Ben in the middle of his chest with such force that it drove him up into the far corner of the ceiling, driving his head through the plasterboard into the timber joists above. Ben dropped to the floor like a rag doll and lay there motionless. Elizabeth lost Ben's thoughts instantly, as if a telephone line had been cut off in mid-sentence. She realised the enormity of the sacrifice that Ben had just made, his life for hers. Elizabeth flew into a black rage. It was the biggest mistake that Dada had made in over 5,000 years of life.

Elizabeth's perception of her environment was heightened by the enormity of her loss. She could literally *see* him clearly now and the lioness was on him. Elizabeth's rage had accentuated her Angel senses, joining them together to form a complete picture. It was almost as if he was in bright sunshine. She wanted revenge for the loss of her cub. The slashes from her cutlass came hard and fast, carving lumps of meat off him. Dada was driven into a state of panic, unable to lift his spear in defence of this hurricane attack. He burst out of the room and ran for his life down the stairs, crashing through the window into the garden. Elizabeth dropped her cutlass and ran to the limp and blood-soaked body of her brother.

In his panic Dada made his second monumental mistake of the night. Instead of running out through the wide open main driveway to the road, he chose the secluded route out through the Robinson's garden. Tini smelt the rancid cocktail of Shadow and blood as Dada turned the corner of the house and he launched himself into attack. Tini's powerful legs, and the madness caused by the scent, drove him towards Dada at impossible speed. When Tini reached the bounds of his tether, the momentum that he had generated snapped the piano wire like cotton and he leapt at the Shadow. Dada saw the dog just in time to raise his spear and met it full on. The razor-sharp blade entered Tini's shoulder and the sheer force of his jump drove it up the full length of his body. It rattled between his ribs and his skin until it exited through his back leg. The power of Tini's attack carried him on up the shaft of the spear until he and Dada were face to face.

Dada's last memory on this Earth, were of the dog's piercing yellow and blue eyes as Tini ripped his throat out.

Elizabeth picked up Ben's slack body and laid him on the bed. Tears of grief were streaming down her blood splattered face. She tenderly swept the blonde curl of hair from his forehead with her delicate fingers and spoke to him as if he was a child.

"Why did you do that Ben when you know that your life is more precious to me than mine?" she was rocking him gently.

"I can't do this without you Ben. They can take me too now, I'm done with this. I've no more fight left."

Elizabeth curled up next to Ben on the blood-soaked bed and laid her head on his chest, completely stricken and defeated. He had sacrificed his life for hers and nothing mattered anymore. The sharp pain that she suddenly felt in her temple brought her to her senses. She lifted Ben's blood soaked shirt to see what it was and her jaw dropped in amazement. Instead of a deep gaping wound, there was a long shallow cut from his navel to his sternum and the broken tip of Dada's spear was still embedded in it. Their increasing bone density had stopped and the blade and saved Ben's life.

After the frenzy of the fight and the shock of Ben's apparently fatal wound, Elizabeth had failed to pick up his vital signs. The bruising on his chest was like he had stopped a cannonball though, and his head was split open from the impact on the timber of the ceiling joists. As she dug the steel splinter from Ben's chest he began his journey back to her. When at last he became fully conscious, he sprang to his feet. Ben was still in the terror of the moment, bewildered and disorientated.

"It's OK Ben, it's OK. We're safe now. Shush."

Elizabeth had to restrain him physically and force him to lie down, soothing him as she did so. Then, only as a woman can change, she vented off at him.

"Don't you ever do something as stupid as that again , or I swear I will kill you myself!"

Then she clung to him like her very life depended on it.

Chapter 18

Corporal Jackson arrived at the Robinson's house earlier than usual. He had slept well for the first time in a long while and was feeling particularly up-beat. He approached from the garden calling Tini. When the dog didn't respond and, he immediately feared the worst. Mike took the pistol from his pocket holster and went forwards cautiously. Normally Tini would have known that he was there as soon as his car pulled up. Something had to be dreadfully wrong. Mike raised his head above the shrubs and saw Tini lying across one of the biggest men that he'd ever seen. It was only when he got closer, that he could see the carnage. Both man and dog were drenched in blood.

As he ran over he could hear Tini whimpering pathetically. The only sign that the dog was able to show to acknowledge his master's presence was the cocking of his ears and a soulful look in his quirky eyes as he looked up at him. Mike was horrified at the sight of Tini's massive wound and felt physically sick. It was heart-breaking. The dog had given everything and more than could have been expected of him. Mike ruffled Tini's head in tender appreciation while his tears flowed freely down his cheeks.

"Good boy," he whispered encouragingly.

His words didn't even begin to commend the duty that the dog had selflessly performed.

He turned his attention to the corpse and recognised the immense black man immediately as Dada; one of the cruellest and most feared Shadows of them all, and across all time. Mike was amazed at the amount of mutilation that he had suffered. Dada had literally been hacked to pieces and his throat ripped out.

After reassuring himself that the Shadow was dead, Mike concentrated on what he could do for Tini. He was impaled on Dada's spear in what was clearly a fight to the death, and Tini was perilously close to that. Mike gently slipped the shaft of the spear out of Dada's dead hand. He was careful to not disturb the wound and encourage more bleeding. Mike gently lifted the impaled Tini to his car and covered him with a rug to protect him from the cold morning air.

Mike dragged Dada's lifeless body into the undergrowth to conceal it and ran to the house. His heart was racing with the effort of moving Dada, but more so because of his fear of what carnage was waiting for him in the house. Judging by the state of Dada, he must have inflicted some horrific injuries, or even death, on Elizabeth and Ben

"It must have been the mother of all fights," Mike thought, feeling nauseous.

Mike entered the Robinson's house through the shattered glazed panel and followed the blood trail upstairs. It was everywhere. A broad red smear zigzagged down the stairs where Dada had used the stump of his left arm to steady him. As he passed the open doors to both Ben's and Elizabeth's bedrooms, he saw the pulled back covers and the familiar pungent smell of cordite stung his nostrils. He hesitated at the next room steeling himself for what he might see and entered cautiously.

When Mike walked in, Elizabeth had already cleaned and sterilised Ben's wound. She was in the process of putting a field dressing on a nasty gash that ran up his stomach. It took several seconds for Mike to take in the enormity of what must have happened in the room. It looked like a scene out of a Hammer horror movie. There were bullet holes and flesh everywhere. Not a wall or drape had escaped a blood drenching. A grotesque, severed hand was on the floor still grasping a gun. It was way past surreal. Elizabeth was smiling back at him through a macabre dried mask of blood. Only her eyes and teeth were still white.

Mike had seen some carnage in his active duty in Afghanistan, but this was on another level. His head was spinning as he sat down next to Elizabeth, thankful to take the weight off his legs. Particularly as he couldn't trust them to keep him up. Elizabeth could see the concern on his face and put her hand on his shoulder. She was strangely calm and controlled.

"It's alright Mike we're both OK."

They quickly agreed on a containment plan. Elizabeth had already conditioned her Aunt and Uncle when they entered her room in a state of panic. She had sent them back to bed believing that nothing had happened and she felt sickened by her deceit. There were bullet holes everywhere and Dada's arterial blood had pumped itself all over the house. Mike made a quick call to his headquarters and a clean-up team was dispatched immediately. Elizabeth and Ben were shocked when they heard just how often *containment plans* had been needed in the past. Angels had their own specific people to help execute them, apparently. They nodded to each other in sad agreement that they would never know the carefree joy and freedom of ordinary life again.

Mike was desolated that he hadn't recognised the Range Rover as a threat when, with hindsight, he absolutely knew that it was.

"You were being controlled Mike, conditioned, just as Elizabeth has done to Aunt and Uncle. It's not your fault. Dada was one of the most powerful of all the Shadows. You didn't stand a chance of resisting him, not a hope. Your honour is intact mate."

Despite his supportive words, Ben could feel the enormity of Mike's hurt.

Mike consciously tried to put the matter behind him and responded positively.

"Between you both, you killed a giant of a man. I just can't believe it. So many have failed against him over the millennia and then two very young and inexperienced people took him, and took him in style. You have my deepest respect for that."

Ben had to speak out on Elizabeth's part.

"I did my bit Mike but it's unbelievable how Lizzie took him to pieces, I mean literally! She has always been the strong one, but I could never have imagined just how strong she could be," then he added in humour, "I pity the man, whoever he is, that gets involved with her!"

There was a pregnant silence and both Elizabeth and Mike looked awkward. Elizabeth turned and walked away. She was thankful for the excuse to leave and continue the smoothing of her aunt and uncle. Ben took the opportunity to ask his question.

"Just in case things get too busy to ask again Mike, do you fancy coming to Lizzie's eighteenth birthday party on Saturday?"

"Well, yes I would love to," Mike answered without hesitation.

Elizabeth was still within earshot and Ben clearly heard Elizabeth's profound thought.

"Yes!"

He was almost sure that she had raised her right forearm, just slightly and clenched her fist at the same time, in that stereotypical winning gesture.

The next and most pressing tasks were to deal with Dada's body and get Tini to a vet. As sickening as it looked, the wound proved to be literally skin deep. The spear had run all the way under his skin with entry and exit wounds missing vital organs and arteries. They decided to leave the spear in, as the trauma of withdrawing it would be huge and could kill Tini. Ben used his hands and mind to slow the bleeding and deliver pain easement. Tini responded quickly and you could be forgiven for thinking that the dog actually looked pleased with himself.

Mike found the Range Rover keys in Dada's pocket and minutes later, he pulled up on the drive with it. Despite their combined Angel strength, it took all their effort to lift the dense bulk of the Shadow's body into the Rover. Mike would deliver the car and body later to Grese's house for her to deal with. The urgency now was to get Tini to the Vet.

As Mike drove out of the drive, a police squad car pulled up alongside their colleague's car and two officers got out. After a brief visual inspection, one of them was on the radio talking urgently.

"Two officers down, it's a mess. Request ambulance and backup. Now!"

Grese heard the screech of the tyres as the black Range Rover pulled up abruptly in her drive. She ran to the window, it was Dada's. She was scared for the first time since she was sentenced to death for her war crimes. When she saw a young man hastily leaving the car and not Dada, Grese was elated. She knew exactly what that meant. Dada was dead! Grese screamed up the stairs to Katya, who came bounding down despite her injuries. Grese threw her arms around her for the first time since she was a baby.

"He's dead Katya, the bastard is dead! Can you imagine how he must have felt being taken by children! Hell's teeth I wish I could've seen it!"

A wry smile crossed Grese's face.

"My position in Adolphius's cell is once again secure."

Grese was licking her upper lip and her hand was stroking her neck erotically.

"And I will now be a member of the Senate!" Katya declared.

Katya looked at her mother and gave her the falsest of smiles as the thought crossed her mind.

"And my rise to Supreme Senator has only just begun."

Corporal Jackson arrived at the Veterinary Hospital with Tini in his arms still. The surgeon was horrified, he had never seen anything to compare. It was beyond his comprehension that anyone could do such a thing. He sedated Tini and then hastily prepared the operating theatre.

"I don't have any staff on this morning, so you are going to have to help me."

He immediately took Mike to get changed and scrub up for the operation. After administrating the appropriate anaesthetic, the surgeon skilfully removed the spear and cleansed the wound along its full length using improvised swabs that he could draw through the path of the spear. He stitched the entry and exit wounds, injected a strong antibiotic and one hour later it was done.

"There's no logical explanation for how your dog could have survived this trauma," the surgeon began, "his blood loss is relatively marginal for this type of wound. That really is most strange. He hasn't gone into shock either, which you would normally expect," he scratched his head in dismay. "I simply can't fathom it."

"The hand of Angels perhaps?" suggested Mike.

"Perhaps so, just perhaps, I have seen some strange things in my time. I'll give you the rest of the antibiotics and something to keep the dog sedated. I know it'll be difficult, but he will need to be kept as still as possible. I will come to your house in three days to change the dressings and save Tini the trauma of the journey."

The surgeon was struggling with the horror of what he had been presented with. It was undoubtedly the most sickening thing that he had ever had to deal with. Mike knew that a little *smoothing* would be necessary to remove the event from his mind. He would have to get Elizabeth or Ben to do that, as it was out of his skill set.

"Have you reported this horrific attack to the police?"

"No but I can assure you that the person concerned has been most severely dealt with and won't be doing anything like it again," there was a wry smile on Mike's face as they wheeled Tini out to his car.

Chapter 19

Elizabeth dealt with the smoothing of her Aunt and Uncle so that they were oblivious to the carnage. They didn't even question why the six man team were about their business in their house. The cleaners were under strict instruction to be finished and gone by Friday afternoon at the latest. That was so the final preparations for Elizabeth's eighteenth birthday party could be made. Aunt Jillie was going through the guest list with Elizabeth. She was making sure that everybody was seated appropriately and next to somebody that they could relate to.

"Oh and Corporal Jackson has confirmed his attendance," Elizabeth said nonchalantly, "he will be sitting between me and Ben." She was taking no chances.

"Good, I have his place name already printed. Doesn't it look grand?" Aunt Jillie handed the ornate seating card to Elizabeth.

She looked at the name on the printed card and her mouth opened in disbelief. It read: *Corporal Michael Alexander Goldberg-Jackson.*

"Oh my God," she thought, "he must be Emanuel Goldberg's son."

"Is there something the matter Lizzie?"

Aunt Jillie was concerned about the sudden change that had come over her.

"No, no not at all, I was just thinking how strange and grand his name was too," then Elizabeth remembered May's comment and her knowing smile when she had said, "I can't even imagine what Emanuel Goldberg's son, Michael will make of you when he sees you!"

Had May been spying on her future? She wondered, feeling a little cross at being manipulated. Elizabeth smelled a rat and decided that she was going to give Corporal Jackson a very hard time indeed and have it out with May.

\--

It was after four o'clock on Saturday afternoon and everything was in place ready for the guests to arrive at six. Elizabeth was in the bathroom making herself look beautiful and Ben was chilling in his room with his game console. He heard Elizabeth scream out in alarm.

"Ben, come here quickly!"

He threw the handset down, reached under the bed for his cutlass then ran down the corridor to her. Ben burst into the bathroom expecting the worst, only to be confronted with Elizabeth in her underwear on the scales with her head in her hands. She was horrified.

"What kind of a girl, who dresses size ten, can weigh in at nearly twelve stone Ben?"

"Lizzie! You scared the crap outta me. Don't you ever do something as stupid as that again," Ben's feelings were a mixture of relief and anger.

"But twelve stone Ben that's as much as a man!"

"Let me try," Ben eagerly stepped onto the scales and the digital display stopped at just over fifteen stone. "Wow, get a load of me. That's some man you're looking at Lizzie!"

Ben was thrilled but Elizabeth was still not quite so sure about being *that* heavy.

Ben dropped his bathrobe. They both stood innocently in their underwear in front of the full-length bathroom mirror, examining their bodies. They were both fully mature with good muscle definition, man and woman; neither had the slightest hint of their childhood remaining.

"It's our genetic acceleration, just as May said. Denser bones and muscles," Ben surmised. "You don't really look that big Lizzie, well except for your arse that is...."

It was only Ben's swift Angel reflexes, which saved him from the slap that he deserved. Elizabeth swivelled her hips towards the mirror just to check and be sure.

"As you've got your shirt off I'll change your bandages."

Elizabeth set about unwrapping him in a business-like fashion. She was still furious. Ben decided that, under the circumstances, it was probably safer just to succumb and keep his mouth shut. As the last wraps came away the shock on Elizabeth's face was apparent. Ben was suddenly deeply concerned.

"What is it Lizzie?"

"Nothing Ben, I mean there's nothing to see. You haven't got a wound, it's gone."

"Gone?" Ben felt around his stomach and chest and then looked closely in the mirror. "There's not even a bruise or a scar Lizzie, but it hasn't even been 24 hours yet?"

"We still have a lot to learn about ourselves Ben and we're going to have to learn fast. We were lucky this time but we need to understand our given weapons more. After the party, we will dedicate all of our time to finding our limits."

Ben agreed.

"But first your party Lizzie; it's getting late and you'd better get moving. Your face still needs a lot of work and I hope your fat arse still fits in that little black dress."

Ben was gone, even before the shampoo bottle exploded on the closing bathroom door.

It had been agreed that Uncle George and Aunt Jillie would receive the first of the guests themselves to allow Elizabeth to be handed by Ben and make a grand entry down the main staircase. The event had been much awaited by the community. By twenty minutes after six, most of the guests had already arrived. They were eagerly awaiting Elizabeth's entrance with their glasses charged ready for the toast. Just before half past six Ben went to collect Elizabeth. He knocked and opened the door. It was a jaw dropping moment and involuntarily Ben whistled.

"Wow!" he said in awe.

Elizabeth's hair was gathered up wildly giving her a much taller appearance. The short black dress, long legs and stupidly high heels accentuated her model looks. Big green eyes, skilfully made up, shone from a perfect face with full red, promising lips. Ben had never seen her remotely like it before. He wondered how something so slender and elegant could have done something as brutal as she had to Dada, only a matter of hours ago. It was a contradiction in terms, a living oxymoron.

162

From Elizabeth's perspective, the man in the tuxedo who had come to present her, was strikingly handsome. Amazingly, he looked in his late teens to early twenties with the build of a rower. His broad shoulders and narrow waist were made more prominent by the well-cut tux, flattering his assets. From where he stood in the doorway, Elizabeth was able to gauge that he was already six feet tall. His blond curly hair, dimpled smile and the mischief in his sparkling blue eyes, was just the knockout punch. No doubt about it, he was drop dead gorgeous and would be breaking a few hearts tonight.

Elizabeth proudly took the arm that Ben proffered and they walked to the grand staircase to make their entrance. Several of the guests had remained in the hallway for an early sighting, and George and Jillie were meeting and greeting the new arrivals. The butler announced each of them as they entered the marquee.

All heads turned as Elizabeth and Ben began their decent. Most all leaned towards their partners and whispered compliments about their appearance. Jillie took George's arm, looked up at him and whispered to him proudly.

"They look stunning," and then slightly jealously. "Was I ever that beautiful George?"

He tenderly cupped her cheeks in his hands and kissed her softly.

"You still are," he said with an honest smile.

Jillie pressed her face into George's broad chest to fight back her tears of happiness.

Elizabeth and Ben stopped at the bottom of the stairs and looked down the hallway towards the old ornate mirror. It was done in the hope that May would be looking back at them through it. They both dearly wished she could have come. Elizabeth felt Ben's particular sadness and linked with his mind.

"May would have found you irresistible Ben, as will all my girlfriends when they see you."

Ben smiled back at her but there was only one girl in this world, or indeed any other, that he really wanted to impress. They crossed the hallway to Uncle George and Aunt Jillie, joined arms and walked into the marquee. The butler called for attention and presented them.

"I give you Elizabeth and Benjamin Robinson."

There was a general mumble of approval and some sideways comments. The guests gave light applause and the music began. Elizabeth and Ben separated and mingled with the guests, greeting each in turn, as was the protocol for a society function. Both were secretly waiting for the formal dinner to be over and the party to begin!

Elizabeth was particularly looking forward to seeing Laura. She would be arriving with her new boyfriend Matt, and she was curious to meet the legend. A brief search proved that Laura had not arrived yet. She was immediately concerned about her having had an accident in Matt's car, knowing how reckless some young boy drivers can be.

"Stop it Lizzie!" she had to say to herself, "you're only just eighteen and already worrying like a mother hen."

However Elizabeth was relieved when she finally heard the butler make his announcement.

"I give you Laura Black and Matthew St John."

She looked up to see Laura looking radiant in a sky blue halter neck dress, with her shining chestnut hair brushed over her left shoulder. She was wearing a powder blue orchid high on her right temple enhancing her exotic look. Laura had possessively linked arms with Matt as a declaration of ownership. Elizabeth had to concede that he looked handsome, if not a little roguish, in his tuxedo.

Elizabeth caught Laura's eye and she immediately steered Matt through the crowd to present him to her.

"Happy birthday Lizzie, and wow you look stunning!"

There was no envy or falseness in Laura's greeting. They threw their arms around each other, faking a kiss so that they didn't smudge lipsticks.

"This is Matt, doesn't he look dashing?"

"Doesn't he just!" Elizabeth confirmed and Matt flinched with the embarrassment of it. "You'd better keep him away from the other girls," Elizabeth jibed.

Laura had only been there for minutes but, like most girls of her age, that was all it took for her to have an in depth awareness of what was going on.

"OMG Lizzie, is that really Ben standing next to your aunt? I hardly recognise him; he's changed so much. He looks so strong and handsome."

Laura noticed Matt's discomfort and rescued herself.

"He's the second most handsome man here, in fact."

Laura squeezed Matt's arm reassuringly and gave him a winning smile that promised the earth in compensation.

Elizabeth could see from their body language how much in love they were. When she overheard Laura's innermost thoughts, she tuned out quickly for fear of blushing openly. To divert herself, she looked at the venomous wound that Katya had inflicted on Laura's neck. Although it had been cleverly camouflaged with makeup, it was still angry and would leave a nasty and permanent scar. Elizabeth felt guilty knowing that she was the cause of that disfigurement. The image of Laura on the life-support machine, with her life slipping away, would be with her for ever. Elizabeth had removed the episode from both Laura's and her family's memories. Nobody should have to carry that baggage around through a lifetime, Elizabeth had decided. She broke the morbid train of thought.

"Help yourself to drinks. I think you'll need one! It's all a bit stiff at the moment. Once we've eaten and Uncle George's business friends have gone, it'll loosen up and we can let our hair down."

There was a mischievous twinkle in Elizabeth's eye that wasn't wasted on Laura.

"There's a live band followed by karaoke then a late disco, so I think you'll need a taxi back."

"I certainly hope so Lizzie!" the statement was reinforced with a conspiratorial grin. "Have you lined up some potential boyfriend material, or are you still saving yourself for a Knight in shining armour?"

"Well there is one possibility, if he should be so lucky. He hasn't arrived yet though."

Elizabeth was becoming slightly concerned about Mike's tardiness.

"Let me know when he does and I'll tell you whether he ticks all the right boxes or not. I do have experience in these things you know."

Laura winked at Elizabeth and they both giggled at the riskiness of it.

Meanwhile, Ben was being mauled by Elizabeth's other friends and the daughters of the Robinson's guests. He only managed to escape them by committing himself to a dance with each later. It should have been heaven but after meeting May, as lovely as some of them were, they couldn't hold a candle to her. Ben knew that May was way out of his league though, but he couldn't get her out of his mind. He was thinking of her even while the other girls were faffing over him.

At last Elizabeth's wait was over and the butler's voice boomed out above the Muzak and chatter.

"Your attention please; I give you Corporal Michael Alexander Goldberg-Jackson."

All heads turned. Corporal Jackson was in his full-dress military uniform. His red tunic was adorned with gold braid and service medals. His breeches bore the regimental red stripe and his ceremonial sword was the killer blow for the ladies. He could have taken his pick.

This hadn't gone unnoticed by Elizabeth. She quickly and strategically took her place beside him, out-ranking all others. After all it was her party. This in fact was entirely unnecessary as Mike had only gone to see her and was oblivious to all the admiring looks that he was getting.

Elizabeth was wilfully standoffish and offhand at the outset.

"Well Michael Goldberg, I'm so pleased that you were able to make it. Let me get you a drink."

She over-stated the word *Goldberg*, testament to how angry she still was about some conspiracy that only *might* exist between May and the Goldbergs. She had taken the stance of judge, jury and executioner, even before she had the facts. But then this wasn't unusual for Elizabeth, nor would it be the first time that it had got her in deep water. Elizabeth shrugged and walked in front of him leading him to the bar. It was fortunate for Elizabeth that Mike couldn't see her face as she was grimacing and rolling her eyes in self-chastisement.

"Where the hell did that shit come from Elizabeth? Are you trying to commit suicide or something?"

Mike followed Elizabeth. He was a little confused and wondered what he had done wrong. Elizabeth was determined to turn the bad start around but at the bar she couldn't help herself and just buried herself deeper. She called the barman over.

"Please arrange a drink for Corporal Goldberg," again she emphasised the *Goldberg* part.

Elizabeth turned to Mike with the intention of being sweet. Then, as the barman handed Mike his champagne, something entirely different came out of her mouth.

"Enjoy. There are a lot of young ladies here just dying to meet you."

She left him at the bar.

"Shit, shit, shit!" Elizabeth said to herself as she walked away, "that's really done it now."

Elizabeth headed as quickly as she could to the bathroom to escape and locked the door behind her. She was so angry with herself, and felt so foolish, that she just burst into tears.

Laura had seen the debonair Corporal arrive and noticed how quickly Elizabeth had appeared at his side.

"Ah so he's the one Matt. Not bad at all Lizzie, well done you!"

Laura was really impressed with his military bearing and roguish good looks.

"He ticks all the boxes and a few more besides." She smiled genuinely at the thought of Elizabeth being in love.

Minutes later, when Elizabeth brushed hurriedly past, Laura knew that something was wrong and followed her out of the marquee to the bathroom.

"Lizzie, it's me Laura, what's the matter? Let me in, open the door."

The lock slid open and Laura stepped in and closed the door behind her.

"What is it Lizzie, is that nasty soldier bothering you?"

It was only meant as a joke but Elizabeth lost it, she was furious.

"He's not nasty at all, you don't even know him. How can you say that and how would you like it if I said that about Matt?"

"Hey, hey steady on girl! You know I wasn't being serious, Jesus...," Laura was taken aback by Elizabeth's sudden onslaught.

"Oh Laura I am so sorry. I know you didn't mean it, only I've made such a fool of myself. It's me who's been nasty."

Elizabeth put her arms out for a cuddle and Laura took the olive branch. After a minute or two Laura prompted her to explain.

"So tell me now what's upset you."

"I wouldn't even know how or where to begin, it's too complicated," Elizabeth was already feeling much calmer now.

"You have only just met him and already it is too complicated?" a look of sudden understanding came on Laura's face, "OMG Lizzie you're pregnant!"

Laura stepped back with her hand covering her mouth in shock.

"God Laura, not everything is about sex," it all suddenly seemed so ridiculous to Elizabeth that she burst out laughing, "I suppose in the grand scale of things I haven't got much of a problem at all, have I?"

Elizabeth reflected for a moment then continued.

"It's just that I treated him so very badly for something that he hasn't even done. God he must think that I am such a fruit-loop."

"Lizzie he's just a man, they're not big on thinking. Just go straight up to him and take his arm, kiss him on the cheek and say sorry then forget it. He will," Laura's uncomplicated understanding of things was so refreshing. "But first Lizzie we have to repair your face".

When they returned Elizabeth had regained her composure and confidence. Mike was with Ben and almost all of the young ladies on the invitation list. They were all over them.

"Right," said Elizabeth, "watch this."

She walked off towards the boys with and exaggerated sway of her hips. Mike saw her coming purposefully towards him and his face showed visible signs of fear.

"Excuse me ladies," Elizabeth said muscling through and linked her arm with Mike's, "this girl needs a drink, are you buying soldier?"

Elizabeth reached up and kissed his cheek, "And that's sorry in spoilt bitch language."

Never had a man looked quite so confused.

May stepped through the old mirror into the Robinson's hallway. She was dressed in a white full length, bias-cut dress that accentuated the curves of her body. Her elegant high-heeled shoes and clutch bag were haute couture, skilfully chosen to set off the sophisticated but slinky dress. May's hair was swirled upwards in a futuristic cone-style that added several inches to her height, further enhancing her svelte appearance. Apart from lip gloss and eye liner, she wore no other makeup, nor needed it. Her smooth tanned skin shone with health, she was the very essence of womanhood.

"My apologies ma'am but I didn't see you arrive," the old butler looked quite startled, "I must be getting old and dozed off. I was by the door and I don't know how I could possibly have missed you."

He was looking quite puzzled and clearly worried about his lapse. May gently reassured him.

"It's alright, I slipped in while you had just turned away but I've forgotten my invitation. Will that be alright?"

"Absolutely no problem at all ma'am; your name will be on my list here. Can I have it?" the butler was clearly relieved that he hadn't nodded off.

"Maelströminha," offered May.

"Let me see. How strange ma'am, you don't appear to be here," the old butler looked crest fallen over the omission.

"Look, there I am," May pointed to some random name.

"Yes of course how silly of me," the old butler had succumbed to a little gentle deception.

"Follow me please Miss and may I be so presumptuous as to say how delightful you look this evening?"

"Why thank you kind sir," May smiled generously.

He was the archetypical butler, a gentle well-bred old man that you could imagine as a devoted Grandfather.

What is your name?" May asked. She was already fond of him.

"Jeeves ma'am."

"Yes of course," she replied and followed him into the marquee.

The guests were already seated and the live band was playing when the butler called for their attention. A hush came over the guests and Jeeves made his announcement.

"I give you Miss Maelströminha."

After an appropriate pause he led her towards the Robinson's table. All heads were turned her way. More than a few wives found it necessary to elbow their husbands to prompt them to avert their stares or lift their chins to close their open mouths. Elizabeth and Ben left their seats the instant they saw May and met her halfway. They embraced as if they hadn't seen each other in a long time. Nobody could have mistaken the sheer joy of that reunion.

"I can't believe that you have actually come, thank you! You've made my party perfect *Miss Maelströminha* and wow, what a name!"

Elizabeth was doing that same little victory dance, completely oblivious to what anybody else might have thought about it.

"Does your name have a meaning?" Elizabeth asked.

"Yes, a silly one though."

May looked reluctant to say, but she could tell from Elizabeth's face that she wasn't going to get away with not.

"*Maelström* means a powerful vortex or storm and the *inha* is the diminutive. So it's Little Storm I guess.

170

"How appropriate;" Elizabeth clapped her hands at the pleasure of it, "and you look astonishing May. So elegant and *I* want that dress!"

"You shall have it Lizzie but please excuse me if it's not right now, right here," May replied jokingly.

"Ben wouldn't have minded," Elizabeth pointed out shooting him a cheeky smile.

Ben derailed the conversation, taking the opportunity to strike back at Elizabeth.

"We will have a place laid for you at the table between Lizzie and me, only I'm afraid that Lizzie has insisted that a certain handsome soldier sits on her other side."

The smile that May returned was all-knowing and showed not the slightest hint of surprise about Lizzie choosing to sit next to the young soldier.

"*Touché,*" thought Elizabeth nodding at Ben in good humour, "I deserved that."

May's lack of surprise was noted by Elizabeth. Never being one to hold her own council, she decided that she would have this spying matter out with her later in the evening.

Throughout dinner, the four of them were engaged in light conversation, not once mentioning the darker side of their lives. That could wait. Tonight was to celebrate an important milestone in Elizabeth's life and it was shaping up to be a great party. Any onlooker couldn't have failed to notice that the four of them were subconsciously coupling up. Often, when May was talking to Ben, she would touch his arm and laugh enthusiastically at his wit. In return Ben was attentive, always leaning closely to listen and he simply couldn't take his eyes off her.

It was clear that Elizabeth had forgiven Mike for whatever it was that he clearly hadn't done. She was helping him through his shyness by encouraging him to talk about himself and his military career. Some of his covert missions left Elizabeth amazed at his bravery and resilience. She was warming to him by the minute and Mike was getting just a little hot under the collar.

Jillie turned to George and pointed to the head table.

"I don't recall a *Miss Maelströminha* on the guest list and I couldn't have failed to remember a name like that."

"Whatever," replied George, "but looking at how Ben's acting, you would have a hard job throwing her out right now."

"Yes, he is quite taken isn't he? What a dark horse that boy is," Jillie looked at George thoughtfully. "Do you know George, that when Miss Maelströminha walked in, every man in the room stared at her?"

"No really?" George's expression was at the very least, guilty.

"Yes really," confirmed Jillie.

"Ah, I see that your glass is empty. I will call the waiter," diverted George.

After dinner, the band began taking requests. Elizabeth leant over towards May and they exchanged whispers then nodded in agreement. They left the table and walked over to the band. After a quick exchange, the saxophonist handed Elizabeth his instrument and May took the microphone from the lead singer. Elizabeth leaned over to speak into the mike and already the guests had begun to pay attention, particularly the men.

"I want to thank you all for coming here this evening to share my birthday with a song. The words to this one seem appropriate to me and where I am at this moment in my life. We would like to play for you *Somewhere over the Rainbow*, in the style of Eva Cassidy. May will do the vocals while I strangle this thing."

Elizabeth began the haunting introduction with such feeling that everybody was immediately attentive and expectant. When May came in with her soulful vocals, they were all swept away in the ecstasy of the moment. At the end, everybody rose to their feet and applauded enthusiastically. Jillie was nonplussed.

"Where did that come from George? Lizzie was always good but never *that* good," but of course Jillie was unaware of the changes that she was going through.

After that, they sang a duet. It was *Perfect by* Fairground Attraction. Elizabeth pointed at Mike as they sang the opening words:

172

*"Don't want half-hearted love affairs
I need someone who really cares....."*

Elizabeth put on a bit of a girlie act for Mike and he responded by whooping back at her. Jillie was horrified. She looked around self-consciously and turned lamely to the lady beside her.

"He's a soldier don't you know?"

At the end, May leaned across to whisper in Elizabeth's ear.

"This is the most fun that I've had in over 5,000 years! I'm not sure that your Aunt is quite as impressed though, perhaps we should tone it down a little?"

They didn't. It finished to another round of applause and calls for more. Elizabeth picked up the microphone and waved the audience to silence with a sweep of her hand.

"Later everybody, can't you see that I have a young soldier who's desperate for a kiss?"

The audience capitulated and watched in anticipation as Elizabeth walked back to Mike who greeted her with open arms and they had their first kiss, and a public one at that, to the cheering of the guests and the reserved judgement of Aunt Jillie.

When May sat down next to Ben, he put his hand naturally over hers. He was clearly impressed, if not just a little inarticulate.

"That was awesome May. I was so proud to be your friend."

"Friend?"

May raised her eyebrow then kissed him on the cheek.

"I'm going to help myself to some more cake. You bring out the hunger in me."

She ran her fingers under his chin as she got up, leaving Ben somewhere between confused and Heaven.

May took the carving knife and measured herself a particularly unfeminine portion. She was about to cut when a sudden feeling of near and present danger came over her, a premonition. Something was dreadfully, dreadfully wrong!

173

Irma Grese was at home with Katya when her mobile phone rang. She looked at the display and it read *the Hydra*. It was a rare occurrence indeed that she would call her directly and it sent a cold chill up her back.

The Hydra was aptly named after the multi-headed serpent in Greek mythology that guarded the entrance to the Underworld. If you cut off one head, then two would grow in its place. Even its poisonous breath would kill. The Shadow Hydra was also known for having scores of identities over the millennia, changing to another each time that the identity was compromised. All feared the Hydra and all obeyed. It was with a sense of great trepidation that Grese accepted the call.

"Grese speaking."

"Ah Grese, I have an opportunity for you that will earn you great favour should you succeed."

The Hydra needed something from her which was an immediate relief.

"I am listening. What is it that you would have me do?"

"I sense that Maelströminha has left the safety of the mother ship. She is here and almost definitely at the Robinson's house. She will have arrived through the portal there. It is a unique opportunity and I want you to kill her and the Robinsons."

"No small task then," Grese thought.

The Hydra continued.

"She will not stay long, maybe only hours if that. She knows that I will sense her presence. I suggest that you consider *the Jackal*, his expertise in this field is second to none."

The Jackal was a highly respected Shadow assassin named after *Carlos the Jackal*, one of the most famous political terrorists of the 20th century, currently serving a life sentence in France for his crimes. Over the centuries, this Jackal had assassinated countless Angels, Heads of State, politicians and the like with impunity.

"That was the name that immediately sprung to my mind," Grese began. "He professes to have resources constantly at hand to act immediately, if needed. Of course there is always the matter of an appropriate fee. I assume that money is not an issue?"

Grese's question was only a formality.

"Not at all Grese; just do it."

The Hydra cut the call without any niceties. Grese looked through her address book, found the Jackal's contact and pressed *select*. The phone rang only twice.

"Jackal here," the voice was cold even for a Shadow.

"I have work for you as a direct request from the Supreme Senator and I want no survivors, not even the men that you take with you. I don't want the possibility of trouble arriving back at my doorstep. Do you understand?"

"Perfectly Grese," his voice was cold and Grese felt the chill of it. "Do you understand just how expensive that would be?"

"If you succeed in your mission, then you can write your own cheque," offered Grese, "and if you fail, the Hydra will have you killed. Now do you understand?"

"Perfectly, who is so important as to command such a price?"

The intrigue in the Jackal's voice was apparent.

"Maelströminha," Grese enjoyed playing her ace.

"The price just went through the roof," the Jackal countered, already deep in thought.

The Jackal's High Mobility Multipurpose Wheeled Vehicle, commonly known as the Humvee, stopped 300 yards from the Robinson's house. Three men dressed in black with SAS style, three-hole balaclavas exited. They were armed with Kalashnikov AK-47 rifles and silenced pistols. Each wore grenade belts and carried rucksacks. Had they not been Shadows, you may well have expected them to be wearing NVGs too, but their eyesight at night was impeccable and needed no optical enhancement.

The two men that the Jackal had chosen were his best. They were battle hardened veterans and experts in most weaponry, including explosives used in covert operations. He had used them in most all of his high significance hits over the last 50 years and would find them hard to replace, but the price was right. After all, they were just Drones, faithful and trusting Drones.

The Jackal squatted with his men and gave them their instructions. They immediately busied themselves preparing the plastic explosives that were cached in their rucksacks. He swapped his AK-47 for the M40A5 sniper rifle with telescopic sight and sound suppressor. He loaded a shell into the breach and set off alone on reconnaissance. The Jackal needed to know exactly what the enemy disposition was; their numbers, armament and location, along with any fall-back possibilities.

His first search of the area was wide to make sure that he wasn't already inside an Angel trap. The Jackal reduced the radius by ten yards each circuit thereafter, until he was inside the Robinson's grounds. He smelt the dog stench on the night air coming from the opposite end of the garden behind the marquee. He needed higher ground to get sight of the dog. Using the down-water pipes from the roof, he scaled the house to the roof. Shadow's power to weight ratio are in line with that of the apes, so the climb only took seconds.

Careful not to show himself on the skyline, he kept lower than the ridge and made his way to the opposite end of the house. There below him, close by the marquee, was Tini's replacement. Another Husky, pacing up and down his run with ears pricked and nose sniffing the chilly night air. The Jackal unslung his sniper rifle and aimed at the top of the dog's head. At this distance he didn't really need the telescopic sight but his professionalism ensured that he meticulously lined up the target in the crosshairs of the sight. He squeezed the trigger gently and the rifle kicked firmly into his shoulder. The high velocity bullet struck home with a sickening thud, removing most of the dog's skull. The Jackal reloaded and waited for any response. None came and he slipped silently away.

The Jackal returned to his men after little more than half an hour and huddled next to the Humvee to brief them. He pulled off his balaclava to cool down after the exertion of the mission. The night air felt invigorating against his face and it concentrated his mind. He had sharp features and his cold, dark eyes flicked around constantly taking in everything around him. His looks coupled with his rangy frame added to the appropriateness of his nickname.

"Well," he began, "this is either the best trap ever set, or our prey truly is totally off guard. There are no soldiers around the perimeter, no surveillance, not even a passing security guard. Nothing except a rancid dog that I've already killed. All the guests are either already drunk or getting there. Maelströminha is partying with some girl singing with the band, it's surreal."

The Drones nodded approvingly, they were already banking their bounty money.

"This will be simple and make us all rich beyond our dreams. Trust me when I say that this will *definitely* be the last hit you ever make."

It was ironic. While his men were prematurely celebrating their wealth, the Jackal was considering how he would kill them later that night.

The plan was set. The Jackal's two men would plant a ring of eight 20 pound packs of C4, radio controlled explosives around the outside of the marquee. Meanwhile, the Jackal would take up his position at the side of the house. From there, he could lay down covering fire if things went wrong and detonate the explosive devices remotely. The two men crossed over to the marquee and worked quickly and efficiently. Their plan was to set the explosives two per side of the marquee, insert the slave detonators and activate them. Both would then return to their agreed stations at opposite ends of the marquee awaiting radio confirmation to evacuate.

From his secure position at the side of the house, the Jackal had his sniper rifle trained on the small strip of garden between the Robinson's back entrance and the marquee. From here he could mitigate the risk of Maelströminha leaving the party early, via the portal in the house. To do this, she would have to cross the divide and he would take her out there. The Jackal glanced down at the master detonator on the ground beside him. The first of the LEDs lit up as the slave was activated. The curtain of explosions, totalling 160 pounds of C4, would leave no recognizable corpses and his men would be just two more unidentified victims in the carnage.

He glanced down again, just as the second LED lit up.

"Just six more to go," he thought with some professional satisfaction.

When he looked up again, he saw a dapper old man walking out into the garden lighting a cigarette. He brought the crosshairs of his sniper rifle on to the old man's head and gently caressed the trigger.

Jeeves had tended to all of the guests' needs up to the end of dinner, so his work was more or less done for the evening. He was looking forward to a long overdue cigarette and walked out into the garden to light up. There was always a little guilt when he allowed himself a cigarette. He remembered how his wife used to chastise him about it and he thought about her fondly.

His mind drifted from work to more pleasurable things. He began to think about Sunday lunch with his son and his family that had been planned for the next day. Jeeves' was approaching seventy. Since his wife had died, three years ago, the thing that brought him the most pleasure in life was to be with his son, daughter-in-law and his two grandchildren. James was nearly four and Bella, just three. They loved him dearly and he doted on them. They were the reason why he couldn't give up. From the minute that he would arrive until the time he left, the children would be all over him, competing for his attention. He needed to stick around to give them all the things that he wasn't able to give to his son. Most particularly, that was his time. He had carried the guilt of this omission for the last 35 years and it still haunted him. This was a way of balancing the books and making it right.

The butler was lost in his happy thoughts about them, when he suddenly remembered that there had been a guard dog in the garden. He took a last puff of his cigarette, stamped it out and returned to the kitchen, looking at his gold pocket watch.

"I have just enough time to get some scraps together for him before my Taxi," he thought and hurried back to the kitchen.

Five minutes later he returned with a generous bowl of various meats and another with water. He walked into the gloom of the garden and called the dog. His old eyes were not good in the dark and he almost fell over the dog before he saw it.

"Here we are boy, I couldn't let you go hungry now could I?"

Jeeves bent down to place the bowls beside the dog but couldn't quite make sense of what he was seeing in the shadows. When at last the

178

enormity of the situation registered he recoiled in horror. He gagged at the sight of the headless dog and ran in panic back to the house for help.

The Jackal released his finger from the trigger as the old man crushed his cigarette under his foot and returned to the house. He clearly hadn't seen anything untoward.

"You will live to die another day old man," he thought and returned his attention to the master detonator.

There were now five LEDs lit up on the display. It was going well; in fact even better than expected. The Jackal allowed himself a smile. Even if his men were discovered now, 100 pounds of explosives was already more than enough to kill everybody in the marquee, including his men. At that moment the sixth LED lit up.

"Just two more to go," he noted.

The Jackal re-focussed his attention on the strip of land between the house and the marquee. At that moment Jeeves came hurrying out of the main house, carrying two steel bowls, then disappeared behind the marquee.

"Big mistake old man," the Jackal muttered and levelled his rifle in anticipation of him discovering the mutilated dog.

Seconds later, Jeeves came running out into view in a state of panic. The Jackal swung the rifle smoothly until the crosshairs were lined up with the glinting gold chain of his pocket watch and squeezed the trigger. The bullet took Jeeves through the chest, just to the left of centre. The eccentric force spun him around, propelling him deep into the shrubbery.

There would be an empty place at the table and two heart-broken children at the family Sunday lunch the next day.

When Elizabeth and May returned to their tables after singing, the band played a slow number. Laura took her opportunity and grabbed Matt's hand. She had a mischievous look in her eyes.

"I want you to dance me real slow Matt."

The music began and Matt took her in his arms. The Champagne had done its trick and they were soon lost in the song, oblivious to their audience. At the end Laura took Matt's arm and led him outside.

"I need a little more kissing."

Her face was upturned and expectant as she pulled him into the shadows at the flank of the marquee.

As the seventh and eighth LEDs lit up on the master detonator, Laura and Matt slipped out of the party and right into the crosshairs of the Jackal's sniper rifle. They were in a lovers embrace and their heads were superimposed in his telescopic sight. Although they would be killed anyway in the explosion, the thought of killing them both with a single shot excited the Jackal. He decided that he would take the shot anyway, for the sake of his professional pride. He would then detonate the bombs immediately afterwards. The Jackal had not the slightest concern that he was about to execute his own men too. After all, their job was done. They were not as useful to him as the money would from the hit. The Jackal put that thought to one side. For now, there was only this shot. He consciously relaxed and exhaled, so that his aim would be perfect. He slowly increased the pressure on the trigger...

May put down the cake knife and returned quickly to the table, where the others were sat in animated conversation.

"Sorry Lizzie but can I borrow Mike just for a moment?"

May's face showed no sign of concern and none was perceived by Elizabeth.

"Of course May, but don't be too long. I shall miss him," Elizabeth said it playfully but May knew that she meant it.

Mike sensed the change that had come over May. She was a paradox and could change from a carefree nymph to the most deadly adversary in the blink of an eye. When they reached the entrance to the marquee, May confided in him.

"I've let my heart rule my head and placed us all in danger. The Hydra must have sensed my presence here."

May was furious with herself. She had behaved like an irresponsible teenager.

"I can sense that there are two Drones outside the tent; one there and one there."

May had a clear mental image of them as she pointed to the opposite diagonals of the marquee.

"They are crouched moving slowly clockwise around us."

"Planting explosives I would guess," Mike's field experience assisted him in imagining what they were about and how.

"I would agree," May could taste the faint bituminous odour of the C4 putty explosive in the air.

"There will be at least one other Shadow out there, controlling the detonation from a remote point. Most likely a member of the Senate, Drones rarely work unsupervised," Mike added.

"Agreed. The Senator is mine, you deal with the Drones. We can't afford the time to brief Elizabeth and Ben and there will be carnage if we evacuate the guests. The party must continue as if normal."

Mike concurred, it was sound thinking. May began her transformation. She changed her appearance before his eyes, controlling not only his perception of her, but that of any onlooker until she finally disappeared.

It was an amazing skill that demanded ultra-high intelligence and advanced brain development. Every mind had to be brought instantly under control at the very moment that they saw her, it was something akin to mass hypnosis but infinitely more advanced. He had seen this done several times but it never ceased to fill him with awe. Mike smelt May's light perfume as she passed by him. It was the only clue of her presence as she walked out into the night.

Mike's diluted Angel skills amounted to only a little one on one mind control, so he had to revert to military tactics of camouflage and some innovation to achieve the same goal. Mike stripped to the waist. His red military tunic, under floodlighting, would have given his position away instantly. He emptied the coffee pot and dumped the wet coffee grains into a bowl, then lifted the top layer off the chocolate cake. He scooped out the rich dark cream and added it to the mix, making a thin brown paste. He took a napkin and drenched it in the slurry, then flannelled himself until all his flesh was stained dark brown.

Mike took the knife and quietly slashed an opening in the side wall of the marquee, furthest away from the last known position of the Drone. He checked that no one was looking and slipped silently out on his belly with the knife gripped between his teeth.

He snaked along the floodlit grass in that classical military way, leaving the side of the tent to a position from which he could observe clearly. He quickly picked up the flashing red LED on the slave detonator by the entrance, then another close to where he had exited. There was a third at the far end of the marquee, but no sign of the Drone who had planted it. Mike needed to circle round to get a view of the other elevation, furthest from the house. This would mean breaking cover and crawling across the floodlit lawn again. It was a risk but Mike had no choice, he would be totally exposed and vulnerable for at least 20 seconds.

Thankful for his decision to discard his red tunic, Mike slithered across the grass towards the single bush, 60 feet away. While he was exposed to sniper fire, the cold claw of fear twisted in his stomach. Once he reached cover and was in control again, the fear evaporated. It was replaced by total analytical concentration and self-belief. As he expected, the Drone was placing another explosive at the mid-point of the far marquee wall.

Mike estimated the distance to the kill as less than 40 feet. Coming out of the blocks, he could do that in just over three seconds, faster than the Drone could reach for his weapon. He waited until the Drone was fully focussed on his work. Mike transferred the knife to his right-hand and springing forwards, his powerful thighs driving him on. When he collided with the Drone, the ten inch blade was travelling at 20 mph with all Mike's weight behind it. It entered the Drone's back, passing through his heart and killed him instantly.

The intensive training that Mike had received kicked in naturally. Without even thinking, he transferred two of the dead Drones grenades to his belt, slung the AK-47 over his shoulder and took the silenced pistol. A quick check of the rucksack showed that this was the last explosive pack. Mike had killed the Drone before he had armed the device. His own experience told him that the Shadow controlling the master detonator would be watching for all slaves to light up on his display. If even one failed, he would have to assume that the mission was compromised and might detonate immediately. Mike expertly set the slave detonator and the LED flashed in confirmation. He hoped that this would buy him valuable minutes.

Mike went down again on his belly and continued his way around the tent. He gagged and almost gasped out loud when he came face to face with the headless body of his dog. He had to fight back the rage mounting within him in order to regain his self-control. In a futile act of compassion he stroked the already cold body of his dog and swore an oath that, whoever did it, would pay with their lives before the night was out.

Mike used his anger to focus his resolve. He pressed on to the corner of the marquee, giving him sight of the last flank of the tent. The second Drone was only ten feet away with his head down facing him. He was concentrating on arming one of the explosive devices and hadn't sensed Mike's presence. When he looked up, all he saw was Mike's demonic face, the flash of gunpowder and then oblivion. The bullet from the silenced gun had taken out the left side of his brain.

"A head for a head," Mike thought in rough justice.

He couldn't risk being seen evacuating the explosives to a safe distance. He just had to trust that May would successfully eliminate the Shadow that had masterminded the assault.

Mike slipped silently into the tree-line at the boundary of the Robinson's house, waiting and praying that the detonation wouldn't happen.

May was stood facing the Jackal, between him and the loving couple who were oblivious to the danger they were in. The Jackal had neither seen her, nor sensed her presence. To him, it was still an easy double-kill. In his mind the rifle was still pointing at the back of Laura's head. He squeezed the trigger with the smooth gentleness of the consummate professional. His rifle convulsed as the firing pin exploded the high velocity shell in its chamber.

The Jackal looked on in disbelief as the bullet simply hung motionlessly, just inches from the end of his rifle. Long seconds passed as he tried to make sense of it. At last, the enormity of his situation hit him and he began to panic. He dropped his rifle and made a grab for the master detonator. Before his hands could close on it, he was wrenched 20 feet into the air, hanging like a puppet with his arms and legs thrashing wildly. May had used her psychokinetic skills, just as she had described to Elizabeth and Ben.

May released his mind to let him see her. It was a sadistic act, unbecoming of her. She had reverted back to her primitive being, that darkness that lurks in all of us in moments of rage. The shock of seeing the Matriarch caused the Jackal's eyes to widen in terror and his bowels to evacuate. His mouth began to contort as the scream inside him mounted and exploded into a single word.

"Maelströminha!" he knew then that he was looking into the eyes of his executioner.

Laura and Matt heard the scream and thought it was directed at them. They ran guiltily back inside, thinking that they had been caught in the act. Both were still flushed with excitement and they giggled at the riskiness of it, oblivious to how close they had come to death.

May could have dashed the Jackal to the ground and killed him outright, there and then. Instead she held his frightened stare. When the Jackal finally realised what she was doing, it was too late to resist. He couldn't look away. May had his mind totally under her control. She began to selectively delete the memories that the Jackal had collected over thousands of years. When his mind was at last unable to pose any threat, May dropped him to the ground. He landed in a heap by her feet in a catatonic state.

Mike arrived with the two rucksacks re-packed with the explosives. He picked up the master detonator and carefully switched it off, then put it in one of the rucksacks.

"I've swept the area and there are no others, this unit was working alone."

Mike's observations were credible and those of a consumate soldier.

"Good work Mike. It would appear that the Drones were no trouble for you?"

May was thankful for his calmness and professionalism, particularly given the crisis scenario that they had found themselves in.

"No trouble at all, they were at least three short of a good fight."

Mike grinned at her boyishly. He was still pumped up from the overdose of adrenaline.

"Now you can give this man his explosives back," directed May.

Mike was shocked by what seemed to be a ludicrous command.

"But you can't possibly do that, I mean why would you want to?"

"He poses no threat to us now, I have dealt with his mind and he knows exactly what he must do. First he's going to tidy up this mess and then there's a certain package to return to sender."

May's smile was vengeful. Her eyes showed not the slightest compassion and Mike shuddered at the coldness of them. It was so alien to all that May was. It gave him a glimpse of the terrible wrath that was in her and demonstrated how desperate the situation between Angels and Shadows was. Mike knew that later, when it was all over, the remorse and guilt would torment her as it always did.

"And we have a party waiting for us so you had better get cleaned up Mike. There's a young lady who will be wondering where you are!"

May gave him a knowing look. Mike knew that he was an open book to her, but then there were none who she couldn't read if she had a mind to.

When May returned to the party, Elizabeth gently chastised her.

"Your moments are very long indeed May. I think you've lost your perspective with all this time travel stuff!"

It was a gentle jibe but Elizabeth had a bigger fish to fry, she needed to get something off her chest and it simply couldn't wait.

"Can we have a moment alone May?"

"Yes of course Lizzie. Shall we go out into the hallway? It's quieter there."

They left the marquee and walked in silence to the hallway. Elizabeth was struggling with what she was about to say or indeed whether she should even say it at all. Finally she decided that she would, as May had probably already read it in her anyway.

"This is difficult but I'm the sort of person that has to say what's on my mind or I can't deal with things. The last time that we met you said that you couldn't imagine what Emanuel Goldberg's son, Michael would make of me when he saw me. Do you remember?"

"Yes I remember Lizzie, as I remember all things," May already did know what was coming.

"Well it occurred to me that you might be spying on my future, otherwise how would you know that I was to meet Mike unless you had made it happen? I don't think I like that and all that it implies."

It was done and already Elizabeth felt better for saying it.

"Lizzie sometimes you have to help people irrespective of whether they consent or not. If you are able to protect them, then you have a responsibility to do so."

May had her elegant hands on her slightly thrust out hips in the authoritative way that a mother does when she chastises her children and her face had taken on a serious look. Elizabeth already knew that she wasn't going to like what she was about to be told.

"A mother naturally assesses the dangers facing her child and instinctively steers them away from them, or removes them. To be able to help, the mother needs to know what the dangers are. Do you not agree Lizzie?"

"Yes, but I am not a child!"

Elizabeth was clearly cross about being compared to a child and her tone said exactly that. May continued calmly but firmly.

"And when that child is a teenager and the mother suspects that she's in bad company and taking drugs or whatever. Should she look for signs, search her bag or her room, would that be alright or would that be spying on her?"

"That's not fair May, it's not even similar. Of course a mother should do those things, because the teenager hasn't yet got the experience to recognise the risk or even know that it is one."

Elizabeth felt trapped. Her stress levels were rising and she was about to vent off. Recognising this May took Elizabeth's hands and immediately the stress left her body allowing her mind to clear.

"It seems to me Lizzie that you agree that it's OK to spy when the person is unable to protect themselves adequately, is that right?"

"Well, yes I suppose so," Elizabeth agreed reluctantly.

"Then I agree with you. I cannot say what your future holds, it is not a given thing; but I can see some of the possibilities and I can help steer you away from the ones that don't end well."

Elizabeth knew exactly what she meant by the words *don't end well* and shuddered at the thought of it. She nodded her head in unsaid consent. May's face lit up with the pleasure of what she was about to do and she led Elizabeth over to the old mirror.

"That's enough of this seriousness Lizzie. Come with me, I've got something very special to show you!"

May took Elizabeth's hand and placed it on the mirror then covered it with hers. The mirror began to vibrate and the reflection of the hallway was replaced by the view of a room that she had never seen before. Elizabeth quickly deduced that this room had to be a place that the mirror had once been, or has yet to be in. There was a young woman sat with her back to the mirror occupied with something. From what Elizabeth could see, she appeared slim with long blonde curly hair tied up in a lose ponytail. The door at the far end of the room opened and a young man carrying a little girl walked in, followed by an older couple. They all looked strangely familiar.

The young blonde girl got up, turned and walked towards the mirror carrying a baby boy in her arms. She was smiling openly into the mirror. The girl raised her right-hand and placed it exactly where Elizabeth's hand was and she felt her touch. Her first reaction was to pull her hand away at the shock of it but May kept it pressed to the mirror.

They were looking directly into each other's eyes, the very same eyes! Elizabeth's legs began to give way under her as she realised that she was looking at herself in another time and another place. As she began to fall her image grasped her hand to support her, so that they were holding hands across dimensions.

"Hello Lizzie," the image said, "let me introduce you to your son Brady, isn't he just adorable?"

Elizabeth simply nodded as she couldn't form any words to reply.

"I want you to meet some dear people."

Her image beckoned the group over to the mirror so that Elizabeth could see them more clearly. When she could, her jaw dropped open in absolute astonishment and disbelief.

"Of course you already know our Mum and Dad, they send their love," Ralph and Jodie both smiled lovingly back at Elizabeth, "and you have already met your husband, although you don't know that yet."

"Mike!" Elizabeth put her other hand over her mouth as he gave her that look that she had already fallen in love with.

"And last but not least, your daughter Edith, whose special talent is stealing hearts."

Edith reached out to touch the mirror and smiled at Elizabeth uncomprehendingly.

"Mummy," she said in puzzlement.

"You have already stolen mine Edith," Elizabeth whispered.

Tears of happiness were running down her face. Her image smiled back as she continued her message.

"This is all that it could be Lizzie, you will be alright and you *will* know what to do. Trust your instincts, your children are worth fighting for. We are all worth fighting for."

"Those words again, always *those* words!" Elizabeth thought.

She turned her gaze to her mother and looked at her longingly. It was as if she could read her mind and she nodded back, her expression said it all. The image began to recede until all that was left were their own images and the reflection of the hallway. Elizabeth was lost in the enormity of it and May waited patiently until she was ready before saying.

"That is only one of your possible futures Lizzie, do you want it?"

"Yes I want it. I want it with all of my heart."

Elizabeth's expression hardened with resolve. If anyone had witnessed it, they would have been in no doubt that she would have moved Heaven and Earth to make it so.

"You can spy on my future whenever the hell you like May; just as much as it takes to make this happen."

They embraced earnestly. After some time Elizabeth broke the hold and held May at arm's length. She looked into those blue eyes that seemed as deep as the ocean itself. Just like the ocean, Elizabeth could see both tranquil calm and raging storm in them. She wondered at the complexity of this woman. May had the ability to be infinitely compassionate but there was also a danger about her. You would be her enemy at your peril; it was no wonder the Shadows feared her so much.

"You will never leave us will you May? We can't do this without you and we have so much to live for."

Elizabeth was almost childlike in her plea. The vision of the children that she was yet to bear was foremost in her mind.

"Never as long as there is breath in my body Lizzie. Now get back to your man!"

May's smile was beyond human boundaries of happiness and pleasure. It brought with it a tangible feeling of promise and hope. Elizabeth felt secure in her love.

"And you to yours?" Elizabeth prompted mischievously, knowing that May would have already known her thoughts.

"Maybe one day Lizzie, if life should be so kind but now is not that time."

There was a touch of sadness in May's voice and emptiness in those perfect blue eyes that were a window to her soul. Elizabeth squeezed May's hand in understanding. They hurried back to the party, both in delicious anticipation of being with their man.

When they arrived the boys were in a full karaoke rendition of the Dire Straits' song *Brothers in Arms*. It possibly wasn't one of the best performances of the night, but there was no doubt that the boys rated it.

The champagne was taking affect and they had their arms around each other's shoulders. They had already sworn lifelong allegiance, as men do on these occasions, particularly when a few drinks have been involved. When they finished, May and Elizabeth joined them on the stage.

189

Elizabeth immediately kissed Mike full on the lips. The impact it had on him was comical; he was all at sea with a puzzled look on his face.

"What've I done to deserve that?"

"It's not what you have done Mike, it is what you *will* do if life is kind to us."

Elizabeth winked conspiratorially at May which left Mike even more puzzled.

The party was in full swing and all thoughts of Angels and Shadows had receded. Tonight was just to have fun.

Ben was having the time of his life. Despite all the attempts by numerous infatuated men to get May to dance with them, she politely declined and re-doubled her attention towards Ben. He desperately wanted to kiss her but he somehow knew that she wasn't ready for that and he didn't want to spoil things. When he looked over at Mike, he could see that he was also unsure of himself.

"Women seemed to have the upper hand in these things," he decided.

May was also seizing the moment as her life seemed to have been lonely for an eon. Since Crystalita had been taken from her, she had no soul mate and her isolation had become profound. She had begun to lose faith in her ability to continue the fight against the Shadows alone. Now that Elizabeth and Ben were in her life, she felt reenergised and she had once again found hope.

May looked at them all having fun, seemingly carefree but the vision touched her with a deep sadness. She had glimpsed scores of their alternative futures through the mirrors and most of them ended in their violent deaths. She knew that their chance of surviving the next several weeks was less than 3%, but then there was at least a chance. She looked particularly sadly at Ben. He had become a man in only a matter days, physically and mentally, but he lacked experience of life itself. That was something that she could not give him. May knew that Ben would be at the biggest risk. He had already almost sacrificed his life for Lizzie and was more than capable of disregarding danger, as adolescent men do.

May walked over to the stage, took the microphone and made her request. The DJ found the track and nodded. She took a deep breath to calm her emotions and then turned to the guests that were already waiting in anticipation.

"This song is especially for Ben. It's *Billy don't be a hero*, by Paper Lace," she smiled across to him, "Listen to the words Ben I have chosen them for a reason."

The introduction began to play that stereotypical staccato military drumbeat...

'The marchin' band came down along Main Street
The soldier-blues fell in behind
I looked across and there I saw Billy
Waiting to go and join the line
And with her head upon his shoulder
His young and lovely fiancée
From where I stood, I saw she was cryin'
And through her tears I heard her say

Billy, don't be a hero, don't be a fool with your life
Billy, don't be a hero, come back and make me your wife
And as he started to go she said "Billy, keep your pretty head lo-o-ow
Billy, don't be a hero, come back to me...'

When she sung the final verse tears began to run down her face.

'I heard his fiancée got a letter
That told how Billy died that day
The letter said that he was a hero
She should be proud he died that way
I heard she threw that letter away'

It was sung beautifully and with total commitment. Probably the only person in the room that didn't get the message was Ben.

Laura and Matt joined them and for the next two hours. They all became lost in dance and party banter. Nobody noticed that May was distant. She was secretly using her heightened senses to scan the horizon for a second attack, which thankfully never came. Finally the DJ called Elizabeth to choose the last slow dance of the night. She knew which one it would be without a moment's hesitation.

"*Dance with my Father*, by Luther Vandross please, it has special memories for me."

She took hold of Mike even more closely and lost herself in the lyrics. In her mind, she replayed that last dance that she had with her father the day before he died, over four years ago.

'Back when I was a child, before life removed all the innocence
My father would lift me high and dance with my mother and me and then
Spin me around 'til I fell asleep
Then up the stairs he would carry me
And I knew for sure I was loved
If I could get another chance, another walk, another dance with him
I'd play a song that would never, ever end
How I'd love, love, love
To dance with my father again

When I and my mother would disagree
To get my way, I would run from her to him
He'd make me laugh just to comfort me
Then finally make me do just what my mama said
Later that night when I was asleep
He left a dollar under my sheet
Never dreamed that he would be gone from me
If I could steal one final glance, one final step, one final dance with him
I'd play a song that would never, ever end
Cause I'd love, love, love
To dance with my father again

Sometimes I'd listen outside her door
And I'd hear how my mother cried for him
I pray for her even more than me
I know I'm praying for much too much
But could you send back the only man she loved
I know you don't do it usually
But dear Lord she's dying
To dance with my father again

Every night I fall asleep and this is all I ever dream...'

When it was finished she looked up into Mike's eyes, her face.

"I will dance with my father again Mike, I swear it to you."

Mike could see by her determined look that she meant it. Behind her obvious display of vulnerability lay a formidable force inside her that she had even yet to explore.

"Yes you will, I have no doubt about it," he thought admiringly.

Ben was also moved by the lyrics of the song and choked by the effect that it was having on his sister. May felt the sadness inside him growing and cupped his head in her delicate hands, kissing him on the forehead. Miraculously the sadness lifted and a feeling of peace and happiness came over him. He wondered at the beauty and skills of this complex woman that was in his arms. He was about to say something when May put a finger to his lips to stop him, she had anticipated his thoughts.

"With good fortune there will be a time for us one day Ben," she smiled up at him and it lifted his spirits, "but that time is not now. You know that don't you Ben?"

May's sadness was almost a physical thing and he nodded reluctantly in understanding.

"But you will wait for me won't you Ben?"

Her concern was clearly evident by the urgent tone in her voice and her eyes were desperately searching his for the truth.

"Forever if that's what it takes May, forever."

She buried her face in his shoulder so that he couldn't see her tears. She knew that what she had promised was almost certain to be a lie. The dangers that faced him would probably be insurmountable. In contrast Ben's face was beaming with happiness. He was oblivious to her fears.

When the guests had all left, the four of them stood in front of the old mirror pondering on the success of the evening and saying their exhaustive goodbyes. Elizabeth enfolded May lovingly in her arms.

"Thanks for coming May, it meant everything to me and I feel that I have another best friend."

"So do I Lizzie. I had absolutely the best time ever, seriously."

She turned to Mike. Her body language had changed dramatically, business like once more.

"Mike I want you to station yourself here with some men every night until this is over."

It was an unnecessary request. Elizabeth and Ben had become too important to him to leave unguarded. He was glad to have the duty of their care.

"I already have just the matter in hand. My old squad is fresh back from their mission in Afghanistan and on their way even as we speak."

May smiled her approval and turned to Ben. She hugged him and planted a kiss on his cheek.

"Thanks for making it so extra special Ben, I will treasure this night for always," she was about to turn to leave and then added, almost as an afterthought. "Please remember the words of the song that I sang for you. I meant them. Don't take any unnecessary chances with your life. Promise me that Ben, I couldn't stand losing you."

May's concern was profound and sincere. She looked almost scared, as if she already knew something that he didn't.

"I promise," Ben reassured her.

She broke the hug leaving him with an unconvinced smile as she walked towards the old mirror.

Elizabeth blew a kiss as May stepped through it, back into to her own world.

They talked for another hour before retiring. Mike related his story about the Shadow attack, much to their amazement, and Elizabeth told

194

of her encounter with her own image in the mirror. Of course she left the bit out about Mike and their children. It seemed too much information right now.

Mike left the house to let the others sleep but his night wasn't over. When he had told Elizabeth and Ben about the Shadows attempt on their lives, he omitted to tell them about the dog. It was unnecessary for them to know, particularly on such a happy occasion.

Dawn was breaking as Mike walked into the garden to tend to the body of his dog. Something caught his eye in the shrubs. It was a man's foot. As Mike got closer the full horror of it hit him. It was the dear old butler. He was lying face down, shot through the chest with a high velocity bullet, leaving him mutilated. Mike would have to deal with this delicately in the morning and arrange some family easement to help them get through.

The moment was poignant and it upset him deeply. To think that this gentle old man would never again see his family, or the dawning of another day, was heartbreaking. He wondered how many more dawning's he could expect, before he too became a casualty of this war against the Shadows.

Mike would have to return with help to deal with the butler. For now, he picked up his mutilated dog and walked to his car. The joy of the party had receded and he was overwhelmed by the reality of death and despair.

The Jackal pulled his Humvee over into the mouth of the Robinson's driveway, jumped out and opened the tailgate and passenger door. He dumped the two heavy rucksacks into the front seat and then hefted the Drones into the back. With his cargo loaded, he returned to the driving seat and set off to execute the second part of his orders. The Jackal's face was expressionless. He was functioning on autopilot as programmed by Maelströminha.

As the Jackal turned into the drive of Grese's unlit house, he pressed the accelerator to the floor. His unblinking eyes were fixed on the heavy oak front door. The Humvee's powerful engine roared as it sped towards the house, crashing through the wall and on into the staircase. The engine was still in gear and racing. The wheels spun on the nylon carpet, filling the room with dense acrid smoke. As if nothing had happened, the

Jackal reached for one of the rucksacks, took out the master detonator and activated it.

Katya's bedroom was upstairs, immediately above the front door. The impact of the two ton Humvee almost threw her out of bed. Unthinkingly, she jumped out and ran to the stairs to confront the intruder. She was halfway down, looking into the Jackal's vacant eyes, when he detonated the bomb. The impact ripped viciously through her hunched body dismembering it instantly and her remains were consumed in the ensuing inferno.

Grese had awoken to the sound of the racing Humvee engine as it approached the house. She instinctively went into self-preservation mode and charged at her bedroom window. The glass shattered at the same instant that the Humvee impacted the front of the house. Grese landed badly on the garage roof then, seconds later, the whole house swelled with the force of the explosion within. The roof and all walls blew out, except for the one supported by the garage, leaving her protected from the blast. The shockwave from the enormous explosion concussed her and for a while she lay disorientated on the flat roof. At last her head cleared and she was able to assess the situation. Katya would be dead, Grese was sure of it.

"No matter," Grese mused. "She had her own agenda, her own hunger for power that didn't include me."

She knew that Katya would have needed to kill her to achieve that.

"Better that you died now than by my hand later."

With that thought, Grese's grieving was done. More importantly to Grese, this was a milestone in their war against the Angels. It was the first proactive strike initiated by them directly against the Senate. The war had changed. They had woken a dangerous beast, something that they might well regret. The Angels will be bringing the war to them from now on, she knew it. The Robinson children now constituted the biggest threat to the Shadow's long-term existence since the birth of Christ.

Grese eased her aching body onto her knees and looked down onto the drive. Thankfully the green Lotus had escaped the blast. She could hear the distant two-tone sirens of the emergency services and needed to be gone before they arrived. There would be some difficult questions to answer, but more importantly, her cover had been blown.

Grese needed to get to a safe house before the Angels returned to complete a job that was so far only half done. Normally she would have jumped down from the roof. Her body was screaming at her not to, so she eased herself gingerly down the rainwater pipe. The spare car keys were in the magnetic box cached under the front bumper for just such an emergency. Seconds later, she was driving south to the small detached safe house that she had already secured on the outskirts of town.

Chapter 20

It was Monday morning following the party weekend. The sun was shining brightly through the music room window where Elizabeth was enduring another class with the obnoxious Mrs Hyde. To be fair though, Elizabeth had noticed that Mrs Hyde's aggression towards her had tempered a little, replaced with a new policy of ignoring her completely.

"Preferable," she concluded.

Perhaps Elizabeth's significant physical changes and newfound confidence had a lot to do with it. Elizabeth wondered and that she had become afraid of her.

At least Elizabeth had enjoyed the ten minutes that preceded the lesson. Lovely Laura had not stopped enthusing about the party throughout. She was particularly amused by Laura's statement, "I understand men you see..." She was referring to the advice that she had given to Elizabeth in the bathroom on how to make it up with Mike, claiming the success as her own.

"Well fair one," Elizabeth thought and her smile broadened.

Then there was Laura's rapture over how wonderful Matt was. You could almost see the stars floating around her head. Finally she had said unashamedly, "By the way Mike ticks every box that I can think of, and then a few more that I shouldn't!"

Elizabeth had blushed openly, much to Laura's delight.

Mike had planned his moment well. The students were in class, teachers about their duties and there had been a recent fire drill. Any reoccurrence would be treated as an emergency, which was exactly what he wanted, organised panic.

He let himself into the storeroom, poured cleaning fluid over the contents and ignited it. The room became an inferno almost immediately and dense smoke spilled out into the empty corridor. Judging the moment, Mike closed the storeroom door to contain the fire and set off the fire alarm. The bells all around the school rang out in unison, it was bedlam. He added to the confusion by screaming out frenzied warnings as he ran through the school banging on the doors. Finally, he positioned himself at the fire exit, nearest to the music room, waiting for the inevitable.

"Fire, Fire! Everybody out!" he yelled, in a suitably panicked voice.

The normally orderly queues leaving the classrooms were more frenzied, due to the reality of the situation. The classes bustled out into the corridor with their responsible teachers leaving the rooms last, after checking that windows and doors were closed. The contents of the school spilled out into the quadrangle. They made their way chattering and squawking to the fire muster station in the sheltered area under the trees, in the car park.

The music class streamed past Mike. Elizabeth caught his eye and immediately read his thoughts and understood what he was doing. She faked losing her shoe and pulled over to the wall so as not to slow the others down. Mrs Hyde elbowed her way past and out into the sunlit quadrangle.

They only saw it for a split second because Mrs Hyde was strategically positioning herself in the crowd. Just as she left the building, and before she blended with the others, the sun caught her alone and out in the open. Mrs Hyde sensed the moment that it happened and turned to face Elizabeth. Her expression could have turned flesh to stone. Elizabeth looked back at her triumphantly. Mike had seen it too, Mrs Hyde was a Shadow!

When the last of the children were out of the building, Mike went back in. He fought the fire, bringing it under control quickly. The damage was confined to the storeroom only. Ironically, it earned him the prestige of being somewhat of a hero for saving the school. Mike Sir accepted the accolade modestly.

That was the last time that any of them saw Mrs Hyde at Northlands school.

It was going to be another sociable evening at the Robinson's. Uncle George's sister Gina was coming to dinner. She had been unable to make it to Elizabeth's party as her shift pattern at the hospital, where she worked as a Ward Sister, did not permit. She had also been on duty when Elizabeth and Ben had their recent episode with the snake venom. She too had to be conditioned afterwards, to erase some unnecessary memories.

Elizabeth and Ben both enjoyed having Auntie Gina round as she was both fun and the family historian. Her retention of past happenings was astounding. They loved her recounting stories about their parents. It comforted them to reaffirm that they once existed. Their own childhood memories were sadly fading so fast. Tonight was going to be extra special as they had some really probing questions to ask. Gina arrived late, as usual, but this was countered by her invitation having already had an allowance factored in for the difference in their respective time zones.

"Sorry I'm late only I had to take Lucky to the vets..."

George cut her off in mid-sentence with a dismissive wave and a smile.

"It doesn't matter Gina, it's just cold meat and salad from yesterday's bash. Can I get you a drink?"

Gina's eyes lit up, she loved a drop of sherry. George went to the kitchen to arrange the drinks. Gina was certainly one of a kind. She had huge compassion for both people and animals and would collect all the waifs and strays in the world if she could. Family was everything to her and she collected their history meticulously. Gina could tell endless tales about each, which was what Elizabeth and Ben were counting on tonight.

Gina's love of the past was probably down to the loss of her own future. She had been a successful equestrienne and had competed at Badminton, amongst the best in the world, until her fall fifteen years ago. She never recovered the level of fitness necessary to compete at the highest level again and fulfil her dreams. Gina was a survivor though. She kept her interest in horses through helping to care for, and by riding her brother's. Over the years, Gina had devoted a lot of her time to coaching her niece and nephew. They owed a lot of their success to her selfless dedication.

Dinner went splendidly. Gina enjoyed the catch up and was particularly enthralled about the two potential new members to the family; Mike and May. She asked lots of questions then decided that she would get to work on finding out more about them as soon as possible. George and Jillie hadn't thought that it might be quite so cut and dried yet and looked at each other as if they might have missed something.

George and Jillie cleared the table and retired to the kitchen. It was Elizabeth and Ben's chance to do a little research into the past. Elizabeth led the conversation.

"Auntie Gina; Ben and me were talking the other day about Mum and Dad and how much we've already forgotten about them, or never knew in the first place. Now we're older, it would be nice to understand what they were like as people, not just as parents."

It was evident by Gina's smile that she was delighted at the invitation.

"Well starting with your mother, Jodie. After leaving college, she worked in Birmingham as a personal secretary at a number of high profile companies, until she moved out into the country. She met your father there. He was a civil engineer at the time, contracted to build some bridges on the Ludlow town bypass. It was love at first sight actually..."

Gina was lost in the story. Amongst the romantic detail, were tangible descriptions of who Jodie really was: a dedicated friend; resilient; often fiery but forgiving; selfless and a brilliant mum. Jodie had inspired Ralph to take risk and as a result they had enjoyed a varied and enviable lifestyle. Jodie was actively involved in the various business adventures, despite being a mother along the way. Elizabeth and Ben were enthralled about who their mother was and what she had done, and all this hidden behind the badge of just being their mum.

"She would have been your best friend if destiny had allowed it Lizzie," a tear of regret ran down Gina's cheek.

Ben diverted her.

"And what about Dad, what kind of man was he?"

Gina's brow furrowed, she appeared to be less sure about him.

"He was a good and caring man, resourceful and popular. But I must confess that there's a lot about him that I never understood, or somehow never even questioned."

Gina was clearly at odds with herself over why she had not questioned, when it was so against her curious nature.

"What do you mean by that?" Elizabeth prompted to encourage Gina to expand on her statement.

"Well, he was different to me and George. But then there were different fathers involved, I suppose, and..."

Suddenly Gina looked stricken about her indiscretion.

"It's alright Auntie, we already know about that," Ben interjected.

Gina looked immensely relieved and surprised that it had actually become public knowledge.

"Oh, I didn't know that..." Gina continued. "Anyway, even when we were children, there were some strange things. If he cut himself, he would heal so quickly and he always knew just exactly what I was thinking, sometimes even before I did."

Gina smiled reflectively at her fond memories.

"Some of his magic tricks were just *too* real, like he could tell you about something that would happen soon and it actually would!"

"So what other *tricks* could he do then Auntie?" Ben asked urging her on.

"So many Ben; he could hold a ball in his hand and it would raise several inches above it. You could even run your hand around it and not feel any strings. Sometimes the ball would turn into a bird, or a mouse. He said he would teach me how one day, but he never did. Once, when I asked him to pass the salt at dinner, he somehow pushed it towards me. I even looked under the table but I couldn't work it out. I was easy to fool I guess, so much younger. He could have done it professionally you know."

Elizabeth and Ben could see by her expression that she didn't really believe that it was just an illusion.

"And what about as a man Auntie, what can you remember?"

This was going so well that Elizabeth didn't want it to stop and she sensed the same from Ben.

"Everything Lizzie and it gets stranger. Your father used to work away regularly, sometimes weeks at a time. He often came back with some really serious injuries that he would justify with all kinds of crazy stories."

Gina looked reflective, she was struggling within herself.

"I don't think that I ever really believed them. I don't really know why, but I never challenged them either. To this day I don't know why, it's not my way you see."

"Can you give any examples Auntie Gina?"

Ben wanted the detail. Even the smallest thing might enlighten them as to their own possibilities.

"Again there were so many Ben. He came back one time, after six weeks away, with a deep cut from his cheekbone down to his chin. It went right through into his mouth and he had three fingers missing on his left hand too. He said that it was a practice sword fight that went wrong. I remember it all clearly. After that I didn't see him for nearly a month, but when I eventually did, he hadn't even got a scar on his face and he had a full hand of fingers."

Gina was shaking her head, still trying to fathom it out. It sounded even more ridiculous when she actually put it into words.

"You must have questioned that Auntie Gina!" Elizabeth said incredulously and Ben's thoughts came to her as she said it.

"That's why Dad kept me interested in sword fencing Lizzie, to help me protect myself!"

Elizabeth nodded in agreement.

"Well of course I did, Gina said indignantly, "I'm a nurse after all."

Gina was slightly miffed at appearing foolish to them, but more so at herself for having let Ralph get away with the nonsense that he had told her. She continued.

"He said that he'd signed up for some top secret medical research and development programme at a London hospital. He said that I shouldn't mention it to anyone, and I never did."

There was a long pause while Elizabeth and Ben evaluated the information. Gina was lost in her own struggle as to why she had not challenged all this before. She could never have known that her brother would have influenced her mind. Ben broke the silence.

"What you've said has reminded me of something that happened when I was about eight years old. I do remember that Dad used to go away a lot and Lizzie and me would wave him goodbye, crying from the lounge window. Dad said that he had to go away to fight the tigers and giants to keep us safe. The fact that we hadn't seen any only showed how good he was at his job, apparently."

Ben exchanged smiles with Elizabeth at the fond memory of it.

"One of his stories was about the *Giant of Obidos*. He told us about how he fought him for six days and seven nights along the battlements of Obidos castle. The villagers had dug a deep pit and Dad lured him into it. Do you remember Lizzie?"

"Do I ever! Then the villagers buried the giant until only his enormous hand was left showing. It eventually turned to stone and is still there to this day. Dad said that the giant would come back to life when the son of his killer sat in the palm of the stone hand."

Gina remembered the fable too.

"Didn't you go to Obidos sometime afterwards, Portugal wasn't it?"

Gina already knew that they had but she was enjoying the story. Elizabeth continued.

"Yes Auntie we did. Dad re-told the tale just before we got there. Ben was old enough at that time to begin doubting the story. In fact he outright said that it was just rubbish, something that Dad had made up."

Elizabeth began laughing and it was several seconds before she could continue. Ben was beginning to regret that he had brought the subject up in the first place.

"You should've seen Ben's face when we came over the hill and Obidos castle was laid out below us, battlements and all, just as Dad had described it! When the statue of a giant hand came into view Ben was bricking it," Elizabeth was in hysterics and nearly fell off her chair. "It was a scream Auntie, when we stopped Ben wouldn't get into the giant's hand until I did first!"

Ben went into defence mode. His tone was a little sulky.

"I was only eight and I wasn't really scared..."

"Ben, you were bricking it," Elizabeth was enjoying making Ben squirm.

"Whatever," he conceded.

Gina diverted the conversation in a move to rescue Ben,

"Anyway he may well have been fighting tigers and giants for all I know, judging by the state he used to come home in sometimes."

Elizabeth and Ben exchanged the same thought.

"Not tigers and giants, he was fighting Shadows!"

Gina got up from the table to help out in the kitchen and prepare the coffees. It gave Elizabeth and Ben a chance to gather their thoughts.

"That's given us a lot to think about Ben. It was a revelation to Auntie Gina though, I don't think that she had ever really considered that things weren't quite right before, or wasn't allowed to perhaps?"

"I think the latter Lizzie. There was evidence of a number of Dad's special abilities in Auntie Gina's story. Telepathy and mind control for sure, healing and regeneration too, if we assume that there was no research and development hospital in London."

"Agreed, and if Dad was able to predict events before they had happened then he either glimpsed the future in the old mirror or he had used the portal to move through time himself."

Elizabeth considered the possibilities.

"If Dad was able to use the portal to travel through time, then there's no reason why we can't. That's what we need to be able to do to, get back to when Mum and Dad were still alive. I know May has already told us that the portals give access to other times in space, but to actually know that Dad has already done this makes it feel more real and doable."

The thought was inspiring.

"Yes that's the goal. We're not ready for that yet though, not until we've developed the other skills May has told us of. According to Auntie Gina's memories, Dad must have had psychokinetic skills too; levitation and shape-shifting are two from what she has described."

"Maybe," Elizabeth wasn't so sure. "Did Dad actually levitate the ball and change it into little animals? Or did he only control Auntie Gina's perception to think so, like when May threw the stone and made us believe that it was a meteor?"

"Fair one Lizzie, or maybe even a mixture of both. I think we have to put some time aside to explore what we can do with our own minds. Anyway whatever, he must have been a hell of a fighter though. Mum must have been scared to death every time he went away. She must have known or at least suspected what he was up to." Ben reconsidered his statement. "Then again maybe she didn't. She may have been conditioned too."

Ben was idly messing with the salt cellar as he was talking. He was thinking of Auntie Gina's comment about Dad pushing it towards her without touching it. Elizabeth caught his thoughts. Ben set it down in the middle of the table.

"You first Ben, push it to me."

Ben focussed all his attention on the salt cellar. After two minutes nothing had happened. Elizabeth linked her mind with his to work together, just as May had told them to. Still nothing happened, nothing at all. Ben's expression clearly showed his disappointment.

"Dad must have only created the illusion and it just appeared to move to Auntie Gina."

"Or we're missing the point Ben. Maybe Dad never pushed it at all. Perhaps he just selected another possibility, another place in space that it could be?"

Elizabeth focussed her concentration on the salt cellar. After several seconds it faded out of sight then reappeared in front of Ben.

"What did you do Lizzie?"

"I didn't push it Ben, I just imagined it in another position that it could possibly be in. Remember May said that the universe had infinite possibilities and that we are living in only one of them."

"And I thought I was the scientist in the family! Hats off Lizzie that was clever!"

Ben was genuinely impressed. He picked up the salt cellar and held it in his open palm. Moments later, it was in the air six inches above it. Ben's face lit up.

"Hey presto! Levitation."

Despite several attempts, neither Elizabeth nor Ben could change the salt cellar into a bird. They had to give up when Gina walked back into the room. Ben let the cellar drop back into the palm of his hand as Gina placed coffees in front of them.

"We can't tell you how much your stories of Mum and Dad have helped us, really we can't, Auntie Gina."

"Oh I haven't finished yet Lizzie, that's not even the half of it!"

Auntie Gina declared and continued to enthral them with family stories for another two hours.

Chapter 21

Adolphius had called an emergency meeting of the remaining Senators. Three senior ranking Shadows had been killed in as many days and the Hydra had lost confidence in his cell. He was facing displacement. They were gathered in the usual drear , but the dynamics were entirely different. Adolphius was not bristling in his usual manner, he was on the back foot needing support and all there knew it. It was not at all like the courtroom scenario of the last meeting, they were sat around a circular table in a symbol of unity. Alexis was sat to Adolphius' right; the perfect implacable enemy.

"The next one to watch," Grese thought. She was going to enjoy this engagement.

"I'm sure that you both know why I've called this meeting, but I will recap to make sure that we are on the same page."

Adolphius was unusually ill at ease in his address. His top lip twitched, giving away his feeling of vulnerability.

"Dada, with all his experience, was hacked to pieces and killed by the Robinson siblings. We must no longer fool ourselves by calling them *children*. They are far from that now, they are adults in everything but years. Maelströminha has clearly taught them well. Their brains will now be highly evolved and their physical development near complete. After they have discovered their full skill-set and learn how to combine their minds, they will be as dangerous to us as Maelströminha herself."

Adolphius waited until Alexis and Grese acknowledged this before continuing.

"The Jackal has let us down and squandered a unique opportunity to take out Maelströminha and the siblings at a single stroke. Grese you are exonerated. You did the right thing in engaging the Jackal and that is endorsed by the Hydra. Maelströminha must have sensed the attack and neutralised it. We only know that the Jackal returned with his men and the explosives to your house Grese, probably under the mind control of Maelströminha. As you all know, he detonated those explosives killing himself, his men and regrettably Katya. For that you have my sympathy, she would have made a good Senator."

Grese nodded at the sentiment. Her lips were thin with spite.

"It will be avenged you can be sure of that."

Adolphius continued his address.

"I'm sure that you will both have noted that this attack on the Grese household is unprecedented. It is the first time that the Angel pacifists have initiated a strike against the Senate on home soil and ironic that they have used our own kind to commit the deed. This act of aggression has changed how we must perceive our enemy. The war will be coming to us now. They are no longer prepared to be the victims. They appear to have adopted a more proactive approach. They will become the aggressors, you can count on it."

Alexis nodded his ancient head. Instinctively Adolphius paused and deferred to Alexis for his experience and direction.

"Our cell is much depleted, weakened by recent events and through in house rivalry. This has rendered us ineffective as an operating unit. Our numbers are no longer sufficient to withstand a coordinated attack by the Angels and be assured that one will come if we appear weak to them."

Alexis could sense their agreement and continued.

"We have globally lost our best Shadows to reinforce the war effort between the capitalists and the fundamentalists. This is something that all other cells are experiencing in every State across the planet. It is time to either amalgamate with another cell or recruit some muscle to use as insurance, which is your choice?"

Alexis' face was devoid of any expression but his eyes bored down into their very psyche. He could see even their most private thoughts and they knew it.

Grese spoke for both herself and Adolphius.

"You know that we do not favour amalgamation. That invariably leads to more rivalry and struggle for leadership."

Grese glanced at Adolphius for his confirmation which he gave from an almost unperceivable nod of his head.

"I personally favour the use of mercenaries. There is something intrinsically honest about prostitution, and the exchange of money makes the boundaries clear."

Grese paused and looked Alexis directly in the eye.

"You never ask a question Alexis, without already knowing the answer. What are your recommendations?"

Quite unusually Grese had gone to the trouble of making herself up. She had applied eye-liner and red lipstick. With her hair up and the soft lighting she looked feminine and indeed quite beautiful. Whatever, it had certainly helped in giving her some new-found confidence. Alexis' grin was without any sign of pleasure, it only expressed his satisfaction at Grese's submissive response. Any endeavour to gain latitude using her feminine charms was wasted on him.

"I have two guests for you to meet this evening as I have taken the liberty of anticipating your reaction."

Alexis banged his fist heavily on the table twice. Two men entered from an adjoining room. The first had a military stride and was tall with angular features. Both Adolphius and Grese recognised him instantly as Otto Adolf Eichmann, often referred to as the architect of the Holocaust. Adolphius, or Adolf, as he was then known, had given him the role of *Transportation Administrator* of the final solution to the Jewish question. This was at the time when anti-Semitic measures became policy in the Second World War. Eichmann saluted Adolphius in the archetypical German style and bowed his head in Grese's direction.

"*Fraulein*," he acknowledged.

The second was a shorter, rotund man. He was fastidiously dressed and balding with the scholastic look of a physician and sly eyes. Neither Adolphius nor Grese recognised him, but they could sense his cruelty. Grese was particularly ill at ease. There was a perverseness about him, something deeply sinister that made even her feel sick inside. His sly eyes were all over her. Instantly Grese regretted having made herself up. She subconsciously folded her arms to conceal her ample breasts as Alexis began his introduction.

"You will already know our comrade Otto Adolf Eichmann. He served as *SS-Obersturmbannführer* under you Adolphius, and of course *Fraulein* Grese, your paths will have crossed in the concentration camps at Auschwitz and Belsen.

Adolphius had good reason to approve of Eichmann's selection. It was Eichmann who had implemented his genocide plans to the letter nearly 70 years ago. Because of his excellent organisational talents and ideological reliability, Adolphius had rescued him from execution in much the same way that he had for Grese, using a double. After the war, Eichmann had been captured in Argentina by the Israeli Mossad. He was taken to Israel to face trial on fifteen criminal charges, including crimes against humanity and war crimes. He was supposedly executed in 1962, but the man hanging on the end of the rope was not Eichmann. Adolphius had made his substitution and the man that now stood in front of him owed him his life.

Adolphius spoke for them both.

"Welcome comrade it is good to see you, it has been too long," it was as genuine a greeting as you might hope to see amongst Shadows. "May I ask why you have joined us Otto?"

Eichmann gave the Nazi salute and clicked his heels sharply.

"I have a debt to repay to you *mein Führer*."

Adolphius nodded his accord and deferred to Alexis. He was particularly pleased with his selection.

"May I now present Sir William Withey Gull, a man of some notoriety in the Whitechapel district of London in the later part of the 19th century. You might say that he had a certain *way* with the ladies," then Alexis added hastily. "Allegedly of course, nothing was ever proven."

Adolphius and Grese immediately knew the name. Sir Gull, or 'Withey', as he was usually called, was the physician-in-ordinary to Queen Victoria. He was implicated in the Masonic/royal conspiracy theory surrounding a series of brutal killings in the slums, in and around Whitechapel, in 1888. The victims were principally young prostitutes from those. In each case, their throats had been cut prior to abdominal mutilations and the removal of their internal organs. The nickname that the public had given to this sadistic serial killer was *Jack the Ripper*.

Grese tried to keep her voice as even as possible and deliberately avoided giving him the dignity of using his knighthood.

"And so Withey, what do you find attractive about joining our cell?"

Grese maintained eye contact with Withey, even though it sickened her stomach to do so.

"I enjoy my work," he said simply.

Withey's mouth was womanly with an incongruous waxed moustache above it. His voice was squeaky, devoid of any emotion. A lascivious grin came over his pudgy face.

"I believe that there is a certain young lady that I would be particularly interested in making acquaintance with. She will already know that I'm coming as I have already met her many times in her dreams."

Withey was looking particularly pleased with himself. He ogled Grese as he spoke and his feminine mouth worked lewdly, as if he was sucking a sweet. Even Grese felt a cold chill run down her spine and she suddenly and uncharacteristically felt sorry for Elizabeth.

"Better that the Robinson girl had died by my hands rather than by those of this despicable monster," Grese thought ruefully.

Chapter 22

Corporal Michael Jackson had spent the last two days driving his inconspicuous white panel van around the town and nearby countryside. He was looking for a particular green Lotus sports car. Since the destruction of her house, Grese had moved to an unknown location. Mike needed to know where that was in order to manage the threat. At the end of the second day, Mike had some unexpected good fortune. He had arrived coincidentally behind a green Lotus, driven by a woman, at the traffic lights in the centre of town. She had turned her head to pull out into the middle lane, giving him a clear view of her profile. It was Grese! Mike followed the car, heading south, until it turned into the drive of a small detached house on the outskirts of town.

Two other men were inside the van with Mike. They wore headsets and were configuring some hi-tech surveillance equipment. Both were dressed in overalls and fluorescent jackets. Mike pulled over. The men put on their hard hats, dragged some orange plastic barriers out of the van and placed them confidently around the nearest manhole. Mike jumped down from the cab with an A3 Ordnance Survey map in his hand and looked around, as if orientating himself. He was actually looking to see if he had a clear line of sight from the tree next to him, to Grese's driveway. He had. While his men continued to busy themselves preparing the decoy manhole, Mike got back in the van and re-parked it on the verge next to the selected tree.

The van was crammed with all the necessary equipment for sophisticated surveillance, both audio and visual. He took the miniature camera and solar power battery pack from the bench where his men had meticulously prepared it and then exited from the side of the van furthest from Grese's house. In less than a minute, Mike had the unit strapped to the tree and camouflaged. He walked over to his men with the open plan and pointed up the road shaking his head as if he had made a mistake. His men gave a brief show of annoyance, before loading the equipment back into panel van and they were gone.

They stopped a half a mile further up the road. One of the men got out and placed a dish on top of the van, while the other switched on one of the monitors. In moments they had a perfect picture of Grese's drive. Her green Lotus was still parked where she had left it and they could see right up to her front door. After agreeing a shift pattern between themselves, Mike and one of the men left the van and walked back towards the town centre. The first part of Mike's plan was in place.

Mike returned at six o'clock that evening to relieve his man. His squad of ex-SAS soldiers numbered four in total. Two of them were under constant guard at the Robinson's house, leaving the other two plus him to monitor Grese's movements 24/7. The plan was that Grese would eventually and unwittingly lead him to the other Shadows.

At seven o'clock, the movement detection mode on the monitor alerted Mike. The miniature camera was picking up Grese leaving the house in his direction. Mike quickly left the van and removed the Snap-On dish, then turned the van around in readiness. Moments later, the green sports car passed his parked van. After allowing a reasonable distance, Mike pulled out and took up pursuit at the limit of his vision.

Grese's route took her through the town and out into the country on the north side. After some twenty minutes, she turned into a secluded drive. It was framed on both sides by avenues of silver birch trees that reflected the dappled light, before opening up into a small courtyard. At the far end, lay a ramshackle but expansive bungalow, nested in amongst overgrown and neglected bushes. Grese parked the Lotus alongside two other cars and entered the house.

Mike parked the van a few hundred yards away. He picked up the laser audio surveillance equipment that he had prepared, and made his way along the boundary hedges back to the bungalow. He set the equipment down at the corner of the garden furthest point from the house. He then worked himself round to the parked cars attaching a tracking device to each. After making a mental note of the registration numbers, he returned to the state of the art laser equipment at the far corner of the garden. Mike put on the headphones and set up the decoder. He pointed the directional laser microphone at each window, until he got the strongest reading. The microphone picked up sounds from inside the rooms by bouncing a laser beam off the window, then detecting and decoding the vibrations in the glass. With the aid of digital enhancement, Mike could hear their conversation as if he was in the room with them. Every word was being recorded to his hard drive for later analysis.

It was an hour later and gloomy, when Mike heard the meeting draw to an end. He repacked the audio surveillance equipment and took out his night vision binoculars with video link, then positioned himself to capture images of them leaving the bungalow. The Shadows obliged him by leaving singularly and he managed to get some really clear video footage. He waited several minutes after they had gone before leaving the safety of his hide. Mike returned to the van, assembled another miniature camera unit and then secreted it amongst the trees in the garden, giving an uninterrupted view of the bungalow's front door.

Mike left with a feeling of deep satisfaction. In a matter of hours, he had uncovered the location of two Shadow houses, placed trackers on three cars and obtained audio and video records of a meeting of the Senate.

"Not bad," he thought to himself," not bad at all."

The week following the party, Elizabeth and Ben had spent all of their spare time researching and practicing their new skills. It was probably the most fun that they had ever had in their lives. As May had told them, their limitations were only those imposed by their own imagination. The sky literally was the limit! Elizabeth had documented their progress and recorded areas for further research. To recount:

Their telepathic skills were so good, both between themselves and their ability to read other people's thoughts, that they needed to agree some privacy rules between themselves. Those rules also needed to be sacrosanct.

In the gym, Ben could bench press over 300kg and that was only limited by what would fit on the bar. Elizabeth could press just over 200. This was significantly above their normal expectations. They knew that they were still evolving. Their bones and muscles were getting denser and they wondered where it would end. Elizabeth continued to monitor her weight with increasing alarm. Hours of practice had developed their levitation skills, such that inanimate objects were no challenge at all. They had actually managed to levitate themselves and each other to some small degree. They both saw amazing potential in this but acknowledged that these skills were immature and not yet ready to use against the Shadows. Their greatest and most developed skill was that of

213

mind control. They could make anybody see exactly what they wanted them too and here the possibilities were endless, just as May had suggested. For example, they could be sat at the table with Uncle George and Aunt Jillie without them being aware of their presence. It was also interesting what you hear when no one knows that you're there!

Some of their abilities were not always a blessing though. Both had trouble sleeping because their heightened hearing gave them no peace, even the ticking of the Grandfather clock in the hallway was bedlam at night. They hadn't yet learnt how to filter out spurious noise. If a dog barked harmlessly anywhere in the neighbourhood, they would both wake up in terror. Elizabeth was finding this particularly hard as it exacerbated the loss of sleep that she was already experiencing with her reoccurring nightmares about her stalker.

Most significantly, and again as May had told them, anything that they did together had the effect of magnifying their ability enormously. They were astounded when they joined minds and successfully moved a parked truck uphill. It did so without the wheels turning, the whole physical system was moving as a single entity and the braked tyres were screaming in protest. They had to stop when the driver, who had been asleep in the cab, woke up. He had jumped out in a state of panic after checking the handbrake and it was on!

One of the most amazing things that they achieved together was the disappearance of Ben's wristwatch. They were sat at the kitchen table, joined minds and simply willed it away. The moment that it happened was a shock to them as they hadn't expected it to work. Neither had they any idea where it had gone nor how to get it back. Ben was particularly disappointed about this whereas Elizabeth was in tears of laughter which didn't help at all, he liked that watch. This was definitely another to follow up with May.

Elizabeth had been wishing the week away. Aunt Jillie had invited Mike to join them for lunch after Ben's cricket training on the Saturday morning and she couldn't wait. Mike arrived with Ben in his car and to say that Elizabeth had spent hours getting ready for him was an understatement. She had tried on every dress she had in front of Jillie and none were quite right. Consequently, Aunt Jillie had to rush her to the shopping precinct on an errand of mercy. After the fourth shop they came to an agreement on just the right thing.

Mike and Ben piled through the front door scrapping playfully over some childish comment that Ben had made about Mike and Elizabeth's relationship. Mike was taking a swipe at the back of Ben's head when he came face to face with Elizabeth, stopping himself in mid-swing. He smiled guiltily and proffered a bunch of flowers to her that had become somewhat bent in the fray. As an act of appeasement, he gave her that sideways look that guaranteed forgiveness and of course Elizabeth obliged.

Lunch went superbly and Elizabeth couldn't have looked more radiant. The full length shoulder-less white dress fully allowed her womanly figure to dominate. Her zany hair and makeup were the finishing touch, accentuating Elizabeth's huge green eyes. Aunt Jillie watched with some pride and amusement at Mike's efforts to stop staring at her. Of course he failed miserably. The banter was good and the Robinson's were second to none at entertaining. Mike truly felt welcome as part of the family and Elizabeth's expectations were at least that. She used those big green eyes on numerous occasions to reinforce it. When the festivities were over, Uncle George and Aunt Jillie retired to clear up and Mike chose that moment to bring Elizabeth and Ben up to date. Mike, as quiet and reserved a person as he was, had excellent timing and an amazing ability to call people to attention when he wanted to. Both Elizabeth and Ben were waiting in anticipation. They had sensed that he had something important to tell them.

"And so to business," began Mike, "I now know where Grese lives and I've placed a surveillance camera there, watching her drive 24/7."

Elizabeth raised a well-groomed eyebrow and they nodded their approval, already feeling safer in knowing that at least she had been found.

"Grese has already led me to the house of Adolphius and I have a camera there too."

Mike was being perfectly professional in his delivery however Elizabeth was watching his beautiful blue eyes, strong brow and long black eyelashes a little too openly.

"Sis! Pay attention for God's sake," Ben's thoughts arrived abruptly in her mind.

"Privacy rules, remember!" Elizabeth countered fixing him with those eyes. Ben backed off while Mike continued obliviously.

"As luck would have it, Alexis was there too. So we now have a fix on all three of them."

"Very impressive Mike, so much intel gathered in only a few days."

Ben was in awe of Mike's covert skills. He wondered what stories he might have to tell them of his past experiences, but that was for another day.

"Are we ready to attack?" Ben added.

Mike held his hand up in the stop manner.

"Not so fast Ben. A soldier only goes to war after he knows his objectives and fully understands his enemy's capability."

Elizabeth chose her moment well and entered the conversation speaking softly and in an understated and confident manner.

"I know exactly what our *objectives* are Mike; Mum said that I would and my image in the mirror confirmed that too. What I don't know is how though. We must work that out together, but later. First I can sense that you have a lot more to tell us Mike."

Mike looked at Elizabeth almost in wonderment. There was a strength and capability in her that almost scared him. The set of her jaw and the intent in her eyes reflected a level of determination that he had seldom seen, even amongst the trained men that had fought beside him. Mike had to force himself back on track.

"Yes Lizzie, you're right. There is more. The Shadow meeting was attended by two new faces, recruits I would guess, to replenish their recent losses. One I know of, is Otto Adolph Eichmann..."

"I know about him too."

Elizabeth was once again reminded of her school studies, but they were somehow enhanced by some other knowledge. She didn't realise it at the time, but the additional knowledge was from the information that May had implanted in her. She shared it with them.

"Eichmann was instrument in executing the Holocaust, the extermination of the Jewish people in the Second World War. He was a military tactician and a staunch ally of Adolf Hitler, an evil man and not one that you would put on your Christmas card list."

"Indeed not," Mike agreed and he bowed his head fractionally in acknowledgement of her wisdom. "This man will have been carefully selected by Alexis, based solely on his ability to deliver. You should give him your deepest respect. Do not underestimate him, or it will cost your life."

Elizabeth and Ben exchanged glances and agreed that the Shadows had just significantly upped the ante.

"The second new arrival is a man called Sir William Withey Gull, but they called him *Withey*. It's not a name that I am familiar with," Mike gave them that quizzical look again but the name wasn't familiar to Elizabeth or Ben either.

"I'll check the name out online now," With that, Ben picked up his laptop and logged on while Mike continued with his brief.

"I managed to get a full audio recording of the meeting and some clear video footage of them leaving. To summarise though, the new boys appear to be mercenaries and their contract is both to defend the cell and to eliminate you two."

Elizabeth and Ben fidgeted nervously at the thought.

"But not if I can help it," Mike continued, "I've got two of the best men that you'll find anywhere watching you around the clock. I've also fitted tracking devices to all the Shadows cars so we will know exactly where they are at all times."

Ben's name search on Google was successful and he interrupted.

"Here, I have it. Sir William Withey Gull, 1st Baronet of Brook Street. He was a physician. Get this; he was linked to the 1888 unsolved Whitechapel murders that were accredited to the legendary *Jack the Ripper*. Can you believe that?"

Elizabeth's skin went ice cold. Jack the Ripper was the secret fear of all women and for Elizabeth he had been the menace of her dreams for the last four years, ever since she saw the movie. That was singularly the worst thing that she ever did! The reoccurring nightmares had blighted her nights ever since, increasing in intensity and detail almost as if it was her destiny.

The dream came rushing back to her. It was always the same. She would be walking through a maze of dark streets, totally lost with a choking feeling of dread. It was chilly, always chilly. There would be a mist at first that steadily thickened into a fog until she couldn't read the street names, or even see where she was going. Then came the footsteps. Elizabeth knew they were going to come, even before they did. She would be listening for them, turning in circles to know which way to run. Her fear would mount inexorably while she waited. They would be slow and measured at first and then quicken. Her fear would turn to panic and she would run aimlessly, somewhere, anywhere. It was always hopeless though. Her feet would feel like they were in treacle and the harder she tried to run, the more her legs would drag.

Elizabeth would try to scream, but no words would leave her mouth and no one was there to listen, even if they did. The footsteps would be at a full run by now, getting closer and closer, louder and louder. But she could never place them. Then suddenly, he would be there right in front of her, immaculately dressed carrying an ornate cane. Elizabeth would freeze, unable to move or even breathe. She could vividly remember every detail of his pudgy face, as time seemed to stand still while she waited for the inevitable. He was balding with leering cold eyes and a woman's mouth, but with a neat moustache above it. She could even remember the acrid sweaty smell about him and she retched involuntarily at the memory of it.

Elizabeth knew in her dream that she had to fight for her life. She would try and thrash out but her blows always landed like butterflies on him. His womanly mouth would smile cruelly at her, as he showed her the blade of his knife that he pulled from the ornate cane. Then his squeaky voice would utter the same words:

"It's alright my little precious I will free you now," then he would draw the razor-sharp blade across her throat...

Elizabeth would then awaken to the noise of her own screams and run to her mother's bedroom where she would lie awake petrified in her arms, listening out for any noises until the morning came. After the accident this unfortunate duty fell on Aunt Jillie who gave her that security and never complained about it.

"All people have their own relationship with and understanding of fear," she had once told her.

Ben and Mike looked with alarm at the sudden change that had come over Elizabeth. They were calling her name urgently but she wasn't hearing them. She was somewhere else. Their alarm turned to fear and Ben started to shake her.

"Lizzie! Lizzie! What's the matter? Lizzie!"

Elizabeth broke free from the memory of her nightmare, gulping air into her empty lungs. She had been unconsciously holding her breath throughout the terrifying episode and felt that she was suffocating. Ben's cries were ringing in her ears and finally her eyes became focussed again but she had lost something inside her, and that was hope.

"He's going to kill me Ben I know it now, I have always known it."

Elizabeth looked distant. She was in shock, hugging herself defensively and rocking. When she spoke it was softly and in a resigned way.

"Those reoccurring nightmares that I have were not just dreams Ben, they were premonitions. My destiny is to die at the Ripper's hands I know that now."

She put her head in her hands and sobbed her heart out.

It took an hour, three cups of tea and a lot of consoling before Elizabeth was able to put the ordeal behind her. Well at least to convince the boys that she had. Mike had brought the video images to show them on a memory stick that he handed to Ben.

"OK it's time to meet our enemy. With the exception of the Hydra, we have them all."

Ben inserted the stick into his laptop and placed it between them. Elizabeth had secretly slipped her hand into Mike's and was enjoying the feeling of safety that it was giving her. She looked up at him and smiled lamely.

"We're lucky that May placed you to protect us Mike. But please be careful. All those who have tried to so far, have died and I couldn't bare it if anything happened to you."

Elizabeth looked into his handsome face and squeezed his hand positively. A single tear let her down, she knew now that it was not meant to be.

Ben opened the video file and with the digital enhancements that Mike had made, the images were crystal clear. The first Shadow to come out of the door was Adolphius. He was immediately recognisable to them all despite his modern makeover. Adolph Hitler's image was prolific and his deeds, infamous. It was Mike who broke their personal thoughts.

"This is the face of the Shadow that killed my father and orchestrated the death of my brother. I would dance on his grave."

Next out was Eichmann and Elizabeth was surprised at how striking he was. Tall, ramrod straight, with well sculptured features. It was not the face that exuded the evil that was within him. Eichmann clicked his heels and saluted Adolphius before entering the car. Grese followed and walked towards her own car without any bids of farewell. She was made up and considerably more attractive than Elizabeth had expected, but the set of her face was either concealing pain, or fear. She was holding herself in that protective way that women do when they are disturbed, and Elizabeth wondered why?

Alexis stepped out and immediately looked around as if sensing danger. He appeared to be looking directly into the camera with those black eyes of his that were deeply recessed in their sockets. It seemed that he was about to walk in the direction of the camera when he was distracted by Adolphius calling him over.

Mike hit the pause key as he realised how close he had come to being discovered.

"Jesus! That was a close escape, he must have sensed me and I didn't notice it at the time!"

Mike was clearly taken aback, he would never have left there alive if Alexis had seen him.

Alexis was the first of the Shadows that none of them had seen previous images of. They were jointly amazed at how old he looked, his face was almost mummified. Alexis was slightly hunched and the night breeze was blowing his thin wispy white hair around his balding pate in a flurry. Although clearly of great age, he moved like a young man with a confident stride and no stiffness in his neck and shoulders, which is typical of older men. Alexis seemed infinitely more aware of his surroundings than the others. He was peering into the darkness and even scenting the air like a gazelle, constantly alert for predators. It was skills such as these that had kept him alive over the millennia.

"Don't underestimate this one," Mike had been fully briefed by May. "I am reliably told that he is still the most feared of all Shadows; cunning, ruthless and as strong as an ox. When you meet him, don't give him any quarter. He will give you none in return."

Mike shuddered as he said it, realising again how close he had come to being exposed by this prolific killer of men. He tapped the play key and instinctively held Elizabeth's hand as the final Shadow appeared in the doorway. Withey stepped out into full view. Physically, he was a nondescript sort of man, fairly short and a little rotund. Dapper would adequately describe his dress style. His grey jacket sported generous lapels over a neat waistcoat with gold watch chain draped in catenary. He wore a bow tie, brimmed hat and carried a short, broad cane which completed his Poirot-esque style.

Mike took control of the keyboard and zoomed in on Withey's face. It was chubby with somewhat womanly features, particularly the bow lips. He had dark eyebrows above cold lecherous eyes and a well groomed and waxed moustache.

"Is that the face of the man in your dreams Lizzie?" Mike asked almost mockingly.

Elizabeth was looking into the face of the same man who had been stalking her in her sleep for almost as long as she could remember. Every single detail of him was precisely as she had seen in her dreams over and over again. She even knew that the knife that was going to kill her was concealed in the cane that he carryied. This was the man that was going to take her life away and rob her of the future that she had glimpsed in the mirror on the night of her eighteenth birthday party. It was with immense effort that Elizabeth broke the inertia within her and dragged her eyes off the image of Withey. She looked up at Mike lovingly, knowing now that she would never have him or his children, Edith and Brady.

"No Mike nothing like him," she lied smiling thinly at him, "nothing like him at all."

Chapter 23

It was Sunday morning on the day following. The household were all sleeping in, except for Elizabeth, who had been up since five o'clock and was already at the stables. She had deliberately not slept, not even a wink and vowed that she would never do so again. Years ago she had seen the movie, *A Nightmare on Elm Street*, where the serial-killer, Freddy Krueger, could enter your dreams and kill you in them. Even though it seemed preposterous, Elizabeth felt that perhaps the Ripper could do the same. After all, what had not seemed preposterous lately? Elizabeth couldn't let the Ripper get her, not yet. First she needed to prepare Ben and Mike to finish their mission without her.

Elizabeth had arranged for Mike and Ben to come and see her later in the day and had prepared something to show them. But for now she just wanted to enjoy the time that she had left to her with her soul mate, Beauty, and lose herself in her. Elizabeth swung effortlessly up onto Beauty's back and galloped off in the direction of the canal to the place where her parents had died. She had some personal goodbyes to make.

Mike arrived at four o'clock in the afternoon. Ben had been like a cat on a hot tin roof waiting for him. When the Jaguar finally growled into the drive, he was off to meet him in a flash. Elizabeth looked out of the window and saw them greet like brothers. Her heart skipped a beat as she thought about how much Ben would need him in the future, when she was gone. Elizabeth had spent ages getting herself ready for him but everything that she tried on looked drab and her hair seemed to have a mind of its own, even her makeup looked flat. It wasn't really the case, only a symptom of the despair that she was feeling inside her. It was her inner beauty and contentment that was missing and Elizabeth knew it.

Mike's pleasure at seeing Elizabeth was apparent. His face was beaming as he crossed the hallway enthusiastically to meet her. He wrapped his arms around her in a loving hug.

"Wow, you look beautiful."

Elizabeth responded in the same manner but her hold on him was just a little too urgent and Mike sensed it.

"Hey, what's the matter Lizzie?"

Mike put his hand under her chin and lifted her head so that he could look into those sparkling green eyes of hers. He could see that she was unusually sad and the fire that normally raged inside her was not there.

"Just tired is all Mike; I didn't sleep last night," Elizabeth put on a brave face and brushed the matter to the side. "Come with me, I've got something to show you both.

"OK but you need a break Lizzie. How about I take you to the movies on Friday so we can chill out, I could do with that too?"

Mike had put himself out on a limb and was hoping that he hadn't misread her feelings for him.

"That would be lovely, and yes, I do need a break. I'll look forward to it."

They went to Elizabeth's room. As she let them in she apologised for the mess.

"Sorry it is a bit of a tip, only I got ready in a hurry."

It was both an understatement and a lie. She had taken hours to get ready and it looked like a bomb had hit the place. Elizabeth scraped some space on the bed and sat them down. She crossed to her dressing table and flipped the mirror over. It took a few moments for the boys to orientate themselves to what they were looking at. Elizabeth had created a storyboard with 'Post-it' notes on the back of the mirror. Across the top, reading from left to right, were the names: Emanuel Goldberg; Mum and Dad; Miss Crystal and David Williams, along with the dates of their deaths. Below that, also on Post-it notes, were the names: Adolphius; Grese; Alexis; Katya and the Hydra. Elizabeth had created links in red ribbon connecting the victims with their killers: Adolphius with Emanuel Goldberg; Grese with Mum, Dad and David Williams and Alexis with Miss Crystal.

Elizabeth let her shock of blonde curls down and shook them free with her long neck. It was something that didn't go totally unnoticed by Mike, but then it wasn't a complete accident on Elizabeth's part either.

"As I see it, we don't want to kill any of these Shadows right now; doing that, would only help to fix the future," the boys looked puzzled.

"No," she continued, "We need to go back in time and take them out before they have killed our loved ones, and there is an order about it. If we go back in time to before Mum and Dad left Uncle George's house and kill Grese then, we not only save their lives but also David's, albeit years later. We know that Alexis killed Miss Crystal, I mean Crystalita, on the same day and we know it was as she left the school. So we have to take Alexis out too sometime before that happens."

Ben and Mike were listening intently and Mike was captivated as usual.

"We know that Mum and Dad left the house at seven o'clock, because I remember Mum saying that, and that they would be back in time to put us to bed. It's only ten minutes to the bend by the canal so they died at about ten past seven. We need to know exactly what time Crystalita was murdered, so that we can prevent that too. May will certainly have felt it, so she can tell us next time we see her."

Elizabeth turned to Mike and smiled at him. It was a brave smile. What she was about to propose would be her parting gift to him, before she succumbed to the inevitability of her destiny.

"Then we go back further in time and kill Adolphius, before he kills your father Mike."

Mike's brow furrowed it was utopia and there was no such thing as perfect. A scenario that gave him back his father and his brother? His immediate reaction was that it was untenable, too good to be true and Elizabeth read it.

"It can be done Mike you just have to trust me. In a world with infinite possibilities, there are an infinite number of outcomes. We just have to engineer the one that we want."

Elizabeth's self-confidence was undeniable but there was the small matter of a cell of cut-throat Shadows to deal with first. That was something that, in Mike's mind, seemed to have been somewhat underplayed in Elizabeth's plan.

"Lizzie all this has to happen on the other side of the mirror. I haven't managed the journey there yet and I don't think that I can. That would mean that you would be on your own, without my protection," Mike looked pained. "It's a brave and noble plan Lizzie but common sense says that we kill them now and protect the future of the Angels. Let the past remain in the past. Think of yourselves and the bigger picture."

It was almost a plea and Elizabeth could tell that he was afraid of losing her and Ben.

"Have faith Mike. We dealt with Dada with only the smallest understanding of our skills. I promise that we won't go until we're truly ready, you know that I wouldn't risk Ben, not for anything."

Ben was was fully on board with what Elizabeth was saying but he was feeling a little left out.

"Don't worry Mike; I will look after Lizzie, when the time comes. After all, it's becoming a bit of a habit," Ben followed that taunt with a cheeky grin and Elizabeth bit.

"In your dreams sunshine, you have always needed mothering by me and you always will!"

Elizabeth realised too late that she had been got but the words were already out there and Ben was looking particularly smug.

"You really can be such a royal pain in the backside Ben. Let's see if you're still so smug when you've got a Shadow snapping at your arse screaming *Lizzie, Lizzie please help me!*"

That turned the situation comical and fell around in fits of laughter at the mental picture conjured up by it; Ben running, looking back over his shoulder, with a Shadow trying to bite a chunk out of his backside.

It released the tension of the moment and they were relaxed and positive again. Ben brought them back to the matter in hand.

"We have to do this Mike, not just for us but May needs Crystalita back. Her life is broken without her sister and the Angel race needs her bloodline. Besides..."

Ben looked a little choked and struggled with his next sentence.

"Besides May said to me that I will help bring Crystalita back to her one day and so we must do as Elizabeth says. We owe it to her."

He looked into Elizabeth's eyes and could feel her reaching into his mind.

"Yes Ben. We must bring them all back, even if it means that we don't make it home ourselves. Agreed?"

"100% Lizzie," was Ben's unspoken reply.

He reached out for her hand. Their fingers entwined and gripped so hard, that their knuckles whitened with the force of it.

"Love you too," Elizabeth confirmed.

The next day was Bank Holiday Monday and the start of half-term. Elizabeth had spent the morning with Auntie Gina at the stables. After tending to the chores, they tacked up Beauty and Laser and took the Ridge circuit. The horses were particularly frisky and up for a gallop. It was two miles from point to point, but Beauty and Laser never tired. The girls screamed with the exhilaration of it. For the first time in a long time, Elizabeth felt totally free of her fears.

Beauty was light on her feet and Elizabeth's skill at moving as one with her, made it easy going for the mare. It was poetry in motion. Then it happened and it was a total shock to Elizabeth. Her mind had connected with Beauty's, in a primordial way. She could sense and share all of Beauty's base emotions. Elizabeth was carried away by the inexplicable want and thrill of the horse just to run and keep running. It was electrifying, the consummate riding experience! Elizabeth's love for Beauty just doubled and re-doubled. Riding would never be the same again for her. It was the most incredible feeling of her life.

When they reached the end of the Ridge, Elizabeth and Gina were breathless. They dismounted and Elizabeth immediately threw her arms around Beauty's neck, kissing her cheekbone and whispering in her ear. Beauty was breathing heavily and snorting, her body wet and steaming from the exertion of it.

They agreed to walk the horses back to rest them, and in moments they were both lost in Gina's tales of the past. Elizabeth was amazed at just how therapeutic visiting and reinforcing your memories could be, particularly now that she realised that she had no future. Elizabeth felt rejuvenated and couldn't wait to meet with May later in the day as planned. She had forced the images of the Ripper out of her mind and for now she was happy and at peace with the world.

Ben had enjoyed a totally different day. He had spent the morning in the surveillance van with Mike and two battle hardened SAS soldiers, learning all he could about the technology and techniques of modern warfare. He was soaking up their knowledge like a dry sponge. Once he was confident that he knew all that he could about surveillance, he moved on to learn about search and destroy, survival and assassination techniques. His Angel brain was absorbing and storing the information on first-pass. Mike looked on in admiration of Ben's application and retention. When Ben's back was turned both soldiers gave the thumbs-up sign to Mike and nodded their approval. Mike knew however, that if Ben was going to survive the next few weeks, he would need all this and a small miracle besides.

Ben was satisfied with the day's progress, he had already learnt enough to put his own private plan together.

"Sometimes," he thought, as youth does, "you've just got to go out there, do it and forget the crap."

Chapter 24

Although it hadn't been long since the party when they last saw May, it seemed ages ago to them and they had missed her so much. Now they were stood in front of the old mirror, full of anticipation and ideas to share with her. Quite coincidentally, their thoughts went back to when they first met May. They smiled at each other at the beautiful memory of it, then held hands and walked into the mirror.

They had expected to arrive as usual in the brightness of the corridor of mirrors but they were somewhere else. It was dark and a warm breeze was caressing their faces, beautiful music was filling their minds and a storm of colours was swirling across the night sky. It was all coming from over the ridge in front of them and they were drawn towards it like moths to a flame. A feeling of *déjà vu* came over them. When they saw May sat on the rock in front of them, there was no feeling of surprise at all. She was playing her lute of light and singing. Her naked lithe body was encrusted with jewels emitting light in every colour of the rainbow, changing with the beat of the music, just as when they had first seen her. Her thick black hair was swept over her shoulder falling to her slim waist and her eyes, set above those high cheekbones, were changing to every possible hue of blue according to the mood of the music. May slid off the rock and began to dance with sensuous, sinuous movements that complimented the music, song and the lights so perfectly.

Suddenly Elizabeth was filled with a great foreboding. Something was dreadfully wrong.

"We have to go Ben, right now before she sees us!"

Elizabeth grabbed Ben's arm and dragged him back to where she knew that the corridor of mirrors would be.

Ben was confused but he could tell by Elizabeth's alarm that he had to comply. They ran back to the corridor with Elizabeth still clasping his hand. The mirrors were flashing their images as they ran by them until they reached their own. Elizabeth literally shoved Ben back into their world.

"What the hell was all that about Lizzie, and what's May going to think of it?"

Ben was trying to catch his breath and his voice was a mixture of disappointment, dismay and anger.

"Don't you see Ben? It wasn't right it wasn't where, I mean *when* we had meant to go. We arrived in the past, back to when it all started. What was the last thing that you were thinking of before we stepped into the mirror?"

Elizabeth was holding Ben by the shoulders willing him to remember.

"About how we had first met May and..." Ben suddenly realised the enormity of it. He nodded, wide-eyed in absolute astonishment. "We went back in time Lizzie; we actually went back in time!"

"Yes, I was thinking about the past too," Elizabeth was so much further ahead of the game. "We accidentally both thought of a specific time and place as we stepped through the mirror and it took us there, just as May said it would."

"Wow it all really works!"

Ben was seriously impressed with Elizabeth's ability to have made such a swift analysis of the situation. Not to mention a little annoyed with himself for not having seen it too. Ben still wasn't quite there though.

"But why did we have to leave so urgently?"

"I'm not totally sure," Elizabeth confessed, "but we were about to create another possibility, another reality and I didn't want it."

Elizabeth was in some kind of personal distress. She was confused but convinced that deep down; she had made the right decision. Mum had already said that she would know and May had said *trust your instincts, they will always be right* and that is what she had done.

"Explain Lizzie, you know that you do know. You always know."

There had never been an occasion in Ben's life where Elizabeth had gone out on a limb for them and been wrong. Elizabeth considered the situation carefully before replying.

"Ben, so much has happened since we first met May. We have survived three major Shadow attacks: Katya with the snake venom; Dada in our house and an attempt by the Jackal to blow us all up. Maybe in another scenario, we wouldn't have made it."

Elizabeth paused and looked at him shyly.

"And maybe we would never have met Mike..."

Ben sensed Elizabeth's vulnerability and the gentleman in him prevailed. He totally agreed with her logic and didn't embarrass her by pressing it further.

"OK let's go back and this time, we had better be bloody sure of what we want and where and when we are going!"

He flashed his cheeky smile at her and they linked minds, thought of May in the present, and then stepped back into the corridor of mirrors.

They found May over the ridge sitting on the same rock as when they first saw her. This time however, she was surrounded by dozens of wild animals from birds to bears, all competing for her affection. Affection that she had in abundance. If the first time that they saw her was amazing, then this just took it totally off the scale. May was talking wordlessly to the animals. She was offering tit-bits and playing with them, sometimes chastising the big ones when they bullied the little ones. You could even see them sulk at her rebuke. It was an orchestration of total love and devotion.

Elizabeth held Ben's arm to stop him from going to meet May and whispered to him.

"No Ben, not yet; this is too beautiful a moment to miss. Let's just enjoy it for a while."

It was magical and they looked on in total awe. May had exchanged her skin of gems for an enchantment of miniature flowers. They were so minuscule, colourful and perfect and they complimented every womanly curve and secret cleft of her body. Elizabeth and Ben gasped at the absolute beauty and perfection of it. They were looking at the summation of everything good about what woman could be; young, beautiful, vital and in empathy with nature.

At last May saw them up on the ridge and her face lit up with her genuine happiness to see them. The tiny rose buds that made up her full red lips bloomed and spread into the most amazing welcoming smile. Her feelings towards them were so intense and infectious, that all the animals simultaneously looked at them in that same moment and none flinched nor tried to run.

They sat on the rock next to May and she cooed softly to them the way that she had done in the beginning.

"Let me introduce you to my adopted family, although perhaps it is they who have adopted me."

May talked about each one of them in turn fondly describing their characters, likes and dislikes. Each had a name and a reason why she had chosen it.

"... and finally the bear. He's a new member to my family. He's young and lost from his own parents, orphaned I think. He's headstrong and stubborn but cuddly and loveable, so I have chosen the name *Ben* for him."

Elizabeth nearly fell of the rock laughing and May joined in joyously. It was several minutes before Ben could get any kind of sense out of them so he contented himself with just watching May and bathing himself in her beauty and fragrance.

At last they were lucid again and Ben's next question was delivered in a matter of fact way.

"You don't by any chance have any orang-utans called *Lizzie* do you?"

Ben howled with laughter at his own joke, while the girls just pretended not to understand.

Elizabeth told May about her riding experience with Beauty and how she had developed an empathy with her and how special that had felt. May had explained that in time, that empathy would extend to all beings as part of her evolution. When Ben told her about the disappearance of his wristwatch, after they had willed it away May was clearly amazed and the tiny blush pink flowers that made up her brow darkened as if furrowed.

"Are you sure that it really physically disappeared Ben?" May asked in disbelief, "or could it be that you just altered your perception of it and simply overlooked it?"

"No, not only couldn't we see it but we couldn't touch it either."

"Well it seems you've moved something significantly through space without using the portal, which means that you could equally have moved it in time too, or even both. There's no difference you see, it's just another dimension."

This was a significant happening in May's mind and her face literally blossomed with the pleasure of it.

"We have moved through time too May," Elizabeth added and related their *déjà vu* experience.

"You were right to abandon the alternative reality Lizzie," May confirmed. "Even though we have no certainty of the outcome of this one, you have already survived so much together and that is not a *given*. The smallest change in what you do causes a divergence. It's like being at a 'Y' junction, your choice of path leads you to a different destination. Life consists of millions of decisions some minor and some major. All affect the ultimate outcome of your lives and you have chosen wisely so far."

May paused to collect her thoughts before continuing.

"Your joint ability to manipulate time and space areimpressive and you are not yet fully formed. If we can keep you safe until your transition is complete, then the Shadows will truly fear you and the sway of power will once more be with us."

A benign expression came over May's perfect face. She continued as if she was somewhere else; in a dream perhaps, "That will be the time when I can fulfil my destiny and mother the next generation. My blood will begin to restore our race's fading abilities and we will be able to protect the human kind from the tyranny of the Shadows once again."

"And if we fail you?" Ben asked hesitantly, although he already knew the answer.

The negative words brought May immediately back from her reverie.

"Then it will be as I have already told you, the Shadows' power will become absolute and they will use up your Earth and discard it. The mother ship will fall into their hands and ultimately they will search the universe for a suitable planet to colonise and it will begin over again. And so it will go on."

The thought was chilling so they all consciously moved the conversation away from their troubles, chatting idly for an hour about everything and nothing. Slowly the animals moved away one by one, some sulkily, at having been displaced by the new arrivals.

Somehow out of nowhere, May produced a jug of iced lemonade and some glasses and they all drank thirstily until they were quenched. Ben was distracted by one of the animals scurrying away then, somehow and inexplicably, May was lying next to him with her head on his lap smiling up at him. He was puzzled at how it could have happened so quickly and without him seeing, but then May had no boundaries as he knew them. He was just happy that it had happened. The smell of her was intoxicating. The riot of fragrances from the miniature flowers of her skin were combining and sending messages to his brain, almost as a language. The words in that scented language were expounding love. If Ben could have chosen a place and a way of spending eternity it would have been right there and right now.

It was getting late and out of necessity the subject changed to their on-going struggle with the Shadows. Ben began his update but May raised her hand to stop him.

"All this I already know from what Mike has told me. He has made significant progress and in such a short time. I feel so much better knowing that he and his men are watching over you now."

Ben was slightly put out as he was looking forward to the telling of it but he didn't let it show, although somehow he felt that she already knew that.

"But how do you know May. Mike says that he can't use the portals? And why can't he, he's Emanuel's son and an Angel himself?"

"Firstly, I'm sorry that I spoilt your story Ben, which was insensitive of me."

May tipped her head submissively and Ben actually felt her regret.

"Mike is the first victim in his family line to suffer the ultimate consequences of the dilution of his bloodline. He has retained all of his physical advantages, albeit to a lesser degree and still has good telepathic skills, particularly when linked to a higher life form." May smiled that irresistible smile and added. "That's a very complicated way of saying that we have our little chats."

Elizabeth searched deeper, driven by more personal matters.

"Does that mean that if Mike has children, they won't be Angels with our skills?"

Her voice was just a little too desperate and she immediately felt foolish. May fielded the question skilfully and Ben was once again gentleman enough not to cash in on the opportunity.

"That would be dependent on the quality of the union. If it was with a partner of earthly blood then there would be only some minor residual abilities, nothing more than that. However, if that union was with the bloodline of the Patriarchs, the elite of the Angels, then an almost full skill-set would result. Not too dissimilar to your own Lizzie."

Elizabeth nodded and tried not to show her obvious relief. The sudden rush of blood that coursed up her neck and flushed her cheeks, let her down though. By way of diversion, Elizabeth began to explain her storyboard and the order in which they needed to kill the Shadows. But Elizabeth was still disorientated and inarticulate.

"The only missing information is the exact time of Crystalita's death."

Elizabeth cringed at the insensitive way that that she had just trivialised Crystalita's life as *missing information*. Then, when she saw the devastating effect that it had on May, she felt ten times worse. All the

233

little flowers that composed her skin had wilted and withered away. Elizabeth was desolated for what she had done and clambered frantically across the rock to reach May. When she got there she threw her arms around her.

"I'm sorry May, so sorry. I didn't mean..."

"Ten past seven Lizzie, coincidentally exactly the same time that your parents died."

May had to choke out the words. She burst into inconsolable tears. Her body convulsed with the waves of emotion that crashed through her. This powerful woman was suddenly a lost child. The remains of the flowers of her skin turned to dust on the wind, leaving her naked and vulnerable in Elizabeth's arms.

Chapter 25

It was Friday morning in the Robinson household and there were great expectations. For Elizabeth it would be her first official date with Mike who was collecting her at seven o'clock that evening. They were to dine first and then go to the cinema. For her the day just couldn't go quickly enough. She had everything planned to the last detail: hair; dress; makeup and even some of the things that she wanted to say to him. Things that she needed to say, before she capitulated to the monster in her dreams. Elizabeth was going to just chill for the day and recoup her strength. It was nearly a week now since she had slept and she wanted to look as good as she possibly could for him. She was ever conscious that each encounter could be her last and she wanted him to remember her at her best. She had even gone as far as considering that she didn't want to die a maiden. That thought alone, raised a dozen others.

Ben was looking forward to something quite different. It was the day of the long awaited under-sixteens fencing championships. He and Uncle George were going together making it a good opportunity for a man to man catch up. Ben had every reason to have high expectations. He had become so superior to the other boys in fencing, that he was now practicing with the old masters instead. With the new skills that he had gained from May's teaching, his ability to assimilate technique proved meteoric. When none could match him with the foil, he began to learn the skills associated with the épée and sabre. Ben was now regarded by his masters as somewhat of a prodigy and they had already contacted the national team about him.

As far as Ben was concerned, there would be no doubt at all as to the the outcome of the championship. There was only one boy that he hadn't yet fenced against and beaten. That boy was also sixteen and his name was Illya Dracul.

The two men fencing were uncle and nephew. Both were wearing their four-piece protective uniforms and helmets with see-through mesh. They looked an unlikely match. One was tall and athletically built and the other, much smaller and slightly hunched with a plume of wispy white hair escaping from his helmet. They had chosen sabres for the bout, where points could be scored by both stabbing and slashing assaults. Each was testing the other. The bout ebbed and flowed as blades flourished in their skilled hands and the clash of sabres was almost musical to the ear.

The bout ceased to the yell of "*touché!*" as the smaller of the men's sabre struck his opponents lame jacket in the centre of his chest. He pulled his helmet off and his thin white hair fell around his balding pate in an almost comical manner.

"Bravo Illya you are becoming quite a challenge!" the old man shook the other approvingly by his shoulders.

Illya took off his helmet revealing a handsome Slavic face with eyes so dark they were almost black. His short cropped blonde hair, pale skin and perfect white teeth were incongruous with the colour of his eyes but completed his striking good looks.

"As you would expect Uncle Alexis, after all I have the best teacher that this world has ever known!" Illya's laugh was spontaneous and full of the confidence and arrogance of youth.

"You are ready Illya. Adolphius has bred a fine son and you will make us both proud today."

Alexis crossed the room to a glass cabinet. He took out a long antique box and opened it in an almost ritualistic manner. Inside were two beautiful old duelling sabres with jewelled, guilt handles and ornately engraved, razor-sharp blades. The notching in the blades was evidence apparent that they had been used in anger. The mysterious blades they kept their dark secret of how many lives had been taken with them. Alexis looked at them lovingly.

"These belonged to an infamous ancestor of ours. You will choose your moment and present these to the Robinson boy. He will not be able to resist a friendly spar with them. It is in his nature after all, and then you will kill him."

The journey to the stadium took a little over an hour. Time however passed rapidly, as Ben and George lost themselves in their enthusiastic conversation over motorbikes and karts. They kept two dirt bikes at the stables. Ben's was a KTM 250cc, four-stroke and George's was the 450cc version of it. Much to Ben's pleasure, they had unanimously agreed that he needed an upgrade, justified by Ben now being bigger and heavier even than George. Better still, they would kick it all off that weekend and put the plan into action!

George, and his brother Ralph had owned the land behind the stables right up to the Ridge. When Ralph died the land had passed to George. The landscape just below the ridge apex lent itself perfectly to the needs of a challenging dirt track and George had created just that. The circuit followed the natural contours of the land giving a demanding combination of uphill and downhill sections, throughout its sinuous three mile length. Once a month, George extended its use to the local bikers and their families and it had quickly become a recognised social event. The women had also come to look forward to it for the festive get together. Some had already started to compete. George bit his bottom lip as he considered the future possibilities.

"Do you think that Lizzie would become interested if we kept your bike for her Ben?"

"Yes, if we can get Mike interested in bikes too. Then you can bet your life on it Uncle. You can also bet that she won't be letting him win either. That's an odds-on certainty!" Ben became reflective, "Besides she could use the distraction right now Uncle."

Ben knew Elizabeth only too well. She had become withdrawn lately and this could be just the fillip that she needed to break out of it. He had no idea though, that her remoteness was driven by her fear of Withey. No idea that she was counting the days left to her, before he was to end her life.

"OK we'll hang onto it then but it's up to you to get Mike interested. I can't imagine that being much trouble for you," George's manner was conspiratorial.

"No trouble Uncle; just leave that to me."

A big smile spread across Ben's face at the thought of having them all race together and him on his new *bad boy* dirt bike too. The others wouldn't have a chance!

Sixteen candidates had been selected across the Counties and they had been divided into two groups, 'A' and 'B'. Ben had been nominated to the group 'B' knock-out matches, where five bouts constituted a match. Ben had won his three matches comfortably at 5-0 in each, taking him into the final where he would face the winner of group 'A'. Ben was looking at the Leader Board with George.

"Looks like game on at last Uncle. I see that this *Illya Dracul* has also had a clean sweep in his group. Win or lose this will be an interesting match, not that there is much chance of losing though!" Ben's attitude was cocky and it irked his uncle.

"Don't be complacent Ben. I've been watching that boy and his wins were every bit as easy as yours. You'll need to be focussed right from the call of *En-guard!*"

"The bigger they are the harder they fall Uncle..."

Ben had that youthful arrogance of supreme confidence and it worried George deeply. The contest had the word *disaster* written all over it.

"Anyway, nearly time to get kitted up again and soundly whip this pretender."

Ben gave his uncle a sweeping bow with an exaggerated flourish of his sword before turning for the change area. As he passed the gymnastics apparatus at the back of the hall, he saw the rings unattended and noted that he still had several minutes to spare. The last time that he had used them, was before meeting May. That was before his recent muscle development and Ben was curious to measure his improvement. He had struggled previously with his boyish power to weight ratio. Ben chalked his hands and approached the apparatus with great expectations.

It would be normal for Ben to be assisted up into the starting position but he sprang up easily, taking the rings in his firm grip. He pressed them down until his arms were straight out from the sides of his body, placing him in the Iron Cross position, a move that takes tremendous upper-body strength to perform. He held that position for several seconds then swung up into a handstand. He then dropped into an Inverted Iron Cross, before putting in a couple of swings into a triple salto dismount, landing feet together. Ben bowed to his imaginary audience and felt pumped up and ready for his match against Illya Dracul!

Dracul was alone in the changing room stripped to the waist. It was plain to see that he had extraordinarily well developed arms and body for a sixteen year old. When Ben entered, he was almost knocked over by the pungent smell of deodorant. He coughed involuntarily, which prompted a friendly response from his opponent.

"Sorry mate. Name's Illya Dracul. I had a can explosion with this bloody thing."

The boy shook the empty deodorant can and tossed it across the room for a perfect hit in the waste bin ten yards away.

"Don't know about fencing mate but you would be a star in the girl's netball team!"

They both laughed and shook hands enthusiastically, Ben felt unusually at ease with this lad.

"Ben Robinson your arch enemy. I'm pleased to meet you Illya."

Illya smiled at the unintended appropriateness of Ben's comment.

"Pleased to meet you too Ben. I was also watching your girlie talents and clearly there won't be many women out there who'd beat you at fencing, that's for sure!" Illya's smile was perfect to the point of being hypnotic.

"*Touché* Illya, I deserved that," Ben gave respect to an equal wit. "Where are you from, your name has never come up in the tournaments before?"

Illya's manner was self-evasive.

"Immigrant family recently arrived from Transylvania. And yes before you become boring, the family name Dracul does go back to the fabled Vlad III Dracul, or Dracula, as he's now commonly known."

Illya smiled easily. His looks were striking, almost mesmerising. His black eyes burnt like coals, contrasting dramatically with his pale face and short cropped blonde hair. Ben averted his eyes, suddenly, conscious that he was staring. There was something strange about this handsome young man, but Ben couldn't quite work out what. The closer that he got to the answer, something seemed to push the thought further from his mind. Ben abandoned his efforts.

"That's just about the coolest thing I ever heard Illya! Do you have a reflection in the mirror?" Ben returned Illya's smile, pleased with his little quip.

"Now you really are getting boring Ben. If I have heard that once, then I've heard it ten thousand times," Illya was still smiling that enigmatic smile and holding Ben's eyes confidently. "It gets better Ben. My ancestor was known as Vlad the Impaler, which incidentally is what's going to happen to you, very shortly."

They both laughed unreservedly at the nonsense of it all. Ben was already looking forward to kicking his arse.

Illya cut the laughter short.

"I however do know exactly who you are Ben and I've been waiting to show you something that only a true lover of the blade would appreciate," Illya took away the towel, exposing an exquisitely carved box and opened it. "You see before you the duelling sabres of the very Vlad himself."

Ben was awestruck and desperate to handle them.

"They've been in my family for generations and killed more men than you've had hot dinners."

Ben was besotted with the legend and the implied power of these swords. He was already seduced.

"The swords of Dracula, can I?" Ben asked reaching for one of the beautiful blades.

"No!" Illya was over-firm and Ben shocked by it. Ben's disappointment was evident on his face. "I mean no, not here. To appreciate them you need to wield them as they were intended. Come on Ben we've still got a few minutes, let's do a little re-enactment in the yard outside."

Ben was sucked in hook, line and sinker. He followed Illya out into the yard as trustingly as a little puppy.

Elizabeth had probably never looked more beautiful. She had taken hours and made herself up to look the perfect femme fatale. He doesn't stand a chance she decided but continued fidgeting and pacing around the room nonetheless. It was still only five o'clock but Mike would be early for her, she just knew it. She looked at her reflection in the mirror for confirmation,

"After all how could he not be?"

Once in the yard, Illya tossed Ben one of the duelling swords. He caught it in the grip with a natural ease and swished in around in a flourish of cuts and thrusts. The finely-honed blade sang in the air hauntingly and its balance of it was exquisite.

They were stripped to the waist and truly looked a duelling pair from days of old. You could imagine that it might over the love of some rare beauty, standing undecided on the side-lines holding her handkerchief to her mouth in delicious dread as they fought for her honour. The young men circled each other and feigned attacks from a distance. There was the occasional clash of blades that rang out clean and pure as they tested each other. The noise of it was delicious and intoxicating to them.

Illya suddenly came in with a coordinated attack that Ben parried with ease.

"Steady Illya, we're not dressed for this."

"Sorry Ben I just got carried away. There's something special about using these swords that makes it all feel real. Imagine the hundreds of victims that died from them, don't you think that's awesome?"

"Awesome and some," Ben agreed. "It makes the swords that we play with feel like toys," Ben was positively beaming at the experience and Illya's enchanting smile never left his face.

Illya attacked again with a vengeance that Ben was totally unprepared for. He parried the first few thrusts, but one went through his defences gouging his right side. Blood welled up immediately and flowed profusely from the angry wound down his leg. Ben became focussed immediately. It was partly through the pain in his side but mostly through the sudden recognition of the faint acrid smell in his nostrils, the same smell that he remembered when Dada had come into their bedroom.

All in a flash he recalled how the changing room had reeked of deodorant. That was no coincidence! It was to corrupt his senses, so that he didn't pick up the Shadow's stereotypical acrid smell. Then, he thought about how he was immediately at ease with Illya and realised that he had fallen under his control. He had been *smoothed*. Illya had used that hypnotic smile on him and had controlled Ben's mind right from the moment he had walked into the changing room. Ben glanced down and his heart sank. He saw just what he hoped that he wouldn't see. There was only one shadow falling to the courtyard floor. It was his!

"I could've killed you there and then Ben Robinson but I've let you live for my further amusement. You will die by a thousand cuts, start counting!"

Illya's beautiful face had turned demonic and his black eyes drilled into Ben's with tangible hatred. Not even a trace of that benign smile remained. He attacked again. It was the same move but on the other hand. Illya's blade cut Ben deeply on his left side. He immediately retreated out of range to taunt him.

"Symmetry Ben; I will create a work of art with your body. They will hang your corpse in a gallery and I will of course sign it with this blade for posterity," Illya's laugh had become almost hysterical.

While Illya was revelling in his success, Ben replayed every move that Illya had made so far and how he had responded unsuccessfully to them. He was *learning* him.

"I can take a few more hits," Ben decided, then went in on full attack.

Ben had been duped and had started behind the curve. Now, blades were fizzing and clashing, but Illya gave no ground. They came up face to face with swords crossed at each other's throats. They were both pressing for a physical advantage, but on that front they were equals. At last they broke free from the stalemate and circled each other like wolves waiting to attack. Ben assessed his opponent.

"He's confident in his own ability and won't give ground, an attacking swordsman," Ben conceded and nodded in respectful admiration.

Illya came on again and this time Ben held his ground. He was soaking up the venomous thrusts either on the blade or through parries. Typical of the taller man, Illya preferred to initiate his attack from on high, forcing his opponent's arm directly above his head. In this defensive position, muscle groups are at their weakest, with no leverage. Conversely, the attacker is at their strongest. Ben indulged this and suffered the consequential raking of his chest and stomach, as the razor sharp blade ran down him. He felt no real pain however, and just clenched his jaw whilst continuing to memorise all Illya's moves. Ben needed to know one more aspect of Illya's game, how he dealt with the low sword. He came in testing under his guard.

"Alleluia he now gives ground!" Ben's relief was tangible.

Uncomfortable with the low assault, Illya broke free and came back in from on high to regain the initiative. Ben simply pulled backwards, withdrawing from the fight and infuriating his opponent. The sword fight was becoming much more balanced now and the tempo rose to a furious pace. The sweat from the sheer exertion was running off their naked torsos, like Gladiators in some Greek arena.

The smug look on Illya's face had wilted to something close to fear as his brash confidence began to desert him. With every passing minute Ben was learning more and more of Illya's skills and technique, until he could anticipate his every move.

"You should've killed me when you had the chance Dracul, because you will feel my blade in your heart soon. You already know that don't you?" Ben taunted through gritted teeth.

When Ben's powerful thrust finally took his opponent through his abdomen and upwards out of his back, Illya's black eyes opened almost as wide as his mouth. He dropped his sword in disbelief as Ben pulled his own sword out with a twisting motion to release the suction. It should have been a mortal wound. The blade had pierced Illya's lung and he was coughing up frothy blood, but Illya was not human. As he regained his balance, his black eyes searched for an escape route. He ran to the yard wall and scaled it, using a wheelie bin as a springboard and he was gone.

All at once, Ben started to feel the effects of blood loss, shock and sheer physical exhaustion. There was nothing left in him for the chase. He let Dracul go and concentrated his mind on stemming the blood flow from his many wounds. Within minutes, he had slowed it to a trickle and was able to turn his concentration to implementing some kind of a damage limitation plan. Ben only had a few minutes to make everything appear normal, before his uncle and the officials would arrive. What he failed to do, would require a little subject smoothing later.

"If Uncle George was to see him in the state he was in, he would've had a fit," Ben realised and needed to sort himself out.

Ben stowed his blood soaked clothing in one of the lockers, then showered. Although the blood had stopped flowing through mind control, the gashes on his body were deep, ugly and wide open. They needed binding, particularly the one from his chest down to his groin, which you could tuck your fingers in. Ben pulled the roller towel off the wall and ripped the linen into two inch strips. He stood in front of the mirror and bound himself up tightly from upper arms to crutch. When it was done, he managed a wry smile at his reflection.

"Not cool. I look like a 20 year old man in a baby-grow," then randomly, "God, I hope May's not watching this somehow!"

He was suddenly looking forward to telling her of the encounter. Of course he would embellish it a little too.

After Ben had dressed himself, he quickly went through Illya's bag and clothes for any useful information. When he found his wallet, there was the usual money, cards and stuff but Ben's jaw dropped when he saw the photograph. It was clearly Illya as a young boy stood between two men. One was an ancient man with white gossamer hair and the other, a pale faced man, with sunglasses and brown hair swept to one side. They were the same men that Mike had captured on his video, Alexis and Adolphius!

"Close escape!" Ben realised.

He suddenly felt vulnerable and started to shake as shock began to set in. Ben realised that he couldn't sort out the rest by himself, so he picked up his mobile phone and called Mike. The call connected and Ben felt immediately relieved.

"Is that you Mike?" his tone was urgent. Mike knew right away that Ben needed his support.

"What is it Ben? Where are you, are you alright?"

"I'm OK just got cut up a little in a sword fight with a Shadow. There's a bit of a mess to tidy up here though. Blood everywhere in fact, and questions are going to be asked that'll need a little smoothing. Can you come? We're still at the stadium. You could be here in 45 minutes in that Jag of yours, if you boot it."

Mike had already handed his Shadow watch over to one of the SAS lads and left immediately. The roads were clear and Mike made good time, but he hadn't a hope in Hell of getting back to pick up Elizabeth at seven o'clock. He decided to call her when he got to the stadium and put their date back to see the late night viewing.

"That should be alright," he thought.

Fortunately the route was mostly motorway. Even with the heavy commuter traffic, typical of that time of day, he was able to average over 100 mph. When he arrived at the stadium there were already two police cars and an ambulance parked out front. Ben had managed to contain the situation at the stadium to a degree by confusing the minds of the police, Uncle George and the sporting officials.

There was blood, but no body or weapon. Ben had secreted the duelling sabres away as *spoils of war* and were now his as victor. There was no way that he was going to part with those. The blood was *apparently* from a cat that an urban fox had savaged in the courtyard and of course nobody had seen the injuries that Ben had sustained.

The stumbling block was the inexplicable disappearance of Illya Dracul, before his well-earned match in the final. Also, that all his kit had been left in the changing rooms. When Mike arrived, he was assertive from the outset and took over as the interface between the emergency services and the stadium officials. He reinforced everything that Ben had told them, lending more credibility and confidence to the explanation. Finally it was agreed that Illya's disappearance was no

244

more than a severe attack of pre-match nerves, reinforced by there being no reports of missing persons. The police left the stadium an hour later, leaving two very exhausted young men and a confused uncle.

Mike suddenly turned pale. His expression was a mixture of guilt and pure fear.

"Oh shit, I didn't call Lizzie!"

Chapter 26

It was evening and seven o'clock came and went. To say that Elizabeth was disappointed was about as big an understatement as could possibly be made. She was furious. Hours, no days, of expectations and planning had gone into preparing for this moment and he had spoiled it. On their very first date too! It was after eight o'clock when Elizabeth finally came downstairs. Aunt Jillie was in the kitchen and was surprised to see her.

"Oh, I thought that you'd left an hour ago Lizzie..." When she saw the expression on Elizabeth's face she hurried across the kitchen and folded her in her arms, "What's happened Lizzie?"

Elizabeth's emotions were running too high for her to even try to speak. It was a mixture of anger and deep disappointment. The phone rang and Elizabeth allowed herself several seconds to compose herself before answering it.

"Hello Elizabeth Robinson speaking," it was Mike.

"Oh Lizzie, I'm so sorry only something really important cropped up. I will be around in an hour and explain. We still have time to go to the late viewing..."

Mike was trying to be positive but Elizabeth cut in.

"Clearly something more important than me. Well don't bother yourself; now or ever!"

She slammed the phone down and burst into tears burying her face in Aunt Jillie's shoulder.

It was a few minutes before Elizabeth could speak again.

"The bastard couldn't even be bothered to ring me beforehand. These things don't just happen you know."

Elizabeth was well past upset. What she felt now was little short of a black rage.

"Let's just wait till we hear what he has to say Lizzie. I expect that there's a good reason," Jillie was trying to be mediatory. "Get changed and join me and Uncle George in the lounge, we can watch a movie at home."

"Good reason my arse. It's taken me hours to get ready to go to the cinema and that is where I'm going, without him. He can go to Hell and stay there!"

Elizabeth turned on her heels and stomped upstairs to repair some facial damage.

Mike looked at his phone disbelievingly and then turned to Ben. He gave that look of his and shrugged his shoulders despairingly.

"She hung up on me Ben. She's really pissed off, I mean really!"

"Not good," Ben pronounced with theatrical effect. "She does *pissed off* really well. I wouldn't want to be in your shoes mate."

"Thanks a bunch for the encouragement Ben. What would she do if I bought her some flowers and chocolates?" Mike was desperately looking for a solution.

"Do you really want to know?" Ben was pointing at Mike's backside.

"Very funny Ben. Anyway, it should be your arse. You're the one who's got me into this mess."

Ben's timing was poor and Mike was struggling to see the funny side of it.

"Look Mike, joking apart, just leave her to calm down. I'll tell her what happened and she will be just fine. Then try the flowers and chocolates with your back to the wall!"

This time Mike laughed with him and they continued with the last stages of the smoothing exercise and damage limitation.

Elizabeth was sat bolt upright on the bus heading into town. Any third party observer couldn't possibly have failed to see the jutted out chin, folded arms and scowl. She was still fuming. Jillie had offered to run her into town but Elizabeth had thanked her and refused.

"I'm best left in my own company for a while," she had said.

Besides, it was only a fifteen minute walk from the bus station to the cinema and it would do her good. Or so she thought.

It was nearly ten o'clock when Elizabeth stepped off the bus. The night had a chill to it and the moist summer air was condensing into a light mist that swirled mystically around her legs as she walked. She was deep in thought and it came as a surprise when she arrived at the cinema. There were only two movies to choose from. One was the latest in the series of *A Nightmare on Elm Street* and the other a Disney adventure. Elizabeth chose the Disney option for obvious reasons.

"I already have one freak in my dreams," she thought, "the last thing I need right now is another!"

The film was about to start. Elizabeth hurriedly collected her ticket along with some comfort food and took her seat just as the film began. Binging on chocolate and Coca-Cola would cheer her up, or so she thought. An hour later, she had neither gained comfort nor diversion from it. Instead it had fuelled the guilt that she was already feeling about her disproportionate reaction to being side-lined by Mike.

The plot was simple to say the least, but Elizabeth wasn't keeping up with it. She was hoping to find escape but found none. Her thoughts were all about how Mike had let her down and how wretched she felt. She was in a state of self-pity and personal turmoil, knowing in her heart that Mike wouldn't have let her down unless there was something really serious for him to deal with. This added to her guilt. She was now worried about what might have happened.

"Was either he or Ben in danger?" Elizabeth wondered.

She would never forgive herself if anything had happened to him and she hadn't been there to help. Elizabeth was angry with herself for not giving Mike the chance to explain. It was self-centred and selfish of her and she regretted it deeply. *Going off on one* was a bad character trait of hers and it only ever served to push the self-destruct button. She vowed that she would deal with things better in future.

It was warm and snug in the gloomy cinema and the music of the soundtrack, soothing. The many sleepless nights had left Elizabeth tired to the point of desperation. She was caught up in a circle of thoughts that she could neither break free of, nor solve. Despite her effort to resist, Elizabeth was slowly succumbing to her tiredness until finally she drifted into a confused, almost feverish sleep.

Her feeling of guilt fuelled her dreams. One after another the faces of her friends and family were appearing in her head, each scalding her about her attitude.

"You've really done it now Elizabeth," one said, looking hatefully at her.

"He won't be coming back!" said another.

It was all becoming frenzied. She was apologising to them and begging for another chance, but nobody would listen. Suddenly, her brother's face was in hers and he was shouting at her.

"You spoil everything for me Lizzie, you always have. He would've been a good friend but you've ruined it!"

Elizabeth was still apologising and pleading with him when his face began to transform. Now he was leering at her through cold eyes with lips pursed like a woman's. Ben spoke but it wasn't his voice; it was squeaky, almost feminine.

"It's alright my little precious, I will free you soon," it was the same face, the same voice and the same words that her stalker had used in her nightmares. It was Withey!

Elizabeth cried out in pure terror of it. She stood up in the middle of the cinema and screamed hysterically, until the lights came on and ushers came running down the aisles to assist her. When they reached out to calm her, she couldn't separate their actions from her dream. Elizabeth cowered away from them, whimpering like a whipped puppy.

"Please no, don't hurt me please, I'll do anything... "

As the dream receded, Elizabeth realised her predicament and began to feel foolish.

"I'm so sorry, really I am... I don't know what... I mean, please excuse me."

Elizabeth turned away with her head bowed low in shame. She clutched the collar around her throat as if she was cold, but the chill was only a physical manifestation of her fear and vulnerability. She ran out passed the ticket office into the now fogbound street, unable to breathe. Eventually, Elizabeth stopped and leant against a wall for support. She was gasping for air, trying unsuccessfully to regain her composure. Elizabeth's nerves and emotions were completely in tatters, and her terror coiled and writhed like a snake within her.

She looked around her to find that the mist had now turned into a thick fog. Even though Elizabeth knew the area quite well, she had difficulty in orientating herself. Lack of sleep and anxiety had dulled her wits. The direction of the traffic in the one-way street confirmed which way she had to go. She headed against it, towards where she knew that the pedestrian area would be. Distance is a hard thing to reconcile in fog, Elizabeth knew that it was a left turn ahead somewhere, but she couldn't tell which one. To make matters worse, the street names were set at the first floor level of the buildings, too high for Elizabeth to read in the ever thickening fog.

"I must have already gone too far," Elizabeth concluded.

She took a left anyway, thinking that at least she would be heading in the right direction. Elizabeth could soon tell that she was, because the roads had become narrow and traffic free, just as she had expected. Elizabeth came unexpectedly to a dead end. She hadn't seen the cul-de-sac sign that was obscured by the fog and the darkness. Cursing her luck, she doubled back on herself taking the first right to work her way around the block. She was desperately hoping to meet someone who actually knew where they were in the almost total black out.

The sound of Elizabeth's stiletto shoes on the pavement was the only sound that she could hear. They seemed to ring out disproportionally in the still night air, as if calling attention to her; calling Withey. Calling the Ripper!

"I'm here, come and get me," they were saying and the thought of it sent a frisson down her spine.

It felt chilly to Elizabeth now; really chilly. A choking feeling of dread began to consume her. It was just as it was in her nightmare. Now she was listening out for those other footsteps, the Ripper's. The feeling of *déjà vu* in her deepened, taking over her mind, driving her inexorably towards insanity.

If it was possible, the fog became even denser and the night darker. Elizabeth nearly missed the right-hand turn. She took it at the last second and quickened her pace as she did so. She was becoming increasingly disorientated in the fog, bumping against the wall constantly and grazing herself as she tried to steer herself along the narrow pavement. Her panic was rising to breaking point. Irrationally, Elizabeth imagined that someone might jump out on her from one of the doorways and stepped out into the middle of the road. She immediately regretted it. Her high heel shoes now made even more noise on the polished cobblestones, shattering the silence of the night, pinpointing her position to any predator. Instinctively she reached down, unhooked the backs of them and kicked them off. She ran on bare footed terrified, driven to the very edge of despair.

Elizabeth's bare feet padded softly against the cobblestones now. She ran on blindly in the night, with no idea of where she was or running to; not even what she was running from. Then she heard it. Rubber soles were slapping the cobbles at the same tempo as hers. Behind her, all around her, she wasn't sure, but ever closer by the second. Elizabeth forced herself to stop and listen to place them. She knew that her life would depend on the decision that she was about to make. She was all alone at a crossroads in the blackness, turning in circles, just as she was in her dreams. Trying to work out which way to run for safety; for her life!

Sir William Withey Gull was already sat in the cinema when Elizabeth entered and took her seat, four rows in front of him. It was obvious to him which film she would choose. He smiled with self-satisfaction at his own perception. He had even guessed where she might choose to sit. The rows between them were empty and Withey could clearly smell Elizabeth's fragrance. He tasted the air and it excited him, enhancing the anticipation of the perverse things that he was going to do to her. He was a nondescript sort of man, fairly short and a little rotund. Dapper would adequately describe his dress style. His grey jacket sported generous lapels over a neat waistcoat with gold watch chain draped in catenary. He wore a bow tie, brimmed hat and carried a short, broad cane which completed his Poirot-esque style.

When Elizabeth left her seat screaming, Withey was in rapture over the powerful physical manifestation of terror that he had instilled in her. Years of careful grooming and planning had led up to this point and he knew that it would all be perfect, just as it had been so many times before. Withey's womanly mouth was salivating as he fondled the handle of the knife concealed in his ornate cane. It was as if it was a living thing, calling him to expose it and bathe it in young virgin blood to quench its thirst. But the knife was insatiable, as it had been over the centuries, and would be for centuries to come.

Withey followed Elizabeth out of the cinema, just outside of her vision. He maintained that close proximity as she stumbled her way towards the bus station. When Elizabeth came to the cul-de-sac and doubled back, she almost walked straight into him. Withey had to side-step to avoid her but, in her fear, Elizabeth remained totally unaware of his presence.

"Not yet my little precious, you are not nearly ready for me. I will only release you when you have lost all control; when you are paralysed by the fear that I have created within you."

Withey was in delicious anticipation of the final act.

"No, not until you are begging me for your worthless life. Only then will I free you Elizabeth Robinson, only then...."

Withey was just yards behind Elizabeth when she kicked off her shoes and began to run up the middle of the road. He was panting with the exertion of trying to keep up with her, and worried that he was about to lose her. His little mouth was working like a baby's sucking at a bottle. Beads of acrid sweat formed like raindrops on his pudgy face. It came as quite some relief when she suddenly stopped at the crossroads.

Elizabeth had started to circle in confused terror, ever conscious of what might be behind her. She moved jerkily, looking over her shoulder just as much as in front. Withey knew that she was listening for him and it fuelled his excitement. He knew too what she was going through, what they had all been through; countless women over countless years.

"Elizabeth would be special though," Withey thought.

He slipped silently by her to take up his position at the place where he knew that she would finally be; the place where he would take her life.

"Soon now Elizabeth," Withey whispered, caressing the handle of his cane, "very soon my little precious," his anticipation was a tangible thing, almost painful and he needed to exorcise it.

As Elizabeth circled at the fogbound crossroads, she thought she heard footsteps. Her head jerked from side to side as she tried to place her stalker, but he had stopped. The silence was deafening. She set off again running blindly, with no idea of whether she was running towards him or away. Elizabeth's fear had risen past terror, shocking her body into paralysis until her legs no longer responded to her commands. It was like she was wading through treacle, just as it was in her dreams. Elizabeth knew that she would meet him very soon now. It would all end for her here, alone in this cold and nameless street. Despair filled her heart. She knew it was hopeless to try and run from him; he would catch her, he always did. This was her destiny and she was resigned to the inevitability of it now, already wishing it over and done with. Elizabeth stopped and capitulated, totally broken. Her head was bowed and she sobbed uncontrollably. It was as she had always known it would be.

Elizabeth looked up and he was there, her master. The man was immaculately dressed with his little waxed moustache, carrying his cane, leering at her through the coldest eyes that she had ever seen. It was Elizabeth's last chance. Even in her numbness she knew that. She began to strike out at him desperately, but just as in her dreams, her fists landed like caresses on him. Withey just smiled cruelly at her and offered his womanly mouth as if to kiss her. Elizabeth could smell the acrid stench of him now and pulled her head back, heaving the contents of her stomach out onto the pavement. Withey showed Elizabeth the ornate cane and slowly withdrew the knife, deliciously watching her as the horror of it twisted her delicate features into a grotesque mask.

Withey's voice sounded shrill in the still night air.

"You have waited patiently for this moment Elizabeth, but it's alright my little precious, I will free you now. You are ready at last".

As he pressed the knife into Elizabeth's throat, her perfect white skin opened, letting the first blood run down her neck. There was only one more thing that he wanted of her that would make it all perfect; it was for her to beg him for mercy.

He knew that he wouldn't be disappointed and it began as Elizabeth stammered her words.

"No, please no. Don't take my future I beg you, I will do anything, anything! Please, just don't hurt me please... "

Withey was fully aroused now. He paused in the cutting stroke to savour the moment. Elizabeth could see by his cruel smile that her plea was futile.

In those last moments that she had left, her short life flashed before her. There were images of her parents smiling down at her when she was small. She knew now that she would never use her special talents to bring them back from their premature and violent deaths. She had failed them and the pain of it hurt more than the knife that was cutting into her throat. Then there was Ben looking so proud after winning the cup for his team, knowing too that he would never survive against the Shadows without her. She saw Mike with his special smile and deeply regretted that they could never be together as one.

All the people she loved flashed through her mind in milliseconds. She felt crushed by their love for her and desolated at how she was letting them all down. Not even fighting for her life; just capitulating to be yet another victim of this despicable man. Elizabeth sought solace from her final thoughts, the ones that would take her into oblivion. In her mind she was riding Beauty, galloping bareback through fields of corn with the wind in her hair. Her final memory was the image of Edith and Brady, her unborn children that she had been given the gift to *glimpse* in the future.

It was like an electric shock. Something deep within her, something primordial and instinctive erupted like a volcano inside her. Energy suddenly flowed into her wasted muscles and her mind sharpened. She was fully focussed again and a rage was upon her as she screamed out.

"No! You will not take them! They will be born to me!"

Elizabeth was free of the chains of terror and inertia now. She was on Withey like a crazed cat, raking at his face with her fingernails, ripping his skin off. Withey was totally taken by surprise. He slashed frantically at Elizabeth with his razor sharp knife, opening her skin to the bone, but she felt nothing. The stabs were going into her body up to the hilt of his knife, then leaving her flesh with a vulgar sucking sound but Elizabeth never slowed her vicious assault. She was in frenzy, fighting for the future of her family and nothing was going to stop her. At last she managed to grab his knife hand, locking it in her vice-like grip, crushing the bones in his wrist like dried twigs. The knife dropped from Withey's useless hand ringing out in the still night as it hit the cobblestones. Withey was beaten and he knew there and then that he was a dead man.

Elizabeth stooped to pick up the knife and was about to use it on the petrified Withey but stopped half way through the act. Somehow she had accidentally linked with his mind and it was a dark and evil place. As she searched his memories his piggy eyes were begging her not to kill him. There were assaults in there, so perverse and disgusting, that nobody should ever witness them, let alone endure them. Elizabeth was seeing the pitiful images of his foul deeds, as if through his eyes. There were the contorted faces of hundreds of terrified women as he mutilated them and the sound of their pitiful and futile pleading was excruciating to her.

Elizabeth lowered the knife and handed it back to the bewildered Withey.

"No Withey," her rage had now turned to deep and profound sadness for all those poor lost souls, "that would be too good for you. You don't deserve to die like this."

The images of what he had done to those women would be in her mind now forever. She looked away, no longer able to bear the sight of him.

"You do it," she said without emotion.

Withey's jaw dropped at the realisation of what was happening, what he was doing to himself. He had turned the knife towards his own stomach and then, inexplicably, he drove it in with both hands. He looked down in horror at what he had done and then back up at Elizabeth shaking his head disbelievingly. His womanly mouth was trying to utter something, a plea.

"Do it Withey!" Elizabeth commanded.

He obediently began to saw around his stomach cavity until he had completed the circle. His entrails dumped themselves onto the street and the stench of it made Elizabeth gag, but she kept him at his task.

"Go on, you know what to do."

Withey nodded in obedience and reached up into the empty space of his body cavity. He took his own beating heart in a firm grip and held the knife against his throat with the other hand. The terror in his eyes was palpable as he waited for Elizabeth to sentence him do death.

"This is for all those women. May they now rest in peace and you rot in Hell!"

In a single act, Withey ripped his own heart out and slashed his throat, cutting right back to the bone. Just for a moment, he stood there in disbelief, staring at the organ that was still beating in his hand. He then fell lifeless, to the floor.

It was over but Elizabeth had been driven to the very edge of her mental and physical tolerance. The rapid loss of blood from the gaping wounds, inflicted by Withey's knife, was too much for her. She began to shake violently as she went into shock. Her senses were reeling and she was losing consciousness. When the blackout came it was so quick that Elizabeth had no time to protect herself. Her head struck heavily against the kerb as she landed in the gutter beside Withey's grotesque corpse. Blood streamed from the back of her skull, adding to the multiple knife wounds. She lay there in the river of her own blood as it drained silently into the gutter.

Elizabeth's phone began to ring and Ben's number flashed up on the LED screen. After a few seconds, it went into answer phone mode.

"You have reached the voicemail of Elizabeth Robinson. Please leave your message after the tone and I'll get back to you."

It was both sad and poignant, a semblance of normality in a surreal scene from the macabre theatre of death. In an almost enchanted manner, a stiff breeze picked up, clearing the fog from the streets and unveiling the full horror of the nightmare. It was carnage. An unfortunate woman walking her dog was the first to happen on the scene. Her screams were so manic, that people poured out of their houses to witness the cause. It was several minutes later when the police arrived. They had been hampered by the ghouls that had collected to gawp in delicious horror at the gruesome spectacle before them. One of the residents, a trainee nurse, had applied a makeshift dressing to Elizabeth's head and bound some of the deeper knife wounds with strips of her own clothing.

She had her fingers jammed in Elizabeth's neck, stemming the blood flow, just as the young WPC pressed through the crowd.

"Oh my God!"

Her voice was aghast and the colour went immediately out of the police woman's face. It took her several seconds even to begin to take in the enormity of the carnage in front of her.

"Jesus," she said, in disbelief and then vomited involuntarily.

It was another ten minutes before the paramedics arrived. When they did, they took control swiftly and professionally. Even with their experience though, the sight of Withey's disembowelled and mutilated body clutching his own heart, was beyond their imagination and training.

"She must have put up a hell of a fight," one of them said in admiration and then turned to his team. "Come on focus now lads, we have to fight for her life just as hard as she must have done."

The paramedic tending Elizabeth's severed carotid artery commended the young trainee for her efforts so far.

"Well done, she would already be dead if you hadn't done what you did for her. If she makes it, she owes it to you."

The paramedics worked frantically on Elizabeth. At last they were able to stabilise her condition, but she had lost a dangerous amount of blood and remained critical. Meanwhile the young WPC cleared the streets and called the Air Ambulance to evacuate Elizabeth from a nearby field. It was going to be touch and go and you could see that written plainly on the paramedics' strained faces.

After leaving the stadium, Ben and Mike were on the pretence of going clubbing while George set off back home alone. Ben needed some medical attention and Mike was taking him to one of their *approved* hospitals. These were places where they were used to dealing with Angels and no questions would be asked. It was after ten o'clock when they finally left the hospital and began the drive back to the Robinson's house. Ben was in deep conversation with Mike about who Illya Dracul was and how he might fit into the bigger picture. Suddenly he felt a sharp pain in his throat and screamed out clutching it instinctively.

"What's wrong?" Mike flashed Ben a concerned look.

"I don't know? Nothing, just a stabbing pain but it's gone now."

Ben was just about to continue with his thoughts on Dracul when he felt the stabbing pains again. He screamed out and grabbed his arm then his stomach, then his arm again, screaming in agony each time.

"What the hell's happening to me?" this time it was his neck and shoulder.

"Ben, what's up?"

"I think its Lizzie Mike, it must be. Something's happening to her I know it, I can *feel* it!"

Ben picked up his phone to call her then screamed out in pain again. He felt like he had been clubbed on the back of his head, even his eyes blurred at the false impact of it. He dialled Elizabeth's number and waited in trepidation for the connection.

"Shit Mike, it's gone to answer phone."

Ben was losing it. He began shaking with real fear for his sister. He could feel the panic rising within himself. Mike recognised the symptoms from his experience of soldiers under stress and took charge of the situation. He needed to divert Ben/

"Call home Ben, your aunt will be there. Maybe she knows something?"

Mike's tone was deliberately calmer than he felt. He needed Ben to remain focussed but could sense that he was on the brink of nervous collapse. He knew that Ben needed to be put to work to orientate himself. Much to Ben's relief Jillie answered on the second ring and it had an immediate calming effect on him. He forced an even tone.

"Where's Lizzie?"

"Oh hello Ben, she went to the cinema but she'll be back soon. Can I give her a message?" Fortunately Jillie hadn't sensed Ben's alarm.

"No message, just ask her to call me as soon as you see her. Only we're thinking of going clubbing and thought she might like to join us, especially as Mike couldn't make it to the cinema this evening."

"OK Ben that'll do her good. Tread carefully though, she's quite upset. Oh, and stay out of trouble. You may look over eighteen but you're still a boy," Aunt Jillie couldn't stop herself from giving some essential parental advice.

"Yes of course Auntie, see you later," he cut the call.

Ben couldn't help thinking that if only she knew the half of it, she would be freaking out right now.

"She went to the cinema Mike, head there first. I'll try the police in case something's been reported."

Ben's call went straight through to the switchboard.

"How can I help you sir?" the young female receptionist asked with a bubbly voice.

My name's Ben Robinson. I'm worried about my sister, Elizabeth. I can't contact her and that's not normal. I just wondered whether there have been any accidents or incidents, I mean... well you know what I mean."

There was a pregnant pause and then the girl replied clearly flustered and her upbeat tone was now false.

"I will connect you to our incidents room sir. Are you are alone?"

Ben knew exactly what that meant and he began to shake even more violently with the fear of what he was about to hear. His voice faltered as he replied.

"No, I'm with my friend Michael Jackson, he's driving at the moment."

"Would you ask him to pull over while I connect you please sir?"

The receptionist put Ben on hold and composed herself before she called the incident room.

"I have a Mr Ben Robinson on the line, he's asking about his sister Elizabeth. Can I put him through?"

Detective Inspector Russell Bates had been in the Serious Crime Division for over fifteen years and this case was singularly the most horrific that he had ever been given. He called out to his team for an update.

"What's the latest on the Robinson girl?"

One of his administrators was quick to respond.

"They've just landed at the Harvey hospital and she's in transit to the Intensive Care Unit there. She's still holding on though sir."

Bates nodded and then answered the receptionist.

"You can put him through now."

"I'm Detective Inspector Russell Bates. Am I talking to Ben Robinson?"

"Yes, that's me," Ben could hardly hold the telephone now.

"What I have to say is going to be very difficult for you Ben. I trust that you are not driving?"

"No sir we're parked. What's happened to my sister?"

The Detective Inspector started with the positives.

"She has just arrived safely at the Harvey hospital and is in good hands there," he put his hand over the mouthpiece and whispered to his colleague, "God I hate this part of the job, how do you tell a boy that his sister is probably going to die or be a vegetable if she doesn't?"

Bates had no idea how acute Ben's hearing was, all he heard was the noise of Ben dropping his mobile.

"Ben, are you still there?"

Ben was ashen; the phone had dropped into the floor-well. He turned to face Mike.

"She's dying Mike, Lizzie's dying," Ben buried his face in his hands and he felt physically sick.

Mike picked up the mobile and took a deep breath to steady himself. Despite his anxiety, he had to hold it all together for all of their sakes.

"Michael Jackson here; I'm afraid that Ben can't speak at the moment, can you tell me what's happened?"

"Well Michael, I can't tell you too much over the phone. An investigation is underway and until we know…"

Mike cut him off in mid-sentence.

"Just tell me what injuries she has, I'm not interested in police protocols."

"Quite. Well, she has sustained multiple knife wounds and a blow to the head. She's lost a lot of blood and has not regained consciousness since she was found."

"Where is she now and have you told her guardians, Mr and Mrs Robinson?" Mike's attitude was firm and analytical.

"At the Harvey hospital and a squad car has been sent to the Robinson's house. We don't like to do these things over the phone you will understand."

Mike considered the situation and then advised the Detective Inspector.

"Perhaps you could radio ahead and tell your officers that George Robinson is on his way home and should be there in 20 minutes. It would be better that you didn't tell his wife, Jillie, until he arrives."

"Yes, and thanks for that. I'm sorry truly I am. Please convey that to Ben for me," Detective Inspector Bates sympathy was clearly heartfelt.

"Yes of course and thank you."

Mike cut the call and tossed the phone onto the back seat. He started the car and re-joined the highway with wheels spinning and a trail of thick white smoke behind them. Ben still had his head in his hands, his stomach was sick and he was in almost physical agony. After a while he looked up totally stricken.

"I can't feel her Mike, I just can't feel her. I think she's gone and I wasn't there for her."

Ben couldn't speak anymore. He had just lost the most precious person in the world to him and he was devastated.

Mike pressed the accelerator to the floor, in hope that he wasn't already too late. He had to see her one more time. He had to say how sorry he was for failing her.

The helicopter journey from the pick-up field to the hospital was only ten minutes. In that time, the paramedics had got Elizabeth on a respirator and plasma drip, supplementing her dangerously high blood loss. The problem was that the knife wounds had severed some of her major veins and arteries and she needed a blood transfusion urgently and even so, she probably wouldn't make it.

They were still unsuccessfully fighting to control the bleeding. The two paramedics knew that they were running out of time and that they were going to lose her, but neither would admit defeat to the other. Elizabeth's vital signs had fallen below any viable levels. It was just before the helicopter landed that a transformation in Elizabeth's medical condition occurred. Her bleeding all but stopped, her heart rate stabilised and she was breathing of her own accord.

The paramedics looked at each other in disbelief, one genuflected but both were in awe of something that was inexplicable. They had either witnessed something supernatural or deeply religious, a miracle perhaps. Whatever it was, both knew that it wasn't in the realms of human possibility.

"She's back Mike! Jesus Christ she's back and fighting. I can feel her again!"

Ben was suddenly energised and aware of his surroundings. He looked around him and realised that Mike was turning into the hospital grounds.

"Are you sure Ben? God don't be wrong please."

Mike was in the depths of despair himself and he simply couldn't bear any false hope.

"I'm sure Mike but she must be in a bad way, I can't read any thoughts maybe she's sedated or something?" Ben suddenly tempered his optimism. "Maybe it was worse than that," he thought but didn't share that with Mike.

Elizabeth was still in theatre when they got to the reception. They were told to sit in the waiting room, until the surgeon had finished and that he would call them to make his report. When George and Jillie arrived, both took the news so badly that Ben had to use his special ability to smooth at least some of their anguish.

George brought Ben and Mike up to date with all that the police were able to reveal to them at the time. Apparently Elizabeth's attacker was killed, possibly by Elizabeth herself, but they were keeping an open mind on it. It appeared that the injuries that he had suffered were extensive and they had considerable doubt as to whether a young woman could have done it, particularly considering the extent of Elizabeth's own injuries. So they were currently looking for a third party. Ben smiled sardonically at Mike and he nodded back in agreement. The police clearly had no idea of what Elizabeth was capable of. It appeared that Dada might have got off lightly!

"Good for you Lizzie," Ben thought and wondered what she must have gone through.

An hour later, they were called to the surgeon's office. He had already changed and was sat at his desk, writing his notes and swigging from a mug of coffee.

"Please sit down. My name is Craig Jamieson. I was a friend of your father's Ben," Craig turned to address George and nodded in recognition. "And of course we have already met, George."

He smiled in acknowledgement at George, who looked somewhat relieved to have a friend of the family on Elizabeth's case.

"It's been four years hasn't it Mike?" Mike raised his eyebrow in the affirmative leaving Ben wondering what connection he had with the surgeon. "Can I arrange coffees for you?"

Craig Jamieson was a man in his late thirties, handsome with a strong chin and bright blue eyes. He was the sort of man who exuded competence and confidence. They all immediately felt reassured knowing that Elizabeth was in his care. Ben and Mike exchanged glances. They were in accord. This man was a fellow Angel, they could both sense it.

They accepted the offer of coffee. When they were all sat, Craig took them through Elizabeth's case notes and prognosis,.

"Firstly, I must put your minds at ease. Elizabeth is out of any immediate danger, although we are still treating her condition as most serious."

There was as a unanimous sigh of relief and a visible release of tension in their body language. Only Ben remained guarded as Craig continued. He had a special insight into Craig's mind and what he was about to say so he had a head start on the others.

"Elizabeth suffered multiple knife wounds and has lost a lot of blood, but her body seems to be coping well with this and I have no doubt that she will make a complete physical recovery. She also suffered a blow to the head, quite possibly from falling. Again, I don't see that she will suffer more than you might expect from moderate concussion."

"Can we see her?" Jillie was desperate. "She needs to know that we are here. Please?"

"Yes of course, but perhaps two at a time. Maybe you and George first?"

Jillie accepted eagerly. Craig led them to the recovery ward, where Elizabeth had just been transferred to.

"I must warn you that Elizabeth is still on oxygen and sedated. It can look a little shocking if you're not prepared for it, but it's just for tonight and it looks much worse than it is. Really."

Craig looked at their stricken faces and smiled reassuringly.

"You can hold her hand and it would be good if you talked to her. Sometimes, patients are much more alert than they appear and it might comfort her."

Craig led them to Elizabeth's bed and drew the curtains around them to give a semblance of privacy. When Jillie saw how pitiful Elizabeth looked, silent tears began running down her face and she covered her mouth with her hands. George put his arm around her to console her, but he was full himself and couldn't trust himself to speak.

"What must she have gone through George? What kind of monster does this? As if the poor little soul hasn't been through enough already, it's sickening."

Jillie reached into her bag and took out Elizabeth's first cuddly toy. She tucked in her arms and began talking to her like she was a child again.

"Look what I brought you Lizzie, it's Floppsy Bunny. Do you remember her? She will be here when you wake up just like she has been every day of your life."

Jillie gently brushed Elizabeth's hair away from her face and looked back at George.

"This doesn't happen in real life George, not to people like us. It's only something that you read about in the papers. How could it have happened?"

"I don't know, but she's a fighter Jillie. We are all fighters and we will get through this. Time will heal the scars and we will get her through the rest."

George was holding Elizabeth's hand almost desperately, as if to let go would be to lose her. Until that moment, he hadn't realised just how much he loved her.

After settling George and Jillie with Elizabeth, Craig returned to his office. He shut the door behind him and sat down. He was about to address them when Ben interjected.

"You can tell us the truth now Craig?"

As guarded as Craig had been, Ben had read his underlying thoughts and had recognised that not everything in the garden was rosy.

"Was I that easy to read?" Craig could see at once that Ben was the son of the father.

"You were to me. I know that you were protecting my aunt and uncle but you have to level with us. So how is it, really?"

Ben had hardened himself for what might be ahead. He knew that he couldn't afford to be weak now. He had to be strong for her, just as Elizabeth had always been for him. Craig resigned himself to the telling of the whole truth.

"I told no lies. Elizabeth will heal fully from the physical wounds and how she controlled the bleeding was little short of miraculous. I have only ever seen that done once before and that was over four years ago when I was on a mission with your father. He was commanding an elite task force to take out an Al Qaeda training camp, in Pakistan. We were just flying out at the end of the mission when we came under enemy fire. The tail gunner took a bullet through his foot and your father got one through his neck."

It was clear from the look on Craig's face that the memory was still traumatic and he was shaking his head as if he was back there in the moment.

"It was a flawed mission, we had an informer amongst us and Ralph walked his men straight into a trap. We lost three good men that night and it was only your father's mind control and his Angel metabolism, inherited from the Patriarchs bloodline that saved him," Craig was unsettled by the recollection and turned to Mike. "You will remember it well Mike we both thought that we'd lost him. I couldn't stem the bleeding and Ralph just did it by himself. It was incredible and now it appears that Elizabeth has inherited that same ability."

Ben was astounded.

"Mike you fought with my father? But you never said, why didn't you tell us such an important thing?"

"Priorities, that's all Ben. There's been too much happening in the present and planning for the future, so the past had to wait."

"You can tell me and Lizzie at the same time when she's got through this," Ben added more positively than he felt. Craig continued.

"There's a lot that we still don't understand about Angels from a physiological point of view, and then there's such variation according to ancestry. How far they are removed from their original blood-line makes significant difference to their mortality," Craig paused to get his words right. "I've run a few initial tests on Elizabeth and her brain activity is considerably lower than I would expect, it's as though she has selectively shut down all non-essential functions and slipped into some shock-induced coma, or..." Craig paused again, agonising with the truth.

"Or what?" demanded Ben.

"Or she has suffered brain damage."

Ben and Mike exchanged looks of horror. Both were choked by the implications of Elizabeth's condition. It was Mike who found his tongue first.

"So what does that mean Craig?"

"Well I must confess that I really don't know. Brain damage can mean anything, but if it's through self-control then we can expect a positive outcome. Shock however is an unknown quantity, there are cases where comas have lasted days and others years, sometimes a lifetime. By all accounts, the crime scene surpasses horrific and we have no idea of what Elizabeth must have gone through. She might have simply retreated from the nightmare of it to find solace."

The word nightmare triggered Ben's response.

"Lizzie has always known that this was going to happen to her. She had dreamt about it for years, she even knew exactly what her attacker was going to look like and none of us believed her. God this is so screwed up," Ben felt the guilt of his omission like an arrow through his heart. Something occurred to him, "Where's the body of her attacker?"

"Well, here in the mortuary but..." Craig was cut off again.

"We need to see it Craig, can you fix that?"

Craig had arranged access for Ben and Mike into the mortuary. This amounted to a colleague taking an unscheduled coffee break and the door being left open. The body was still police evidence, subject to an autopsy and was therefore totally out of bounds. Breaking this protocol was a sacking offence, so they were about their task in a business-like manner to be out again at the soonest. Craig led them down the corridor of steel cabinets until he came to the one he was looking for. After a quick check to confirm that they were alone, he slid the drawer open. The body was orientated head outwards and was covered by a clean green sheet. A black plastic sack was tied up and placed at the corpse's feet.

Ben slowly pulled back the sheet uncovering the corpse's face then stepped back in shock.

"Withey!"

Despite the massive mutilation to his face through Elizabeth's clawing, he was exactly as they had seen in Mike's video. It was undisputedly Withey.

"Jesus, Lizzie has almost ripped his face off."

Withey's face had been lacerated by Elizabeth's fingernails so severely, that it looked like he had been attacked with a garden rake. His sightless eyes were opaque and staring, and his squat tongue was protruding out of the cupid bow of his lips beneath his still immaculately waxed moustache.

"You know this man?" Craig's surprise was evident.

"Yes we know of him Craig. He is, or should I say was, a hired mercenary working for Adolphius. God Mike, Lizzie must have known all along that it was the man in her dreams from the moment you showed her that video. Why didn't she say?"

"Because we wouldn't have believed her I expect. It is way beyond what we perceive as credible and she would have felt a fool. I can't begin to imagine how terrified she must have been this last week knowing that he really was out there, let alone when it actually happened."

Mike was burdened with the guilt of not having been there for her and it was weighing heavily on his heart. He pushed the thought away.

"Come on Ben, take the sheet off and let's see what else she did to him."

"Christ!" the three of them said in unison.

"She must have disembowelled him and cut his throat," Mike said, stating the obvious. "What the hell was in her head? That plastic sack must contain his entrails."

That thought of that was eclipsed by what they saw next. His heart, with torn veins and arteries, was placed incongruously in the void of his stomach cavity.

"God she must've ripped the bastard's heart out too," Ben added.

He was in awe of what his sister had endured and done to save her life. It even surpassed all that Dada had thrown at her. This encouraged some typical Robinson irony.

"I hope she's not still pissed off with you when she wakes up Mike."

Although it was sick, it was the first time that they had allowed themselves the luxury of a laugh since the news broke. Craig shook his head in disbelief at what he was looking at.

"Any woman who can do this, with the injuries that she had sustained, is strong enough to recover. My guess is that she's just taking time out."

"I hope so Craig, I hope to God it's only that."

Ben was cautiously optimistic. He knew the enormity of his sister's inner strength. If anybody could get through this, it was Elizabeth. In that moment, he swore a silent oath to seek revenge for what they had done to her. Ben was already planning how he was going to do that and decided to bring his personal strike against the Shadows forward.

On the way back, Craig briefed them on what needed to be done for Elizabeth in the short term.

"I have arranged for Elizabeth's transfer to one of *our* hospitals. In less than 48 hours, Elizabeth's physical wounds will all but have disappeared, which will raise some serious questions here. I want you to put together all that she will need for an extended stay and plan some kind of rota between you to visit her. Sometimes just being there helps. Even in a coma, some patients can sense this."

The thought of an *extended stay*, sent a cold shiver of dread through them all.

When they arrived at the recovery ward, George and Jillie were still sitting with Elizabeth. Craig let them in to the tented area to join them. It was a sad and sorry sight and Craig's heart went out to them. This kind of situation always made him realise just how much his line of work had hardened him. He had become accustomed to serious injury, mutilation and death but had never even got close to being immune to the suffering and grieving of their loved ones. Craig again fixed on the positives.

"That's exactly the right thing to do Jillie, keep talking to her. As I have told the boys, I want you to keep a bedside vigil doing just that until she responds, which I believe with your support, she will."

From Mike's point of view it was an unnecessary request. He had no intention of leaving Elizabeth's side, no matter how long it would take. It never would have happened if he had been there in the first place. He swore that if she made it through, he would never leave her again until this was all over.

A week had passed since Withey's assault. Although Elizabeth's physical wounds had healed, without leaving so much as a scar, she remained in a coma. Thankfully the MRI scan she had undergone supported Craig's belief that the coma was only shock-induced and not worse. He was however uncomfortable with the fact that she hadn't yet regained consciousness. Mike had been true to his word, and had remained at Elizabeth's side throughout.

Mike had delegated authority to one of his SAS team, who was maintaining their surveillance regime 24/7. It worried him though that there had been no Shadow activity over the last week and that it might well be a symptom of the enemy readying themselves for a major assault. Mike just had to trust in his men's insight and judgement; after all they were consummate professionals and used to working alone in the field.

Ben had visited Elizabeth every day. He spent hours at a time trying to reach into her mind but it was like her very spirit had been erased. There was nothing to access and he was despairing of it. He wanted revenge and he wanted it now. His plans were almost complete. Soon he would be able to go out and wreak the vengeance that Adolphius' cell deserved.

Chapter 27

Ben had spent most of his spare time with Mike's SAS team and was fully briefed on the current status quo:

Of the known cell, all but Grese had taken up residence at Adolphius' house. Eichmann had taken on the responsibility of their security and he had installed nine highly trained Drones. They were working in three shifts of three to give them round the clock protection. The Drones were armed with AK-47 rifles and grenades, in the same way that the Jackal and his men had been. It was standard issue for Shadows and their mercenaries.

Eichmann, Alexis and Adolphius seldom left the house and Grese had only been a daily visitor until recently. It had been observed and recorded that Withey had left the house on the Friday and not returned. He was therefore categorised as being *at large* and as such an immediate threat. It wasn't until Mike had confirmed the identity of the man lying in the hospital morgue, that the SAS boys had the pleasure of changing his category to *deceased*. When they had heard precisely how he had died at the hands of Elizabeth, they were blown away. Even by their standards, it was inventive to say the least!

Since the death of Withey, Grese had begun to stop over and evident to them all that this was no coincidence. Clearly, even the infamous Grese had her own standards. None however could have truly known how deep her fear and revulsion of him was. There had been a new arrival at the house, a blonde haired youth with an affliction or favouring an injury. Ben deduced that this must be Illya Dracul, someone he had some unfinished business with and was looking forward to their re-match.

Ben had convinced the SAS team that it would be appropriate for him to be armed at home from now on. After some basic training on the ranges, he was handed a flak jacket and a Heckler & Koch MP5 9mm submachine gun, complete with sound and flash suppression. Having a firing rate of 800 rounds per minute, made it the coolest toy that Ben had ever been given. He was looking forward to using it in anger against the Shadows.

Ben had studied the plans outlining the grounds and buildings that comprised Adolphius' expansive homestead. Through sound surveillance, they were able to determine which Shadow was sleeping in which bedroom and where they congregated for their discussions. They had determined that Eichmann was working on a master plan and that he had already begun to resource it. Although they had full sound surveillance, often the discussions were around some plan or chart. Without actually seeing that chart, the Shadows' conversation was open to a high degree of interpretation.

The SAS team had also recorded the positions of the three Drones guarding the homestead, the times of the changing guard and their individual patrol routes. Ben memorised these, along with dozens of pages of specific recordings in the surveillance log. It was all that Ben needed to know, in order to execute his own plan. Although he understood Elizabeth's rationale that Adolphius, Alexis and Grese needed to be killed backwards in time, before they had committed their crimes against their loved ones, this did not include Eichmann. To kill Eichmann, their strategist, in their own grounds would send a shockwave through the rest of them and make them think twice about going out hunting Angels!

Stealth and silence were to be the key elements of Ben's assault. There were two things that Ben still needed to achieve that; his father's hunting bow and knife. The machine gun was just for insurance in case things went wrong...

Adolphius, Alexis, Grese and Dracul were sat facing the whiteboard in the war room and Eichmann was about to present. He called them to attention.

"The plan remains the same. It is still four squads but Illya now heads up the fourth. Personally I think Dracul will be an asset. I have always had misgivings about Withey's leadership ability in a fight. He was too much of a *one trick pony*."

Grese couldn't help herself and put her own spin on it.

"Withey was a pervert! He preyed on the weakness of women on his own despicable terms and for his sole vulgar gain. Nothing about what he has ever done has been to support our objectives," Grese's tone was past disdainful. "For the first time I applaud the resolve of an Angel. Elizabeth has done the world a great favour!"

Grese had revelled in the news of Withey's death and had the strongest admiration for Elizabeth's metal in dealing with him. In fact Grese's admiration was bordering on respect. Grese knew that if they were to defeat Elizabeth, it would only be through an insurmountable, coordinated act of force. This was exactly what was being proposed by Eichmann.

Eichmann continued with only the faintest nod of acknowledgement. He focussed them on the aerial view photograph taped to the whiteboard.

"We have assumed the most likely case scenario, which is all four Robinsons and Jackson in the house plus three soldiers in the van outside. We should also assume that within ten minutes of the start of our assault, that a further six SAS will arrive plus a police response to the incident."

Eichmann was an inspirational orator, just as Adolphius had been as Hitler in the Second World War. He had their undivided attention.

"So we have ten minutes from start to finish to eliminate all of them. That includes getting out afterwards. To recap then, each squad will consist of one of you plus six Drones. Each of you will be responsible for the training, coordination and application of your own squad. You will meet with them covertly and drill them until you have full confidence in their ability. Each squad will operate independently of the others and individual squads will not be briefed of the existence of the others or the location of the target, until the day of the operation. Is that clear?"

It was clear. Each member of the Senate fully understood the need to minimise the possibility of a breach of security. For the first time, the whole of the Senate would be exposing themselves as one. If it went wrong, and the Angels were prepared for them, they would be walking into a trap of their own making. It would be carnage for them. Eichmann continued.

"Each squad arrives separately as a unit, staggered in 30 second intervals so within two minutes all squads will be deployed. Alexis; you and *Red Squad* will be first in with shoulder-fired missiles. Your men take up these six positions marked in red targeting these windows which are the principal rooms of the house. Alexis, you will be here sighting the SAS van. After exactly 30 seconds you fire in unison and retreat to the fence line to take care of any unexpected new arrivals and anyone fleeing the house. Clear?"

"Crystal," was Alexis' stoic response.

"Dracul and *Blue Squad*; you go in next, taking up these blue positions at the front of the house, two by each of the blown out windows. You lay down machine gun fire driving anyone still alive, to the back of the house. Got it?"

"I understand," he replied respectfully.

Dracul was clearly honoured by the opportunity and responsibility that he had been given. Eichmann addressed Adolphius next.

"Adolphius and *Green Squad*; you are next, coming in by helicopter onto the roof as Blue Squad open fire. Rope access to these six upstairs windows, grenades in and you follow flushing anyone there downstairs into Blue Squad's fire. Any questions?"

"None," returned Adolphius.

"Grese and *Yellow Squad*; you come in last taking these six positions at the back of the house, grenades through these windows and then blanket fire. At precisely three minutes after the initial missile attack, you go in at the back here and Blue Squad in the front here. Drones are expendable. They go in first as there will be a high risk of being caught in our own cross-fire. I'm looking for positive IDs and confirmed kills for each of the targets. You don't leave until that is done or you don't leave at all. Now is that totally clear?"

Grese answered for all of them.

"If anyone leaves before then, I will kill them myself," the expression on Grese's face was such that none doubted it.

"OK questions then," Eichmann's manner was business-like.

Adolphius was the first up.

"I'm sure that you will already have considered that Elizabeth and Ben might go out via the portal as a last resort. Perhaps you would clarify your instructions in that event?"

"Quite. If they are not amongst the body count then you destroy the mirror and send them into oblivion. If they are dead and the mirror is not already broken in the cross-fire, then you take it out with you. If that's not practical then you destroy it anyway."

"Any more questions?" Eichmann searched their faces for any uncertainty. "Yes Grese?"

"What about our exit plan?"

Eichmann had this unambiguously covered.

"All our dead and seriously wounded, are to be drenched in petrol and torched. Helicopter picks up team leaders at plus nine minutes and Drones leave out through the back garden to vehicles already parked in the streets."

Alexis had held his council throughout but when he began to talk, all gave their undivided attention.

"What you are proposing is a complete departure from all protocols and the *modus operandi* that we have meticulously employed for thousands of years. It is only our low impact approach to these things that has kept our anonymity and enabled us to walk amongst the humans undetected. The act that you propose has the potential to expose us and all the repercussions that would go with that."

Alexis was only saying what the others already knew, but it underlined the magnitude of what they were about to undertake. He also knew that the mission had the highest possible endorsement. He was uncomfortable about it though, and wanted an *eyes open* dialogue and continued.

"An act of open warfare like this in a quiet suburban town will invite a massive investigation and media attention. Are we ready for that?"

Adolphius' response was tempered with the respect that he had for Alexis' seniority and wisdom.

"It is a good question to ask Alexis and I know why you have chosen to do so. A heavy responsibility falls on us all to succeed in this mission. The potential consequences of failure are unthinkable. We would be sought out as intruders, vilified and persecuted. It would herald the end of our reign of power on this Earth and we do not yet have control of the mother ship to escape to another."

Alexis nodded his aged head in agreement.

"And would you share with us the Hydra's thoughts about this unveiled attack against the Angels?"

"Of course."

Adolphius welcomed the opportunity to air the Hydra's endorsement and the trust that she had placed in him.

"Drastic times call for drastic measures. The Hydra sees the ascension of the Robinson siblings to full Angel status and power, as singularly the biggest threat to the Shadow race since the birth of Christ. That was the last time that power had shifted in favour of the Angels. It has taken two thousand years to wrest it back. Our attempts to surgically remove the siblings have proven futile and costly and they become stronger and more resourceful each day. The Hydra believes that it is only a matter of time before they fully empower Maelströminha with all the consequences that would bring. You can rest assured that the Hydra is fully committed to this attack."

Alexis leaned back in his chair, his face implacable. He had asked the question and now they were all aware of the seriousness of their endeavour and the ultimate cost of failure.

"It would not be my way," he thought and smiled to himself wryly as he considered the unlikelihood of any other Shadow ever reaching his 8,000th year.

Chapter 28

Ben had spent most of the day at the hospital with Elizabeth and Mike. It was the ninth day since the attack and there had been no signs of any improvement. Mike hadn't left the hospital throughout, so Ben had brought him yet another change of clothes. Mike had been living on fast food and coffee and looked dreadful. He could take a shower at the hospital, but hadn't shaved or slept properly. Mike was starting to look a bit like Robinson Crusoe.

Ben had tried relentlessly to get through to Elizabeth, but she was somewhere so isolated, that it was proving futile. Mike seemed to have drifted so deeply into despair himself, that Ben was having almost as much trouble getting through to him. When Ben left the hospital in the late afternoon, he was depressed and his rage and hatred towards the Shadows was a physical thing. He knew he couldn't wait any longer. He wanted blood revenge and he wanted it today!

It was after four o'clock, when Ben got back home. His aunt and uncle had taken a weekend break, so he had the house to himself. Ben had decided to bring his strike forwards by a week to that very night, because he physically couldn't support his anger any longer. The Drones at Adolphius' house changed guard at midnight. He had chosen to attack an hour and a half before that, to coincide with the lethargy that normally kicks in towards the end of a shift. He knew that the darkness would not be entirely in his favour. Shadows had acute night vision, but then again his was now impeccable too.

Ben prepared himself to go into battle almost as if he was a samurai. He bathed meticulously and prepared his mind by playing out every act that he had planned in his head. It was almost like he was already there in the grounds around the house. When he was satisfied that he had enacted every possible scenario, he laid out his flak jacket and clothes on the bed. Ben had meticulously chosen these too, both for practicality and look. If this was to go wrong, it would matter very much to Ben how he was found. The trousers were Quiksilver camouflage combat pants in greens and browns and the mountain jacket, by Abercrombie & Fitch, was in distressed military green. The jacket had two deep pockets, ideal to accommodate six magazines in each for his machine gun. By the time Ben was dressed, it was 9.30 pm and already nearly dark. He picked up the gun, wrapped it in a black bin liner and slipped out the back door. He had some killing to do.

Elizabeth had been given a private room at the hospital. The nurses had done their rounds at 9.30 pm and wouldn't be back again until midnight. That gave Mike three hours to try and catch up on some much needed sleep. It was set to be another long night. The room was warm and dimly lit and so Mike had no trouble drifting off in the easy chair at the foot of Elizabeth's bed.

It was an hour later, with nobody around to witness it, that Elizabeth's eyelids began to flicker wildly as her brain restarted. Half an hour later she sat up, eyes wide open with a startled expression on her face.

"Ben?" she whispered, as if he was there.

Elizabeth could never have known it, but that was the precise second that Ben had committed himself to his one man assault on the Shadows.

Elizabeth looked around the unfamiliar room. Even though the lamps were dimmed, the light was painful to her unaccustomed eyes. She found Floppsy Bunny and kissed him fondly on the nose and hugged him to her breast. Elizabeth could see the bearded man asleep in the gloom at the bottom of her bed and wondered who he was and why he was there. She slowly worked out that she was in some hospital and that the sleeping man must have been there to watch over her.

"And not a very good at it either," she thought.

As her vision sharpened Elizabeth realised that this dishevelled man looked familiar and then all at once she recognised him.

"Mike!" she called out.

Still he slept. She knelt up and gazed at him in astonishment. He had a beard! She wondered how long she had been there, more than a week, perhaps two? She called his name again, but still he slept. When

Floppsy Bunny hit him squarely between the eyes, he was on his feet in a moment, alarmed and confused.

"Wake up stupid, I'm starving!" Elizabeth had her hands on her hips and a mock petulant look on her face. "You owe me a dinner; remember?"

Once Mike had convinced himself that he wasn't dreaming, he threw himself onto the bed bowling Elizabeth over. They were in a heap laughing and kissing.

"God Lizzie I thought you were never coming back to us. I thought I'd lost you," Mike had to stop talking before his voice faltered and let him down.

Elizabeth sensed that and rescued him by doing the talking.

"You have a habit of underestimating me Mike," then maliciously, as only women can be in tender moments like this, she added, "and another of not turning up on dates that you make!"

That hurt, and Mike was immediately on the defensive.

"But I had no choice I..."

"Only teasing you Mike. Besides, some fella tried to pick me up on the way home, so at least I got some male attention that night."

Elizabeth was laughing at him and Mike, quite shocked. The Robinson's sick sense of humour took a little getting used to.

"How can you even joke about a thing like that Lizzie? He nearly killed you."

Elizabeth put her finger on his lips to shush him.

"Only nearly, I think he came second.

Mike still looked shocked.

"It's just gallows humour Mike. Making light of a bad situation is good for your soul, you should try it sometime," she kissed him and then became philosophical. "What doesn't kill you makes you stronger, right?. What happened needed to happen, now I'm free of him and I feel so good, I just can't tell you how good. That was like two years dream free sleep in..."

Elizabeth stopped in mid-sentence and looked slightly panicked.

"How many days have I lost?"

"Days? It would have been two years to the day tomorrow," Mike lied convincingly. "We had something planned here for you, but thank God I can cancel it now."

Elizabeth's chin dropped and her eyes opened wide at the shock of it. She looked at the back of her hands.

"Oh My God I'm twenty already!" she shook her head in disbelief. So much lost youth. "What about Ben?"

Mike was learning *sick* really quickly.

"Ben had to leave school after he got a girl pregnant. He joined the RAF to sort it, but he's doing just fine now and he's got a lovely little boy. His name's Finlay."

"Oh Jesus no, the stupid bastard!" Elizabeth was horrified. "What about you Mike; what have you been doing all that time?"

Elizabeth was buying it all. She was scared about what he might say, as he was already looking guilty.

"Well, I waited for you for the first year but the doctors said that you wouldn't make it back..."

"And!" Elizabeth demanded.

"And I met someone. We got married last summer and now we have a little girl."

Elizabeth's hands went up to her mouth. She was just about to burst into tears when she *read* him.

"You bastard! You absolute bastard!" Elizabeth rained down punches on him, half laughing and half crying. "Where in your small brain did you ever think that might be funny?"

"Hey, hey, what happened to gallows humour being good for your soul and, *you should try it sometime?*"

"Count yourself lucky that I've had a good sleep or I mightn't have found that so funny," Elizabeth had to acknowledge that she had been well and truly got. "So how many days was it then?"

"It was nine Lizzie, only nine," Mike gave her that look and of course he was forgiven.

"Dick," was all that Elizabeth said.

Ben knew exactly where the SAS boys would be and managed to leave the house without them knowing. It was only ten minutes brisk walk to the Robinson's stables where Ben had already cached the knife and hunting bow, with its quiver of arrows. Ben had spent hours practicing with his father's bow. Its maximum killing range was 40 yards and. He was finally satisfied, when he could regularly put three arrows in a beer mat at that distance.

Ben checked the fuel in his KTM, slung the bow and quiver over one shoulder and his machine gun over the other. He was just about to mount the bike when he thought of one final thing. Ben found the boot black amongst the cleaning equipment, as he had expected. He inserted two fingers into the cream and drew stripes down his cheeks. He justified it to himself as completing his camouflage, but in fact it was a vanity thing. It rather completed his *Rambo* look which he checked out approvingly in the mirror.

It was now nearly ten o'clock, which left Ben a good 30 minutes to be in position at Adolphius' house. As his KTM wasn't street legal, and there was a little matter of not having a licence or insurance too, Ben took the unlit back roads. As is often the case when you depart from the straight and narrow for the first time in your life, it went wrong. Ben picked up a blue light. At first the police car had been drawn to Ben's motorcycle for not having lights. When they saw the bow and machine gun slung across his back, the pursuit took on a whole new dimension.

Ben knew that he wouldn't lose the police tail on the roads, as his bike was and better suited to the track. He gunned the 450cc KTM engine regardless and leant the bike hopelessly around the sinuous country lanes. His ability to escape was further limited by not having lights and knew that it would only be a matter of time before he misjudged a turn and dropped the bike.

Ben slowed down as if to concede defeat, while his eyes searched for a gap or thinning in the hedgerow. Luck was with him and he saw what he was looking for ahead. Ben dropped two gears and gave the KTM full throttle. Using the verge as a ramp, he jumped the hedge into the field beyond. The bike landed awkwardly and Ben had to fight desperately to control it. Finally it responded to a fist full of power and snaked itself up the wet grass to the top of the hill. Ben pulled up into a broadside skid, stopping to look back down at the police car. The policemen were out of their car. One was on the radio, obviously calling for support. Ben raised his right arm with his fist clenched in triumph then opened the throttle, wheelieing away audaciously.

Ben was stoked which further fed his blood lust. He was riding dangerously high on a heady cocktail of emotion and adrenaline. The bad boy in him was well and truly out tonight.

It was at exactly 10.30 pm when Ben took his position in the undergrowth at the grounds of Adolphius' house, fully committed to his assault.

Elizabeth dressed hurriedly and discharged herself, much to the displeasure and concerns of the night receptionist. Mike wasn't too sure about the wisdom of it either.

"If you don't feed me soon Michael Alexander, I will pull the biggest strop that you have ever seen. Trust me when I say that you wouldn't want that!" Elizabeth was past insistent and Mike left in no doubt that she meant it.

"Pizza?" Mike offered in capitulation with that look and lopsided smile.

"That'll do for a start," Elizabeth conceded.

She linked arms with him and strode purposely out of the hospital, leaving an extremely bewildered clerk standing at reception.

Elizabeth didn't trouble with elegant, and devoured the first pizza before Mike had much more than dented his.

"Delish," Elizabeth sighed as she called the waiter over for another.

Mike was bursting to know the full story behind Withey's attack and his death but Elizabeth wouldn't be drawn in.

"I only want to tell that story once and then never think of it again, so you will have to wait until Ben is with us," Elizabeth said adamantly.

"So why did you stand me up on our date?" Elizabeth asked cramming another slice of Pizza in her mouth looking up at him.

"Well," began Mike, "that story belongs to Ben and he would kill me if I told you."

"And I will kill you if you don't," Elizabeth was pointing her knife at him menacingly. "Where is Ben anyway?" a shadow had come over Elizabeth's face as she suddenly remembered that, when she had awoken, her mind was filled with a sort of premonition about him.

"At home like he always is at eleven o'clock at night," Mike was surprised at her question.

Elizabeth thought hard about it.

"No he's not Mike, that's what must have woken me. Something's going on. He's up to something, I just know it."

"I'll call my men and get them to check the house," Mike reached for his mobile but Elizabeth stopped him.

"There's no point Mike Ben's not there. He's somewhere dark and dangerous, experiencing a mixture of excitement and fear I can feel it," Elizabeth was mentally searching for him, trying to get into his mind. "Where are you Ben, talk to me please talk to me."

Elizabeth's stomach somersaulted and she felt sick with fear for him. She could tell he was deliberately blocking her out of his mind. Mike suddenly left his seat as he realised what was going on.

"I know where he's gone. It's exactly where I would have gone if I was him. Get your coat!"

Elizabeth obeyed unquestioningly and ran out after him to the car. She was barely in, Mike accelerated away. They sped past the angry restaurateur who was shaking his fist at them for leaving without paying.

"Where are we going?" Elizabeth asked.

She hadn't yet caught up, which was unusual for her and a symptom of the ravages of her long sleep.

"He's gone to kill the Shadows in revenge for what they did to you Lizzie. He will be at Adolphius' house taking them on alone. I'm just as sure of that as you were that he wasn't at home."

Mike was dialling up his SAS team on Bluetooth as he spoke. The call connected and without any niceties Mike gave his orders.

"Get to the Shadow's house now and wait for me and Elizabeth. Ben's gone in without support. Repeat, Ben has gone in. Prepare for evacuation and have medics on standby."

"Understood. We will rendezvous at the crossroads on the south side, with full assault kit for the both of you."

Mike cut the call.

"I hope we're not already too late," Mike cringed and regretted his words the moment that they left his mouth.

Elizabeth just stared ahead in silence.

From Ben's chosen position, he could see two out of the three Drone guards. Eichmann had chosen their positions well. It was clear that the Drones had line of sight between themselves and, even without looking, he knew that the third Drone would also have sight of the other two. That wasn't obvious on the plans and Ben needed to rethink the order in which he would take them out.

His objective was to bring Eichmann out into the open alone. To achieve that, he needed to kill the last Drone immediately after he had raised the alarm. Ben was counting on Eichmann's professionalism to deal with this himself and not risk the other Shadows. If he was wrong about this and they all came out together, he would be a dead man.

Ben needed to wait until one of the Drones was completely distracted, then he would be the easy one to kill second. He would at best be oblivious to the attack and at worst slow to respond. That would leave the third to raise the alarm before Ben killed him too. The next bit would be a little trickier; a game of cat and mouse in the jungle-like garden against a Shadow war veteran...

Right now, Ben needed to get within 40 yards of his first two targets. That meant breaking cover from the dense trees and bushes that formed the outer perimeter of the grounds. Then crossing the garden lawn, where he would be totally exposed. The lawn effectively gave the house a *sterile zone,* protecting it from covert attack.

Again, it wasn't quite as Ben had imagined. The chances of getting across the open space without being seen were slim. He started to work his way around the edge of the lawn in the cover of the small shrubs. He was looking for a position that would afford him sight of two of the Drones, at less than the 40 yard killing range of his compound bow. By absolute chance, the moonlight picked out the dew drops that had condensed on the otherwise invisible wire that skirted the edge of the lawn. It was a tripwire and Ben had almost triggered it. But triggered what? He looked more closely and then saw the array of 1,000 watt Halogens set to illuminate the open ground and building.

Ben went weak at the knees. If he had tried to cross the lawn, he would have been in the middle of no-man's land, lit up like a Christmas tree and cut down by AK-47s. It was a sobering thought. His fear factor went through the roof, but at the same time, his excitement factor went viral as adrenaline pumped through his veins. It was in that same moment, that Elizabeth woke and tuned in to his thoughts. He had to quite literally squeeze her out to concentrate on the job in hand.

"Sorry Sis, not now," he said under his breath.

Ben needed to keep a clear head, but the knowledge that she was back, manifested itself in a smile that split his face from ear to ear.

He proceeded more cautiously now. His lack of experience had already nearly got him killed, so he looked carefully before placing each step. The soil immediately in front of him seemed more friable than that surrounding it, as if it had been recently dug.

"To plant something perhaps?" Ben puzzled.

He gently brushed away the top inch of soil, finding exactly what he had feared. It was a landmine and it sent a cold shiver down his back. He looked behind him with a sinking feeling in his stomach and saw several other freshly dug patches that he had only missed by pure chance. It was Ben's second lucky escape and he was only ten minutes into his mission. The realisation of just how out of his depth and ill prepared that he really was, hit Ben hard. He knew that he should quit while he still could, but something inside him wouldn't let him. It was pride!

Quite randomly, the chorus of a song came into Ben's head. It was the one that May had sung for him at Elizabeth's party, *Billy don't be a hero.* Suddenly he knew why she had chosen it. She must have known that he would do something crazy like this and she was warning him. Ben was just about to make the sensible decision and leave, when he saw the garage ahead set apart from the main house. The roof would be perfect for his shot at less than 40 yards away with an elevated view of two of the Drones.

"Sorry May," he murmured, "but this is for Lizzie."

Ben pressed ahead stealthily, keeping himself below the shrub-line. He was now truly in the zone. The near misses had focused him and his Angel senses had become heightened, making him realise just how numb he must have been at the outset. The fear had melted away and was now replaced by confidence and another huge adrenaline rush.

He reached the drive that led up to the detached garage and this time, stopped to assess the situation before acting. Ben searched around for any hazards. Satisfied that there were none, he continued his assessment. Ben was relieved when he found that the drive was paved and not gravelled. That would mean that his footsteps would fall silently as he made his approach. Then there was another obstacle that his sharp eyes picked out; approach lighting with a PIR photocell sensor. The garage was about 30 yards away. The plastic PIR sensor, measuring about three inches square, was screwed to the wooden facia board above the doors. It would be a tough shot, but an essential one. Ben unslung his father's compound bow and nocked an arrow. He sighted his target whilst still allowing his peripheral vision to monitor the leaves in the adjacent tree, as they responded obediently to the light night breeze. At the very moment that the leaves stilled, Ben loosed the arrow. With no more than a swish and a thud, the arrow found its mark and impaled the PIR to the facia. Randomly, Ben wondered if his father could ever have pulled off that shot. This served to harden his resolve as in part, this mission was another step towards bringing him back.

Ben made it from his cover, up the open drive to the side of the garage, in several seconds. He pressed himself up against the wall furthest from the house with his weapon ready, waiting for any signs that he had been detected. Satisfied that he was not, Ben scaled the wall onto the pitched roof, then up to the ridge until he could clearly see his two targets.

The Drones were dressed in black jackets and pants with their AK-47 rifles held at the port arms position in readiness. Ben was immediately taken aback by how human they looked and was at odds with his own humanity. He was going to kill these men taking away their hopes and aspirations. At that moment one of them received a phone call and the glow from the display lit his face hauntingly. It was just the distraction that Ben needed though to execute his plan. He put all thoughts of humanity out of his mind. They were not human, and he became analytical again.

Ben took the bow and nocked another arrow and aimed at the other Drone. There would be no turning back from when he loosed the next arrow and it had to be a clean kill. The night breeze was from behind him now, so there was no need for wind correction. Ben estimated the distance as less than 30 yards. It would be an easy shot technically, but the enormity of taking a life was not and his hands were shaking. It was only after enormous concentration that Ben was able to slow his heart rate down to enable the shot. When he let go, the arrow left the bow truly. It found the un-expecting Drone's larynx in the blink of an eye, severing his spine, before partly exiting the back of his neck. He died instantly and slumped to the floor. The second Drone was still totally engaged in his conversation, oblivious to his colleague's death. He would never even have felt the next arrow as it passed through his mobile phone into the cavity of his ear, then deep into his skull.

The third Drone must have raised the alarm, as moments later the house and lawns were floodlit. Ben sacrificed valuable seconds waiting for sight of him and the kill, before conceding that it wasn't going to happen. Just as Ben slid from the roof, the third Drone came into view and opened fire. It split the air above him and it was another lucky escape. Ben hit the ground running and disappeared into the trees at the back of the garden.

"Damn!" Ben cursed.

He needed all three Drones down to stand a chance against Eichmann in what was to ensue. He quickly decided on his next course of action, a deadly game of hopscotch with the Drone through the minefield. Ben's powers of retention, since his initiation as an Angel were astounding. He was about to gamble his life on just how good his memory really was. He replayed the route that he had taken through the trees and shrubs to get to the garage and pictured the positions of all the mines that he had seen. If that wasn't hard enough he had to then picture it backwards. He would be running at full speed in the opposite direction to which he came, with an angry Drone on his tail. Just for a split second, Elizabeth's words came into his mind and he smiled at the unintended truth of it.

"Let's see if you're still so smug when you've got a Shadow snapping at your arse screaming Lizzie, Lizzie please help me!"

Ben re-focussed. He was more or less happy in his mind about where all the mines were that he *had* seen but what was really scaring him were all those that he hadn't. He needed his luck to hold out just a little longer. Ben made his way back to the point where he had left the shrubs to run up the drive. He needed to draw the Drone to this exact position and then get him to follow him into the minefield. Ben unslung his bow and quiver and laid them on the drive where they could be seen clearly.

There were six halogen lamps illuminating the area. Ben took them out with six short bursts from his gun. He had deliberately removed the sound and flash suppression, so that the enemy could pinpoint his position more easily. It almost worked too well. The bushes around him erupted as the automatic fire tore through the vegetation. A bullet went through his jacket pocket into the spare magazine clips destroying two of them. Ben used the opportunity and screamed out in agony encouraging the Drone to come in and finish the kill. It worked. Ben could hear the Drone's heavy boots slapping down the drive towards him.

Ben let the Drone get just a glimpse of him before he turned and ran flat out through the minefield. He never looked down, trusting in the map that was in his head, even though his heart was in his mouth. He snaked through the trees and bushes, occasionally leaping when his natural stride would have taken him on top of a mine. Ben could hear the Drone hot on his heels and was amazed at his speed and agility.

"The Drone must have had superior eyesight, as the gap between them was closing to only yards," Ben deduced.

He could hear him readying his gun. The explosion that followed was massive. It bowled Ben over and over, disorientating him and covering him in the blood of the Drone's blast-torn body. For a split second, Ben thought it was his blood. Then he saw the mutilated Drone barely alive and whimpering like a dog struck by a car. It was pitiful and so far outside of Ben's experience that he nearly vomited. He took his hunting knife and crossed over to the dying Drone. As he drew the knife across his throat, he simply said, "Sorry," and the whimpering stopped. Ben felt bereft. Not for the death of the Drone though, it was for the death of his own innocence and humanity. He knew that the stain would be on him now and for all eternity.

The explosion had given Ben mild concussion and he lost valuable minutes while he re-orientating himself. Ben knew that Eichmann and possibly the others, would now be out in the grounds searching for him and his current position must have just been made patently clear to them. He checked time. It was now 11.15 pm, giving him another 30 minutes to complete his mission, before the replacement guards would arrive. Less if they had been summoned to arrive prematurely. He hefted the corpse onto his shoulder, picked up his AK-47 and slipped through the trees and back to the perimeter to get ready to take on Eichmann.

Eichmann was stood at his whiteboard, fine-tuning his plan when his radio burst into life.

"Guards down sectors one and two!"

The voice of the third Drone sounded breathless. There was a short burst of automatic fire and the radio blared out again.

"Enemy position, garage roof; can only see one. Wait, he's off the roof now, moving back into the south-east area of the garden."

Eichmann threw the switch to the halogens and the house and grounds lit up. His instructions to the Drone were simple.

"Kill him!"

The other Shadows mustered in the room. Grese crossed immediately to the gun cabinet and took out AK-47s for each of them, handing them around with spare magazines. Eichmann was already on the telephone calling in the other guards. With that done, he turned to address them. He was clear in the knowledge that their security was his responsibility.

"We have to hold out for 20 minutes. Enemy numbers are unknown, only one confirmed so far. Two guards are down and the third is engaging now." Eichmann's address was succinct, "I need you all to take up positions at the top of the stairs, away from the windows. Lock all doors to the landing and be prepared for an attack."

"And you comrade?" Adolphius invited.

"My duty is out there *mein Führer*," Eichmann gave the Nazi salute and clicked his heels sharply.

He left the building by the door furthest from the garage, just as the landmine exploded. He had personally laid each of them and the guards had all been thoroughly briefed and shown their positions. It was therefore unlikely in his mind that the guard would have set the mine off, but it had to remain a possibility until proven otherwise. Eichmann made his way to the outermost part of the garden to make sure that he started his search with nobody behind him. He was dressed in military fatigues and armed with his AK-47, grenades and knife.

Eichmann skirmished through the trees and shrubs towards the garage with his rifle held at high port. It was a skill that he had learnt thoroughly through numerous campaigns. He was almost invisible as he passed silently through the trees, hardly disturbing the foliage. Eichmann reached the garage and surveyed the area. His sharp eyes soon picked up the hunting bow and quiver at the side of the drive. It was too obvious and clearly put there to be found. Eichmann proceeded with extra caution and immediately found the two sets of boot-marks entering the mined zone. By the length of the strides Eichmann could tell that both hunter and hunted were running at full speed through the minefield.

"It would be remarkable if they were not both killed," he mused.

When he came to the crater left by the exploded mine, the trees around it were still wet with the blood of the casualty. Eichmann checked the boot prints. Only one set left the crater but they were deeper than before and headed away from the house. Clearly the survivor was carrying the other which meant that his guard had to be the one killed, otherwise it would not make sense. There had to be a purpose for removing the Drone's body and Eichmann was intrigued. This had all the hallmarks of a singleton attack. There was nothing to suggest otherwise. A coordinated attack would have taken out all three guards at the same time, followed by an assault on the house.

"No this is a spontaneous attack, probably borne out of vengeance for Withey's attack on Elizabeth," Eichmann thought and a smile flickered on his lips. "Benjamin Robinson!"

Ben reached the perimeter and dumped the Drone's corpse onto the ground and dragged it under a bush so that only his lower back and legs were exposed. Ben then took his Heckler & Koch submachine gun and set it in the Drone's arms, as if the body was in a concealed firing position. Ben was fast running out of time. It was 11.25pm so he only had 20 minutes left, at best, before the changing of the guard. He cursed himself for having given himself such limited time. Ben needed to draw Eichmann to this position quickly so he let a single shot go from the AK-47, hoping that this would be interpreted as a mercy killing. He made some final adjustments to the Drone's position to make it look more authentic and then slipped into the treeline.

Eichmann heard the shot and was able to place it quite accurately. He avoided the temptation to go directly to it and chose to circle backwards and around instead. Too many of the Senate had already lost their lives to these *children* by underestimating them, and he wasn't about to make it another. Eichmann ran silently along the back fence line. His keen senses quickly picked up the smell of death on the night breeze, giving him a precise direction to follow. Then he saw it, a man half concealed in the bushes by the fence line in the classic sniper's prone position. He moved to within 30 feet and stopped to observe every detail of the sniper and his surroundings. First he concentrated on the sniper himself. He was dressed in a green jacket and camouflage pants with his head and shoulders obscured in the bush. It appeared that the sniper had chosen his position by the fence expecting his quarry to come from the front, where he would have been all but invisible to them.

Eichmann stayed observing for a full five minutes before he was satisfied that the sniper was alone and that there was nothing untoward. Then he moved in swiftly for the kill. He covered the ground silently in a matter of seconds and emptied the magazine of his AK-47 into the green jacket.

It had been so simple. Eichmann felt in some way disappointed but then after all, it was just an inexperienced boy. He stooped down and dragged the body out of the bushes by the boots and rolled it over to take a look at his victim's face. A look of consternation came over him. It was the face of a man, not a boy. Even with the mutilation of the blast, he could see that it was clearly his guard. His clothing wasn't green any more either, somehow it was black. Eichmann stood up slowly as the enormity of what he was seeing hit him. He heard the sound of an AK-47 being made ready and turned to face Ben Robinson. Ben had used his ability of mind control to create that simple illusion and now he was about to kill his first full-blooded Shadow.

"*Für Elise*," Ben said simply.

His voice was icy cold as his finger began to squeeze the trigger. Eichmann begged for his life.

"No Ben, please no! I'm a father I have children..."

Ben hesitated. It was only for a split second, but that was all that it took. Eichmann used a high kick and sent the AK-47 spinning from Ben's hands and his knife was drawn in an instant. He launched himself at Ben. Ben stepped back, only just avoiding the first thrust taking his father's hunting knife from his belt as he did so. They were bent forwards towards each other, faces only inches apart circling. Each was feigning, making false attacks as one tried to measure the other. Ben was thankful for his swordsmanship skills that gave him the quickness of eye and agility of foot, but cursed his stupidity for putting himself in this mess in the first place. May's words came hauntingly into his mind for the second time that night.

"If you have the chance to kill a Shadow and you hesitate, even for one moment, then it will probably cost you your life," the thought of never seeing May again reinforced his resolve.

Ben desperately tried to regain control of Eichmann's mind but the Shadow was too guarded and focussed now that they were locked in battle. It was futile. Time was on Eichmann's side and Eichmann knew it. Ben attacked relentlessly but the Shadow just backed away giving ground at each onslaught. Ben consistently failed to get Eichmann to engage, he was clearly playing for time. Ben decided to goad him to try and get a reaction.

"Man against a boy and you back away, what kind of pussy are you? Come on where's the soldier in you *Obersturmbannführer* Otto Adolf Eichmann!"

290

Eichmann wasn't taking the bait but Ben could tell that he was irked though. His black eyes were almost reptilian, devoid of any compassion. They were focussed only on his prey and that was Ben. The look on Eichmann's face was murderous. Ben kept on goading him, working him closer and closer towards the minefield.

"There's no fight in you Eichmann, no backbone," Ben was relentless. "Gassing innocent Jews at Auschwitz was more your measure, I bet you got off on that!"

Ben touched a nerve. Eichmann suddenly slashed wildly at him taking him unawares, opening up a six inch gash in Ben's left shoulder. Eichmann quickly regained his self-control and retreated again. The pain was excruciating but Ben never showed it.

"A soldier executes his orders nothing more."

Eichmann was clearly a proud and professional man, but Ben had found the chink in his armour. He continued to drive his opponent ever closer to the mines.

"You are no soldier. You're no better than Withey, who preys on vulnerable young women," Ben's tone was derisive.

Again, it got the reaction that he wanted. This time though, Ben managed to avoid Eichmann's flashing blade.

"I am nothing like Withey!" Eichmann was furious at the comparison.

He struggled to regain his self-control, backing away as he did so playing out the time. He knew that it could only be a matter of minutes now, before his guards arrived and that there was nothing to be gained by risking his life to this boy.

The minefield was now only a few feet away. Ben continued with his distraction.

"At least Withey had the courage to use his knife."

Ben slashed at the Shadow's face adding venom to his words. His hunting knife found the softness of Eichmann's mouth and the blade rattled against his teeth. Eichmann's lower lip dropped to his chin exposing his blooded teeth giving him a maniacal look and incensing him beyond the bounds of his self-control.

Sometimes you have to be careful what you wish for. Eichmann was literally spitting blood. He launched himself at Ben with a fierceness that Ben hadn't reckoned on. When their chests clashed together, all the air was driven out of Ben leaving him winded and stunned. Eichmann followed up with a two-handed stab to Ben's chest. Ben had to drop his own knife to use both hands and all his strength to absorb the lethal thrust. The momentum of Eichmann's assault went on to take Ben off his feet. He landed painfully on his back next to one of the mines with the Shadow on top of him. Ben was astonished at the weight and strength of the man and realised that he had recklessly ignored another of May's warnings; not to choose to fight the Shadows at night, when their powers were enhanced. Ben was literally inches from the minefield but it was too late, Eichmann was slowly pressing the knife down towards his throat and there was nothing he could do about it.

In those final moments Ben could hear Elizabeth knocking at the door of his mind again. This time he let her in to say goodbye to her...

Elizabeth suddenly sat bolt upright in the passenger seat and screamed out.

"Ben!"

She had a vision of him in the last throws of a death struggle. She could see Eichmann's twisted and blooded face bearing down on her as if through Ben's eyes. She could feel Ben's power to resist him evaporating by the second.

"What is it Lizzie?"

The transformation in her was so sudden and enormous, that it shocked Mike. Elizabeth was in a trance-like state and he couldn't get through to her. Even the violent movement of the Jaguar through the tortuous bends had no effect on her. She was like a statue.

Ben felt the force of Elizabeth's mind joining his like an adrenaline shot. His tired muscles began to respond to his desperate commands, just as Eichmann's knife pierced the skin of his throat. Elizabeth had stimulated the anaerobic combustion of carbohydrates in his body, giving him an immediate flow of energy to his screaming muscles. It was an instant transformation and Ben was able to press the point of the knife back out of his throat. It was a pivotal moment and Eichmann sensed the shift of power. When he saw Ben's eyes come back into focus he knew there and then, that his life would now purely depend on the arrival of his guards. For now all he could do was just hold on. Ben could feel his body recharging and he waited for as long as he could to maximise his muscle power, he would need it.

Ben became conscious of the imminent arrival of the guards and the need to end this struggle now. He was left with only one option but it might kill them both.

The plan was desperate indeed. Ben needed to flip Eichmann over, landing him on his back on top the mine next to them. At the same time, he needed to be perfectly in-line above him so that Eichmann took the full blast. If Ben got it wrong then at best he would lose limbs but probably his life too. It was likely that the mine would rip right through Eichmann and Ben was counting on his flak jacket to do the rest. In much the same way that a skateboarder can get air by ollieing his skateboard, Ben raised his legs and kicked them down into the dirt letting the stiffness and flex of his body, spring him upwards. At the same time he wrenched his body around creating massive torsion, flipping them both over and sideways.

The manoeuvre took Eichmann completely by surprise. He landed on his back and immediately heard the metallic click of the detonator. It was only for a matter of milliseconds, but Eichmann knew exactly what had happened and his pupils contracted in alarm. The TS-50 anti-personnel mine beneath his spine erupted and the full force of the Composition B explosive tore through his back, cutting him in half. The blast went on upwards to thump into Ben's stomach with the force of a charging bull, throwing him several feet into the air before dumping him rudely in the crater that had been formed by the explosion.

Elizabeth's eyes came back into focus and her body relaxed, she was with Mike again.

"Ben's down Mike but he's not out. We have to get to him. I don't know how bad it is or who else is there."

"We're already at the rendezvous Lizzie."

293

Mike skidded to a halt next to the SAS van. It only took seconds to transfer and then they sped off towards Adolphius' house several hundred yards ahead, donning their flak jackets on the way.

Ben had no idea of how long he had lost consciousness for. All he knew was that he hurt all over and his ears were blown out. He frantically checked his body over to prove his limbs and almost cried with relief when he found them intact. Although he was confused and disorientated, Ben knew that he had to get away but he couldn't see where to go. Everything had gone black. In his concussed state, he couldn't work out what could've happened to make it so. Finally the realisation that he was blind hit him like an express train. Ben felt his eyes. They were running with blood triggering a vomiting spasm as he staggered aimlessly away from the crater. It was only by chance that he headed towards the road and not deeper into the minefield.

The SAS van screeched around the final bend before the drive to the house. Only the driver's quick reactions and skill, avoided them hitting the seemingly drunken man who was staggering down the middle of the road towards them.

"Ben!" screamed Elizabeth, "Its Ben!"

Mike slid the side door open and dragged him in while the van was still movin.

"Go, go, go!" Mike shouted.

The driver floored the accelerator. Just seconds after they passed the drive to Adolphius' house, a Ford Transit minibus, with six armed guards, slewed in.

"That was close!" Mike said as he turned to face Elizabeth.

He could see that her face was stricken and her words were hollow.

"Look at his eyes Mike, just look at his eyes!"

Elizabeth nursed Ben like he was a baby, talking to him softly as he drifted into shock induced unconsciousness.

The Air Ambulance landed in the paddock at the Robinson's stables at 20 minutes after midnight. The two paramedics worked swiftly. Ben was assessed and ready for transfer in only another five. The jargon that they used to describe his eye injuries over the radio was *blast-related ocular trauma*. Because of the seriousness of the injuries, they were instructed to fly directly to the London Heliport for onward transfer to the Moorfields Eye Hospital, at City Road. Elizabeth flew with him while Mike put the wheels in motion for some additional Angel specialist medical support. His first call was to Craig Jamieson, the surgeon who had put Elizabeth back together.

"Craig, its Mike Jackson."

"Oh Mike, good to hear from you. How's Elizabeth?" Craig was not expecting a business call.

"Fine but listen there's no time to explain. Ben has just been air lifted to the Moorfields Eye Hospital, with blast-related ocular trauma. He's in a mess Craig and I don't think it's going to be good news."

Mike was emotional and, in admitting the obvious, his words came out with great difficulty. Craig's response was all that Mike could have hoped for; commanding and positive.

"By good fortune I'm in London right now on a conference and can get to Moorfields sooner than Ben. I've got contacts there and will get involved. Not as the surgeon of course, as eyes are not my speciality, but I am able to coordinate *certain things* shall I say."

Craig was putting an action plan together in his head as he spoke.

"It would be handy if you could be here Mike."

"Try and stop me. Thanks Craig," he cut the call.

After briefing his men, Mike headed out toward the motorway taking the southbound carriageway London-bound. He felt guilty, again. Mike knew that he had taken his eyes off the ball again because of his feelings for Elizabeth. His closeness was affecting his effectiveness. Ben's condition was partly because of that. He vowed that he would never be so derelict in his duty again.

Mike had seen bomb victims, who had suffered eye trauma before. None had looked this bad, and all had suffered permanent blindness as a result.

"I should've been there for him," Mike admitted gritting his teeth as he thumped the steering wheel in self-remorse, "I've failed both of them now."

Elizabeth and Mike were in the waiting room at Moorfields. Ben had been sedated more than four hours earlier and was still in theatre. The long wait was intolerable. They had run out of positive things to say to each other and the silence had become pregnant. When Craig entered the room, their relief was paplable. Elizabeth and Mike immediately stood up in hopeful expectation.

"Ben is out of any danger and is on his way to the recovery ward as we speak."

Craig had chosen his opening address carefully, so as to stay in the positive.

"Would you like to join me in one of the spare offices for coffees?"

Elizabeth was avoiding any mind contact with Craig. She was too fearful of what he might have to say to risk pre-empting any bad news. Mike simply nodded and took Elizabeth's hand supportively. They were sat around Craig's desk with their coffees. It felt like *déjà vu* for Mike, the only difference being an exchange of siblings. It was surreal. Mike was in deep personal despair, he was involved in something that was too big to fix. He knew that one day or another he would lose both of them, as the odds were hopelessly stacked against their continued survival. All he could really do was delay the inevitable.

Craig began with a summary of Ben's condition.

"It would appear from Ben's injuries, that he was in very close proximity to an explosion after what appears to have been a knife fight. He has minor blade wounds to his arms and throat. One is particularly deep on his left shoulder, but none of these are of any real concern."

That was the easy bit.

"The explosion has blown out his ear drums and damaged the ossicles in his middle ear. He will be temporarily deaf but a little surgical help and some Angel regeneration should bring about a full recovery. So again you shouldn't worry too much about this in the longer term."

Elizabeth cut him short.

"His eyes Craig, what about his beautiful eyes?" Elizabeth looked in pain.

The pause that followed said it all and Elizabeth held her breath as dread filled her heart.

Craig cleared his throat nervously before continuing.

"Fortunately there was no mechanical perforation to the eyes so Ben's injuries are confined to what we call *closed-globe* and they have managed to save the organs."

"*Save the organs?* What kind of a positive comment was that?" Elizabeth thought.

She was subconsciously squeezing Mike's hand in anticipation of what was to come next. Her fingernails were starting to draw blood but Mike ignored the pain.

"Ben has suffered hyphema, which is bleeding from the front chamber of his eyes. The force of the explosion has gone on to cause vitreous haemorrhage and retinal detachments. It's too soon to be sure at this stage, but there may also be damage to both optical nerves."

Craig was about to move on to the prognosis but Elizabeth had seen it coming.

"Which means that he will probably never see again," she stated helplessly.

Elizabeth was feeling the enormity of it. The realisation crushed her chest so that she couldn't breathe. She thought that she was going to pass out.

"Well yes I'm afraid that is very likely, perhaps certain. Even with his special powers of regeneration, it would be a big ask. I'm truly sorry," Craig looked desolated for them.

Elizabeth was already thinking ahead positively. The prognosis just wasn't acceptable.

"*Sorry* is just not enough Craig. I want Ben ready to travel as soon as he's well enough and I want to be with him when he wakes up."

"Where will you be taking him?" Craig asked incredulously, as Elizabeth got up to go to Ben.

"To the only person on Earth that might be able to save his eyes, Maelströminha!"

It was another two hours before Ben began to emerge from the morphine induced sleep. Ironically his awaking dream was in vivid Technicolor.

Ben was swimming under water, over a coral reef, with myriad colourful fish around him. He felt weightless and in total peace and harmony with his surroundings. The warm, crystal clear water was caressing his body, soothing him. When he finally felt the need to breath, he looked up and swam towards the sun that danced on the choppy surface above him. Ben broke the surface, exhaled and opened his eyes waking as he did so. Instead of being in the bright sunshine he was in a dark place. Moments later, the memory of the explosion hit him and he reached for his bandaged eyes in panic. Elizabeth caught his wrists.

"Easy Ben, it's alright I'm here and you're safe."

"Lizzie, is that you?" Ben's voice was urgent. "Where am I?"

"You're at the hospital and Craig is looking after you," she released his wrists and began running her fingers soothingly through the hair at Ben's temples.

Ben realised that Elizabeth was talking to him through her mind and not her voice.

"Talk to me Lizzie, I want to hear your voice," it was a plea rather than a preference as he had already sensed that there was a reason for it.

"Craig says that it will be a while before you can hear again Ben but you will hear, you will."

Silent tears of grief rolled down Elizabeth's face. Ben touched the bandages covering his eyes with trembling hands. All at once he clearly recalled the tremendous impact of the explosion and his bleeding, sightless eyes.

"Will I see again Lizzie?"

It was an emotional moment. Elizabeth faltered just too long before finding the right words to say. By then, Ben already knew the answer.

"It's alright Lizzie I already know."

Ben reached out to find Elizabeth's hand. She took it desperately and choked back her tears. She didn't want him to feel her despair.

The drive back to the Robinson's house was almost in silence. Elizabeth just had to see May and she was totally consumed by the possibilities of that reunion. There had to be a solution and May would have it. This all couldn't end like this with Ben condemned to a life of darkness, it just couldn't.

George's car was in the drive when they arrived. Mike dropped Elizabeth off, turned the car around, and headed straight back to London to be with Ben. George and Jillie had just returned from a long weekend away and were still stood in the hallway, when Elizabeth entered.

"Lizzie!" Jillie had missed her and it showed in her greeting.

To their astonishment, Elizabeth just walked straight by as if unaware of them. Jillie was just about to protest at her rudeness, when she disappeared into the mirror without so much as a backward glance.

Chapter 29

May was sat cross legged on the floor in front of her mirror. She was looking into an empty family room that reflected the emptiness of her life. The similarity was poignant.

May had lived every painful moment of Elizabeth and Ben's traumatic journeys. She had felt Elizabeth's mind numbing terror when she faced

Withey, the man who had terrorised her for years in her dreams. She had felt every slash of the knife as it tore into Elizabeth's soft flesh and followed her to the very edge of her sanity and into the oblivion that ensued. May had felt Ben's heady cocktail of excitement and fear, when he was one on one against Illya Dracul, and the excruciating pain when the cold steel ripped through his sides and shoulder. She had felt every moment of Ben's dual with Eichmann and his desperation that culminated in an act of almost certain suicide. She felt the blast rip through his eyes and ears, as if it were her own body, and she could feel the isolation and despair that he was suffering now.

Throughout all of this, May had felt impotent. In their hour of need, she could be no more than a spectator as they played out their parts in the most dangerous game on Earth. May knew that they had to find the strength and innovation within themselves, by themselves. They had to learn it all the hard way, through experience. What they were going through tortured May. It had only just begun for them and she knew that things would get much worse before they got any better. She knew too that they would never be safe again. It was a miracle that they had both got this far and most unlikely that they would get much further.

But it was too much for May. Her evolution had taken her way past this barbarity and she wasn't emotionally equipped for the pain and suffering of it. Thousands of years of life had been a curse not a blessing. So many times she had grown close to and even to love people, only to see them mutilated or killed. Even the ones that had survived the war with the Shadows had been lost to her through illness and age. She was in a prison, partly of her own making and the loneliness and futility of it crushed her. The responsibility of the survival of her people hers and hers alone and the responsibility was unsupportable.

May curled up like a cat on the floor in front of the portal that now looked into her empty past. She wished that she could just die and be free of it. May even wondered how she might do that, and sobbed uncontrollably. The guilt she felt knew no bounds, and her desolation and isolation was absolute. At last, total mental exhaustion extinguished the pain and she locked herself away in a coma-like sleep that she wanted to last forever.

Elizabeth saw May on the floor the second she passed through the portal and ran down the corridor of mirrors to her. She was scared of what she might find and knelt beside her. Instinctively she checked for the pulse in her neck and breathed a sigh of relief when she felt the steady rhythm of a young and healthy heart. Elizabeth lifted May's head into her lap and caringly brushed the hair from her tear ravaged face, while she tried to take in the situation. May was clearly exhausted and remained unaware of Elizabeth's presence. The floor was wet with her tears and she appeared to have wasted away. There was nothing of her. Elizabeth looked into the mirror of May's past, but the image was just of an empty room.

"Like her life." Elizabeth guessed.

She could feel May's isolation and despair through her own senses. Elizabeth picked her up like a sleeping child and carried her out into the sunshine. Elizabeth laid her down by the rock that had become their meeting place, and sat beside her.

She looked at her critically. Even in her personal crisis, May's features were beautiful beyond words. Her face was timeless and her skin, flawless. Her long black hair shone with health in the morning sunshine and fell in natural waves down her shoulders and back. She was dressed in a black cat suit that was quite literally more cat than suit. It even had the look and texture of black leopard skin. Quite strangely, it looked part of her rather than a garment that she was wearing. Even her hands and feet were petite and perfectly manicured.

"She looks more like a doll than a woman," Elizabeth thought in wonderment.

She moved on to think about what might fill May's daily life. She was more or less in exile, and had been so for at least a thousand years. Now, since the death of Crystalita, she was totally alone without companions. Elizabeth knew that in some way, May coordinated the fight against the Shadows. That was remotely though, using her telepathic abilities. There was little or no personal contact. That thought reminded her of how she had accused May of spying on her future and then the profound realisation came to Elizabeth.

"May can probably feel our pain and suffering. Maybe even our emotions telepathically!"

The implications of that were huge. It would mean that she would have gone through all of her and Ben's sufferings, not to mention those of the people that were close to her over past generations. All at once Elizabeth understood the change that had come over May. For someone with her capacity for love and compassion, it would have been unbearable for her to stand by and watch the horrific things that had just taken place. She knew too that May was particularly fond of them and perhaps in love with Ben.

"Yes that was it," Elizabeth concluded. "She had come to the end of her resilience. Perhaps she had given up hope altogether," she wondered.

Elizabeth wasn't sure whether these were her own deductions or an empathy that she now shared as a fellow Angel. Either way, she knew that she needed to know more about May as a person and share her burden. She vowed to herself that from today onwards, she would be a better friend and that would start with fattening her up. Despite her beauty, May was looking ragged. Elizabeth lay with May for the next few hours waiting patiently for her to awaken. When at last she did, the joy on May's face at seeing her was profoundly honest and heart-touching. May sat up and put her arms around Elizabeth.

"Sorry," was all that she could find to say.

"Sorry for what May? Elizabeth didn't get it. "You didn't cause any of this. Without your help and guidance, we would already have been killed; just like they killed Mum and Dad."

Elizabeth pushed May back to an arm's length and held her by the shoulders, keeping eye contact to add weight to her words.

"You have blessed us with a fighting chance against the Shadows and the possibility of bringing our parents back. We are prepared to die for that. Don't give up on us now May, We need you to help us finish this."

There was no doubt of the earnestness and desperation of Elizabeth's plea. May was still in a bad place though and the deep regret and guilt showed on her face.

"I'm sorry that I wasn't there to protect you Lizzie, and sorry that Ben will never see again. It's my fault and I can't live with it anymore," May looked devastated and Elizabeth angry.

"Now you listen to me Miss Maelströminha! You didn't volunteer for this but neither did we. And you haven't fought all your life to give up now. You can't quit and neither can we; too much depends on us!"

It was shock treatment but Elizabeth meant every word that she said.

"Everybody despairs sometimes May, but sometimes you can't afford the self-pity and now is when you cannot. We're almost there May we know the enemy and we have a plan."

May still wasn't receptive. Elizabeth had to harden her line still further.

"Give Ben his eyes back and we'll bring back Crystalita, Emanuel, David and our parents. I swear it to you!"

Elizabeth was the empowered one now; it was complete role reversal. May was still negative and lacking in faith. What Elizabeth was asking of her, was beyond even her ability.

"Lizzie. You know that I would do absolutely anything if I could, but I'm not a magician and certainly no surgeon," May looked beaten. "The mother ship has a fully equipped operating theatre and stem cells, kept in cryopreservation, that are over 5,000 years old. I don't have the necessary skills to help Ben though Lizzie. I wish I had, but I don't."

Elizabeth interrupted.

"But your father does May. You told us that he was a renowned surgeon and an expert in cryogenics."

Elizabeth frowned. She suddenly realised that something didn't add up.

"Why have you never visited you parents May?"

"For many reasons Lizzie," May seemed lost in her thoughts, "I have already told you that we cannot co-exist near our past or future life-forms. It would cause a fatal instability and besides..."

May stopped mid-sentence. Elizabeth pressed her for an answer.

"Besides what, May?"

"Besides, I cannot burden the last happy years of their lives. How can I tell them that the evacuation to Earth was a disaster? That the Shadows are taking over, that everyone they knew is dead, including Crystalita. It would be too cruel Lizzie, I just couldn't do that."

There was a gaping flaw in May's logic and Elizabeth was on it in a flash.

"Do you not think that, as one of Angelos' top scientists, your father wouldn't have already known for hundreds of years about the fate of Angelos?" Elizabeth leveraged the statement. "And maybe it would be comforting for him to know that you and Crystalita made it to Earth and had 5,000 of life that you would not have had?”

The concept was something of a revelation to May and she felt foolish for not having considered it before.

“No strangely and perhaps even stupidly. I haven’t considered that,” she looked embarrassed. “Sometimes, when you’re really close to something, you just don’t see the full picture.”

May looked for another reason to excuse herself and then added defensively:

“Besides Lizzie, I couldn’t co-exist near my life-form anyway, so it would have been too dangerous.”

“You don’t have to May, I could bring him here!”

Immediately after the guards had secured the surrounding grounds, Adolphius called a crisis meeting. The bodies of the three Drones and Eichmann had been recovered and disposal arrangements made. The four of them were armed and mustered in the war room. Adolphius addressed them starting with an update. He was still bristling with rage at the audacity of the attack.

“I have doubled the guard and in future, one of us will be on duty at all times,” there was a consensus of agreement and Adolphius continued. “It appears that it was a single assassin. As the girl is hospitalised, we can assume that it was either the boy or Jackson.”

Alexis nodded in agreement. He knew exactly what had happened. Somehow he always did and he enlightened the others.

“Eichmann was killed by one of his own mines. There is a blood trail leaving the area that could not possibly be his. So we can assume the assassin is injured, how badly we cannot tell. My guess is that it was the boy, a revenge attack following the Withey fiasco.”

Alexis’ assumption went uncontested. Adolphius continued.

“This means that we conceivably have both siblings hospitalised with injuries and therefore cannot depend on either being at home across the coming week or so. Our strategy to eliminate them dictates that they are all back at the household in an established routine. So for now, we just need to observe until that happens. Have you got any comments or questions?"

Grese was the only one to respond.

"Does that mean our plan goes ahead unchanged, other than the date of it?" her confidence had enjoyed another boost through the loss of Eichmann, who had outranked her.

"Absolutely Grese. Eichmann's plan was built around four assault squads headed by each of us. I see no reason to change that. The only unknown is when. Angels heal fast, so I anticipate that they will be home within two weeks. That means I want your squads trained and ready to employ in ten days."

They were stood in the corridor of mirrors animatedly discussing how it would go. May was as excited and as nervous as a puppy.

"What will they think of me Lizzie? Oh God they will be disappointed. Look at me I'm so thin; they'll think I look like a boy. What should I wear; something little girlish maybe? No, that wouldn't be right at all, perhaps I could..."

May was all at sea and couldn't put any coherent thoughts together.

"What should I say to them Lizzie? I'll just babble on, I know I will. They will think I'm a fool..."

"May stop it!" Elizabeth's head was spinning with the panicked rubbish that May was talking. "You are babbling and you are nobody's fool. Just relax and be yourself. They will be proud of you. I promise."

Elizabeth had taken control and May was thankful for her taking the decisions away from her.

"You will dress elegantly. Perhaps the same outfit that you wore to my party, but with your hair down and soft," then Elizabeth added as an afterthought, "and maybe less aggressive lipstick this time?"

"Was I really that brash?"

May put her hand to her mouth in a gesture of mock horror.

"Well it certainly worked on Ben!" Elizabeth jibed.

"Did it really?" May's attempt at surprise was thinly veiled.

Elizabeth put her hands on her hips and tilted her head in an accusing manner.

"You know fine well that it did and you should be ashamed of yourself. You're old enough to be his mother!"

"I think his great, great, great grandmother to the power of n would be more accurate," May countered.

They burst into unrestrained laughter as they walked down the corridor to prepare May for her monumental meeting.

Mike was sat with Ben, listening to him relate the story of his epic battle against the Shadows. Ben's memory for detail made it a splendid tale and Mike was totally engrossed in it. He was particularly impressed with Ben's marksmanship with the bow and had enthused with him.

"They were impossible shots Ben. Even your father would've been hard pressed to have made them!"

The part where Ben had memorised the layout of the minefield backwards and had run full speed through it with a Shadow on his tail, was bordering on fiction.

"Awesome and ballsy," was all Mike could muster by way of comment.

The *pièce de résistance* had to be Ben's shit or bust decision to flip Eichmann on top of the landmine, which also blew Mike away.

"Remind me not to play poker with you Ben. That was an *all chips in* decision, fair play to you!"

Mike was impressed by how resourceful Ben had been in the field, particularly having had no formal training or experience. It was the mark of a true soldier.

"Hats off to you Ben, you can be in my squad anytime."

"Not much call for a blind soldier though is there Mike?" Ben was slipping towards the tragic.

Mike derailed his line of thought.

"I dunno. Someone has to shake the tin can for beer money on a Friday night, lol."

Despite himself, Ben did laugh out loud.

"You've been spending too much time with my Sis, Miss Inappropriate, learning *sick*!"

Ben was suddenly serious again, sensing that Mike had momentarily regretted making the joke.

"I will be alright with this Mike. I can and will cope and I don't really regret what I did. It's strange, hard to explain really. I needed to do it for Lizzie and for me, whatever the consequence. Does that make any kind of sense?"

"Yes Ben, it does," Mike had already seen what men will volunteer for in the theatre of war, "I know just what you mean and I've seen your father do the same. He would have done just what you did Ben; be proud."

"You know Mike I'm lucky, I don't need my ears to hear your thoughts and all my senses will eventually work together to make pictures that my eyes can't see,"

Ben's positivity dried up and the words that he wanted to say stuck in his throat. Tears ran down his cheeks from his sightless eyes and his expression was tragic.

"The only thing is that I'll never again see how beautiful May is, not ever again."

Elizabeth had spent several hours trying to put the most perfect woman in the world together for her meeting with her parents. It should have been easy but she was dealing with the fads, fantasies and temperament of an emotionally retarded teenager. It had gone way past intolerable. At last Elizabeth's proclamation was a mixture of both belief and the loss of will to live.

"That's it May you look stunning and you'll knock them out for sure. I bet your Dad says that you look just like your mother did when he first met her."

Elizabeth was more than happy with their work or was it re-work or re-re-work? May however was still at sixes and sevens and really anxious about meeting her parents.

"It's not too much is it Lizzie?"

May gave a pirouette in an elegant black dress that was coincidently modelled on the one that Elizabeth had worn at her eighteenth birthday party.

"Don't answer that. It's just that I feel like I'm going out on a date," May added awkwardly.

Elizabeth smiled at her anxious face affectionately.

"You are May, what *date* do you have in mind?"

After some thought May returned her smile.

"I was thinking the month before we left Angelos for Earth. I would have been just eighteen, like you are now Lizzie. It's likely to be a time when they would be in despair of our future. Perhaps the news will comfort them. That's if the shock of seeing you appear in their front room doesn't kill them first!"

May laughed nervously but it showed that she was beginning to relax a little.

They stood in front of the portal and May took a deep breath.

"Here goes."

She placed her hand on the glass letting her thoughts take herself back. At last the mirror displayed the image that she wanted.

"Perfect. It's the equivalent of your Sunday after lunch," May said.

It was a relaxed family moment. May's parents were sat on the sofa, leaning against each other. They were looking at something that resembled a magazine, but the pages were like films of light emitting plastic. May and Crystalita were engaged in what looked like a conspiratorial discussion about something that might be *risqué*, judging by their expressions and body language.

"Typical girls," Elizabeth said admonishingly.

"Excuse me!" May faked insult.

"What are your parents' names and will they understand what I'm saying?" Elizabeth asked.

With all the fuss of getting May ready, she hadn't thought too much about her own role in this.

"My Father is Jorall and my mother Zita. They won't totally understand you at first Lizzie, but don't worry about it. I'm guessing that they will hold your hands and join your mind to find what you want to say. After that, they will know your language thoroughly. It's much simpler than ours. Much."

At that moment, the girls stood up and crossed the room to Zita. There was a brief exchange followed by kisses and then they walked out. They were clearly on some kind of a nefarious mission.

"I remember this," May's smile was nostalgic. "We had plotted to go to see a somewhat *avant-garde* show on the pretence of seeing something, should I say *more compatible* with parental thinking. Not easy when your parents can usually read you like a book!"

"So I wasn't wrong when I thought *typical girls* then, was I?" Elizabeth teased which brought May guiltily back to the present.

"Anyway, you have them to yourself for hours if need be Lizzie. Remember, for me time will effectively stop. You will come back to the same point in time that you left, wiping out anything that happens afterwards. I won't even know that you were gone."

May fidgeted, a sign that she was still really nervous about what was to come. In the next instant, she would be meeting her parents for the first time in over 5,000 years.

"OK then May prepare yourself and wish me luck!"

With that Elizabeth took a brave step into the unknown.

Elizabeth suddenly appeared in May's parents' front room. Jorall left his seat at the shock of it, quickly positioning himself protectively between her and his wife Zita.

"Who are you, what do you want here?"

There was no semblance of hostility, as that emotion had been lost to evolution countless millions of years ago. From Jorall's par, his reaction was purely surprise and fear of the unknown.

Elizabeth had no understanding of the words that Jorall had said, but she handled the situation well. She just smiled with her hands up and bowed her head in submissive manner. She waited like that until Jorall came over to her. He immediately sensed Elizabeth's humility and peaceful intent. He took her hands and led her to the sofa, sitting her between himself and Zita, who had already sensed that the visitor had come as a friend.

Jorall appeared to be in his late thirties, according to our earthly years. He was tall and athletic, with angular features, wide mouth and kind blue eyes. He spoke some sentences then quickly realised that Elizabeth was not of them.

Just as May had guessed, they linked hands with her and gazed into her eyes. Elizabeth was startled by the comfort that she felt in what would, in any other situation, be bizarre. Language barriers disappeared. They were talking to each other freely without words about nothing in particular and everything in general; who Elizabeth was, where she came from, any brothers or sisters, ambitions, so much and only in moments.

Zita was an elegant willowy woman, with long black hair and doll-like features. She had a gentleness about her and looked more like May's older sister than her mother. She shared the same child-like smile and demureness. It came as a complete shock to Elizabeth when Zita talked to her in the most perfect English.

"You are sad and troubled Lizzie. Why have you come to us?"

Zita's inexplicable understanding of Elizabeth's emotional turmoil was so perceptive and compassionate that Elizabeth immediately felt able to open up her heart to them without embarrassment. Elizabeth let it all go. Recognising her distress, Zita took Elizabeth in a motherly embrace and shushed her. Elizabeth felt that same flow of positive energy that she had from May, when she had comforted her. It was a feeling special beyond words. The pain and uncertainty left her and Elizabeth was ready to make her request.

"Thank you Zita," Elizabeth smiled openly at her, "that was just how your daughter Maelströminha comforted me and my brother a few months ago, when we were sad."

"You know our daughter?" Jorall interjected, it didn't equate. "A few months ago, how could that be?" his face showed both perplexity and concern. Elizabeth knew that if they had wanted to, they could have interrogated her mind for all the answers, but they were giving her the courtesy of her privacy. Elizabeth began her story.

"Well it was a few months ago for me, but for you, more than 5,000 years in the future."

"Maelströminha is still alive 5000 years from now?" Jorall was elated.

His face lit up in the same bioluminescent way that May had radiated light when she was joyous.

"That means that the expedition to your planet Earth was a success. They made it!" Jorall clasped Zita's hand who was already crying at the relief of it.

Elizabeth sensed their next question. It would be about Crystalita. Elizabeth couldn't bear to answer it so she derailed the conversation instead.

"Maelströminha wants to tell you the whole story herself and she is waiting for you on the other side of the portal."

"Why did she not come?" Zita asked.

Her face was wet with tears, but radiating relief and happiness such that Elizabeth could feel the warmth and inner peace of it.

"For many reasons Zita that she will tell you. One is that she cannot co-exist in close proximity to her counterpart, so she needs you to go to her," Elizabeth paused then added imploringly, "and I need you to go there to help my brother. He needs you Jorall, I want you to save his eyes."

Elizabeth told Jorall all she knew about Ben's injuries and the prognosis that he had been given. When he said the words, "It's not so serious Lizzie," she could have kissed him.

"We will pack some things to take with us. Make yourself at home Elizabeth, we will only be a few minutes," Zita said, taking Jorall's hand to leave the room.

Elizabeth looked around the ultra-modern living room. The geometric styling was in discrete monochrome décor with strategically placed ornaments, pictures and drapes in bright primary and secondary colours. The contrast gave the room lift, depth and identity. The theme was predominantly blues and greens which worked well. In her idleness Elizabeth imagined how different the room would look if they had chosen reds and oranges instead. To her absolute astonishment, the décor changed to suit her visualisation of it.

"Awesome!" Elizabeth said out loud. "Now I'm an interior decorator, how cool is that?"

Elizabeth spent the next ten minutes changing the colours of the walls and even the floor covering to her fancy. She suddenly panicked that she might not be able to get it back as it was but fortunately it wasn't difficult. She wondered whether anything had actually physically changed at all and that it was only her perception of it that had changed. Her reality.

Jorall and Zita returned with their hastily packed bag chatting animatedly to each other. Elizabeth could feel their joy. It was like an aurora that transcended their physical beings, a spiritual thing. It was a special gift that she now shared with them as part of her own personal renaissance.

Jorall took Zita's hand as they crossed to the mirror. Zita glanced back at Elizabeth for reassurance, with a nervous but grateful smile on her face. Jorall placed his hand on the mirror and the portal opened for them. They stepped through time and space, straight into the outstretched and welcoming arms of their daughter.

The reunion was way past emotional and an unimaginable contradiction. On the one side there was a daughter who hadn't seen her parents for more than 5,000 years. On the other, her parents, who hadn't lost her yet but feared that they soon would and never see her again. Elizabeth watched in tearful happiness as they hugged, cried and laughed. Every emotion was coursing through them. May finally had to tell them the whole of her story. She told them in the same way that she had done with Elizabeth and Ben, by stimulating all of their senses. It was a spectacle to watch and it took Elizabeth back to the night when she had performed for them and wondered that it already seemed a lifetime ago.

Because of May's highly evolved audience, the transfer of information only took minutes. During that episode, her bioluminescence lit her up like a torch and the mood of her story was reflected by the degree of light and animation of her parents. Elizabeth knew the precise moment that May had told them of Crystalita's death as the lights went out and grief flowed out of them like a river of darkness. May must have then said something profound, Elizabeth thought, as the mood became up-tempo again. When May finished, there were smiles on their faces again. May turned to Elizabeth with a look of deep contentment, the like of which Elizabeth had never seen in her before.

"I have told them everything that has happened," May was calm but Elizabeth could sense guiltiness about her, "I had to tell them that Crystalita died more than two Earth years ago and that was the hardest thing that I have ever had to do. They were devastated."

May couldn't face Elizabeth for what she had to say next. She looked down at her feet and continued.

"Until I told them how you and Ben will bring her back to us."

Elizabeth's jaw dropped in disbelief at the responsibility that May had placed on her and Ben. There was no certainty of anything. They were living their lives from day to day on a knife-edge. Elizabeth was aghast.

"How could you promise such a thing?"

"Because, with Ben back you will do it Lizzie. You must."

Mike had made the difficult decision to leave Ben at the hospital under guard. He needed to take control of his squad again and direct and support the surveillance operation that he had so far neglected, albeit for good reason. He was in the white SAS van, sifting through all the data that had been captured so far. He was trying to make sense of it all. There was clearly a substantial strike planned on the Robinsons' house. Unfortunately, technical problems with the laser audio surveillance equipment had resulted in some extensive gaps in their intelligence. What they did know with some degree of certainty was:

- There would be a four phased attack, using squads of six Drones each commanded by one of the remaining Shadows.

- Those Shadows were: Adolphius, Alexis, Grese and a new edition, Illya Dracul.

- The first attack would be Red Squad led by Alexis with shoulder-fired missiles.

- There would be three other attacks of unknown manner across the next two minutes (loss of audio system denying details).

- A helicopter was in the plan so that meant that they should consider that at least one squad could attack from the air.

- The brief was no survivors and that included the Shadows own seriously injured.

- Secondary objective, was to capture or destroy the portal, depending on whether or not Elizabeth or Ben had escaped through it.

- Exodus was by air and road.

- Timeframe was ten to fourteen days.

"Plenty to go on Jake."

Mike's summation was directed at the burly Sergeant Major who had led the operation in his absence. Jake was a rough *old-school* soldier and was of another mind-set.

"Enough to know we should go in tonight and kill 'em all in their beds sir," Jake replied. "Just give the order and it'll be done."

Jake was tired of all this surveillance bullshit. As a trained killer and a simple thinker, the solution was obvious to him.

"Oh that it was so simple Jake, but there is a time and a place for them all to die and that's not here and it's not now."

"Aye as you bid sir. But I've been a soldier all me life and you take 'em when you can or you regret it later."

"Perhaps Jake but humour me for now. How would you have the four squads attack us if you were them?"

It was bread and butter stuff for Jake and he was back in the positive again.

"Assuming they know the layout of the house, and they will from council drawings. And assuming they know we've got the place watched, and again they will..."

Red Jake had fair skin that showed the ravages of his recent tour in the Middle East. His pale blue eyes darted around as he tugged at his short cropped and greying red beard, while he considered the scenario.

"...then the first rocket attack will take out our van and all major rooms in the downstairs level. Next I'd drop men on the roof to take the upstairs, grenades in through all windows."

Red Jake was only confirming what Mike had already thought.

"Roof squad go in next, following the grenades. They clear any survivors on the upstairs level. The third squad opens up with machine gun fire at the downstairs front blown out windows," Jake nodded to himself in self-approval. "The fourth squad tidies up any *runners*, while the first squad stands by to take out any unwanted visitors."

Jake smiled almost toothlessly at Mike. He had the face of a man with too many pub brawls under his belt.

"That's how a soldier'd do it sir. Eichmann, evil bastard that he was, is known for his tactical skills as a soldier. You can't odds that."

It was more or less exactly as Mike had read it too and confirmed and validated Mike's next moves.

"Short of an all-out air strike Jake, I agree. Anyway, they wouldn't have four squads in the first place if that was their plan. They would just level the building."

Mike considered why they wouldn't choose that easy option.

"If they used an air-strike, they wouldn't be able to account for the bodies to confirm the success or otherwise of their mission. That must be unacceptable to them. Also, the mirror would be lost to them at the very least. No, an air strike wouldn't be their best option, hands down."

The next question posed by Mike, was why ten to fourteen days? It was a simple operation that only needed days to train and deploy. Mike continued.

"From the broken audio recordings, it's reasonable to assume that they know they've injured both Elizabeth and Ben. They must know that they are recuperating elsewhere and their plan demands that we are all back in the same place for a single kill."

It was a simple deduction and Jake concurred.

"Ten days can only be their best guess sir based on gut feeling and that was yesterday's intel. So we've only nine days to plan our counter-attack... or defence," Jake added reluctantly.

"Sorry Jake it will be defence this time, all part of the bigger picture. We can't risk the lives of the Robinsons, they have an important job to do and they're not ready yet."

"Then they better bloody well soon be sir. We can't nursemaid 'em forever, these guys mean business and they simply will not stop."

Jake's words always came straight from the shoulder, even to his commander and he wasn't through yet.

"And another thing sir. You need to get their Aunt and Uncle to a safe house before it kicks off, 'cos it's not gonna be no place for them neither."

Mike already had that covered. He knew that Elizabeth and Ben owed them the respect of an honest reason for being evacuated and without any smoothing this time.

"Not an enviable task," he thought wryly, cocking an eyebrow.

Elizabeth had returned from her meeting with May and was sat with Ben beside his hospital bed. Craig had just left the room to meet George and Jillie, who were sat anxiously in the waiting room. They had so far only been told that Ben had been close to an explosion and that had suffered damage to his hearing and sight but was out of any real danger.

"Ben," Elizabeth began, "we owe it to them to come clean about everything. They are in as much danger as we are and it's not fair to organise their minds to just accept it."

"I feel the same Lizzie, only how much can we say? It's all so incredible, preposterous even. They'll think we're mad," Ben couldn't realistically see how their aunt and uncle could possibly buy it. "If someone told me the story, I would think they were barking."

"Maybe they will. Perhaps we have to do it the same way that May did to us in the beginning and tell the whole story. Well maybe not in all the detail that she did, but all of it through our minds."

Elizabeth would dearly have loved to have seen Ben's response eye to eye instead of looking down at his bandaged head. She felt his isolation and loneliness. Ben forced a smile, knowing that she would be watching his face.

"OK then, but you take the lead. I'm just a little compromised at the moment, as you can see."

"Cop out! You've always got an excuse Ben," Elizabeth teased.

Uncle George and Aunt Jillie entered the room, clearly worried about what they would find.

"Ben!" Jillie crossed the room and took his hand urgently, "What happened?" she saw his head swathed in bandages, covering his eyes and ears and naturally panicked. "Oh God what have you done Ben, can you hear me, its Auntie?"

He squeezed her hand and a broad smile dimpled his cheeks. The simple act somehow seemed to make his injuries seem even more tragic.

"Hey it's OK Auntie. Don't worry, I'm going to be fine I promise. It looks worse than it is, really."

George sat down beside the bed and took Ben's other hand, "Can't leave you alone for five minutes can we son?" the sarcastic words were cover for how wretched George was feeling and Ben sensed it.

"Just trying to get a little attention Uncle and its going well so far..." Ben reassured them with another smile.

Even in the emotion of the moment George laughed but it was a hollow and unconvincing laugh. This was the second time in less than two weeks that they had been told, "It looks worse than it is, really," the only difference being the one in bed was Ben this time.

Elizabeth usurped the moment.

"We have an incredible story to tell you that will stretch the very bounds of your belief but every word will be true we swear."

What George said next floored both of them.

"Will it go some way to explain why you have both changed so much and why there are more deaths around here than in an episode of *Midsomer Murders*?" George quizzed and shot her a knowing glance.

The look of disbelief on Elizabeth's face was epic. George continued allowing Elizabeth time to recover.

"We're not as obtuse as you seem to think. Remember my brother was involved in all this stuff before you ever came along," George's smile was provocative.

"What do you know then Uncle?" Elizabeth was still in shock at what he had just said and needed more time to compose herself.

"Not enough and little more than either you or Ralph has allowed us, but over a lifetime you can't hide it all," George looked at Jillie who nodded encouragingly. "That time in the graveyard, when you first asked me about the old ornate mirror was the moment that I knew that you had become involved in its dark secrets, just as your father was."

Elizabeth shook her head in disbelief. They had known all along. George continued.

"I always knew that Ralph was different from other people. He would know what you were thinking before you knew yourself and he was too strong for his age, far too strong. If he hurt himself he healed too quickly, so many things. But most of all he was too secretive, just as you are," his look was accusational.

It was a subtle telling off. Elizabeth was about to tell their story when Aunt Jillie interjected.

"Before you tell us Lizzie I want to know what happened to you Ben and I want to know if you're going to be alright and I want the truth this time," Aunt Jillie held Ben's hand a little tighter to encourage him.

"Well Auntie, it won't make much sense until you know the whole story so this is going to be a little back to front but I was in a fight and there was an explosion close to my face. The injuries that I have to my eyes and ears would normally be permanent but as you already know, we are not entirely normal. There is a surgeon, one of our kind, that can fix all of this and then I will be able to see and hear again. Honestly you don't have to worry."

Jillie picked up on the inconsistency straight away.

"Hear again Ben? What on Earth do you mean by that?"

"It's going to sound strange. I'm not hearing you Auntie; I'm picking up your thoughts."

Jillie pulled away at the shock of it and Elizabeth stepped in quickly.

"I think that we need to start from the beginning Auntie," Elizabeth took George and Jillie's hands. "Take Ben's hands, we're going on a *Magical Mystery Tour* that's going to take you away. Just as the Beatles said it would!"

Under the pretence of building a conservatory, Mike had arranged for several hundred dense blocks to be delivered to the Robinson's house, along with sand and cement. Cached in the deliveries was an arsenal of weapons and ammunition. Enough for a small war. Mike had doubled the guard already and it was to be re-doubled before the earliest planned attack in eight days' time. Mike had considered increasing the numbers further, but twelve would be an optimum and discrete number that could be supported in the ruse of a construction project. The six currently in operation, led by Jake were posing as builders. They never left the house, day or night though.

George had refused outright to be confined to a safe house. He was coordinating the construction of the blast walls that were to be placed three yards back from each of the principal windows upstairs and down.

319

George was somewhat of a technophobe. He had dedicated the rest of his time to helping Jake set up CCTV in all the principal routes and locations, inside and outside the house. All these fed into the control room, situated in the cellar, that was to become their own *war room*. George and Red Jake quickly became unlikely friends as they were forced together, working around the clock to achieve their goal.

On the Friday evening of the fourth day, they had completed the blast walls and their war room was operational. That left them four clear days to set up a few surprises of their own, before the earliest attack date of the Tuesday following. George and Jake were sat in the cellar that now displayed twelve functioning VDUs and a central communication unit.

"Tomorrow, we plant the explosives at the selected points and you'll detonate them here George using this console," Jake ran through the console functions. "You'll be our eyes George, the only one of us that'll see the whole picture. Your judgement and timing will either save our souls or send us to Hell."

"No pressure then?" George said in mock earnest.

"Y' know I like you George, I just hope that I still do after you've blown our bloody arses off."

It was banter. Jake was the consummate soldier and a good judge of character. He had given George the job for two reasons. Firstly because there was no one that he believed would do it better and secondly because George really wanted it. That impressed him. Jake produced a bottle of whisky and two glasses from his kit bag.

"What's it they say about all work and no play?" Jake had the devil in his eye.

"Dunno Jake, something about making hay while the sun shines isn't it?" the devil had a twin.

"Close enough," Jake let out a bawdy guffaw as he poured a couple of stiff ones. "Here's to my father, whoever he was," he said and they downed them in one.

"So what does that make you Jake?"

George took the bottle and re-charged their glasses. They downed the second.

"Your friend and the most despicable bastard you could ever meet," Red Jake laughed heartily at his own joke and prompted George. "You going to pour another drink or what?"

It was Saturday morning. They were gathered in front of the old mirror and the atmosphere was charged with expectation. Ben was out of bandages and his sightless eyes were hidden by his Oakley sunglasses. As usual, he had spent some time getting his appearance just right for May. Ben had trusted in Elizabeth to make sure that he hadn't made any colour coordination errors. She was secretly enjoying the fact that she had childishly given him one black and one pink sock.

Elizabeth held Ben's arm, giving emotional rather than physical support while. Mike, George and Jillie were there to wish Ben good luck. George and Jillie's farewells were as if they wouldn't see Ben for some time, based on their perception of it. Elizabeth needed to correct that or otherwise they would have been in for the shock of their lives.

"When we go through the portal time will appear to stop for you, as we will return to this exact time. No matter how long the operation and convalescence takes, we will be back in the same second and whatever did happen in between will be erased."

Elizabeth smiled at their astonished expressions as they looked back in disbelief. There was no way that they could truly understand the concept of time-travel and what that would mean in physical terms.

"God willing, it will be with Ben as good as new."

It was at exactly quarter past nine, that Saturday morning, when with a mocking, "Hey presto!" they stepped into the corridor of mirrors to meet Jorall.

Chapter 30

May and her parents were passing, time looking through the mirrors back into the history of their world and others. It was relaxing, after 48 hours of non-stop work preparing the theatre and stem cells for Ben's operation. May was at the far end of the corridor, when Elizabeth and Ben stepped through the portal. She immediately screamed, "Ben," and ran bare footed to them. May threw her arms urgently around him, almost taking him off his feet. She was babbling again.

"Oh Ben! I'm so sorry; I've been so scared for you. I nearly lost you. Why did you do that? I just knew you would do something stupid…"

Ben shut her up the only way that he could think of, by smothering her mouth with a kiss. May's knees gave way beneath her as she swayed confused and helpless in his arms. It had seemed to Ben like he had waited a lifetime to do that, and it felt so good. It took May a long moment to regain her self-control and she reluctantly pushed Ben away.

"If you ever do anything like that again, I swear I'll kill you myself!"

A panicked expression came over her face. She was flustered, thinking that Ben might take that the wrong way.

"No, I don't mean the kiss. Not the kiss. You can do that anytime, I mean the stupid thing that you did, the risk you took…"

May suddenly felt hugely embarrassed at her wanton behaviour in front of her parents. She was relieved that at least Ben couldn't see her blushing. Without a word being spoken, May looked back at her parents and communicated her thoughts.

"I will explain later."

The smile she received was all-knowing and confirmed that no further explanation was necessary.

May's parents greeted Ben as if they had known him for a lifetime. It occurred to Elizabeth that here in the corridor of mirrors, perhaps they already did? They spent some time discussing Ben's condition and the procedures they would use in the operation. They answered his questions and relieved his concerns so that he was completely at ease about it all. May didn't leave Ben's side throughout. It was only when Jorall said, "Can you not give the man a little space?" that she backed away petulantly.

Jorall and Zita meticulously prepared Ben for his operation. Instead of bathing him in water, he was undressed and placed in a cubicle that bathed him in a blue light that cleansed him of all bacteria. Next, they dressed him in a light cotton robe and cap before taking him into theatre.

Zita had been Jorall's assistant long before they had become romantically involved. She took Ben's blood samples, then put him through a whole body scanner and reviewed the report with Jorall. While they talked over the findings, Ben listened to their conversation. Although it was in their language, it was rapidly becoming familiar to him. Even to the point that he raised his questions in their tongue. He was continuously being amazed at the depth and complexity of the new abilities that had been bestowed on them.

Jorall was ready for his summation.

"So Ben," he began. "The operation will take about four hours for your eyes and a further three for your ears. You will then be kept sedated in a regeneration incubator for a further three days. There won't be any pain or discomfort during or after the operation, on that you can be sure of. Do you have any questions before we begin?"

"What can I expect at the end of three days? Oh, and will I be able to eat then? You've starved me for a day already."

"On the medical front, your hearing will be adequate. Full recovery however, will take another week or so while the stem cells continue to regenerate your damaged organs. All we will need to do is keep you in relative peace and quiet for a few days, which probably means away from the girls," Ben couldn't see Jorall's smile so the quip was wasted on him.

"The surgery on your eyes will be more intrusive, as the damaged organs are more complex. After three days your retinas will have regenerated and fully attached themselves and the optic nerve will be functioning again. All good news Ben and you have nothing to worry about. Your eyes will need to remain wrapped for a further week, until the healing process is complete."

Jorall was still reading the report and adding notes while he talked. He looked up at Ben and continued.

"When the bandages come off, your vision will be fully restored. We will however need to keep you in controlled conditions with a regime of antibiotics and anti-rejection treatment for a further week."

Jorall smiled thoughtfully, then teased him.

"Then you will be able to gaze into my daughter's eyes as handsomely as ever you did."

"Am I really that obvious?" Ben asked innocently.

"No Ben, but she is. She has waited more than 5,000 of your years for love Ben and you now hold the key to her heart, her hopes and her dreams. Are you big enough for that responsibility?"

Ben Replied without a moment's hesitation.

"I want that more than my sight."

The sincerity of it touched Jorall and he nodded thoughtfully.

"Perhaps you can have both Ben, perhaps both."

Jorall called May and Elizabeth to give their good luck wishes before sedating Ben. As he succumbed to the narcotic, Ben slipped into a dream filled unconsciousness, fuelled by all the mad events of the last few months.

Elizabeth and May watched in amazement from the overhead viewing gallery. They were holding hands tightly as if that could make the operation more successful.

"It does seem scary Lizzie, but this is what Dad does every day. Ben will be fine," none the less they held hands a little tighter just in case.

The operating theatre was a shining, metallic dome bathed in the same sterilising blue light that cleansed Ben during his pre-op. The operating table was like an altar in the middle of the dome, surrounded with robotic arms and medical paraphernalia that defied description. Ben was in a tank, totally immersed in a luminous green fluid that must have been oxygenated, as he breathed it in and out quite naturally. Mechanical arms worked silently and remotely, as if of their own accord and Jorall was at the control panel. Zita competently tended to Ben's vital needs, using the complex life-support system, just as she had done when she first met Jorall. The atmosphere was calm and confident. Elizabeth watched in wonderment at just how far their civilization had come. She wondered still more, that she was now part of it.

"What's happening May, why is Ben in that green liquid?"

"It's a highly oxygenated amniotic fluid Lizzie. It contains pluripotent stem cells that are able to differentiate into various types of tissue. Ben can breathe this fluid, which will sustain his oxygen needs and it's laced with an anaesthetic that will keep him free of pain. My father will make the necessary incisions via the robotic arms to affect any mechanical repairs to Ben's eyes and ears, and then the stem cells in the amniotic fluid will do the rest."

May smiled encouragingly, Elizabeth could see how immensely proud she was of her father and his skills.

"Ben will make a full recovery Lizzie I promise. Then we can all move on."

Elizabeth returned her smile.

"You love him don't you May?" she said in a matter of fact way

"As I love you Lizzie."

May replied defensively and fidgeted slightly, giving away her poor attempt at deception.

"No May, I mean that you *love* him."

May was silent for a long moment and looked sad.

"I'm not sure that I know what that is Lizzie. It's been so long for me and I'm just confused is all, perhaps scared and a little lonely."

"In love is what you are May, and yes, that feels confusing but you can't fight it. Even I already know that."

It was strange, Elizabeth thought. In these things, May could be so naïve, so immature. Their roles had reversed in this respect so that she was the big sister.

"I must fight against it Lizzie. He's so young and I am, well damaged. All I bring to anyone is danger," there was an air of hopelessness about her. "I'm cursed Lizzie and Ben deserves better. You know he does."

"Ben is no longer a boy May. What you initiated in us has grown us up. He is a man now, with wants and needs the same as you and he wants you May. Anyway, he looks the same in our years as you do in yours and his mind has advanced way beyond his years. He would die for you and you know that, as you would for him."

Elizabeth could see May's distress and she held her for a while to comfort her. Not for the first time, her thoughts turned to how complex this being in her arms truly was, a living contradiction. She was such a mixture of woman and child. Part of her had grown up strong and resourceful, able to compartmentalise her feelings, plan and fight to the death if necessary. Then there was the emotional side that had been stunted, not allowed to blossom. In these things, she had no experience or skill at all and was vulnerable and without confidence. The years of isolation had taken their toll, even on such an evolved being as May. Elizabeth knew that she would eventually give up the fight or die if she never found the love that she so craved, just as Crystalita had needed love.

Elizabeth suddenly became aware that May had been listening to her thoughts.

"Am I really such a mess Lizzie?"

"Not a mess May, but you are *damaged*. Ben can heal you if you let him, just as your father is healing him now. Sometimes we have to reach out and take help when and where we can."

May considered that for a while, then forced a confident smile.

"I have waited so long Lizzie and I can wait a little longer still. I will be fine, please don't worry about me," she had clearly decided that it was the end of the conversation.

"Perhaps you can May, perhaps. But I really don't think that Ben can."

Alexis had been uncomfortable ever since the single-handed attack on them. In fact it was before that. He recalled their initial meeting there with Eichmann and Withey, he had sensed something was wrong then, but Adolphius had distracted him. Alexis was furious with himself for not having followed his instincts through at the time. While he could accept that it was probably a spontaneous act of revenge for Withey's attack, it also begged a number of questions. Up until that point they were confident of being secure in an unknown location. If that was wrong, then who else knew about their location and how much more intel had they got on them? Potentially the flood gates were wide open.

It was dusk when Alexis stepped outside into the cool evening breeze. He cast his mind back to the night of that meeting. He recalled that he had followed Grese out of the house to where he was now and that something didn't feel right but he wasn't sure what. Stood there now, he had that same feeling that something was out there at the furthest corner of the garden. This time, it was stronger and he knew that he was being watched.

Alexis walked out into the garden aimlessly as if stretching his legs, so that if he was under surveillance, he would appear oblivious of it. He walked up the drive to the main gate without turning his head to the left or right but his black eyes were darting around taking everything in. Then he saw it, the reflection of one of the floodlights in the lens of a small camera secreted in one of the trees. Alexis walked on without showing any signs of his discovery, stretching out his long wiry arms casually as he did so.

At the end of the drive, he turned right and strolled along the fence line towards the furthest corner of the grounds. He heard what sounded like a man leaving hastily through the hedge. He maintained his casual and steady pace. At the corner, he turned right again without hesitation but his eyes had already picked up the three dents in the grass where the legs of a tripod had been, and the break in the hedge onto the road.

"Laser sound surveillance," he spat venomously. "They know everything."

Ben began to regain consciousness on the afternoon of the third day and Elizabeth was with May at his side. It was a slow awakening, as he kept drifting back into the most weird drug induced dreams. The last one was possibly the most bizarre of them all. He was walking down the corridor of mirrors and behind each was someone that he loved.

Their faces were contorted into horrific masks by the terror that consumed them. They were banging their fists against the glass screaming at him to help them get out. Ben kicked frantically at the mirrors to break them, but his kicks lacked any power. All he could do was look despairingly back at them mouthing the words, "Sorry, I'm so sorry..."

At the next mirror, Elizabeth and May were desperately screaming his name. Their hands and faces were pressed and distorted against the glass.

"Ben! Ben!" they called, terrified beyond words.

Close behind them were Withey, Alexis and Grese. They were trapped and Ben was their only hope. He charged at the mirror over and again, but it resisted him. He tried smashing at it with his fists until they bled, but that too was futile. Ben could only watch helplessly as the Shadows grabbed Elizabeth and May, pulling them back from the mirror. Their arms were pathetically extended towards him and they were still desperately screaming out his name.

"Ben! Ben it's OK we're here shush. It's OK you're safe," Elizabeth pressed his shoulders down and continued to utter soothing words.

"Lizzie! How did you escape, where's May? I'm sorry, I tried but I couldn't..."

"I'm here Ben. You were just having a bad dream. We've both been here waiting for you to come back to us," May squeezed his hand reassuringly.

"God, have I had the weirdest of dreams. I thought I'd lost you both to the Shadows," his tone reflected the depth of his relief.

Ben was still groggy from the anaesthetic and struggled to remember where he was. At last his mind cleared.

"How did it go?"

"It went very well Ben," Elizabeth assured, then couldn't help herself. "You're just a week away from seeing the girl of your dreams again."

Elizabeth gasped at the sheer force of May's elbow and withering glance.

"I think what your clumsy sister is trying to say, is that we are both really happy to have you back and that the operation went well and you are doing fine."

They talked for the next two hours. It was apparent that Ben's hearing was already as acute as it was before his new abilities had been bestowed upon him. If that was as good as it ever got, Ben would have regarded it as a result. It was the first time that the three of them had been together since their ordeals and it gave them a chance to tell their stories. As Ben had centre stage, he began by first recounting his duel with Illya Dracul. May was clearly impressed, but Ben couldn't be sure of just how much of it she already knew.

"Illya Dracul is Adolphius' son and Alexis' nephew," May began. "He will have been coached and mentored by Alexis himself, who is probably the best swordsman of all time. You did well to better him Ben."

"I would have killed Dracul if he hadn't run away like a girl!" then after a moment's thought added a caveat to his remark. "Present company excluded that is ladies," Ben used his brilliant smile to its best effect to disarm his audience.

"I'm sure you haven't completely missed your chance Ben but be careful what you wish for!" Elizabeth warned.

"Quite, no more heroics please Ben, I don't think that either of us could stand it again," May added more in optimism than belief.

Then Ben recounted the episode about his assault on the Shadow's house beginning with the police chase and how he jumped the hedge to escape them.

"It was just like Steve McQueen's motorcycle jump in *The Great Escape*. I wish you could've seen it!" Ben was really enjoying his moment of stardom and it brought out the boy in him.

"Yeah I'm sure it was great. Right up to the point where you nearly got your bloody head blown off Ben," Elizabeth pointed out sardonically.

They could all laugh about it now but a week ago it wasn't quite so funny.

"It was pretty cool actually," Elizabeth added reluctantly in admiration.

Ben beamed with pride and May was certain that he wasn't even close to having learned his lesson. They listened attentively to the full story but both, in one way or another, had lived part or all of it with him. The sprint through the minefield had the girls holding their breath. They couldn't believe that a sane person would have even considered that as an option in the first place. The final death struggle with Eichmann eclipsed the rest of the story. Ben's *shit or bust* decision to gamble all on

329

detonating the mine was all the confirmation that Elizabeth needed to prove her brother was a nut-nut.

Ben looked reflective and had to concede one thing though.

"It was a little bleak when Eichmann had me pinned down, pressing his knife into my throat. I was happy that you butted in at that point Lizzie."

"I saved your backside again Ben, just like I told you I would. Shadows snapping at your arse and all that," Elizabeth enjoyed rubbing it in.

May stepped in a little too defensively.

"We all need each other and that's how we are going to get through this."

It was a rebuke and a little possessive of her. Elizabeth let it go though. She was just happy that May felt that way about her brother.

This protective intervention was followed by a display of double standards as May took her turn to have a go at Ben.

"Did you understand nothing when I sang that song for you at Lizzie's party?" May's expression was cross and although Ben couldn't see it, he certainly felt it. "I knew that you would do something crazy like that, I just knew it."

"Guilty as charged May and I'm sorry and I know that you went through it all with me. Those words did cross my mind but I was already too committed..."

"Is there any point in asking you not to do it again?" May's tone had mellowed.

It was clear to them both how deep her feelings were for Ben.

"Can I plead the fifth amendment on that one?

Ben smiled revealing his dimples and straight white teeth. He was immediately forgiven, as usual.

It was an opportune moment for Elizabeth to change the subject and tell the story of her own encounter with Jack the Ripper. It was a complete revelation to Ben. Despite how close he and Elizabeth were, he had no idea of how desperately scared she had been for the last several years.

When Elizabeth told her story, it was clear that the scars hadn't yet healed. Even in the telling of it, she looked stricken. The fact that she owed her own survival to the maternal protection of her unborn children was deeply profound and emotional. The big shock for Ben was yet to come. He hadn't realised until then that Elizabeth had made Withey take his own life in such a violent manner.

"Two nut-nuts in the family," he thought, "but this one was not the kind to piss off."

May took their hands and smiled at them fondly.

"I'm so proud of what you've become. Already the Shadows fear you and know unquestionably, that together you have the ability to sway the balance of power back towards our kind."

May had become somehow whole again and the confident Matriarch once more. Elizabeth wondered if it had anything to do with her at last accepting her feelings towards Ben?

May's body language changed unexpectedly and she became serious. They sensed it and listened attentively, realising that what she had to say to them might prove pivotal to their chances of survival.

"In as few as three days, after you return to your place and time, you will be under siege by the combined forces of Adolphius' cell. Mike has already uncovered their plan and is preparing for that attack. It will be the mother of all battles. Your abilities have grown. You have both done some amazing things and shown outstanding resourcefulness but you are not yet ready for your mission, nor will you be in only three days. Your last encounters were successful but they required too much luck, they could equally have cost your lives."

May had to be cruel to be kind and tell it as it was. Ben had already demonstrated how dangerous over-confidence can be. She continued.

"They will somehow separate you and their experience will count in the final showdown. As things stand now, you would lose," May paused to let their mortality sink in. "But time stands still for you here. I need three months of your time, after Ben's bandages come off, to prepare you for their attack. This way, you will at least have that *fighting chance* that you spoke of Lizzie."

May smiled at them thinly through her guiltiness. She omitted to tell them that, in their absence, Mike and his men would have fought the Shadows and all souls would surely have died a terrible death at the house. Although the future would be re-written when Elizabeth and Ben returned, giving them a second chance, May knew that they would not have accepted these terms if they knew.

Ben sent Elizabeth a silent message and squeezed her hand, "All the way Sis, no matter what?"

"All the way Ben, all the way..."

The week passed quickly for all of them. May took the opportunity to reintegrate with her parents and the experience of their unconditional love made her feel complete once more. She visibly blossomed, as her self-confidence was restored. For Jorall and Zita, it was something more profound. They had known for centuries that their own world was doomed and had lived in the shadow of that. Meeting their daughter more than 5,000 years in the future, had made the prospect of what was coming feel less hopeless. Now that the conduit back to May had been proven, they had planned to maximise their time with her before the predicted asteroid impact. Time spent on Earth would be at zero cost to their own time, which meant that they could spend long periods together. In fact they could conceivable extend their lives immeasurably.

Jorall and Zita had quickly grown to love May's new friends as an extension to their own family. This was deeply enhanced in the knowledge that they were about to risk their own lives to bring Crystalita back to them. When May had told her parents, they were elated beyond words but May had to temper this later. She warned them that, although the probability of Elizabeth and Ben surviving their mission had increased, it was still less than 10%. They were stunned and humbled that the Robinsons would do this for their daughter, even though it was only as part of a greater plan to bring back other loved ones.

May's parent's couldn't help but notice that May had special feelings for Ben but also deep guilt and misgivings over them. After considerable reluctance to talk about it, May finally bared her heart to them.

"He's so young and I'm so old it doesn't seem right, not here on Earth anyway," May began.

Jorall immediately countered her statement and put the situation into perspective.

"You are in uncharted territory May. From the moment you made the decision to awaken their Angel genes, you committed them to accelerated evolution. You cannot any longer measure their mental and physical maturity in human years."

May knew what her father was saying was right, but she needed to hear it from him. It was beginning to make sense to her and she conceded at last.

"Yes, but it's not just that Dad. I bring danger and death to everybody that I love or have ever loved," her despair was palpable. "I already love him too much and if things get more involved and I lost him, well I just wouldn't be able to go on."

Jorall considered what May had said carefully before replying and folded her in his strong arms as he did so. It was something that she had missed for what seemed an eternity. It felt so good and the smell of him was nostalgic and emotive.

"You are also still young in our terms May and your forced isolation has stunted your emotional development. I can see you are confused and probably out of your comfort zone for only the second time in your life. The first being when you left Angelos, but you cannot deny yourself love. Your friends were in mortal danger even before you met them. You are not the cause May, but you are their hope for salvation. From what I can see, they would already have been assassinated but for your intervention. They need you every bit as much as you need them."

Jorall held his daughter at arm's length to look into her eyes.

"You live but once little one, and you only take your experiences and memories on to eternity. Bank your dreams, they will be all that you have and your regrets will be your nightmares. You alone can choose which of these Ben will be for you."

May looked into her father's eyes that were as deep blue as the ocean. She knew there and then which it would be.

It was Saturday morning and Alexis had called another extraordinary meeting of the cell. They were gathered in the war room in front of the whiteboard, waiting for him to address them. The atmosphere was tense. Alexis would certainly have something profound to say and they sensed it in him. He had deliberately waited until the morning, so that their observers would not be suspicious and make the connection between this meeting and his walk in the gardens the previous evening.

Alexis began to write on the whiteboard without speaking.

'We are being watched and recorded and must assume that the enemy already knows our plan.'

They exchanged glances but remained quiet. Adolphius got up and crossed over to the board taking another marker pen.

'Abort the plan?'

Alexis shook his head and wrote again.

'No accelerate it, double the force. Increase squads to twelve and spread disinformation that we are doing the opposite. They are expecting Tuesday earliest. Can we accelerate to tomorrow morning?'

Each of them nodded positively. Alexis wrote his final comment.

'OK we will start the meeting now. Just go along with a deferment initiative and be vocal.'

Alexis asked each of them in turn for a progress report. One after another, they painted a picture of technical difficulties and resource problems. At last Alexis summed up the situation.

"So it seems that none of you have achieved your objectives. You are fortunate that Eichmann is not around to hear it, or you would have felt his wrath!" Alexis continued in the theatrical and then added, "You have two weeks and then we go in. Don't disappoint me again!" Alexis left the room and slammed the door in fake rage.

The SAS operator ripped off his earphones at the painful sound of the slamming door but he had already heard enough. He quickly closed down his surveillance equipment and silently left the grounds to report the new deferred attack date. He had completely missed their subterfuge and was about to feed the intended disinformation back to Mike.

There was an air of expectancy amongst them. They were all stood around Ben while Jorall slowly removed the bandages from his eyes. The lighting was purposely subdued to reduce the shock on the delicate photosensitive cells of Ben's new retinas.

"Perfect," whispered Elizabeth almost to herself as the last wrap fell away. "Just perfect," her relief was echoed by them all.

Ben brought the world slowly into focus and his eyes immediately fell on May. She had chosen to dress for him as she had done in one of their first meetings. Her skin of brilliant diamonds and sapphires, combined with her own bioluminescence, lit her up so that at first he couldn't fathom out what he was looking at. The shimmering image, with a mane of spun-gold, began to take human shape as his eyes focussed. Moments later Ben realised that it could only be one person on this planet, the one that he desperately wanted. He stretched out his arms and called her to him. May was shaking with anticipation when he took her in his strong arms.

"You are the most beautiful creature that I have ever seen May. I had almost forgotten just how lovely you truly are. The perfect image to be my first with my new eyes," then without the slightest hint of embarrassment he added. "Can I ask that you still be there with me when I see my last?" Ben flashed a cheeky smile that clearly hit May in an almost physical way.

She was noticeably flustered. Once she had composed herself, she diverted and avoided her direct response.

"Well you will have to ask my father," she teased and pecked him on the mouth which was a big yes as far as Ben was concerned. "But don't let the two occasions be too close together; please!"

"Yuck!" Elizabeth said in mock disdain. "Can't you at least wait until you are alone?" it wasn't jealousy but she suddenly really missed Mike.

Thankfully Jorall brought the matter back to business.

"Excuse me, but the patient is not yet discharged. Now will you kindly leave the room while Zita and I conduct our examination? Thank you."

They spent the next hour running a variety of tests and scans to prove Ben's audio-visual responses. Jorall described his progress as, "More than satisfactory". In fact it was better than that. Ben had made near complete recovery. Such were the wonders of the advanced Angel medical techniques and Ben's own powers of regeneration.

Jorall took the opportunity to have a *father and son* talk with Ben before discharging him.

"You have made it clear to all that you are rather fond of our daughter Ben and it would appear that your feelings are reciprocated," Jorall looked up from his notes to catch Ben's reaction.

Ben was surprisingly relaxed with his response. But then it was hard to take a fellow Angel by surprise as they have certain communication advantages.

"It's true from my part, but then not so clear to me about May's feelings. I think that she has deep reservations."

"Perhaps so and you have none?" probed Jorall.

"None whatsoever Jorall. Those that I did have were to do with my age but the speed that I've changed, grown up if you like, has closed that gap. After meeting your daughter, there just couldn't be anyone else for me; ever."

May had been on his mind every day since he met her. She was perfection in Ben's mind.

"She doesn't even have a clue about how special and lovely she really is. It's almost perfect naivety," Ben added.

"What you say is true Ben. She has beauty and power but she will be a big responsibility too. Her importance to the survival of our race is pivotal. As powerful as May is, she is also emotionally fragile and immature. Could you give her the strength to be all that she needs to be?"

Ben's response was unequivocal.

"Nobody can be sure of the future Jorall, not even May with the power of the portals. I do know that I would die for her trying though."

"I believe you Ben. How you got yourself into this operating theatre in the first place, is testament to that. As for May's reservations, I believe they are receding but she will need time, months perhaps even years. Could you cope with that?"

Ben's reply was philosophical.

"I have no choice Jorall because I love her. I had no choice from the day I met her."

Chapter 31

It was late summer. The Grecian evenings near Mount Olympus were still warm and balmy. The three of them were sat on the rock that had become their natural meeting place. They were talking about all they had achieved over the last two and a half months with May refining their skills, readying them for their imminent fight against the Shadows. Although this in itself constituted amazing progress, it was still insignificant compared to power that still lay within them, yet to discovered.

May decided that they were at last ready to know the full extent of the Angels' powers over Nature. Up until now, they would have been shocked at the destructiveness that was within her; within them all. So far, they had seen May as something more than a mortal, but much less than a god. However after tomorrow, they might well reappraise that divide. May had planned a demonstration to awaken their minds to the magnitude of their ability to affect Nature, almost placing them amongst the mythical gods of this very Greece. A vision was forming in her mind and it was founded on a distant memory.

"What better place could there be to display this might than Mount Olympus itself?" May thought, "The fabled Seat of Zeus, king of gods, god of the sky and thunder and ruler of Olympus!"

They left the mother ship before dawn the following morning to embark on the 20 hour hike to Mytikas, the highest peak of Mount Olympus. It was an arduous, but non-technical hike that ended in a final challenging climb from Skala to the fabled palace of the Dodekatheon, or Twelve Olympian Gods. Mytikas, in mythological days, was the top of the then known world and commanded the dread of all in Greece. Along the way, they stopped and enjoyed the views across the 52 peaks that constituted the massif itself. They extended across the border of Thessaly and Macedonia, looking out towards Thessaloniki, Greece's second largest city.

May told them her first hand stories of how the myths were first implanted into the minds of the then primitive Greek people.

"Belief in the gods has always been a way to control the direction of primitive races," she began. "We used it here some eight centuries before the birth of Christ. It was a tool that the Patriarchs used for the better good. At the same time, the Shadows were corrupting people's religious beliefs to control them and gain power."

May was momentarily sad and reflective and seemed to be lost in her memories.

"You still see examples of this all around you with Al Qaeda and Islamists, but any faith can be manipulated by them. This was also the case in the Catholic Inquisitions that spanned six centuries. The Shadows had infiltrated the Vatican, resulting in the torture and execution of millions of innocent humans and Angels," the memory clearly pained May and again she seemed lost. "But I digress. Through implanting the belief of all seeing and all powerful gods, we were able play out the scenarios of all human emotion. Give them a code of conduct, if you like. All wrapped up in a wonderful story."

May became pensive again as she led them ever upwards towards Olympus. Ben watched her as she led them up the track that had been etched into the mountain by the hooves of myriad goats over the millennia. May moved gracefully and effortlessly and Ben was lost in her. She turned suddenly and caught him looking at her and smiled knowingly at him. There was just the hint of a smirk on her face. Ben realised that his mind had wandered, perhaps inappropriately and he was embarrassed. He had been found out. He never saw the smile of joy that was on May's face when she turned away from him though.

May subconsciously quickened the pace spurred on by the fillip of Ben's idle thoughts and she continued her story.

"In Greek mythology, the ruling powers were the Titans. They were a primeval race of powerful deities, descended from Heaven and Earth that ruled in the legendary Golden Age. They were huge immortal beings, all powerful that none challenged. Not until Zeus and his eleven siblings dared to confront them in a war that lasted ten years. It became known as the War of Gods and they became the Twelve Olympian Gods who took dominion over the world."

They had reached the lesser summit of Skala and looked up to their destination, the summit of Mytikas. May pointed towards it and reminisced.

"The Palace of Zeus stood there once," she began. "I was there 2,800 years ago with Crystalita and ten others of Patriarch descent. We staged an act of the gods before an audience of more than 500 people that were stood right here where we are now. It was the birth of their belief in the Olympian Gods. Homer the famous philosopher and another of the Patriarchs, was there too. He recorded the event and those writings have lasted to this day."

The memory had clearly brought back happy thoughts as May's skin began to glow in that tell-tale way that gave insight to her inner being.

"Homer's works went on to become models in persuasive speaking and writing that were emulated throughout the ancient and Medieval Greek worlds. They influenced behavioural patterns and thinking over the next three thousand years."

"What did you do that inspired the Greeks to believe you?" Elizabeth was captivated. It was beyond her imagination that May could have been there so long ago.

"We shook heaven and earth is what we did but that is for later!"

May's smile was mischievous. She knew that she had raised their expectations and left them unfulfilled. They would be rewarded soon though. May hurried them on.

"Come on we must get there before dark."

May quickened the pace still further and continued to enjoy Ben's eyes on her as she led them up the final leg of their journey. She could hear them chattering together, trying to make sense of it all and it amused her.

May began to sing, which further demonstrated her happiness. Her enchanting voice rang out clearly in the rarefied mountain air and reflected back from the mountainous peaks that surrounded them. Her voice brought them peace and raised their spirits. Elizabeth and Ben were consumed by the natural beauty surrounding them, whilst still being charged with a mixture of expectancy and dread.

It was dusk when they finally reached the summit. They stood there on what would once have been considered the top of the world, marvelling at the lesser peaks that clawed their way up into the low mountain cloud. They could feel an almost holiness about the place, as if the myths had left their mark there for all time. The Nightjars were singing, hailing the coming of the night and their song was a cacophony of voices. May spread her arms palms down to invite them to sit and hear her story.

"On that day, we took on the roles of the Twelve Olympians. We were dressed like the gods that we represented. Crystalita was Aphrodite, daughter of Zeus, goddess of love, beauty, and desire. I remember how thrilled she was to get the part and how fittingly she played it. I was another daughter of Zeus, Athena. She was the virgin goddess of wisdom, defence and strategic warfare. So like me don't you think?" May laughed like a school girl, "The virgin bit has been a little hard to handle at times though."

She shot Ben a glance that caused him to blush uncontrollably and Elizabeth to fall off the rock that they were sat on.

"Penny for your thoughts Ben," Elizabeth teased without the need for words, leveraging the moment.

"Boil your head Sis."

Ben couldn't help himself from smiling though. He was much relieved when May continued her story, without labouring the point.

"We had taken some of the elders and scholars of Athens with us to this summit to recount what they had seen with their own eyes. Each of these became believers and priests after what they saw."

May was eking it out painfully. Elizabeth and Ben had become desperate for the climax. It was particularly too much for Elizabeth, with the impatience and curiosity of women.

"May! Just tell us what happened here 2,800 years ago that was *so* important for you to bring us to this place."

Elizabeth's expression was imploring but May was not going to be hurried.

"The twelve of us shook the very foundations of Mount Olympus itself, that's what happened! But why should I tell you when I can show you?" May's manner was theatrical now adding to their suspense.

"Show us?" Elizabeth could see nothing but the heavens and the mountains. "Show us what, where?"

"Show you what power lies within us that we can summon at will!"

May stretched her arms up above her head and began to circle them slowly. The Nightjars silenced immediately and sped off on urgent wings, sensing that something malevolent and dangerous was about to happen.

At first they thought they were imagining it, but soon they were sure. A light breeze had picked up swirling around them centred on May. Black tendrils of hair began to flick around her temples and she began to glow like the embers of a fire being encouraged by the wind. Slowly, almost indiscernibly, she increased the speed of her circling arms. The wind picked up accordingly until they were in a vortex that drove a plume of dust up into the sky. May now glowed red hot like the coals in a furnace. It had become scary. Elizabeth and Ben clung together to resist the wind, but more particularly, for the reassurance it gave them.

May appeared to be in a trance. The wind increased to hurricane force at the outside of the vortex and clouds began to appear in the skies above them, forming a dense black thunderhead. May's hair was now swirling around her face in a wild frenzy. Minutes later, hailstones the size of golf balls began to fall as thunder rumbled around the peaks of Olympus. They watched in awe as May became a white beacon of light. Then, when it happened, Elizabeth and Ben were paralysed with fear. It was biblical! Bolts of lightning came from her palms, fire and brimstone, smiting the rock wherever she pointed splitting huge boulders into gravel. It felt like the day of reckoning; Armageddon!

She called them to her. At first they wouldn't go for fear of their lives but her call was not a request, it was a command that they couldn't disobey. They walked to her obediently and took the hands that she offered them and were instantly engulfed in the same brilliant white light.

"Give me your minds!" May screamed above the deafening roar of the wind.

When they did, the earth shook violently beneath them and rented asunder, leaving deep crevices that could swallow a man. May had made her point and she let the storm subside until all was calm and they were left clinging together breathlessly. Nobody spoke.

They were drained beyond exhaustion and slipped to the floor where they lay amongst the melting hailstones. Despite the coldness, they slept there until the sun rose above the peaks drenching them in her warm rays.

Ben was the first to awaken. There had been a frost overnight and he was chilled to the bone. He was confused and disorientated, still in that zone somewhere between sleep and awake. He wondered whether it had all been a dream. His eyes could just make out the newly broken boulders and the deep crevices in the bedrock that they had wreaked, decimating the landscape, proof of what had happened.

He squinted in the half-light and looked at the fragile creature that lay there with him. She was a paradox. May had the gentleness and compassion of a saint, mixed with the dreadful power of destruction and ruthlessness of Zeus himself. Ben realised for the first time just how deeply in love he was with her and he had a crushing urge to hold her to him. He picked May up easily and cradled her in his arms. She was completely unaware, just as children are when you pick them up in sleep. May's skin was still warm to touch.

"Part of her advanced physiology," Ben thought idly.

It prompted him to think about the violent storm that she had created and the destruction that she had caused. It was impossible to fathom. Her science and evolution was beyond human bounds of understanding. The rule book no longer applied, nor had any meaning, it had to be discarded but for what?

It was at that moment that Ben fully understood why May had taken them there. It was because there was no rule book, she was showing them that. The rules were theirs to make and theirs alone. She was telling them that their limitations were only those that they gave themselves.

"Yes Ben that's why she has brought us here," Elizabeth had woken and was watching him, listening to his thoughts.

His eyes were still struggling in the low morning sun. Elizabeth continued where he left off.

"She is preparing us for what we must do and the self-belief and imagination that we will need to do it. But it has cost her Ben, cost her dearly. Just look at her."

Ben nearly dropped May at the shock of what he saw. Her thick lustrous black hair was now brittle and shot through with grey. Wrinkles had appeared at the corners of her eyes and lips and her skin had lost its youthful shine. The morning sun was falling unkindly on her aged face. Tears flowed down Ben's face in rivulets. He felt like he had been kicked in the stomach. May had sacrificed so much for their enlightenment, far too much for Ben.

"No!" Ben shouted holding May up towards the heavens as if begging the Gods to make it not so.

May's eyes flickered open and she put her hand to his face and smiled at him.

"Shush don't cry for me Ben, I'm tired is all and I have never been happier," her smile was still as beautiful as ever it was, even though she had lost her youth. "I'm happy because you now both have my gift, a part of me that might make the difference in your darkest hour. Things will become clearer to you now and you will learn faster. If the gods are kind then you will return to me. I pray that it be so."

Neither Elizabeth or Ben could bring themselves to tell May about the physical change that she had undergone and seemed unaware of. The next few minutes seemed an eternity. May, however, had assumed that their quietness was down to their coming to terms with all that had happened.

She left them to it. May went down the mountain to recharge their water bottles from the crystal clear water that percolated through the fissures in the bedrock. On the way she foraged for berries and roots until she had sufficient for the three of them, singing happily as she went. She was oblivious to the trauma that her body had suffered.

Elizabeth and Ben sat huddled together for warmth and comfort, watching the sun chase the night shadows away. The shock of what had happened was profound and Elizabeth had become philosophical. She pointed at the orange globe in front of them.

"That would have been Helios, the Titan god of the sun, before the War of Gods when Apollo took power under Zeus."

Elizabeth recalled her learning's from the project that she had done on Greek history at school.

"The power of darkness and god of the underworld would have been Hades, who was banished from Olympus by his brother Zeus."

It reminded Ben of a poem that their father had written for Elizabeth when she was a little girl.

"Lizzie, do you remember that when you were studying Greek mythology, Dad was away for weeks at a time and he sent you a poem to help your imagination? What was it called?"

Ben asked the question, even though he already knew the answer. It was just to distract them from the grief that they were both feeling for May.

"It was The *Battle of the Titans*. Do you think he knew that I would be here one day?"

"I think I would believe anything right now Lizzie. Not even the impossible is anymore. So much has happened to us since then Lizzie, so much," Ben wondered how much was still to come and it chilled him to the very depths of his soul. "Can you still remember the words?"

"I'll remember them forever Ben. I used to say them to myself at night to ward off the evil dreams through those dark and desperate *Withey* nights. It was as if the words would call Dad back to come and protect me."

Elizabeth began. Her emotions were a mixture of happiness and sorrow as she spoke the words:

"In the stillness of the evening the battle rages on,

'Tween advancing soldiers of darkness and the weakened falling sun.

At last the fight is over and Lord Darkness takes his throne,

While the sun lies bleeding in the winter skies banished, all alone.

No more the warming golden rays that kept cruel frost at bay,

His icy whiteness freed at last to swiftly engulf his prey.

So crushing is his victory, there's no will left to fight,

All things on Earth have thus become, prisoners of the night.

When it seems there is no hope and no one hears their plight,

The night is torn by spears and swords of brilliant, blinding light.

Dawn has come! The rescue sure, salvation now in sight,

As night gathers up his cloak of darkness and scurries off in flight.

The sun is borne in skies serene, the day begins anew.

The cruel clasp of frost's wintry grip now gently turns to dew.

As life awakes, with smiles and songs and children at their play,

Rejoice mankind Rejoice! Is dawned another day."

"That was beautiful Lizzie and so appropriate right now."

May applauded. She had arrived without them even noticing as they were lost in the words of the poem, the magnificent sunrise and their sadness for May.

"I know that your father loved you very much Lizzie, and that those words would've been written with you in his heart. They are special Lizzie, very special."

Elizabeth nodded her acknowledgement and smiled back at May, but she couldn't trust herself to speak. Her emotions were running far too high.

May laid the bizarre collection of fruits and tubers in front of them. Elizabeth and Ben ate cautiously at first and then enthusiastically.

"Mm it's really good May, well if you don't look at it that is," Elizabeth conceded, finding her voice at last.

She was now over the initial shock of May's demonstration and ready to talk.

"What happened to us last night and what has happened to you now?"

May looked puzzled at first and then shocked as she read their thoughts. She pulled her long hair in front of her face and looked aghast at the change that had taken place. Its lustrous, silky blackness had gone and it was now dry, lifeless and grey. She felt her face then looked at the back of her hands. Her jaw dropped in horror, she had always known that it could happen with the exertion of what she had done, but the extent of her aging was more than a thousand years in her terms. She looked up at them in desolation.

"I don't look good in the mornings," she said lamely and forced a pathetic smile, which melted almost immediately. "I look like a witch, don't I?" she asked and began sobbing.

They came to her side to comfort her and Ben tried to be reassuring.

"No May just different."

"Oh Ben!" May threw her arms around his neck and clung to him urgently. "I'm so sorry I've spoilt everything for us. That was so stupid. How will you ever be able to forgive me?"

May was shaking violently with the grief and shock of it; mourning the death of all that could have been.

"There's nothing to forgive May. Everything that you've ever done has been to give us the best possible chance of survival. It's us that owe you May, you have enlightened us please believe that. Nothing has changed," Ben implored.

May looked Ben directly in the eye and smiled at him thinly.

"Yes it has Ben. You will never look at me again, the way that you did when we were climbing the mountain. And you will never again have the thoughts of me that you were thinking."

Her words hit Ben like a physical blow. He put his head in his hands to stifle the sobs. May's heart went out to him and she put her hand on his shoulder to comfort him.

"But we will be best friends Ben, always."

Chapter 32

It was seven o'clock in the morning. Demitri Papandreou was on the balcony of his luxury town house in Thessaloniki, breakfasting in his white silk robe as was usual. The five million Euro house looked out southwards across the foothills that grew into the peaks that finally formed Mount Olympus itself. The sun was low in the south eastern skies bathing him in a warm orange light. His *aide-de-camp* poured the hot sweet Turkish coffee and passed him the morning paper, along with his journal.

"Your observations have been confirmed in today's Athens News *Kyrie*. Apparently they felt the tremor even there. It has prompted immediate fears of an eruption," his aide was fidgeting, clearly worried about it himself.

"They are all fools Vassos, just like you. If the gods really existed, their laughter would be heard like thunder across the heavens," Demitri exuded power, corrupt power and his aide was humble in his presence.

"Olympus is not volcanic and this was not an act of nature! Get the Hydra on the phone I want to talk to her immediately."

The order had an immediate impact on the young blonde and fair skinned Vassos, a withdrawn but able young man. He left in dread of the call that he had to make. Nobody made demands of the Hydra!

Demitri turned his powerful telescope on the fabled mountain. At a distance of some 60 miles, he had no expectations of seeing anything. It helped to focus his mind though.

Demitri was tall and muscular in the middle of his age. Black stubble darkened his strong chin and he was ruggedly handsome. There was a hint of Arab in his psyche that further fuelled his inherent chauvinism. This was not a man to confront, much less to disobey. Greece was, and always had been, a perfectly corruptible country. Plenty of bureaucracy, no functioning justice system, laws with numerous loopholes and an already corrupt Government.

Demitri was directly related to the former Premier Andreas Papandreou. He was the founder of Pasok, the most infamous political mafia on Earth. The Pasok Mafiosi initiated their own impunity and immunity through government cronyism. They were operating way beyond the law, which ironically also happened to be on the payroll. In the latest phase of embezzlement, Demitri and his cronies had relieved the Greek Treasury of more than 300 billion Euros, including international bailouts from the IMF and ECB, leaving Greece bankrupt. This money was distributed across 2,062 separate Swiss bank accounts, comprising only a part of the trillion Euro scandal. The Hydra enjoyed a 50% cut of all illegal gain as funding towards the greater initiative of globalised financial control. Demitri's undeniable success placed him in great favour with her.

Vassos was still trembling from his ordeal when he returned. He proffered the phone to his master and his relief to be rid of it was palpable as Demitri took it from his slim well-manicured hand.

"Hydie! It's been so long, you've been neglecting me for months and I'm hurt," this familiar and disrespectful address would have meant a death sentence to any other man but Demitri was not just any other man.

"Age has not diminished your charm *agápe mou* and neither your insolence," she laughed girlishly enjoying his flirtatiousness. It reminded her of how it was in their youth.

Things could have turned out so differently, she mused and with some regret. The Hydra had to consciously pull herself together. She hated herself for still letting him have that effect on her.

"You haven't called to flatter me, so what is it Demitri?"

Demitri smiled to himself and it was a smile of deep satisfaction. He was still special to her, he could tell. She wasn't over him nor ever would be. As father of her son, they would have a special bond for all time.

"No, my love; I will reserve that for another day. You can count on it."

He knew that she would be smiling, enjoying being charmed. The thought of it aroused him. He still remembered how stunningly beautiful she was in her day.

"There was a happening last night Hydie. One that you should be aware of," Demitri paused just long enough to manipulate the response that he was after.

"Don't spoon feed me Demitri, and save your flirting for those drab girls in Athens. Now get on with it!"

Demitri took brief pleasure in his success at goading her and then came directly to the point.

"Do you recall the last time that we were on Mount Olympus Hydie, and what happened there?"

The Hydra's eyes softened as the memory came back to her and her pulse quickened.

"Do you mean when we conceived our son Anaxis? But that was more than 1,000 years ago."

Demitri put his hand over the mouthpiece of the phone and cursed his own clumsiness.

"I beg your pardon Hydie but I was referring to the time before that. It was in the presence of the Patriarchs, the Twelve Olympians."

Demitri's indirect reference to their late son was unsettling for the Hydra. She kept her own council, forcing Demitri to continue.

"We were stood on the lesser peak of Skala, looking up at Mytikas, to where they performed the act of the *Wrath of the Gods.*"

"Go on," encouraged the Hydra.

"Last night, at about ten o'clock there was a reoccurrence. It was not of the same magnitude, but the aftershock was felt as far away as Athens."

"That bitch has left the safety of the mother ship again and she's showing off to those spoilt brats!" there was no longer any trace of softness in her manner.

"What would you have me do *agápe mou*?" the question was purely rhetorical.

"Kill them! Kill them all, just as she killed our son. Avenge Anaxis for me!"

Vassos had already anticipated his master's next move and had set up a videoconference in the den. He had three Senators on hold and their cells on standby. It was now nearly eight o'clock. Demitri knew that their window of opportunity was numbered in hours only and even minutes were valuable. He took his place at the conference table, without acknowledging the diligence and foresight of his aide. This off-handedness was entirely business as usual and Vassos had got used to it.

Demitri was now cleanly shaven, commanding and debonair in an almost piratical way. Vassos looked at his master and had to hide the crush that he had on him. It wasn't only women who found him irresistible. Demitri was a ruthless killer, unscrupulous businessman and a danger to all women. They were drawn to him helplessly, like moths to a flame. His countless conquests all despised themselves for it afterwards, but they never despised him.

Demitri initiated the conference. His screen split into four, each of them occupying one quarter. They were local cells and all of them cutthroats. Demitri's problem wasn't to get them to kill, only to get them to work together as a team.

Demitri got straight to the point and made his opening address.

"There is no time for niceties. We have a rare opportunity, one that hasn't presented itself in the last millennium. Maelströminha has left the mother ship and is right now somewhere on or around Mount Olympus."

There was a nervous shuffling amongst the attendees. They all knew what was coming. They were going to war against a legend and it was probably a death sentence for them.

"It is likely that she is not alone, probably with Ralph Robinson's teenagers. You all know the father only too well and just to make you pay a little more attention, these two together are almost as dangerous as Maelströminha herself."

None ventured to reply and all were waiting to hear the price tag that went with their obvious task.

"We know that she, or more probably they, were at the Seat of Zeus last night. The tremor that you will have felt was caused by Maelströminha there and we assume that it was as some kind of initiation of the Robinsons," Demitri paused to let them calculate the value of the task ahead of them. Greed always fuelled their appetites.

"An act of this magnitude will have depleted her. It is likely that they will have stayed the night on the mountain, so they are probably starting their return to the mother ship even as we speak. We know that the ship is secreted to the south of Olympus and probably no more than 100 kilometres from it. You will need to secure all roads and tracks leaving southwards. They will need water, so include any natural springs or brooks in your plans,"

Demitri could see that they were ready to know the price that was associated with the risk that they were about to take.

"The bounty on the heads of each of these is ten billion Euros."

The effect on his audience was monumental and Demitri's eyes were smiling at it but his face remained implacable. Yiorgos Zacharias was the first to find his voice while the others were still blown away by the enormity of the bounty.

He was an insignificant man, short and stocky with long hair, balding pate and shifty eyes. He had none of the attributes that you might associate with a shipping tycoon, but nothing entered or left Greece by sea or air without suffering from a hefty *Zacharias tax*. This man was one of the richest men on Earth. He posed his question.

"I am assuming that the sum is payable to each of us, irrespective of who *pulls the trigger* so to speak?" Yiorgos was pushing out the boundaries of opportunity.

Demitri's eyes narrowed. He hated greed when it wasn't his own and this man was his equal in wealth.

"You assume correctly Yiorgos. You will all share in the bounty at the going rate if you succeed," Demitri grinned sadistically and added, "just as you will all share the death penalty if you don't"

None of them doubted it and there was suddenly an air of uneasiness about them.

"Your window of opportunity is certainly less than 24 hours. Don't fail me!"

Demitri cut the call.

The downhill return to the mother ship was much more arduous than the climb. It was illogical but the pain in their hearts was tangible and weighed heavily upon them. In their own ways, Elizabeth and Ben were trying to come to terms with what had happened to May, but neither had the courage to approach her and discuss it. Finally Ben couldn't stand the strain any longer. He had to ask her outright.

"Why did you do that May? Didn't you know the risk that you were taking?"

May didn't look at Ben when she replied as she couldn't bear to have his eyes upon her.

"I miscalculated Ben. I wanted to show you what your possibilities were to make you believe in yourselves but I took it too far," May continued to look ahead, denying Ben her presence; shutting him out. "The special things that we do, take a toll on us Ben. We have powers of regeneration that quickly rejuvenate us and the younger we are the more quickly we regenerate."

May forced herself to look at Ben, struggling to not let herself break down with the finality of what she was about to say.

"You need to understand that Angels age exponentially and in the final third of our lives we don't regenerate at all. I misjudged the effort needed to create such destruction and I have taken myself past the point of regeneration. This is now the best that I will ever look."

May involuntarily hid her face so that they couldn't see the profound guilt and shame that she was feeling. She looked even more desolate than she had before. The burden of what she was about to say was insupportable.

"Much worse than this Ben, I've sentenced the Angel race to death by an act of my own stupidity."

The enormity of her mistake caused May to choke on her next words.

"I will be barren now, and there will be no mothering of the new race, no renewal just death and destruction."

"No May there must be something. Maybe your father..." Ben was desperate and clutching at straws.

May cut him off cruelly.

"My father's a doctor Ben, not a bloody magician! Now grow up and get used to it like I'll have to," she turned away and ran on ahead to distance herself.

Ben was about to run after her, when Elizabeth grabbed his arm.

"No Ben, that's not the way. She's hurting and needs to be alone. May will hate herself for what she just said. Give her time, that's all she needs for now, space and time."

"I still love her Lizzie. It doesn't matter what's happened I can live with that."

Elizabeth could tell that he really meant it, "I think you could Ben, I really do. But I don't think that May can."

Elizabeth and Ben walked together, with May far ahead and out of sight. The conversation was strained and they couldn't be objective about anything. Each attempt at positivity ended in the heartbreak that they were both feeling for May. It was dusk when they finally found her curled up in the foetal position, asleep under a tree. Her ravaged face was evidence that she had cried herself to sleep there.

They decided not to wake her. Sleep would be the thing that she would need most to be able to cope, so they lay beside her and huddled to keep her warm. Elizabeth succumbed to a death-like sleep almost immediately, seeking solace in oblivion but Ben couldn't shut down he was searching for a solution.

"It couldn't end like this," he thought, "it just couldn't!"

Ben went over everything that had happened since they met May, looking for some glimmer of hope. Some tangible happening that he could build on. Everything led to a dead end but then suddenly the idea struck him.

"Wake up Lizzie, wake up!" Ben shook her urgently.

Just for a moment she thought it was Withey.

"God Ben you scared the crap out of me! What the hell's the matter?"

"You're going to think I'm crazy but we can fix her. It's not hopeless, not hopeless at all."

"Ben you've been dreaming. Go back to sleep," Elizabeth snuggled a little closer to May and put her arm protectively over her.

"No Lizzie I'm serious, listen to me! Why did May take us to the top of Mount Olympus?"

"You know the answer to that already Ben," Elizabeth was becoming impatient.

"Humour me," Ben urged.

"To show us the magnitude of the power that's within us."

"Yes and what is it that limits us and what are the rules?" Ben was pressing her to shake off her sleepiness and engage.

"Only our imagination and self-belief limit us. There are no rules, you know that."

Elizabeth was irritated by Ben's persistence. She was still desperately tired and confused and needed to sleep.

"Precisely Lizzie, we make the rules. We are the gods if you like; the Olympians," Ben was becoming almost fanatical as his vision was unfolding. "May told us that we live in our own reality tunnels and the limits of our understanding are only the limits that we impose on ourselves within our own tunnels, based on our limited experience and vision."

The full understanding of their situation was only just precipitating on Ben. He was almost diagnosing and inventing as he was going along.

"The truth is only as we see it Lizzie; in the eye of the beholder if you like. If we witness it, then it's true and if we don't then it may never have even happened. We never accept or explore the possibilities of what could have happened. May takes us beyond that. Her powers are a result of both her evolution and her ability to expand and exploit science and reality, exploring those infinite possibilities that she told us of. Now we need to liberate our perception of reality by accepting possibility and meet her in the new world that she has created for us.

We've already proven our power over physical systems, people's minds, and even the chemistry of our own bodies; like self-healing and regeneration. If you take that to its logical conclusion then we can apply that to other people's bodies too, May's for example. We are limitless."

"Go on Ben," Elizabeth was beginning to see the possibilities and was now wide awake and fully engaged.

"When we first met May, she somehow stimulated our dormant Angel genes to change our physiology resulting in the people that we have now become. She must have altered our genetic code by using the power of her mind alone. There was no physical intervention so it had to be that. Then, when we were in that hospital dying from the snake venom, she appeared in our minds, remember? She said that all we needed to create antivenom, was already in the chemicals and molecules of our own bodies. All we needed to do was to open our minds to that possibility and make it happen."

Ben was still thinking the detail through.

"What if we joined the power of our minds with May's and evoked the possibility of repairing her damaged DNA from within her and then we stimulate her own ability to rejuvenate. Expanding reality... perhaps? It would be almost like creating stem cells to promote new growth. We could turn back the clock... maybe?"

Ben began to lose his confidence, afraid that it was just a desperate wish and he began to doubt his own propaganda. It was Elizabeth's turn to be positive.

"Yes Ben maybe, all we would need to do is bring her back from the brink, wind back the years to where her own body could take over. Success might depend on how much she miscalculated; how far past her ability to regenerate she took herself. You mustn't hold out too much hope though."

Ben cut Elizabeth off in mid-sentence.

"No Lizzie you're still missing the point. It's all about self-belief. The rules are ours to make, we have to push the boundaries until we finally find our limits, if indeed they exist. Until then we must believe that *everything* is possible otherwise it just won't work, and that includes giving May back her youth."

They spent the next hour discussing the possibilities and how they might do it. After lengthy debate they concluded that it would be much the same as how Ben had done it in the hospital for them, just by believing and focussing his mind on the task. The rest seemed to be automated. The only difference this time, would be that they would join together first, begin the process, and then bring in the immense power of May's mind. In truth they hadn't a clue, but they now trusted that their minds and bodies did.

"Are you ready?" Ben asked and Elizabeth nodded.

Their hearts were pounding as the adrenaline began to pour into their bloodstreams.

"OK Lizzie focus on what success looks like. Picture May just as she was at your party and I will do the same."

"Here goes everything then Ben."

With that, they linked hands and took the sleeping May's doll like hands into theirs. Their minds began interacting with each other. At first Ben took the lead taking them to a higher state of consciousness. Then Elizabeth's mind morphed into his, increasing their combined brain power exponentially until their brain activity became so intense that it stimulated their bioluminescence. They began to glow. At first lighting up the area around them like a camp fire, then the intensity increased as the electrical synapses in their brains mounted to impossible levels.

When May's mind joined theirs, their collective brain activity went viral, searching for the genetic key to unlock May's power of regeneration. She had even become hot to touch. The DNA in all her cells began to respond to the coded commands to restructure and she lit up, just as she had on the top of Olympus. Together they shone like a beacon. Their combined brilliance illuminated everything for 500 yards around them and the air became dense with moths attracted to the brilliance of it. Their union lasted almost until morning, when the fire within them began to die. Finally they were left in the dark, mentally exhausted and spent. None of them were aware of the finishing of it as they were asleep before the darkness came over them.

The sun had set in the western skies almost an hour earlier and it was now fully dark. The single-engine Cessna Skyhawk banked hard to port and began its return from a fruitless search of the southern peaks and foothills of the massif. Yiorgos Zacharias had taken it on himself to do the reconnaissance. The others had little more than their lives to lose, whereas he had billions. He yawned and ran his stubby fingers through his long, thinning black hair as he put his plane through the turn. He had the look of a human in his mid-forties, but Yiorgos had been around since the birth of Christ. He was a survivor against impossible odds. Yiorgos had weathered all adversities and adversaries over two millennia including war, military coups, pestilence and worst of all, rivalry. Currently, Yiorgos had no rivals as they had all been disposed of; except for Demitri Papandreou that is.

The corpulent pilot had never considered Demitri Papandreou a rival. In fact they had enjoyed some highly lucrative joint ventures, but now the multi-billionaire had reason to be afraid. He knew that Demitri had a special relationship with the Hydra and that made him dangerous beyond all others. Yiorgos was lost in his thoughts of how he would *retire* Demitri before he could no longer take the initiative to do so. Their personal wealth was not too dissimilar, but Demitri held sway over the government, military and police. He however had the best links into the Greek underworld despite Demitri's Mafia connections.

Yiorgos concluded that it would be too close to call and best avoided altogether. It would be almost safer to take on Maelströminha herself!

357

It was only a flicker in the corner of his eye and Yiorgos nearly missed it as he was so deeply immersed in his thoughts. He levelled the aircraft, dropped to 2,000 feet and turned to starboard to take a second look. A beacon of light split the night sky, too intense to look at. Yiorgos shielded his eyes but could not make sense of what he saw. In all his experience, which crossed millennia, there was nothing to compare but given the current scenario, he had struck gold! Yiorgos used the on-board video cameras to record the phenomenon then pressed *send*. In an instant, the images and their coordinates arrived on the screen in Demitri's den where the faithful Vassos was waiting to receive them.

Vassos, although a shy and retiring young man with more personal issues than his councillor could cope with, was blessed with an empirical understanding of systems and numbers. Coupled with this, he had an intuition that was almost at the level of prophecy. Other people just called him autistic. Within minutes, Vassos had applied every form of digital analysis and enhancement to the video that was available on software, plus some of his own special effects. Twenty minutes later, the images that Demitri received by media message were of two women and one man with hands joined in an almost trancelike attitude. They were blurred out by intense light and a storm of insects, but it was enough to be certain. He picked up the phone and called Vassos.

Without the need to engage in any greetings, Vassos simply imparted what he knew.

"I have given them the enemy's position *Kyrie* and they are mobilising now. Expected engagement will be shortly after dawn tomorrow and it will be a coordinated attack by air and ground based missiles."

Demitri cut the call without any acknowledgement, direction, dialogue or praise.

Vassos stared crestfallen at the silent phone in his hand. He wondered if there would ever be anything that he could do that might result in just one word of commendation from his master to give him hope. Vassos put the phone back on its cradle wiping the tears from his eyes. It would be yet another lonely night of misery. He reached for the pills that would help him get through until dawn, when it would begin all over again.

May was the first to awaken but she had no recollection of what had happened. She was just happy that they had found her and was determined to be more positive now. Elizabeth and Ben needed her to be at least that. She left them sleeping and walked down to the mountain stream that they had been following. None of them had eaten for 24 hours and they needed protein. Angel metabolism was far faster than human and May knew that they were becoming dangerously depleted. She saw the trout in mid-stream, sheltering beneath a slab of rock that protruded into the river. They were angling themselves against the brisk current with only their flicking tails giving them away. May waded out and took up a position behind them and reached gently under the belly of one of them and began to stroke it. The trout succumbed in moments and went into a trance-like state, at which point May grabbed it and tossed the trout onto the bank where it thrashed in protest. After ten minutes she had three beauties, weighing over two pounds each.

May smiled at the thought of the meal that she would prepare for them while she threaded her catch on to a reed to carry them. She re-filled the water bottles and headed back to her sleeping beauties. It was just then, that the earth shook. The shockwaves from two enormous explosions, ripped through the still mountain air concussing her ears and filling her heart with dread.

Yiorgos called in the long overdue favour from his friend General Spiros Kallas of the Hellenic Air Force. Through his connections, Yiorgos had afforded the General diplomatic immunity when an illegal arms deal almost literally blew up in his face. The disgrace and scandal would have ruined the General. Now, it was his turn to repay that favour.

It was six o'clock in the morning. The two, twin-engine Boeing AH-64 Apache attack helicopters were ready for take-off at Macedonia, Thessalonikis' International Airport. Pilots and gunners were running through their weapons checks and the computer guided, Hellfire missiles were armed and ready. Each delivered a payload of high-explosive warheads, powerful enough to burn through the heaviest tank armour.

For lighter targets close up, the Apache sported an M230, 30mm automatic cannon, capable of delivering 650 rounds of high-explosive cartridges a minute. Essentially, the Apache was a flying tank, designed to survive heavy attack and inflict massive damage. This was exactly the plan scheduled for 0700 hours that morning at a location 45 kilometres southwest of Mount Olympus at coordinates 39°51′N 21°52′E, near Kotroni.

Both pilots signalled to the man in the blue trench coat, stood with his hands jammed in his pockets peering out at them from under the brim of his hat. Their command to go, was just a simple, almost imperceptible nod of his head. The twin turbo-shaft engines responded eagerly to the throttle and the four variable pitch rotors began to thump the air. The pilots increased the power and pitch of the blades, lifting them off the apron in tandem. The helicopters slewed towards the south, then headed off towards Olympus, leaving the General with his coat-tails slapping and hanging on to his hat.

He watched as they picked up speed and climbed noisily to their cruising altitude. Now sure that they were fully committed, he turned his back and walked away muttering bad-temperedly.

"This is going to bite me right in the arse," and he cursed Yiorgos and Demitri for foisting it on him.

General Spiros Kallas wasn't the only one having a bad day. The two other Senators present at Demitri's videoconference had their own misgivings. They knew that despite their shoulder-fired missiles and support from the Apache attack helicopters, that they were no match for Maelströminha if they lost the element of surprise.

The legend, that was Maelströminha, had spanned the millennia and her powers of destruction were fabled. Although the legend had placed herself in exile for the last thousand years, both Nicos Papos and Takis Petrides were old enough to have seen her and others of pure Angel blood at war. It was enough to know that you should never meet them head on. Their weakness was only their compassion and that they were not the aggressors.

Their plan was simple. There was no point throwing numbers at the attack as that would only negate the possibility of surprise. They had elected to go as two, two man teams in Land Rovers with rocket launchers. Nicos Papos would be coming in from the north and Takis Petrides, from the south. The Javelin missiles, fired from shoulder held launch tubes, had a range of 2,500 yards, enough to afford some safety of distance. They would coordinate their attack with the Hellfire missiles, fired from the Apache attack helicopters. Their escape routes would be north and south from where they came. That would at least give one of the teams a chance to escape, if it all went tits up.

They had chosen their operating bases from the Ordnance survey map, using the coordinates given to them by Yiorgos Zacharias. The topography was ideal for an ambush, with high ground at both locations. Clearly the enemy hadn't chosen their campsite from a strategic defence point of view, which meant that they hadn't considered an attack in the first place. All good news for the anxious Papos and Petrides!

It was just after dawn when they took up their places with the Javelin missiles armed and ready. They both had clear site of their quarry and were in contact via shortwave radio. The Apaches were now only five minutes away and everything was looking good.

"Nicos are you receiving me? Over."

"Loud and clear Takis and ready for action. Over."

"Here too. ETA Apaches five minutes. We strike first to give them an easy target to spot, then we get the hell out of here! Understood. Over."

"Roger that. What head count have you got Nicos? I see only two/ Over."

"Same here, they must have split up. What do we do? Over."

"We hit as soon as the Apaches are overhead, then run whatever happens and hope to god the third one isn't anywhere nearby. Good luck. Over and out."

They turned simultaneously to their Drones with their shoulder mounted weapons, and ordered them to engage. The Drones obediently sighted their targets, using the *lock-on-before-launch* command. The missiles were then programmed to automatically seek their targets when fired. Nicos lit his cigar. It looked like a soft target and he allowed himself a cruel smile.

It was hard to see how this could possibly go wrong.

Ben woke with an inexplicable feeling of alarm and foreboding and shook Elizabeth to alert her.

"She's gone!"

Elizabeth couldn't separate herself from her dream at first and her response was confused.

"Who's gone where Ben?"

"Lizzie wake up. May has gone. She's left us!"

It was just after dawn. They were once again bathed in that surreal orange light that added to Elizabeth's drowsy confusion. She had to consciously fight to clear her mind.

"Easy Ben, she won't have gone far. She's probably gone to the loo or to find us some breakfast, like she did before."

Elizabeth was trying to be rational, but deep inside her she felt it too. Something like a premonition, *déjà vu.*

It had now become second nature to them and they joined their minds focussing all their senses on their surroundings. The first thing they noticed was the absence of a dawn chorus. This was typical of when a natural habitat has been rudely violated and it added to their mounting dread. The northerly breeze was tainted with the acrid smell of an over-hot engine and sweet smell of tobacco smoke, wafting in on the air. In the distance, they could hear the rhythmic thumping of helicopters approaching. This was all they needed to confirm their fears. An attack was imminent.

Nicos was first to hear them approach, as they were coming in rapidly from the north. He picked up the radio with shaking hands.

"Takis are you there; can you hear me? Thirty seconds to missile launch."

Radio protocols were lost in the urgency of the moment.

"Got that Nicos; firing in thirty," Takis cut the radio.

Beads of sweat were literally popping out of his thick set, almost apelike brow. He tugged at the neck of his shirt as if it was starving him of air. The terror of the moment was asphyxiating. Nicos counted them down.

"....four, three, two, one fire!"

Javelin missiles have a soft launch that ejects the missile from the tube without excessive noise and recoil. Then the second stage ignites, sending the guided missile relentlessly to its target. The instant that the second stages ignited, the missiles were committed and their targets doomed. Both missile crews immediately dropped their launching tubes and ran for their Land Rovers. At that very moment, the Apache strike helicopters appeared in the sky above them. The fire power they brought with them, was enough to take out a small army and the outcome was obvious to the pilots as they prepared to engage.

Elizabeth and Ben stood back to back, facing north and south. Inexplicably they knew exactly where the attacks were going to come from. Each was focused on the two outcrops of rock that concealed the threat. Although they were functioning as individuals, they were mentally linked. Their bodies were somehow becoming charged with static electricity. They didn't know it but they were attracting a sea of electrons. The earth around them took on an enormous negative charge and began to hum like a high voltage transformer. The hair on their heads stood up in comical fashion as the static charge continued to mount. The primary charges of the two Javelin missiles ignited and they felt the percussive shock wave hit them giving them first sight of the missiles. The secondary's ignited simultaneously moments later and the Javelins were homing in on them, accelerating by the second.

It was beyond credibility. Neither Elizabeth nor Ben was the slightest bit afraid. Somehow, they knew that they had the solution within them, it was all about belief just as Ben had said. In tandem they thrust out their arms towards the speeding missiles. The huge potential difference between them and the oncoming missiles caused the air between them to ionise, creating plasma closing the electrical circuit. A blue flash instantaneously and momentarily joined them with the oncoming missiles. The massive negative potential around them discharged itself through the plasma, detonating the missiles. The force of the explosions ripped through the trees and bushes throwing them to the ground leaving them bruised and concussed. It was just then that the Apache attack helicopters arrived overhead, ready to fire their Hellfire missiles.

The explosions released a fury in May that was beyond measure and alien to her nature. They had dared to attack her dearest friends in her company and, for all she knew, had killed them too. There would be no enemy survivors. Whoever had committed this crime against her would pay with their lives, from the doers to the organisers. They would all die. Tears of rage streamed from her eyes blurring her vision as she sped through the trees back to where she had left them.

It had only taken moments to get back and Elizabeth and Ben were still writhing on the ground, clasping their ears in the agony. They were completely removed from the battle, prey for the taking. Above them, were two helicopters deploying their warheads, in seconds the whole area would be consumed in explosive Hell-fire!

May's eyes and head cleared instantly and her expression was murderous. The black rage of revenge was upon her and she wanted blood. She stopped in her tracks and bowed her head in concentration with her fists clenched and arms slightly away from her sides. Suddenly May thrust her hands towards the deadly war machines above her. The compression wave that left them, impacted the air gathering force, compressing it between her and the Apache helicopters, turning it from gaseous state through liquid into solid. The Hellfire missiles, that were still only tens of yards from the Apaches, exploded on impact against what was literally a wall of ice, consuming the helicopters in a fireball. The burnt out hulks crashed into the hillside, testament to the almost limitless power that Maelströminha had over Nature and her elements.

Elizabeth and Ben were on their knees but had recovered sufficiently to have witnessed May's awesome strike. They were still out of the game though, unable to assist. May turned her attention to the two Land Rovers speeding away in diametrically opposite directions. Again she bowed her head in concentration, adopting that manner with her fists clenched and arms slightly away from her sides. An expression of horror came over Ben's face. For the first time since they had met her, he could see no beauty in her, none whatsoever. Only malevolence and it scared him beyond words.

They had barely made it to their Land Rovers when the Javelin missiles detonated. For a target at over two kilometres away that was too soon, much too soon and it filled them with dread. Something had gone wrong and that was confirmed by the massive explosions above them. Nicos looked up just in time to see the Apache nearest him turn into a fireball as its armoury of Hellfire missiles ignited. The burning carcass of the helicopter dropped out of the sky with its rotors still turning in pathetic futility. It crashed 100 yards from him, spitting fire as the 30mm explosive cartridges from the M230 cannon began to ignite in the intense heat. He jumped into the driving seat and was underway in moments, leaving his Drone to drag himself in to the moving car. Nicos had little concern whether he made it or not, in truth he would have preferred that he didn't. It would have slowed down the enemy dealing with him. It was a similar scenario for Takis, only his Drone didn't make it. Takis had shot him to make sure of it.

The two Land Rovers sped away from each other, hoping to divide Maelströminha's attention, but it needed much more than hope. Both drivers pulled up suddenly on their brakes without understanding why, then found themselves inexplicably engaged in three point turns to take the opposite directions.

"What the hell are you doing?" the Drone asked in disbelief.

He looked in puzzlement for some obstruction blocking their way, but there was none. He looked at Nicos Papos and saw the change that had come over him. He was in some other place, certainly not there with him. As the Land Rover began to accelerate he took one last despairing look at Nicos then bailed out of the door, landing heavily among the boulders in the verge.

Both Rovers were almost flat out on the narrow dirt track road when they first had sight of each other. In the last moments the drivers floored their accelerators and stared implacably at each other, as if they were strangers. Over five tonnes of metal collided head on at a combined speed of 160 mph, crushing the Land Rovers and sending a ball of flames 50 feet into the air. Death was instantaneous.

May relaxed from her aggressive pose. Her hands dropped to her sides but her head remained bowed. She was ashamed of herself and avoided looking at Elizabeth and Ben. It was partly because she felt ugly in spirit and guilty for her inhumanity but it was more than that; she felt ugly as a person. Ben was about to go over to her but Elizabeth took his arm and held him back. Once again her perception was more acute than Ben's.

"Not yet Ben, she's not ready," Elizabeth whispered and Ben conceded.

May was silhouetted against the mystical orange dawn glow. That, combined with the burning hulks of the Apache helicopters and twisted Land Rovers, gave the scene a surreal feeling. Occasionally cartridges exploded in the inferno of the burning wreckage painfully impacting on their already traumatised ears. It was like something out of the movies and only needed Bruce Willis to walk out of the carnage to complete the Hollywood scene. It was several long minutes before May turned to face them. At the very same moment, the sun offered its crescent above the hills in the east, spilling its white light over the land and falling gently on May's face.

"I'm sorry," she began ashamedly. "That was Neanderthal," she lamented.

The look of guilt was plain on her face, but something else was too and they were awestruck by it. May could see their reaction and immediately mistook it for horror and hid her face again. Elizabeth reached into her waist bag, took out her makeup mirror, and walked over to her.

"Look at yourself May."

Elizabeth offered the mirror but May pushed it away in anger.

"I don't need those anymore, how could you be so cruel?"

"Just look!" Elizabeth insisted. It was no longer a request.

May reluctantly took the mirror and looked at her reflection. An expression of sheer disbelief came over her face and she hesitantly touched her cheek with those long elegant fingers. May hastily pulled a handful of silky black hair in front of her eyes and, for final proof, looked at the backs of her hands. Her scream of joy echoed around the mountains and she began jumping around, waving her arms like an over-excited school girl. She was whooping and stamping her feet which stimulated her bioluminescence so that she looked like some dancing deity, which was in stark contrast to the scene of death and destruction that surrounded them. It was so infectious that they all joined in.

Any spectator looking at them dancing and shouting in the middle of what was a battlefield, would have thought that they had lost their minds. They were crying and laughing all in the same moment. May was back with a vengeance and if anything, more beautiful than ever.

It ended suddenly as May focussed on their vulnerability.

"Quickly we must leave. It's not safe here, we can celebrate later."

She took them back to the stream, collected the fish and water bottles then led them at a full run back towards the direction of the mother ship. They kept that pace going for two hours before she considered it safe enough to stop for their long overdue breakfast. The lactic acid had built up painfully in their muscles, exacerbated by their low blood-sugar levels. Both Elizabeth and Ben were glad to just sit and watch while May collected wood and set the campfire. Within a half an hour she had the fresh trout baking in the embers and the smell was just to die for.

There was a lot to discuss but that would be for later, first they needed protein and sleep. While they ate, May enjoyed having Ben's eyes on her. It amused Elizabeth just how many times she giggled, pouted or flicked her hair or pulled it over her shoulder to tumble down over her breast. May was oblivious to her flirtatiousness, being totally naïve in the ways of the world. There must have been half a dozen opportunities for Ben to have put his arm around her and he missed each of them.

"I will have to have a little chat with him later," Elizabeth decided.

They slept through the heat of the mid-day under a shady tree. Elizabeth was the first to wake. She had clearly misjudged her brother, as he was asleep face to face with May in a mutual cuddle. Elizabeth smiled for them and then felt sad that Mike wasn't with her. The weeks had passed slowly and she was really missing him. Ben was over his operation now, so she decided that they would go back home as soon as they could after their return to the mother ship.

They continued their journey at a slower pace, deep in conversation, exchanging their experiences and asking questions of each other. This time, it was May who was the most anxious to know what had happened to her.

"How did this happen?" May asked.

She touched her face and looked at her hands for reassurance that it wasn't just a dream. She was still beaming at the miracle of it.

"We had a good teacher May, and we were creative!" Ben replied and May tipped her head at the compliment. "We used your teachings and the learning from our experiences so far; like creating remedies from within our own bodies, the principals of rejuvenation, expanding possibility and most of all self-belief. You said that together we would have almost full Angel ability. We thought that if we could join our minds with the power of yours, then together we could stimulate the re-building of your damaged DNA to the point where your own body could take over and do the rest. And it must have worked because you look pretty good to me!"

Ben smiled proudly and May was choked with happiness and pride in what they had become but not least from the direct compliment that Ben had paid her.

"What you have both achieved in such a short period of time humbles me and fills me with pride. I was truly blessed to have met you and the Angel race is fortunate to have you."

The feeling was mutual and Elizabeth spoke for them both.

"I think we were blessed too May. You have equipped us for the fight ahead. When Katya came with her venom, you gave us the solution and when Dada came to take us in our beds, you made the difference. One by one the Shadows have fallen to us. Today we had the solution, only because of what you showed us on Mount Olympus. Don't you see that you are keeping us one step ahead of the game, otherwise we would have had no chance?"

Ben struggled to be manly in the flood of emotion and chose science and pragmatism as his escape.

"I think I understand the physics behind how we neutralised the oncoming missiles through creating a potential difference, just as you did on Olympus, but how did you take out the helicopters?"

"I would be lying if I said anything else other than that it was a creation arising out of pure rage," May shook her head soulfully in regret for her barbarity. "I could've dealt with the whole incident in other ways that wouldn't have cost life, but I don't seem to look for that option anymore. I am corrupted just as they are."

"No!" Elizabeth was furious, "you are not corrupt. Maybe it's just that you have never loved and protected so much before. It's a primordial thing that you cannot be guilty of."

Ben steered the situation back on track.

"You haven't answered the question May, what did you do?

"In scientific terms, it was no more than schoolboy physics Ben; Charles's Law in fact. I used the relationship between pressure, temperature and the volume of a thermodynamic system, causing phase transitions between gaseous, liquid and solid states of matter," May was clearly playing with Ben in her explanation, "I created an exponentially increasing shock wave through the air that changed the variables affecting the physical system. Are you with me?" May was teasing him and Ben knew it.

"Yes May, you squashed the air between you and the missile causing it to freeze and now you're just showing off complicating the hell out of it!"

Their laughter was spontaneous but May quickly became serious again.

"These are not abilities that we can show to others. Your own kind could potentially become a greater danger to you than the Shadows. If they knew what you could do, they would either hunt you down and kill you out of fear, or try to control you and turn you into war machines. In part that is why I have chosen to isolate myself, but I wouldn't wish that on you."

It was a sobering thought and something that they would have to consider for the rest of their lives.

The rest of the journey back to the mother ship went without incident and the conversation was confined to idle chatter around the hopes and plans of normal young people. It was refreshing and cleansing. By the time they arrived at the mother ship, they had exorcised the trauma of all that had happened on that mythical mountain that is Mount Olympus.

Chapter 33

When they stepped back through the portal into the Robinson's hallway, it was still exactly quarter past nine on the same Saturday morning, even though a month had passed. All that had happened in that month for those in the hallway now never did. It had been erased and they were about to embark on another possibility. Their future was to be re-written from that moment onwards. Thankfully, Elizabeth and Ben would never have known that they had all died horribly in that alternative life.

The expression on George, Jillie and Mike's faces when they re-appeared a split second after leaving was something to behold. Elizabeth and Ben were bronzed by the sun and dressed in different clothes from those that they had left in. Ben was no longer wearing his Oakley sunglasses and his bright blue eyes shone with health.

Mike was the first to find his voice as it wasn't quite the unique experience for him that it was for the others. However, he still found it awesome.

"That's some quick fix Ben. I was expecting you back with a white stick!" Mike joked.

He took Ben in a welcoming embrace. They were like brothers now.

"And I can see that you are still just as ugly!" Ben returned his jibe and reinforced it with a brilliant smile.

It had been weeks since the injury and since Ben had actually seen them all. His emotions were running high so that when his aunt and uncle took their turn in embrace, his happiness was evident and he felt somehow secure in their love for him.

Elizabeth waited patiently for some attention from Mike. To her, it had been a long time. She had missed him so much, but he was making no obvious moves to welcome her back. She was beginning to feel hurt and cross and then realised that for him, it was only a moment ago that he had last seen her. There was nothing to miss on his part. Elizabeth immediately forgave him but decided to give him a hard time about it anyway.

"So where's my welcome then Mike? I've been gone a month and you don't seem the slightest bit concerned about it."

Mike was puzzled.

"A month? But, well you haven't really been gone a month. I mean... well, how did it go?" Mike was floundering and didn't quite know what to say so Elizabeth ended his misery.

"Just a kiss and a cuddle will do for now," Mike gladly took the lifeline that was offered.

They breakfasted for the second time that morning. Ben recounted the story of his operation. He told them how Jorall and Zita had immersed him in amniotic fluid that literally re-grew his damaged organs. George and Jillie were amazed at the medical advancements that had been made by this alien nation and Gillie saw some possibilities and tested the waters for the possibility of a little cosmetic surgery.

"Do you think he could push back time a little for me?" she asked.

Jillie was only half joking.

"I don't know if I should," Elizabeth warned. "He's seriously handsome you know, and you and a new body. Well, what would George say?"

"Now I absolutely insist that you ask him!" Jillie teased but she had a mischievous look in her eye as she smiled innocently back at George.

Elizabeth took them on the roller coaster ride that was their journey to Mount Olympus. It was so far beyond their comprehension though, preposterous even. Jillie shuddered at the thought of the dangers that would now face them for the rest of their lives and the knowledge that she and George were now a part of it.

Mike was blown away by the part where they took out the Apache strike helicopters and Javelin missiles. There was also more than a hint of jealousy that he wasn't there with them. Mike was the eternal soldier.

"It makes the escapade that I had with your father in the desert seem almost irrelevant," Mike conceded.

Elizabeth put her hand on his arm reassuringly.

"No Mike, not irrelevant at all just, order of magnitude versus ability. I know that what you did put yours and Dad's lives at risk many times. I doubt if any of us would still be here today if you hadn't."

Mike smiled appreciatively at Elizabeth's support and sincerity. Her comment about them maybe not being here today but for his efforts, prompted him to turn current dangers.

"OK that's enough reminiscing for now. We have to prepare for a war. Latest intel, received earlier this morning, is that the Shadows have delayed their attack by two weeks. Apparently it was because the Senators all failed to meet their personal objectives. Alexis ran roughshod over them and to say that he was angry would be an understatement."

"But you said that we've got another two weeks. What's the hurry?" Ben was enjoying being the centre of attention and reluctant to draw it to a close.

"If there's one thing that you can count on about the Shadows, it's that you can't count on them at all. None of us can afford to rest until this house is as safe as we can make it, and in as short a period of time as possible," Mike turned his attention to George. "I want you to continue your work with Jake on creating a full network of surveillance cameras and on planting explosives at all windows and doors. I want them all linked back to your war room ready for detonation at the soonest." Upon reflection he added, "Oh and at the top of the stairs too. Configure it so that there's no danger of damaging the old mirror in the hall, or you might condemn Elizabeth and Ben to oblivion."

George frowned in consternation. He couldn't see why the two were mutually dependent and looked at Elizabeth for an explanation.

"As you already know Uncle, it's our way in and out of here. Although we've said that time effectively stands still for you while we are in transit, well it doesn't actually. Time continues but we come back to the point that we left, erasing that possibility. If the mirror breaks while we're away then there is no way back for us; ever."

"Then move the bloody mirror now, it might get hit in the crossfire anyway," George's empirical logic stopped them in their tracks.

"Well... yes I hadn't thought of that," Elizabeth was still off balance.

Ben took over to give her some thinking space.

"Good clear thinking Uncle, we'll move it out to the stables today. It can go in the garage there with Dad's old Harley. You would've made a great Angel!"

"I can't really picture myself sitting on a cloud all day playing a harp Ben, so maybe not," George's smile was easy and confident.

Ben was amazed that his uncle had not been phased or afraid of any of the madness that was thrust on him. For the first time he realised that there was much more to this man than just plain Uncle George. Ben was suddenly filled with pride and a deep respect for a man that he clearly didn't really know.

Chapter 34

It was late Saturday afternoon when Mike called George and his six man SAS squad for an update on their state of readiness. He had been agonising over the new intel. The idea that a simple assault operation could be significantly delayed through the incompetence of all four Senators was unlikely at best. It just didn't stack up in his mind. They were sat with mugs of tea, exhausted by the relentless pace of the day. All were anticipating Mike's praise for it and to be stood down as a reward. Mike began his address.

"How would we stand if the attack came now?"

"Up shit creek without a paddle," offered Jake. "They better bloody well not!"

"Well I think that they *bloody well* might Jake," Mike cocked that quizzical brow of his. "What could take war hardened veterans, with a cumulative experience of several thousand years, more than 48 hours to put an attack like this together?"

Jake considered the question and was clearly annoyed with himself for his own lack of foresight. He had the face of a street fighter. Jake shook his bullish red head as if recovering from yet another punch.

"It's a load of bollocks ain't it sir; disinformation?" he grunted. "They're coming for us and they're coming bloody soon."

At that moment everyone at the table knew that it was true. Mike continued.

"OK, here's how it goes," Mike was right in his comfort zone now. This was what he lived for. "We planned on twelve SAS but six are in transit from Afghan, arriving Monday. We'll assume that's too late and if not then we'll bank that luxury. I'll take Nath and Ruben off surveillance duties at Adolphius' house from midnight tonight. Bringing them in will significantly increase our fire power and besides, their job there is virtually over anyway."

There was a tangible sense of relief around the table at the prospect of much needed reinforcement. Nath and Ruben were two of the most experienced soldiers amongst them and had proved themselves in numerous missions. There was an unstated agreement that they could change the outcome of the fight.

"You will be up against four Senators and 24 well prepared and heavily armed Drones, but you know how and where they will attack," Mike cocked that look at them. "What could you get done before first-light tomorrow morning that would give us a better chance?"

Mike watched as they strategized and went through the logistics of what they still had to do. The odds weren't good, but the six SAS commandos were of the best in the elite force. Mike knew that some or all of them would be lost in the next few days or even hours. It prompted him to think of who they were as people, not just as soldiers:

Red Jake, his second in command, was a bull of a man closer to 50 than 40 and unlikely to make 60. This was down to the attrition of his lifestyle rather than the dangers of his job. He was a fighter, drinker, insomniac and a paradox. He was fearless and ruthless, but Mike had often heard him in his room late at night crying over some chick flick movie. Mike remembered him out in Afghanistan with the orphaned kittens that he had befriended. Jake had fed them with his own rations until they were old enough to fend for themselves. He had made a home for them in an open kitbag on the floor of their Jackal rapid assault vehicle. Conversely, this same man wouldn't think twice about cutting another's throat.

Chas and Joey were Paratroopers. They were devoted brothers that had joined less than a year apart and inseparable in service. Each owed his life to the other, on more than one occasion. It was their back-watching and total commitment to each other that had been their salvation. Mike knew that if he was to lose one defending the house, then he would probably lose the other. That would either be in support of his brother, or in mindless revenge.

James was a 39 year old Weapons Technician, whose skills with explosives were currently second to none. He had the accolade of being the most prolific surviving bomb disposal expert in the combined armed forces. James had commanded two Explosive Ordnance Disposal units in Iraq and Afghanistan. He and his team were tasked with the disabling of roadside IEDs, investigating the aftermath of roadside car bombings, and searching the villages door to door to uncover bomb-makers at their homes. James had probably spent more time in a bomb suit than any other living soldier. This understated, solitary man was nerveless and Mike was grateful to have him in his squad. The explosives that he would set around the Robinson's house would ultimately count for at least half of the Shadow assault force, leaving realistic odds for their unit to face.

That left the Marines Zak and Rudy, both dangerous men on and off the battlefield. They were a wild pair in their late twenties and highly charged with testosterone. Mike dreaded them being off-duty, as it invariably meant that he would have to negotiate their release from the local gaols the next day. Mike cocked an eyebrow and nodded in respect, as he thought about how these men could turn a fight around.

Jake brought Mike back from his thoughts and to the task in hand.

"Well sir; for starters, we can place most of the explosives at the doors and windows and a few in the gardens by then and maybe arm and prove some back to the war room for George to deploy."

George cut in with new found authority.

"How about you just dig the bloody holes and place all of them, leaving the clever stuff to me?"

George had already seen how it was done and didn't need overseeing. His rebuke was only slightly intended in humour, but the intent was crystal. He continued with that same authority.

"That way, we can get them *all* armed and proven, not just some of them."

The big Sergeant Major looked at him with a hardened military eye considering whether he could trust his life to this man? When it came, the nod was almost imperceptible but George received it loud and clear.

"It's all yours George but make sure I don't see you in Hell!" the mutual respect was also loud and clear.

Only time would tell if that trust was misplaced. Mike continued his brief.

"Righ,t you know what's required. I want this complete by 0400 hours tomorrow morning. That gives you ten hours. You can sleep at your posts after that in shifts of three, until the reinforcements come, or the attack, whichever is first."

Mike could see that the threat of imminent engagement had given them metal and driven away their tiredness. They were itching to get on with it.

"I'll get Jillie to prepare some food and you eat in pairs. From now on, it will be guns at hand at all times. George, you prepare the war room and make sure that you're fully briefed by Jake on how and when to detonate the explosives. Jillie stays down there with you until this is over, understood?"

George nodded his confirmation and Mike continued.

"Jake; familiarise him and Jillie with the use of a machine gun, in case the enemy make it to the war room. I'll open the arsenal and lay out weapons and ammunition at the agreed places, then brief Elizabeth and Ben. After that, we'll take that mirror down to the stables."

Mike was thinking on his feet. He was conscious that even the smallest oversight by him could cost them the war.

"Do we have perimeter alarms set Jake?"

"All set sir and fed back to George's war room. Oh, and we've got Tini back on duty, he's tied up on his run. He'll let us know when they're coming better'n any surveillance can."

Red Jake gulped back the last mouthful of sweet tea and stood up to address his men.

"OK lads you know what to do. Get moving. Full muster and drill at 0400 hours and that's all of us, the Robinsons too."

They wrapped the old mirror in blankets and lifted it onto the flatbed truck. Mike took the route that would take them past the builders' merchants, which would appear reasonable to any onlooker. When they were confident they hadn't picked up any unwanted attention, Mike took a left taking them round the back of town out towards the stables.

Ben unlocked the garage that housed his father's Harley V-Rod. The remote garage had been its keeping place since even before the accident, as Jodie had hated the sight of it.

"It's a bloody killing machine," she had said, "and I want no part of it."

So out of sight, out of mind was Ralph's solution. It was still immaculate and Ben had kept it so in memory of him. The Harley was left on constant trickle charge and Ben would start it up regularly to keep it moving and George would take it out for a run periodically. Ben was looking forward to being old enough to take his motorcycle test and regarded the bike as part of his inheritance.

Ben couldn't resist starting it up. He straddled it, turned on the ignition and the beast burst into life at the command of the start button. The V-Rod was a Harley/Porsche collaboration and its 1100 cc liquid-cooled V-twin Revolution engine delivered 115hp to the chunky back wheel. The exhaust note from the Screaming Eagles Siamese pipes was awesome and Elizabeth cringed at the cacophony of it.

"Stop it! Won't you ever grow up?" Elizabeth covered her ears at the pain of it.

Ben reluctantly cut the engine.

"I hope not," Ben smirked.

He took the keys out, tossed them in the air and bounced them off his bicep into his hand, grinning cheekily. Elizabeth turned away shaking her head and tutting in despair.

With the mirror safely stowed, they began their journey back home. It was then that Mike dropped the bombshell.

"I don't want you around for this fight. At the first sign of attack I want you out of there, even sooner if possible."

Mike kept his eyes firmly on the road ahead, but he could feel Elizabeth's eyes drilling into him. She was livid.

"You've gotta be kidding me! If you think for one moment that…"

Mike cut her off.

"For once in your life will you just bloody listen to me woman?" Mike stared her down, helped by Ben's hand on Elizabeth's shoulder, prompting her to let Mike speak.

"Thank you," Mike acknowledged. "Don't let your emotions cloud your judgement Lizzie. You have to keep thinking of the bigger picture. If we lose you, then there's no way back for your parents, Crystalita or my brother and father and that's just a small part of the bigger picture."

Mike paused just long enough for that to sink in but not long enough to let Elizabeth back in.

"Worse. If you are lost then you condemn May and the rest of the Angel race to eventual extinction, along with all those that you have ever loved. That's how the Shadows work and you know it. Your aunt and uncle, along with me would be casualties along the way whatever the outcome of this attack. We can only prevail if you survive this."

Mike was undeniably right and they both knew it. Elizabeth didn't argue it further.

"What are your chances of surviving the attack without us, I mean honestly?"

The hostility had gone out of Elizabeth and her shoulders and chin had dropped displaying her capitulation.

"Honestly? Well we're going to need a certain amount of luck that's for sure. If it's at dawn tomorrow, like I suspect, then maybe our chances are evens. If it's later, when the other SAS boys have arrived, then odds on that we take them," Mike even managed an encouraging smile.

"That's not good enough Mike. Those are nothing but losing odds," Elizabeth put her hand on his arm and turned to Ben. "Ready or not, we're going back in time at midnight tonight Ben and were going to fix this mess."

Elizabeth could sense Ben's agreement just as she could sense the fear inside him that matched her own, but they really had no other choice. They both knew that Mike and his brave men had no chance against the Shadows and that was why he wanted them out of it. There was no doubt in their minds that they would all die in a few hours' time unless they could stop the attack ever happening in the first place.

"If we succeed in our mission Mike, then whatever the outcome of tomorrow's fight is, it will be as if it never happened and we will all have our loved ones back," Elizabeth struggled to utter her next sentence lest it gave substance to the possibility of it. "And if we don't, then history will record that we all die. You, Uncle George, Aunt Jillie and the lads here massacred in the early hours of tomorrow morning and us..." Elizabeth looked like her soul had been sucked out of her, "well we will have died a little over four years ago, two nameless people in some unknown place."

Chapter 35

Alexis called Adolphius into conclave. He had chosen the gardens for their seclusion and certainty of not being overheard.

"Walk with me a while Adolphius. It is a most pleasant afternoon would you not agree?"

The invitation was for the benefit of the enemy's concealed recording equipment and only warranted a nod from Adolphius. They began their stroll, taking a route that took them away from the perimeter, away from the surveillance equipment. Alexis wasted no time.

"As I understand it we are ready to go; is that not so?" it was a rhetorical question.

Adolphius indulged it with an answer.

"The four squads have been augmented from the original six to twelve in each as you have asked and they are fully trained with all logistics in place for immediate deployment."

Adolphius took some professional pleasure in his brief. He had taken on the responsibility since Eichmann had fallen to the boy. Now they were meticulously prepared.

"Excellent Adolphius, sometimes we have to employ ourselves when the consequences of failure are unacceptable. You have once again proven your worthiness," Alexis was clearly impressed. "You have always been safe hands Adolphius. The world would be a better place now, if your generals had not failed you in the early forties."

That was the closest that Alexis had come to fully endorsing Adolphius' work in centuries, and it was intended as an overt declaration of his allegiance. There comes a time, and in Alexis' case an age, when you need to begin to accumulate your allies.

"I have simply fulfilled my duty that is all," Adolphius sighed.

They looked an unlikely couple as they walked in the picturesque grounds. The stooped and wizened Alexis, with his aged face, white pallor and wispy white hair, had an almost Troll-like look about him. In contrast, Adolphius was upright and up to date in appearance. He sported mirrored, aviator sunglasses, jeans and trainers. Alexis continued with his questions, regarding their state of readiness.

"You said *immediate deployment* Adolphius. Can I take that as meaning that it would be possible to bring the mission forwards to midnight tonight?" Alexis looked at his watch thoughtfully and his face remained implacable as ever. "That would give you eight hours."

"That would certainly be a challenge Alexis, but an achievable one. Of course I would need to give the order immediately. You would not be asking me unless you had great reason. I trust that you will share it with me?"

"Quite so Adolphius and you should know. You do not get this old without acquiring some wisdom and insight and my intuition tells me that it is the right thing to do."

Alexis' eyes were continuously searching while they walked. Even at his advanced age his predatory instinct was keen and evident. He was still singularly the most dangerous of his kind.

"There are things that we can sense without any rational explanation, but we somehow know them to be true," Alexis began. "I am certain that the disinformation that we have given is doubted. This tactic is common ploy in warfare and it won't have been the first time that Corporal Jackson will have encountered it. He will have had time to consider it and will undoubtedly have come to the conclusion that it is rubbish."

Alexis stopped and turned to face Adolphius. His skin was like screwed up parchment but his eyes still burned with fanaticism.

"They are nobody's fools Adolphius. The longer we wait, the more we play into their hands. What is their current disposition?"

"All that you say supports our latest intelligence Alexis. There are six *builders* working at the house, around the clock. All Robinsons are back there and the Corporal almost never leaves it. I agree that this is not a scenario of ignorance and complacency."

They walked in silence for several minutes each considering their own part in the strategy and the preparations that needed to be made. Adolphius broke the silence.

"I was able to recruit three Shadows and the fallen Angel, Sean O'Malley, to augment and command the newly assigned Drones. That will allow us to stand back from the frontline and set up a command and control point to coordinate the attack. O'Malley will fly the helicopter of course, and he has been actively involved in training the squads because of his oprevious siege experience."

"Quite rightly so comrade. Under his direction, our enhanced 48 man squad should quickly overwhelm them, particularly if we take the midnight initiative."

Alexis pulled at his unshaven chin as he mulled over the scenario. He was still uncomfortable about the enemies' disposition.

"It doesn't make sense Adolphius. They know that we are coming, yet they number only seven as fully trained soldiers. Why would the Corporal risk that Adolphius?"

"Perhaps he has no choice Alexis; or maybe reinforcements are already on their way?"

"That would be my guess too, and it supports the need for us to strike tonight. Come Adolphius, let us return to the house and put this plan into action. The world might be a different place by morning."

It was twenty minutes to midnight and Jillie was on yet another coffee run. The work had been relentless, but she had succeeded in getting them flying high on caffeine. The men had bettered their own expectations by four hours and all explosives were set and proved back to the remote detonators in the war room. Arms and ammunition were cached in all the appropriate places and George and Jillie were fully briefed on how to use them.

Elizabeth and Ben had been helping with preparing the house for siege and hardly had time to even begin to think about their own imminent mission. It was only after that last coffee, that they went to their rooms to get themselves ready to leave. Ben was going through the same ritual that he had, when he prepared himself to take on Eichmann. It gave him a strange feeling of calm and empowerment.

In contrast, Elizabeth had just thrown everything that she could think of on the bed but still couldn't make any decisions. It was like her brain had stalled. She was preoccupied by the thought that they were going to abandon them all and leave them to die in the most horrific and terrifying manner. She feared, no she knew in her heart, that she would never see Mike again. For a full ten minutes she sat on the bed and sobbed at the hopelessness and injustice of it, before the set of her chin changed.

Elizabeth got up, wiped the tears from her face with the back of her sleeve and put on some makeup. She went directly to find Mike, as if she was on a mission. She was! Elizabeth found him helping James set the explosives at the top of the stairs. Mike set the switch on the slave detonator to the *on* position and the LED began to pulse. He looked up and saw her.

"Lizzie, why aren't you getting ready? It's a quarter to twelve and I thought that we had agreed..."

Elizabeth put her finger on his lips to silence him and spoke to him softly.

"Shush, I've got something that I want to share with you," she took his hand and led him back to her room.

When they were inside Elizabeth shut the door and leant against it. The image of her two unborn children appeared in her mind, just as she had seen them in the mirror on the night of her party. Her sadness was deepened by the unlikelihood of it and she brushed her tear away along with the thought. That was for later now it was all about her and Mike.

"This might be the last time we ever see each other Mike and I want to share some precious moments with you. Create some memories that we can both take with us to eternity; if that's what awaits us."

Elizabeth's green eyes were big and they had a softness about them that Mike had never seen before. She tilted her head to one side inviting him over and he was drawn to her surrender. They locked in an urgent embrace just as the night air was torn by Tini's frantic barking.

Ruben was ensconced in his hide at the north-east corner of the garden at Adolphius' house, tending the equipment. He and Nath, were splitting the surveillance into eight hour shifts to limit the number of changeovers as they were the high risk times of exposure. Eight hours was as long as a man could reasonably lie in one position and still be able to get up and walk at the end of it. Ruben was into his eighth hour and his body was screaming to get up and leave. The last hour was always a mental challenge that took Ruben to the very edge of his tolerance. He had to play mind games to get through it.

Ruben was distracting himself from the pain in his muscles by playing virtual noughts and crosses in his head. He was just placing the final cross when the bullet from Alexis' silenced pistol took out the back of his brain.

It had only taken them a few hours after Alexis had discovered the camera in the gardens of Adolphius' house to find where the SAS team had been parking their surveillance van. It had to have been close enough to pick up the audio/visual signals and not too far to come and go from. For the days that followed they had maintained a close watch on it waiting their time.

"They had chosen well," Grese thought as she walked down the dimly lit road.

It was parked amongst several other white vans on a small industrial estate, close to Adolphius' house.

"A wolf hiding amongst the sheep," she smirked.

Grese looked at her watch it was just coming up to the time agreed with Alexis, eleven thirty. She slid the package under the van and walked on past. Thirty seconds later, the bomb exploded throwing the van twenty feet in the air in a ball of flames. Nath never even emerged from his dream; his death was instant.

Sean O'Malley lifted the Lynx AH9 utility helicopter with its cargo of five men, from the field at the side of Adolphius' house. At that precise moment, a convoy of three minibuses led by a Range Rover, left the drive and turned in the direction of the Robinson's house.

Adolphius was at the wheel of the Rover with Alexis, Grese and Dracul as passengers. They were dressed in black and armed with AK-47s and grenades. Their task was to set up a forward control point and help O'Malley to coordinate the 47 man squad. All had been meticulously briefed and were linked audio and visually, with relay back to the comms panels in the Rover and helicopter cockpit. The assault force would be double the strength that the enemy were expecting, and the attack significantly earlier than Corporal Jackson could have reasonably anticipated, or prepared for. Under the circumstances, they could not have been better prepared nor have achieved a better element of surprise. There was every reason to believe that their attack would be totally overwhelming.

O'Malley was under instructions to stay out of earshot until the rocket attack, which would be his signal to come in and come in fast. He followed the convoy as agreed, up until the vehicles extinguished their headlights at the two mile point. It would be approximately another seven minutes before the attack and until then, his job was just to stand by.

Hovering there, O'Malley had time to reflect on the sequence of events that had led to his descent into dishonour. It was ironic that he was on a mission to kill the children of the very man who had stood by him throughout his chequered career in the SAS. He had been the pilot on most of Ralph Robinson's desert sorties and was there on his last, when he took a bullet through the neck.

It had all started when he had lost control of his gambling addiction. O'Malley had kept it from his family, always hoping for the big win that would make it alright. Of course the big win never came and he was about to lose everything; house, car, wife, kids and his career. It was then, when his life had hit an all-time low, that he was approached by the Shadows. They had a solution and money would never again be a problem, but everything comes at a price...

Many years ago, O'Malley had been chosen, or more correctly inserted, by the Shadow Senate as part of an elite SAS strike force led by Ralph Robinson. Their objective was to liberate the hostages held by siege at the Iranian Embassy in South Kensington, London in 1980. He recalled that the six armed militia, campaigning for the autonomy of Iran's Khūzestān Province, had taken 26 hostages. On the sixth day, they had begun killing hostages after failing to negotiate the release of Arab prisoners and their own safe passage. O'Malley went in with Ralph's squad, abseiling from the roof to the windows, blowing them out and storming the house. It only took seventeen minutes and that was long enough to kill five out of the six terrorists, with the loss of only one hostage.

They were immediately embraced as heroes by the nation, but subsequently faced accusations that they had unnecessarily killed two of the terrorists. O'Malley himself was implicated. It was Ralph who had convinced the judges at his court martial that he had acted appropriately and in self-defence. The truth was sinister. O'Malley was under payback instructions to execute the two terrorists who were flying in the face of Shadow explicit directive. The Khūzestān issue was muddying the waters of a much greater Shadow initiative, which was nuclear escalation in the melting pot that was the Arab nation.

O'Malley hadn't yet lost all of his humanity but tonight was going to take him way past redemption. He hated himself for it and that he was now owned by the Shadows. There would always be another demand, and he was on a fast track to Hell.

The shockwave from the coordinated rocket attack on the Robinson's house, literally rocked the Lynx helicopter in the air and brought O'Malley back to the present. He dipped the nose of the helicopter and brought it up to full speed heading out towards the bombed out, burning shell that was the Robinson's household.

The blacked out convoy cut their engines as they came into the Robinson's road and freewheeled the last 500 yards, arriving in silence. Adolphius turned to Grese.

"There will be a dog. There is always a dog."

"I'll deal with it," Grese volunteered, "I already know where the beast will be tied."

She had used the dog to warn the Robinson children when Dada had made his attempt to assassinate them. The memory of Dada's mutilated body caused Grese to smile but it was a smile just as empty as her soul. The dog would be in the same place, she was sure of it.

"You carry on setting up the forward control point and deploy the men. Don't wait on me, it will only take minutes."

Grese chose to circle and come in from the west to put the gusty wind in her favour. She looked at her watch; it was twelve minutes to midnight, minute perfect so far. The dog stench was on the night air and she could easily position it, using her highly developed sense of smell. Taking the silenced pistol from her webbing, she vaulted the six foot fence and landed just downwind of Tini's run. It was just at that moment that the gusty wind shifted and Tini got scent of her. He began to bark, crazed as the acrid chemicals pervaded his olfactory system. Grese cursed at her bad luck, and only just had enough time to level her gun at the maddened dog racing towards her. The bedlam only lasted for a few short seconds before Grese's pistol spat three bullets into Tini's head killing him instantly.

The barking stopped as suddenly as it had begun and meant only one thing to Mike. Tini was already dead.

"It's started Lizzie! Get Ben and get the hell out of here. Now!"

Mike ran out of the room shouting to his men to take up their positions, leaving Elizabeth bewildered and disorientated. She knew then, that she would never see him again and her desolation was immense. Elizabeth had to function and fought off the numbness that had befuddled her. Seconds later, she ran out of her room to find. He was already leaving his room, carrying two machine guns and webbings with spare magazines and grenades

386

"Take these Lizzie we've got to get out and down to the stables while we still can. Perhaps it wasn't such a good idea to move the mirror there," it was a statement rather than a question.

"We've got to make sure that Auntie and Uncle are armed and safely in the war room before we go Ben or they won't stand a chance," Elizabeth pleaded.

She had already shaken off the chains of stupor that had bound her, and was now fully focused on their task. They ran passed the SAS brothers, Chas and Joey, who were coming up the staircase to take their battle stations on the landing. In their haste Elizabeth and Ben only narrowly missed stepping on the explosives that were placed on the tread of the second step. Ben's blood ran cold at the thought of it. It was much too soon to use up any luck. It reminded him of his careless actions when he took on Eichmann. The thought made him shudder. They crossed the hallway to the stairs leading to the basement, or war room as it was now known as, and heard Mike shouting orders to his men.

"Stay behind the blast walls, attack imminent!"

Mike's voice was clear, calm and confident. It gave his men unity and belief, something that only comes with the respect and trust of past skirmishes endured. Jake spat out his chewing tobacco and turned his ruddy red head towards Mike.

"You were right boss, and looks like Nath and Ruben are done for or they would've blown the whistle."

Mike didn't need to answer and all of the SAS boys were already thinking the same. The odds had lengthened, but they had done enough work in the last six hours to at least make a fist of it.

Elizabeth and Ben poured down the stairs into the war room. They were relieved to see George and Jillie already at their stations. George had his submachine gun levelled at their waists.

"Jesus I could've killed you! How about knocking next time?"

George was clearly on edge, but then they all were. He looked up at the VDU's and gasped.

"Christ, they're everywhere. Dozens of them!"

Red Squad went in first taking their positions with shoulder held rocket launchers. They were being coordinated by Alexis at the forward control point, with O'Malley watching them and feeding back by air. They circled the front and sides of the house in pairs, standing ten yards back giving them a safe distance from their own rocket blasts.

As they knelt in front of their designated targets in that classic easy firing stance, Dracul mobilised Blue Squad. Moments' later, they were spilling into the garden taking up their places behind Red Squad, ready to follow up the rocket attack with machine gun fire. Alexis was just about to give the command to launch the rockets, when the night air was split by three consecutive explosions decimating the outer ranks of Dracul's men. Six of them went down in the blasts. One of them pulled the trigger of his AK-47 as his body convulsed in death spasms, killing the Drone next to him and fatally injuring two others.

Alexis bellowed his command over the radio.

"Fire you buffoons!"

Simultaneously, the twelve rockets loosed with the sound of thunder. They tore into the fabric of the Robinson's house, sending a ball of fire high into the night sky. Seconds later O'Malley appeared above the burning ruins of the Robinson house in the helicopter with its blades thumping the night air heavily.

Adolphius immediately gave the command to O'Malley.

"Deploy Green Squad!"

Almost immediately, the five men in the Lynx began to abseil down on to the roof, arriving above their stations in a matter of seconds. They stayed hooked onto their ropes and dropped down to the upstairs window level. Each tossed a grenade through the window next to them and then rolled to the side for cover. Seconds after the detonations, they released their ropes and were in.

The three survivors from Blue Squad, reinforced by seven of O'Malley's land-based force, ran through the retiring rocket squad to take up their machine gun positions at the blown out doors and windows. As they opened fire, a Mexican wave of explosions went around the front of the house as the concealed explosives were detonated. Of the initial ten, only four of Blue Squad was left standing. The survivors began blindly emptying their magazines through the gaping holes in the side of the house. They were hoping for a lucky hit and to drive the enemy out the back of the house, straight into Grese's squad for the kill.

Alexis saw the carnage on his monitors and immediately spat out orders for Red Squad to take up the positions of the fallen gunners. He looked hatefully at Adolphius.

"Less than two minutes in and we are fifteen men down, nearly one third of our contingent. Be ready with your weapons, it looks like we are going in after all."

Above the machine gun fire, they could hear explosions in the upstairs section of the house but there was too much smoke to make any sense of the images from Green Squad's head cams. Dracul was feeling the pressure and addressed the squad in a clearly panicked voice.

"Engage the enemy! Sweep them out into the machine gun fire. Do it now!"

His voice was an octave above normal and he came across as a screaming fishwife and knew it. He also realised, but too late, that he had given orders to his father's squad and Adolphius was livid.

"The next time you disrespect me will cost you your life boy. Do you understand?"

Adolphius' black eyes were devoid of any fatherly love and his face was twisted in anger. Dracul dropped his head in submission and all could sense his shame.

The four Senators watched the burning house from the Range Rover. The helicopter was bathed in orange light. Its powerful rotors were fanning the black smoke and flames down the building rather than up in a surreal manner. It was carnage and the neighbourhood was waking up to it. Lights were coming on in the surrounding houses and people began spilling into the roads.

Grese gauged the moment well. She signalled Yellow Squad to come in from the back of the house to drop grenades in the back windows and then execute any enemy driven out by machine gun fire from the front. As they deployed, she heard three more explosions at the back of the house. When she looked at the monitors in the Range Rover, five of the comms units were dead. Then a fourth explosion split the night and two more comms units went down. As far as she could tell, none of them had got their grenades to the back windows. Grese couldn't afford to lose the remaining five of her squad or the back of the house would be open to escape. She flicked the comms switch to the *on* position.

"Yellow Squad pull back to a safe distance and take them as they are driven out."

She turned to the other Senators and summed up the situation.

"Our losses so far are twenty Drones and two Shadow commanders but that's acceptable. We are in and advancing our positions. Despite our heavy losses, we still have more than our originally planned force available, albeit with only one Shadow in command on the ground and O'Malley in the air," she looked at her watch. "Time is still good Adolphius, but we need a result in less than seven minutes or the emergency services will be arriving."

Adolphius was about to agree when O'Malley's broad Irish voice boomed out over the radio.

"Come in forward command."

"Receiving you O'Malley," Adolphius had assumed command.

"You've got to get your men at the front of the house inside now, while any survivors are still concussed. It has to be hand to hand stuff from here on or we'll time out, understood, over?"

"Roger that; understood and out."

Adolphius gave the order. Several seconds later they had augmented the five Drones upstairs with a further fifteen to go in at the ground floor. Their objective being to cleanse the building room by room. That left five outside at the back sweeping up. It was an insurmountable force, even for a squad as highly skilled and battle hardened as the corporal's.

Even in shock George scanned the bank of screens in front of him, dragging his mind back into focus. He had played out a dozen different *what if* scenarios in his mind, preparing for this moment. When his brain suddenly cleared Elizabeth and Ben immediately saw that change that had come over him. George flicked quickly and efficiently between screens, taking in the content of each. He was building a picture in his head of the enemy attack from a holistic view. He switched the comms on and saw that he had seven green lights, Mike and all six commandos were online. He was their eyes and ears and began his commentary to orientate them.

"OK men listen. We've got twelve enemy with rocket launchers at the front of the house, taking to their knees now... Range Rover in the drive with three or maybe four passengers, looks like a control point. Wait, twelve more baddies coming in to reinforce the positions and in our mined zone now. Detonating mines 13, 14 and 16."

George pressed the detonators on his consul. The shock wave shook the building, breaking glass at several of the windows. A single machine gun spat out its deathly rattle.

"Bingo! Nine down!" George checked the monitors frantically, "Brace yourselves. Enemy preparing for rocket fire... launching now!"

Moments later the house rocked on its foundations as twelve rockets ripped into it. George and the others in the basement fared the best, but the others in the body of the house were concussed at the massive shockwave. The newly built blast walls had done their job though and were still standing.

"Head count?" radioed George. His voice was urgent.

One by one they all checked in, groggy with the after-shock of the missile attack. He continued flicking through the monitors to update the enemy's position and continued his commentary.

"External camera picking up men on the roof now, five I think... Down at window level now."

George watched as the windows blew out and the intruders entered.

"Chas, Joey they're in! Good luck."

That was all George could do for them. He turned his attention back to his other monitors.

"Ten enemy approaching the front of the house with machine guns... They're at the doors and windows now. Detonating mines 1 through 8."

George pressed the buttons and the explosions rippled around the building. The screams of the dying and injured rang out in the night, each ending with the sound of a single shot.

"Bloody Hell, they're executing their own injured!" George looked at the monitors in horrified astonishment. "That's another six down for the bad guys."

Elizabeth and Ben exchanged glances and nodded in agreement. Uncle George was a one man demolition squad.

"Remind me not to piss you off in future Uncle!" Ben joked in typical Robinson style.

"Let's hope we all have one Ben," George never looked up from the monitors. "Attention men, there's another squad coming in from the back of the house, ten or twelve of them..."

Elizabeth turned to Ben.

"How many more have they got out there? We'll never get passed them and out to the stables. Never."

"We don't' have to Lizzie, we just have to make it up into the loft somehow."

"Of course, Emanuel Goldberg's portal! Why didn't I think of that?"

"Because you're blonde Lizzie, it goes with the territory..."

The smile that complimented Ben's quip was little more than a grimace. He knew that in a matter of minutes or even seconds, the house would be overrun with Shadows. Even getting to the loft, might be just as impossible as getting out to the stables. George was about to update the status quo when machine gun fire began upstairs. The brothers, Chas and Joey, had engaged the enemy. He muttered under his breath, "Be lucky boys," and then turned back to his radio.

"It's twelve not ten. They're coming in towards the back windows with grenades at hand. In range now, detonating mines 18 through 21," George's voice remained level and emotionless.

He seemed to have a natural ability to remain calm and focussed. The explosions rang out but there was no screaming, they were all clean kills.

"Seven more enemy down and they're pulling back!"

For a moment George thought that they were in full retreat and the tone of his last message reflected that. They stopped at the fence however and crouched facing the house with their AK-47s at the ready.

"Sorry lad's premature joculation. Five of them have taken up firing positions against the back fence. Looks like they're expecting you to leave by the back door lads so don't please them eh?"

George sequenced the monitors until he had full view of the front of the house again.

"They're regrouping out front. More than a dozen of them, less than twenty it's hard to say; there's so much smoke. Looks like they're coming in lads and I don't have any more toys except the one on the landing. God be with you."

George cut the radio and turned to Elizabeth and Ben.

"If you don't leave the house now then you never will. God only knows how though. They'll cut you down as soon as you get out there."

"We don't have to Uncle. Emanuel Goldberg's portal is in the loft so we've just got to get there unseen," Ben briefly embraced his uncle and added in parting. "You were awesome Uncle and you've given Mike and the lads a chance that they never really had. Now you've got to hold that stairway until Mike clears the enemy."

Ben kissed Aunt Jillie and whispered something to her that prompted a brave smile. Elizabeth said her goodbyes just as swiftly and couldn't help her tears. They all knew that they were leaving them to die. As they turned for the stairs, leading up to the hallway, Elizabeth looked guiltily back over her shoulder.

"We will fix this and meet again, I promise."

"You better bloody well had Lizzie," was Jillie's hollow response.

The unit had been well drilled with each knowing exactly what was expected of them. The brothers Chas and Joey were the most obvious pairing and they swiftly climbed the stairs to defend the first floor. The doors in the house were solid oak and all but two screws had been removed in each, to enable them to be ripped off their hinges easily and used for cover if required. There were six rooms that opened into the spacious hallway, three on each side. Chas and Joey tore the doors off and laid them three deep at each end of the corridor, before taking up their positions behind them. The combined thickness gave them four and a half inches of protection, enough to withstand machine gun fire and even a light grenade. The positioning of the barricades was chosen to create a killing field between them that the enemy had to enter in order to gain access to the staircase.

Zak, Rudy and Jamie's brief, was to secure the front rooms of the house. To afford them cover, they toppled the oak dresser in the lounge and laid the heavy table on its side in the dining room. They took up their positions at the furthest point from the front wall. Zak and Rudy took the lounge, with its pair of magnificent bay windows and James the smaller dining room, with its single bay. The blast walls took away their view of the gardens, so all they could do was wait in nervous anticipation for the imminent rocket attack.

Because of lack of resource, Mike had made the conscious decision to sacrifice the back of the house on the ground floor level. This was based on any assault coming from that direction could only gain access to the rest of the house via the hallway that would be defended by him and Jake. The hallway was the atrium of the house and gave access to the lounge, dining room, kitchen, study, front and back doors and to the grand staircase. It was a strategic position and whoever controlled it, controlled the house. They could not afford to lose it. The hallway was their *Alamo* and where they would all fall-back to for their final stand.

There were two other windowless rooms that had doors into the hallway, the cloakroom and washroom. From these positions, Mike and Red Jake were going to stake their ambush. The rooms would afford them protection from the initial rocket attack, and concealment from the enemy. George's final act would be to monitor the hallway and orientate them. They would then know the precise positions of the enemy before breaking cover. Of course that assumed that the cameras weren't destroyed in the blast.

They were all in place with their ear defenders on and as prepared as they could be. A lot would depend on the five-block thick blast walls in front of the doors and windows, resisting the initial rocket attacks. Each knew that the fate of all of them, would be determined in the next few minutes. Tini's brief early warning had given them just enough time to make their preparations; otherwise it would have all been over in moments. The house was in total silence and their nerves were already strained to breaking point. George's voice came in clearly over their comms, almost startling them.

"OK men listen. Twelve enemy with rocket launchers at the front of the house, taking to their knees now..."

Yakov Yurovsky cut the engine of his black sixteen seater Mercedes-Benz minibus and coasted the last 500 yards to the Robinson's house. In front of him, were the four Senators in the Range Rover and following behind, was the remainder of the Drone assault force led by two experienced Shadow commanders. Yurovsky had been given the command of the Red Squad rocket attack, so he was to be first to deploy. The rocket attack was an arm's length assault. This enabled Blue Squad to go in with machine guns hands-on. If the mission went as expected, then they probably wouldn't need to get their own hands dirty after that.

Yakov Yurovsky was no stranger to the elimination of whole family units, nor indeed their whole bloodline. Genocide had been his speciality, which had gained him favour amongst his fellow Shadows over the centuries. He was known as *The Executioner*. The elimination of the Robinson bloodline, would rate as an even more prestigious achievement than when he executed the entire Russian Imperial Romanov family.

Yurovsky's orders had come from Lenin himself, one of the ruling Senators at the time. On the night of 16th July 1918, Yurovsky had led a squad of Bolshevik secret police to a house in the Ural Mountains. The deposed Tsar, Nicholas II, along with his wife Alexandra, son Alexei and their four daughters: Olga; Tatiana; Maria and Anastasia, were taken to a sub-basement in the house and brutally executed by him.

Yakov Yurovsky smiled at the memory. He was a devoted Marxist who cruelly manipulated regimes for power and money. He was an inscrutable man with an evil set to his eyes, a shock of black hair and a heavy moustache over a thick ducktail beard. Yurovsky had hated the Romanovs and all that they stood for, which had made it even easier to kill them. They were supporters of the Angel-led White Movement, opposed to the Red Army and the Bolsheviks. Their doctrine was for law and order and the salvation of Russia. Their White Army had fought against traitors and barbarians and proclaimed a united multinational Russia. This was in direct contrast to the Shadow's manifesto.

The Range Rover ahead pulled up just short of the targeted house and Grese left the car moments later, disappearing into the gardens of a neighbouring property.

"Dogs," Yurovsky assumed and signalled his men to hold.

Less than a minute later Grese returned and Alexis' voice broke the radio silence.

"Red Squad advance to your positions!"

Yurovsky pulled on his black balaclava and led Red Squad to their positions. They were dressed in black night tactical gear, with AK-47s slung over their shoulders and SMAW rocket launchers at hand. Each had six NATO L2A2 frag grenades in the pouches of their webbing and a dozen spare magazines. They were armed to the teeth. The squads ran in single file following the Range Rover until it pulled into the drive of the Robinson's household. Yurovsky and Red Squad continued on to their positions. They knelt in front of the impressive homestead shouldering their rocket launchers, waiting for the command to attack.

Blue Squad, led by Boris Stein, began spilling into the space behind them readying themselves to take up small arms against the enemy. Stein was a last minute junior substitute for Heinrich Bloom who was one of the most powerful Shadows of the 21st century. Heinrich Bloom also enjoyed the ear of the Hydra herself. Bloom had been taken out of the frame at the last minute on her orders. The justification that was given was, "Needed for other essential duties," but they all knew that the truth was that he was too valuable to lose. It also underpinned Adolphius' belief that the Hydra had little faith in his cell's ability to achieve its objective.

Yurovsky was just about to give the command to launch the rocket attack, when the earth erupted behind him. Three almost simultaneous ear-splitting blasts ripped through Blue Squad decimating the unit, taking six out instantly. One of the blast victims spiralled in his death throws, emptying the magazine of his AK-47, taking out three others in the convulsion. One of them was Boris Stein, not dead but seriously wounded.

"Minefield!" yelled Yurovsky. He was a veteran and naturally took charge of the leaderless squad. He swiftly regrouped the remains of Blue Squad and augmented it with O'Malley's land-based standby unit.

"Fire you buffoons!" Alexis' voice came thundering across the radio,

Yurovsky was not amused and simply shouted abuse back at the man he called a *white haired old freak*. He then switched his radio off in contempt. Red Squad launched their twelve rockets in unison and the house seemed to swell under the enormity of the explosion. The ground floor doors and windows at the front and flanks were now gaping holes Flames and smoke from the drapes and soft furnishings were licking up the outside walls. At that moment, O'Malley arrived in the air above them with men already abseiling from the five dangling ropes. It was precision flying and skilled rope work. Seconds later grenades were through the upstairs windows and they were in.

"Anyone in those rooms, upstairs or down will not have survived, so the task is probably already at least half done," Yurovsky surmised as he signalled Blue Squad forwards.

They slid through the retiring rocket launchers and took their places in front of the gaping openings. The enemy's meticulous level of preparedness became suddenly apparent to Yurovsky. A rapid series of explosions rippled around the building taking six of his men down, some of them screaming in agony. Those that were still standing began emptying their AK-47s into the building, while Yurovsky went around executing those that hadn't been killed outright. His last bullet was for Boris Stein who looked up at him pleadingly. A lifetime of association meant nothing to Yurovsky. He dispatched him without a word. Machine guns began their menacing chatter in the upstairs section of the house, shortly followed by three explosions at the back of it that sounded nothing like grenades.

"More mines," Yurovsky thought ruefully, no longer under-estimating the strategic ability of his enemy. "They were well prepared indeed," he acknowledged.

Yurovsky re-activated his comms set and chose to direct his communication at O'Malley rather than Alexis and the other Senators, snubbing them overtly.

"O'Malley do you read me?"

"Loud and clear, go ahead Yurovsky."

"What's the status of the assault at the back of the house?"

"Failed. We suffered multiple deaths. They have aborted and have taken up firing positions along the back fence. Over."

"OK understood. I'm sending Red Squad in at the front with the four remaining gunners. Let your men upstairs know so we don't get any *black on black* casualties.." then, as an afterthought knowing that Alexis would be listening. "Oh yes, and tell that white-headed poison dwarf too. Out."

"It looks like I'll be earning my money tonight after all," Yurovsky mused.

His pulse quickened with the delicious anticipation of it.

Chas and Joey felt the floorboards under them lift with the force of the rocket explosions below. Cracks that you could put your hands in appeared simultaneously up the walls and smoke began to billow up the stairwell. Almost at once, grenades went off in the bedrooms to the sides of them, followed by rapid automatic fire. The intruders were clearly spraying the rooms with lead for a lucky kill.

"Keep your head down Bro, don't get yourself killed by a lucky shot," Chas as ever wasn't too concerned about his own safety but he was always scared for his brother.

"You're worse than Mum, you just worry about yourself Chas. This'll be a walk in the park anyway," it was the usual squaddie banter that somehow calms soldier's nerves before the fray.

Three Drones spilled into the corridor from the blown out bedrooms. Their AK-47s were spitting venomously to encourage any enemy to take cover rather than return fire. It was unprofessional and clumsy. They were now in the killing zone, disorientated in the smoke, and without sight of their enemy.

Chas and Joey opened up together aiming slightly upwards so as to not catch each other in friendly fire. Their machine guns, capable of delivering their 9mm bullets at a rate of 800 rounds per minute, literally cut the three men down in seconds.

The two remaining Drones were alerted by the exchange of fire ending with the definitive sound of the Heckler & Kochs. Based on that, it was easy for them to conclude that their comrades were dead. They were also able to place the machine gun fire as coming from both ends of the corridor. After a brief dialogue over their head comms, they had formed their strategy. Both Drones ripped mirrors off the bedroom walls and slid them out into the hallway. Chas and Joey almost immediately shot the glass out of them, but it was too late. The Drones had already seen what they needed. They had them positioned and sight of the oak doors that were giving them cover.

The Drones each took a frag grenade from their webbing, pulled the pins from the fly-off levers, and tossed them to the far ends of the hallway. The thickening smoke had obscured the act, so the first that Chas knew of the grenade's arrival, was the heavy thump as it hit the thick oak door. Fortunately it had fallen on the safe side. He screamed out a warning to his brother.

"Get down Joey, grenades!"

The frag grenades were on four second fuses and that was all the warning they had. Both detonated simultaneously. Chas felt the door crash into him with enormous force, driving him against the wall. Fortunately the lamination of sturdy doors had served their purpose. He desperately called out to his brother.

"Joey! Joey!"

But there was no reply. One of the Drones stepped out into the corridor with his AK-47 blazing, taking Chas in the upper chest. It would have stopped a bull, but Chas was demented and kept coming. He was screaming at the Drone as he unloaded his magazine into him, sending him spinning back into the room.

Blood was pumping out of Chas's chest and boiling out of his mouth as he staggered down the corridor towards his brother. He was mouthing Joey's name over and over but no air came out of his lungs to sound the words. It was just as he saw Joey's mutilated and dismembered body, that the bullets ripped through his back and the base of his neck. His lifeless corpse fell like a puppet with its strings cut across his brother's, uniting them in death.

The last of the five Drones ejected the spent magazine as his victim collapsed over the remains of his comrade. It had been costly, but they had succeeded in securing the first floor. As the Drone walked towards the stairs he called O'Malley on his head comms.

"O'Malley, are you reading me?"

"Loud and clear. Over"

"We've taken the first floor. Two enemy down and our losses are four. I'm taking position at the top of the staircase now waiting on ground support to come in. Out."

The Drone had no concerns over the loss of the others in his squad. It was just collateral damage to him. The macabre scene of the two SAS soldiers next to him, tangled in death, amused him. The smile was still on his face as he took up his position at the top of the stairs, waiting for his next kill.

James was behind the heavy Regency oak dining table. He had laid it on its side across the corner of the room nearest the door into the hallway. From this position he would stand the best chance of retreating into the atrium when the time came. He had gambled a couple of valuable minutes wedging three grenades close to the door and window. James had attached draw cords to the grenade pins and ran them back to his position. The gamble had paid off. He had just finished and got back to his retreat, when he heard the rockets ignite in their launch tubes.

The impact was massive. The dense block blast wall partly disintegrated under the force of it, showering him in debris. But other than cuts and bruises, he was uninjured. Machine gun fire from outside the house began ripping through the room, destroying everything. Hundreds of rounds thumped harmlessly into the sturdy old table and soft furnishings. Randomly the scene reminded him of the movie *Mr and Mrs Smith*, where Brad Pitt and Angelina Jolie were under siege in much the same manner.

"They got through it," James thought wryly and promised himself a repeat viewing if he was lucky enough to get through his ordeal.

The automatic fire abated. The first of the Drones stepped in through the window and crouched behind the cover of what was left of the blast wall. He was still trying to make sense of what he was looking at when the fly-off lever of the first grenade dropped at his feet. His last image in this world, was of the grenade inches from his face as it detonated.

Zak and Rudy had decided to use a decoy tactic. The toppled wardrobe at the back of the room was an obvious stronghold and would automatically attract the enemy's attention and most likely their combined fire power. Instead of using the cover of the wardrobe, they had chosen to take up positions in the corners of the lounge, either side of the double bay windows. The downside was that they only had the sturdy lounge chairs to protect them from the blast.

They were banking their hopes on the blast wall taking the main impact of the rocket attack, with minimal sideways transferred shock. They were also gambling that the residual shock could be absorbed by the heavy armchairs. From their lateral positions they would remain unsighted and could take any intruder the instant they entered the room.

Their greatest risks were hitting each other in the crossfire, and the enemy getting smart and taking them out with secondary rocket fire.

"OK Zak let's run through it one more time. After impact we stand back from the front wall a yard or two giving us an oblique line of fire. that way you won't shoot my arse off."

Rudy winked at his partner in crime. His broad smile was unlikely in the last seconds before all Hell was about to let loose.

"Got it Rudy. Let them get all the way in before we hit them, so they don't go running off telling tales about where we are."

Just as they settled into their cover positions behind the generous leather armchairs, George's voice came in across their comms sets.

"Brace yourselves. Enemy preparing for rocket fire... launching now!"

The air was filled with the rush of multiple incoming rockets. The house shook on its foundations as the missiles thumped into the dense block blast walls, cracking them and shoving them physically towards the back of the lounge. The armchairs served their purpose in absorbing the shockwave, but the force was so great that it rammed them against the walls. They were both left slightly concussed and winded, fighting for breath. The blast was immediately followed by the rattling of AK-47s, as they slashed in arcs around the spacious lounge ripping the room to pieces. The random shredding of the room with automatic fire gave Zak and Rudy just enough time to recover their breath and gather their wits.

Two Drones stepped in unison through the remains of the blown out windows, concentrating their fire into the dresser as expected. Zak and Rudy opened fire from their oblique positions and caught the Drones unaware in their united crossfire, driving them back out through the window like lifeless ragdolls. As their corpses dropped, two more Drones pressed through and were immediately cut down and dispatched in the same manner.

The firing stopped and nearly a minute passed.

"I don't like it Rudy. They're up to something, more rockets maybe?"

"Yeah, let's get the hell outta here while we still can!"

Zak was the furthest from the door. He had to make it past the two blown out windows to get to the hallway and needed cover. Rudy edged over to the window and poked the barrel of his submachine gun out and randomly squeezed off a magazine. A single scream signalled a lucky hit, as Zak ran doubled up passed the windows. Seconds later they were in the hallway just as a second volley of rockets crashed into the lounge, taking out the front wall. It was a narrow escape. Rudy raised an eyebrow and flashed a cheeky smile at Zak as they ran to take up their positions to defend the atrium.

Yakov Yurovsky had already lost four men in the assault on the Robinson's lounge and wasn't about to lose any more in the same way. He pulled his men out and re-deployed the rocket launchers. Just before the launch one of the SAS soldiers opened fire from the broken downstairs bay window. The fire was undirected, but it caught the Drone next to him through the gut. He screamed out in agony. Yurovsky was unsympathetic and simply put a single bullet through the back of his head in perfunctory manner, then gave the order to launch.

The front wall of the house blew out and the unsupported room above fell in on it. Yurovsky ordered three Drones in to leverage the advantage, despite the risk of further collapse. At the same time, he deployed the rest of his force at the front door and dining room window.

Yurovsky had heard the exchange between O'Malley and the surviving Drone from the first floor assault and had already made his decision. The upstairs needed reinforcing or they could lose the initiative if the remaining Drone couldn't hold the stairway. He quickly appraised the front of the house. The rainwater downpipes were cast iron and looked well fixed. One of them was close to an upstairs, blown out window which would give him easy and silent access in. Decision made, Yurovsky quickly and effortlessly scaled the side of the building. Whereas this would have been a significant feat for a human, his natural power to weight ratio as a Shadow made this task simple. In less than a minute he was in.

Elizabeth and Ben disappeared through the doorway, leading up to the hallway as George turned his attention back to his screens. Jillie came to his side. She had a feeling of intense foreboding and somehow knew that they were spending their last few moments together. When she looked at the screen the hallway was deserted.

"Mike and Jake must already be in their hideaways," George observed without looking up, and then added. "Look there's Elizabeth and Ben."

They were making their way cautiously to the main staircase with their weapons at the ready. George flicked the screen to the stair camera and gasped in horror. There was a Drone knelt at the top of the stairs with an automatic weapon trained at the bottom opening.

"Christ!" he shouted and hit the detonate button.

Unfortunately, it was at the precise moment that Elizabeth and Ben came into view. The sound of machine gun fire from the Drone and the explosion seemed simultaneous and the stair camera went dead. They looked at each other with shocked expressions, neither knowing for sure what had happened. All possibilities were open, including that George had killed them all.

"I have to go to them Jillie, I have to." George said solemnly.

He stood and reached for his submachine gun and webbing belt. Jillie threw her arms desperately around him to stop him leaving.

"No! You can't George. If you do, I know I won't see you again. Please..."

"I have to Jillie. I couldn't live with myself otherwise. Besides Mike will take care of things you know that."

They held each other only briefly but desperately. George broke the moment. He visibly gathered himself and crossed to the stairs. The thin smile that he gave Jillie as he left said it all. He wasn't coming back.

Elizabeth and Ben let themselves cautiously into the grand hallway. The rocket attack had filled it with debris from the shattered blast wall. Family pictures and ornaments were smashed and strewn around without sentiment. Ben's eyes involuntarily fell on the light patch on the wallpaper that betrayed where the old antique mirror had been hung. It was all that remained as evidence of how this nightmare had begun.

Momentarily he wondered if that was all that it was, just a bad dream that he would awaken from shortly with the most fantastic story to tell. He was brought back to reality as machine gun fire spewed into the hallway and buzzed around their heads like demented bees. Several holes appeared where the mirror had been hung, underpinning their good decision to have moved it.

Elizabeth helped break Ben's inertia.

"Come on Ben quickly! We have to make it to the stairs and get out of here before it's too late."

They had to cross the hallway to the other side without any cover from the automatic fire. Surviving the next few moments would just be a question of luck.

Elizabeth and Ben reached the staircase unscathed and turned to go up it. They froze on the bottom step, as they met by the cold stare of a Drone on the landing, as he squeezed the trigger of his AK-47.

Suddenly, the staircase erupted as the C4 explosive detonated to George's command. The Drone's rifle emptied its magazine harmlessly into the walls and ceiling but the blast threw them back into the hallway and the incoming machine gun fire. Fortunately it was being aimed randomly about four feet above the floor and fizzed harmlessly above them.

They snaked on their bellies back towards the cover of the blown out stairwell and climbed up through the debris. When they reached the top, neither was prepared for what they saw. They gasped at the sheer horror of it and Elizabeth turned away retching uncontrollably. Each time she breathed in the smoke filled air chocked her, making her heave even more. Ben had to shake her firmly to break the cycle of it.

The mutilated bodies of Chas and Joey were at their feet, entangled in the confusion of an undignified death. Chas's blood-soaked corpse was sprawled across the pitiful remains of his brother, seemingly protecting him even after death. Perhaps it was the deep shock of it all, but neither was aware of Yurovsky as he stood there next to them with his weapon levelled at their waists.

George burst through the doorway into the smoke-filled hallway with his submachine gun at the ready. Incoming fire was all around him. It was faceless though, just guns blindly pointed into the hall by their operators staying out of harm's way, hoping for a random kill. George was out in the open and instinctively threw himself to the floor. It turned out to be a life-saving decision, confirmed by a burst of automatic fire that ripped into the wall only inches above his head. George used his elbows and knees to get to the protection of the heavy ship's chest on the opposite side of the hall. He raised himself on to his haunches and pressed himself against the wall, keeping his head below the level of the top of the chest.

At the same time Zak, Rudy and James left the front rooms of the house, moments before a second volley of rockets tore into the lounge and dining room. The Drones, firing into the hallway, had pulled back to allow the attack. It had given them a valuable window of opportunity to take cover in the other doorways leading off the hallway.

Mike's voice came across their comms.

"Head count and whereabouts?"

Mike held his breath in trepidation and was relieved as each signed in. When there was no response from Chas, none were surprised when Joey failed to call in too. It was how they had all expected it to be in the end; brothers fighting for each other's lives, or vengeance for the first to fall.

The loss hit them all hard and it took valuable moments before Mike could trust his voice again.

"OK let's do this for Chas and Joey. We have to assume that we've lost the first floor and enemy fire will be coming from there too. George is here with us so we won't get a heads up to tell us when they're in and where we want them..."

Jillie's voice cut in sharply.

"Just keep your heads down and I'll tell you when they are committed and in mid-hallway. You just kill the bastards!"

For some reason Mike momentarily felt like a naughty boy and couldn't think of anything else to say but, "Copy that."

His men were waiting on orders from Mike, as soldiers do in the heat of battle. It gives them clarity of mind and almost automates their responses taking away fear.

"Grenades at the ready," Mike began. "Hold until Jillie positions them for us. George you're closest. Open the door at the back of the hall and leave it wide open. I want it to look like we've already left the house that way. Hopefully they'll go straight to it. Make Chas and Joey proud of us lads!" Mike cut the communication.

George began snaking his way to the end of the hall on his belly, even before Mike had finished his brief. The incoming fire was relentless but unimaginative, all aimed at waist height above the floor. George reached up to the door lever and committed his weight to it, just as a burst of automatic fire smashed into the oak door, shattering his hand and the cast bronze door lever. He stifled the scream that welled in his throat. George desperately tried to push the door open but the catch had re-engaged with the door in the shut position. Waves of pain and nausea crashed through his body but he couldn't and wouldn't let himself succumb to it. All their lives could depend on such a simple illusion as an open door.

George snaked back fifteen yards up the corridor, biting his lip and drawing blood in an effort to divert the pain from his mutilated hand. He waited for a pause in the automatic fire and prepared himself for the sprint. When that pause came, George left the floor as if under starter's orders. Seconds later, with bullets fizzing around him, he crashed into the solid door. The sound of his collar bone breaking as the door jamb gave was every bit as loud as the gunfire but he never heard it nor felt it. A short spurt of machine gun fire tore into George's back and opened it up like a zipper, killing him instantly. His lifeless body spewed in through the open doorway kicking and convulsing in the almost comical spasms of death.

Jillie saw George's brave run at the door on the screen in front of her. She lost sight of him just as the Drones spilled in through the front door, with their AK-47s blazing. Her heart literally stopped with the dread and fear of not knowing whether he had made it to safety or not. Then a feeling of finality came over her and she knew, there and then that she had lost him. She forced herself to focus one last time.

"They're in maybe eight of them, mid-hallway now! God bless you..."

Jillie cut the call. She was in shock. Something had happened and she sensed it, like part of her had died. Irrationally she turned all the screens off. It was symbolic, almost an act of closure. Jillie picked up the machine gun and walked robotically to the stairs.

Alexis was still seething from the public abuse that he'd got from Yurovsky. He vowed that if Yurovsky didn't die in this assault, then he would kill him anyway. It was now a question of honour. Nobody had disrespected him in the past and lived to gloat about it, but that was for later. He looked at his wristwatch. They had been engaged for six minutes, it was too long but at last the ground assault was going in.

"Illya, take half of Grese's squad from the back and start piling our dead on the front lawn. Then douse and burn them, were running out of time."

Alexis had usurped Grese's authority but there was no challenge, this was an accepted entitlement earned through age and experience.

"Adolphius. We can expect unwanted visitors within the next five minutes. All the Drones are deployed, so we'll need to dispel them ourselves. Perhaps you could use one of the rocket launchers and take out the lead vehicle, that's all it will take to make them stand back."

It was an order politely phrased as a suggestion and Adolphius went to his task without question or resentment. Alexis turned his attention to the radio.

"O'Malley, do you read me?"

"Go ahead Alexis."

"They've mined the gardens, so check out a suitable spot in the road and land there in precisely four minutes. Be prepared to touchdown and go."

"Understood and out."

Alexis turned to Grese.

"We'll take anyone that comes out the front way. Stay on the drive or the footpath, that's all we can trust to be explosive free."

Grese picked up her AK-47 without hesitation. She had a score to settle for Katya that could only be achieved by some Angel blood-letting. She subconsciously licked her upper lip in that lascivious, idiosyncratic manner of hers.

Alexis and Grese took their positions either side of the Robinson's front door and Adolphius took his on the road, ready to take on the first vehicle that approached. O'Malley began his sweep of the avenue. He could imagine just what Mike and his SAS team were going through as he had been there before. The feeling of guilt was crushing him. He was not only a traitor to those dying soldiers, but a traitor to his own race and the future of it. The urge to plunge his helicopter into the three Senators and end it all, was almost overwhelming. It would have been so easy. But then that would have taken courage, something he once had in abundance but lost somewhere along the way. Instead, O'Malley continued obediently searching for a safe landing place and cursed his own weakness. He had sentenced himself to a life in Purgatory and his friends, to death.

"Deploy grenades now!"

Mike's command was clear and unequivocal. The remaining five of them tossed their grenades in unison into the smoke filled hallway and took cover behind the heavy oak doors.

There were six Drones in mid-hallway when the TNT powered NATO frag grenades came in. Each had a killing radius of 30 feet and the fuses set for only four seconds. Unfortunately for Mike and his men, that was enough time for three of the Drones to distance themselves and find the meagre cover that the hallway offered. The other three were obliterated in the combined blast leaving the hall strewn with body parts. Zak, Rudy and James were the first to leave their cover. With their backs to the front door, they began laying down fire up the hallway. They were shooting blindly in the smoke that was now even denser after the multiple grenade attack.

Zak bellowed urgently down his comms to Mike and Jake, coughing violently as he did so.

"Stay under cover 'till we clear the hallway, then come out and watch our backs for anything coming in from the front. We will clear the way out to the back door. Do you copy that?"

"Understood Zak. Good hunting!"

Mike cut the radio. He could hear the AK-47s returning fire, confirming that the grenades hadn't taken out at least two of the enemy. It was going to be a random shoot out and the outcome would just be who got lucky. The dense, choking smoke made it almost impossible to breathe in hallway. Zak, Rudy and James knew that they had to finish this in less than a minute, or they would become smoke victims anyway. Their coughing was almost as raucous as the machine gun fire.

James was first to pass the blown out stairwell and see the tell-tale barrel flares from the two AK-47s ahead. Two short blasts came from his machine gun, aimed just above the flares, silencing their deathly rattles immediately.

"Two down!" James coughed out his words. "Hallway cleared."

Choking and retching, Zak and Rudy hurried towards James and the back door desperate to fill their lungs with something that resembled air. None of them had noticed the third Drone, who had taken cover and remained unengaged in the upper part of the stairwell. One long burst from his AK-47 was all that it took to deny all three of them the fresh air that they had so desperately craved.

Elizabeth and Ben suddenly became aware of an intense malevolence and the acrid smell of Shadow. They turned slowly to face the heavily bearded man with his AK-47 standing uncomfortably close to them. There was an almost maniacal glint in his black eyes that sent a shiver through them. The man was holding their gaze confidently. It came as no surprise when they realised that he was holding their minds too. He was enjoying the moment and seemed in no hurry to squeeze the trigger. The horror of the deaths of Chas and Joey had momentarily paralysed their consciousness allowing him in to their minds, giving him the upper hand. They were fully in the grip of his mind control, unable to resist.

"So you are what all the fuss is about? Pathetic, what a disappointment," Yurovsky turned his black shaggy head and spat on the floor in contempt. "Even the Romanov aristocrats put up a better fight, before I executed them in that dark cellar in the Urals. Perhaps you can better their screams for mercy though!"

He laughed and turned his cold eyes to Ben.

"You can watch your sister die first..."

Ben was transfixed, powerless to move as he watched the bearded menace increase the pressure on the trigger of his assault rifle that was now pointed between Elizabeth's eyes. In that same moment the air was split by the combined explosion of grenades in the downstairs hallway. The shockwave drove up the stairwell with such force, that they were all bowled over and slammed into the wall, concussing them. Valuable seconds passed as each tried to recover their senses. Yurovsky was the first to find his feet and he stood above Elizabeth and Ben grinning with his rifle once again trained on them and his finger committed to the trigger.

There was a metallic click as the safety catch on Yurovsky's AK-47 moved of its own accord from the *fire* position to *weapon safe*. A bemused expression came over his face that slowly changed into realisation and then fear.

"Telekinesis!" he gasped in astonishment.

They were more advanced than he could have imagined. Yurovsky had squandered his opportunity to kill them out of his own vanity. He had lost the initiative in the chaos of the explosion. The combined power of Elizabeth and Ben's minds, had taken control of his and it was insurmountable. Yurovsky just stood there unable to function. The fear inside him writhed and churned in his stomach and he knew that his vanity had just cost him his life.

Machine gun fire had begun in earnest downstairs. Ben knew that they had a minute at most to get to Emanuel Goldberg's portal in the loft. He jumped up and punched the loft hatch away then turned to Elizabeth.

"Give me a leg up Lizzie," moments later he was in reaching down to Elizabeth. "Quickly take my hand."

Ben hauled Elizabeth up with considerably more effort than he had imagined.

"You're stacking on a bit Sis," Ben said with typical Robinson sarcasm.

Despite all the horror that was going on around her, Elizabeth rose to the gibe and cussed him like any woman scorned might and Ben reeled at the mouthful.

"Alright, steady on Lizzie, it was only a joke!"

Ben turned his attention back to the trembling Shadow below them.

"What's your name?" he demanded.

"Yakov Yurovsky," was the obedient reply.

Ben had either read about the history of the Romanovs, or he had learned of them through May's teachings. He wasn't sure.

"Well Yurovsky, go and meet the Romanovs. I'm sure they're looking forward to seeing you again."

Ben and Elizabeth turned to face each other and nodded in agreement as they exerted the power of their combined minds. Seconds later there was a metallic clattering on the floor around Yurovsky. He looked down in horror at the six grenade fly-off levers at his feet. His hands groped in panic at the now primed grenades in the pockets of his webbing, trying to rid himself of them. Yurovsky had just enough time to look up and see the smiling faces of the Robinsons as they closed the loft hatch above him, before he was torn in half by his own grenades and sent into oblivion.

Mike tried desperately to reach his men over the comms but there was no response from any of them except Jake. The last round of automatic fire was from an AK-47, not from one of the Heckler & Kochs. This had to mean that he'd lost them all. George hadn't responded earlier either and Jillie had left the radio. There was a sudden explosion upstairs, which meant that there were still enemy up there which didn't bode well for Elizabeth and Ben. It had all gone FUBAR.

Mike called Jake back again on the comms.

"Come in Jake, we've got to take this fight outside to give Jillie a chance," then he added more in hope than belief, "Lizzie and Ben too, if it's not already too late. We go out the back on three, got it?"

"Loud and clear Mike."

Jake had dropped the *sir*. Now they were just two friends fighting desperately for their lives.

They burst out into the smoke filled hallway and made a run for the back door. They were blindly stepping over bodies and never even realised that one of them was George. The smoke was burning their eyes and choking their lungs. They needed to get outside whatever the risk. Jake wrenched the back door open. With their machine guns blazing, they ran straight into enemy fire.

As far as Mike could make, out there were four of them. Both he and Jake trained their weapons on the barrel flares coming from the back of the garden. As experienced soldiers, they naturally assumed who were whose targets. Two enemy guns fell silent almost immediately, but the intense incoming fire drove them back towards the house. They had almost made it through the threshold, when Mike screamed out in agony as a bullet took him in the upper thigh. Red Jake put his massive arm around him and pulled him out of the doorway into the cover of the kitchen, taking a bullet in his shoulder as he did so. Although Jake cursed through clenched teeth, the bull of a man shrugged off the pain and maintained a firm hold on his injured friend.

"We'll have to try the front way Mike," Red Jake decided for them.

He had risen to his new responsibility as protector of his commanding officer and friend.

The brief spell in the night air had given their lungs some respite from the smoke though, enough to see them back through to the front of the house if needed.

"Can you stand?" Red Jake asked.

"Yes, if I can lean on you Jake," Mike's leg was almost useless and he needed a few moments to steel himself so he distracted Jake. "Did you ever see the movie, *Butch Cassidy and the Sundance Kid*, their last stand?"

"Saw it boss. You thinkin' of when Butch and Sundance were all shot up and left the house, guns blazing with half the Bolivian army out there?"

"Yeah that's the one. How did it end for them?"

"Badly boss. You ready?" despite all, Jake still had a devilish twinkle in his eye and total a distain of death.

"Badly eh?" Mike gave him that cheeky sideways look. "Come on Red Jake, let's go and re-write history!"

Jake took Mike's weight and drove him forward like they were in a three-legged race. They ran through the kitchen and into the now blazing hallway. As they burst through the blown out front door into the garden their clothes were on fire and they were partially blinded by the smoke and heat. Oblivious to the pain, Mike laid down automatic fire to his right, in a broad aimless arc and Jake did the same to his left. There was a single pained scream that rose even above the noise of the gunfire indicating a hit. It was meagre comfort for two men who were literally running blind into the arms of the enemy.

They never saw the ambush, and made only twenty yards before Alexis and Grese opened up with their AK-47s from behind them, scything them down mercilessly. Mike and Jake's bodies danced a comical jig to the close range onslaught of lead and then collapsed together in a burning heap in the middle of the Robinson's lawn.

When Jillie reached the top of the stairs and let herself into the hallway, all guns had fallen silent. To the left of her, the hall was ablaze and impassable. She knew that when she'd last seen George, he was headed the other way though, towards the back of the house. The smoke was dense forcing her down on her hands and knees, to get below the worst of it. She felt her way along the hallway towards the back of the house. Jillie found George almost immediately; lying face down just inside the kitchen. His back was ripped open and his shirt, drenched in blood. She gently turned his head to face her and began speaking softly to him, as if he could hear her.

"George it's me Jillie. I'm here now it's OK."

George's sightless eyes were looking directly at her and his mouth was still in the grimace of a silent, agonised scream. She kissed him tenderly and stroked his hair with the back of her hand.

"Wait for me George, I'm coming now."

She was suddenly aware of the Drone, who had been in the stairwell until then. He crouched next to her with the barrel of his rifle only inches from her face, but she showed no fear. Then, as she silently pulled the pins from two of the hand grenades in George's webbing, she whispered tenderly to him.

"I'm bringing someone with me..."

Elizabeth and Ben fumbled their way in the pitch darkness of the loft until they found the mirror. When Elizabeth placed her hand on the glass it began to vibrate and her relief was beyond immense.

"It works Ben," the comment was unnecessary and Elizabeth felt a little silly for saying it.

She took her hand off the mirror suddenly as if it had burnt her.

"We've got to both be really sure that we know where and when we're going to Ben. Remember what happened last time."

"Yes, too well! If we get this wrong then it's all been for nothing."

Ben paused for thought. He was trying to clear his head to remember the detail.

"So, the accident was February 18th 2009 for sure. I remember that clearly. It was only two days after my twelfth birthday," Ben had a peg to hang it on and besides, they had already past four anniversaries since then. "And we know that Mum, Dad and Crystalita all died at ten minutes past seven. To stand the best chance against Grese and Alexis, we need to take each of them on together, that way we have infinitely more power. We can't afford the risk of being separated. May said that if the odds were one on one, then their experience would count in the end."

"Agreed, we have to stay together at all cost. If we go to the school first and stop Crystalita from leaving when she did and falling into Alexis' trap, then we don't even need to take the risk of fighting Alexis. Hher death just won't happen. Then, we both deal with Grese before Mum and Dad get to the canal bend. We can work out *how* later. Maybe we could even use these machine guns and Crystalita's help?"

"Perfect Lizzie and its low risk. Avoiding taking Alexis on is simply inspirational! Anyway, we can't go to our house first in case we meet ourselves. You know, that thing about not being able to co-exist in the same place?"

Ben was once again in awe of Elizabeth's quick thinking.

"OK so what time and where?" Ben asked.

"The stables. We need transport and you've always wanted to ride Dad's Harley! An hour or so before should be OK. Say quarter to six, February 18th 2009?"

They held hands to be sure that they left as one and placed the other on the mirror. It began to vibrate and became fluid.

"Concentrate Ben, quarter to six in the evening of February 18th 2009 at the stables," with that they pushed through into the past.

It was already ten minutes since the initial rocket launch. Illya Dracul, with his two Drones were piling their dead on the front lawn. Some of them had been dismembered and it was a gruesome task. He dowsed the corpses in gasoline, ready to torch them. Adolphius had taken his position at the top of the drive with a rocket launcher, awaiting the long overdue emergency services. Alexis and Grese were in their positions either side of the Robinson's front door.

Alexis looked anxiously at his wristwatch. It had taken too long and they still didn't have a result. He could only give it another minute or so at best, before they would need to pull out and abandon the mission.

It was at that precise moment, that two burning men staggered out of the house firing their automatic weapons in what was clearly random manner. He saw Adolphius go down screaming as he and Grese opened up with his AK-47s. They emptied their magazines into the backs of the men, cutting them down and sending them sprawling face down across the lawn. Alexis crossed over to the two burning bodies while Grese covered his back. He kicked the back of their heads to turn their faces towards him.

"One's Jackson, the others a nobody," he drove his boot into Jackson's scorched face in anger. "But it's not what we came here for!"

The ground floor was now fully ablaze and smoke was billowing out of the upstairs windows. Without taking her eyes off the front of the hous,e Grese offered her opinion.

"Nobody could still be alive in there Alexis, the ground floor is an inferno and anyone still upstairs would have died of smoke inhalation. We know that they keep the portal in the hall and that couldn't possibly have escaped the automatic fire or it's burning now anyway. If the Robinsons escaped through it, then they are already in oblivion."

Alexis rubbed his rheumy eyes that were now sore with the effects of the smoke and considered Grese's summation. His white hair was a storm around him in the down-draft of the landing helicopter.

"Perhaps Grese and perhaps not, but we have run out of time anyway."

He turned to Dracul who was tending his father's injury.

"We're leaving. Torch the rest of the bodies and get him in the helicopter," he turned to Grese. "Surviving Drones leave in the Range Rover and the hired minibuses stay."

Alexis' fury was tangible. None of them dared to so much as look at him, lest he turned on them.

"It's a bloody shambles we've left our DNA all over the place. When the Hydra hears of this, heads will roll, mark my words!"

Alexis coughed as he breathed in the smoke that swirled around him and added venomously.

"We will go down in history as the clowns that blew the Shadow's anonymity, after 5,000 years of stealth. Or more precisely Adolphius will!"

Detective Inspector Russell Bates hated working nights. Even after fifteen years in the Serious Crime Division, he still hadn't got used to it.

If something really dreadful was going to happen, it would invariably happen in the early hours when he had little or no support.

His phone rang, it was Mary the receptionist.

"Sir, the switchboard has gone mad. I've got something coming in about some attack on a house in Queensway. Some militia with automatic weapons, explosives, helicopter and I don't know what else. The house is on fire and it sounds like there's an all-out war going on."

"Is it a hoax Mary? What cars have we got on tonight?" the detective was shocked into action.

"No hoax, and just three cars sir."

"Get them there, but tell them to stand back and not to engage. Just observation and public safety for now, got it? I want fire tenders and ambulances there straight away and get me Brigadier Clifton-Holt on the line. Tell him that I don't care what time it is!"

"Right away sir."

"Oh and Mary, what house number is it?"

"Number 53 sir."

The address was familiar to Bates, "53, isn't that the Robinson girl's address? You know the one who was stabbed in town recently."

"Um, yes it is sir. Unlucky coincidence perhaps?" Mary offered.

"I wonder? I'm not big on coincidences Mary. Get me all you can on Elizabeth Robinson and anyone else that lives there. Oh and tell CID that it's top priority."

The emergency services arrived just as the helicopter and Range Rover left the scene with rotors thumping and wheels spinning. The firemen immediately ran out their hoses and within minutes the teams were at their stations fighting the fire. People were spilling out of their houses and the three squad cars had their hands full dealing with the rubberneckers.

Detective Inspector Bates arrived fifteen minutes later and got a quick briefing from one of his constables.

"Whoever was here just left in a helicopter and black Range Rover. We have the licence number and are running a plate check now. There's a pile of maybe 30 burning bodies in the garden dowsed in petrol, and there's two more dead bodies burning on the lawn. Fire brigade are putting those fires out now. Most of the doors and windows are blown out and we've got several discarded rocket launchers. The gardens are covered in craters from explosions, mines maybe. Fire-fighters are sticking to the pathways just in case, and they're going to work from the extendable ladders on the tenders for safety. What do you make of it sir?"

"World War III. God knows what went on in the house but both sides were well prepared for it."

Bates was at a loss. This was outside of anything that he had ever experienced and probably outside of anyone else's.

"Can we save the house? I need some forensics," he asked the young policeman.

"Fire Chief says not the ground floor for sure as it's already gutted but the roof and some of the upstair, maybe."

"OK good brief constable, carry on."

Detective Inspector Bates no longer had any doubt that there was some connection between the attack on Elizabeth Robinson and this unprecedented full-scale military assault on her family home.

Chapter 36

Elizabeth and Ben appeared from nowhere outside the stable next to the paddock. Their sudden appearance startled the horses, sending them galloping off to the far side of the field. Ben's sigh of relief at arriving at their chosen destination, was audible even above the near gale-force wind that whipped around them. He turned to Elizabeth with his easy smile and was stopped in his tracks when he saw the look of devastation on her face. She looked like her soul had just been ripped out of her.

"What's the matter Lizzie?" Ben's arms were spread palms upwards and his bewilderment evident. "We made it. I don't understand."

Words wouldn't form in Elizabeth's mouth. Ben held her and let her sob until the storm inside her began to abate.

"So what is it Lizzie?" Ben stroked her tangle of blonde curls reassuringly.

"Just as we entered the portal, I felt Mike die," Elizabeth leaned against Ben to steady herself. "And if Mike is dead, then they probably all are; Uncle and Auntie too."

They remained silent for some minutes as each tried to come to terms with it and control their emotions. At last Ben broke the silence.

"Lizzie, if we're honest with ourselves we knew this would happen, even though we couldn't admit it," Ben had to be strong for both of them now. "It's only all over if we let it be so Lizzie. We can create a new possibility here and now, just like May has shown us. We've just got to stay focussed and do what we came here for."

"May and her kind were focussed on changing the course of events that led up to the atom bomb attacks on Hiroshima and Nagasaki," Elizabeth countered, "but they failed, why should we do any better?"

Elizabeth's negativity was uncharacteristic of her and it caused a vitriolic onslaught from Ben, designed to shock her into action. His deep blue eyes narrowed and hardened.

"How dare you feel sorry for yourself Lizzie? I have lost them all too but I intend to give them another chance, either with you or without you!"

Ben turned away from her and he hated himself for what he had said. It was contrary to all that he felt, but he needed her back from that dark place that she was now in.

"No Ben, don't leave me please! I can still do this... No, I will do this!" Elizabeth was desperate.

The determined look on Elizabeth's face showed Ben that she meant it. The fire of revenge was back in those green eyes that shone like cut emeralds, and the set of her jaw was once again resolute. She was ready to fight tooth and nail for her loved ones and he had no doubt about it.

"Come on Lizzie we've got wrongs to right and we need transport. That Harley's been begging me to thrash it for a long time!"

The spare key to the stables was exactly where they had expected it to be, hung on a nail on the inside of the barge boarding above the stable door. Ben let them in and went straight to the garage end of the stable, where their father's Harley was parked under its dustcover. Ben smiled in delicious anticipation as he rolled back the cover, slowly revealing the shiny Harley V-Rod. Right out of the blue, Elizabeth interrupted him. She was pointing at the digital clock on the wall. Her concern was obvious from the desperation in her voice.

"Look what time it is Ben."

Ben looked at the clock and his blood ran cold. It read 18:50, February 18th 2009. He instinctively pulled his sleeve back to look at his wristwatch but of course it was showing the time that they left, not when they arrived.

"Christ, were an hour late!" Ben struggled to understand the reason why. "We entered the portal with quarter to six in the evening, February 18th 2009 clearly in our minds, how then…"

Elizabeth interrupted.

"Oh Ben it must be my fault, I lost the plot. When I felt Mike dying, I don't know what I was thinkin. We can go back and…"

"To where Lizzie, a burning house surrounded by Shadows?"

There was no sign of anger or disappointment in Ben's voice; it was just a statement of fact. He could see the despair in Elizabeth's face and he still needed to think for her.

"We can only get back to our own time using the same portal, Emanuel's mirror. As it is, if the fire brigade don't get there and our house burns down, then we won't exist anyway and that could easily happen in the next half-hour."

Ben was forming a plan in real time as he spoke.

"We only have one chance Lizzie and that's still to finish this," Ben's manner hardened with his resolve.

"Mum, Dad and Crystalita die in twenty minutes, unless we change history."

Elizabeth nodded as she considered their predicament. She was thankful that Ben was still on top of his game.

"The odds just went their way big time Ben. Twenty minutes isn't enough time to get to both places together and fight them with our united powers. It'll have to be one on one, a level playing field at best. It's just what May told us *not* to do."

"Yes, you're right. But we have no choice Lizzie. I'll take on Alexis then."

Ben was adamant. Alexis was the more powerful of the two by far and it wasn't up for debate. It was Ben's time to become his sister's protector, just as she had been his over the last four and a half years.

"I think I can get to the school in time on the Harley and we've got these," Ben shook his machine gun like a radicalised zealot.

"And if Beauty will run like the wind for me, I could get to the bend by the canal, going the cross-country route," Elizabeth added but it was a big *if*.

Ben glanced at the clock on the wall.

"We've got nineteen minutes, go!"

Beauty had galloped to the far end of the paddock along with her siblings when Elizabeth and Ben had literally appeared out of thin air, startling them. Elizabeth knew Beauty only too well, and that she would spook if she approached her too quickly. It would take valuable minutes, but she couldn't take the risk of it turning into a game of chase. Elizabeth wished that she had thought about taking a few slices of apple to entice her. Then there was an added problem. Elizabeth had changed dramatically in her appearance, and would be a complete stranger to Beauty now.

Elizabeth was halfway across the paddock when, to her surprise, Beauty came cantering over of her own accord. Her tail was swishing and she was snorting and whinnying in her way of greeting. It came as a profound shock to Elizabeth, as she realised that Beauty had engaged her spirit with Elizabeth's, in that primordial way. Beauty wasn't duped by appearance; she knew exactly who Elizabeth was. When Beauty arrived, she nuzzled Elizabeth trustingly, taking in her scent and snorting her approval. Elizabeth couldn't understand why, but Beauty seemed to understand what was wanted of her, better than she did herself. Elizabeth placed little kisses gently on Beauty's muzzle and cheek and then whispered in her ear.

"I need you to run for me like you've never run before. Will you do that for me Beauty?"

Beauty tossed her handsome head and raked the ground with her hoof in a declaration of consent. There was no time to saddle up. Elizabeth threw herself up onto Beauty's back, turned her towards the four-bar fence on the west side and then encouraged her into a breath-taking gallop. Beauty was fully committed. She jumped the fence with the ease of a thoroughbred steeplechaser. Elizabeth steered Beauty with just the subtle pressure of her knees, and headed out towards the canal.

The Harley engine caught instantly and growled menacingly. Ben was taken by surprise at its response to the throttle and left the garage with the back wheel spinning on the smooth garage floor. When the smoking tyre bit on the rough concrete of the drive, he nearly lost it and had to lean over the front forks to keep both wheels grounded. He took the bend leading out towards the main road with considerably more respect for the Harley's brute power and glanced briefly at his wristwatch as he did so.

"Less than sixteen minutes left," he thought ruefully.

It was going to be too late to forewarn Crystalita. At best he would get to her as she walked out of the school gates.

It was worse than that; Ben was most likely to get there too late. Although the Harley had phenomenal acceleration, its long-wheelbase made it a bitch to get around the tight country bends. Ben was risking all to make up time and the inevitable finally happened. He was flat out going downhill into a U-bend, leaving his breaking late. He hit a patch of wet autumn leaves, causing the bike to straight-line and skid off the road. It was purely as a matter of good fortune, that there was a gate access into a field ahead that the farmer had laid to fallow. The gate was old and heavily wormed. At a speed 40 mph and a combined weight of nearly half a tonne, rider and bike hit the gate splintering it like matchwood. Ben fought for control as the bike snaked its way across the field. He knew the land well, as it backed onto his uncle's. If he could just keep the bike upright, it would be a significant shortcut saving probably two miles of torturous country lanes.

With his heart in his mouth, Ben accelerated until he was literally flying over the ditches and undulations.

"It's a shit-load easier on my dirt bike," he cussed as he fought the ungainly lump of chrome over yet another obstacle.

At the far end of the field, the farmer had just opened the gate and was about to drive his tractor in. He looked up and saw some idiot coming towards him on a shining bucking bronco, looking more out of control than in. He opened his mouth to yell rebuke but before he could, the rider smiled disarmingly and shouted back at him.

"Thanks Mr Simons!" as he slewed sideways out of the gate onto the road.

Elizabeth melted herself into Beauty's powerful gallop and became as one with her. She was almost laid across her back with one arm around her neck and her face close to Beauty's ear whispering words of encouragement.

"Run for me Beauty run!"

Their connection was much more than a physical and sensory thing. They were bonded through their base instincts as creatures that shared the same Mother Earth and there was an understanding, one for the other. Beauty could sense the urgency of Elizabeth's request and the burden and sadness that she was carrying in her heart and so she ran to please her, despite the increasing pain and danger of the challenge. The machine gun was bouncing painfully on Elizabeth's back distracting her and disrupting the connection that she had made with Beauty. She was tempted to discard it but instead risked her free arm to control it, glimpsing her watch as she did so. Eight minutes left and Beauty was already tiring under the strain.

Elizabeth reached under Beauty until she could feel her heart. It was beating impossibly. She needed to rest her and soon, but rest was out of the question.

"I need more Darling," she called out despairingly.

423

Elizabeth used her mind to stimulate Beauty's heart muscles. The affect was immediate. The contractions of her heart became faster and more powerful; raising her blood pressure to dangerous levels, driving more oxygen into Beauty's screaming muscles. The tears were streaming down Elizabeth's face. She knew that she was sentencing little Beauty to death and that Beauty knew it too. Elizabeth had never felt so wretched since the day that she lost her parents. She felt the surge of power as Beauty's heart responded to the increased levels of adrenaline. Beauty thundered on with new vigour, each powerful stride taking them ever closer to the canal bend.

Beauty's hide was soaked through with sweat so that Elizabeth was sliding precariously on her back, unable to get a secure grip. Her powerful chest was pumping like foundry bellows and the hot air that surged as steam from her flared nostrils gave her the appearance of a fire-breathing dragon. They were still a good three minutes away from the canal when Beauty's heart began to fail. Elizabeth reached down to her chest again and encouraged her body to produce still more adrenaline. Between sobs she was imploring Beauty to run on.

"Please Beauty don't stop now, run for me Beauty. Run!"

Beauty shook her head and snorted as she reapplied herself, but she was blown and each stride was clearly excruciating for her.

"I'm sorry Beauty, I'm so sorry. Please forgive me, please..."

Through her tears Elizabeth saw a dark-blue car appear over the ridge, about a mile away to her left. As it started to wind itself down towards the canal the distinctive exhaust note confirmed that it was the Porsche and her heart missed a beat. She held her breath in trepidation, praying that the green sports car wouldn't mount the ridge too. After twenty seconds her hopes were dashed and the little sports car arrived at speed, accelerating down the hill in pursuit of her parents.

"Run damn you Beauty. Run!"

Elizabeth was desperate; her window of opportunity was closing. She immediately felt dreadful for cussing Beauty and caressed her cheek guiltily. Beauty responded with an extra turn of speed, but it was going to be right down to the wire. Elizabeth wrestled with the strap of the Heckler & Koch trying to get the gun into a firing position but she'd got it tangled in the race and couldn't free it. Beauty was at full gallop, only yards from the road as the midnight blue Porsche growled by with driver and passenger engaged in conversation, oblivious to their arrival.

Beauty's pounding heart couldn't take anymore. Elizabeth had driven her systolic blood pressure too high and for too long. The faithful horse's aorta burst and arterial blood pumped into her chest cavity, killing her almost instantly. Beauty's legs folded under her and she skidded across the road behind the Porsche on her knees and belly. Beauty hit the verge and cartwheeled over her own head, sending Elizabeth sprawling into the trees before landing winded and disorientated near the water's edge.

Ralph mounted the crest of the hill and began the long winding run down to the canal. It was his favourite stretch of road and he gunned the Porsche down through the sweeping bends taking the racing line as usual. They had been silent for several miles. Neither he nor Jodie had come to terms with the profound danger that their family was now in. Ralph was deep in thought about how he was going to transition their lives to the new secure regime and Jodie, the eternal mother, how she could keep the family positive and happy.

She looked up at Ralph and saw his pained expression. He was exhausted by the guilt of what he had brought on the family but she knew that it was not of his making. He was only a chess piece on the board of a much greater game. They were just collateral damage in the grand scheme of things.

"Ralph, I do have faith."

Jodie had always supported Ralph's decisions and they always turned out to be good ones, in part because of her unerring support.

"I know that you will turn all this around and times will be good for us again. Stay strong for us Ralph. We need you to be that and more."

Jodie leaned across to kiss his cheek and Ralph turned his head to face her. She looked up into his deep blue eyes. Ralph was distracted and he never saw the green sports car coming up behind him at breakneck speed. Nor did he see the frantic rider on the galloping horse to his side, as it collapsed and skidded across the road behind them.

The green Lotus was a good twenty seconds behind the Porsche when it reached the crest, before the winding drop down to the canal bend. Grese cursed the performance of her Lotus, pitted against the Porsche and she had to drive like a lunatic to make up ground. When she reached the crest, Grese cursed again. Inexplicably her quarry had accelerated down the hill but she was sure that it wasn't because Ralph had seen her. Grese couldn't have anticipated that it was the stretch of road that always brought out the boy racer in Ralph. She had to close the gap before they reached the sweeping right-hander down by the canal, where she had planned to take them off the road. It meant that she had to risk all to do it. Grese drove in blind hope that there was nothing on the other side of the road coming towards her.

Grese's luck held out and she gained those valuable seconds. She was perfectly placed to make her killer move and pulled out committing herself to the manoeuvre. Suddenly, out of nowhere, a girl on horseback came crashing to the ground from her right skidding across the road only yards in front of her. Grese had no choice but to swerve to her left. The horse would have weighed little less than a tonne and at 90 mph the impact would have been fatal. Grese swerved and crashed into the woodland, taking out several small trees. She was concussed as the car continued down the steep bank and plunged into the canal. The shattered windscreen gave in to the force of the bow wave of water created by the impact, flooding the passenger compartment instantly.

When Grese recovered her senses, the car had already sunk level with its roof and she was fully submerged. The seatbelt pre-tensioners had activated and Grese was cinched into her seat. She struggled frantically to release herself. After what felt like an age, the belt obliged and she began to make her way out through the front windscreen. It came as a total shock when Elizabeth's hand clasped around hers crushing it in her vice-like grip. She screamed underwater at the pain of it as she hopelessly tried to wrench it free.

"Stay there and die you bitch!" Elizabeth yelled venomously, and the roar of it was audible even underwater.

"It had to be the rider of the horse, a girl," Grese deduced. "But who and who could have a grip like this? Only an Angel that was for sure."

The girl's hold on her was relentless. Grese resorted to chewing at her attacker's fingers, but the girl was resolute. Even when she severed one of them, there was no relaxing of her grip. The fight was rapidly draining Grese of valuable oxygen. At this rate, she could only last a minute or two at best. Grese felt the cold snake of fear began to slither in her gut as the remaining seconds of her life ticked by.

Ben's unintentional shortcut had gifted him valuable minutes and the road opened up and straightened in his favour. He maxed out at 150 mph on the one mile straight leading into town. The adrenaline pumping in his veins made him light-headed and euphoric, suppressing the fear that was trying to rise like bile within him. He was conscious that he would be arriving with no coherent plan and that he was literally flying by the seat of his pants into unknown danger. He was going to have to depend solely on his reflexes and his machine gun!

The back of the Harley kicked out violently as Ben threw the cumbersome bike into the school approach road. He reversed the steering and increased the power driving out of the skid, allowing himself the luxury of a "whoop" as he did so.

Ben looked up and saw Crystalita leaving the school gates some 500 yards ahead and gunned the Harley onwards. A white haired old man was stood by a black panel van and Ben recognised him immediately as Alexis. Suddenly and theatrically, the old man clutched his chest and fell backwards against the van, as if in deep distress. Crystalita started running urgently towards the stricken old man. It was all playing out in front of him and Ben was too far away to stop it. He shouted out desperately to her.

"No Crystalita, it's a trap!" but his voice was lost on the wind and the roar of the Harley.

Ben was only 50 yards away but it might as well have been 50 miles. Crystalita was now only a few yards away from her killer and he wasn't going to make it. Ben frantically stabbed at the switches on the unfamiliar handlebars trying to find the horn. Luckily, he found it on the fourth attempt. As it blared out he aimed at the gap between victim and assassin.

Crystalita stopped in her tracks at the sound, and saw the speeding motorcycle coming straight at her. She tried in vain to back-pedal but the handlebars of the Harley clipped her on the hip, spinning her like a top and sending her head first into a lamp post. The other side of the handlebars caught Alexis in the abdomen. It drove the wind out of him and sent him flying backwards into his van, leaving him gasping for air. The sudden deceleration of the Harley threw Ben over the handlebars but his dirt biking experience came to the fore. He quick-wittedly tucked himself into a ball and rolled to absorb the force of the impact and was back on his feet in one fluid move. Ben swung his weapon up into the firing position as he ran back towards the motionless body of Crystalita.

Alexis stayed in the van desperately trying to recover his breath as six armed Drones spilled out into the street. Before they had time to orientate themselves, Ben mowed them down with a long burst from his machine gun. He crossed to Crystalita and checked her quickly. She was bleeding profusely from a head wound, but her breathing was steady. She was probably going to be alright he decided and turned to face Alexis.

Alexis had recovered enough to sit on the step-up into the side of the van, but he was still bent double fighting for his breath. When he turned his head to face Ben he was looking down the barrel of his machine gun. Alexis fixed Ben with a murderous stare and his eyes were as cold as a Siberian winter.

"Ben Robinson isn't it?" Alexis presumed.

Alexis' intuition was faultless. The family resemblance was undeniable but he was no longer a boy. The man in front of him was from the future. There was no other explanation for it.

"So you have learned how to use the portals then Ben? It was always just a matter of time before you did," the old man was philosophical about it.

Although Ben was the one with the machine gun, he felt the lesser of the two men. He knew that he shouldn't listen to the old man, but somehow he couldn't help himself. He was caught in his stare.

"So this is how it is to end then?" Alexis' rheumy eyes were as mesmerising as a snake's, "the cowardly assassination of an unarmed old man."

"And stabbing an unarmed woman would have been different?"

Ben held Alexis' cold eyes, but he was foolishly allowing dialogue.

"A Matriarch is never unarmed, as they hold the power of nature in their hands. A true Angel would never resort to such cowardly methods as you are about to Ben Robinson," Alexis was feeding Ben the bait. "But then you have your father's blood and he is a coward too." Alexis goaded.

"He was not!" Ben was enraged, "he was worth a thousand of you."

"Ah, was?" Alexis' face showed surprise followed by amusement. "How interesting that you talk of him in the past Ben. That can only mean that Grese has succeeded in killing him."

"She did but Elizabeth will change that today, just as I have changed the outcome here," Ben blurted.

He instantly hated himself for his sudden show of emotion and loss of control.

"I hope she does. I look forward to putting him to the sword myself," Alexis continued to goad Ben. "Your father fancied himself as a swordsman but he was clueless, as I expect are you."

"I kicked your nephew's arse only months ago! He's only alive because he ran away like a girl," Ben had taken the bait now, hook, line and sinker.

"Illya is a boy. Do you only fight boys?" Alexis sneered.

He reached into the van and produced a long antique box and opened it. Inside were two beautiful old duelling sabres with jewelled guilt handles and ornately engraved, razor-sharp blades.

"These have been in my family for hundreds of years and are still salty with the blood of Angels like you," Alexis proffered one of them to Ben and he took it.

"I have seen them before and they don't only favour Shadows. Illya cried like a stuck pig when I stabbed him with one of them!"

Ben smiled his easy smile, swished the sabre flamboyantly and tossed his machine gun away.

"*En-guard!*"

Alexis sprang to his feet as nimbly as an athlete and wielded the blade around him with the flourish of a master swordsman. There was not even a hint of stiffness to betray his great age.

"You are a fool Ben Robinson, a thousand times a fool! You should have killed me when you had the chance. I haven't lost a sword fight in seven thousand years and this one will be no exception, just the icing on the cake for me."

"You haven't won it yet Alexis. I will go easy on you at first, you being an old age pensioner and all that."

Ben began to circle the white haired relic and wondered at how something so ancient could still have a pulse. He never even saw it coming. Alexis struck almost instantly like a cobra and stabbed him in his left side, just below his ribs. It was only a flesh wound but Ben gasped at the pain of it.

"That was just to wake you up boy. Can't have you sleeping on the job now can we?" Alexis' almost toothless smile was devoid of any humour and his eyes never left Ben's.

Ben retreated a step and tried to re-run Alexis' move in his mind but he hadn't been focussed enough to remember it. In fact, he felt mentally clumsy. Ben used the pain to concentrate his attention, knowing that he needed to learn from every mistake if he was going to survive this duel. He fleetingly thought of May. If he was lucky enough to survive this, and she ever found out that he had been stupid enough to give the most deadly Shadow of them all a chance like this, she would probably kill him anyway. The words of her song came back to him hauntingly and it spurred him on.

"Silly Billy," he mused.

Ben began to test the footwork of the old man, thinking that at his age he must have some difficulties in manoeuvring. He feigned some advances and retreats but to his alarm, the white haired fossil scuttled backwards and forwards in an almost comical manner, using the textbook stance of the professional. His weight was evenly placed over his feet, front foot pointed towards his opponent with knees flexed and his back foot at the classic 45 degrees away. His right elbow was tucked in to his body with his forearm parallel to the ground and his left arm curled upwards behind him. From this perfectly balanced position he could scuttle forward in short rapid steps, extend his arm into a lunge and retreat quickly and efficiently.

Alexis came in suddenly with a low assault that Ben only just read and was able to parry at the last second.

"Yes I have the height advantage so he will probably prefer coming in low," Ben though.

Ben countered, coming at his opponent with a concentrated overhead attack. He wielded the jewelled sabre forcefully, cutting down towards Alexis' neck, left and right. Alexis parried each slash with ease, as if he knew in advance what Ben was going to do.

Ben feigned another high attack then came in low trying to get under his guard, but Alexis was ready. He cut him away with a vicious parry that ran down the full blade length of Ben's sabre, then across his chest, opening a gash across it as the cold steel of Alexis' sabre rattled across his ribs. Ben had to stifle his scream. The first slithering signs of fear began in his stomach, like a snake wakening slowly from a deep sleep.

"He's reading me like an open book," Ben realised.

Alexis had smoothed him just as his nephew Illya Dracul had done in the changing room when they met at the county fencing championships.

Alexis had gained access into Ben's mind and was now able to anticipate his every move and stifle his innovation. He was first in with his powerful mind, blocking Ben's ability to use his Angel skill-set. Ben was now lethargic and slow witted by comparison. He was furious with himself for letting the same thing happen twice. He also knew that, without Elizabeth's intervention to break his mind free, he would not stand a chance against Alexis.

The old man was toying with him in the sadistic way that a cat does with a mouse and Ben knew it. It would just be a matter of time before Alexis would tire of the amusement and end it. Ben needed to join minds with Elizabeth to empower himself to break free of the inertia that Alexis had instilled in him. This at least would give him a fighting chance.

Once again Alexis' sabre found Ben's flesh. It was a simple advance but again he didn't read it and blood began to flow freely down Ben's left arm. He instinctively knew that Alexis had chosen to just wound him rather than end it and he desperately reached out to Elizabeth across the space between them, hoping that he had sufficient free will left to alert her.

"Elizabeth!"

The last thing that Elizabeth saw as she and Beauty slid across the road behind her father's Porsche, was the shocked expression on Grese's face. She was frantically braking and swerving, which sent the green sports car out of control and into the trees. At the same moment, Beauty's head buried itself into the verge sending them both cartwheeling into the trees. When Elizabeth had recovered her wits, the green sports car had already sunk up to its windows in the murky canal.

She eased herself up painfully and looked over to where Beauty lay. She was looking back at Elizabeth through sightless eyes with her head at an impossible angle. The force of the collision with the bank had broken her neck and ripped her jaw off, making her ugly in death. It was the final humiliation.

"Oh my Darling, what have I done to you?" Elizabeth was in shock.

Tears of anguish streamed down her bruised face as she began to walk stiffly over to the pitiful corpse of her beloved horse. Just then a hand appeared out of the sinking car.

"Over my dead body!" Elizabeth screamed.

She sprinted towards the canal. All symptoms of the trauma of her fall and Beauty's appalling death were side-lined by this sudden rush of anger. Elizabeth leapt from the bank landing on the back of the sinking car. She scrambled across its slippery roof and grabbed Grese's wrist, pressing her back into the car.

"Stay there and die you bitch!" Elizabeth yelled.

She struggled with the woman who was now fighting desperately for her life. The car sank more quickly under their combined weight and Elizabeth was soon up to her neck.

Grese sank her teeth into Elizabeth's fingers ripping at her like a crazed Rottweiler. The pain was excruciating, but there was no way that Elizabeth was going to let go. She took one final deep breath before her head went under and the car sank silently to the canal bed settling there in the soft silt.

"I must wait her out," Elizabeth thought to herself.

She began to slow her heart rate and metabolism down to conserve oxygen and energy. The pain in her hand as Grese chewed at it, gave her something to focus on. She could feel the strong pulse in Grese's wrist which gave her a physical way of monitoring her death. All Elizabeth had to do now was hold on until she could no longer feel that pulse. Grese was using up her resources fast in the struggle. At last Elizabeth began to feel the throbbing begin to slow. Elizabeth was amazed at the strength of this woman, who fought on relentlessly.

The seconds turned into minutes. Elizabeth was beginning to feel the overpowering urge to breathe but at last Grese's pulse rate began to plummet, she was spent. Elizabeth waited on with her lungs bursting until Grese's heart finally flat-lined.

Satisfied that there were no signs of life, Elizabeth scrambled upwards, gulping in precious air the instant that her head broke surface. The struggle had taken its toll and Elizabeth was used up too. She could barely swim the few yards to the bank. Her machine gun was like an anchor dragging her down and it took all her remaining energy to pull herself up out of the water. She collapsed immediately afterwards and rolled over onto her back. Her chest heaved as she tried to re-oxygenate herself and the pain in her hand was excruciating.

Elizabeth had been driven past exhaustion, almost to delirium. When at last she looked up and saw Grese standing there in front of her, holding a rock the size of pillow above her head, she thought that she was only dreaming. It was surreal. The madness was augmented by the impossible sound of Ben's voice calling out to her in desperation.

"Elizabeth!"

Grese knew she would never shake of the powerful grip of her attacker. She also knew that the longer she struggled, the faster she would use up her rapidly depleting oxygen reserves. The girl seemed oblivious to the pain that she was inflicting on her, so it left only one alternative, to feign death.

Grese began to shut down her normal aerobic respiratory system, reverting to anaerobic respiration. This was a legacy from primitive times, before evolving to exist in the oxygen rich atmosphere of Angelos. It was now a significantly reduced ability and energetically much less efficient than breathing, but it would sustain her essential needs; for hours if necessary. Her heart slowed until it stopped beating altogether. To another, all her vital signs would have appeared to have ceased. At last the girl released her wrist. Grese was in no hurry to surface though.

She would reserve the element of surprise, besides she would need time to re-oxygenate.

Grese anticipated that her enemy would also need to recover from her ordeal and would be at her most vulnerable during the next few minutes. She left the car through the collapsed windscreen and swam underwater to the bank. Grese eased her head up above the rushes and saw the girl lying on her back breathing heavily and oblivious to everything around her.

Grese ventilated herself before slithering up the bank as silently as a snake and crossed stealthily towards her quarry. There was a boulder set in the bank that was at least as heavy as a man. She pulled it out of the earth with ease and the girl remained totally unaware of her approach. Grese was stood over her with the rock held high above her head, ready to slam it into her face. Just as she was about to hurl the rock she paused and gasped incredulously in recognition but it couldn't be. It was a woman beneath her, not a child. Grese involuntarily shouted her name at the shock of it.

"Elizabeth!"

Ben joining Elizabeth's mind so suddenly and desperately was like an electrical discharge in her head. Her eyes flew open in alarm.

"Ben!" she screamed.

But it wasn't Ben in front of her. Somehow it was Grese holding a huge rock above her. The piled up blonde hair had sagged over her high forehead and mascara was streaming from her black eyes. Her cruel mouth was twisted in an astonished snarl as she spat out Elizabeth's name disdainfully.

The revelation had unbalanced Grese, albeit only for a split second. It was long enough. Elizabeth grabbed her machine gun releasing the safety catch in one fluid move and emptied the magazine into the surprised Grese's body. The combined upward force of the 9mm bullets took Grese off her feet and catapulted her backwards into the canal. The weight of the rock drove her straight to the bottom of the canal.

"Stay there and rot you bitch!" Elizabeth cursed before collapsing on the bank.

At that momen,t the enormity of what she had achieved dawned on her, Grese was dead and her parents saved!

Her euphoria lasted but seconds, before her mind was filled with her brother's thoughts. She could sense his fear and feel his pain but more than that, she could see Alexis through his eyes.

Ben felt Elizabeth join him and his loneliness and desperation immediately abated, but his fear of the Troll-like old man in front of him was still mounting by the second.

Alexis was a highly evolved killing machine and Ben couldn't even begin to guess how many lives he must have ended in a similar bloody scenario. Elizabeth's union had an immediate effect on Ben. He instantly felt unencumbered, free of Alexis' control, but he was still unable to call upon his special skills. The danger that Alexis imposed was too intense and consuming to allow him any latitude to divert his attention, not even for one second. Full union with Elizabeth was therefore impossible. Alexis sensed the change in his opponent and retreated strategically to reassess the situation. He was an analytical man and never allowed himself the luxury of spontaneity which was the killer of young men.

They circled each other in the middle of the wide road. The shorter, white-haired old man's thin hair was dancing around his head, tinged orange in the setting sun. It looked as if it was on fire, making him look still more menacing. In contrast the tall, blond and athletic frame of Ben towered above the short stocky man, making them look like a comical David and Goliath. Dead bodies were randomly strewn around the black van, leaking blood into the gutter and Crystalita was lying in an undignified state on the pavement, bleeding profusely from a gash to her head. Elizabeth took it all in through Ben's eyes.

People were beginning to collect at a safe distance to watch in delicious fear as the two duelled in the street, like gladiators in some ancient arena. They were too scared to come any closer and much too intrigued to be concerned for their own safety and leave.

Alexis manoeuvred Ben until he had the brilliant setting sun behind him, dazzling Ben and obscuring his intent. He advanced suddenly and lunged at Ben as fast as a lizards tongue. Ben's parry was almost quick enough and Alexis' sabre only just grazed him. Ben's riposte was so swift and natural that it took Alexis by surprise. Ben's blade drew its first blood and Alexis retreated paying no attention to the blood that flowed down the front of his crisp white shirt. His implacable eyes remained fixed on Ben like those of a cat on its prey. He sensed the dangerous change that had come over his opponent and that could only mean one thing.

"Welcome aboard Elizabeth! Now you can watch me kill your little brother," Alexis hissed.

They continued circling and testing each other, each trying to manoeuvre the other up against an obstacle to prevent them from retreating. If achieved, it would enable an easy kill. Both were wise to this empirical ploy though and neither succeeded. When one attacked, the other was quick to parry and riposte, then immediately attack himself usurping the initiative as good swordsmanship strategy dictates. Alexis was always the quickest and most innovative of the two swordsmen and Ben was collecting multiple minor hits as a consequence. Each wound was taking its toll though, slowly draining his energy and resolve.

"I can't hold him off much longer Lizzie he's relentless and has no weaknesses, none at all. He's gonna kill me!"

Ben's thoughts were showing the first signs of despair. Elizabeth read them clearly, even over the miles that separated them and she needed to quell them.

"Only if you let him, damn you Ben. Man up!"

Elizabeth had been running across the fields towards the town for several minutes trying to get to Ben. She knew in her heart though that it would be over, one way or another, before she got there. Elizabeth had to keep Ben focussed and confident.

"Everybody has weaknesses Ben you just have to find them."

Elizabeth could see Alexis through Ben's eyes as clearly as if she was there and his face was a mask of pure hatred. Every time his sword found its mark, she felt the sting of it in her own flesh and it served to drive her onwards to her rapidly fatiguing brother. She tried to enter his mind still more to unleash the powers within him, but Alexis was there holding her back just enough to prevent it. Ben couldn't afford to lose his immediate focus to help her in either.

"Concentrate Ben, watch him and learn him. He must have trigger moves, something that gives him away."

She was analysing every move Alexis made herself, in case she could see what Ben couldn't. She felt the sting as Alexis found flesh yet again and the pain sharpened her awareness.

"There it is Ben, there! His pupils contract just before he advances. Focus on his eyes Ben, feel his mind."

It was that glimmer of hope that Ben needed to clear his own mind and raise his game, and he did. With it, came an essential rush of adrenaline that rejuvenated his cramping muscles and quickened his reflexes. Alexis came scuttling forwards rapidly staying low to come in under Ben's guard, ready to lunge upwards into his exposed belly. It would have been the killer move. Ben had read Alexis' eye reflex though, and was ready to parry the attack. As he did so, he used his opponent's momentum to pirouette on his front foot and delivered a spinning kick to the side of the old man's head. Alexis was sent sprawling and lost grip of his sabre. Defenceless and vulnerable now, he looked up at Ben resignedly, awaiting his execution.

Inexplicably, Ben kicked the sabre over to his helpless opponent.

"Get up!" he ordered with a confidence in his voice that had not been there before. "That's not how Angels do it, taking a blade to a defenceless person, like you were going to do to Crystalita."

"Twice the fool then Ben Robinson!" Alexis spat.

He picked the sabre up in his right-hand and produced a six inch stiletto knife in the other.

"Ben what the hell are you doing? Kill him now!" Elizabeth's voice was screaming in Ben's mind.

"Sorry Lizzie it's not my way, this has to end with honour," Ben watched Alexis like a hawk as he rose to his feet, "*En-guard* old man."

Having the stiletto changed Alexis' technique. It brought out an element of the street fighter in him. Now, mixed with his finely honed swordsmanship skills, came the wild and lethal stabs and slashes from the knife, worthy of the best that the ghettos in Harlem could boast. All fear had now left Ben, which allowed him clarity of thought and action. Conversely, sensing this, Alexis was showing signs of desperation and frustration in his attacks. Ben had to sacrifice his left forearm to fend off the stiletto. He managed to isolate the pain from his mind and stem the flow of precious blood into it. They continued in their deadly circling manner, each looking to press home any advantage.

It came as an epiphany to Elizabeth when she realised it but it had been so obvious. How could they both have missed it? She wondered as she watched them circle through Ben's eyes. Alexis would regularly take quick steps to the left or right but for no obvious purpose. It was the orange light that lit up his cragged face that alerted her to it.

"Ben! Keep him facing the sun he can't see you there."

Shadows are genetically adapted to sombre conditions. With his aging eyes, Alexis' vision was severely challenged when forced to look into the setting sun.

Ben began to manoeuvre the old warrior until he had his own back to the sun and then kept him there squinting, desperately trying to turn the fight back to his own advantage. Alexis didn't see the advance until it was too late. Ben came in low in a lunging run. It was quick and deadly, coming up under Alexis' guard. The point of his sabre entered Alexis' chest just below his sternum and buried itself up to the hilt until they were face to face. The sabre and stiletto dropped from Alexis' trembling hands. He placed them on Ben's shoulders to support himself in his dying moments. The anger had gone out of his face and, replaced with an almost peaceful but surprised expression. He no longer looked the formidable adversary, just an extremely frail old man.

"Bravo Ben Robinson, a worthy opponent at last," Alexis coughed up thick dark blood and continued, struggling to form his words. "Your father will be proud of you, as I now respect you as my killer."

Alexis' words were fading such that Ben had to draw closer to hear him.

"I am tired Ben Robinson. 8,000 years is too long for a man to live, much too long and I have seen too much. You will be blessed with much less time. Perhaps you will use it wisely and heal the divide between our races?"

Alexis' life passed with those meaningful words.

Ben let him slip slowly to the floor, removing his sword gently and respectfully as he did so. He laid the old warrior on his back, crossing his arms on his chest and closed his staring eyes. Tears ran down Ben's face over the taking of another's life. He considered what the old man had said and he knew that those words would never leave him.

"That must be my cause old man, rest in peace."

Elizabeth both saw and sensed the passing of Alexis, and like Ben her emotions were a mixture of triumph and regret. It would be so easy for them to lose their humanity in the struggle that lay ahead. It was a dilemma. Without strength and resilience, there would be defeat and death, but at what cost? This was something that only Maelströminha herself could counsel them on. It would be high on her agenda for their next meet.

Thankfully Elizabeth was now able to slow the pace of her run into town. Even with her gifted strength, the ordeal with Grese followed by the frantic run, had drained her. With those distractions now gone, she suddenly became aware of the excruciating pain in her mutilated left hand. Her ring finger on her left hand was severed above the knuckle and it prompted idle thoughts of Mike and a marriage that would never be.

She wondered whether what they had done would make any difference as to seeing him again. It was at best unlikely. She pushed the thought from her mind, focussing on the present. Elizabeth tore the hem off her T-shirt as she ran and bound the wound. She remembered how Auntie Gina had told her that her father's fingers had regenerated quite quickly and hoped that it wasn't just a tale.

Ben was still knelt next to Alexis when Elizabeth arrived. Crystalita's petite body was rudely sprawled on the pavement, bleeding profusely and it sent a shudder of dread through her. She ran to her side, scared that the injury might be fatal. Instinctively she placed her hand on the head wound and felt the warm flow of energy from her into Crystalita. She was alive. The effect was almost immediate, the blood stopped flowing and Crystalita's eyes flickered but it was a couple of minutes before she was lucid.

"Elizabeth! Is that really you?"

"Shush little one, go slowly. You've had a bad fall and yes it's me. A little older and much wiser, but it's me," Elizabeth wiped the tears from her eyes with the back of her rudely bandaged hand.

"But why the tears Lizzie?" Crystalita asked selflessly.

"Because I lost you once and now I have you back. The tears are of joy, I promise."

The crowd of people had sensed the safe resolution of the conflict and had begun to move in, driven by their curiosity. Police sirens were approaching fast too, prompting Elizabeth to get Crystalita to her feet.

"Ben we have to get out of here now, before we have all this to explain!"

Ben was still deep in remorse. It was only at the second time of asking, that he responded. They took Crystalita between them and fled the scene. They chose to go out through the crowd and into the back streets, sweeping the injured girl with them such that her feet hardly touched the ground.

"Ben, we have to get to Emanuel's house quickly before the Police find us."

Elizabeth knew exactly what they must do which was fortunate as Ben was still lost in battle.

"But Emanuel will already be dead. Why?"

"His portal Ben, we have to get to his portal!"

Elizabeth knew that they were all just living on adrenaline and needed medical attention soon, particularly Crystalita. They had one final thing to do though before they themselves could rest, but they needed to get Crystalita into the safe hands of May first.

When they arrived at Emanuel Goldberg's house, it was taped off with crime scene bunting. They approached the policeman guarding the door confidently.

"I'm sorry but I can't let you in," the tall, dark and almost ridiculously young policeman said.

His palm was extended, as if to physically block their path. His jaw almost hit the floor when his eyes took in the full extent of the injuries that the three had sustained and he gasped out loud.

"Christ, what's happened to you?"

Elizabeth took his outstretched hand and began to smooth him.

"It's OK, we're detectives on this case. You can let us in," Elizabeth's smile alone was winning even without the gentle manipulation of his perception. "See, here's my ID."

The young policeman saw everything that he wanted to see although Elizabeth held out nothing. He let them in dutifully.

They went straight to Emanuel's office. The room was dowdy, with rows of bookcases along three of the walls and an enormous antique mirror on the other. Displays of antique guns, axes, swords and cutlasses filled all other available gaps. It was like a room out of the old colonial days. The carpet in the corner of the room was heavily stained with a thick, dark reddish brown substance and they all averted their eyes simultaneously. It was Emanuel's life blood and it stimulated the primitive instinct of revenge in Elizabeth.

"Let's do this," Elizabeth's face was etched with determination as she touched the mirror. "The time is now and the place is the mother ship."

It was said to make absolutely sure that their thoughts were aligned. Then they stepped through the portal leaving the room and its horrors behind them.

Crystalita was fading on them and they had to carry her down the corridor of mirrors. It came as no surprise to them, that May had anticipated their arrival and was hurrying up the corridor towards them. She was ethereal, almost divine, and so different from how they had ever seen her before. It was such a contrast to the cruel and violent world that they had just left and it brought peace to their hearts.

May was translucent and her skin was of the finest silver gossamer. Only her pale blue robe of sheer silk, with the substance of shadows, was there in an attempt to hide her modesty. Her catlike curves were on show to all, but she was without the slightest hint of shyness over her near nakedness. Her long silver hair had been braided in African style with jewels and pearls that danced around her as she ran towards them. But all of this was exceeded by the sheer beauty of her face that even the most eloquent poet could not describe nor compare.

It was the strangest reunion, but then it wasn't a reunion at all. In terms of time it was their very first meeting with May as there was not yet any history between them. They would have been strangers to each other, but for the mirror and the endless possibilities that it gave them.

"Thank you, I will take her now."

May swept little Crystalita up into her arms effortlessly, which visually looked both bizarre and impossible. It was incredulous that such massive strength could exist in her petite frame. Her immediate concern was for her sister.

"I do know who you are and what you have done, but I have to tend to Crystalita. And I can sense that you have not finished whatever it is that you are doing. I will be here waiting for you when it is done, I promise. We can talk then."

With that she turned away and hurried down the corridor, murmuring to Crystalita like a mother does to her baby.

Elizabeth and Ben just stood there bereft, astonished at May's haste and lack of emotion towards them. But they were playing within the circles of time where the logical order of things no longer existed. Ben's heart almost burst with the disappointment of it. Inexplicably, May stopped in her tracks, turned towards them and hurried back. She kissed Ben urgently on the cheek.

"Be patient with me Ben it will happen, it was always meant to. Sometimes you just have to believe in destiny, otherwise none of it makes sense. You are my destiny Ben I know it and I look forward to getting to know you," she turned to Elizabeth with a smile that shone as brightly as the Moon. "And you will be my best friend, I just know it."

The kiss that she and Ben had shared sparked a storm of light under her translucent skin, classically giving her emotions away. There was just the faintest sign of a blush running up her neck into her cheeks as she realised it and Ben's heart leaped. May turned and left them confused but intrigued. They were walking between worlds, with the power to change history. It was too heady a cocktail. Elizabeth brought them back to their Earth with a bump.

"OK Ben let's do it for Mike. We're going back to Emanuel's house to the time just before Adolphius killed him."

Elizabeth suddenly looked guiltily at Ben. In the frenzy of all that was going on she hadn't really appraised the extent of his injuries. He had literally been hacked to pieces by Alexis.

"Can you do this Ben? Maybe we should get you fixed first."

"This isn't over until it is over Sis and I want it finished now," Ben was adamant. "Besides there are two of us now, how hard can it be?"

He flashed his winning smile as he took Elizabeth's arm and steered her back to Emanuel's portal. It was second nature to them now. They both put their hands on the mirror and recalled the events leading up to Emanuel's assassination. The mirror reflected their thoughts and moments later they were looking at their father shaking hands with Emanuel as he bade him goodbye. When he turned towards the door to leave, he briefly looked up into the mirror and raised a brow. It was as if he had seen them. It was such a shock that they recoiled involuntarily. It was Ben who put their thoughts into a question.

"No that's not possible... is it Lizzie? He can't possibly have known that we would be here, could he?"

"Ben I don't know what to believe anymore. Come on we've got to go. Look who's just arrived. It's all about us now Ben and what we can do."

They linked hands and stepped back into Emanuel's office.

Adolphius was in the act of taking the sword down from the wall, when Elizabeth and Ben appeared before him in Emanuel's office. The shock of it twisted his face into a cruel snarl and his black eyes widened in astonishment. Emanuel however, was still oblivious to it all and continued to arrange his papers on the oak desk. It took only seconds before Adolphius realised who the two intruders were, as their appearance had changed so significantly. He was looking exactly at what they had so desperately tried to prevent. Their evolution!

Sometimes a man knows when he is going to die, when the odds are insurmountable and there's nowhere to turn. Adolphius had none of those receptors. He launched himself at them, wielding the sword in frenzy. To his dismay the sword just clashed against something invisible but solid around them, some kind of force field that was impenetrable. Emanuel Goldberg, suddenly alerted by the fray, spun on his heels to face Adolphius. His agility was not as you might expect of an old man, but then he was of the Patriarch bloodline. Adolphius lunged at him with his sword. Elizabeth and Ben were about to respond to protect him, when Adolphius' hand opened and spilled the sword harmlessly to the floor. Emanuel had commanded it and Adolphius was powerless to resist his mind.

Adolphius' eyes darted around the room, searching for an escape route. The open window was his only option. His speed across the floor was supernatural. He dived head first at the opening and would have made it, had not Emanuel slammed the heavy wooden shutters closed with a simple jerk of his head.

Adolphius' face took the full impact. His nose broke audibly and his front teeth were driven back into his mouth. Adolphius picked himself up and turned to face his enemies. Blood flowed freely from his nose and mouth and dripped off his jowl beard, down his chest. He spat his teeth out onto the carpet and glared at them.

"Do your worst," he said hatefully.

"Oh we'll do better than that." Ben said pointing at the old weaponry displayed on the wall.

He swung his hand forcefully in Adolphius' direction. The collection of swords, spears and axes flew off the wall and impaled him against the shutters. None of the wounds was singularly fatal but collectively Adolphius would die of them, slowly and in excruciating pain.

Emanuel picked up the sword that Adolphius had intended to kill him with and crossed over to him.

"I will afford you the compassion that you never gave to the millions that have died through your deeds."

Adolphius didn't acknowledge nor react to the statement. Instead he chose defiance.

"You are a weak, misguided race and you don't understand the people of this planet. Man has always needed a firm hand. They are slaves by nature and need war and crave strong leadership. You bring nothing to the table and you will not prevail over the Shadows, because you don't have the courage to sacrifice the few for the better future of the many."

Adolphius spat a mouthful of his blood into Emanuel's face in contempt. Emanuel held Adolphius' stare as he located the tip of his sword beneath his sternum then pressed it up into his heart. The final *coup de grâce*. Even in death, Adolphius' eyes remained full of hatred.

Emanuel turned to Elizabeth and Ben. He instinctively knew who they were, even though their appearance had changed. He too was an adept of the mirrors.

"So," Emanuel acknowledged each with a nod of his white shaggy head, "I suppose this means that I owe you my life?"

"It was a pledge that we made to your son Mike over four and a half years from now," Elizabeth explained.

It felt bizarre talking about something there in the past that was going to happen in the future, but clearly none of this was strange to Emanuel.

"Does it all turn out alright, and what becomes of Michael?" Emanuel asked running his fingers through his shock of white hair.

Elizabeth almost doubled up at the pain that his name caused her, and her words came with difficulty.

"I don't know, I really don't know. I mean I think so, but we left Mike and the others in a lot of trouble..."

Emanuel crossed to her and folded her in his ample arms. He was a bear of a man and it felt so comfortable and secure there. It was the first time that Elizabeth had felt safe in a long time and she just let go and sobbed her heart out.

When the pent up emotions inside her had been exorcised, Emanuel turned her chin up and looked into her startling green eyes. As one of true blood, he had the power to read her and it only took moments for him to know it all. His face paled as the enormity of their quest unfolded in his mind. His mouth dropped involuntarily in awe of it all.

"Oh Elizabeth, how have you both endured so much?" Emanuel was humbled. It challenged everything that was reasonably possible. "It's beyond fiction and beyond imagination Lizzie."

The last time that Emanuel had seen them, they were mere children and now he marvelled at the powerful and confident people that they had become.

"Your journey is almost over but you must continue to have faith. You have already endured the impossible, so go and reap your reward but come to me again when you are back in your time. I will be waiting for you; we have so much to talk about."

Elizabeth kissed him and Ben locked his hand in a firm shake. They were in awe of the strength and uniqueness of this man that they had only ever known as just Emanuel Goldberg. Ben spoke for them both.

"Now I know why Dad spoke so highly of you Emanuel. Although it will be over four and a half years for you, we will see you in only a couple of days. Meanwhile shall we take out the rubbish?"

Ben jerked his head towards the blood soaked corpse of Adolphius that was nailed to the shutters.

"Would you be so kind?" Emanuel mocked.

Ben hefted Adolphius' body over his shoulder and crossed the room to the old mirror. There was one thing more to tell Emanuel though.

"Dad will be coming back through that door in a few moments. He forgot his phone you see," Ben pointed to the oak table. "But we don't want him to see us like this. Will you explain and send them our love and prepare him and Mum for when they see us. Tell them that it will be Sunday 8th September 2013 and it might be fitting to throw a party that day. Elizabeth will need a dress, about a size fourteen I think..."

"Ten!" corrected Elizabeth and shot Ben a murderous look.

Ben smiled mischievously.

"Oh and can you tell Mum that we will be starving?"

Emanuel nodded in understanding.

"I will be waiting for you here on that day," Emanuel acknowledged, with his usual affable smile as they stepped back into the corridor of mirrors.

They both knew without saying where Adolphius would spend eternity. Ben shrugged the corpse into one of the broken mirrors that consumed it instantly, and then took a hasty step backwards to give the portal a respectful distance. They exchanged astonished looks. The portals had a dreadful power and their blood ran cold, even at the thought of it.

Elizabeth looked at her brother. It was clear that he had held himself together for as long as he could but now he was rapidly becoming undone. His loss of blood had taken its toll and his eyes were sinking into their sockets. The crooked smile that he flashed at her was only bravado and the lights went out in the making of it. Elizabeth only just caught him before he hit the floor.

May was with Crystalita, at her favourite spot where they had first met. Crystalita was still unconscious and May was bathing her wound with the stem cell enriched amniotic fluid. She was murmuring soothing and encouraging words to her. When she looked up and saw Elizabeth carrying Ben's limp body urgently towards her, she panicked and ran to meet them.

"What's happened? Ben, Ben! Please no..." May was shaking like a leaf, almost too scared to look at him.

"He's alive May but only just. He needs blood and he needs it now."

Elizabeth wore large, diamond shape silver earrings. May tore one off her, causing Elizabeth to cry out in pain and clasp her ear.

"What the hell..."

Elizabeth quickly saw that it was no random act. May pulled a reed out of the bank, laid it on the rock and sliced it obliquely at each end with the sharp earring. Kneeling at Ben's side, she slashed the vein in her forearm and inserted the reed. Blood immediately began spurting copiously out of the other end in rhythm with her heartbeat. She opened Ben's vein in the same way but only a trickle of blood oozed reluctantly from it. May inserted the other end of the reed into Ben's arm and pulled the silk shroud from her shoulders offering it to Elizabeth.

"Bind our arms together Lizzie and pray it's not too late!"

May had transformed. The translucent almost ethereal being was just simple flesh and blood now as her deception of clothing had disappeared under the intense concentration of her task. She was naked and oblivious to it.

"Elizabeth, listen carefully I don't have much time," she had locked on to Elizabeth's eyes and there was no doubt as to the urgency of her request, "I will pass out when my blood levels can no longer support me. You must separate us then and bind our wrists with bandages soaked in the amniotic fluid, if you don't we will bleed to death. Do you understand?"

Elizabeth nodded. Pre-empting the situation she ran to where Crystalita was and prepared the bandages. When she returned May was already in a trance-like state as she concentrated all her energy into forcing her blood into Ben's body. It happened faster than Elizabeth could have expected and collapse came in moments. Elizabeth looked at May aghast at the change that had come over her.

The transfusion had gone too fast and too far. May's life force was swiftly ebbing away. She had decided to give it all up for Ben. May's skin had turned as white as the snow and her vivid blue eyes were dulled and wide open in shock. Ben was more than twice her size and she had given him all that she could. There was a smile of contentment on her face though, as if she knew that he would be alright now.

Elizabeth bound Ben's gashed vein with the soaked bandage just as May had instructed, but instead of binding May's, she ripped off her other earring and slashed her own vein and inserted the reed. Elizabeth used the other bandage to bind their arms together so that they could not be separated and then laid down next to her.

She kissed her and whispered.

"Thank you for Ben's life."

Elizabeth put her arm lovingly around May's cold body and talked to her quietly, as if she was reading a bedtime story to a child. It was now for the gods to decide who was to live and who was to die.

Ben woke from the deepest, dreamless sleep feeling on top of the world. His arm was bandaged and a luminous green fluid was oozing from it. He immediately recognised it as the same amniotic fluid that he was immersed in by Jorall and Zita, to regenerate his damaged ears and eyes. He pushed his aching and torn body up until he was on his haunches.

Ben looked around, taking in the situation. Elizabeth and May were lying together sleeping and Crystalita was over by the rock, with her head bandaged, apparently sleeping too. Ben was about to lay back and join them, when he somehow sensed that all was not well and immediately feared for Crystalita. He sprang to his feet and crossed over to where she lay. Ben quickly established that she was stable and out of danger and deduced that this couldn't have been what had raised the alarm in him. He ran back to where Elizabeth and May were lying, with a sense of dread. When he saw them he screamed out loud in despair.

"No! No please God no."

They were both cuddled together in the rigor of death. Elizabeth's eyes were still open and flies were already crawling over her final gaze. Ben turned and vomited into the shrubs. His whole world came crashing in on him. He picked up his sister by the shoulders and shook her forcefully screaming at her staring face as if it might make a difference.

"Wake up! You can't die we've come too far Lizzie. It's over don't you see, it's all over! We have done everything that we wanted to."

Ben pulled her into his chest and the sobs of grief racked his body. He was talking to her as if she could still hear him and all he wanted to do was die with her. May's eyes were closed and she looked peaceful in death, with what looked like a smile of satisfaction on her face.

Ben looked at his bandaged arm and then at the reed that joined Elizabeth and May. He suddenly understood. May had given her life for his and Elizabeth must have risked hers trying to save May. It was the saddest but most noble thing.

"But my life was not worth the two of you, damn your stupidity!" Ben cursed them both, even in death.

There could be no darker place than where Ben was at that moment and his despair was beyond endurance. He wanted to end it and join them in eternity there and then. The blood-soaked earrings that had been used to cut their veins were lying discarded on the sand, beckoning him to do the same. He picked one up and kissed Elizabeth on the cheek, then May on the mouth. He looked up into the clear blue Grecian sky for the last time and slashed his wrist.

"I will be with you soon," were his final words to them.

Peace came to Ben slowly as his blood drained inexorably into the parched earth. His head was filled with flashing images of the happy moments in his life. There was his father throwing him in the air and catching him as a child and he felt the delicious fear and exhilaration of it. Then there was his mother's face close to his, as she carried him through the park animatedly telling him of the adventures that lay just on the other side of the bushes. She promised a world filled with pirates and fairies, both good and bad, and mysterious animals that were just waiting for him to tame to be his pets... Incongruously, Elizabeth's face suddenly appeared in his vision, scalding and rebuking him.

"You bloody fool! Use your brain for once in your life, damn you Ben. You weren't born to just give up on me. Fight for us for God's sake!"

It wasn't really Elizabeth's voice; it was his subconscious guilt coming to the fore. It was the instinct for survival that was nagging him out of capitulation, literally a wakeup call. Ben needed help, he had to think fast. Even moments would make the difference. He fought desperately to clear the clouds that were shrouding his mind.

"Jorall!" he called.

Ben dragged himself to his feet. He ripped a strip off his shirt and tied it around his arm as a tourniquet, to stem the blood-flow. He prayed that he wasn't already too late. Ben was dying and he knew it, but he had to live just a little longer, he just had to. Ben ran drunkenly towards the mother ship, willing his tired legs onwards. When he finally got to the corridor of mirrors, he was already delirious. He tried desperately to find the one that would lead him to May's father, but they all looked the same to him.

Everything began to turn black as Ben edged ever closer to unconsciousness. He knew now that he had failed them. After all they had been through; he had failed them at the last hurdle. Ben's legs gave way beneath him and he fell against one of the mirrors. It was smooth and afforded him no grip as he fought to stay on his feet. He slipped helplessly to the floor, hanging on to the last precious moments of life.

A strong hand took Ben's arm and pulled him to his feet. The sudden shock of it brought Ben back to a state of semi-consciousness. It was beyond Ben's ability to comprehend, the arm supporting him had no body to it. He was still trying to make sense of it as the rest of Jorall stepped through the mirror.

"Jorall! But how..."

"Easy Ben I sense you have little time left. What must I do?"

There was a strength and understanding about Jorall that was indescribable. Maybe it was just where evolution takes us, but Ben was thankful for his fatherly strength. It gave him the stimulation that he needed to eke his life out just that little bit further.

"I'm dying Jorall as you already know."

Jorall nodded solemnly.

"I will be here at your passing Ben, have strength and faith."

That simple statement of inevitability choked Ben and it took him valuable seconds to compose himself.

"I'm sorry about what I have to say and there is no time to say it kindly. May and my sister Elizabeth are both dead. They died sharing their blood to save me, and Crystalita is suffering from a severe head wound."

Jorall's face paled. He looked stricken, totally devastated. His mouth opened to find words that just weren't there. His professionalism came to his rescue and he became objective; once again the pragmatic physician.

"I can still save Crystalita, where is she?"

"No Jorall, that's not the way to do it. Trust me."

Jorall looked at Ben uncomprehendingly. He was about to protest, when Ben cut in. This time, his voice was hardly audible and Jorall had to lean in closely to hear him.

"You can save all of us Jorall, but today is too late. You must leave this place and return yesterday, before it all happens. Make your theatre ready for us and help us when we arrive. You can change all this Jorall, you must. You can create another possibility just as we have," Ben squeezed Jorall's hand and added. "One day you will know that I love your daughter."

With that Ben passed calmly in Jorall's arms.

"Go in peace son," Jorall said fondly, as he closed Ben's eyes for the final time.

Jorall had just finished tending to Crystalita when he saw Ben heft Adolphius's body into the broken portal and the black hole that lay behind it. Moments later, he saw Ben collapse into Elizabeth's arms. Jorall ran down the corridor to them and helped Elizabeth with her unconscious brother.

"Jorall?" Elizabeth exclaimed in disbelief.

"There's no time to explain Elizabeth. I have everything prepared for you just as Ben asked, but we must hurry your brother's blood level is dangerously low."

"Just as Ben asked? But how could he…"

"I said there's no time," Jorall insisted.

He pulled away from Elizabeth suddenly as the pungent smell of rotting flesh hit him. He grabbed her bandaged hand and looked at her veins running up her arm. The tell-tale signs of mortification were already spreading and his concern was written clearly across his face.

"I'm sorry Elizabeth but you may have already lost this arm. Mortification inhibits regeneration but I will try of course. You may still be lucky."

"Just forget about me Jorall, until Ben's safe. Is that perfectly clear?"

It came across more severely than Elizabeth meant it to but Jorall could read the fear that was in her on both counts. He just smiled back in conciliatorily response.

When they arrived in the operating theatre, May was tending a very conscious Crystalita and was clearly having problems keeping her put.

"Don't you dare!" were the words that Elizabeth heard as May pointed accusingly at her sister then hurried to meet them.

Jorall was the consummate and unflustered professional and he put May straight to work.

"I will deal with Ben. I want you to cut away as much rotten flesh as you can from Elizabeth's hand. Go right back to the uncorrupted flesh, and further if you think necessary. Then you massage any poison that you can out of her veins and wrap the wound in dressings of amniotic fluid. There are strong antibiotics in that cabinet. Give her a 50 cc shot, the rest you already know."

The rest was bio-physical intervention. Quite simply that meant that May would link her mind with Elizabeth's and encourage her own immune system to fight the poison within her, much the same as she and Ben had done when Katya had inflicted the snake venom.

Jorall turned briefly to Elizabeth.

"I'm sorry but there will be no time for anaesthetic, you will just have to deal with it."

It was perfunctory, but Elizabeth understood. May busied herself cleaning the mess that was once her hand. She sang to Elizabeth as she worked, cutting away the infected flesh and somehow her melodious voice took away the pain of it. Elizabeth watched May's face in fascination as she frowned and smiled according to her progress until finally she began to wrap her hand in the bandages, drenched in the stem cell enhanced amniotic fluid.

"I'm no doctor but in my perfectly unprofessional capacity, I would say that you will do just fine!"

The operating table was already fully prepared and the mother ship had a good stock of cryogenically preserved blood. Jorall introduced the catheter and within a minute the lifesaving blood was flowing freely into Ben's starved body.

Even in his weakened state, Jorall was amazed at how Ben had controlled the blood-flow to his many and serious wounds. It had quite simply saved his life. He tended to each of them and then wrapped them in bandages soaked in the rejuvenating fluid. An hour later he turned to May who was biting her bottom lip.

"He will be just fine," Jorall said in matter of fact manner.

"Daddy!"

May threw her arms around him and smothered him in kisses.

Chapter 37

It was going to take a while to fully recover from their injuries, particularly mentally. It would give them time though to get to know each other in the context of their present and future selves.

They were once again at May's favourite place by the rock next to the ridge, drinking fresh lemonade and enjoying the warmth of the Greek sun. The breeze was just cool enough to be refreshing, without chilling them and there was an atmosphere of perfect calm and gaiety. May was braiding Crystalita's beautiful blonde hair, which shone in the sun like threads of spun platinum. They were giggling like school girls. May was pretending to be shocked at what her sister was secretly telling her.

Crystalita's skin glowed with the health of youth and she had enhanced it with glitter that reflected rainbows of light. Her body was svelte and promising and her laughter, enchanting. She looked at Ben periodically through her startling blue, mischievous eyes. Periodically she would whisper in May's ear, each time getting a playful slap on her back from a most disapproving sister. It was clear to Elizabeth and probably invisible to Ben, that Crystalita was teasing May; probably making some risqué innuendos. She smiled knowingly at how girls are and enjoyed the moment with them. Elizabeth also noticed that May hadn't missed a trick either. She had never looked more stunning. Her hair was piled on top of her head in a chaos of black curls and her eyes were strategically lined to maximise their size. In case Ben still wasn't paying attention, the colour of her irises were cycling enticingly between greens and blues.

It amused Elizabeth and a thought crossed her mind.

"There was far too much oestrogen going on here," she noted and caught May's gaze at the same instant.

It was almost comical how quickly May averted her eyes, then looked back giving Elizabeth the most lascivious smile. Crystalita had read it too and hooted with laughter, then openly flirted with Ben to infuriate her sister still more.

Elizabeth felt the envy rise inside her. Her thoughts turned to Mike and how they had left him and the others in an impossible situation. They will all have died. She knew that had to be true and a single tear ran down her cheek, betraying her emotions. The trauma of the last few months for Elizabeth and Ben had left deep scars that would take time to heal, considerably longer than their wounds. May sensed this and was conscious not to hurry them into the telling of their story. Elizabeth pushed the bleak thoughts away and immersed herself in the pleasure of watching May and Crystalita laughing and chatting together. It was strange, and hard to imagine, that May would not experience the loss of her sister now that they had prevented it.

May must have read her thoughts and she voiced her reply.

"I do know what you have both done for us," May was humbled and her head was bowed. "But I don't know how, nor what it has cost you to do it. I only know from the mirrors, that it was beyond all reasonable likelihood of success."

May's guilt over what her future self must have made them do, suddenly became unbearable and she was overcome by it.

"The future *me* must have sentenced you to probable death. How could I have done that and how can you ever forgive me?"

To Elizabeth's relief, Ben grasped the moment and crossed to May taking her into his arms.

"It's not like that May, that's not how it happened at all. We had already become targets and you came to our rescue. It was you that taught us how to access our powers and how to use them to our best advantage. It wasn't a death sentence that you gave us May, far from it. It was an opportunity to survive, another possibility."

May felt safe in Ben's powerful arm. He kissed the top of her head as he continued.

"We all needed something May. For us it was our parents back, Mike his father and brother and you needed Crystalita."

May looked up into Ben's eyes and there was no doubting the intensity of the love and gratitude that she had for him. The kiss that followed was pure and powerful and it completely disorientated Ben.

"Ahem, children present!" Crystalita said and then laughed hysterically at the unprecedented behaviour of her sister.

May had lit up in that bioluminescent way that she had no control over. The light that was pulsating in sympathy with May's impossibly high heart-rate only served to heighten her embarrassment and Crystalita's glee.

"Oh Ben, whatever happened to that little boy that I used to teach?"

Crystalita preened openly. The look that May returned, couldn't have said, "Back off sister!" any louder and Crystalita retreated instantly. It was all hugely amusing to Elizabeth and almost totally lost on Ben.

It wasn't just to change the subject but it was altogether a useful distraction and May took the opportunity.

"Are you ready to tell us what happened?" May had parked the slightly embarrassing affair and was eager to hear their story.

Elizabeth looked at Ben and answered for them both.

"Before we tell you, we're both curious to know how you always know so much about us whether that be in the past or in an alternative future."

May looked a little awkward, perhaps even guilty.

"Well I have been manipulating alternative outcomes using the portals over the millennia. It's how we manage the threat of the Shadows. Just like you met the reflection of your future self in the old mirror on the night of your party, I have been doing the same with mine and we share knowledge, emotions and memories. Those memories even become as real as my own, as if they actually happened to me. So in fact I know everything up until the last time you met me in your own time."

"Spying on us," accused Elizabeth.

"Yes, if you like but we've been there before haven't we?"

It was proof absolute.

"Yes, as well you know May. And yes you are perfectly forgiven for it!" there was a tangible sense of relief on May's part, now that obstacle had been removed.

"So tell us of your adventures!"

May and Crystalita were dying of curiosity. Elizabeth began their story.

"After our parents were killed by the Shadows..."

"No, not that way," interjected May, "I want to experience it all with you. We have missed so much, and it will take you forever to tell only part of it otherwise."

She took Elizabeth and Ben's hands and Crystalita completed the circle.

"Let us into your minds please," May reached back into their memories to when they had returned from Mount Olympus with her future self. She knew everything up until then and that was the starting point of their latest struggle against the Shadows. Their story played out moment by moment but it only took minutes in the telling.

Elizabeth and Ben watched the changes that came over the two exotic maidens in front of them, as the magnitude of the story unfolded. They responded in colour and brightness according to the emotion that it evoked in them. They clearly lived their journey. The pain they had suffered, the fear and sometimes even the joy, passed fleetingly across their faces. Tears of both happiness and sadness flowed profusely down their angelic faces.

At last it was over and they broke the circle. May looked open-mouthed at Crystalita with eyes as big as saucers. The enormity of what their friends had been through for them; hit them so dramatically, that they had no words to describe how they felt. It was all beyond belief. May bowed her head and averted her eyes in almost inconsolable guilt, while Crystalita embraced her and tried to take away the pain in the way that only Angels can.

It was a deeply personal moment and Elizabeth and Ben both sensed that it was time to leave them to come to terms with it all. Ben took Elizabeth's hand and led her out into the forest. They walked in silence for some time. It was strange, but in letting them access their minds, they too had relived it all in those few minutes. The experience was both mind numbing and exorcising.

It was Ben who finally broke the silence.

"We did it Sis, we did the impossible and we lived to tell the tale," Ben reconsidered the accuracy of his statement, "Well we died and then lived, to tell the tale to be more exact," Ben flashed his confident and perfect smile at Elizabeth.

She looked back at him and wondered how it could be the same insecure boy that she had mothered for over four years. He was every inch a man now and she felt somehow safe having him around.

"Yes we did it Ben and I'm proud of you. You were awesome. When Dad hears what you've done, he'll retire and pass the tiger and giant fighting stuff over to you."

Elizabeth tucked her head into his neck and felt the protection that she had only ever felt before from her father. They even smelt the same. It was a really safe and secure place to be and she could have stayed there forever. Ben sensed it and remained quiet to let her enjoy the peace of it.

After a while he confessed to her openly and without shame.

"There were several times that I wouldn't have made it without you Lizzie. If I was awesome then you were right off the Richter scale. From the very start you had it nailed. Even Dada didn't stand a chance, when you were just a novice. He must have wondered where the hell you came from!"

Elizabeth smiled appreciatively at the compliment but her mind had moved on.

"You say that we did it Ben, but did what? Elizabeth was suddenly filled with doubt. "Yes we've changed events Ben, created that alternative possibility that we wanted. But when we return to our time, it will be over four years later. So much could have happened in that time. What's to say that they haven't all been killed by some other Shadow plot, or died in a plane crash or..."

"Well thanks for the cup half empty Lizzie. Excuse me while I just cut my wrists... again."

"No, I'm just saying don't get your hopes up," Elizabeth stopped realising her negativity. "Oh shit what rubbish is that? If it happens then we just have to go back in time again and sort it out and find another possibility don't we?" Elizabeth's smile said it all. The fight was back in her again.

"That's more like it Lizzie. Anyway, I think it's time to leave here. We've waited too long for what's only just moments away. Besides, I think that the girls need some space too."

They walked back slowly and it was like the world had come off their shoulders. They talked animatedly of the future which was immensely therapeutic, as only hours ago they didn't think they had one. They felt young again and both yearned to see their parents.

"Do you think they will recognise us when we return? We will have changed so much Ben," Elizabeth asked with real concern.

They both knew that when they returned through the same portal to the same time that they had left, it would over-write events and their counterparts would cease to be.

"Mum and Dad's experiences and ours over the last few years will be completely different. We will be almost strangers to them."

Ben put his arm around her reassuringly.

"You have so many doubts Lizzie. Was Emanuel unable to understand when we met him?"

He looked into Elizabeth's big green eyes and saw the shadows of doubt in them. Elizabeth shook her head and he continued.

"No, because he is a Patriarch as Dad is. And, if you remember, I asked him to explain things to them before we arrive back in our time. I even gave him the date that they could expect us."

Elizabeth smiled back at him reassured by his common sense.

"So we've got nothing to worry about then Ben, eh? Well I think Mum will freak out big time."

Elizabeth kissed his cheek then turned away so that he couldn't see that she was still worried. Their mother wasn't of Angel blood and wouldn't be able to cope with losing the children that she had known and loved, in exchange for two near strangers. Whether they would ever see Uncle George, Aunt Jillie, Mike and the others again, was also far from being a given. It could still all go so desperately wrong.

When they returned to May and Crystalita, May was in a much more positive mood. She had already organised her head with the idea that they would now be living in the alternative future that her counterpart *of* the future had initiated. However it was still hard to imagine that she could have been without her sister had Elizabeth and Ben not intervened. It made her painfully aware of their vulnerability. Although May was still uncomfortable about having put Elizabeth and Ben at such risk, she realised that her options in the future must have been extremely limited and was thankful for that almost divine intervention.

Crystalita was still a little in shock that her life would have ended there on the street at the hand of Alexis. It was beyond belief that the two young children that she had been sent to keep a watchful eye on, in the guise of their music teacher, could have the resourcefulness to change history and save her life. The debt of gratitude that she owed them could never be repaid. She vowed to herself that she would watch over them for the rest of their lives.

May sensed the change that had come over Elizabeth and Ben and sighed resignedly.

"So you have decided that it is time to leave us then?"

They nodded guiltily and Ben responded positively.

"But we will come back tomorrow it's just that we have waited so long to see..."

May interrupted as she needed no explanation.

"Indeed you have and you deserve the reward that lies on the other side of the portal. It's right that you go now," May averted her gaze and there was a shyness about her. "Will you walk with me a while before you go Ben? Only tomorrow for you will be more than four years for me," May couldn't hold back the tears any longer and they ran down her face in rivulets. She looked crest-fallen. Ben's heart went out to her as he took her in his arms.

"Not much of a Matriarch am I?" she reached up to hold his face forcing a smile, "I'm sorry that's not fair, only I panicked about you leaving me after I've only just found you. You must still walk with me though Ben because there's a lot that I want you to know."

Ben looked at Elizabeth and she smiled encouragingly, fully understanding what it was that May wanted to say to him.

"Take all the time that you need Ben. Miss Crystal and me have a lot to catch up on."

They took the old hunting track through the forest that took them out towards the northeast. When the forest cleared they looked out across the peaks that rose up to Mount Olympus itself. They hadn't spoken until then. It was sufficient to just enjoy the peace and tranquillity of the forest and the feeling of closeness. At last Ben broke the silence. He was gazing out towards Olympus full of regret.

"It saddens me that we created so many memories together over the last several months and now they will only be mine."

May turned him to face her and held him in her serene gaze.

"You were not listening to me were you Ben. Do you really think that is true?"

"Well it has to be, you were never there, how could you..."

May couldn't help her amusement and smiled guiltily at him.

"There is still so much that you don't know about the Angels and more particularly the female ones."

Her laughter was both musical and compelling. Ben couldn't resist putting his arm around her waist and holding her to him, which of course was May's intention.

"Enlighten me," Ben was intrigued.

"Well when we linked together to hear your story we took more than that from you. We lived it moment by moment as if we were there with you. Your memories are now our memories."

That news was so elating, that Ben compulsively kissed her full on the lips. Just for a split second a strange look flickered in May's eyes. It was almost like a cloud passing across the blue heavens, but he saw it and she knew it. She looked like a child caught stealing sweets.

"There's more isn't there May?"

May wanted to say, "No", but lying didn't come naturally to her kind so she confessed her sin.

"Despite the millions of years more evolution that we have, there are some things that you just can't change about a women and that is her curiosity and insecurity."

"And?" prompted Ben.

May flushed with embarrassment. It triggered her bioluminescence which damned her even more.

"I looked into your heart."

Ben could see that she was squirming, but he wasn't going to let her off the hook.

"And what did you find there?"

"Me," she said timidly and hung her head in shame.

Ben's joyous laughter rang out loud, echoing around Olympus. The love of the women in his arms made him feel as the mighty as Zeus himself!

It was two hours later when they reappeared at the edge of the forest. Their arms were linked and she was subconsciously leaning into him as women do when they are in love. May was looking up into Ben's face and they were talking animatedly, oblivious to their audience. Crystalita and Elizabeth watched them in amusement as they meandered down towards them. It was clear by the change in them that their love for each other had evolved.

"It's a primitive feeling but I'm so jealous of her!" Crystalita's body language was evidence that she really was. "We don't do very well on the male front in our family."

There was a semi-incoherent mumbling and Elizabeth thought that she heard her say, "More's the pity."

"Have you not met David Williams, the young sports teacher at school? He's really fit you should check him out; seriously!"

Crystalita looked puzzled.

"David Williams? There wasn't anyone there of that name in my time."

"Oh, perhaps he came after you died..." Elizabeth cringed at the crassness of her statement, "Sorry," to Elizabeth's relief Crystalita wasn't precious about it.

"Anyway even if he was there Lizzie, May wouldn't have approved..."

"Excuse me Crystalita! Take a look at that. I don't think that May has that moral high-ground anymore," Elizabeth saw the expression on Crystalita's face and understood immediately. "It's not May stopping you is it?"

Crystalita looked awkward and reluctant to answer, but eventually capitulated.

"No it's me. I've spent too much time here alone with May and I just don't have that kind of confidence. Anyway, what if I did meet him and he refused me?"

"Refuse you?" Elizabeth was shocked that Crystalita could even think such a thing, "You need to spend a bit more time in front of the mirror girl! Your only problem might be that you are just *so* beautiful, that men might be afraid to ask you in case you refused them."

Crystalita still didn't seem too convinced. She was glad that the others had arrived to get her off the hook.

Elizabeth wasn't going to let it be that easy for her though. She took May and Crystalita's hands to get their attention.

"Listen both of you. We will be having a party on Sunday 8th September 2013 and you are invited. I will make sure that Crystalita has some attentive company and winked at her conspiratorially."

Crystalita looked like she was going to die of embarrassment and couldn't look Elizabeth in the eye.

"Well, if you would rather I didn't..." Elizabeth tested.

"No, I didn't say that..."

Her reply was just a little too hasty and too urgent. It betrayed her true feelings and she looked like a rabbit caught in the headlights of a car. It didn't help when Elizabeth and May began laughing, mocking her plight.

All that Ben could add was, "What's so funny?"

Chapter 38

When they stepped through the mirror into Emanuel's office it was fourteen minutes after midnight on the Sunday morning. That was exactly the same time they had entered it in the Robinson's loft on the night of the Shadow's attack. They were once again in their own time, but about to live another possibility, or so they hoped.

Emanuel was sat at his desk waiting for them. When they stepped through the portal, his smile lit up the room.

"True to your words, welcome home both of you!"

He stood up with his arms open to receive them and they embraced with genuine heart-felt emotion.

"My word you look different to the wretched battle-scarred souls that were here a few years ago," Emanuel shook his big white shaggy head in wonderment of it. "I did worry that you might not survive your injuries Ben. You really did look dreadful but I never told your parents that."

"It's a long story Emanuel but in truth, I didn't."

Emanuel's white eyebrows rose in consternation. Ben's comment had made no sense to him. He was about to ask for an explanation, but Elizabeth diverted the conversation to a matter more pressing.

"We'll tell you it all later, but first what of Mum and Dad?" Elizabeth held her breath before saying it. "Are they alive?"

Emanuel smiled at her and answered tantalisingly.

"Now it's my turn to be evasive. There has been a surprise party arranged for you at your Uncle and Aunt's house, to start at three o'clock this afternoon. That is exactly what it will be, a surprise party! All you need to prepare for it is upstairs ready for you."

They talked the night away. By morning, Elizabeth had finally forgiven Emanuel for his mental cruelty and was deliciously anticipating the party. Emanuel had been true to his word. There was a collection of dresses and shoes to choose from with a definite hint of Aunt Jillie's good taste about it. Some of the dresses were so daring, she wondered whether she could pull off wearing one. She decided of course that she could, and would! To her delight, someone had chosen her favourite makeup from the Christian Dior collection and *Naughty Alice* perfume by Vivienne Westwood.

"That *someone* had to be Aunt Jillie", Elizabeth mused.

They had three hours left to get ready and she was going to enjoy every minute of it!

Ben had a selection of Gucci tuxedos in various sizes and cuts to choose from. Clearly Emanuel had some doubts over Ben's size and had guessed all but one on the small side. Fortunately the one that did fit was absolutely perfect and the selection of shirts, exquisite. Ben prepared himself for a shower. After he had undressed he stood in his briefs in front of the full length mirror and appraised himself. The attritions of the last few days had burnt off any trace of fat in his tissue. His muscle definition was that of an athlete, not a body builder. Lean and mean. He would have looked good but for the dozen or so blood stained bandages tinged with the green amniotic fluid.

"I'm not going to the party dressed as a bloody mummy!" Ben grunted.

He began to carefully un-wrap the bandages. It was an almost religious experience and Ben was awestruck at what he finally saw. The deep wounds inflicted by Alexis' sabre had all but disappeared. Even the heavy raking his left forearm had suffered, fending off the stiletto knife, were now just red wheals.

"Lizzie!" he shouted as he ran to her room and burst through her door. "Look at my wounds!"

"Ben!" she grabbed her dress and held it to her in an attempt to hide her modesty. "Didn't you think about knocking?"

"Sorry Lizzie but look at my wounds, they've all but gone!" he was positively beaming. "Just like Dad's did, and in no time at all."

"A-M-A-Z-I-N-G," Elizabeth expounded and subconsciously felt her own bandaged hand. She had been seriously concerned about the amount of heat exuding from it and feared that it could be mortifying.

"Do you think...? Elizabeth said hesitantly.

"Take a look Lizzie if it's not alright you can always bandage it up again."

Elizabeth was just about to then she stopped and offered her hand to Ben.

"I don't think I can bear to look at it Ben. Will you do it?"

"Of course you wimp."

Ben began to un-wrap the bandages gently removing each layer until her hand was completely revealed.

"Oh shit no!" he exclaimed and recoiled in fake shock.

"What is it Ben!" Elizabeth's panic was palpable.

She was too scared to look at her hand so her eyes sought Ben's face for an explanation.

"Nothing, it looks perfect to me..."

His smirk said, "gotcha!" Elizabeth was beyond furious. It was quite possibly the fastest that any man had ever left a beautiful girl's room.

At was half past two and Emanuel had the car waiting at the front door for them. He called upstairs in mocked formal manner.

"Your limousine awaits you."

Emanuel Goldberg was not prepared for the vision that appeared at the top of the stairs. In his old-fashioned way he removed his trilby hat and held it to his chest and simply said, "Oh my."

Elizabeth had chosen the long black, backless dress with a wide vent up the side that exposed the whole of her leg to her hip as she came down the stairs. If that wasn't enough to make you pay attention, then the plunging neckline down to her naval certainly would. It was the kind of dress that invited a wardrobe malfunction. She had already decided that she should perhaps stay on the right side of drunk tonight, or the boys would be in for a treat. The elegant high-heeled silver Charles Jordan shoes, set off the feminine turn of her ankle and the matching clutch bag, provided the essential girl's accessory. Elizabeth's blonde hair was piled up wildly on top of her head and her large green eyes shone like cut emeralds from her tanned face. The bright red lipstick she wore with confidence, made the smile that she gave Emanuel irresistible. He was totally enchanted by her.

Emanuel bowed to her expansively with a flourish of his hat and serenaded her with an improvised line from a famous Simon and Garfunkel song.

"And here's to you Miss Robinson, someone will love you more than you will know. Wo, wo, wo..."

Elizabeth curtsied to him at the bottom of the stairs and couldn't help but think that he had someone particular in mind. Ben appeared at the top of the stairs adjusting his cuff. He paused for just long enough, then smiled at them and swaggered down the stairs, in a practiced James Bond style. He didn't fail to catch his own reflection in the mirror as he passed and cocked an approving eye.

Elizabeth put two fingers in her mouth and turned her head pretending to gag.

"You don't need a girlfriend Ben, you're much too in love with yourself," Elizabeth rebuked.

Ben simply smiled in agreement offering his arm and Elizabeth took it elegantly.

"Are you ready Lizzie?"

"Scared shitless actually Ben, but hey-ho."

They followed Emanuel out to the car, bursting with anticipation.

George and Jillie had gone to great lengths to throw the garden party of the decade. As before there was the marquee, band, caterers and a butler. It was nearly three o'clock. Jillie was still faffing over minor detail, but it was all to hide her own nervousness. It was driving George nuts.

"For God's sake woman, will you not just relax?" George appeared calm but he too didn't quite know what to expect.

Emanuel had explained that they would appear *different* and that their alternative life experience would make that even more apparent. He had assured them that intrinsically they would be the same people, just a little more battle hardened. He had also told them about the assassination of Ralph and Jodie, over four years ago in another life. And that they were essentially the only parents that they now knew. That would mean that Elizabeth and Ben would have a special bond with them, even though that might not be reciprocal. Jillie was worried that she would be a disappointment to them and simply couldn't get her head around the principal of alternative futures.

As if all of that wasn't impossible enough to take in for Jillie, to be told that their home had been the site of full scale warfare, burnt down and all of them murdered, well it was beyond any sane person's ability to comprehend. Even that became almost plausible, compared to the thought of Angels and Shadows walking our Earth and Elizabeth and Ben travelling through time and changing the order of things. This was going to be the most monumental day of their lives and only a fraction of the people invited would ever know that.

"What will the non-family guests make of it, them looking different I mean?"

Jillie had asked Emanuel but he had assured them that Angels have a way to deal with these things. All in all, Jillie had every right to be faffing around. The guests had been asked to arrive at half past two, so that the party would be underway when Elizabeth and Ben arrived with Emanuel. Ralph and Jodie were to arrive a half an hour after that, so that they could enjoy their reunion without the chaos of social formalities. Jillie checked the invitations with the butler. So far, three guests had failed to show up. That was two foreign sounding girls with strange names, Maelströminha and Crystalita and Emanuel's son Michael. He had been on active service overseas and they had failed to get his invitation to him.

Emanuel pulled up in front of the Robinson's house and opened the back door of the limousine for Elizabeth. Her first task, with the radically cut dress was to get out of the limousine gracefully. She made a good fist of it, while Emanuel averted his eyes helping her achieve that goal. Ben alighted from the other side and came around quickly to take her arm. The butler was waiting for them in the hallway, adjusting his tie in the old mirror. He turned to greet them and Elizabeth saw his dear old face.

"Jeeves!" Elizabeth's genuine surprise and glee took the old man by surprise. "Oh I can't tell you how nice it is to see you again."

"I'm sorry ma'am but I wasn't aware that we had met. It is most remiss of me not to remember such an attractive and charming woman," Jeeves looked extremely uncomfortable about his omission.

"You have grandchildren don't you? James and Bella isn't it? They would be about four and three I believe. How are they?"

Jeeves was positively infatuated by Elizabeth's charm and her clear recollections of what he must have told her, but forgot. His face was a picture.

"Yes, how well remembered ma'am. They are fine thank you for asking, and I cannot imagine that I will forget you again Miss Elizabeth." Jeeves bowed respectfully. "May I present you to your guests?"

"Yes of course," Elizabeth replied and added hopefully. "Has a Michael Jackson arrived yet Jeeves?"

"No miss, I'm sorry but apparently he's late returning from overseas. I don't think that the invitation even got to him."

Elizabeth looked crestfallen. Ben squeezed her hand supportively.

"I know you're disappointed Lizzie, but at least it proves that he's still alive."

Elizabeth managed a thin smile as Jeeves led them down the hallway to the marquee. Most of the guests had already seen them enter before Jeeves even called for their attention.

"Ladies and gentlemen may I have your attention please. I present to you our guests of honour, Elizabeth and Ben Robinson."

There was a stir amongst the guests as they passed comments to each other about the striking couple's appearance. It was a mixture of admiration and disbelief.

"That can't possibly be them can it?" a close friend of Jillie asked her husband who was still gawping at Elizabeth.

"She's growing up quite splendidly isn't she?" he replied absentmindedly.

It was said with a little too much enthusiasm, which earned the most disparaging look from his wife.

"Men," she muttered.

George and Jillie immediately made their way to the suave young couple.

"Oh wow!" Jillie proclaimed as she took Elizabeth's outstretched hands. "Just look at you! I absolutely knew that you would choose that dress!"

They hugged carefully but warmly so as not to smudge or wrinkle each other's works of art. George was already in a bear hug with Ben and it was really quite emotional. When they separated, they remained holding each other by the shoulders appraising one another. It was George who spoke first.

"What happened to the boy that I saw yesterday?" he smiled knowingly, nodding his head in approval. "That's going to take some explaining to most of the people here, not to mention how Elizabeth got those dangerous bends overnight!"

"Don't worry Uncle we're working on it. They will come to terms with it over the course of the afternoon and then never question it again."

Ben's cheeky smile lit up his face but it was quickly followed by a more solemn expression as the memories of the night of the Shadow attack filled his head. He could see Uncle George clearly in the war room detonating the explosives and a supernatural like chill ran up his back.

"There are things that happened here that I will regret forever and I need to share them with you Uncle, or I'll never be free of the guilt."

There was no doubting the trauma that Ben had suffered and George could see that, but now wasn't the time and so he put Ben's conscience at ease.

"All's well that ends well eh Ben? You just enjoy your homecoming today. We can save all that until another time but just remember that the end often justifies the means."

Ben was grateful for his uncle's understanding and pragmatic words.

"You were a real hero though Uncle, awesome in fact."

George and Jillie revelled in the company of their now very much adult nephew and niece. It was going to take a lot of getting to know them again and they were looking forward to it with the greatest of pleasure. Between exchanges, Elizabeth and Ben were looking amongst the guests for the two people they had hoped would be there but they were not.

Elizabeth began to feel the doubt rising within her and sought Ben's take on it.

"Do you think that maybe it didn't happen for Mum and Dad and they died somehow?" Elizabeth looked desperate.

"I don't think Emanuel would have let us come here unaware and unprepared for that, do you?"

It was nonsense and Elizabeth knew it deep down. Then the moment that they had waited so long for, finally came.

"Ladies and gentlemen may I have your attention please. I present to you Ralph and Jodie Robinson."

More than four and a half years of grief had built up in them and those words released an avalanche of different emotions, including fear of rejection. Elizabeth thought that she was going to be sick or feint. She reached out for Ben to steady her as her knees began to buckle under her.

"Steady Lizzie you can do this."

Ben was secretly glad that she needed help, as it diverted him from his own nervousness and inertia.

471

Elizabeth's legs began to find traction as adrenaline began coursing through her veins.

"Mum!" she screamed.

She let go of Ben's hand and ran to her mother who was waiting with outstretched arms.

Ralph and Jodie had spent the whole day with their teenage children spoiling them and enjoying every last second. They let them choose whatever they wanted to have or do. Elizabeth and Ben were having the time of their lives enjoying all the close attention. Elizabeth more than Ben, had sensed a sadness within their parents, but when she challenged her mother, she simply denied that there was anything to worry about.

"Just preoccupied, that's all," she had said.

That evening, Jodie had been upstairs for nearly an hour saying her goodnights. Eventually Ralph called up to her.

"Jodie, it's time to leave them now!" Ralph was suffering too and he needed her company.

Jodie left Ben's room after kissing him goodnight for the umpteenth time, re-confirming that she loved him. She ignored Ralph's pleas and went to Elizabeth's room to do the same.

"What is it Mum?" Elizabeth wanted answers. "You and Dad have been acting strangely all day. Actually not just today but for quite a while, truth be known."

Jodie couldn't help the tear that squeezed out of the corner of her eye and she wiped it away with her finger, hoping that Elizabeth hadn't seen it.

"It's just that you and Ben are growing up so fast and soon we will lose you forever."

It was at least half the truth. Jodie turned to leave but just as she did Elizabeth called out to her.

"Whatever it is that you are *really* worrying about will turn out fine. I just know it. Goodnight, love you Mum."

"Love you too Lizzie."

Jodie had to press her hand to her mouth to suppress the sobs welling up inside her and hurried downstairs. She ran across the room to Ralph and buried her head in his shoulder. Her heart was breaking and she cried like she had never cried before.

It was at exactly fourteen minutes after midnight, the same time that Elizabeth and Ben's counterparts walked back through the mirror into their own time, that Jodie woke with a start. She threw off the bedcovers and ran to Elizabeth's room screaming out her name and then into Ben's doing the same. Their beds were unruly but empty, just like her heart. She dropped to her knees stricken, shaking her head in disbelief. Strong arms lifted her to her feet and Ralph turned her towards him. She looked like something had died within her.

"My babies have gone Ralph. They've taken my babies."

Ralph had anticipated how devastated Jodie would be and had prepared a sedative to help her through the rest of the night. It was after midday when she began to waken. He at least could understand the principal of what had happened and why and what their children must have endured to do it. For Jodie though, it was different. To her, she had simply lost her children. Or at least the ones that she knew. The possibility that they still existed somewhere else and were the same people, just didn't equate. She was bereft and it all felt hopeless.

Jodie took a shower to refresh and clear her head. As the hot water ran over her flat belly she was suddenly reminded of showering in her pregnancies. Her hands automatically fell to her stomach and the poignancy of it was excruciating for her.

"I've lost you. How can you ever forgive me for that?"

Jodie slid down the wall until she was sat in the shower tray with the water cascading heavily on her head, washing the streaming tears from her face. She sat there in a trancelike state for nearly half an hour. The hot water had long since run out and she was oblivious to the cold water that was dangerously numbing her brain and body. Ralph found her there, shaking from the cold and shock of her loss. He lifted her out and wrapped her in towels, then placed her gently on the king-size bed. He spoke to her softly, reassuring her, but she was in some place that he couldn't reach. Jodie was perilously close to slipping into madness.

"I'm not too old to still have babies am I?" she was in delirium looking at Ralph but not really seeing him.

It broke his heart to watch her suffering and was in his own personal dilemma. Ralph had vowed when they first met, that he would never take advantage of her mind with his special abilities. He wanted her to be a free spirit. But now, with her at the very edge of her sanity, he had to do something before she lost her mind. Ralph cupped her face with his hands and drew her to him until their foreheads touched and let her thoughts join his. It was all darkness and despair. She was going through living Hell, struggling with her guilt and helplessness. In her mind, she had failed to protect her children, but that wasn't how it really was. Ralph needed to show her how things really were and make her understand.

He had almost left it too late to find any part of her mind that was still coherent. At last he did, and it was a foothold to begin her climb out of despair. At first he used joint happy memories to bring her back into a calm and receptive state, before demonstrating to her the pivotal decisions that they had made in their lives. How each changed the outcome of things. He was establishing the theory of infinite possibilities to her and how they were only living in one of them.

When Ralph felt that she was lucid and ready to talk he withdrew from her mind and began conventional dialogue.

"In answer to your question about being *too old to still have babies*, well no you are not."

Jodie smiled contently for the first time and Ralph continued.

"But why would you want a baby when the two children that you already have will soon be giving you grandchildren?"

Jodie didn't reply for a couple of minutes.

"You really do believe that they are still alive don't you Ralph?"

"I couldn't be more certain and they are waiting for you at my brother's house right now. They just took a different path than us to get there, that's all."

Ralph let her consider that for a while.

"The path that we took, over four years ago killed us and left them orphans. They have risked their lives to change things and give us the lives that we have now. God knows what they must have endured to do that. Well, it's just simply impossible to imagine. They must have needed us so badly that they fought for us. Are you going to fight for them now?"

Ralph could see the clouds of uncertainty clearing from her eyes. Jodie's pupils suddenly contracted in alarm and her voice was panicked.

"What time is it? When have we got to be there?" Jodie was suddenly alert.

"Eh, just after two thirty and we meet them at three thirty…"

"Jesus Christ Ralph! Why didn't you sort me out earlier? I can't let them see me like this."

Jodie jumped off the bed and ran into the bathroom. Seconds later Ralph could hear the annoying noise of the hairdryer. He knew that she was going to be just fine now.

"It was always his fault when something wasn't going too well," he mused.

Forty minutes later, they got into the Porsche. Jodie looked radiant in her slinky red dress, looking like she was still in her late twenties. Ralph nodded at her appreciatively and gave her a cheeky smile.

"You will look like sisters," he assured her.

She knew that he meant it and blushed just slightly.

Ralph had less than twenty minutes to get to his brother's house, so he took the route that enabled him to get the best out of the Porsche and headed out towards the canal. On the way up to the top of the hill that led down to the sweeping bend, Jodie began to have some personal doubts.

"What if they don't like me? Maybe they've spent enough time away that they don't need me anymore. Besides they probably regard George and Jillie as their parents now..."

"Jodie, it will be just fine. They will adore you, just like they always have and always will. Can you not imagine how desperately they must have missed us these last four years?"

Ralph went over the brow of the hill then gunned the engine, maxing out through his favourite bends leading down to the sweeping right-hander by the canal. He was enjoying the delicious thrill of it and had just committed the car fully into the bend, when Jodie yelled out in panic. Startled by Jodie's outburst, Ralph took the power off which was exactly the wrong thing to do and he fought desperately to keep control of the car. The wheels were in the verge kicking up debris. Jodie screamed out in terror, holding her head in her hands, anticipating the impact. It was more by luck than judgement, that Ralph managed to keep the Porsche on the road and they exited the bend with their hearts in their mouths.

"Jesus that was close! What was all that about? You nearly got us killed!" Ralph chastised.

He didn't mean to be so harsh, but it had scared the life out of him.

"I'm sorry, I don't know. I just had the most dreadful feeling of malevolence, a premonition or something."

They drove in silence for a few minutes while they both came to terms with their narrow escape. Jodie turned earnestly to Ralph.

"Something evil happened there Ralph. Evil and deeply sinister, I can sense it. I've had a bad feeling ever since they found Beauty's broken body in the trees there. I can't explain it Ralph but I never want any of us to go near there again... ever!"

They pulled up in George's drive and Ralph squeezed Jodie's hand to encourage her. She looked a beautiful bag of nerves.

"Are you ready?" Ralph prompted and Jodie nodded back unconvincingly.

"Remember they may look very different but they are the same people, your babies."

Ralph's words and boyish smile bolstered her up. Jodie was as ready as she would ever be, when Jeeves greeted them in the hallway.

"You must be the proud parents. Everyone is waiting for you."

It was the first tangible confirmation that her children still existed, and was the immediate fillip that Jodie needed to reenergise her.

"Take us through now please Jeeves and hurry would you?" she turned to Ralph, running her fingers across his chin. "I can't wait!"

Ralph smiled with relief at the positive change that had come over her. Jeeves led them to the Marquee. As they entered, Jodie's eyes searched the crowd for her children.

The butler's voice suddenly boomed out above the animated chatter.

"Ladies and gentlemen may I have your attention please. I present to you Ralph and Jodie Robinson."

All faces turned towards them. With a mother's instinct, Jodie picked them out immediately, even though they had changed immeasurably.

"There they are Ralph!" she pointed to them and opened her arms in welcoming fashion.

Elizabeth was clearly unbalanced holding on to Ben for support and Jodie immediately saw her distress.

"Something's wrong with Lizzie!" the tremor in her voice showed the depth of her concern.

Jodie was about to run to her, when Ralph restrained her.

"She's just nervous, that's all. Let her find her balance," Ralph had read it perfectly.

Seconds later, Elizabeth had regained her composure.

"Mum!" she screamed.

She let go of Ben's hand and ran straight into her mother's open arms. Ralph joined in enfolding both of them in his embrace. Tears of joy and relief streamed from the girl's faces. Even Ralph had to force himself to show some metal.

Ben had the good grace to stand back and let Elizabeth enjoy her special moment but was secretly aching for his turn. Ralph broke free and crossed over to Ben. He was looking awkward and self-conscious and grinning nervously.

Ralph stopped when they were only a couple of feet apart and looked Ben up and down nodding appreciatively. His son had changed almost beyond recognition. He was much taller, more muscular and stood before him as a man. It was only his boyish smile that gave him away.

"Been working out have you son?" Ralph smiled fondly.

"Not really Dad, just had a few tough days lately is all. I was glad that you showed me a few things with the bow and sword though. That seemed to have made the difference in the end." Ben grinned at his father impishly. "Anyway old man, you used to look this good before you got poorly."

Ben was using one of his father's well used lines against him and it brought a nostalgic smile to his father's face.

"Perhaps we could spend some father and son time in the gym together Ben? Of course you would need to go easy on me though, being an *old man* and all that."

"Sure thing Dad, would love to," Ben respectfully held his hand out in greeting.

"You must be joking son!" Ralph exclaimed and surprised Ben with a bear hug and a kiss. "God I'm so happy to see you Ben and I couldn't be more proud of how you've turned out and what you've done. When this party's over I want to hear it all. I'm sure it would make a fantastic book!"

"'Fantastic' doesn't even come close to it Dad. And another thing, don't ever even think about pissing Lizzie off. She goes way past dangerous!"

"Takes after her mother then eh?" Ralph mused.

Jodie picked up their conspiratorial looks, as only a woman can. She walked over to them arm in arm with Elizabeth. Jodie dismissed Ralph with a mocking cast of her eyes.

"He's always much braver when you're around Ben."

Ben couldn't wait any longer and threw his arms around his mother and the flood gates opened.

"When we lost you it was the end of my world Mum. I've missed you so, so much. I only survived it because Lizzie and Aunt and Uncle kept me together. Especially Lizzie. I don't know how she coped with me, how any of them did."

Ben had to stop talking to steady his voice and prevent himself from crying publically. Jodie sensed it and held him closer. She shushed him and he felt the calmness of her, like he always had in the past. Ben was soon able to continue.

"All the way through this impossible ordeal, I've been afraid of one thing. That is that you wouldn't want us or that we would be strangers to you."

Jodie pushed him gently away so that he could look into her face and know that what she was about to say was true.

"Oh Ben; I had those fears too, which makes me just as stupid. We are the family that might never have been but for your and Elizabeth's love and courage," she searched Ben's eyes for his recognition of her love. "You and Lizzie made this day happen and although I don't really understand that, your father does. I'm only just beginning to realise how lucky we are, but you'll have to go slowly with me and help me understand."

Jodie broke the solemnity and took Elizabeth and Ben's arms. She smiled proudly up at them.

"I seem to have missed out on your growing up! You must have lots to tell me, but I suppose we ought to share you with the others for a while," Jodie looked around, suddenly aware of all the astonished guests. "Besides, I think that's enough entertainment for the crowd for now, don't you?"

It was a most bizarre spectacle for all those present and it had caused great consternation amongst them. It appeared to be a family reunion but nothing added up. Nobody had left to return and Elizabeth and Ben were clearly not who they purported to be.

"It's a Theme Party, a game," one woman had suggested. "It'll become clearer later, when their real children turn up. But well-acted though don't you think?"

The conjecture was rife at first. After a while though, any reference to their strange looks and behaviour receded until they were all oblivious to it. Elizabeth and Ben's smoothing was going just fine.

Lovely Laura was in animated conversation with George. She wore a simple clinging burgundy dress, with low laced back and a flattering neckline. The dress emphasised the curves of her youthful body and she looked great. Her luscious chestnut hair hung naturally around her shoulders and she had strategically chosen burgundy lipstick of the exact shade of her dress. Elizabeth saw her and hurried excitedly over to her. Uncle George graciously made his excuses to leave, to let them catch up.

"Laura I've missed you! I can't tell you just how much."

Elizabeth threw her arms around Laura and held her tightly, like a long-lost friend.

"That's weird Lizzie. It's only been a day for God's sake!"

Elizabeth let her go awkwardly.

"I think it's time you got yourself a boyfriend Lizzie," Laura had that mischievous grin on her face, "and I've got a good feeling about this party!"

Elizabeth's eyes fell on Laura's simple pearl necklace and it triggered the memory of Katya's venomous attack.

"Laura your neck! Elizabeth exclaimed, and then felt foolish. "Well it's perfect, I mean."

There was no sign of the ugly scaring, but of course it never happened in this life. Laura's hand went automatically to her neck and she looked surprised. "It really is time we got you a boyfriend Lizzie."

"I already have one Laura. Well at least I think I do," Lizzie was still recovering from being just a little bit embarrassed. "Have you met Matt yet?"

"Matt who?"

"Matthew St John," Elizabeth could tell by the look on her face that she had not.

"Lizzie, you're acting very strange and something's different about you. Is there anything the matter?"

Laura hadn't yet completely succumbed to the smoothing process and she was struggling to work out what was wrong. Elizabeth diverted her.

"Look, there's someone I want you to meet and you will just love him I promise. You can trust me on this one!"

Elizabeth gave her a brief hug and left the marquee. Laura turned back to George with a puzzled look on her face.

"What's wrong with Lizzie?"

Elizabeth stood in the grand hallway by the open front door. She turned the pages of the telephone directory until she found St John. She knew roughly where he lived, as she recalled Laura saying, *Mother of course does not approve. He's from the wrong side of town apparently.* That could only mean Stanhope. There were only two listing under *St John*. Elizabeth dialled the first number.

"Hello, can I speak to Matt please?"

"Sorry you must have the wrong number," the woman hung up abruptly.

At Elizabeth's second attempt it was a man who answered the phone.

"Hello."

"Do I have the right number for Matthew St John?" Elizabeth had subconsciously crossed her fingers.

"Yes, just a minute please. Matt! It's for you."

Moments later Matthew St John picked up the phone.

"Yes Matt here, who is it?"

"Elizabeth Robinson but you don't know me. Look, I know this is quite random but would you like to come to a party?" Elizabeth still had her fingers crossed.

"When and why me?" Matt's voice was guarded.

He was expecting someone to try and sell him something, and was ready to put the phone down. Elizabeth sensed it.

"Don't hang up Matt. It's today and now, and it's because we need men."

Elizabeth put her hand over the mouthpiece and cringed.

"That must have sounded dreadful," she thought.

"I mean it's a posh do, and the tables are socially unbalanced. I was told that you were the right kind of person to invite."

Elizabeth was jigging up and down in nervous anticipation.

"No sorry, I've got things planned for today; perhaps another time?"

"I was hoping that you would do it the easy way Matt. Let me put it to you again."

Elizabeth's voice was no longer conciliatory and she was about to take an unfair advantage of him.

"You are coming to this party now and it's at 53 Queensway on the east side of town. You can't miss the marquee in the garden. Do you have a tuxedo?"

"No but I can hire one."

"Get it," Elizabeth cut him off. "Job done!" she thought, and smiled at the possibility that she had created.

Elizabeth turned and walked down the hallway, looking appreciatively at her own image as she approached the old ornate mirror. She was staggered at how much she had changed over the last few months. The last time that she had studied herself closely in it, was when she was little more than a girl. That was before her encounter, when it had all begun. Something caught her eye. It was the refection of a big dog sat in the garden.

Elizabeth turned and walked back curiously towards the open front door. There was a big Husky sitting on the lawn, next to something and he was looking at her expectantly. She quickened her pace as she realised that the *something* was a man lying face down, dressed in military uniform. He appeared to be unconscious. Elizabeth knelt beside him and the dog nuzzled her. Strangely it had one blue and one yellow eye. It reminded her of a dog that she had once known.

"Tini?" she said in wonder.

The dog looked trustingly back at her with his quizzical expression. She checked for a pulse in the soldier's neck and was relieved when she felt a strong and steady throbbing. Elizabeth lifted and turned his face gently out of the grass and gasped when she saw it.

"Mike!"

She dropped his head heavily on the ground at the shock of it. She couldn't have possibly known that he was lying in the precise place that he and Red Jake had fallen, as their flaming bodies were cut down by Alexis and Grese. Mike's eyes flickered then opened myopically at the rude impact. He looked confused and disorientated as Elizabeth checked him over for any injuries.

"What are you doing, who are you?"

Mike sat up startled, but Elizabeth pressed him down again.

"Easy soldier, stay down until we know what's happened to you."

"It's nothing I must have feinted that's all. Just as I got here the strangest feeling came over me and the world seemed to turn upside-down. I'm normally tougher than that..." he added lamely, raising a brow and flashing his crooked smile.

"I do hope so," Elizabeth mocked, noticing the sergeant's stripe on his arm for the first time, "When did you get promoted?"

"Just. How did you know that I had been?"

"Newly sewn on," she lied and changed the subject as she began fussing the dog. "Why did you bring Tini?"

"I just got back from overseas and I had nobody to leave him with. Normally he would stay with Dad or my brother but they are both here, I think."

Elizabeth knew instinctively that the overseas job would have been some dangerous mission and she shuddered at the thought of how easily she could still lose him.

"Yes Emanuel and David are already here and they will be happy that you made it," Elizabeth was trying to be off-hand.

"How did you know that my dog was called Tini?" Mike looked at her suspiciously.

"It's on his collar," Elizabeth said in a matter of fact way.

"No it's not."

"Then it should be! That's perfectly irresponsible of you," Elizabeth employed attack as her best means of defence, then she added as an afterthought. "You must have called his name when you were coming to."

"Yes perhaps."

Mike let it go for now. But even if that was true, it didn't explain how she knew who his father and brother were.

"I'll take Tini and tie him up by the marquee and give him a drink while you go to the bathroom and tidy yourself up. See you later then soldier boy," Elizabeth turned her back on him and went about her duties in a business like way. "Come on Tini, good boy."

Tini went to her side obediently and walked to heel looking up at her with his tongue hanging out, panting faithfully.

"And that's not right either," Mike thought. "Tini *never* goes to a stranger and certainly not that eagerly. It was as if he already knew her."

When Elizabeth returned to the party, she was elated at having found Mike, and relieved that he had endured. She only felt slightly guilty about the game that she was playing with his mind.

"Anyway there would be plenty of time to explain later, and what harm could it possibly do?" she thought.

Elizabeth sought out her mother and quickly became animatedly engaged in conversation and her childish misdemeanour was quickly forgotten. She was part telling their story, restricted information weighs heavily on a woman's mind, and there was a consensus between them not to wait. They were cut off in mid-flow when Jeeves voice boomed out above the Muzak and chatter.

"Ladies and gentlemen may I have your attention please. I present to you Sergeant Michael Alexander Goldberg-Jackson".

Elizabeth had a compelling urge to go over to him, but Emanuel had already usurped the initiative followed by his elated brother David Williams.

"Or would that be Goldberg-Williams?" she wondered idly.

Mike was in his full-dress military uniform, with a red tunic adorned with gold braid and service medals. His breeches bore the regimental red stripe and he wore his ceremonial sword. The effect that a young man in dress uniform has on women should never be underestimated. It immediately attracted the girls to him like flies around a honeypot, forcing Emanuel and David to beat a hasty retreat.

Jodie immediately saw the change that had come over Elizabeth and smiled knowingly.

"He's the one isn't he?"

"Is it that obvious?" Elizabeth looked concerned at her own transparency.

"Yes, and then some," Jodie confirmed looking at Mike approvingly over the rim of her champagne glass. "Oh my, he is rather dashing though isn't he?"

"Yes but he hasn't got a clue about it either. That's what makes it such fun," Elizabeth returned a conspiratorial smile.

The girls were starting to paw over him, touching his medals and asking what they were for, without really listening to the answer. One rather stunning brunet took hold of the hilt of his sword and thrust her chin out towards his face laughing provocatively. Elizabeth heard her clearly.

"Have you ever used this in anger?" this time the innuendo wasn't missed, even by Mike.

Jodie watched Elizabeth's face becoming slowly enraged. She couldn't have known that for Elizabeth it was a feeling of *déjà vu* but she did know that Elizabeth needed to deal with it and encouraged her to do so.

"I wouldn't have given any girl this much opportunity when I first saw your father Lizzie. In fact I didn't. Strangely enough he didn't have a clue either."

Jodie recalled the event fondly and raised her glass at Ralph who had coincidentally just looked up and was smiling broadly back at them. He was oblivious to their exchange.

"And he still doesn't Lizzie," she smiled sweetly back at him over the rim of her champagne glass.

"Excuse me for a minute please Mum."

Elizabeth strode purposefully over to the girls competing for Mike's attention. She was perfectly aware that the last time she did this, she hadn't handled it too well and was conscious not to mess it up this time.

"Sorry girls you're outranked, my party," she turned to Mike. "You were about to ask me for a dance."

"Was I?" Mike looked confused.

Elizabeth's chin hardened. She looked like one not to mess with.

"I mean I was," Mike added and smiled lamely.

"Well, aren't you going to ask me then?" Elizabeth gave the illusion of impatience.

"Um, would you like to dance?" Mike gestured towards the dance floor.

"No not just yet, but you can get me a drink though," she took Mike's outstretched arm and led a very confused soldier to the bar.

The champagne flowed freely and they were all sharing their attentions gregariously. Even Elizabeth occasionally risked leaving Mike to the charms of the predatory women. She was secure in her considered opinion that the others weren't even in her league. That was largely underpinned by having a little peek into his mind, something that she had learnt from May and was feeling a little guilty about. Elizabeth had decided not to tell Mike their story until they had got to know each other better, or he might just think that she was a crackpot. Besides, she was having far too much fun playing with his head.

Laura was enjoying yet another glass of champagne and Ben's attention, coming on to him just a little too obviously. Elizabeth could see that her brother needed rescuing and made her excuses to Mike once again.

"Mike, would you fix me another drink please while I just have a quick chat with Laura?" Elizabeth pecked him on the cheek leaving him just a little astonished.

"Ben, will you excuse us?" Elizabeth took Laura's arm and steered her away from her relieved brother.

"What did you do that for?" Laura was miffed, "I was doing really well and he's turned into such a hunk don't you know?"

"Trust me, you weren't Laura. He prefers older women."

"But I am older!" Laura protested.

"But I'm talking positively ancient here," Elizabeth added.

Well it was partly true if not somewhat unfair, she justified.

"Oh dear, poor boy," Laura conceded with a disdainful look on her face.

"Anyway, I've fixed you a date. His name is Matt St John and he can't wait to see you."

"Really, how interesting...," her mischievous smile lit up her face.

"Yes, well; the moment that Jeeves announces his arrival, you go straight to him before the others get a look in OK? You will be several glasses of champagne ahead of him so use them wisely!"

They parted with a hug. Elizabeth smiled as she saw Laura go straight towards the entrance of the marquee, to take up her strategic position. She didn't have to wait long. Almost immediately, Jeeves entered with a rather soave young man at his side.

"Ladies and gentlemen may I have your attention please. I present to you Matthew St John".

The poor young man didn't stand a chance. Laura had got him by the arm and was already steering him towards the bar chatting animatedly to him. As she passed Elizabeth Laura turned her head and gave her an appreciative wink and silent scream.

They had spent so much time socialising, that it was nearly six o'clock before Elizabeth and Ben got a chance to talk to each other. By then, there was no question that any of the guests were suspicious of them.

The party was in full swing and about to change phase into dinner and live music. May and Crystalita hadn't shown up and Ben's disappointment was profound.

"What could have happened to them?" he asked. "They've waited more than four and a half years for this day?"

Elizabeth was also a little anxious, but wasn't actually surprised.

"I expect that they have planned to get here late Ben. They would have the good grace to let us enjoy our reunion with Mum and Dad first."

Elizabeth was only half convinced of what she said but the more she thought about it the more likely it seemed.

"Perhaps we should prepare Mum and Dad before they arrive, only it's going to seem a bit bizarre when they do come and you are all over May like a rash," Elizabeth teased.

Elizabeth enjoyed his awkwardness and glanced around to find their parents. When her eyes found them, she could see that they had been watching them. Jodie had linked arms with Ralph and their faces showed their pride and contentment as they walked across to join them.

When they gave a potted history of how they had met May and Crystalita and that they were Matriarchs of another race, well it was beyond Jodie's comprehension. It was also more than Ralph could have expected, even with his inside knowledge.

Jodie latched on to the love story bit though, and was excited about meeting Ben's first girlfriend.

"Will I approve?" Jodie asked, already intrigued by the brief story.

Elizabeth answered for Ben.

"Stunning, gentle and intelligent; you will love her!"

Jeeves was stood in the hallway looking out of the front door, waiting for the last two guests to arrive. He looked at his watch, concerned that he would have to leave his *meet and greet* duties to supervise dinner before the last guests had arrived. Jeeves was old school, and considered not welcoming the guests as dereliction of duty. He reluctantly turned around to return to the marquee and almost walked straight into them.

"Goodness me!" he was startled when he came face to face with May and Crystalita. "I'm sorry ladies but I didn't see you arrive. Have you come in through the back way?"

"Yes Jeeves, parking you know?" May smiled at him fondly.

"Quite so ma'am," although Jeeves couldn't quite see the relevance of it, but of course one never questions a lady. "You appear to know my name ma'am?"

"Mutual friends Jeeves, Elizabeth and Ben Robinson and of course we have met before."

"Indeed," Jeeves nodded.

He led them through to the marquee. He was still perplexed as to how he had failed to recognise Elizabeth, when she so clearly knew him and now another rare beauty escapes his memory.

"I must be getting old," he conceded.

Jeeves led them to the marquee and announced them.

"Ladies and gentlemen may I have your attention please. I present to you Miss Maelströminha and Miss Crystalita".

All heads turned and remained turned. Two such beauties arriving together had got all talking, male and female. Both had chosen their dresses to suit the evening and late party. May had chosen a black, ankle length dress cut off the shoulder with low back but fairly modest bust line, conscious that she would be meeting Ben's parents for the first time. The material was clinging and so sheer that she wore a shawl of the finest black silk to give the illusion of conservatism. This of course could be abandoned as the night progressed. Her outfit was finished off with black open-toed high heel shoes and matching bag by Christian Louboutin.

That was just the packaging. Her slender body, sleek black hair swept over her shoulder and the face of an angel, had her audience completely transfixed.

Crystalita had spent over four years planning for this night and wasn't going to let modesty get in her way! Her daring and slinky low-cut pastel pink catsuit, zipped to the crotch with high heels and clasp bag of haute couture, was a real head-turner. She had pulled her long blonde hair up into a high ponytail with a ribbon that matched the colour of her catsuit. Her big blue eyes were cleverly made up to enhance the feline look, and she used them liberally to their best effect. She stood there epitomising the image of youth and vitality.

Elizabeth glanced over to David Williams. His dark handsome face had lit up into an appreciative smile that showed off his dimples and even teeth. His eyes followed Crystalita as she walked confidently over to Elizabeth and Ben. She accentuated the sway her hips tantalisingly and Elizabeth wondered where that confidence had come from, then she read Crystalita's face. It was window dressing. Inside she was shaking like a leaf!

It took all of May's discipline not to run straight over to Ben. She could sense that he was feeling that same urge too and flashed him a smile and it said, "Wait," Ben took several deep breaths to help him control his emotions and nodded his understanding.

Jodie watched with Ralph as the late guests met with Elizabeth and Ben in the middle of the marquee. The re-union was emotional but controlled. Even so, they could see how deeply in love their son was with the dark-haired girl and that it was reciprocated.

"They are both stunning Ralph," Jodie's face was a picture as she admired them. "Obviously the girl with the black hair is May but she looks four or five years older than Ben though. Wouldn't you agree?"

"Try four or five thousand years, that would be closer to the truth," Ralph corrected.

He was amused by the look of consternation on Jodie's face.

"Don't be ridiculous Ralph, and anyway what man doesn't like a little experience?" Jodie admonished but with a twinkle in her eye.

Ralph thought that this probably wasn't the right time or place to explain.

May and Crystalita sat at the head table with Elizabeth and Ben, Ralph, Jodie, George and Jillie. Auntie Gina arrived just in time for dinner and joined them. Once again her hospital duties had delayed her, but it turned out that she had also stopped by at the stables to tend their new arrival.

"Elizabeth, Ben! Just look at you, what a difference a day makes," Gina's face was the very picture of surprise. "Sorry I'm late but I just had to stop by the stables and see little 'Blackie' on the way."

"Blackie?" Elizabeth returned a surprised expression. "Who is Blackie?"

"You are joking? Our new foal silly," Gina looked strangely at Elizabeth. "You can't have forgotten already, that's not..."

A little smoothing was in order and Elizabeth helped her out.

"Tell me more about Blackie, Auntie."

That was all it needed. Gina told the story in her own meticulous way, not missing any detail until she finally summed it up with obvious pride.

"Blackie has exactly the same temperament as Beauty did. She will make the family complete again, filling that gap since we lost Beauty down by the canal in such a terrible way. That would be over four years ago now."

Elizabeth welled up with the pain and guilt of what she had done to Beauty and it took several minutes for her to calm down and come to terms with it. In fact it was only when May, seeing her distress, reached across and took her hand that the anguish abated.

For an uninterrupted hour, they were all able to get to know each other and get an overview of what had happened in their alternative lives. It was a heady cocktail. By the end of it, the only thing that both Jodie and Jillie were sure of was how much they liked these two exotic and slightly strange maidens. Between stories, Elizabeth and Crystalita were conspiratorial. Emanuel was on another table with his two sons. The girls were taking it in turns to see if they were getting any admiring looks from the boys. Neither was disappointed.

"What do you think of David then?" Elizabeth whispered to Crystalita lasciviously.

"Gorgeous! Is he looking?" Crystalita's concern was showed in her face and voice.

"Only just about all of the time," Elizabeth confirmed.

"Oh God what do I do?"

"Catch him out and smile back at him. I'll tell you when he's looking... OK now."

Crystalita turned her head and tilted it towards David returning his gaze, smiling at him and confirming her interest. David's smile by comparison was self-conscious and he turned away to continue talking to his father, thankful for the diversion.

"How did that go?" Crystalita said looking doubtful. "He probably thinks I'm simple."

"Just fine," Elizabeth said reassuringly. "He took the bait. Now all we have to do is wind him in."

"We do?"

Crystalita hadn't imagined that it could be quite so easy, although she hadn't got a clue about just how you *wind them in.*

Elizabeth got to her feet.

"Go to the bar and I'll meet you there with the boys in a couple of minutes."

Crystalita's nerves were apparent. She had waited a long time for this moment and her legs had gone weak.

"What will I say?"

"Just relax he'll be feeling just the same way too. We'll just muddle through."

Elizabeth left her with a reassuring smile, but *muddling through* didn't seem much of an exact science to Crystalita.

"Sorry Emanuel, can I take these two good-looking young men to frame me at the bar? It does wonders for a girl's ego you know and there's a lot of competition here today."

"Please be my guest Lizzie," Emanuel spread his arms expansively in submission.

He had already seen Crystalita go to the bar and you didn't have to have the insight of an Angel to see what they were up to. Emanuel's knowing smile said it all and Elizabeth just grinned back mischievously as she swept the boys towards the bar.

Crystalita was busying herself with a glass of champagne when they arrived, trying to look as nonchalant and composed as she could. She was completely unaware of just how stunning she looked in the catsuit and that it wasn't only David who was looking at her.

"Ah Crystalita, there you are!" Elizabeth said with mock surprise. "Have you met David and Mike, Emanuel's sons?"

"No I haven't, but I do know your father. He's a fine man," Crystalita's smile was friendly and inviting.

She wasn't sure whether to offer her cheek for a kiss or her hand to shake. Her fear of rejection favoured the latter. She thrust her arm out awkwardly and immediately regretted the decision. Fortunately David Williams was a perceptive man and took her hand bowing gallantly with his disarming smile then kissed it.

"*Enchanté.*"

David held her hand for just long enough to show his interest but not so long as to be uncomfortable.

"Of course we know of you and your sister. Dad has enthused a great deal over the years and now I can see why."

"Well played!" Elizabeth thought to herself as Crystalita blushed demurely.

"Excuse me," Mike leant between them and kissed Crystalita on the cheek, "I'm Mike, a little rougher around the edges than my brother *Don Juan* here but hey-ho..."

Elizabeth took Mike's arm in the typically territorial way that women do, and they naturally paired off in conversation. Crystalita was far too beautiful for Elizabeth to take any chances.

"The alcohol will do the rest," Elizabeth thought.

She picked up a glass of champagne and silently toasted Crystalita, who returned the gesture with a wink of her eye.

"Second job done!" Elizabeth sighed with satisfaction.

After coffees, Jeeves ordered the tables to be cleared and the band changed tempo to encourage the guests to the dance floor. David was quick to invite Crystalita to dance but Mike needed considerably more encouragement. He finally got the message after the fifth number.

Laura leveraged the opportunity of Elizabeth and Mike taking to the floor to encourage Matt into doing the same.

"Come on Matt, let's join Lizzie and Mike," Laura wasn't the kind to wait all night to be asked.

Elizabeth had tired of her cat and mouse game with her unenlightened soldier. She needed to bring him up to speed, back to how they were before the Shadows had invaded their home. Simply, she needed his love. From Mike's point of view he needed to know what game Elizabeth was playing with him. She had lied about how she knew his dog's name and how she knew who his father and brother were. She was flirting outrageously with him, and that didn't make sense either.

"This girl was up to something", he had decided.

Elizabeth had deliberately chosen a slow number to tell Mike the whole truth while he had her in a close hold. It was the perfect moment and she was enjoying it more than just a little. Elizabeth was just about to tell him, when he beat her to it. She was cross with herself for letting it happen that way. To make it worse, he was accusing in manner, having the moral high ground over her.

"So when are you going to tell me the truth Elizabeth?" Mike was firm but fair.

Elizabeth foolishly went on the defensive.

"The truth? But I haven't..."

Mike was having none of it.

"The truth Elizabeth!"

"It's Lizzie actually. You have always called me Lizzie," her tone was off.

Elizabeth pushed Mike away. It was only inches but it marked a change in her body language. He stopped dancing immediately, took Elizabeth's hand and led her over to an empty table. She felt like a naughty schoolgirl.

"I have never called you anything. I want the truth Elizabeth, all of it and I want it now."

The look on Mike's face was that of a man losing his patience. Elizabeth regretted letting her game go this far and uncharacteristically apologised.

"I'm sorry Mike. I've been really quite childish. Can we start again?"

Mike gave her that sideways glance and raised his eyebrow. The memory of it melted Elizabeth's heart. Tears instantly welled in her eyes. Mike was immediately concerned that he had been too hard on her and was about to apologise. Elizabeth had read his thoughts and put her finger to his lips stopping him.

"No Mike let me talk. I have a story to tell you that you couldn't possibly believe, but every word will be true, I swear."

Mike nodded and took her hands in his, sensing that this was going to be difficult for her.

"My tears are because I remember the first time that you used that smile on me. It was some months ago now, but I will remember that moment for the rest of my life. And I cried because when I left you here I thought that I would never see you again."

"But Lizzie, we have never met."

Mike could see that she was sincere but these were ramblings.

"Not in this life Mike but we did in another and I think you died here at a little after midnight on this day."

"I died?" it was getting crazier.

The girl in front of him was either a great actress or she believed the nonsense that she was saying.

"Yes, I think so. This house was under heavy attack by Shadows. You and six of your SAS boys had made it a fortress but there were too many of them. The Shadows had rocket launchers and helicopters, it was impossible. We had to leave you still fighting them with Uncle George and Aunt Jillie in the basement. The house was on fire and we left through your father's portal that was being stored in the loft."

"You know about Shadows and the mirrors?"

For the first time, Mike realised that there might be at least some truth in what she was saying.

"But why would my father's portal be in your loft?" he gave her that quizzical look again.

Elizabeth was suddenly lost for words, how could she tell him that his father had died too?

"It just was," she replied lamely but Mike wasn't going to let it go.

"No Lizzie, why was it in the loft here?"

Elizabeth took a deep breath.

"It was there for safekeeping because the Shadows had killed your father. They later killed our parents, your brother David and Crystalita. I'm sorry but you did ask," Elizabeth looked at him soulfully. "We left the house while you, your men, Auntie Jillie and Uncle George were fighting for your lives. I will never forgive myself for doing that."

"Why did you then?" Mike's tone was respectful.

He could tell that truth or not, Elizabeth certainly believed what she was saying.

"To change history and we did. Us being here tonight is an alternative outcome," all at once Elizabeth felt foolish. "You think I'm nuts don't you?"

It was a tricky question. Mike replied honestly.

"Well not completely."

He quickly followed the statement up with that *look* as a safety net. It worked as usual.

"I wouldn't blame you if you did and I wonder sometimes whether I will wake up to find that it was just a dream."

The association prompted Elizabeth's next question.

"When you feinted out there on the lawn you said, *the world seemed to turn upside-down*, can you be more specific? What exactly did you feel?"

Mike became pensive for a while, trying to piece it together.

"I felt intense heat and I couldn't breathe. Then intense pain, in my back I think. Oh and quite strangely I thought about Jake, a fellow comrade in arms, and I haven't thought about him in ages."

Elizabeth's jaw dropped and she covered her mouth at the shock of it.

What's the matter Lizzie, you look like you've seen a ghost.

"No, but I think you have Mike! On that night, last night in fact, this house was on fire. You couldn't have stayed much longer after we left, because of the smoke and flames. It was choking. There were only two ways out, the backdoor or the front and both were heavily guarded by Shadows. You and Red Jake had taken your positions to defend the hallway..."

The enormity of what must have happened took the air out of Elizabeth's lungs and she couldn't speak. She was consumed by the guilt of having left them to die and in such a terrifying way. Mike dragged her back from wherever it was that she had retreated to.

"And what?"

"You and Red Jake must have died right there on the lawn, where I found you lying with Tini."

Mike was suddenly aware that they were attracting an audience. He encouraged Elizabeth to her feet and hurried her out of the marquee towards the house. When they entered the hallway they met Jeeves. Elizabeth burst into tears again at the sight of him. Mike hurried her past the bewildered old butler, towards the cloakroom.

"What the hell was all that about?"

"He died to," Elizabeth choked at the memory.

Mike bustled her through the door, locked it and passed her a towel to dry her eyes. He filled the glass tumbler with water and Elizabeth drank thirstily. Mike was worried that he might not be able to contain the situation but, to his relief, Elizabeth recovered quickly. It had been almost like an exorcism for her. Her demons were out now in full view and she could cope again.

Elizabeth looked at herself in the mirror. She was immediately glad of the high quality Christian Dior makeup that had been chosen for her and was able to make a reasonable crash repair.

"Come with me to where I found you and I will tell you it all and then you will see for yourself."

Elizabeth took Mike's hand and led him out through the hallway. She stopped at the old mirror.

"It all began here four years after the Shadows murdered Mum and Dad. I was looking into this mirror remembering them. Somehow Mum reached out to me telling me that *I would know what to do.* Some days later, Ben had a similar experience. Come with me."

Elizabeth led him out to the front door passing a very concerned old butler.

"Is madam feeling a little better?"

"Yes thank you Jeeves. Reunions, you know how it is?"

"Yes of course ma'am."

"Will you see that the dog is fed and watered please?"

Jeeves was clearly relieved that Elizabeth had recovered.

"Well I must confess to having already spoiled him somewhat. I do hope you don't mind?"

"No not at all Jeeves, not at all and thank you."

They left the old man and walked out onto the lawn to where Mike had laid next to Tini. Elizabeth reached up and took his face in her cupped hands.

"Now I'm going to tell you it all in a way that Maelströminha taught us, but I need your permission first."

"Why would you want that?" Mike still wasn't quite sure where all this was going.

"Because, you will live all of my memories and they will become yours as if they happened to you and we will no longer be strangers. Could you take that chance?"

"Just as long as you don't turn me into a nutcase too," Mike jibed.

He was quite surprised at the force of the playful slap that he got on his cheek from her cupped hand, but managed to *man up* without making too much of a fuss about it.

Elizabeth tipped Mike's forehead down to touch hers and held his gaze.

"Be prepared for the ride of your life!"

"Really?" Mike quipped with that look of his.

The second slap that he got was significantly less playful than the first.

Mike's mind was quickly drawn into hers. The shock of it manifested itself physically at first, as his muscles went into contraction. That passed swiftly and a calmness came over him. It started with Elizabeth's despair as she stood in front of the old ornate mirror and moved on to her first meeting with May. He could hear the lute and every note that she sang, see every jewel on her body and the sky behind her that was lit up like the northern lights. He was astonished when her memories became of him starting with their first encounter, after Katya's venomous attack then again in the aftermath of Dada's attempted assassination. The vision of her soaked in Dada's blood sat on her bed, tending Ben's wounds, exceeded gruesome. When he heard of Tini being impaled full length by Dada's spear after ripping the Shadow's throat out, tears ran down his face. He was relieved that there was no image to go with it, as Elizabeth had never actually seen it.

He learned that Ben had duelled with Illya Dracul and it had nearly cost his life. Then nearly cost Elizabeth hers as he wasn't there to protect her against Withey, the Ripper. When those images flashed through his mind, he began to convulse at the horror of it. Elizabeth had to erase some of them, as it was too much even for a battle hardened soldier like Mike. The episode where Ben had taken on the Shadows in their own territory alone and was blinded after throwing himself and Eichmann onto a landmine, was bravery bordering on stupidity and beggared belief. All this was almost trivialised by the powers that they had learned and used at Mount Olympus, rendering the earth asunder and taking out helicopters and Hellfire missiles. This was the stuff that would have graced the pages of the finest science fiction story.

He saw the images of the siege on the Robinson's burning house with its blown out doors and windows, then the mutilated bodies of the brothers Chas and Joey on the landing. It was all heart breaking. He witnessed the way that Elizabeth and Ben had dealt with Yurovsky, by detonating the grenades in his own webbing. It showed just how ruthless that they had become.

Mike lived every moment of all this with her and it really was the *ride of his life* and it was relentless. Mike rode on the back of Beauty as if he was there with Elizabeth, feeling the dangerous exhilaration of it and the pain and guilt that she suffered for what she did to her beloved horse. The fight to the death that followed with Grese, deep underwater on the canal bed and then afterwards on the bank, that so nearly ended in disaster. Then he actually felt Ben calling out to her in desperation as he was losing his duel with Alexis. Mike could feel through her, every cut that Ben received from Alexis' sabre and he involuntarily grabbed his left forearm as Alexis seemed to be raking it to pieces with his stiletto.

He was there in Emanuel's office with them when they dealt with Adolphius, one of the most dangerous and despicable men in history. But possibly the most excruciating and heart breaking thing of all, was when Mike learned that Elizabeth, Ben and May had died, each selflessly sacrificing their life for the other. That Ben, despite his injuries and despair, had the foresight to call on Jorall for help in their hour of need, was inspirational and testament to their resourcefulness and determination.

This was just the action that Mike had lived through with Elizabeth. He was not prepared for what came next, the emotional impact of the journey. Mike had become party to the experiences that Elizabeth had with him. Including every thought, every kiss, caress and cross word. He felt her fears, his fears, their hopes and their dreams. He had now shared the last several months of her life, as if he was there with her. Now her memories were *their* memories.

When it was over, Mike was both speechless and in love. He quite naturally took Elizabeth in his arms and kissed her passionately. Elizabeth felt giddy and went weak at the knees so that Mike had to support her. It was all that she had waited desperately for and was lost in the moment.

What Mike said to her next brought her tumbling down to earth.

"Christ girl, you're heavy!"

He impressively ducked the playful slap that had just a little too much venom in it.

"Angels are heavy, you knob," Elizabeth said disdainfully.

She linked arms with him and walked him back towards the marquee.

"I'm sorry Lizzie."

"For calling me heavy?" she quizzed.

"No, for not being there when you needed me, when you were alone in the cinema and Withey attacked you."

"So you should be and don't you ever stand me up again."

"Again? That's hardly fair..."

Elizabeth cut him off in mid sentence.

"My rules and you better get used to it."

It was said with a smile but Mike knew that she meant it and thought to himself, "Feisty madam".

"You betcha!"

Elizabeth had read his thought. Mike realised in that moment, that this was going to be far from easy...

When they returned to the dance floor, they were no longer newly acquainted. Mike found the conversation much easier now and more natural. They were animatedly discussing their adventures and what was going to happen next, when Mike dropped the bombshell.

"So when are we having Edith and Brady?"

Elizabeth was literally gobsmacked and couldn't hide her embarrassment. She blushed outrageously. She had forgotten that when she had let Mike into her mind, he had seen her most intimate secrets too. Mike enjoyed the moment. All that Elizabeth could say through the hand that was now covering her mouth was "Oh my God, no..."

Mike took her back in hold and smiled knowingly at her.

"Just tell me when you're ready," he smirked.

Elizabeth just buried her head in his shoulder, wishing that the Earth would swallow her up.

Ralph had noticed the change that had come over Elizabeth and Mike since returning from their brief absence. He turned to Jodie to point it out. Jodie simply nodded back at him before he had even said a word. She had noticed it too.

"Angels don't waste much time do they?" she said with a knowing smile.

"No indeed not, and this one isn't going to either!"

Ralph stood up and crossed the dance floor to the band leader handing him a memory stick. There was a brief nodding of heads and Ralph returned to Jodie. The band went silent and the guests returned to their tables. Ralph offered Jodie his outstretched hand.

"Would you do me the honour of joining me for the next dance?"

Ralph's smile still showed the same love for her that it did when they had first met. Jodie took his hand with a modest curtsey and Ralph led her to the centre of the dance floor. All eyes were on them in anticipation, as most of them had seen this before. The near silence was broken by the opening chords to *La Cumparsita*, one of Tango's most famous songs.

The Argentine Tango is one of the most sensual and challenging dances. Jodie acted it well without even a hint of shyness. The excitement in the marquee was mounting as the story of the song unfolded. Every move, counter-move and look was passionate and honest, building the tension between them. Only Ralph and Jodie knew the lyrics behind the song:

'If you knew that still in my soul I cherish that love that I had for you...

Who knows, if you knew that I have never forgotten you.

Remembering your past you would remember me...'

Ralph was the perfect partner. He led her through each mood of the dance, expertly creating the passion and tension that makes this one of the most watchable dances of all time. When it was over, Jodie still flushed with the exertion and passion of the dance, threw her arms around Ralph's neck.

"I love it when you dance me like that Ralph, it's so honest," she held on to him desperately, oblivious to the admiring but intruding eyes of their audience.

Elizabeth walked over to them. There was something that she had longed for and she couldn't wait a second longer.

"Ahem," she interrupted theatrically. "Can I have an *excuse me* dance please Dad?"

Jodie bowed out gracefully. Elizabeth had a brief word with the band leader and then returned to her father. She looked into his deep blue eyes as he took her in hold.

"I have wished this moment to happen for more than four and a half years. You can't imagine just how much."

She laid her head into his shoulder and felt safe there as she always used to.

"Sometimes Daddy, dreams really do come true if you want something badly enough."

The track that she had chosen was, *Dance with my Father*, by Luther Vandross. When the song began she was lost in the lyrics. Tears ran down her face from the beginning to the end and she just held on tighter and tighter. Her mind went back to the day before he had died, when they were dancing together at home with her mother playing the piano. That was the happiest day of her life, until today:

'Back when I was a child, before life removed all the innocence
My father would lift me high and dance with my mother and me and then
Spin me around 'til I fell asleep
Then up the stairs he would carry me
And I knew for sure I was loved
If I could get another chance, another walk, another dance with him
I'd play a song that would never, ever end
How I'd love, love, love
To dance with my father again...'

Although Elizabeth never looked up throughout the dance, Ralph could feel the emotion deep within her. It was like a stormy sea crashing against the rocks. By the end of the song, the storm had abated and the calm that followed was the peace in her very soul. It was an exorcism and she knew that she could move on now.

"Daddy, just wait here a moment."

Elizabeth exchanged words with the band leader then hurried across to her mother and led her on to the dance floor to re-join her father.

"This is your song and it brings back fond memories for me."

It was *Lady in Red*, by Chris de Burgh. The moment that the song began Jodie exchanged a grateful smile with Elizabeth. As they danced Jodie posed the question to Ralph.

"Do you know why Lizzie has chosen this song for us Ralph?"

The slant of Ralph's head showed that he did not, or at least that he wasn't about to steal her thunder.

"When she was small we were all on a cruise docking at Santander. It was my birthday, the cabaret had just finished and we were watching the couples dancing. I was wearing a red dress that night and, little as she was, she asked the band to play this for us. I will remember it forever."

Elizabeth watched them with deep pride as they circled the dance floor. She felt that the family was whole again and how apt that her mother had chosen to wear a red dress tonight!

Their dances were a catalyst for the party and the dance floor was packed for the next hour. Ben took his mother's hand and led her to the floor.

"Wow, you and Dad can still really cut the mustard!"

It was sincerely meant even though it did come across somewhat patronisingly. Jodie countered his remark.

"What was it that George Bernard Shaw said about *youth being wasted on the young*? Your Dad and me could still give you and Lizzie a run for your money, you can be sure of that! But thanks anyway for the back handed compliment," Jodie's smile was only playfully admonishing.

Somehow, Jodie had come to terms with the changes that had come over her children. Whether that was by nature or by some Angel nurture, she would never know. Whatever, she couldn't remember ever being happier than she was at that moment.

"I like May very much Ben but there's something quite extraordinary about her that I can't quite put my finger on."

Jodie was searching for the right words but they eluded her. The closer she got, the further away they became. It was like chasing shadows.

"She's really special to you isn't she?" Jodie added thoughtfully.

"She is Mum and that *extraordinary* thing about her is just simply because she *is* extraordinary and that's the bit that makes her special to me."

Jodie understood.

"There was always something extraordinary about your father too Ben and I don't doubt that there's not some connection. Perhaps you'll explain it all to me one day," Jodie's smile suggested that it was a demand rather than a request.

"I don't know how much you already understand but when we lost you, she was the one who taught us the way back to you. This life that we are now living is as much to do with her as us."

"Intriguing, I look forward to her joining us for dinner soon so we can get to know each other."

Ben couldn't help laughing and Jodie looked puzzled.

"What's so funny about that?"

"I don't know Mum, but the idea of having Maelströminha, a girl from out of space, around for dinner just knocks me out."

Jodie joined in laughing at the very nonsense of it.

"Don't be ridiculous, a girl from out of space, really?"

Crystalita and David hadn't left the dance floor since their first dance. They talked animatedly between numbers and during the slower tracks. Crystalita's fears about not having anything to say seemed to have evaporated. Stopping her would have been harder. Elizabeth couldn't help but admire just how striking and contrasting the couple were. David was tall, dark and particularly handsome. Women of all ages were smitten by him. On the other hand, Crystalita was a petite but curvy blonde, literally with the face of an angel. She knew just how to use the catsuit to its best advantage too, which wasn't wasted on David. Indeed not by the other men in the marquee either. Elizabeth conceded that they would be a tough act to beat but she was going to give it a go anyway and looked around for Mike.

May was patiently waiting for Ben to devote his full attention to her. She could tell that he wanted that too, but he had to share his favour, which was understandable but not entirely acceptable. She decided that he needed a little encouragement and had just the idea. She exchanged a few brief words with Elizabeth and Crystalita on the dance floor then crossed over to the band leader who nodded at her request and began searching for the track. It was *I will survive*, by Gloria Gaynor and it had some tenuous links with their own journey.

The three girls took to the stage and to say that they made a stunning group was an understatement. All eyes were on them, both male and female. The piano introduction started with the well-known opening chords and ascending notes, then the girls came in with gusto:

"At first I was afraid I was petrified

Kept thinking I could never live without you by my side

But then I spent so many nights thinking how you did me wrong

And I grew strong and I learned how to get along

And so you're back from outer space..."

When that line came, the words were particularly appropriate and Elizabeth pointed at May and Crystalita accusingly. The chorus was even more evocative for them and they sang it with even more gusto:

"...Did you think I'd crumble; did you think I'd lay down and die?

Oh no not I, I will survive, oh as long as I know how to love

I know I'll stay alive; I've got all my life to live

I've got all my love to give and Ill survive

I will survive, hey hey."

After all they had been through, the words that proclaimed survival were particularly poignant to them all. They conjured up a sequence of grotesque pictures in Elizabeth's mind, like a slide show. The images only took seconds to run through, but they were devastating. It was small wonder that May had judged their chances of survival as slim at best but just as the song said, "*I will survive*," and they had!

When the song ended, everyone called for more but Elizabeth passed her microphone to May and ran to Ben. She threw her arms around him. It was the first time that she dared to admit it to herself, lest it all turned out to be a dream.

"We did it Ben. We did the impossible!"

Ben could sense Elizabeth's heady cocktail of emotions.

"Yes we really did Lizzie. Look around you. So many people here just wouldn't be if we had failed, including us!"

May tapped Elizabeth on the shoulder and she moved over to let May into their circle. They wrapped their arms around each other's shoulders and drew themselves in tightly until their faces were almost touching. May had something profound to say.

"I couldn't help but tune into your thoughts, they were so intense. And yes what you have achieved was more or less impossible. Even when I searched the portals for possible outcomes, none of them included both of you surviving," that guilty look came over her face again. "But then if I had let you do nothing you would have both died at the Shadow's hands anyway. Catch-22 if you like."

May looked admiringly over at Crystalita dancing with David Williams. The smile of sheer joy that was on her face prompted her bioluminescence to spark off under her skin like little explosions of light. To an onlooker it would just have seemed like she was wearing glitter that reflected the spotlights.

"You made that possible for me and I have never seen her more radiant and happy in millennia. I can never repay that gift."

Elizabeth angled their circle until May was directly facing Ralph and Jodie.

"Look May, you already have."

Elizabeth graciously withdrew from the circle and left Ben and May dancing closely to the slow number that followed. The champagne was starting to cloud her mind and her feet were killing her. She saw her father talking to Emanuel. Elizabeth suddenly needed some air and quality father-daughter time. She linked her arm with her father's.

"Sorry Emanuel. Can you walk with me a while Daddy? It's just that the champagne and the dancing..."

"Of course darling. Emanuel will you excuse us?"

As soon as they got outside Elizabeth kicked off her heels and sighed at the sheer pleasure of it. The grass felt cool and refreshing under her feet. Tini was tied to one of the guy ropes waiting patiently. They could see that Jeeves had indeed spoiled him by the various dishes and bones that surrounded him. Elizabeth untied him.

"Tini can walk with us," she decided and fussed him a little.

"We have so much to tell you Dad. Tini saved our lives twice in that other life. It almost cost him his own the first time and I think that it probably did on the second."

They walked around the house in silence at first just enjoying the closeness. Elizabeth began to open up.

"It defies understanding but we were here less than 24 hours ago, when this whole house was under siege and ablaze," Elizabeth shuddered at the thought.

"Go on," prompted Ralph.

"We were attacked by Adolphius and his cell, along with 40 or 50 Drones. Mike knew they were coming and he and his six SAS boys turned this garden into a minefield and the house into a fortress. They had come a few days earlier than expected. It was midnight last night in fact, before Mike's reinforcements had arrived."

The memory was still painful and Elizabeth had to collect herself before she could continue. It seemed impossible to her that this was really only last night, it felt a lifetime ago.

"Take your time Lizzie," Ralph could feel the regret in her.

"They came at us in waves. They blew out all the downstairs doors and windows with rockets then others came in from the air and went in through the upstairs windows. Uncle George and Aunt Jillie were in the basement that Mike had converted into a war room."

Elizabeth allowed herself a smile.

"Uncle George was amazing, you should've seen him kick Shadow arse! He controlled all the explosions from there and took out at least half of the Drones and gave the boys a fighting chance at least..."

Elizabeth stopped as she remembered the faces of the men who must have died there.

"Who were the SAS boys?" Ralph asked anticipating her thoughts.

"There was Red Jake, Mike's second in command. He was a big man so strong and dangerous but a contradiction really, I've heard him crying over late night movies."

"Yes I know him well. He's the first man you would choose to watch your back, as he has mine on many an occasion. And who else?"

"There was James. He was the bomb head. It was his mines that decimated the enemy. Then there was Zak and Rudy, two Marines that seemed to live to fight," Elizabeth grinned. "I think they had a bit of an eye for the girls too."

"I know them all and yes they do have an eye for the ladies, good lads all of them. Who were the other two?".

These were also men that had fought alongside him.

The image of the mutilated bodies of Chas and Joey at the top of the stairs was indelibly printed on her mind and it made the telling of the next bit difficult.

"They were the brothers Chas and Joey."

Ralph nodded his approval.

"Mike chose his men well."

"Mike wouldn't let us stay when they attacked. Somehow we had to get to Emanuel's portal that had been stored in the loft after he died."

Elizabeth saw the expression change on her father's face at the mention of Emanuel's death.

"But that's another story for later Dad. We left Uncle George and Aunt Jillie in the war room, knowing that they would probably die there. God forgive us."

Elizabeth's voice faltered under the feeling of remorse that she felt. Ralph took her hands and waited until she was ready to talk again.

"Go on."

"We found Chas and Joey at the top of the stairs, lying together. They had been mutilated beyond recognition. It was horrible. The whole house was burning and there was machine gun fire downstairs so that meant they were already in the house."

Elizabeth shivered, but it wasn't just the cool night breeze, it was reliving the terror of that night. Ralph encircled her in his arms to keep the night chill off her.

"Keep going Lizzie. You'll feel better when you get it off your chest."

"We were just about to get into the loft when the Shadow, Yurovsky, had us at gunpoint. He had come in through the upstairs window. We hadn't sensed him because of the shock of seeing the brothers that way."

Elizabeth looked into her father's eyes with a vengeful look in her own.

"He was a fool, too theatrical. He waited too long to kill us. There was an explosion downstairs that came up the stairwell, knocking us to the ground and he lost the initiative."

"Yakov Yurovsky, the murderer of the Romanovs? Well he showed them no mercy, so what did you do?"

"We killed him horribly," Elizabeth said without emotion, "and then we left through Emanuel's portal.

"That must have been one hell of a fight Lizzie if I know those boys."

"But in my heart Daddy I know that they all died trying to save us, even Uncle and Auntie who were innocent of it all."

Ralph considered his next words carefully.

"You can't carry the guilt of that night with you Lizzie. You must park it. You and Ben did the right thing. If you had stayed, then none of us would be here today. Now that you have found out who and what you are, I'm sorry to say but these decisions of great magnitude will be the norm for you, not the exception. You had better start getting used to it."

Elizabeth nodded reluctantly accepting the truth. Ralph felt uncomfortable for telling it that way, but it just had to be said, "Your birth-right comes with a lot of baggage Lizzie, but you will always have the ability to make a difference and that makes it all worthwhile. You and Ben have a long journey ahead of you, I have always known that. Your combined possibilities will give you both power and powerful enemies. You must stay alert and live every moment Lizzie like your Mum and I have."

"And what of the SAS boys now, are they alive and safe?" Elizabeth had subconsciously crossed her fingers.

"Yes, except for James. His luck ran out on him in Afghan last month disarming an IED. I'm sorry."

Elizabeth didn't have time to voice her regrets. At that same moment Tini went mental and ran to the drive. A black limousine was cruising slowly by and the back window was open. Tini snapped viciously at the open space, trying to get at the passengers in the back seat. Just for a moment those passengers were illuminated by the streetlight. There was an elegant woman sat between two men, one of them young and the other in the middle of his life. The woman touched the driver on his shoulder and the powerful limo accelerated away into the night.

"Mrs Hyde!" Elizabeth exclaimed in surprise. Her mouth remained open, testament to her genuine astonishment.

Ralph looked at her in consternation.

"Mrs Hyde? Who is Mrs Hyde?"

"My music teacher."

Her father's expression told her that it was more than just that.

"You were looking into the eyes of the Hydra herself Lizzie. The others were her lover Demitri Papandreou, a megalomaniac if there ever was one, and Illya Dracul, son of Adolphius and just about as nasty."

512

"But she is my music teacher, how could I not have…"

Ralph interrupted.

"Lizzie, have you never heard the expression *keep your friends close and your enemies even closer?*"

Elizabeth nodded and snuggled into her father's protective arms instinctively calling Tini to her side.

"You were being watched Lizzie, probably to get to May."

They returned to the marquee. The experience of meeting the very Hydra herself was a monumental experience for Elizabeth and with it came a feeling of vulnerability and inevitability. In that moment, she made a profound decision and that was to *live for today* and every day as it came from now on. She had already experienced too much for her tender years and had seen how it could all change in a moment. Inexplicably the image of her unborn children, Edith and Brady, came into her mind which reinforced that decision.

Elizabeth shared a parting kiss with her father and went directly to Mike who was talking animatedly with Ben. It was as if they were brothers and had known each other a lifetime. The honesty of the moment touched Elizabeth deep within her being. She wondered what joys and dangers they would share in the future. They would be inseparable, she was sure of it, and that thought comforted her.

"Ben will you excuse us?"

Elizabeth's smile was somehow different from any other that Ben had ever seen from her and he capitulated graciously.

Elizabeth took Mike's hand and led him out of the Marquee into the garden, stopping just before the house. Mike instinctively knew that it was the right time to hold her and he took her into his arms. He felt her trembling and her heart was beating impossibly. It was a tender moment and Mike sensed that Elizabeth was in personal turmoil and had something profound to say.

"Mike, my memories are now your memories and they are precious above all else but they are far from complete."

Elizabeth searched Mike's deep blue eyes for understanding but he was clearly unenlightened.

"This was going to be difficult," she thought.

"Do you remember that just before the Shadows attacked our house that we were together in my room?"

Mike smiled and gave her that look.

"How could I not? It's astonishing but yes somehow I do remember, clearly."

"And I said that I wanted to share precious moments with you and create memories that we could both take with us to eternity. Do you remember that too?"

Mike nodded and saw that Elizabeth's green eyes had that same softness in them that they had that night and her neck was tilted in the same act of submission.

"Make those memories with me now Mike, who knows what tomorrow brings?"

They were both charged with expectation and fell into a lover's embrace that was honest and urgent and couldn't be delayed. Mike took Elizabeth's hand and led her through the hallway to the stairs that led up to her room. As they passed the mirror, they were oblivious to the reflection of the old butler. He was smiling to himself as he observed their blind passion. The vision stirred his own memories of long ago and he continued smiling about the impetuousness of youth.

The Hydra had seen enough and signalled for the driver to leave. The black limousine accelerated smoothly away from the Robinson's house and was out of sight in seconds. She turned to Demitri.

"*Agápe mou*, all is as you have told me," she took his hand affectionately, "but they are complacent Demitri and I have a plan for complacency."

She smiled up at him sweetly but her eyes were cold.

"The Mullah Ismael Alansari came the closest so far to achieving our goal. Perhaps he deserves another chance?"

Demitri nodded his silent agreement and the Hydra leant across to the driver.

"Get me Mullah Ismael Alansari on the line now."

She turned back to Demitri and the words that she uttered were bitter and vengeful.

"This is not the end!"

THE END

AUTHOR's NOTE

Well that is the end of 'Angels & Shadows', but the second and third books in the series, 'Forsaken' and 'Scorned', are now available on Amazon. They are harder hitting as the story grows up. I hope that you enjoy them as much as I enjoyed writing them for you.

The fourth, 'The Assassin', will be available at the end of 2018.

If you did enjoy 'Angels & Shadows' I would be forever grateful if you would leave a review on Amazon. This is essential to help me up the 'search engine' and be noticed as a writer. Without that 'Angels & Shadows' is almost invisible. If you could recommend a friend too, then that would be immense.

Thank you,

Chris Savage.

34852823R00299

Printed in Great Britain
by Amazon